THE COMPANIONS OF JEHU

THE WORKS OF

ALEXANDRE DUMAS

IN THIRTY VOLUMES

❧

THE

COMPANIONS OF JEHU

❧

Fredonia Books
Amsterdam, The Netherlands

The Companions of Jehu

by
Alexandre Dumas

ISBN 1-58963-249-4

Copyright © 2001 by Fredonia Books

Reprinted from the 1902 edition

Fredonia Books
Amsterdam, The Netherlands
http://www.fredoniabooks.com

CONTENTS

THE COMPANIONS OF JEHU

AN INTRODUCTORY WORD TO THE READER

JUST about a year ago my old friend, Jules Simon, author of "Devoir," came to me with a request that I write a novel for the "Journal pour Tous." I gave him the outline of a novel which I had in mind. The subject pleased him, and the contract was signed on the spot.

The action occurred between 1791 and 1793, and the first chapter opened at Varennes the evening of the king's arrest.

Only, impatient as was the "Journal pour Tous," I demanded a fortnight of Jules Simon before beginning my novel. I wished to go to Varennes; I was not acquainted with the locality, and I confess there is one thing I cannot do; I am unable to write a novel or a drama about localities with which I am not familiar.

In order to write "Christine" I went to Fontainebleau; in writing "Henri III." I went to Blois; for "Les Trois Mousquetaires" I went to Boulogne and Béthune; for "Monte-Cristo" I returned to the Catalans and the Château d'If; for "Isaac Laquedem" I revisited Rome; and I certainly spent more time studying Jerusalem and Corinth from a distance than if I had gone there.

This gives such a character of veracity to all that I write, that the personages whom I create become eventually such integral parts of the places in which I planted them that, as a consequence, many end by believing in their actual existence. There are even some people who claim to have known them.

(3)

In this connection, dear readers, I am going to tell you something in confidence—only do not repeat it. I do not wish to injure honest fathers of families who live by this little industry, but if you go to Marseilles you will be shown there the house of Morel on the Cours, the house of Mercédès at the Catalans, and the dungeons of Dantès and Faria at the Château d'If.

When I staged "Monte-Cristo" at the Theâtre-Historique, I wrote to Marseilles for a plan of the Château d'If, which was sent to me. This drawing was for the use of the scene painter. The artist to whom I had recourse forwarded me the desired plan. He even did better than I would have dared ask of him; he wrote beneath it: "View of the Château d'If, from the side where Dantès was thrown into the sea."

I have learned since that a worthy man, a guide attached to the Château d'If, sells pens made of fish-bone by the Abbé Faria himself.

There is but one unfortunate circumstance concerning this; the fact is, Dantès and the Abbé Faria have never existed save in my imagination; consequently, Dantès could not have been precipitated from the top to the bottom of the Château d'If, nor could the Abbé Faria have made pens. But that is what comes from visiting these localities in person.

Therefore, I wished to visit Varennes before commencing my novel, because the first chapter was to open in that city. Besides, historically, Varennes worried me considerably; the more I perused the historical accounts of Varennes, the less I was able to understand, topographically, the king's arrest.

I therefore proposed to my young friend, Paul Bocage, that he accompany me to Varennes. I was sure in advance that he would accept. To merely propose such a trip to his picturesque and charming mind was to make him bound from his chair to the train.

We took the railroad to Châlons. There we bargained with a livery-stable keeper, who agreed, for a consideration of ten francs a day, to furnish us with a horse and carriage. We were seven days on the trip, three days to go from Châlons to Varennes, one day to make the requisite local researches in the city, and three days to return from Varennes to Châlons.

I recognized with a degree of satisfaction which you will easily comprehend, that not a single historian had been historical, and with still greater satisfaction that M. Thiers had been the least accurate of all these historians. I had already suspected this, but was not certain. The only one who had been accurate, with absolute accuracy, was Victor Hugo in his book called "The Rhine." It is true that Victor Hugo is a poet and not a historian. What historians these poets would make, if they would but consent to become historians!

One day Lamartine asked me to what I attributed the immense success of his "Histoire des Girondins."

"To this, because in it you rose to the level of a novel," I answered him. He reflected for a while and ended, I believe, by agreeing with me.

I spent a day, therefore, at Varennes and visited all the localities necessary for my novel, which was to be called "René d'Argonne." Then I returned. My son was staying in the country at Sainte-Assise, near Melun; my room awaited me, and I resolved to go there to write my novel.

I am acquainted with no two characters more dissimilar than Alexandre's and mine, which nevertheless harmonize so well. It is true we pass many enjoyable hours during our separations; but none I think pleasanter than those we spend together.

I had been installed there for three or four days endeavoring to begin my "René d'Argonne," taking up my pen, then laying it aside almost immediately. The thing would not go. I consoled myself by telling stories. Chance willed that I should relate one which Nodier had told me of four young men affiliated with the Company of Jehu, who had been executed at Bourg in Bresse amid the most dramatic circumstances. One of these four young men, he who had found the greatest difficulty in dying, or rather he whom they had the greatest difficulty in killing, was but nineteen and a half years old.

Alexandre listened to my story with much interest. When I had finished: "Do you know," said he, "what I should do in your place?"

"What?"

"I should lay aside 'René d'Argonne,' which refuses to materialize, and in its stead I should write 'The Companions of Jehu.'"

"But just think, I have had that other novel in mind for a year or two, and it is almost finished."

"It never will be since it is not finished now."

"Perhaps you are right, but I shall lose six months regaining my present vantage-ground."

"Good! In three days you will have written half a volume."

"Then you will help me."

"Yes, for I shall give you two characters."

"Is that all?"

"You are too exacting! The rest is your affair; I am busy with my 'Question d'Argent.'"

"Well, who are your two characters, then?"

"An English gentleman and a French captain."

"Introduce the Englishman first."

"Very well." And Alexandre drew Lord Tanlay's portrait for me.

"Your English gentleman pleases me," said I; "now let us see your French captain."

"My French captain is a mysterious character, who courts death with all his might, without being able to accomplish his desire; so that each time he rushes into mortal danger he performs some brilliant feat which secures him promotion."

"But why does he wish to get himself killed?"

"Because he is disgusted with life."

"Why is he disgusted with life?"

"Ah! That will be the secret of the book."

"It must be told in the end."

"On the contrary, I, in your place, would not tell it."

"The readers will demand it."

"You will reply that they have only to search for it; you must leave them something to do, these readers of yours."

"Dear friend, I shall be overwhelmed with letters."

"You need not answer them."

"Yes, but for my personal gratification I, at least, must know why my hero longs to die."

"Oh, I do not refuse to tell you."

"Let me hear, then."

"Well, suppose, instead of being professor of dialectics, Abelard had been a soldier."

"Well?"

"Well, let us suppose that a bullet—"

"Excellent!"

"You understand? Instead of withdrawing to Paraclet, he would have courted death at every possible opportunity."

"Hum! That will be difficult."

"Difficult! In what way?"

"To make the public swallow that."

"But since you are not going to tell the public."

"That is true. By my faith, I believe you are right. Wait."

"I am waiting."

"Have you Nodier's 'Souvenirs de la Révolution'? I believe he wrote one or two pages about Guyon, Leprêtre, Amiet and Hyvert."

"They will say, then, that you have plagiarized from Nodier."

"Oh! He loved me well enough during his life not to refuse me whatever I shall take from him after his death. Go fetch me the 'Souvenirs de la Révolution.'"

Alexandre brought me the book. I opened it, turned

over two or three pages, and at last discovered what I was looking for. A little of Nodier, dear readers, you will lose nothing by it. It is he who is speaking:

The highwaymen who attacked the diligences, as mentioned in the article on Amiet, which I quoted just now, were called Leprêtre, Hyvert, Guyon and Amiet.

Leprêtre was forty-eight years old. He was formerly a captain of dragoons, a knight of St. Louis, of a noble countenance, prepossessing carriage and much elegance of manner. Guyon and Amiet have never been known by their real names. They owe that to the accommodating spirit prevailing among the vendors of passports of those days. Let the reader picture to himself two dare-devils between twenty and thirty years of age, allied by some common responsibility, the sequence, perhaps, of some misdeed, or, by a more delicate and generous interest, the fear of compromising their family name. Then you will know of Guyon and Amiet all that I can recall. The latter had a sinister countenance, to which, perhaps, he owes the bad reputation with which all his biographers have credited him. Hyvert was the son of a rich merchant of Lyons, who had offered the sub-officer charged with his deportation sixty thousand francs to permit his escape. He was at once the Achilles and the Paris of the band. He was of medium height but well formed, lithe, and of graceful and pleasing address. His eyes were never without animation nor his lips without a smile. His was one of those countenances which are never forgotten, and which present an inexpressible blending of sweetness and strength, tenderness and energy. When he yielded to the eloquent petulance of his inspirations he soared to enthusiasm. His conversation revealed the rudiments of an excellent early education and much natural intelligence. That which was so terrifying in him was his tone of heedless gayety, which contrasted so horribly with his position. For the rest, he was unanimously conceded to be kind, generous, humane, lenient toward the weak, while with the strong he loved to display a vigor truly athletic which his somewhat effeminate features were far from indicating. He boasted that he had never been without money, and had no enemies. That was his sole reply to the charges of theft and assassination. He was twenty-two years old.

To these four men was intrusted the attack upon a diligence conveying forty thousand francs of government money. This deed was transacted in broad daylight, with an exchange of mutual courtesy almost; and the travellers, who were not disturbed by the attack, gave little heed to it. But a child of only ten years of age, with reckless bravado, seized the pistol of the conductor and fired it into the midst of the assailants. As this peaceful weapon, according to the custom, was only charged with powder, no one was injured; but the occupants of the coach quite naturally experienced a lively fear of reprisals. The little boy's mother fell into violent hysterics. This new disturbance created a general diversion which dominated all the preceding events and particularly attracted the attention of the robbers. One of them flew to the woman's side, reassuring her in the most affectionate manner, while complimenting her upon her son's precocious courage, and courteously pressed upon her the salts and perfumes with which these gentlemen were ordinarily provided for their own use. She regained consciousness. In the excitement of the moment her travelling companions noticed that the highwayman's mask had fallen off, but they did not see his face.

The police of those days, restricted to mere impotent supervision, were unable to cope with the depredations of these banditti, although they did not lack the means to follow them up. Appointments were made at the cafés, and narratives relating to deeds carrying with them the penalty of death circulated freely through all the billiard-halls in the land. Such was the importance which the culprits and the public attached to the police.

These men of blood and terror assembled in society in the evening, and discussed their nocturnal expeditions as if they had been mere pleasure-parties.

Leprêtre, Hyvert, Amiet and Guyon were arraigned before the tribunal of a neighboring department. No one save the Treasury had suffered from their attack, and there was no one to identify them save the lady who took very good care not to do so. They were therefore acquitted unanimously.

Nevertheless, the evidence against them so obviously called for conviction, that the Ministry was forced to appeal from this decision. The verdict was set aside; but such was the government's vacillation, that it hesitated to punish excesses that might on the morrow be regarded as virtues. The accused were cited before the tribunal of Ain.

in the city of Bourg, where dwelt a majority of their friends, relatives, abettors and accomplices. The Ministry sought to propitiate the one party by the return of its victims, and the other by the almost inviolate safeguards with which it surrounded the prisoners. The return to prison indeed resembled nothing less than a triumph.

The trial recommenced. It was at first attended by the same results as the preceding one. The four accused were protected by an alibi, patently false, but attested by a hundred signatures, and for which they could easily have obtained ten thousand. All moral convictions must fail in the presence of such authoritative testimony. An acquittal seemed certain, when a question, perhaps involuntarily insidious, from the president, changed the aspect of the trial.

"Madam," said he to the lady who had been so kindly assisted by one of the highwaymen, "which of these men was it who tendered you such thoughtful attention?"

This unexpected form of interrogation confused her ideas. It is probable that she believed the facts to be known, and saw in this a means of modifying the fate of the man who interested her.

"It was that gentleman," said she, pointing to Leprêtre.

The four accused, who were included in a common alibi, fell by this one admission under the executioner's axe. They rose and bowed to her with a smile.

"Faith!" said Hyvert, falling back upon his bench with a burst of laughter, "that, Captain, will teach you to play the gallant."

I have heard it said that the unhappy lady died shortly after of chagrin.

The customary appeal followed; but, this time, there was little hope. The Republican party, which Napoleon annihilated a month later, was in the ascendency. That of the Counter-Revolution was compromised by its odious excesses. The people demanded examples, and matters were arranged accordingly, as is ordinarily the custom in strenuous times; for it is with governments as with men, the weakest are always the most cruel. Nor had the Companies of Jehu longer an organized existence. The heroes of these ferocious bands, Debeauce, Hastier, Bary, Le Coq, Dabri, Delbourbe and Storkenfeld, had either fallen on the scaffold or elsewhere. The condemned could look for no further assistance from the daring courage of these exhausted devotees, who, no longer capable of protecting their own lives, coolly sacrificed them, as did Piard, after a merry supper. Our brigands were doomed to die.

Their appeal was rejected, but the municipal authorities were not the first to learn of this. The condemned men were warned by three shots fired beneath the walls of their dungeon. The Commissioner of the Executive Directory, who had assumed the rôle of Public Prosecutor at the trial, alarmed at this obvious sign of connivance, requisitioned a squad of armed men of whom my uncle was then commander. At six o'clock in the morning sixty horsemen were drawn up before the iron gratings of the prison yard.

Although the jailers had observed all possible precautions in entering the dungeon where these four unfortunate men were confined, and whom they had left the preceding day tightly pinioned and heavily loaded with chains, they were unable to offer them a prolonged resistance. The prisoners were free and armed to the teeth. They came forth without difficulty, leaving their guardians under bolts and bars, and, supplied with the keys, they quickly traversed the space that separated them from the prison yard. Their appearance must have been terrifying to the populace awaiting them before the iron gates.

To assure perfect freedom of action, or perhaps to affect an appearance of security more menacing even than the renown for strength and intrepidity with which their names were associated, or possibly even to conceal the flow of blood which reveals itself so readily beneath white linen, and betrays the last agonies of a mortally wounded man, their breasts were bared. Their braces crossed upon the chest—their wide red belts bristling with arms—their cry of attack and rage, all that must have given a decidedly fantastic touch to the scene. Arrived in the square, they perceived the gendarmerie drawn up in motionless ranks, through which it would have been impossible to force a passage. They halted an instant and seemed to consult together. Leprêtre, who was, as I have said, their senior and their chief, saluted the guard with his hand, saying with that noble grace of manner peculiar to him:

"Very well, gentlemen of the gendarmerie!"

Then after a brief, energetic farewell to his comrades, he stepped in front of them and blew out his brains. Guyon, Amiet and Hyvert assumed a defensive position, their double-barrelled pistols levelled upon their armed opponents. They did not fire; but the latter, considering this demonstration as a sign of open hostility, fired upon them. Guyon fell dead upon Leprêtre's body, which had not moved. Amiet's hip was broken near the groin. The "Biographie des Contemporains" says that he was executed. I have often heard it said that he died at the foot of the scaffold. Hyvert was left alone, his determined brow, his terrible eye, the pistol in each practiced and vigorous hand threatening death to the spectators. Perhaps it was involuntary admiration, in his desperate plight, for this handsome young man with his waving locks, who was known never to have shed blood, and from whom the law now demanded the expiation of blood; or perhaps it was the sight of those three corpses over which he sprang like a wolf overtaken by his hunters, and the frightful novelty of the spectacle, which for an instant restrained the fury of the troop. He perceived this and temporized with them for a compromise.

"Gentlemen," said he, "I go to my death! I die with all my heart! But let no one approach me or I shall shoot him—except this gentleman," he continued, pointing to the executioner. "This is an affair that concerns us alone and merely needs a certain understanding between us."

This concession was readily accorded, for there was no one present who was not suffering from the prolongation of this horrible tragedy, and anxious to see it finished. Perceiving their assent, he placed one of his pistols between his teeth, and drawing a dagger from his belt, plunged it in his breast up to the hilt. He still remained standing and seemed greatly surprised. There was a movement toward him.

"Very well, gentlemen!" cried he, covering the men who sought to surround him with his pistols, which he had seized again, while the blood spurted freely from the wound in which he had left his poniard. "You know our agreement; either I die alone or three of us will die together. Forward, march!" He walked straight to the guillotine, turning the knife in his breast as he did so.

"Faith," said he, "my soul must be centred in my belly! I cannot die. See if you can fetch it out."

This last was addressed to his executioner. An instant later his head fell. Be it accident or some peculiar phenomenon of the vitality, it rebounded and rolled beyond the circle of the scaffolding, and they will still tell you at Bourg, that Hyvert's head spoke.

Before I had finished reading I had decided to abandon René d'Argonne for the Companions of Jehu. On the morrow I came down with my travelling bag under my arm.

"You are leaving?" said Alexandre to me.

"Yes."

"Where are you going?"

"To Bourg, in Bresse."

"What are you going to do there?"

"Study the neighborhood and consult with the inhabitants who saw Leprêtre, Amiet, Guyon and Hyvert executed."

There are two roads to Bourg—from Paris, of course; one may leave the train at Mâcon, and take stage from Mâcon to Bourg, or, continuing as far as Lyons, take train again from Lyons to Bourg.

I was hesitating between these two roads when one of the travellers who was temporarily occupying my compartment decided me. He was going to Bourg, where he frequently had business. He was going by way of Lyons; therefore, Lyons was the better way.

I resolved to travel by the same route. I slept at Lyons, and on the morrow by ten in the morning I was at Bourg.

A paper published in the second capital of the kingdom met my eye. It contained a spiteful article about me. Lyons has never forgiven me since 1833, I believe, some twenty-four years ago, for asserting that it was not a literary city. Alas! I have in 1857 the same opinion of Lyons as I had in 1833. I do not easily change my opinion. There is another city in France that is almost as bitter against me as Lyons, that is Rouen. Rouen has hissed all my plays, including Count Hermann.

One day a Neapolitan boasted to me that he had hissed Rossini and Malibran, "The Barbiere" and "Desdemona."

"That must be true," I answered him, "for Rossini and Malibran on their side boast of having been hissed by the Neapolitans."

So I boast that the Rouenese have hissed me. Neverthe-less, meeting a full-blooded Rouenese one day I resolved to discover why I had been hissed at Rouen. I like to under-stand these little things.

My Rouenese informed me: "We hiss you because we are down on you."

Why not? Rouen was down on Joan of Arc. Neverthe-less it could not be for the same reason. I asked my Rou-enese why he and his compatriots were ill-disposed to me; I had never said anything evil of apple sugar, I had treated M. Barbet with respect during his entire term as mayor, and, when a delegate from the Society of Letters at the unveiling of the statue of the great Corneille, I was the only one who thought to bow to him before beginning my speech. There was nothing in that which could have rea-sonably incurred the hatred of the Rouenese.

Therefore to this haughty reply, "We hiss you because we have a grudge against you," I asked humbly:

"But, great Heavens! why are you down on me?"

"Oh, you know very well," replied my Rouenese.

"I?" I exclaimed.

"Yes, you."

"Well, never mind; pretend I do not know."

"You remember the dinner the city gave you, in connec-tion with that statue of Corneille?"

"Perfectly. Were they annoyed because I did not re-turn it?"

"No, it is not that."

"What is it then?"

"Well, at that dinner they said to you: 'M. Dumas, you ought to write a play for Rouen based upon some sub-ject taken from its own history.'"

"To which I replied: 'Nothing easier; I will come at your first summons and spend a fortnight in Rouen. You can suggest the subject, and during that fortnight I will write the play, the royalties of which I shall devote to the poor.'"

"That is true, you said that."

"I see nothing sufficiently insulting in that to incur the hatred of the Rouenese."

"Yes, but they added: 'Will you write it in prose?' To which you replied— Do you remember what you answered?"

"My faith! no."

"You replied: 'I will write it in verse; it is soonest done.' "

"That sounds like me. Well, what then?"

"Then! That was an insult to Corneille, M. Dumas; that is why the Rouenese are down on you, and will be for a long time."

Verbatim!

Oh, worthy Rouenese! I trust that you will never serve me so ill as to forgive and applaud me.

The aforesaid paper observed that M. Dumas had doubtless spent but one night in Lyons because a city of such slight literary standing was not worthy of his longer sojourn. M. Dumas had not thought about this at all. He had spent but one night at Lyons because he was in a hurry to reach Bourg. And no sooner had M. Dumas arrived at Bourg than he asked to be directed to the office of its leading newspaper.

I knew that it was under the management of a distinguished archeologist, who was also the editor of my friend Baux's work on the church of Brou.

I asked for M. Milliet. M. Milliet appeared. We shook hands and I explained the object of my visit.

"I can fix you perfectly," said he to me. "I will take you to one of our magistrates, who is at present engaged upon a history of the department."

"How far has he got in this history?"

"1822."

"Then that's all right. As the events I want to relate occurred in 1799, and my heroes were executed in 1800, he will have covered that epoch, and can fur-

nish me with the desired information.   Let us go to your
magistrate.''

On the road, M. Milliet told me that this same magis-
terial historian was also a noted gourmet.   Since Brillat-
Savarin it has been the fashion for magistrates to be epi-
cures.   Unfortunately, many are content to be gourmands,
which is not at all the same thing.

We were ushered into the magistrate's study.   I found
a man with a shiny face and a sneering smile.   He greeted
me with that protecting air which historians deign to assume toward poets.

''Well, sir,'' he said to me, ''so you have come to our
poor country in search of material for your novel?''

''No, sir; I have my material already.   I have come
simply to consult your historical documents.''

''Good!   I did not know that it was necessary to give
one's self so much trouble in order to write novels.''

''There you are in error, sir; at least in my instance.   I
am in the habit of making exhaustive researches upon all
the historical events of which I treat.''

''You might at least have sent some one else.''

''Any person whom I might send, sir, not being so
completely absorbed in my subject, might have overlooked
many important facts.   Then, too, I make use of many localities which I cannot describe unless I see them.''

''Oh, then this is a novel which you intend writing yourself?''

''Yes, certainly, sir.   I allowed my valet to write my last;
but he had such immense success that the rogue asked so
exorbitant an increase of wages that, to my great regret, I
was unable to keep him.''

The magistrate bit his lips.   Then, after a moment's silence, he said:

''Will you kindly tell me, sir, how I can assist you in
this important work?''

''You can direct my researches, sir.   As you have com-
piled the history of the department, none of the important

events which have occurred in its capital can be unknown to you."

"Truly, sir, I believe that in this respect I am tolerably well informed."

"Then, sir, in the first place, your department was the centre of the operations of the Company of Jehu."

"Sir, I have heard speak of the Companions of Jesus," replied the magistrate with his jeering smile.

"The Jesuits, you mean? That is not what I am seeking, sir."

"Nor is it of them that I am speaking. I refer to the stage robbers who infested the highroads from 1797 to 1800."

"Then, sir, permit me to tell you they are precisely the ones I have come to Bourg about, and that they were called the Companions of Jehu, and not the Companions of Jesus."

"What is the meaning of this title 'Companions of Jehu'? I like to get at the bottom of everything."

"So do I, sir; that is why I did not wish to confound these highwaymen with the Apostles."

"Truly, that would not have been very orthodox."

"But it is what you would have done, nevertheless, sir, if I, a poet, had not come here expressly to correct the mistake you, as historian, have made."

"I await your explanation, sir," resumed the magistrate, pursing his lips.

"It is short and simple. Elisha consecrated Jehu, King of Israel, on condition that he exterminate the house of Ahab; Elisha was Louis XVIII.; Jehu was Cadoudal; the house of Ahab, the Revolution. That is why these pillagers of diligences, who filched the government money to support the war in the Vendée, were called the Companions of Jehu."

"Sir, I am happy to learn something at my age."

"Oh, sir! One can always learn, at all times and at all ages; during life one learns man; in death one learns God."

"But, after all," my interlocutor said to me with a gesture of impatience, "may I know in what I can assist you?"

"Thus, sir. Four of these young men, leaders of the Companions of Jehu, were executed at Bourg, on the Place du Bastion."

"In the first place, sir, in Bourg executions do not take place at the Bastion; they execute on the Fair grounds."

"Now, sir—these last fifteen or twenty years, it is true—since Peytel. But before, especially during the Revolution, they executed on the Place du Bastion."

"That is possible."

"It is so. These four young men were called Guyon, Leprêtre, Amiet, and Hyvert."

"This is the first time I have heard those names."

"Yet their names made a certain noise at Bourg."

"Are you sure, sir, that these men were executed here?"

"I am positive."

"From whom have you derived your information?"

"From a man whose uncle, then in command of the gendarmerie, was present at the execution."

"Will you tell me this man's name?"

"Charles Nodier."

"Charles Nodier, the novelist, the poet?"

"If he were a historian I would not be so insistent, sir. Recently, during a trip to Varennes, I learned what dependence to place upon historians. But precisely because he is a poet, a novelist, I do insist."

"You are at liberty to do so; but I know nothing of what you desire to learn, and I dare even assert that, if you have come to Bourg solely to obtain information concerning the execution of—what did you call them?"

"Guyon, Leprêtre, Amiet, and Hyvert."

"You have undertaken a futile voyage. For these last twenty years, sir, I have been searching the town archives, and I have never seen anything relating to what you have just told me."

"The town archives are not those of the registrar, sir;

perhaps at the record office I may be able to find what I am seeking."

"Ah! sir, if you can find anything among those archives you will be a very clever man! The record office is a chaos, a veritable chaos. You would have to spend a month here, and then—then—"

"I do not expect to stay here more than a day, sir; but if in that day I should find what I am seeking will you permit me to impart it to you?"

"Yes, sir; yes, sir; and you will render me a great service by doing so."

"No greater than the one I asked of you. I shall merely give you some information about a matter of which you were ignorant, that is all."

You can well understand that on leaving my magistrate, my honor was piqued. I determined, cost what it might, to procure this information about the Companions of Jehu. I went back to Milliet, and cornered him.

"Listen," he said. "My brother-in-law is a lawyer."

"He's my man! Let's go find the brother-in-law."

"He's in court at this hour."

"Then let us go to court."

"Your appearance will create a sensation, I warn you."

"Then go alone—tell him what we want, and let him make a search. I will visit the environs of the town to base my work on the localities. We will meet at four o'clock at the Place du Bastion, if you are agreed."

"Perfectly."

"It seems to me that I saw a forest, coming here."

"The forest of Seillon."

"Bravo!"

"Do you need a forest?"

"It is absolutely indispensable to me."

"Then permit me—"

"What?"

"I am going to take you to a friend of mine, M. Leduc, a poet who in his spare moments is an inspector."

"Inspector of what?"

"Of the forest."

"Are there any ruins in the forest?"

"The Chartreuse, which is not in the forest, but merely some hundred feet from it."

"And in the forest?"

"There is a sort of hermitage which is called La Correrie, belonging to the Chartreuse, with which it communicates by a subterranean passage."

"Good! Now, if you can provide me with a grotto you will overwhelm me."

"We have the grotto of Ceyzeriat, but that is on the other side of the Reissouse."

"I don't mind. If the grotto won't come to me, I will do like Mahomet—I will go to the grotto. In the meantime let us go to M. Leduc."

Five minutes later we reached M. Leduc's house. He, on learning what we wanted, placed himself, his horse, and his carriage at my disposal. I accepted all. There are some men who offer their services in such a way that they place you at once at your ease.

We first visited the Chartreuse. Had I built it myself it could not have suited me better. A deserted cloister, devastated garden, inhabitants almost savages. Chance, I thank thee!

From there we went to the Correrie; it was the supplement of the Chartreuse. I did not yet know what I could do with it; but evidently it might be useful to me.

"Now, sir," I said to my obliging guide, "I need a pretty site, rather gloomy, surrounded by tall trees, beside a river. Have you anything like that in the neighborhood?"

"What do you want to do with it?"

"To build a château there."

"What kind of a château?"

"Zounds! of cards! I have a family to house, a model mother, a melancholy young girl, a mischievous brother, and a poaching gardener."

"There is a place called Noires-Fontaines."

"In the first place the name is charming."

"But there is no château there."

"So much the better, for I should have been obliged to demolish it."

"Let us go to Noires-Fontaines."

We started; a quarter of an hour later we descended at the ranger's lodge.

"Shall we take this little path?" said M. Leduc; "it will take us where you want to go."

It led us, in fact, to a spot planted with tall trees which overshadowed three or four rivulets.

"We call this place Noires-Fontaines," M. Leduc explained.

"And here Madame de Montrevel, Amélie and little Edouard will dwell. Now what are those villages which I see in front of me?"

"Here, close at hand, is Montagnac; yonder, on the mountain side, Ceyzeriat."

"Is that where the grotto is?"

"Yes. But how did you know there was a grotto at Ceyzeriat?"

"Never mind, go on. The name of those other villages, if you please."

"Saint-Just, Tréconnas, Ramasse, Villereversure."

"That will do."

"Have you enough?"

"Yes."

I drew out my note-book, sketched a plan of the locality and wrote about in their relative positions the names of the villages which M. Leduc had just pointed out to me.

"That's done!" said I.

"Where shall we go now?"

"Isn't the church of Brou near this road?"

"Yes."

"Then let us go to the church of Brou."

"Do you need that in your novel?"

"Yes, indeed; you don't imagine I am going to lay my scene in a country which contains the architectural masterpiece of the sixteenth century without utilizing that masterpiece, do you?"

"Let us go to the church of Brou."

A quarter of an hour later the sacristan showed us into this granite jewel-case which contains the three marble gems called the tombs of Marguerite of Austria, Marguerite of Bourbon, and of Philibert le Beau."

"How is it," I asked the sacristan, "that all these masterpieces were not reduced to powder during the Revolution?"

"Ah! sir, the municipality had an idea."

"What was it?"

"That of turning the church into a storage house for fodder."

"Yes, and the hay saved the marble; you are right, my friend, that *was* an idea."

"Does this idea of the municipality afford you another?" asked M. Leduc.

"Faith, yes, and I shall have poor luck if I don't make something out of it."

I looked at my watch. "Three o'clock! Now for the prison. I have an appointment with M. Milliet at four on the Place du Bastion."

"Wait; there is one thing more."

"What is that?"

"Have you noticed Marguerite of Austria's motto?"

"No; where is it?"

"Oh, all over. In the first place, look above her tomb."

"'Fortune, infortune, fort'une.'"

"Exactly."

"Well, what does this play of words mean?"

"Learned men translate it thus: 'Fate persecutes a woman much.'"

"Explain that a little."

"You must, in the first place, assume that it is derived from the Latin."

"True, that is probable."

"Well, then: 'Fortuna infortunat—' "

"Oh! oh! 'Infortunat.' "

"Bless me!"

"That strongly resembles a solecism!"

"What do you want?"

"An explanation."

"Explain it yourself."

"Well; 'Fortuna, infortuna, forti una.' 'Fortune and misfortune are alike to the strong.' "

"Do you know, that may possibly be the correct translation?"

"Zounds! See what it is not to be learned, my dear sir; we are endowed with common-sense, and that sees clearer than science. Have you anything else to tell me?"

"No."

"Then let us go to the prison."

We got into the carriage and returned to the city, stopping only at the gate of the prison. I glanced out of the window.

"Oh!" I exclaimed, "they have spoiled it for me."

"What! They've spoiled it for you?"

"Certainly, it was not like this in my prisoners' time. Can I speak to the jailer?"

"Certainly."

"Then let us consult him."

We knocked at the door. A man about forty opened it. He recognized M. Leduc.

"My dear fellow," M. Leduc said to him, "this is one of my learned friends—"

"Come, come," I exclaimed, interrupting him, "no nonsense."

"Who contends," continued M. Leduc, "that the prison is no longer the same as it was in the last century?"

"That is true, M. Leduc, it was torn down and rebuilt in 1816."

"Then the interior arrangements are no longer the same?"

"Oh! no, sir, everything was changed."

"Could I see the old plan?"

"M. Martin, the architect, might perhaps be able to find one for you."

"Is he any relation to M. Martin, the lawyer?"

"His brother."

"Very well, my friend, then I can get my plan."

"Then we have nothing more to do here?" inquired M. Leduc.

"Nothing."

"Then I am free to go home?"

"I shall be sorry to leave you, that is all."

"Can you find your way to the Bastion without me?"

"It is close by."

"What are you going to do this evening?"

"I will spend it with you, if you wish."

"Very good! You will find a cup of tea waiting for you at nine."

"I shall be on hand for it."

I thanked M. Leduc. We shook hands and parted.

I went down the Rue des Lisses (meaning Lists, from a combat which took place in the square to which it leads), and skirting the Montburon Garden, I reached the Place du Bastion. This is a semicircle now used as the town market-place. In the midst stands the statue of Bichat by David d'Angers. Bichat, in a frockcoat—why that exaggeration of realism?—stands with his hand upon the heart of a child about nine or ten years old, perfectly nude—why that excess of ideality? Extended at Bichat's feet lies a dead body. It is Bichat's book "Of Life and of Death" translated into bronze. I was studying this statue, which epitomizes the defects and merits of David d'Angers, when I felt some one touch my shoulder. I turned around; it was M. Milliet. He held a paper in his hand.

"Well?" I asked.

"Well, victory!"

"What is that you have there?"

"The minutes of the trial and execution."

"Of whom ?"

"Of your men."

"Of Guyon, Leprêtre, Amiet—!"

"And Hyvert."

"Give it to me."

"Here it is."

I took it and read:

REPORT OF THE DEATH AND EXECUTION OF LAURENT GUYON, ETIENNE HYVERT, FRANÇOIS AMIET, AN-TOINE LEPRÊTRE. Condemned the twentieth Thermidor of the year VIII., and executed the twenty-third Vende-miaire of the year IX.

To-day, the twenty-third Vendemiaire of the year IX., the government commissioner of the tribunal, who received at eleven of the evening the budget of the Minister of Jus-tice, containing the minutes of the trial and the judgment which condemns to death Laurent Guyon, Etienne Hyvert, François Amiet and Antoine Leprêtre;—the decision of the Court of Appeals of the sixth inst., rejecting the appeal against the sentence of the twenty-first Thermidor of the year VIII., I did notify by letter, between seven and eight of the morning, the four accused that their sentence of death would take effect to-day at eleven o'clock. In the interval which elapsed before eleven o'clock, the four accused shot themselves with pistols and stabbed themselves with blows from a poinard in prison. Leprêtre and Guyon, according to public rumor, were dead; Hyvert fatally wounded and dying; Amiet fatally wounded, but still conscious. All four, in this state, were conveyed to the scaffold, and, living or dead, were guillotined. At half after eleven, the sheriff, Colin, handed in the report of their execution to the Munici-pality for registration upon the death roll:

The captain of gendarmerie remitted to the Justice of the Peace a report of what had occurred in the prison, of which he was a witness. I, who was not present, do certify to what I have learned by hearsay only.

(Signed)   DUBOST, Clerk.

Bourg, 23d Vendemiaire of the year IX.

Ah! so it was the poet who was right and not the his-torian! The captain of gendarmerie, who remitted the report of the proceedings in the prison to the Justice of the Peace, at which he was present, was Nodier's uncle. This report handed to the Justice of the Peace was the story which, graven upon the young man's mind, saw the light some forty years later unaltered, in that masterpiece entitled "Souvenirs de la Révolution." The entire series of papers was in the record office. M. Martin offered to have them copied for me; inquiry, trial and judgment.

I had a copy of Nodier's "Souvenirs of the Révolution" in my pocket. In my hand I held the report of the execution which confirmed the facts therein stated.

"Now let us go to our magistrate," I said to M. Milliet. "Let us go to our magistrate," he repeated.

The magistrate was confounded, and I left him convinced that poets know history as well as historians—if not better.

ALEX. DUMAS.

PROLOGUE

THE CITY OF AVIGNON

W E DO not know if the prologue we are going to
present to our readers' eyes be very useful, nevertheless we cannot resist the desire to make of
it, not the first chapter, but the preface of this book.

The more we advance in life, the more we advance in
art, the more convinced we become that nothing is abrupt
and isolated; that nature and society progress by evolution
and not by chance, and that the event, flower joyous or sad,
perfumed or fetid, benificent or fatal, which unfolds itself
to-day before our eyes, was sown in the past, and had its
roots sometimes in days anterior to ours, even as it will
bear its fruits in the future.

Young, man accepts life as it comes, enamored of yester-
een, careless of the day, heeding little the morrow. Youth
is the springtide with its dewy dawns and its beautiful
nights; if sometimes a storm clouds the sky, it gathers,
mutters and disperses, leaving the sky bluer, the atmosphere
purer, and Nature more smiling than before. What use is
there in reflecting on this storm that passes swift as a caprice,
ephemeral as a fancy? Before we have discovered the secret of the meteorological enigma, the storm will have
disappeared.

But it is not thus with the terrible phenomena, which at
the close of summer, threaten our harvests; or in the midst
of autumn, assail our vintages; we ask whither they go, we
query whence they come, we seek a means to prevent them.

To the thinker, the historian, the poet, there is a far
deeper subject for reflection in revolutions, these tem-

pests of the social atmosphere which drench the earth with blood, and crush an entire generation of men, than in those upheavals of nature which deluge a harvest, or flay the vineyards with hail—that is to say, the fruits of a single harvest, wreaking an injury, which can at the worst be repaired the ensuing year, unless the Lord be in His days of wrath.

Thus, in other days, be it forgetfulness, heedlessness or ignorance perhaps—(blessed he who is ignorant! a fool he who is wise!)—in other days in relating the story which I am going to tell you to-day I would, without pausing at the place where the first scene of this book occurs, have accorded it but a superficial mention, and traversing the Midi like any other province, have named Avignon like any other city.

But to-day it is no longer the same; I am no longer tossed by the flurries of spring, but by the storms of summer, the tempests of autumn. To-day when I name Avignon, I evoke a spectre; and, like Antony displaying Cæsar's toga, say:

> "Look! in this place ran Cassius' dagger through;
> See what a rent the envious Casca made;
> Through this the well-beloved Brutus stabbed—"

So, seeing the bloody shroud of the papal city, I say: "Behold the blood of the Albigenses, and here the blood of the Cevennais; behold the blood of the Republicans, and here the blood of the Royalists; behold the blood of Lescuyer; behold the blood of Maréchal Brune."

And I feel myself seized with a profound sadness, and I begin to write, but at the first lines I perceive that, without suspecting it, the historian's chisel has superseded the novelist's pen in my hand.

Well, let us be both. Reader, grant me these ten, fifteen, twenty pages to the historian; the novelist shall have the rest.

Let us say, therefore, a few words about Avignon, the

place where the first scene of the new book which we are offering to the public, opens. Perhaps, before reading what we have to say, it would be well to cast a glance at what its native historian, François Nouguier, says of it.

"Avignon," he writes, "a town noble for its antiquity, pleasing in its site, superb for its walls, smiling for the fertility of its soil, charming for the gentleness of its inhabitants, magnificent for its palace, beautiful in its broad streets, marvellous in the construction of its bridge, rich because of its commerce, and known to all the world."

May the shade of François Nouguier pardon us if we do not at first see his city with the same eyes as he does. To those who know Avignon be it to say who has best described it, the historian or the novelist.

It is but just to assert in the first place that Avignon is a town by itself, that is to say, a town of extreme passions. The period of religious dissensions, which culminated for her in political hatreds, dates from the twelfth century. After his flight from Lyons, the valleys of Mont Ventoux sheltered Pierre de Valdo and his Vaudois, the ancestors of those Protestants who, under the name of the Albigenses, cost the Counts of Toulouse, and transferred to the papacy, the seven châteaux which Raymond VI. possessed in Languedoc.

Avignon, a powerful republic governed by podestats, refused to submit to the King of France. One morning Louis VIII., who thought it easier to make a crusade against Avignon like Simon de Montfort, than against Jerusalem like Philippe Auguste; one morning, we say, Louis VIII. appeared before the gates of Avignon, demanding admission with lances at rest, visor down, banners unfurled and trumpets of war sounding.

The bourgeois refused. They offered the King of France, as a last concession, a peaceful entrance, lances erect, and the royal banner alone unfurled. The King laid siege to the town, a siege which lasted three months, during which, says the chronicler, the bourgeois of Avignon returned the

French soldiers arrow for arrow, wound for wound, death for death.

The city capitulated at length. Louis VIII. brought the Roman Cardinal-Legate, Saint-Angelo, in his train. It was he who dictated the terms, veritable priestly terms, hard and unconditional. The Avi nonese were commanded to demolish their ramparts, to fill their moats, to raze three hundred towers, to sell their vessels, and to burn their engines and machines of war. They had moreover to pay an enormous impost, to abjure the Vaudois heresy, and maintain thirty men fully armed and equipped, in Palestine, to aid in delivering the tomb of Christ. And finally, to watch over the fulfillment of these terms, of which the bull is still extant in the city archives, a brotherhood of penitents was founded which, reaching down through six centuries, still exists in our days.

In opposition to these penitents, known as the "White Penitents," the order of the "Black Penitents" was founded, imbued with the spirit of opposition of Raymond of Toulouse.

From that day forth the religious hatreds developed into political hatreds. It was not sufficient that Avignon should be the land of heresy. She was destined to become the theatre of schisms.

Permit us, in connection with this French Rome, a short historical digression. Strictly speaking, it is not essential to the subject of which we treat, and we were perhaps wiser to launch ourselves immediately into the heart of the drama; but we trust that we will be forgiven. We write more particularly for those who, in a novel, like occasionally to meet with something more than fiction.

In 1285 Philippe le Bel ascended the throne.

It is a great historical date, this date of 1285. The papacy which, in the person of Gregory VII., successfully opposed the Emperor of Germany; the papacy which, vanquished in matters temporal by Henry IV., yet vanquished him morally. This papacy was slapped by a simple Sabine gentleman, and the steel gauntlet of Colonna reddened the cheek of Boniface VIII. But the King of France, whose hand had really dealt this blow, what happened to him under the successor of Boniface VIII.?

This successor was Benedict XI., a man of low origin, but who might perhaps have developed into a man of genius, had they allowed him the time. Too weak for an open struggle with Philippe le Bel, he found a means which would have been the envy of the founder of a celebrated order two hundred years later. He pardoned Colonna openly.

To pardon Colonna was to declare Colonna culpable, since culprits alone have need of pardon. If Colonna were guilty, the King of France was at least his accomplice.

There was some danger in supporting such an argument; also Benedict XI. was pope but eight months. One day a veiled woman, a pretended lay-sister of Sainte-Petronille at Perugia, came to him while he was at table, offering him a basket of figs. Did it conceal an asp like Cleopatra's? The fact is that on the morrow the Holy See was vacant.

Then Philippe le Bel had a strange idea; so strange that it must, at first, have seemed an hallucination.

It was to withdraw the papacy from Rome, to install it in France, to put it in jail, and force it to coin money for his profit.

The reign of Philippe le Bel was the advent of gold. Gold! that was the sole and unique god of this king who had slapped a pope. Saint Louis had a priest, the worthy Abbé Suger, for minister; Philippe le Bel had two bankers, two Florentines, Biscio and Musiato.

Do you expect, dear reader, that we are about to fall into the philosophical commonplace of anathematizing gold? You are mistaken.

In the thirteenth century gold meant progress. Until then nothing was known but the soil. Gold was the soil converted into money, the soil mobilized, exchangeable, transportable, divisible, subtilized, spiritualized, as it were.

So long as the soil was not represented by gold, man,

like the god Thermes, that landmark of the fields, had his feet imprisoned by the earth. Formerly the earth bore man, to-day man bears the earth.

But this gold had to be abstracted from its hiding-place, and it was hidden far otherwise than in the mines of Chile or Mexico. All the gold was in the possession of the churches and the Jews. To extract it from this double mine it needed more than a king; it required a pope.

And that is why Philippe le Bel, that great exploiter of gold, resolved to have a pope of his own. Benedict XI. dead, a conclave was held at Perugia; at this conclave the French cardinals were in the majority. Philippe le Bel cast his eyes upon the Archbishop of Bordeaux, Bertrand de Got, and to him he gave rendezvous in a forest near Saint-Jean d'Angely.

Bertrand de Got took heed not to miss that appointment.

The King and the Archbishop heard mass there, and at the moment when the Host was elevated, they bound themselves by this God they glorified to absolute secrecy. Bertrand de Got was still ignorant of the matter in question. Mass over, Philippe le Bel said:

"Archbishop, I have it in my power to make thee pope."

Bertrand de Got listened no longer, but cast himself at the King's feet, saying:

"What must I do to obtain this?"

"Accord me the six favors which I shall ask of thee," replied Philippe le Bel.

"It's for thee to command and for me to obey," said the future Pope.

The vow of servitude was taken.

The King raised Bertrand de Got, and, kissing him on the mouth, said:

"The six favors which I demand of thee are these: First, thou shalt reconcile me completely with the Church, and grant me pardon for the misdeed that I committed toward Boniface VIII. Second, thou shalt restore to me and mine the right of communion of which the Court of Rome deprived me. Third, thou shalt grant me the clergy's tithe in my kingdom for the next five years, to help defray the expenses of the war in Flanders. Fourth, thou shalt destroy and annul the memory of Pope Boniface VIII. Fifth, thou shalt bestow the dignity of cardinal upon Messires Jacopo and Pietro de Colonna. As to the sixth favor and promise, that I shall reserve to speak to thee thereof in its time and place."

Bertrand de Got swore to the promises and favors known, and to the promise and favor unknown. This last, which the King had not dared to mention in connection with the others, was the abolition of the Knights Templar. Besides the promises made on the Corpus Domini, Bertrand de Got gave as hostages his brother and two of his nephews. The King swore on his side that he should be elected pope.

This scene, set in the deep shadows of a crossroad in the forest, resembled rather an evocation between magician and demon than an agreement entered upon between king and pope.

Also the coronation of the King, which took place shortly afterward at Lyons, and which began the Church's captivity, seemed but little agreeable to God. Just as the royal procession was passing, a wall crowded with spectators fell, wounding the King and killing the Duc de Bretagne. The Pope was thrown to the ground, and his tiara rolled in the mud.

Bertrand de Got was elected pope under the name of Clement V.

Clement V. paid all that Bertrand de Got had promised. Philippe was absolved, Holy Communion restored to him and his, the purple again descended upon the shoulders of the Colonna, the Church was obliged to defray the expenses of the war in Flanders and Philippe de Valois's crusade against the Greek Empire. The memory of Pope Boniface VIII. was, if not destroyed and annulled, at least besmirched; the walls of the Temple were razed, and the Templars burned on the open space of the Pont Neuf.

All these edicts—they were no longer called bulls from

the moment the temporal power dictated them—all these edicts were dated at Avignon.

Philippe le Bel was the richest of all the kings of the French monarchy; he possessed an inexhaustible treasury, that is to say, his pope. He had purchased him, he used him, he put him to the press, and as cider flows from apples, so did this crushed pope bleed gold. The pontificate, struck by the Colonna in the person of Boniface VIII., abdicated the empire of the world in the person of Clement V.

We have related the advent of the king of blood and the pope of gold. We know how they ended. Jacques de Molay, from his funeral pyre, adjured them both to appear before God within the year. *Η το γερων σιβυλλια*, says Aristophanes. "Dying hoary heads possess the souls of sibyls."

Clement V. departed first. In a vision he saw his palace in flames. "From that moment," says Baluze, "he became sad and lasted but a short time."

Seven months later it was Philippe's turn. Some say that he was killed while hunting, overthrown by a wild boar. Dante is among their number. "He," said he, "who was seen near the Seine falsifying the coin of the realm shall die by the tusk of a boar." But Guillaume de Nangis makes the royal counterfeiter die of a death quite otherwise providential.

"Undermined by a malady unknown to the physicians, Philippe expired," said he, "to the great astonishment of everybody, without either his pulse or his urine revealing the cause of his malady or the imminence of the danger."

The King of Debauchery, the King of Uproar, Louis X., called the Hutin, succeeded his father, Philippe le Bel; John XXII. to Clement V.

Avignon then became in truth a second Rome. John XXII. and Clement VI. anointed her queen of luxury. The manners and customs of the times made her queen of debauchery and indulgence. In place of her towers, razed by Romain de Saint-Angelo, Hernandez de Héredi, grand master of Saint-Jean of Jerusalem, girdled her with a belt of walls. She possessed dissolute monks, who transformed the blessed precincts of her convents into places of debauchery and licentiousness; her beautiful courtesans tore the diamonds from the tiara to make of them bracelets and necklaces; and finally she possessed the echoes of Vaucluse, which wafted the melodious strains of Petrarch's songs to her.

This lasted until King Charles V., who was a virtuous and pious prince, having resolved to put an end to the scandal, sent the Maréchal de Boucicaut to drive out the anti-pope, Benedict XIII., from Avignon. But at sight of the soldiers of the King of France the latter remembered that before being pope under the name of Benedict XIII. he had been captain under the name of Pierre de Luna. For five months he defended himself, pointing his engines of war with his own hands from the heights of the château walls, engines otherwise far more murderous than his pontifical bolts. At last forced to flee, he left the city by a postern, after having ruined a hundred houses and killed four thousand Avignonese, and fled to Spain, where the King of Aragon offered him sanctuary.

There each morning, from the summit of a tower, assisted by the two priests who constituted his sacred college, he blessed the whole world, which was none the better for it, and excommunicated his enemies, who were none the worse for it. At last, feeling himself nigh to death, and fearing lest the schism die with him, he elected his two vicars cardinals on the condition that after his death one of the two would elect the other pope. The election was made. The new pope, supported by the cardinal who made him, continued the schism for awhile. Finally both entered into negotiations with Rome, made honorable amends, and returned to the fold of Holy Church, one with the title of Archbishop of Seville, the other as Archbishop of Toledo.

From this time until 1790 Avignon, widowed of her popes, was governed by legates and vice-legates. Seven sovereign pontiffs had resided within her walls some seven decades; she had seven hospitals, seven fraternities of penitents, seven monasteries, seven convents, seven parishes, and seven cemeteries.

To those who know Avignon there was at that epoch—there is yet—two cities within a city: the city of the priests, that is to say, the Roman city, and the city of the merchants, that is to say, the French city. The city of the priests, with its papal palace, its hundred churches, its innumerable bell-towers, ever ready to sound the tocsin of conflagration, the knell of slaughter. The town of the merchants, with its Rhone, its silk-workers, its crossroads, extending north, east, south and west, from Lyons to Marseilles, from Nimes to Turin. The French city, the accursed city, longing for a king, jealous of its liberties, shuddering beneath its yoke of vassalage, a vassalage of the priests with the clergy for its lord.

The clergy—not the pious clergy, tolerantly austere in the practice of its duty and charity, living in the world to console and edify it, without mingling in its joys and passions—but a clergy such as intrigue, cupidity, and ambition had made it; that is to say, the court abbés, rivalling the Roman priests, indolent, libertine, elegant, impudent, kings of fashion, autocrats of the salon, kissing the hands of those ladies of whom they boasted themselves the paramours, giving their hands to kiss to the women of the people whom they honored by making their mistresses.

Do you want a type of those abbés? Take the Abbé Maury. Proud as a duke, insolent as a lackey, the son of a shoemaker, more aristocratic than the son of a great lord.

One understands that these two categories of inhabitants, representing the one heresy, the other orthodoxy; the one the French party, the other the Roman party; the one the party of absolute monarchy, the other that of progressive constitutionalism, were not elements conducive to the peace and security of this ancient pontifical city. One understands, we say, that at the moment when the revolution broke out in Paris, and manifested itself by the taking of the Bastille, that the two parties, hot from the religious wars of Louis XIV., could not remain inert in the presence of each other.

We have said, Avignon, city of priests; let us add, city of hatreds. Nowhere better than in convent towns does one learn to hate. The heart of the child, everywhere else free from wicked passions, was born there full of paternal hatreds, inherited from father to son for the last eight hundred years, and after a life of hate, bequeathed in its turn, a diabolical heritage, to his children.

Therefore, at the first cry of liberty which rang through France the French town rose full of joy and hope. The moment had come at last for her to contest aloud that concession made by a young queen, a minor, in expiation of her sins, of a city and a province, and with it half a million souls. By what right had she sold these souls in æternum to the hardest and most exacting of all masters, the Roman Pontiff?

All France was hastening to assemble in the fraternal embrace of the Federation at the Champ de Mars. Was she not France? Her sons elected delegates to wait upon the legate and request him respectfully to leave the city, giving him twenty-four hours in which to do so.

During the night the papists amused themselves by hanging from a gibbet an effigy of straw wearing the tri-color cockade.

The course of the Rhone has been controlled, the Durance canalled, dikes have been built to restrain the fierce torrents, which, at the melting of the snows, pour in liquid avalanches from the summits of Mt. Ventoux. But this terrible flood, this living flood, this human torrent that rushed leaping through the rapid inclines of the streets of Avignon, once released, once flooding, not even God Himself has yet sought to stay it.

At sight of this manikin with the national colors, dancing at the end of a cord, the French city rose upon its very foundations with terrible cries of rage. Four papists, suspected of this sacrilege, two marquises, one burgher, and a workman, were torn from their homes and hung in the manikin's stead. This occurred the eleventh of June, 1790.

The whole French town wrote to the National Assembly that she gave herself to France, and with her the Rhone, her commerce, the Midi, and the half of Provence.

The National Assembly was in one of its reactionary moods. It did not wish to quarrel with the Pope; it dallied with the King, and the matter was adjourned. From that moment the rising became a revolt, and the Pope was free to do with Avignon what the court might have done with Paris, if the Assembly had delayed its proclamation of the Rights of Man. The Pope ordered the annulment of all that had occurred at the Comtat Venaissin, the re-establishment of the privileges of the nobles and clergy, and the reinstallation of the Inquisition in all its rigor. The pontifical decrees were affixed to the walls.

One man, one only, in broad daylight dared to go straight to the walls, in face of all, and tear down the decree. His name was Lescuyer. He was not a young man; and therefore it was not the fire of youth that impelled him. No, he was almost an old man who did not even belong to the province. He was a Frenchman from Picardy, ardent yet reflective, a former notary long since established at Avignon.

It was a crime that Roman Avignon remembered; a crime so great that the Virgin wept!

You see Avignon is another Italy. She must have her miracles, and if God will not perform them, so surely will some one be at hand to invent them. Still further, the miracle must be a miracle pertaining to the Virgin. La Madonna! the mind, the heart, the tongue of the Italians are full of these two words.

It was in the Church of the Cordeliers that this miracle occurred. The crowd rushed there. It was much that the Virgin should weep; but a rumor spread at the same time that brought the excitement to a climax. A large coffer, tightly sealed, had been carried through the city; this chest

had excited the curiosity of all Avignon. What did it contain? Two hours later it was no longer a coffer; but eighteen trunks had been seen going toward the Rhone. As for
their contents, a porter had revealed that: they contained
articles from the Mont-de-Piété that the French party were
taking with them into exile. Articles from the Mont-de-
Piété, that is to say, the spoils of the poor! The poorer
the city the richer its pawn-shops. Few could boast such
wealth as those of Avignon. It was no longer a factional
affair, it was a theft, an infamous theft. Whites and Reds
rushed to the Church of the Cordeliers, shouting that the
municipality must render them an accounting.

Lescuyer was the secretary of the municipality. His
name was thrown to the crowd, not for having torn down
the pontifical decrees—from that moment he would have
had defenders—but for having signed the order to the
keeper of the Mont-de-Piété permitting the removal of
the articles in pawn.

Four men were sent to seize Lescuyer and bring him
to the church. They found him in the street on his way to
the municipality. The four men fell upon him and dragged
him to the church with the most ferocious cries. Once
there, Lescuyer understood from the flaming eyes that met
his, from the clinched fists threatening him, the shrieks
demanding his death; Lescuyer understood that instead of
being in the house of the Lord he was in one of those circles of hell forgotten by Dante.

The only idea that occurred to him as to this hatred
against him was that he had caused it by tearing down the
pontifical decrees. He climbed into the pulpit, expecting
to convert it into a seat of justice, and in the voice of a man
who not only does not blame himself, but who is even ready
to repeat his action, he said:

"Brothers, I consider the revolution necessary; consequently I have done all in my power—"

The fanatics understood that if Lescuyer explained, Lescuyer was saved. That was not what they wanted. They

flung themselves upon him, tore him from the pulpit, and thrust him into the midst of this howling mob, who dragged him to the altar with that sort of terrible cry which combines the hiss of the serpent and the roar of the tiger, the murderous zou! zou! peculiar to the people of Avignon.

Lescuyer recognized that fatal cry; he endeavored to gain refuge at the foot of the altar. He found none; he fell there.

A laborer, armed with a stick, dealt him such a blow on the head that the stick broke in two pieces. Then the people hurled themselves upon the poor body, and, with that mixture of gayety and ferocity peculiar to Southern people, the men began to dance on his stomach, singing, while the women, that he might better expiate his blasphemies against the Pope, cut or rather scalloped his lips with their scissors.

And out of the midst of this frightful group came a cry, or rather a groan; this death groan said: "In the name of Heaven! in the name of the Virgin! in the name of humanity! kill me at once."

This cry was heard, and by common consent the assassins stood aside. They left the unfortunate man bleeding, disfigured, mangled, to taste of his death agony.

This lasted five hours, during which, amid shouts of laughter, insults, and jeers from the crowd, this poor body lay palpitating upon the steps of the altar. That is how they kill at Avignon.

Stay! there is yet another way. A man of the French party conceived the idea of going to the Mont-de-Piété for information. Everything was in order there, not a fork or a spoon had been removed. It was therefore not as an accomplice of theft that Lescuyer had just been so cruelly murdered, it was for being a patriot.

There was at that time in Avignon a man who controlled the populace. All these terrible leaders of the Midi have acquired such fatal celebrity that it suffices to name them for every one, even the least educated, to know them.

This man was Jourdan. Braggart and liar, he had made the common people believe that it was he who had cut off the head of the governor of the Bastille. So they called him Jourdan, Coupe-tête. That was not his real name, which was Mathieu Jouve. Neither was he a Provencal; he came from Puy-en-Velay. He had formerly been a muleteer on those rugged heights which surround his native town; then a soldier without going to war—war had perhaps made him more human; after that he had kept a drink-shop in Paris. In Avignon he had been a vendor of madder.

He collected three hundred men, carried the gates of the town, left half of his troop to guard them, and with the remainder marched upon the Church of the Cordeliers, preceded by two pieces of cannon. These he stationed in front of the church and fired them into it at random. The assassins fled like a flock of frightened birds, leaving some few dead upon the church steps. Jourdan and his men trampled over the bodies and entered the holy precincts. No one was there but the Virgin, and the wretched Lescuyer, still breathing. Jourdan and his comrades took good care not to despatch Lescuyer; his death agony was a supreme means of exciting the mob. They picked up this remnant of a sentient being, three-quarters dead, and carried it along, bleeding, quivering, gasping, with them.

Every one fled from the sight, closing doors and windows. At the end of an hour, Jourdan and his three hundred men were masters of the town.

Lescuyer was dead, but what of that; they no longer needed his agony. Jourdan profited by the terror he had inspired to arrest or have arrested eighty people, murderers, or so-called murderers of Lescuyer. Thirty, perhaps, had never even set foot within the church. But when one has such a good opportunity to be rid of one's enemies, one must profit by it; good opportunities are rare.

These eighty people were huddled into the Trouillas Tower. Historically it is known as the Tower de la Glacière; but why change this name of the Trouillas Tower? The name is unclean and harmonizes well with the unclean deed which was now to be perpetrated there.

It had been the scene of the inquisitorial tortures. One can still see on the walls the greasy soot which rose from the smoke of the funeral pyre where human bodies were consumed. They still show you to-day the instruments of torture which they have carefully preserved—the caldron, the oven, the wooden horse, the chains, the dungeons, and even the rotten bones. Nothing is wanting.

It was in this tower, built by Clement V., that they now confined the eighty prisoners. These eighty men, once arrested and locked up in the Trouillas Tower, became most embarrassing. Who was to judge them? There were no legally constituted courts except those of the Pope. Could they kill these unfortunates as they had killed Lescuyer?

We have said that a third, perhaps half of them, had not only taken no part in the murder, but had not even set foot in the church. How should they kill them? The killing must be placed upon the basis of reprisals. But the killing of these eighty people required a certain number of executioners.

A species of tribunal was improvised by Jourdan and held session in one of the law-courts. It had a clerk named Raphel; a president, half Italian, half French; an orator in the popular dialect named Barbe Savournin de la Roua, and three or four other poor devils, a baker, a pork butcher—their names are lost in the multitude of events.

These were the men who cried: "We must kill all! If one only escapes he will be a witness against us."

But, as we have said, executioners were wanting. There were barely twenty men at hand in the courtyard, all belonging to the petty tradesfolk of Avignon—a barber, a shoemaker, a cobbler, a mason, and an upholsterer—all insufficiently armed at random, the one with a sabre, the other with a bayonet, a third with an iron bar, and a fourth with a bit of wood hardened by fire. All of these people were chilled by a fine October rain. It would be difficult to turn them into assassins.

Pooh! Is anything too difficult for the devil?

There comes an hour in such crises when God seems to abandon the earth. Then the devil's chance comes.

The devil in person entered this cold, muddy courtyard. Assuming the features, form and face of an apothecary of the neighborhood named Mendes, he prepared a table lighted by two lanterns, on which he placed glasses, jugs, pitchers and bottles.

What infernal beverage did these mysterious and curiously formed receptacles contain? No one ever knew, but the result is well known. All those who drank that diabolical liquor were suddenly seized with a feverish rage, a lust of blood and murder. From that moment it was only necessary to show them the door; they hurtled madly into the dungeon.

The massacre lasted all night; all night the cries, the sobs, the groans of the dying sounded through the darkness. All were killed, all slaughtered, men and women. It was long in doing; the killers, we have said, were drunk and poorly armed. But they succeeded.

Among these butchers was a child remarked for his bestial cruelty, his immoderate thirst for blood. It was Lescuyer's son. He killed and then killed again; he boasted of having with his childish hand alone killed ten men and four women.

"It's all right! I can kill as I like," said he. "I am not yet fifteen, so they can do nothing to me for it."

As the killing progressed, they threw their victims, the living, dead and wounded, into the Trouillas Tower, some sixty feet, down into the pit. The men were thrown in first, and the women later. The assassins wanted time to violate the bodies of those who were young and pretty. At nine in the morning, after twelve hours of massacre, a voice was still heard crying from the depths of the sepulchre:

"For pity's sake, come kill me! I cannot die."

A man, the armorer Bouffier, bent over the pit and looked down. The others did not dare.

"Who was that crying?" they asked.

"That was Lami," replied Bouffier. Then, when he had returned, they asked him:

"Well, what did you see at the bottom?"

"A queer marmalade," said he. "Men and women, priests and pretty girls, all helter-skelter. It's enough to make one die of laughter."

"Decidedly man is a vile creature," said the Count of Monte-Cristo to M. de Villefort.

Well, it is in this town, still reeking with blood, still warm, still stirred by these last massacres, that we now introduce two of the principal personages of our story.

CHAPTER I

A TABLE D'HÔTE

THE 9th of October, 1799, on a beautiful day of that meridional autumn which ripens the oranges of Hyères and the grapes of Saint-Peray, at the two extremities of Provence, a travelling chaise, drawn by three post horses, galloped at full speed over the bridge that crosses the Durance, between Cavailhon and Château-Renard, on its way to Avignon, the ancient papal city which a decree, issued the 25th of May, 1791, eight years earlier, had reunited to France—a reunion confirmed by the treaty signed in 1797, at Tolentino, between General Bonaparte and Pope Pius VI.

The carriage entered by the gate of Aix and, without slackening speed, traversed the entire length of the town, with its narrow, winding streets, built to ward off both wind and sun, and halted at fifty paces from the Porte d'Oulle, at the Hotel du Palais-Egalité, which they were again beginning to quietly rename the Hotel du Palais-Royal, a name which it bore formerly and still bears to-day.

These few insignificant words about the name of the inn, before which halted the post-chaise which we had in view, indicate sufficiently well the state of France under the government of the Thermidorian reaction, called the Directory.

After the revolutionary struggle which had occurred between the 14th of July, 1789, and the 9th Thermidor, 1794; after the days of the 5th and 6th of October, of the 21st of June, of the 10th of August, of the 2d and 3d of September, of the 21st of May, of the 29th Thermidor and the 1st Prairial; after seeing fall the heads of the King and his judges, and the Queen and her accusers, of the Girondins and the Cordeliers, the Moderates and the Jacobins, France experienced that most frightful and most nauseous of all lassitudes, the lassitude of blood!

She had therefore returned, if not to a need of monarchy, at least to a desire for a stable government, in which she might place her confidence, upon which she might lean, which would act for her, and which would permit her some repose while it acted.

In the stead of this vaguely desired government, the country obtained the feeble and irresolute Directory, composed for the moment of the voluptuous Barrès, the intriguing Sièyes, the brave Moulins, the insignificant Roger Ducos, and the honest but somewhat too ingenuous Gohier. The result was a mediocre dignity before the world at large and a very questionable tranquillity at home.

It is true that at the moment of which we write our armies, so glorious during those epic campaigns of 1796 and 1797, thrown back for a time upon France by the incapacity of Scherer at Verona and Cassano, and by the defeat and death of Joubert at Novi, were beginning to resume the offensive. Moreau had defeated Souvarow at Bassignano; Brune had defeated the Duke of York and General Hermann at Bergen; Masséna had annihilated the Austro-Russians at Zurich; Korsakof had escaped only with the greatest difficulty; the Austrian, Hotz, with three other generals, were killed, and five made prisoners. Masséna saved France at Zurich, as Villars, ninety years earlier, had saved it at Denain.

But in the interior, matters were not in so promising a state, and the government of the Directory was, it must be confessed, much embarrassed between the war in the Vendée and the brigandages of the Midi, to which, according to custom, the population of Avignon were far from remaining strangers.

Beyond doubt the two travellers who descended from the carriage at the door of the Hotel du Palais-Royal had reason to fear the state of mind in which the always excitable papal town might be at that time; for just before reaching Orgon, at a spot where three crossroads stretched out before the traveller—one leading to Nimes, the second to Carpentras, the third to Avignon—the postilion had stopped his horses, and, turning round, asked:

"Will the citizens go by way of Avignon or Carpentras?"

"Which of the two roads is the shorter?" asked the elder of the two travellers in a harsh, strident voice. Though visibly the elder, he was scarcely thirty years of age.

"Oh, the road to Avignon, citizen, by a good four miles at least."

"Then," he had replied, "go by way of Avignon."

And the carriage had started again at a gallop, which proclaimed that the citizen travellers, as the postilion called them, although the title of Monsieur was beginning to reappear in conversation, paid a fee of at least thirty sous.

The same desire to lose no time manifested itself at the hotel entrance. There, as on the road, it was the elder of the two travellers who spoke. He asked if they could dine at once, and the way this demand was made indicated that he was ready to overlook many gastronomical exigencies provided that the repast in question be promptly served.

"Citizens," replied the landlord, who, at the sound of

carriage wheels, hastened, napkin in hand, to greet the travellers, "you will be promptly and comfortably served in your room; but if you will permit me to advise—" He hesitated.

"Oh, go on! go on!" said the younger of the travellers, speaking for the first time.

"Well, it would be that you dine at the table d'hôte, like the traveller for whom this coach, already harnessed, is waiting. The dinner is excellent and all served."

The host at the same time indicated a comfortably appointed carriage, to which were harnessed two horses who were pawing the ground, while the postilion sought patience in the bottle of Cahors wine he was emptying near the window-ledge. The first movement of him to whom this proposal was made was negative; nevertheless, after a second's reflection, the elder of the two travellers, as if he had reconsidered his first decision, made an interrogative sign to his companion, who replied with a look which signified, "You know that I am at your orders."

"Very well, so be it," said the other, "we will dine at the table d'hôte." Then, turning to the postilion, who, hat in hand, awaited his order, he added, "Let the horses be ready in a half hour, at the latest."

And the landlord pointing out the way, they both entered the dining-room, the elder of the two walking first, the other following him.

Every one knows the impression generally produced at a table d'hôte by new-comers. All eyes were bent upon them and the conversation, which seemed to be quite animated, stopped.

The guests consisted of the frequenters of the hotel, the traveller whose carriage was waiting harnessed at the door, a wine merchant from Bordeaux, sojourning temporarily at Avignon for reasons we shall shortly relate, and a certain number of travellers going from Marseilles to Lyons by diligence.

The new arrivals greeted the company with a slight inclination of the head, and sat down at the extreme end of the table, thereby isolating themselves from the other guests by three or four empty places. This seemingly aristocratic reserve redoubled the curiosity of which they were the object; moreover, they were obviously people of unquestionable distinction, although their garments were simple in the extreme. Both wore hightop boots and breeches, long-tailed coats, travelling overcoats and broad-brimmed hats, the usual costume of the young men of that day. But that which distinguished them from the fashionables of Paris, and even of the provinces, was their long straight hair, and their black stocks buckled round the neck, military fashion. The Muscadins—that was the name then given to young dandies—the Muscadins wore dogs' ears puffing at the temples, the rest of the hair combed up tightly in a bag at the back, and an immense cravat with long floating ends, in which the chin was completely buried. Some had even extended this reaction to powder.

As to the personality of the two young men, they presented two diametrically opposite types.

The elder of the two, he who, as we have already remarked, had taken the initiative several times, and whose voice, even in its most familiar intonations, denoted the habit of command, was about thirty years of age. His black hair was parted in the middle, falling straight from his temples to his shoulders. He had the swarthy skin of a man who has travelled long in southern climes, thin lips, a straight nose, white teeth, and those hawk-like eyes which Dante gives to Cæsar. He was short rather than tall, his hand was delicate, his foot slender and elegant. His manner betrayed a certain awkwardness, suggesting that he was at the moment wearing a costume to which he was not accustomed, and when he spoke, his hearers, had they been beside the Loire instead of the Rhone, would have detected a certain Italian accent in his pronunciation.

His companion seemed to be some three or four years younger than he. He was a handsome young man with a rosy complexion, blond hair and light blue eyes, a straight, firm nose and prominent but almost beardless chin. He was perhaps a couple of inches taller than his companion, and though his figure was somewhat above medium height, he was so well proportioned, so admirably free in his movements, that he was evidently if not extraordinarily strong, at least uncommonly agile and dexterous. Although attired in the same manner and apparently on a footing of equality, he evinced remarkable deference to the dark young man, which, as it could not result from age, was doubtless caused by some inferiority of position. Moreover, he called his companion citizen, while the other addressed him as Roland.

These remarks which we make to initiate the reader more profoundly into our story, were probably not made as extensively by the guests at the table d'hôte; for after bestowing a few seconds of attention upon the new-comers, they turned their eyes away, and the conversation, interrupted for an instant, was resumed. It must be confessed that it concerned a matter most interesting to the travellers—that of the stoppage of a diligence bearing a sum of sixty thousand francs belonging to the government. The affair had occurred the day before on the road from Marseilles to Avignon between Lambesc and Pont-Royal.

At the first words referring to this event, the two young men listened with unmistakable interest. It had taken place on the same road which they had just followed, and the narrator, the wine merchant of Bordeaux, had been one of the principal actors in the scene on the highroad. Those who seemed the most curious to hear the details were the travellers in the diligence which had just arrived and was soon to depart. The other guests, who belonged to the locality, seemed sufficiently conversant with such catastrophes to furnish the details themselves instead of listening to them.

"So, citizen," said a stout gentleman against whom a tall woman, very thin and haggard, was crowding in her terror. "You say that the robbery took place on the very road by which we have just come?"

"Yes, citizen, between Lambesc and Pont-Royal. Did you notice the spot where the road ascends between two high banks? There are a great many rocks there."

"Yes, yes, my friend," said the wife, pressing her husband's arm, "I noticed it; I even said, as you must remember, 'Here is a bad place; I would rather pass here by day than at night.'"

"Oh! madame," said a young man whose voice affected to slur his r's after the fashion of the day, and who probably assumed to lead the conversation at the table d'hôte, on ordinary occasions, "you know the Companions of Jehu know no day or night."

"What! citizen," asked the lady still more alarmed, "were you attacked in broad daylight?"

"In broad daylight, citizeness, at ten o'clock in the morning."

"And how many were there?" asked the stout gentleman.

"Four, citizen."

"Ambushed beside the road?"

"No; they were on horseback, armed to the teeth and masked."

"That's their custom," said the young frequenter of the table d'hôte, "and they said, did they not: 'Do not defend yourself, we will not harm you. We only want the government money.'"

"Word for word, citizen."

"Then," continued this well-informed young man, "two dismounted from their horses, flinging their bridles to their comrades, and commanded the conductor to deliver up the money."

"Citizen," said the stout man astonished, "you describe the thing as if you had seen it."

"Monsieur was there, perhaps," said one of the travellers, half in jest, half in earnest.

"I do not know, citizen, whether in saying that you intend a rudeness," carelessly observed the young man who had so pertinently and obligingly come to the narrator's assistance, "but my political opinions are such that I do not consider your suspicion an insult. Had I had the misfortune to be among those attacked, or the honor to be one of those who made the attack, I should admit it as frankly in the one case as in the other. But yesterday at ten o'clock, at precisely the moment when the diligence was stopped, twelve miles from here, I was breakfasting quietly in this very seat. And, by-the-bye, with the two citizens who now do me the honor to sit beside me."

"And," asked the younger of the two travellers who had lately joined the table, whom his companion called Roland, "how many men were you in the diligence?"

"Let me think; we were—yes, that's it—we were seven men and three women."

"Seven men, not including the conductor?" repeated Roland.

"Yes."

"And you seven men allowed yourselves to be plundered by four brigands? I congratulate you, gentlemen."

"We knew with whom we had to deal," replied the wine merchant, "and we took good care not to defend ourselves."

"What! with whom you had to deal?" retorted the young man. "Why, it seems to me, with thieves and bandits."

"Not at all. They gave their names."

"They gave their names?"

"They said, 'Gentlemen, it is useless to defend yourselves; ladies, do not be alarmed, we are not bandits, we are Companions of Jehu.'"

"Yes," said the young man of the table d'hôte, "they warned you that there might be no misunderstanding. That's their way."

"Ah, indeed!" exclaimed Roland; "and who is this Jehu who has such polite companions? Is he their captain?"

"Sir," said a man whose dress betrayed somewhat the secularized priest, and who seemed also to be, not only an habitual guest at the table d'hôte, but also an initiate into the mysteries of the honorable company whose merits were then under discussion, "if you were better versed than you seem to be in the Holy Scriptures, you would know that this Jehu died something like two thousand six hundred years ago, and that consequently he cannot at the present time stop coaches on the highways."

"Monsieur l'Abbé," replied Roland, who had recognized an ecclesiastic, "as, in spite of the sharp tone in which you speak, you seem a man of learning, permit a poor ignoramus to ask you a few details about this Jehu, dead these two thousand six hundred years, who, nevertheless, is honored by followers bearing his name."

"Jehu!" replied the churchman, in the same sour tone, "was a King of Israel anointed by Elisha, on condition that he punish the crimes of the house of Ahab and Jezebel, and put to death the priests of Baal."

"Monsieur l'Abbé," replied the young man laughing, "I thank you for the explanation. I don't doubt it is correct, and, above all, very learned. But I must admit it doesn't tell me much."

"What, citizen!" exclaimed the abbé, "don't you understand that Jehu is his Majesty Louis XVIII., anointed on condition that he punish the crimes of the Revolution and put to death all the priests of Baal; that is to say, all those who had taken any part whatsoever in the abominable state of things which, for these last seven years, has been called the republic?"

"Yes, indeed!" exclaimed the young man; "of course I understand. But among those whom the Companions of Jehu are appointed to fight, do you reckon the brave soldiers who have repulsed the enemy along the frontiers of France, and the illustrious generals who have commanded the armies of the Tyrol, the Sambre-and-Meuse, and of Italy?"

"Why, beyond doubt, those foremost and before all."

The young man's eyes flashed lightning; his nostrils quivered and his lips tightened. He rose from his chair, but his comrade touched his coat and forced him to sit down again, while with a single glance he silenced him. Then he who had thus given proof of his power, speaking for the first time, addressed the young man of the table d'hôte.

"Citizen, excuse two travellers who are just arrived from the end of the earth, from America, or India as it were. Absent from France these last two years, we are completely ignorant of all that has occurred here, and most desirous to obtain information."

"Why, as to that," replied the young man, to whom these words were addressed, "that is but fair, citizen. Question us and we will answer you."

"Well," continued the dark young man with the eagle eye, the straight black hair, and the granite complexion, "now that I know who Jehu is, and to what end his company was instituted, I should like to know what his companions do with the money they take."

"Oh! that is very simple, citizen. You know there is much talk of the restoration of the Bourbon monarchy?"

"No, I did not know it," replied the dark young man, in a tone which he vainly strove to render artless; "I am but just arrived, as I told you, from the end of the earth."

"What! you did not know that? Well, six months hence it will be an accomplished fact."

"Really!"

"I have the honor to tell you so, citizen."

The two soldier-like young men exchanged a glance and a smile, though the young blond one was apparently chafing under the weight of his extreme impatience.

Their informant continued: "Lyons is the headquarters of the conspiracy, if one can call conspiracy a plot which was organized openly. 'The provisional government' would be a more suitable word."

"Well, then, citizen," said the dark young man with a politeness not wholly exempt from satire, "let us call it 'provisional government.'"

"This provisional government has its staff and its armies."

"Bah! its staff perhaps—but its armies—"

"Its armies, I repeat."

"Where are they?"

"One is being organized in the mountains of Auvergne, under the orders of M. de Chardon; another in the Jura Mountains, under M. Teyssonnet; and, finally, a third is operating most successfully at this time, in the Vendée, under the orders of Escarboville, Achille Leblond and Cadoudal."

"Truly, citizen, you render me a real service in telling me this. I thought the Bourbons completely resigned to their exile. I supposed the police so organized as to suppress both provisional royalist committees in the large towns and bandits on the highways. In fact, I believed the Vendée had been completely pacificated by Hoche."

The young man to whom this reply was addressed burst out laughing.

"Why, where do you come from?" he exclaimed.

"I told you, citizen, from the end of the earth."

"So it seems." Then he continued: "You understand, the Bourbons are not rich, the émigrés whose property was confiscated are ruined. It is impossible to organize two armies and maintain a third without money. The royalists faced an embarrassing problem; the republic alone could pay for its enemies' troops and, it being improbable that she would do so of her own volition, the shady negotiation was abandoned, and it was adjudged quicker to take the money without permission than to ask her for it."

"Ah! I understand at last."

"That's very fortunate."

"Companions of Jehu then are the intermediaries between the Republic and the Counter-Revolution, the tax-collectors of the royalist generals?"

"Yes. It is not robbery, but a military operation, rather a feat of arms like any other. So there you are, citizen, and now you are as well informed on this point as ourselves."

"But," timidly hazarded the wine merchant of Bordeaux, "if the Companions of Jehu—observe that I say nothing against them—want the government money—"

"The government money, no other. Individual plunder on their part is unheard of."

"How does it happen, then, that yesterday, in addition to the government money, they carried off two hundred louis of mine?"

"My dear sir," replied the young man of the table d'hôte, "I have already told you that there is some mistake. As surely as my name is Alfred de Barjols, this money will be returned to you some day."

The wine merchant heaved a sigh and shook his head, as if, in spite of that assurance, he still retained some doubts. But at this moment, as if the promise given by the young noble, who had just revealed his social position by telling his name, had stirred the delicacy of those whom he thus guaranteed, a horse stopped at the entrance, steps were heard in the corridor, the dining-room door opened, and a masked man, armed to the teeth, appeared on the threshold.

"Gentlemen," said he, in the profound silence occasioned by his apparition, "is there a traveller here named Jean Picot, who was in the diligence that was held up yesterday between Lambesc and Pont-Royal?"

"Yes," said the wine merchant, amazed.

"Are you he?" asked the masked man.

"I am."

"Was anything taken from you?"

"Oh, yes, two hundred louis, which I had intrusted to the conductor."

"And I may add," said the young noble, "that the gentleman was speaking of it at this very moment. He looked upon it as lost."

"The gentleman was wrong," said the masked unknown, "we war upon the government and not against individuals. We are partisans and not robbers. Here are your two hundred louis, sir, and if a similar mistake should occur in the future, claim your loss, mentioning the name of Morgan.''

So saying, the masked individual deposited a bag of gold beside the wine merchant, bowed courteously to the other guests, and went out, leaving some terrified and others bewildered by such daring.

CHAPTER II

AN ITALIAN PROVERB

ALTHOUGH the two sentiments which we have just indicated were the dominant ones, they did not manifest themselves to an equal degree in all present. The shades were graduated according to the sex, age, character, we may almost say, the social positions of the hearers. The wine merchant, Jean Picot, the principal personage in the late event, recognizing at first sight by his dress, weapons, mask, one of the men who had stopped the coach on the preceding day, was at first sight stupefied, then little by little, as he grasped the purport of this mysterious brigand's visit to him, he had passed from stupefaction to joy, through the intermediate phases separating these two emotions. His bag of gold was beside him, yet he seemingly dared not touch it; perhaps he feared that the instant his hand went forth toward it, it would melt like the dream-gold which vanishes during that period of progressive lucidity which separates profound slumber from thorough awakening.

The stout gentleman of the diligence and his wife had displayed, like their travelling companions, the most absolute and complete terror. Seated to the left of Jean Picot, when the bandit approached the wine merchant, the husband, in the vain hope of maintaining a respectable distance between himself and the Companion of Jehu, pushed his chair back against that of his wife, who, yielding to the pressure, in turn endeavored to push back hers. But as the next chair was occupied by citizen Alfred de Barjols, who had no reason to fear these men whom he had just praised so highly, the chair of the stout man's wife encountered an obstacle in the immovability of the young noble; so, as at Marengo, eight or nine months later, when the general in command judged it time to resume the offensive, the retrograde movement was arrested.

As for him—we are speaking of the citizen Alfred de Barjols—his attitude, like that of the abbé who had given the Biblical explanation about Jehu, King of Israel, and his mission from Elisha, his attitude, we say, was that of a man who not only experiences no fear, but who even expects the event in question, however unexpected it may be. His lips wore a smile as he watched the masked man, and had the guests not been so preoccupied with the two principal actors in this scene, they might have remarked the almost imperceptible sign exchanged between the eyes of the bandit and the young noble, and transmitted instantly by the latter to the abbé.

The two travellers whom we introduced to the table d'hôte, and who as we have said sat apart at the end of the table, preserved an attitude conformable to their respective characters. The younger of the two had instinctively put his hand to his side, as if to seek an absent weapon, and had risen with a spring, as if to rush at the masked man's throat, in which purpose he had certainly not failed had he been alone; but the elder, who seemed to possess not only the habit but the right of command, contented himself by regrasping his coat, and saying, in an imperious, almost harsh tone: "Sit down, Roland!" And the young man had resumed his seat.

But one of the guests had remained, in appearance at least, the most impassible during this scene. He was a man between thirty-three and thirty-four years of age, with blond hair, red beard, a calm, handsome face, with large blue eyes, a fair skin, refined and intelligent lips, and very tall, whose foreign accent betrayed one born in that island of which the government was at that time waging bitter war against France. As far as could be judged by the few words which had escaped him, he spoke the French language with rare purity, despite the accent we have just mentioned. At the first word he uttered, in which that English accent revealed itself, the elder of the two travellers started. Turning to his companion, he asked with a glance, to which the other seemed accustomed, how it was that an Englishman should be in France when the uncompromising war between the two nations had naturally exiled all Englishmen from France, as it had all Frenchmen from England. No doubt the explanation seemed impossible to Roland, for he had replied with his eyes, and a shrug of the shoulders: "I find it quite as extraordinary as you; but if you, mathematician as you are, can't solve the problem, don't ask me!"

It was evident to the two young men that the fair man with the Anglo-Saxon accent was the traveller whose comfortable carriage awaited him harnessed in the courtyard, and that this traveller hailed from London, or, at least, from some part of Great Britain.

As to his remarks, they, as we have stated, were infrequent, so laconic, in reality, that they were mere exclamations rather than speech. But each time an explanation had been asked concerning the state of France, the Englishman openly drew out a note-book and requested those about him, the wine merchant, the abbé, or the young noble to repeat their remarks; to which each had complied with an amiability equal to the courteous tone of the request. He had noted down the most important, extraordinary and picturesque features of the robbery of the diligence, the state of Vendée, and the details about the Companions of Jehu, thanking each informant by voice and gesture with the stiffness peculiar to our insular cousins, replacing his note-book enriched each time by a new item in a side pocket of his overcoat.

Finally, like a spectator enjoying an unexpected scene, he had given a cry of satisfaction at sight of the masked man, had listened with all his ears, gazed with all his eyes, not losing him from sight until the door closed behind him. Then drawing his note-book hastily from his pocket—

"Ah, sir," he said to his neighbor, who was no other than ·the abbé, "will you be so kind, should my memory fail me, as to repeat what that gentleman who has just gone out said?"

He began to write immediately, and the abbé's memory agreeing with his, he had the satisfaction of transcribing literally and verbatim the speech made by the Companion of Jehu to citizen Jean Picot. Then, this conversation written down, he exclaimed with an accent that lent a singular stamp of originality to his words:

"Of a truth! it is only in France that such things can happen; France is the most curious country in the world. I am delighted, gentlemen, to travel in France and become acquainted with Frenchmen."

The last sentence was said with such courtesy that nothing remained save to thank the speaker from whose serious mouth it issued, though he was a descendant of the conquerors of Crecy, Poitiers and Agincourt. It was the younger of the two travellers who acknowledged this politeness in that heedless and rather caustic manner which seemed habitual to him.

" 'Pon my word! I am exactly like you, my lord—I say my lord, because I presume you are English."

"Yes, sir," replied the gentleman, "I have that honor."

"Well! as I was saying," continued the young man, "I am delighted to travel in France and see what I am seeing. One must live under the government of citizens Gohier, Moulins, Roger Ducos, Sièyes and Barras to witness such roguery. I dare wager than when the tale is told, fifty years hence, of the highwayman who rode into a city of thirty thousand inhabitants in broad day, masked and armed with two pistols and a sword at his belt, to return the two hundred louis which he had stolen the day previous to the honest merchant who was then deploring their loss, and when it is added that this occurred at a table d'hôte where twenty or twenty-five people were seated, and that this model bandit was allowed to depart without one of those twenty or twenty-five people daring to molest him; I dare wager, I repeat, that whoever has the audacity to tell the story will be branded as an infamous liar.''

And the young man, throwing himself back in his chair, burst into laughter, so aggressive, so nervous, that every one gazed at him in wonderment, while his companion's eyes expressed an almost paternal anxiety.

"Sir," said citizen Alfred de Barjols, who, moved like the others by this singular outburst, more sad, or rather dolorous, than gay, had waited for its last echo to subside. "Sir, permit me to point out to you that the man whom you have just seen is not a highwayman."

"Bah! Frankly, what is he then?"

"He is in all probability a young man of as good a family as yours or mine."

"Count Horn, whom the Regent ordered broken on the wheel at the Place de Grève, was also a man of good family, and the proof is that all the nobility of Paris sent their carriages to his execution."

"Count Horn, if I remember rightly, murdered a Jew to steal a note of hand which he was unable to meet. No one would dare assert that a Companion of Jehu had ever so much as harmed the hair of an infant."

"Well, be it so. We will admit that the Company was founded upon a philanthropic basis, to re-establish the balance of fortunes, redress the whims of chance and reform the abuses of society. Though he may be a robber, after the fashion of Karl Moor, your friend Morgan—was it not Morgan that this honest citizen called himself?"

"Yes," said the Englishman.

"Well, your friend Morgan is none the less a thief."

Citizen Alfred de Barjols turned very pale.

"Citizen Morgan is not my friend," replied the young aristocrat; "but if he were I should feel honored by his friendship."

"No doubt," replied Roland, laughing. "As Voltaire says: 'The friendship of a great man is a blessing from the gods.'"

"Roland, Roland!" observed his comrade in a low tone.

"Oh! general," replied the latter, letting his companion's rank escape him, perhaps intentionally, "I implore you, let me continue this discussion, which interests me in the highest degree."

His friend shrugged his shoulders.

"But, citizen," continued the young man with strange persistence, "I stand in need of correction. I left France two years ago, and during my absence so many things have changed, such as dress, morals, and accents, that even the language may have changed also. In the language of the day in France what do you call stopping coaches and taking the money which they contain?"

"Sir," said the young noble, in the tone of a man determined to sustain his argument to its end, "I call that war. Here is your companion whom you have just called general; he as a military man will tell you that, apart from the pleasure of killing and being killed, the generals of all ages have never done anything else than what the citizen Morgan is doing?"

"What!" exclaimed the young man, whose eyes flashed fire. "You dare to compare—"

"Permit the gentleman to develop his theory, Roland," said the dark traveller, whose eyes, unlike those of his companion, which dilated as they flamed, were veiled by long black lashes, thus concealing all that was passing in his mind.

"Ah!" said the young man in his curt tone, "you see that you, yourself, are becoming interested in the discussion." Then, turning to the young noble, whom he seemed to have selected for his antagonist, he said: "Continue, sir, continue; the general permits it."

The young noble flushed as visibly as he had paled a moment before. Between clinched teeth, his elbow on the table, his chin on his clinched hand, as if to draw as close to his adversary as possible, he said with a Provençal accent, which grew more pronounced as the discussion waxed hotter: "Since *the general* permits"—emphasizing the two words—"I shall have the honor to tell him and you, too, citizen, that I believe I have read in Plutarch that Alexander the Great, when he started for India, took with him but eighteen or twenty talents in gold, something like one hundred or one hundred and twenty thousand francs. Now, do you suppose that with these eighteen or twenty talents alone he fed his army, won the battle of Granicus, subdued Asia Minor, conquered Tyre, Gaza, Syria and Egypt, built Alexandria, penetrated to Lybia, had himself declared Son of Jupiter by the oracle of Ammon, penetrated as far as the Hyphases, and, when his soldiers refused to follow him further, returned to Babylon, where he surpassed in luxury, debauchery and self-indulgence the most debauched and voluptuous of the kings of Asia? Did Macedonia furnish his supplies? Do you believe that King Philip, most indigent of the kings of poverty-stricken Greece, honored the drafts his son drew upon him? Not so. Alexander did as citizen Morgan is doing; only, instead of stopping the coaches on the highroads, he pillaged cities, held kings for ransom, levied contributions from the conquered countries. Let us turn to Hannibal. You know how he left Carthage, don't you? He did not have even the eighteen or twenty talents of his predecessor; and as he needed money, he seized and sacked the city of Saguntum in the midst of peace, in defiance of the fealty of treaties. After that he was rich and could begin his campaign. Forgive me if this time I no longer quote Plutarch, but Cornelius Nepos. I will spare you the details of his descent from the Pyrenees, how he crossed the Alps and the three battles which he won, seizing each time the treasures of the vanquished, and turn to the five or six years he spent in Campania. Do you be-

lieve that he and his army paid the Capuans for their sub-
sistence, and that the bankers of Carthage, with whom he
had quarrelled, supplied him with funds? No; war fed
war—the Morgan system, citizen. Let us pass on to
Cæsar. Ah, Cæsar! That's another story. He left for
Spain with some thirty millions of debt, and returned with
practically the same. He started for Gaul, where he spent
ten years with our ancestors. During these ten years he
sent over one hundred millions to Rome, repassed the Alps,
crossed the Rubicon, marched straight to the Capitol, forced
the gates of the Temple of Saturn, where the treasury was,
seized sufficient for his private needs—and not for those of
the Republic—three thousand pounds of gold in ingots;
and died (he whom creditors twenty years earlier refused
to allow to leave his little house in the Suburra) leaving
two or three thousand sesterces per head to the citizens, ten
or twelve millions to Calpurnia, and thirty or forty millions
to Octavius; always the Morgan system, save that Morgan,
I am sure, would die sooner than subvert to his personal
needs either the silver of the Gauls or the gold of the capital. Now let us spring over eighteen centuries and come
to the General Buonaparté.'' And the young aristocrat,
after the fashion of the enemies of the Conqueror of Italy,
affected to emphasize the *u*, which Bonaparte had elimi-
nated from his name, and the *e*, from which he had removed
the accent.

This affectation seemed to irritate Roland intensely. He
made a movement as if to spring forward, but his companion
stopped him.

"Let be," said he, "let be, Roland. I am quite sure that
citizen Barjols will not say the General Buonaparté, as he
calls him, is a thief."

"No, I will not say it; but there is an Italian proverb
which says it for me."

"What is the proverb?" demanded the general in his
companion's stead, fixing his calm, limpid eye upon the
young noble.

"I give it in all its simplicity: 'Francesi non sono tutti ladroni, ma buona parte'; which means: 'All Frenchmen are not thieves, but—'"

"—A good part are?" concluded Roland.

"Yes, 'Buonaparté,'" replied Alfred de Barjols.

Scarcely had these insolent words left the young aristocrat's lips than the plate with which Roland was playing flew from his hands and struck De Barjols full in the face. The women screamed, the men rose to their feet. Roland burst into that nervous laugh which was habitual with him, and threw himself back in his chair. The young aristocrat remained calm, although the blood was trickling from his brow to his cheek.

At this moment the conductor entered with the usual formula:

"Come! citizen travellers, take your places."

The travellers, anxious to leave the scene of the quarrel, rushed to the door.

"Pardon me, sir," said Alfred de Barjols to Roland, "you do not go by diligence, I hope?"

"No, sir, I travel by post; but you need have no fear; I shall not depart."

"Nor I," said the Englishman. "Have them unharness my horses; I shall remain."

"I must go," sighed the dark young man whom Roland had addressed as general. "You know it is necessary, my friend; my presence yonder is absolutely imperative. But I swear that I would not leave you if I could possibly avoid it."

In saying these words his voice betrayed an emotion of which, judging from its usual harsh, metallic ring, it had seemed incapable. Roland, on the contrary, seemed overjoyed. His belligerent nature seemed to expand at the approach of a danger to which he had perhaps not given rise, but which he at least had not endeavored to avoid.

"Good! general," he said. "We were to part at Lyons, since you have had the kindness to grant me a month's furlough to visit my family at Bourg. It is merely some hundred and sixty miles or so less than we intended, that is all. I shall rejoin you in Paris. But you know if you need a devoted arm, and a man who never sulks, think of me!"

"You may rest easy on that score, Roland," exclaimed the general. Then, looking attentively at the two adversaries, he added with an indescribable note of tenderness: "Above all, Roland, do not let yourself be killed; but if it is a possible thing don't kill your adversary. Everything considered, he is a gallant man, and the day will come when I shall need such men at my side."

"I shall do my best, general; don't be alarmed."

At this moment the landlord appeared upon the threshhold of the door.

"The post-chaise is ready," said he.

The general took his hat and his cane, which he had laid upon the chair. Roland, on the contrary, followed him bareheaded, that all might see plainly he did not intend to leave with his friend. Alfred de Barjols, therefore, offered no opposition to his leaving the room. Besides, it was easy to see that his adversary was of those who seek rather than avoid quarrels.

"Just the same," said the general, seating himself in the carriage to which Roland had escorted him, "my heart is heavy at leaving you thus, Roland, without a friend to act as your second."

"Good! Don't worry about that, general; seconds are never lacking. There are and always will be enough men who are curious to see how one man can kill another."

"Au revoir, Roland. Observe, I do not say farewell, but au revoir!"

"Yes, my dear general," replied the young man, in a voice that revealed some emotion, "I understand, and I thank you."

"Promise that you will send me word as soon as the affair is over, or that you will get some one to write if you are disabled."

"Oh, don't worry, general. You will have a letter from

me personally in less than four days," replied Roland, adding, in a tone of profound bitterness: "Have you not perceived that I am protected by a fatality which prevents me from dying?"

"Roland!" exclaimed the general in a severe tone, "Again!"

"Nothing, nothing," said the young man, shaking his head and assuming an expression of careless gayety which must have been habitual with him before the occurrence of that unknown misfortune which oppressed his youth with this longing for death.

"Very well. By the way, try to find out one thing."

"What is that, general?"

"How it happens that at a time when we are at war with England an Englishman stalks about France as freely and as easily as if he were at home."

"Good; I will find out."

"How?"

"I do not know; but when I promise you to find out I shall do so, though I have to ask it of himself."

"Reckless fellow! Don't get yourself involved in another affair in that direction."

"In any case, it would not be a duel. It would be a battle, as he is a national enemy."

"Well, once more—till I see you again. Embrace me."

Roland flung himself with passionate gratitude upon the neck of the personage who had just given him this permission.

"Oh, general!" he exclaimed, "how happy I should be —if I were not so unhappy!"

The general looked at him with profound affection, then asked: "One day you will tell me what this sorrow is, will you not, Roland?"

Roland laughed that sorrowful laugh which had already escaped his lips once or twice.

"Oh! my word, no," said he, "you would ridicule me too much."

The general stared at him as one would contemplate a madman.

"After all," he murmured, "one must accept men as they come."

"Especially when they are not what they seem to be."

"You must mistake me for Œdipe since you pose me with these enigmas, Roland."

"Ah! if you guess this one, general, I will herald you king of Thebes! But, with all my follies, I forgot that your time is precious and that I am detaining you needlessly with my nonsense."

"That is so! Have you any commissions for Paris?"

"Yes, three; my regards to Bourrienne, my respects to your brother Lucien, and my most tender homage to Madame Bonaparte."

"I will deliver them."

"Where shall I find you in Paris?"

"At my house in the Rue de la Victoire, perhaps."

"Perhaps—"

"Who knows? Perhaps at the Luxembourg!" Then throwing himself back as if he regretted having said so much, even to the man he regarded as his best friend, he shouted to the postilion, "Road to Orange! as fast as possible."

The postilion, who was only waiting for the order, whipped up his horses; the carriage departed rapidly, rumbling like a roll of thunder, and disappeared through the Porte d'Oulle.

CHAPTER III

THE ENGLISHMAN

ROLAND remained motionless, not only as long as he could see the carriage, but long after it had disappeared. Then, shaking his head as if to dispel the cloud which darkened his brow, he re-entered the inn and asked for a room.

"Show the gentleman to number three," said the landlord to a chambermaid.

The chambermaid took a key hanging from a large black wooden tablet on which were arranged the numbers in white in two rows, and signed to the young traveller to follow her.

"Send up some paper, and a pen and ink," Roland said to the landlord, "and if M. de Barjols should ask where I am tell him the number of my room."

The landlord promised to obey Roland's injunctions and the latter followed the girl upstairs whistling the Marseillaise. Five minutes later he was seated at a table with the desired paper, pen and ink before him preparing to write. But just as he was beginning the first line some one knocked three times at the door.

"Come in," said he, twirling his chair on one of its hind legs so as to face his visitor, whom he supposed to be either M. de Barjols or one of his friends.

The door opened with a steady mechanical motion and the Englishman appeared upon the threshold.

"Ah!" exclaimed Roland, enchanted with this visit, in view of his general's recommendation; "is it you?"

"Yes," said the Englishman, "it is I."

"You are welcome."

"Oh! if I am welcome, so much the better! I was not sure that I ought to come."

"Why not?"

"On account of Aboukir."

Roland began to laugh.

"There are two battles of Aboukir," said he; "one which we lost; the other we won."

"I referred to the one you lost."

"Good!" said Roland, "we fight, kill, and exterminate each other on the battlefield, but that does not prevent us from clasping hands on neutral ground. So I repeat, you are most welcome, especially if you will tell me why you have come."

"Thank you; but, in the first place, read that." And the Englishman drew a paper from his pocket.

"What is that?" asked Roland.

"My passport."

"What have I to do with your passport?" asked Roland, "I am not a gendarme."

"No, but I have come to offer you my services. Perhaps you will not accept them if you do not know who I am."

"Your services, sir?"

"Yes; but read that first."

Roland read:

In the name of the French Republic—The Executive Directory hereby orders that Sir John Tanlay, Esq., be permitted to travel freely throughout the territory of the Republic, and that both assistance and protection be accorded him in case of need. (Signed) FOUCHÉ.

And below:

To whom it may concern—I recommend Sir John Tanley particularly as a philanthropist and a friend of liberty.
(Signed) BARRAS.

"Have you read it?"

"Yes; what of it?"

"What of it? Well, my father, Lord Tanlay, rendered M. Barras some services; that is why M. Barras permits me to roam about France. And I am very glad to roam about; it amuses me very much."

"Oh, I remember, Sir John; you did us the honor to say so at dinner."

"I did say so, it is true; I also said that I liked the French people heartily."

Roland bowed.

"And above all General Bonaparte," continued Sir John.

"You like General Bonaparte very much?"

"I admire him; he is a great, a very great, man."

"By Heavens! Sir John, I am sorry he is not here to hear an Englishman say that of him."

"Oh! if he were here I should not say it."

"Why not?"

"I should not want him to think I was trying to please him. I say so because it is my opinion."

"I don't doubt it, my lord," said Roland, who did not see what the Englishman was aiming at, and who, having learned all that he wished to know through the passport, held himself upon his guard.

"And when I heard," continued the Englishman with the same phlegm, "you defend General Bonaparte, I was much pleased."

"Really?"

"Much pleased," repeated the Englishman, nodding his head affirmatively.

"So much the better!"

"But when I saw you throw a plate at M. Alfred de Barjols' head, I was much grieved."

"You were grieved, my lord, and why?"

"Because in England no gentleman would throw a plate at the head of another gentleman."

"My lord," said Roland, rising with a frown, "have you perchance come here to read me a lecture?"

"Oh, no; I came to suggest that you are perhaps perplexed about finding a second?"

"My faith, Sir John! I admit that the moment when you knocked at the door I was wondering of whom I could ask this service."

"Of me, if you wish," said the Englishman. "I will be your second."

"On my honor!" exclaimed Roland, "I accept with all my heart."

"That is the service I wished to render you!"

Roland held out his hand, saying: "Thank you!"

The Englishman bowed.

"Now," continued Roland, "as you have had the good taste, my lord, to tell me who you were before offering your services, it is but fair that, since I accept them, I should tell you who I am."

"Oh! as you please."

"My name is Louis de Montrevel; I am aide-de-camp to General Bonaparte."

"Aide-de-camp to General Bonaparte. I am very glad."

"That will explain why I undertook, rather too warmly perhaps, my general's defence."

"No, not too warmly; only, the plate—"

"Oh, I know well that the provocation did not entail that plate. But what would you have me do! I held it in my hand, and, not knowing what to do with it, I threw it at M. de Barjols' head; it went of itself without any will of mine."

"You will not say that to him?"

"Reassure yourself; I tell you to salve your conscience."

"Very well; then you will fight?"

"That is why I have remained here, at any rate."

"What weapons?"

"That is not our affair, my lord."

"What! not our affair?"

"No; M. de Barjols is the one insulted; the choice is his."

"Then you will accept whatever he proposes?"

"Not I, Sir John, but you in my name, since you do me the honor to act as my second."

"And if he selects pistols, what is the distance to be and how will you fight?"

"That is your affair, my lord, and not mine. I don't know how you do in England, but in France the principals take no part in the arrangements. That duty devolves upon the seconds; what they decide is well decided!"

"Then my arrangements will be satisfactory?"

"Perfectly so, my lord."

The Englishman bowed.

"What hour and what day?"

"Oh! as soon as possible; I have not seen my family for two years, and I confess that I am in a hurry to greet them."

The Englishman looked at Roland with a certain wonder; he spoke with such assurance, as if he were certain that he would not be killed. Just then some one knocked at the door, and the voice of the innkeeper asked: "May I come in?"

The young man replied affirmatively. The door opened and the landlord entered, holding a card in his hand which he handed his guest. The young man took the card and read: "Charles du Valensolle."

"From M. Alfred de Barjols," said the host.

"Very well!" exclaimed Roland. Then handing the card to the Englishman, he said: "Here, this concerns you; it is unnecessary for me to see this monsieur—since we are no longer citizens—M. de Valensolle is M. de Barjols' second; you are mine. Arrange this affair between you. Only," added the young man, pressing the Englishman's hand and looking fixedly at him, "see that it holds a chance of certain death for one of us. Otherwise I shall complain that it has been bungled."

"Don't worry," said the Englishman, "I will act for you as for myself."

"Excellent! Go now, and when everything is arranged come back. I shall not stir from here."

Sir John followed the innkeeper. Roland reseated himself, twirled his chair back to its former position facing the table, took up his pen and began to write.

When Sir John returned, Roland had written and sealed two letters and was addressing a third. He signed to the Englishman to wait until he had finished, that he might give him his full attention. Then, the address finished, he sealed the letter, and turned around.

"Well," he asked, "is everything arranged?"

"Yes," said the Englishman, "it was an easy matter. You are dealing with a true gentleman."

"So much the better!" exclaimed Roland, waiting.

"You will fight two hours hence by the fountain of Vaucluse—a charming spot—with pistols, advancing to each

other, each to fire as he pleases and continuing to advance
after his adversary's fire."

"By my faith! you are right, Sir John. That is, indeed,
excellent. Did you arrange that?"

"I and M. de Barjols' second, your adversary having
renounced his rights of the insulted party."

"Have you decided upon the weapons?"

"I offered my pistols. They were accepted on my word
of honor that you were as unfamiliar with them as was M. de
Barjols. They are excellent weapons. I can cut a bullet
on a knife blade at twenty paces."

"Peste! You are a good shot, it would seem, my
lord."

"Yes, I am said to be the best shot in England."

"That is a good thing to know. When I wish to be
killed, Sir John, I'll pick a quarrel with you."

"Oh! don't pick a quarrel with me," said the Englishman, "it would grieve me too much to have to fight you."

"We will try, my lord, not to cause you such grief.
So it is settled then, in two hours."

"Yes, you told me you were in a hurry."

"Precisely. How far is it to this charming spot?"'

"From here to Vaucluse?"

"Yes."

"Twelve miles."

"A matter of an hour and a half. We have no time to
lose, so let us rid ourselves of troublesome things in order
to have nothing but pleasure before us."

The Englishman looked at the young man in astonishment. Roland did not seem to pay any attention to this
look.

"Here are three letters," said he: "one for Madame de
Montrevel, my mother; one for Mlle. de Montrevel, my sister; one for the citizen, Bonaparte, my general. If I am
killed you will simply put them in the post. Will that
be too much trouble?"

"Should that misfortune occur, I will deliver your

letters myself," said the Englishman. "Where do your mother and sister live?"

"At Bourg, the capital of the Department of Ain."

"That is near here," observed the Englishman. "As for General Bonaparte, I will go to Egypt if necessary. I should be extremely pleased to meet General Bonaparte."

"If you take the trouble, as you say, my lord, of delivering my letters yourself, you will not have to travel such a distance. Within three days General Bonaparte will be in Paris."

"Oh!" said the Englishman, without betraying the least surprise, "do you think so?"

"I am sure of it," replied Roland.

"Truly, he is a very extraordinary man, your General Bonaparte. Now, have you any other recommendations to make to me, M. de Montrevel?"

"One only, my lord."

"Oh! as many as you please."

"No, thank you, one only, but that is very important."

"What is it?"

"If I am killed—but I doubt if I be so fortunate."

Sir John looked at Roland with that expression of wonder which he had already awakened three or four times.

"If I am killed," resumed Roland; "for after all one must be prepared for everything—"

"Yes, if you are killed, I understand."

"Listen well, my lord, for I place much stress on my directions being carried out exactly in this matter."

"Every detail shall be observed," replied Sir John. "I am very punctilious."

"Well, then, if I am killed," insisted Roland, laying his hand upon his second's shoulder, to impress his directions more firmly on his memory, "you must not permit any one to touch my body, which is to be placed in a leaden coffin without removing the garments I am wearing; the coffin you will have soldered in your presence, then inclosed in an oaken bier, which must also be nailed up in your presence.

Then you will send it to my mother, unless you should prefer to throw it into the Rhone, which I leave absolutely to your discretion, provided only that it be disposed of in some way."

"It will be no more difficult," replied the Englishman, "to take the coffin, since I am to deliver your letter."

"Decidedly, my lord," said Roland, laughing in his strange way. "You are a capital fellow. Providence in person brought us together. Let us start, my lord, let us start!"

They left Roland's room; Sir John's chamber was on the same floor. Roland waited while the Englishman went in for his weapons. He returned a few seconds later, carrying the box in his hand.

"Now, my lord," asked Roland, "how shall we reach Vaucluse? On horseback or by carriage?"

"By carriage, if you are willing. It is much more convenient in case one is wounded. Mine is waiting below."

"I thought you had given the order to have it unharnessed?"

"I did, but I sent for the postilion afterward and countermanded it."

They went downstairs.

"Tom! Tom!" called Sir John at the door, where a servant, in the severe livery of an English groom, was waiting, "take care of this box."

"Am I going with you, my lord?" asked the servant.

"Yes!" replied Sir John.

Then showing Roland the steps of his carriage, which the servant lowered, he said:

"Come, M. de Montrevel."

Roland entered the carriage and stretched himself out luxuriously.

"Upon my word!" said he. "It takes you English to understand travelling. This carriage is as comfortable as a bed. I warrant you pad your coffins before you are put in them!"

"Yes, that is a fact," said Sir John, "the English people understand comfort, but the French people are much more curious and amusing—postilion, to Vaucluse!"

CHAPTER IV

THE DUEL

THE road was passable only from Avignon to l'Isle. They covered the nine miles between the two places in an hour. During this hour Roland, as he resolved to shorten the time for his travelling companion, was witty and animated, and their approach to the duelling ground only served to redouble his gayety. To one unacquainted with the object of this drive, the menace of dire peril impending over this young man, with his continuous flow of conversation and incessant laughter, would have seemed incredible.

At the village of l'Isle they were obliged to leave the carriage. Finding on inquiry that they were the first to arrive, they entered the path which led to the fountain.

"Oh! oh!" exclaimed Roland, "there ought to be a fine echo here." And he gave one or two cries to which Echo replied with perfect amiability.

"By my faith!" said the young man, "this is a marvellous echo. I know none save that of the Seinonnetta, at Milan, which can compare with it. Listen, my lord."

And he began, with modulations which revealed an admirable voice and an excellent method, to sing a Tyrolean song which seemed to bid defiance to the human throat with its rebellious music. Sir John watched Roland, and listened to him with an astonishment which he no longer took the trouble to conceal. When the last note had died away among the cavities of the mountain, he exclaimed:

"God bless me! but I think your liver is out of order."

Roland started and looked at him interrogatively. But seeing that Sir John did not intend to say more, he asked:

"Good! What makes you think so?"

"You are too noisily gay not to be profoundly melancholy."

"And that anomaly astonishes you?"

"Nothing astonishes me, because I know that it has always its reason for existing."

"True, and it's all in knowing the secret. Well, I'm going to enlighten you."

"Oh! I don't want to force you."

"You're too polite to do that; still, you must admit you would be glad to have your mind set at rest about me."

"Because I'm interested in you."

"Well, Sir John, I am going to tell you the secret of the enigma, something I have never done with any one before. For all my seeming good health, I am suffering from a horrible aneurism that causes me spasms of weakness and faintness so frequent as to shame even a woman. I spend my life taking the most ridiculous precautions, and yet Larrey warns me that I am liable to die any moment, as the diseased artery in my breast may burst at the least exertion. Judge for yourself how pleasant for a soldier! You can understand that, once I understood my condition, I determined incontinently to die with all the glory possible. Another more fortunate than I would have succeeded a hundred times already. But I'm bewitched; I am impervious alike to bullets and balls; even the swords seem to fear to shatter themselves upon my skin. Yet I never miss an opportunity; that you must see, after what occurred at dinner. Well, we are going to fight. I'll expose myself like a maniac, giving my adversary all the advantages, but it will avail me nothing. Though he shoot at fifteen paces, or even ten or five, at his very pistol's point, he will miss me, or his pistol will miss fire. And all this wonderful luck that some fine day when I least expect it, I may die pulling on my boots! But hush! here comes my adversary."

As he spoke the upper half of three people could be seen ascending the same rough and rocky path that Roland

and Sir John had followed, growing larger as they approached. Roland counted them.

"Three!" he exclaimed. "Why three, when we are only two?"

"Ah! I had forgotten," replied the Englishman. "M. de Barjols, as much in your interest as in his own, asked permission to bring a surgeon, one of his friends."

"What for?" harshly demanded Roland, frowning.

"Why, in case either one of you was wounded. A man's life can often be saved by bleeding him promptly."

"Sir John," exclaimed Roland, ferociously, "I don't understand these delicacies in the matter of a duel. When men fight they fight to kill. That they exchange all sorts of courtesies beforehand, as your ancestors did at Fontenoy, is all right; but, once the swords are unsheathed or the pistols loaded, one life must pay for the trouble they have taken and the heart beats they have lost. I ask you, on your word of honor, Sir John, to promise that, wounded or dying, M. de Barjols' surgeon shall not be allowed to touch me."

"But suppose, M. Roland—"

"Take it or leave it. Your word of honor, my lord, or devil take me if I fight at all."

The Englishman again looked curiously at the young man. His face was livid, and his limbs quivered as though in extreme terror. Sir John, without understanding this strange dread, passed his word.

"Good!" exclaimed Roland. "This, you see, is one of the effects of my charming malady. The mere thought of surgical instruments, a bistoury or a lance, makes me dizzy. Didn't I grow very pale?"

"I did think for an instant you were going to faint."

"What a stunning climax!" exclaimed Roland with a laugh. "Our adversaries arrive and you are dosing me with smelling salts like a hysterical woman. Do you know what they, and you, first of all, would have said? That I was afraid."

Meantime, the three new-comers having approached within earshot, Sir John was unable to answer Roland. They bowed, and Roland, with a smile that revealed his beautiful teeth, returned their greeting. Sir John whispered in his ear:

"You are still a trifle pale. Go on toward the fountain; I will fetch you when we are ready."

"Ah! that's the idea," said Roland. "I have always wanted to see that famous fountain of Vaucluse, the Hippocrene of Petrarch. You know his sonnet?

> " 'Chiari, fresche e dolci acque
>   Ove le belle membra
>   Pose colei, che sola a me perdona.'

This opportunity lost, I may never have another. Where is your fountain?"

"Not a hundred feet off. Follow the path; you'll find it at the turn of the road, at the foot of that enormous bowlder you see."

"My lord," said Roland, "you are the best guide I know; thanks!"

And, with a friendly wave of the hand, he went off in the direction of the fountain, humming the charming pastoral of Philippe Desportes beneath his breath:

> " 'Rosette, a little absence
>   Has turned thine heart from me;
>   I, knowing that inconstance,
>   Have turned my heart from thee.
>   No wayward beauty o'er me
>   Such power shall obtain;
>   We'll see, my fickle lassie,
>   Who first will turn again.' "

Sir John turned as he heard the modulations of that fresh sweet voice, whose higher notes had something at a feminine quality. His cold methodical mind understood nothing of that nervous impulsive nature, save that he had under his eyes one of the most amazing organisms one could possibly meet.

The other two young men were waiting for him; the

surgeon stood a little apart. Sir John carried his box of pistols in his hands. Laying it upon a table-shaped rock, he drew a little key from his pocket, apparently fashioned by a goldsmith rather than a locksmith, and opened the box. The weapons were magnificent, although of great simplicity. They came from Manton's workshop, the grandfather of the man who is still considered one of the best gunsmiths in London. He handed them to M. de Barjols' second to examine. The latter tried the triggers and played with the lock, examining to see if they were double-barrelled. They were single-barrelled. M. de Barjols cast a glance at them but did not even touch them.

"Our opponent does not know these weapons?" queried M. Valensolle.

"He has not even seen them," replied Sir John, "I give you my word of honor."

"Oh!" exclaimed M. de Valensolle, "a simple denial suffices."

The conditions of the duel were gone over a second time to avoid possible misunderstanding. Then, these conditions determined, the pistols were loaded. They were then placed, loaded, in the box, the box left in the surgeon's charge, and Sir John, with the key in his pocket, went after Roland.

He found him chatting with a little shepherd boy who was herding three goats on the steep rocky slope of the mountain, and throwing pebbles into the fountain. Sir John opened his lips to tell Roland that all was ready; but the latter, without giving the Englishman time to speak, exclaimed:

"You don't know what this child has been telling me, my lord! A perfect legend of the Rhine. He says that this pool, whose depth is unknown, extends six or eight miles under the mountain, and a fairy, half woman half serpent, dwells here. Calm summer nights she glides over the surface of water calling to the shepherds of the mountains, showing them, of course, nothing more than her head with its long locks and her beautiful bare shoulders and arms. The fools, caught by this semblance of a woman, draw nearer, beckoning to her to come to them, while she on her side signs to them to go to her. The unwary spirits advance unwittingly, giving no heed to their steps. Suddenly the earth fails them, the fairy reaches out her arms, and plunges down into her dripping palaces, to reappear the next day alone. Where the devil did these idiots of shepherds get the tale that Virgil related in such noble verse to Augustus and Mecænas?"

He remained pensive an instant, his eyes bent upon the azure depths, then turning to Sir John:

"They say that, no matter how vigorous the swimmer, none has ever returned from this abyss. Perhaps were I to try it, my lord, it might be surer than M. de Barjols' bullet. However, it always remains as a last resort; in the meantime let us try the bullet. Come, my lord, come."

Then turning to the Englishman, who listened, amazed by this mobility of mind, he led him back to the others who awaited them. They in the meantime had found a suitable place.

It was a little plateau, perched as it were on a rocky proclivity, jutting from the mountain side, exposed to the setting sun, on which stood a ruined castle where the shepherds were wont to seek shelter when the mistral overtook them. A flat space, some hundred and fifty feet long, and sixty wide, which might once have been the castle platform, was now to be the scene of the drama which was fast approaching its close.

"Here we are, gentlemen," said Sir John.

"We are ready, gentlemen," replied M. de Valensolle.

"Will the principals kindly listen to the conditions of the duel?" said Sir John. Then addressing M. de Valensolle, he added: "Repeat them, monsieur; you are French and I am a foreigner, you will explain them more clearly than I."

"You belong to those foreigners, my lord, who teach us poor Provençals the purity of our language; but since you so courteously make me spokesman, I obey you." Then exchanging bows with Sir John, he continued: "Gentlemen, it is agreed that you stand at forty paces, that you advance toward each other, that each will fire at will, and wounded or not will have the right to advance after your adversary's fire."

The two combatants bowed in sign of assent, and with one voice, and almost at the same moment, they said:

"The pistols!"

Sir John drew the little key from his pocket and opened the box. Then approaching M. de Barjols he offered it to him open. The latter wished to yield the choice of weapons to his opponent; but with a wave of his hand Roland refused, saying in a tone almost feminine in its sweetness:

"After you, M. de Barjols. Although you are the insulted party, you have, I am told, renounced your advantages. The least I can do is to yield you this one, if for that matter it is an advantage."

M. de Barjols no longer insisted. He took one of the two pistols at random. Sir John offered the other to Roland, who took it, and, without even examining its mechanism, cocked the trigger, then let it fall at arm's-length at his side.

During this time M. de Valensolle had measured forty paces, staking a cane as a point of departure.

"Will you measure after me?" he asked Sir John.

"Needless, sir," replied the latter: "M. de Montrevel and myself rely entirely upon you."

M. de Valensolle staked a second cane at the fortieth pace.

"Gentlemen," said he, "when you are ready."

Roland's adversary was already at his post, hat and cloak removed. The surgeon and the two seconds stood aside. The spot had been so well chosen that neither had any advantage of sun or ground. Roland tossed off hat and coat, stationed himself forty paces from M. de Barjols, facing him. Both, one to right the other to the left, cast a glance at the same horizon. The aspect harmonized with the terrible solemnity of the scene about to take place.

Nothing was visible to Roland's right and to M. de Barjols' left, except the mountain's swift incline and gigantic peak. But on the other side, that is to say, to M. de Barjols' right and Roland's left, it was a far different thing.

The horizon stretched illimitable. In the foreground, the plain, its ruddy soil pierced on all sides by rocks, like a Titan graveyard with its bones protruding through the earth. Then, sharply outlined in the setting sun, was Avignon with its girdle of walls and its vast palace, like a crouching lion, seeming to hold the panting city in its claws. Beyond Avignon, a luminous sweep, like a river of molten gold, defined the Rhone. Beyond the Rhone, a deep-hued azure vista, stretched the chain of hills which separate Avignon from Nimes and d'Uzes. And far off, the sun, at which one of these two men was probably looking for the last time, sank slowly and majestically in an ocean of gold and purple.

For the rest these two men presented a singular contrast. One, with his black hair, swarthy skin, slender limbs and sombre eyes, was the type of the Southern race which counts among its ancestors Greeks, Romans, Arabs and Spaniards. The other, with his rosy skin, large blue eyes, and hands dimpled like a woman's, was the type of that race of temperate zones which reckons Gauls, Germans and Normans among its forebears.

Had one wished to magnify the situation it were easy to believe this something greater than single combat between two men. One might have thought it was a duel of a people against another people, race against race, the South against the North.

Was it these thoughts which we have just expressed that filled Roland's mind and plunged him into that melancholy revery.

Probably not; the fact is, for an instant he seemed to have forgotten seconds, duel, adversary, lost as he was in

contemplation of this magnificent spectacle. M. de Barjols' voice aroused him from this poetical stupor.

"When you are ready, sir," said he, "I am."

Roland started.

"Pardon my keeping you waiting, sir," said he. "You
should not have considered me, I am so absent-minded. I
am ready now."

Then, a smile on his lips, his hair lifted by the evening
breeze, unconcerned as if this were an ordinary promenade,
while his opponent, on the contrary, took all the precaution
usual in such a case, Roland advanced straight toward M. de
Barjols.

Sir John's face, despite his ordinary impassibility, betrayed a profound anxiety. The distance between the opponents lessened rapidly. M. de Barjols halted first, took
aim, and fired when Roland was but ten paces from him.
The ball clipped one of Roland's curls, but did not touch
him. The young man turned toward his second:

"Well," said he, "what did I tell you?"

"Fire, monsieur, fire!" said the seconds.

M. de Barjols stood silent and motionless on the spot
where he had fired.

"Pardon me, gentlemen," replied Roland; "but you
will, I hope, permit me to be the judge of the time and
manner of retaliating. Since I have felt M. de Barjols'
shot, I have a few words to say to him which I could not
say before." Then, turning to the young aristocrat, who
was pale and calm, he said: "Sir, perhaps I was somewhat
too hasty in our discussion this morning."

And he waited.

"It is for you to fire, sir," replied M. de Barjols.

"But," continued Roland, as if he had not heard, "you
will understand my impetuosity, and perhaps excuse it, when
you hear that I am a soldier and General Bonaparte's aide-
de-camp."

"Fire, sir," replied the young nobleman.

"Say but one word of retraction, sir," resumed the young

officer. "Say that General Bonaparte's reputation for honor and delicacy is such that a miserable Italian proverb, inspired by ill-natured losers, cannot reflect discredit on him. Say that, and I throw this weapon away to grasp your hand; for I recognize in you, sir, a brave man."

"I cannot accord that homage to his honor and delicacy until your general has devoted the influence which his genius gives him over France as Monk did—that is to say, to reinstate his legitimate sovereign upon the throne."

"Ah!" cried Roland, with a smile, "that is asking too much of a republican general."

"Then I maintain what I said," replied the young noble. "Fire! monsieur, fire!" Then, as Roland made no haste to obey this injunction, he shouted, stamping his foot: "Heavens and earth! will you fire?"

At these words Roland made a movement as if he intended to fire in the air.

"Ah!" exclaimed M. de Barjols. Then with a rapidity of gesture and speech that prevented this, "Do not fire in the air, I beg, or I shall insist that we begin again and that you fire first."

"On my honor!" cried Roland, turning as pale as if the blood had left his body, "this is the first time I have done so much for any man. Go to the devil! and if you don't want to live, then die!"

At the same time he lowered his arm and fired, without troubling to take aim.

Alfred de Barjols put his hand to his breast, swayed back and forth, turned around and fell face down upon the ground. Roland's bullet had gone through his heart.

Sir John, seeing M. de Barjols fall, went straight to Roland and drew him to the spot where he had thrown his hat and coat.

"That is the third," murmured Roland with a sigh; "but you are my witness that this one would have it."

Then giving his smoking pistol to Sir John, he resumed his hat and coat. During this time M. de Valensolle picked up the pistol which had escaped from his friend's hand, and brought it, together with the box, to Sir John.

"Well?" asked the Englishman, motioning toward Alfred de Barjols with his eyes.

"He is dead," replied the second.

"Have I acted as a man of honor, sir?" asked Roland, wiping away the sweat which suddenly inundated his brow at the announcement of his opponent's death.

"Yes, monsieur," replied M. de Valensolle; "only, permit me to say this: you possess the fatal hand."

Then bowing to Roland and his second with exquisite politeness, he returned to his friend's body.

"And you, my lord," resumed Roland, "what do you say?"

"I say," replied Sir John, with a sort of forced admiration, "you are one of those men who are made by the divine Shakespeare to say of themselves:

> " 'Danger and I—
> We were two lions littered in one day,
> But I the elder.' "

CHAPTER V

ROLAND

THE return was silent and mournful; it seemed that with the hopes of death Roland's gayety had disappeared.

The catastrophe of which he had been the author played perhaps a part in his taciturnity. But let us hasten to say that in battle, and more especially during the last campaign against the Arabs, Roland had been too frequently obliged to jump his horse over the bodies of his victims to be so deeply impressed by the death of an unknown man.

His sadness was due to some other cause; probably that which he confided to Sir John. Disappointment over his own lost chance of death, rather than that other's decease, occasioned this regret.

On their return to the Hotel du Palais-Royal, Sir John mounted to his room with his pistols, the sight of which might have excited something like remorse in Roland's breast. Then he rejoined the young officer and returned the three letters which had been intrusted to him.

He found Roland leaning pensively on a table. Without saying a word the Englishman laid the three letters before him. The young man cast his eyes over the addresses, took the one destined for his mother, unsealed it and read it over. As he read, great tears rolled down his cheeks. Sir John gazed wonderingly at this new phase of Roland's character. He had thought everything possible to this many-sided nature except those tears which fell silently from his eyes.

Shaking his head and paying not the least attention to Sir John's presence, Roland murmured:

"Poor mother! she would have wept. Perhaps it is better so. Mothers were not made to weep for their children!"

He tore up the letters he had written to his mother, his sister, and General Bonaparte, mechanically burning the fragments with the utmost care. Then ringing for the chambermaid, he asked:

"When must my letters be in the post?"

"Half-past six," replied she. "You have only a few minutes more."

"Just wait then."

And taking a pen he wrote:

MY DEAR GENERAL—It is as I told you; I am living and he is dead. You must admit that this seems like a wager. Devotion to death.

Your Paladin,

ROLAND.

Then he sealed the letter, addressed it to General Bona-parte, Rue de la Victoire, Paris, and handed it to the chambermaid, bidding her lose no time in posting it. Then only did he seem to notice Sir John, and held out his hand to him.

"You have just rendered me a great service, my lord," he said. "One of those services which bind men for all eternity. I am already your friend; will you do me the honor to become mine?"

Sir John pressed the hand that Roland offered him.

"Oh!" said he, "I thank you heartily. I should never have dared ask this honor; but you offer it and I accept."

Even the impassible Englishman felt his heart soften as he brushed away the tear that trembled on his lashes. Then looking at Roland, he said: "It is unfortunate that you are so hurried; I should have been pleased and delighted to spend a day or two with you."

"Where were you going, my lord, when I met you?"

"Oh, I? Nowhere. I am travelling to get over being bored. I am unfortunately often bored."

"So that you were going nowhere?"

"I was going everywhere."

"That is exactly the same thing," said the young officer, smiling. "Well, will you do something for me?"

"Oh! very willingly, if it is possible."

"Perfectly possible; it depends only on you."

"What is it?"

"Had I been killed you were going to take me to my mother or throw me into the Rhone."

"I should have taken you to your mother and not thrown you into the Rhone."

"Well, instead of accompanying me dead, take me living. You will be all the better received."

"Oh!"

"We will remain a fortnight at Bourg. It is my natal city, and one of the dullest towns in France; but as your compatriots are pre-eminent for originality, perhaps you will find amusement where others are bored. Are we agreed?"

"I should like nothing better," exclaimed the Englishman; "but it seems to me that it is hardly proper on my part."

"Oh! we are not in England, my lord, where etiquette holds absolute sway. We have no longer king nor queen. We didn't cut off that poor creature's head whom they called Marie Antoinette to install Her Majesty, Etiquette, in her stead."

"I should like to go," said Sir John.

"You'll see, my mother is an excellent woman, and very distinguished besides. My sister was sixteen when I left; she must be eighteen now. She was pretty, and she ought to be beautiful. Then there is my brother Edouard, a delightful youngster of twelve, who will let off fireworks between your legs and chatter a gibberish of English with you. At the end of the fortnight we will go to Paris together."

"I have just come from Paris," said the Englishman.

"But listen. You were willing to go to Egypt to see General Bonaparte. Paris is not so far from here as Cairo. I'll present you, and, introduced by me, you may rest assured that you will be well received. You were speaking of Shakespeare just now—"

"Oh! I am always quoting him."

"Which proves that you like comedies and dramas."

"I do like them very much, that's true."

"Well, then, General Bonaparte is going to produce one in his own style which will not be wanting in interest, I answer for it!"

"So that," said Sir John, still hesitating, "I may accept your offer without seeming intrusive?"

"I should think so. You will delight us all, especially me."

"Then I accept."

"Bravo! Now, let's see, when will you start?"

As soon as you wish. My coach was harnessed when you threw that unfortunate plate at Barjols' head. However, as I should never have known you but for that plate, I am glad you did throw it at him!"

"Shall we start this evening?"

"Instantly. I'll give orders for the postilion to send other horses, and once they are here we will start."

Roland nodded acquiescence. Sir John went out to give his orders, and returned presently, saying they had served two cutlets and a cold fowl for them below. Roland took his valise and went down. The Englishman placed his pistols in the coach box again. Both ate enough to enable them to travel all night, and as nine o'clock was striking from the Church of the Cordeliers they settled themselves in the carriage and quitted Avignon, where their passage left a fresh trail of blood, Roland with the careless indifference of his nature, Sir John Tanlay with the impassibility of his nation. A quarter of an hour later both were sleeping, or at least the silence which obtained induced the belief that both had yielded to slumber.

We shall profit by this instant of repose to give our readers some indispensable information concerning Roland and his family.

Roland was born the first of July, 1773, four years and a few days later than Bonaparte, at whose side, or rather following him, he made his appearance in this book. He was the son of M. Charles de Montrevel, colonel of a regiment long garrisoned at Martinique, where he had married a creole named Clotilde de la Clémencière. Three children were born of this marriage, two boys and a girl: Louis, whose acquaintance we have made under the name of Roland, Amélie, whose beauty he had praised to Sir John, and Edouard.

Recalled to France in 1782, M. de Montrevel obtained admission for young Louis de Montrevel (we shall see later how the name of Louis was changed to Roland) to the Ecole Militaire in Paris.

It was there that Bonaparte knew the child, when, on M. de Keralio's report, he was judged worthy of promotion from the Ecole de Brienne to the Ecole Militaire. Louis was the youngest pupil. Though he was only thirteen, he had already made himself remarked for that ungovernable and quarrelsome nature of which we have seen him seventeen years later give an example at the table d'hôte at Avignon.

Bonaparte, a child himself, had the good side of this character; that is to say, without being quarrelsome, he was firm, obstinate, and unconquerable. He recognized in the child some of his own qualities, and this similarity of sentiments led him to pardon the boy's defects, and attached him to him. On the other hand the child, conscious of a supporter in the Corsican, relied upon him.

One day the child went to find his great friend, as he called Napoleon, when the latter was absorbed in the solution of a mathematical problem. He knew the importance the future artillery officer attached to this science, which so far had won him his greatest, or rather his only successes.

He stood beside him without speaking or moving. The young mathematician felt the child's presence, and plunged deeper and deeper into his mathematical calculations, whence he emerged victorious ten minutes later. Then he turned to his young comrade with that inward satisfaction of a man who issues victorious from any struggle, be it with science or things material.

The child stood erect, pale, his teeth clinched, his arms rigid and his fists closed.

"Oh! oh!" said young Bonaparte, "what is the matter now?"

"Valence, the governor's nephew, struck me."

"Ah!" said Bonaparte, laughing, "and you have come to me to strike him back?"

The child shook his head.

"No," said he, "I have come to you because I want to fight him—"

"Fight Valence?"

"Yes."

"But Valence will beat you, child; he is four times as strong as you."

"Therefore I don't want to fight him as children do, but like men fight."

"Pooh!"

"Does that surprise you?" asked the child.

"No," said Bonaparte; "what do you want to fight with?"

"With swords."

"But only the sergeants have swords, and they won't lend you one."

"Then we will do without swords."

"But what will you fight with?"

The child pointed to the compass with which the young mathematician had made his equations.

"Oh! my child," said Bonaparte, "a compass makes a very bad wound."

"So much the better," replied Louis; "I can kill him."

"But suppose he kills you?"

"I'd rather that than bear his blow."

Bonaparte made no further objections; he loved courage instinctively, and his young comrade's pleased him.

"Well, so be it!" he replied; "I will tell Valence that you wish to fight him, but not till to-morrow."

"Why to-morrow?"

"You will have the night to reflect."

"And from now till to-morrow," replied the child, "Valence will think me a coward." Then shaking his head, "It is too long till to-morrow." And he walked away.

"Where are you going?" Bonaparte asked him.

"To ask some one else to be my friend."

"So I am no longer your friend?"

"No, since you think I am a coward."

"Very well," said the young man rising.

"You will go?"

"I am going."

"At once?"

"At once."

"Ah!" exclaimed the child, "I beg your pardon; you are indeed my friend." And he fell upon his neck weeping. They were the first tears he had shed since he had received the blow

Bonaparte went in search of Valence and gravely explained his mission to him. Valence was a tall lad of seventeen, having already, like certain precocious natures, a beard and mustache; he appeared at least twenty. He was, moreover, a head taller than the boy he had insulted.

Valence replied that Louis had pulled his queue as if it were a bell-cord (queues were then in vogue)—that he had warned him twice to desist, but that Louis had repeated the prank the third time, whereupon, considering him a mischievous youngster, he had treated him as such.

Valence's answer was reported to Louis, who retorted that pulling a comrade's queue was only teasing him, whereas a blow was an insult. Obstinacy endowed this child of thirteen with the logic of a man of thirty.

The modern Popilius to Valence returned with his declaration of war. The youth was greatly embarrassed; he could not fight with a child without being ridiculous. If he fought and wounded him, it would be a horrible thing; if he himself were wounded, he would never get over it so long as he lived.

But Louis's unyielding obstinacy made the matter a serious one. A council of the Grands (elder scholars) was called, as was usual in serious cases. The Grands decided that one of their number could not fight a child; but since this child persisted in considering himself a young man, Valence must tell him before all his schoolmates that he regretted having treated him as a child, and would henceforth regard him as a young man.

Louis, who was waiting in his friend's room, was sent for. He was introduced into the conclave assembled in the playground of the younger pupils.

There Valence, to whom his comrades had dictated a speech carefully debated among themselves to safeguard the honor of the Grands toward the Petits, assured Louis that he deeply deplored the occurrence; that he had treated him according to his age and not according to his intelligence and courage, and begged him to excuse his impatience and to shake hands in sign that all was forgotten.

But Louis shook his head.

"I heard my father, who is a colonel, say once," he replied, "that he who receives a blow and does not fight is a coward. The first time I see my father I shall ask him if he who strikes the blow and then apologizes to avoid fighting is not more of a coward than he who received it."

The young fellows looked at each other. Still the general opinion was against a duel which would resemble murder, and all, Bonaparte included, were unanimously agreed that the child must be satisfied with what Valence had said, for it represented their common opinion. Louis retired, pale with anger, and sulked with his great friend, who, said he, with imperturbable gravity, had sacrificed his honor.

The morrow, while the Grands were receiving their lesson in mathematics, Louis slipped into the recitation-room, and while Valence was making a demonstration on the blackboard, he approached him unperceived, climbed on a stool to reach his face, and returned the slap he had received the preceding day.

"There," said he, "now we are quits, and I have your apologies to boot; as for me, I shan't make any, you may be quite sure of that."

The scandal was great. The act occurring in the professor's presence, he was obliged to report it to the governor of the school, the Marquis Tiburce Valence. The latter, knowing nothing of the events leading up to the blow his nephew had received, sent for the delinquent and after a terrible lecture informed him that he was no longer a member of the school, and must be ready to return to his mother at Bourg that very day. Louis replied that his things would be packed in ten minutes, and he out of the school in fifteen. Of the blow he himself had received he said not a word.

The reply seemed more than disrespectful to the Marquis Tiburce Valence. He was much inclined to send the insolent boy to the dungeon for a week, but reflected that he could not confine him and expel him at the same time.

The child was placed in charge of an attendant, who was not to leave him until he had put him in the coach for Mâcon; Madame de Montrevel was to be notified to meet him at the end of the journey.

Bonaparte meeting the boy, followed by his keeper, asked an explanation of the sort of constabulary guard attached to him.

"I'd tell you if you were still my friend," replied the child; "but you are not. Why do you bother about what happens to me, whether good or bad?"

Bonaparte made a sign to the attendant, who came to the door while Louis was packing his little trunk. He learned then that the child had been expelled. The step was serious; it would distress the entire family, and perhaps ruin his young comrade's future.

With that rapidity of decision which was one of the distinctive characteristics of his organization, he resolved to ask an audience of the governor, meantime requesting the keeper not to hasten Louis's departure.

Bonaparte was an excellent pupil, beloved in the school, and highly esteemed by the Marquis Tiburce Valence. His request was immediately complied with. Ushered into the governor's presence, he related everything, and, without blaming Valence in the least, he sought to exculpate Louis.

"Are you sure of what you are telling me, sir?" asked the governor.

"Question your nephew himself. I will abide by what he says."

Valence was sent for. He had already heard of Louis's expulsion, and was on his way to tell his uncle what had happened. His account tallied perfectly with what young Bonaparte had said.

"Very well," said the governor, "Louis shall not go, but you will. You are old enough to leave school." Then ringing, "Bring me the list of the vacant sub-lieutenancies," he said.

That same day an urgent request for a sub-lieutenancy was made to the Ministry, and that same night Valence left to join his regiment. He went to bid Louis farewell, embracing him half willingly, half unwillingly, while Bonaparte held his hand. The child received the embrace reluctantly.

"It's all right now," said he, "but if ever we meet with swords by our sides—" A threatening gesture ended the sentence.

Valence left. Bonaparte received his own appointment as sub-lieutenant October 10, 1785. His was one of fifty-eight commissions which Louis XVI. signed for the Ecole Militaire. Eleven years later, November 15, 1796, Bonaparte, commander-in-chief of the army of Italy, at the Bridge of Arcola, which was defended by two regiments of Croats and two pieces of cannon, seeing his ranks disseminated by grapeshot and musket balls, feeling that victory was slipping through his fingers, alarmed by the hesitation of his bravest followers, wrenched the tri-color from the rigid fingers of a dead color-bearer, and dashed toward the bridge, shouting: "Soldiers! are you no longer the men of Lodi?" As he did so he saw a young lieutenant spring past him who covered him with his body.

This was far from what Bonaparte wanted. He wished to cross first. Had it been possible he would have gone alone.

Seizing the young man by the flap of his coat, he drew him back, saying: "Citizen, you are only a lieutenant, I am commander-in-chief! The precedence belongs to me."

"Too true," replied the other; and he followed Bonaparte instead of preceding him.

That evening, learning that two Austrian divisions had been cut to pieces, and seeing the two thousand prisoners he had taken, together with the captured cannons and flags, Bonaparte recalled the young man who had sprung in front of him when death alone seemed before him.

"Berthier," said he, "tell my aide-de-camp, Valence, to find that young lieutenant of grenadiers with whom I had a controversy this morning at the Bridge of Arcola."

"General," stammered Berthier, "Valence is wounded."

"Ah! I remember I have not seen him to-day. Wounded? Where? How? On the battlefield?"

"No, general," said he, "he was dragged into a quarrel yesterday, and received a sword thrust through his body."

Bonaparte frowned. "And yet they know very well I do not approve of duels; a soldier's blood belongs not to himself, but to France. Give Muiron the order then."

"He is killed, general."

"To Elliot, in that case."

"Killed also."

Bonaparte drew his handkerchief from his pocket and passed it over his brow, which was bathed with sweat.

"To whom you will, then; but I want to see that lieutenant."

He dared not name any others, fearing to hear again that fatal "Killed!"

A quarter of an hour later the young lieutenant was ushered into his tent, which was lighted faintly by a single lamp.

"Come nearer, lieutenant," said Bonaparte.

The young man made three steps and came within the circle of light.

"So you are the man who wished to cross the bridge before me?" continued Bonaparte.

"It was done on a wager, general," gayly answered the young lieutenant, whose voice made the general start.

"Did I make you lose it?"

"Maybe, yes; maybe, no."

"What was the wager?"

"That I should be promoted captain to-day."

"You have won it."

"Thank you, general."

The young man moved hastily forward as if to press Bonaparte's hand, but checked himself almost immediately. The light had fallen full on his face for an instant; that instant sufficed to make the general notice the face as he had the voice. Neither the one nor the other was unknown to him. He searched his memory for an instant, but finding it rebellious, said: "I know you!"

"Possibly, general."

"I am certain; only I cannot recall your name."

"You managed that yours should not be forgotten, general."

"Who are you?"

"Ask Valence, general."

Bonaparte gave a cry of joy.

"Louis de Montrevel," he exclaimed, opening wide his arms. This time the young lieutenant did not hesitate to fling himself into them.

"Very good," said Bonaparte; "you will serve eight days with the regiment in your new rank, that they may accustom themselves to your captain's epaulets, and then you will take my poor Muiron's place as aide-de-camp. Go!"

"Once more!" cried the young man, opening his arms.

"Faith, yes!" said Bonaparte, joyfully. Then holding him close after kissing him twice, "And so it was you who gave Valence that sword thrust?"

"My word!" said the new captain and future aide-de-camp, "you were there when I promised it to him. A soldier keeps his word."

Eight days later Captain Montrevel was doing duty as staff-officer to the commander-in-chief, who changed his name of Louis, then in ill-repute, to that of Roland. And the young man consoled himself for ceasing to be a descendant of St. Louis by becoming the nephew of Charlemagne.

Roland—no one would have dared to call Captain Montrevel Louis after Bonaparte had baptized him Roland—made the campaign of Italy with his general, and returned with him to Paris after the peace of Campo Formio.

When the Egyptian expedition was decided upon, Roland, who had been summoned to his mother's side by the death of the Brigadier-General de Montrevel, killed on the Rhine while his son was fighting on the Adige and the Mincio, was among the first appointed by the commander-in-chief to accompany him in the useless but poetical crusade which he was planning. He left his mother, his sister Amélie, and his young brother Edouard at Bourg, General de Montrevel's native town. They resided some three-quarters of a mile out of the city, at Noires-Fontaines, a charming house, called a château, which, together with the farm and several hundred acres of land surrounding it, yielded an income of six or eight thousand livres a year, and constituted the general's entire fortune. Roland's departure on this adventurous expedition deeply afflicted the poor widow. The death of the father seemed to presage that of the son, and Madame de Montrevel, a sweet, gentle Creole, was far from possessing the stern virtues of a Spartan or Lacedemonian mother.

Bonaparte, who loved his old comrade of the Ecole Militaire with all his heart, granted him permission to rejoin him at the very last moment at Toulon. But the fear of arriving too late prevented Roland from profiting by this permission to its full extent. He left his mother, promising her—a promise he was careful not to keep—that he would not expose himself unnecessarily, and arrived at Marseilles eight days before the fleet set sail.

Our intention is no more to give the history of the campaign of Egypt than we did that of Italy. We shall only mention that which is absolutely necessary to understand this story and the subsequent development of Roland's character. The 19th of May, 1798, Bonaparte and his entire staff set sail for the Orient; the 15th of June the Knights of Malta gave up the keys of their citadel. The 2d of July the army disembarked at Marabout, and the same day took Alexandria; the 25th, Bonaparte entered Cairo, after defeating the Mamelukes at Chebreïss and the Pyramids.

During this succession of marches and battles, Roland had been the officer we know him, gay, courageous and witty, defying the scorching heat of the day, the icy dew of the nights, dashing like a hero or a fool among the Turkish sabres or the Bedouin bullets. During the forty days of the voyage he had never left the interpreter Ventura; so that with his admirable facility he had learned, if not to speak Arabic fluently, at least to make himself understood in that language. Therefore it often happened that, when the general did not wish to use the native interpreter, Roland was charged with certain communications to the Muftis, the Ulemas, and the Sheiks.

During the night of October 20th and 21st Cairo revolted. At five in the morning the death of General Dupey, killed by a lance, was made known. At eight, just as the revolt was supposedly quelled, an aide-de-camp of the dead general rode up, announcing that the Bedouins from the plains were attacking Bab-el-Nasr, or the Gate of Victory.

Bonaparte was breakfasting with his aide-de-camp Sulkowsky, so severely wounded at Salahieh that he left his pallet of suffering with the greatest difficulty only. Bonaparte, in his preoccupation forgetting the young Pole's condition, said to him: "Sulkowsky, take fifteen Guides and go see what that rabble wants."

Sulkowksy rose.

"General," interposed Roland, "give me the commission. Don't you see my comrade can hardly stand?"

"True," said Bonaparte; "do you go!"

Roland went out and took the fifteen Guides and started. But the order had been given to Sulkowsky, and Sulkowksy was determined to execute it. He set forth with five or six men whom he found ready.

Whether by chance, or because he knew the streets of Cairo better than Roland, he reached the Gate of Victory a few seconds before him. When Roland arrived, he saw five or six dead men, and an officer being led away by the Arabs, who, while massacring the soldiers mercilessly, will sometimes spare the officers in hope of a ransom. Roland recognized Sulkowksy; pointing him out with his sabre to his fifteen men, he charged at a gallop.

Half an hour later, a Guide, returning alone to headquarters, announced the deaths of Sulkowksy, Roland and his twenty-one companions.

Bonaparte, as we have said, loved Roland as a brother, as a son, as he loved Eugène. He wished to know all the details of the catastrophe, and questioned the Guide. The man had seen an Arab cut off Sulkowsky's head and fasten it to his saddle-bow. As for Roland, his horse had been killed. He had disengaged himself from the stirrups and was seen fighting for a moment on foot; but he had soon disappeared in a general volley at close quarters.

Bonaparte sighed, shed a tear and murmured: "Another!" and apparently thought no more about it. But he did inquire to what tribe belonged these Bedouins, who had just killed two of the men he loved best. He was told that they were an independent tribe whose village was situated some thirty miles off. Bonaparte left them a month, that they might become convinced of their impunity; then, the month elapsed, he ordered one of his aides-de-camp, named Crosier, to surround the village, destroy the huts, behead the men, put them in sacks, and bring the rest of the population, that is to say, the women and children, to Cairo.

Crosier executed the order punctually; all the women and children who could be captured were brought to Cairo, and also with them one living Arab, gagged and bound to his horse's back.

"Why is this man still alive?" asked Bonaparte. "I ordered you to behead every man who was able to bear arms."

"General," said Crosier, who also possessed a smattering of Arabian words, "just as I was about to order his head cut off, I understood him to offer to exchange a prisoner for his life. I thought there would be time enough to cut off his head, and so I brought him with me. If I am mistaken, the ceremony can take place here as well as there; what is postponed is not abandoned."

The interpreter Ventura was summoned to question the Bedouin. He replied that he had saved the life of a French officer who had been grievously wounded at the Gate of Victory, and that this officer, who spoke a little Arabic, claimed to be one of General Bonaparte's aides-de-camp. He had sent him to his brother who was a physician in a neighboring tribe, of which this officer was a captive; and if they would promise to spare his life, he would write to his brother to send the prisoner to Cairo.

Perhaps this was a tale invented to gain time, but it might also be true; nothing was lost by waiting.

The Arab was placed in safe keeping, a scribe was brought to write at his dictation. He sealed the letter with his own seal, and an Arab from Cairo was despatched to negotiate the exchange. If the emissary succeeded, it meant the Bedouin's life and five hundred piastres to the messenger.

Three days later he returned bringing Roland. Bonaparte had hoped for but had not dared to expect this return.

This heart of iron, which had seemed insensible to grief, was now melted with joy. He opened his arms to Roland, as on the day when he had found him, and two tears, two pearls—the tears of Bonaparte were rare—fell from his eyes.

But Roland, strange as it may seem, was sombre in the midst of the joy caused by his return. He confirmed the Arab's tale, insisted upon his liberation, but refused all personal details about his capture by the Bedouins and the treatment he had received at the hands of the doctor. As for Sulkowsky, he had been killed and beheaded before his eyes, so it was useless to think more of him. Roland resumed his duties, but it was noticeable his native courage had become temerity, and his longing for glory, desire for death.

On the other hand, as often happens with those who brave fire and sword, fire and sword miraculously spared him. Before, behind and around Roland men fell; he remained erect, invulnerable as the demon of war. During the campaign in Syria two emissaries were sent to demand the surrender of Saint Jean d'Acre of Djezzar Pasha. Neither of the two returned; they had been beheaded. It was necessary to send a third. Roland applied for the duty, and so insistent was he, that he eventually obtained the general's permission and returned in safety. He took part in each of the nineteen assaults made upon the fortress; at each assault he was seen entering the breach. He was one of the ten men who forced their way into the Accursèd Tower; nine remained, but he returned without a scratch. During the retreat, Bonaparte commanded his cavalry to lend their horses to the wounded and sick. All endeavored to avoid the contagion of the pest-ridden sick. To them Roland gave his horse from preference. Three fell dead from the saddle; he mounted his horse after them, and reached Cairo safe and sound. At Aboukir he flung himself into the mêlée, reached the Pasha by forcing his way through the guard of blacks who surrounded him; seized him by the beard and received the fire of his two pistols. One burned the wadding only, the other ball passed under his arm, killing a guard behind him.

When Bonaparte resolved to return to France, Roland was the first to whom the general announced his intention. Another had been overjoyed; but he remained sombre and melancholy, saying: "I should prefer to remain here, general. There is more chance of my being killed here."

But as it would have appeared ungrateful on his part to

refuse to follow the general, he returned with him. During
the voyage he remained sad and impenetrable, until the
English fleet was sighted near Corsica. Then only did he
regain his wonted animation. Bonaparte told Admiral
Gantheaume that he would fight to the death, and gave
orders to sink the frigate sooner than haul down the flag.
He passed, however, unseen through the British fleet, and
disembarked at Frejus, October 8, 1799.

All were impatient to be the first to set foot on French
soil. Roland was the last. Although the general paid no
apparent attention to these details, none escaped him. He
sent Eugène, Berthier, Bourrienne, his aides-de-camp and
his suite by way of Gap and Draguignan, while he took the
road to Aix strictly incognito, accompanied only by Roland,
to judge for himself of the state of the Midi. Hoping that
the joy of seeing his family again would revive the love of
life in his heart crushed by its hidden sorrow, he informed
Roland at Aix that they would part at Lyons, and gave
him three weeks' furlough to visit his mother and sister.

Roland replied: "Thank you, general. My sister and
my mother will be very happy to see me." Whereas formerly his words would have been: "Thank you, general.
I shall be very happy to see my mother and sister again."

We know what occurred at Avignon; we have seen with
what profound contempt for danger, bitter disgust of life,
Roland had provoked that terrible duel. We heard the
reason he gave Sir John for this indifference to death. Was
it true or false? Sir John at all events was obliged to
content himself with it, since Roland was evidently not disposed to furnish any other.

And now, as we have said, they were sleeping or pretending to sleep as they were drawn by two horses at full speed
along the road of Avignon to Orange.

CHAPTER VI

MORGAN

OUR readers must permit us for an instant to abandon Roland and Sir John, who, thanks to the physical and moral conditions in which we left them, need inspire no anxiety, while we direct our attention seriously to a personage who has so far made but a brief appearance in this history, though he is destined to play an important part in it.

We are speaking of the man who, armed and masked, entered the room of the table d'hôte at Avignon to return Jean Picot the two hundred louis which had been stolen from him by mistake, stored as it had been with the government money.

We speak of the highwayman, who called himself Morgan. He had ridden into Avignon, masked, in broad daylight, entered the hotel of the Palais-Egalité leaving his horse at the door. This horse had enjoyed the same immunity in the pontifical and royalist town as his master; he found it again at the horse post, unfastened its bridle, sprang into the saddle, rode through the Porte d'Oulle, skirting the walls, and disappeared at a gallop along the road to Lyons. Only about three-quarters of a mile from Avignon, he drew his mantle closer about him, to conceal his weapons from the passers, and removing his mask he slipped it into one of the holsters of his saddle.

The persons whom he had left at Avignon who were curious to know if this could be the terrible Morgan, the terror of the Midi, might have convinced themselves with their own eyes, had they met him on the road between Avignon and Bédarides, whether the bandit's appearance was as terrifying as his renown. We do not hesitate to assert that the features now revealed would have harmonized so little with the picture their prejudiced imagination had conjured up that their amazement would have been extreme.

The removal of the mask, by a hand of perfect whiteness and delicacy, revealed the face of a young man of twenty-four or five years of age, a face that, by its regularity of feature and gentle expression, had something of the character of a woman's. One detail alone gave it or rather would give it at certain moments a touch of singular firmness. Beneath the beautiful fair hair waving on his brow and temples, as was the fashion at that period, eyebrows, eyes and lashes were black as ebony. The rest of the face was, as we have said, almost feminine. There were two little ears of which only the tips could be seen beneath the tufts of hair to which the Incroyables of the day had given the name of "dog's-ears"; a straight, perfectly proportioned nose, a rather large mouth, rosy and always smiling, and which, when smiling, revealed a double row of brilliant teeth; a delicate refined chin faintly tinged with blue, showing that, if the beard had not been carefully and recently shaved, it would, protesting against the golden hair, have followed the same color as the brows, lashes and eyes, that is to say, a decided black. As for the unknown's figure, it was seen, when he entered the dining-room, to be tall, well-formed and flexible, denoting, if not great muscular strength, at least much suppleness and agility.

The manner he sat his horse showed him to be a practiced rider. With his cloak thrown back over his shoulders, his mask hidden in the holster, his hat pulled low over his eyes, the rider resumed his rapid pace, checked for an instant, passed through Bédarides at a gallop, and reaching the first houses in Orange, entered the gate of one which closed immediately behind him. A servant in waiting sprang to the bit. The rider dismounted quickly.

"Is your master here?" he asked the domestic.

"No, Monsieur the Baron," replied the man; "he was obliged to go away last night, but he left word that if Monsieur should ask for him, to say that he had gone in the interests of the Company."

"Very good, Baptiste. I have brought back his horse in good condition, though somewhat tired. Rub him down with wine, and give him for two or three days barley instead of oats. He has covered something like one hundred miles since yesterday morning."

"Monsieur the Baron was satisfied with him?"

"Perfectly satisfied. Is the carriage ready?"

"Yes, Monsieur the Baron, all harnessed in the coach-house; the postilion is drinking with Julien. Monsieur recommended that he should be kept outside the house that he might not see him arrive."

"He thinks he is to take your master?"

"Yes, Monsieur the Baron. Here is my master's passport, which we used to get the post-horses, and as my master has gone in the direction of Bordeaux with Monsieur the Baron's passport, and as Monsieur the Baron goes toward Geneva with my master's passport, the skein will probably be so tangled that the police, clever as their fingers are, can't easily unravel it."

"Unfasten the valise that is on the croup of my saddle, Baptiste, and give it to me."

Baptiste obeyed dutifully, but the valise almost slipped from his hands. "Ah!" said he laughing, "Monsieur the Baron did not warn me! The devil! Monsieur the Baron has not wasted his time it seems."

"Just where you're mistaken, Baptiste! if I didn't waste all my time, I at least lost a good deal, so I should like to be off again as soon as possible."

"But Monsieur the Baron will breakfast?"

"I'll eat a bite, but quickly."

"Monsieur will not be delayed. It is now two, and breakfast has been ready since ten this morning. Luckily it's a cold breakfast."

And Baptiste, in the absence of his master, did the honors of the house to the visitor by showing him the way to the dining-room.

"Not necessary," said the visitor, "I know the way. Do you see to the carriage; let it be close to the house with the door wide open when I come out, so that the postilion can't see me. Here's the money to pay him for the first relay."

And the stranger whom Baptiste had addressed as Baron handed him a handful of notes.

"Why, Monsieur," said the servant, "you have given me enough to pay all the way to Lyons!"

"Pay him as far as Valence, under pretext that I want to sleep, and keep the rest for your trouble in settling the accounts."

"Shall I put the valise in the carriage-box?"

"I will do so myself."

And taking the valise from the servant's hands, without letting it be seen that it weighed heavily, he turned toward the dining-room, while Baptiste made his way toward the nearest inn, sorting his notes as he went.

As the stranger had said, the way was familiar to him, for he passed down a corridor, opened a first door without hesitation, then a second, and found himself before a table elegantly served. A cold fowl, two partridges, a ham, several kinds of cheese, a dessert of magnificent fruit, and two decanters, the one containing a ruby-colored wine, and the other a yellow-topaz, made a breakfast which, though evidently intended for but one person, as only one place was set, might in case of need have sufficed for three or four.

The young man's first act on entering the dining-room was to go straight to a mirror, remove his hat, arrange his hair with a little comb which he took from his pocket; after which he went to a porcelain basin with a reservoir above it, took a towel which was there for the purpose, and bathed his face and hands. Not until these ablutions were completed—characteristic of a man of elegant habits—not until these ablutions had been minutely performed did the stranger sit down to the table.

A few minutes sufficed to satisfy his appetite, to which youth and fatigue had, however, given magnificent proportions; and when Baptiste came in to inform the solitary guest that the carriage was ready he found him already afoot and waiting.

The stranger drew his hat low over his eyes, wrapped his coat about him, took the valise under his arm, and, as Baptiste had taken pains to lower the carriage-steps as close as possible to the door, he sprang into the post-chaise without being seen by the postilion. Baptiste slammed the door after him; then, addressing the man in the top-boots:

"Everything is paid to Valence, isn't it, relays and fees?" he asked.

"Everything; do you want a receipt?" replied the postilion, jokingly.

"No; but my master, the Marquise de Ribier, don't want to be disturbed until he gets to Valence."

"All right," replied the postilion, in the same bantering tone, "the citizen Marquis shan't be disturbed. Forward, hoop-la!" And he started his horses, and cracked his whip with that noisy eloquence which says to neighbors and passers-by: "'Ware here, 'ware there! I am driving a man who pays well and who has the right to run over others."

Once in the carriage the pretended Marquis of Ribier opened the window, lowered the blinds, raised the seat, put his valise in the hollow, sat down on it, wrapped himself in his cloak, and, certain of not being disturbed till he reached Valence, slept as he had breakfasted, that is to say, with all the appetite of youth.

They went from Orange to Valence in eight hours. Our traveller awakened shortly before entering the city. Raising one of the blinds cautiously, he recognized the little suburb of Paillasse. It was dark, so he struck his repeater and found it was eleven at night. Thinking it useless to go to sleep again, he added up the cost of the relays to Lyons and counted out the money. As the postilion at Valence passed the comrade who replaced him, the traveller heard him say:

"It seems he's a ci-devant; but he was recommended from Orange, and, as he pays twenty sous fees, you must treat him as you would a patriot."

"Very well," replied the other; "he shall be driven accordingly."

The traveller thought the time had come to intervene. He raised the blind and said:

"And you'll only be doing me justice. A patriot? Deuce take it! I pride myself upon being one, and of the first calibre, too! And the proof is— Drink this to the health of the Republic." And he handed a hundred-franc assignat to the postilion who had recommended him to his comrade. Seeing the other looking eagerly at this strip of paper, he continued: "And the same to you if you will repeat the recommendation you've just received to the others."

"Oh! don't worry, citizen," said the postilion; "there'll be but one order to Lyons—full speed!"

"And here is the money for the sixteen posts, including the double post of entrance in advance. I pay twenty sous fees. Settle it among yourselves."

The postilion dug his spurs into his horse and they were off at a gallop. The carriage relayed at Lyons about four in the afternoon. While the horses were being changed, a man clad like a porter, sitting with his stretcher beside him on a stone post, rose, came to the carriage and said something in a low tone to the young Companion of Jehu which seemed to astonish the latter greatly.

"Are you quite sure?" he asked the porter.

"I tell you that I saw him with my own eyes!" replied the latter.

"Then I can give the news to our friends as a positive fact?"

"You can. Only hurry."

"Have they been notified at Servas ?"

"Yes; you will find a horse ready between Servas and Sue."

The postilion came up; the young man exchanged a last glance with the porter, who walked away as if charged with a letter of the utmost importance.

"What road, citizen ?" asked the postilion.

"To Bourg. I must reach Servas by nine this evening: I pay thirty sous fees."

"Forty-two miles in five hours! That's tough. Well, after all, it can be done."

"Will you do it."

"We can try."

"And the postilion started at full gallop. Nine o'clock was striking as they entered Servas.

"A crown of six livres if you'll drive me half-way to Sue without stopping here to change horses!" cried the young man through the window to the postilion.

"Done!" replied the latter.

And the carriage dashed past the post house without stopping.

Morgan stopped the carriage at a half mile beyond Servas, put his head out of the window, made a trumpet of his hands, and gave the hoot of a screech-owl. The imitation was so perfect that another owl answered from a neighboring woods.

"Here we are," cried Morgan.

The postilion pulled up, saying: "If we're there, we needn't go further."

The young man took his valise, opened the door, jumped out and stepped up to the postilion.

"Here's the promised ecu."

The postilion took the coin and stuck it in his eye, as a fop of our day holds his eye-glasses. Morgan divined that this pantomime had a significance.

"Well," he asked, "what does that mean ?"

"That means," said the postilion, "that, do what I will, I can't help seeing with the other eye."

"I understand," said the young man, laughing; "and if I close the other eye—"

"Damn it! I shan't see anything."

"Hey! you're a rogue who'd rather be blind than see with one eye! Well, there's no disputing tastes. Here!"

And he gave him a second crown. The postilion stuck it up to his other eye, wheeled the carriage round and took the road back to Servas.

The Companion of Jehu waited till he vanished in the darkness. Then putting the hollow of a key to his lips, he drew a long trembling sound from it like a boatswain's whistle.

A similar call answered him, and immediately a horseman came out of the woods at full gallop. As he caught sight of him Morgan put on his mask.

"In whose name have you come?" asked the rider, whose face, hidden as it was beneath the brim of an immense hat, could not be seen.

"In the name of the prophet Elisha," replied the young man with the mask.

"Then you are he whom I am waiting for." And he dismounted.

"Are you prophet or disciple?" asked Morgan.

"Disciple," replied the new-comer.

"Where is your master?"

"You will find him at the Chartreuse of Seillon."

"Do you know how many Companions are there this evening?"

"Twelve."

"Very good; if you meet any others send them there."

He who had called himself a disciple bowed in sign of obedience, assisted Morgan to fasten the valise to the croup of the saddle, and respectfully held the bit while the young man mounted. Without even waiting to thrust his other foot into the stirrup, Morgan spurred his horse, which tore the bit from the groom's hand and started off at a gallop.

On the right of the road stretched the forest of Seillon, like a shadowy sea, its sombre billows undulating and moaning in the night wind. Half a mile beyond Sue the rider turned his horse across country toward the forest, which, as he rode on, seemed to advance toward him. The horse, guided by an experienced hand, plunged fearlessly into the woods. Ten minutes later he emerged on the other side.

A gloomy mass, isolated in the middle of a plain, rose about a hundred feet from the forest. It was a building of massive architecture, shaded by five or six venerable trees. The horseman paused before the portal, over which were placed three statues in a triangle of the Virgin, our Lord, and St. John the Baptist. The statue of the Virgin was at the apex of the triangle.

The mysterious traveller had reached his goal, for this was the Chartreuse of Seillon. This monastery, the twenty-second of its order, was founded in 1178. In 1672 a modern edifice had been substituted for the old building; vestiges of its ruins can be seen to this day. These ruins consist externally of the above-mentioned portal with the three statues, before which our mysterious traveller halted; internally, a small chapel, entered from the right through the portal. A peasant, his wife and two children are now living there, and the ancient monastery has become a farm.

The monks were expelled from their convent in 1791; in 1792 the Chartreuse and its dependencies were offered for sale as ecclesiastical property. The dependencies consisted first of the park, adjoining the buildings, and the noble forest which still bears the name of Seillon. But at Bourg, a royalist and, above all, religious town, no one dared risk his soul by purchasing property belonging to the worthy monks whom all revered. The result was that the convent, the park and the forest had become, under the title of state property, the property of the republic; that is to say, they belonged to nobody, or were at the best neglected. The republic having, for the last seven years, other things to think of than pointing walls, cultivating an orchard and cutting timber.

For seven years, therefore, the Chartreuse had been completely abandoned, and if by chance curious eyes peered through the keyhole, they caught glimpses of grass-grown courtyards, brambles in the orchard, and brush in the forest, which, except for one road and two or three paths that crossed it, had become almost impenetrable. The Correrie, a species of pavilion belonging to the monastery and distant from it about three-quarters of a mile, was mossgrown too in the tangle of the forest, which, profiting by its liberty, grew at its own sweet will, and had long since encircled it in a mantle of foliage which hid it from sight.

For the rest, the strangest rumors were current about these two buildings. They were said to be haunted by guests invisible by day, terrifying at night. The woodsmen and the belated peasants, who went to the forest to exercise against the Republic the rights which the town of Bourg had enjoyed in the days of the monks, pretended that, through the cracks of the closed blinds, they had seen flames of fire dancing along the corridors and stairways, and had distinctly heard the noise of chains clanking over the cloister tilings and the pavement of the courtyards. The strong-minded denied these things; but two very opposite classes opposed the unbelievers, confirming the rumors, attributing these terrifying noises and nocturnal lights to two different causes according to their beliefs. The patriots declared that they were the ghosts of the poor monks buried alive by cloister tyranny in the In-pace, who were now returned to earth, dragging after them their fetters to call down the vengeance of Heaven upon their persecutors. The royalists said that they were the imps of the devil, who, finding an empty convent, and fearing no further danger from holy water, were boldly holding their revels where once they had not dared show a claw. One fact, however, left everything uncertain. Not one of the believers or unbelievers—whether he elected for the souls of the martyred monks or for the Witches' Sabbath of Beelzebub—had ever had the courage to venture among the shadows, and to seek during the solemn hours of night confirmation of the truth, in order to tell on the morrow whether the Chartreuse were haunted, and if haunted by whom.

But doubtless these tales, whether well founded or not, had no influence over our mysterious horseman; for although, as we have said, nine o'clock had chimed from the steeples of Bourg, and night had fallen, he reined in his horse in front of the great portal of the deserted monastery, and, without dismounting, drew a pistol from his holster, striking three measured blows with the butt on the gate, after the manner of the Freemasons. Then he listened. For an instant he doubted if the meeting were really there; for though he looked closely and listened attentively, he could perceive no light, nor could he hear a sound. Still he fancied he heard a cautious step approaching the portal from within. He knocked a second time with the same weapon and in the same manner.

"Who knocks?" demanded a voice.

"He who comes from Elisha," replied the traveller.

"What king do the sons of Isaac obey?"

"Jehu."

"What house are they to exterminate?"

"That of Ahab."

"Are you prophet or disciple?"

"Prophet."

"Welcome then to the House of the Lord!" said the voice.

Instantly the iron bars which secured the massive portal swung back, the bolts grated in their sockets, half of the gate opened silently, and the horse and his rider passed beneath the sombre vault, which immediately closed behind them.

The person who had opened the gate, so slow to open, so quick to close, was attired in the long white robe of a

Chartreuse monk, of which the hood, falling over his face, completely concealed his features.

CHAPTER VII

THE CHARTREUSE OF SEILLON

BEYOND doubt, like the first affiliated member met on the road to Sue by the man who styled himself prophet, the monk who opened the gate was of secondary rank in the fraternity; for, grasping the horse's bridle, he held it while the rider dismounted, rendering the young man the service of a groom.

Morgan got off, unfastened the valise, pulled the pistols from the holsters, and placed them in his belt, next to those already there. Addressing the monk in a tone of command, he said: "I thought I should find the brothers assembled in council."

"They are assembled," replied the monk.

"Where?"

"At La Correrie. Suspicious persons have been seen prowling around the Chartreuse these last few days, and orders have been issued to take the greatest precautions."

The young man shrugged his shoulders as if he considered such precautions useless, and, always in the same tone of command, said: "Have some one take my horse to the stable and conduct me to the council."

The monk summoned another brother, to whom he flung the bridle. He lighted a torch at a lamp, in the little chapel which can still be seen to the right of the great portal, and walked before the new-comer. Crossing the cloister, he took a few steps in the garden, opened a door leading into a sort of cistern, invited Morgan to enter, closed it as carefully as he had the outer door, touched with his foot a stone which seemed to be accidentally lying there, disclosed a ring and raised a slab, which concealed a flight of steps leading down to a subterraneous passage. This passage had a rounded roof and was wide enough to admit two men walking abreast.

The two men proceeded thus for five or six minutes, when they reached a grated door. The monk, drawing a key from his frock, opened it. Then, when both had passed through and the door was locked again, he asked: "By what name shall I announce you?"

"As Brother Morgan."

"Wait here; I will return in five minutes."

The young man made a sign with his head which showed that he was familiar with these precautions and this distrust. Then he sat down upon a tomb—they were in the mortuary vaults of the convent—and waited. Five minutes had scarcely elapsed before the monk reappeared.

"Follow me," said he; "the brothers are glad you have come. They feared you had met with some mishap."

A few seconds later Morgan was admitted into the council chamber.

Twelve monks awaited him, their hoods drawn low over their eyes. But, once the door had closed and the serving brother had disappeared, while Morgan was removing his mask, the hoods were thrown back and each monk exposed his face.

No brotherhood had ever been graced by a more brilliant assemblage of handsome and joyous young men. Two or three only of these strange monks had reached the age of forty. All hands were held out to Morgan and several warm kisses were imprinted upon the new-comer's cheek.

" 'Pon my word," said one who had welcomed him most tenderly, "you have drawn a mighty thorn from my foot; we thought you dead, or, at any rate, a prisoner."

"Dead, I grant you, Amiet; but prisoner, never! citizen —as they still say sometimes, and I hope they'll not say it much longer. It must be admitted that the whole affair was conducted on both sides with touching amenity. As soon as the conductor saw us he shouted to the postilion to stop; I even believe he added: 'I know what it is.'

'Then,' said I, 'if you know what it is, my dear friend, our explanations needn't be long.' 'The government money?' he asked. 'Exactly,' I replied. Then as there was a great commotion inside the carriage, I added: 'Wait! first come down and assure these gentlemen, and especially the ladies, that we are well-behaved folk and will not harm them—the ladies, you understand—and nobody will even look at them unless they put their heads out of the window.' One did risk it; my faith! but she was charming. I threw her a kiss, and she gave a little cry and retired into the carriage, for all the world like Galatea, and as there were no willows about, I didn't pursue her. In the meantime the guard was rummaging in his strong-box in all expedition, and to such good purpose, indeed, that with the government money, in his hurry, he passed over two hundred louis belonging to a poor wine merchant of Bordeaux.''

"Ah, the devil!" exclaimed the brother called Amiet—an assumed name, probably, like that of Morgan—"that is annoying! You know the Directory, which is most imaginative, has organized some bands of chauffeurs, who operate in our name, to make people believe that we rob private individuals. In other words, that we are mere thieves."

"Wait an instant," resumed Morgan; "that is just what makes me late. I heard something similar at Lyons. I was half-way to Valence when I discovered this breach of etiquette. It was not difficult, for, as if the good man had foreseen what happened, he had marked his bag 'Jean Picot, Wine Merchant at Fronsac, Bordeaux.'"

"And you sent his money back to him?"

"I did better; I returned it to him."

"At Fronsac?"

"Ah! no, but at Avignon. I suspected that so careful a man would stop at the first large town to inquire what chance he had to recover his two hundred louis. I was not mistaken. I inquired at the inn if they knew citizen Jean Picot. They replied that not only did they know him, but in fact he was then dining at the table d'hôte. I went in.

You can imagine what they were talking about—the stoppage of the diligence. Conceive the sensation my apparition caused. The god of antiquity descending from the machine produced a no more unexpected finale than I. I asked which one of the guests was called Jean Picot. The owner of this distinguished and melodious name stood forth. I placed the two hundred louis before him, with many apologies, in the name of the Company, for the inconvenience its followers had occasioned him. I exchanged a friendly glance with Barjols and a polite nod with the Abbé de Rians who were present, and, with a profound bow to the assembled company, withdrew. It was only a little thing, but it took me fifteen hours; hence the delay. I thought it preferable to leaving a false conception of us in our wake. Have I done well, my masters?"

The gathering burst into bravos.

"Only," said one of the participants, "I think you were somewhat imprudent to return the money yourself to citizen Jean Picot."

"My dear colonel," replied the young man, "there's an Italian proverb which says: 'Who wills, goes; who does not will, sends.' I willed—I went."

"And there's a jolly buck who, if you ever have the misfortune to fall into the hands of the Directory, will reward you by recognizing you; a recognition which means cutting off your head!"

"Oh! I defy him to recognize me."

"What can prevent it?"

"Oh! You seem to think that I play such pranks with my face uncovered? Truly, my dear colonel, you mistake me for some one else. It is well enough to lay aside my mask among friends; but among strangers—no, no! Are not these carnival times? I don't see why I shouldn't disguise myself as Abellino or Karl Moor, when Messieurs Gohier, Sieyès, Roger Ducos, Moulin and Barras are masquerading as kings of France."

"And you entered the city masked?"

"The city, the hotel, the dining-room. It is true that if my face was covered, my belt was not, and, as you see, it is well garnished."

The young man tossed aside his coat, displaying his belt, which was furnished with four pistols and a short hunting-knife. Then, with a gayety which seemed characteristic of his careless nature, he added: "I ought to look ferocious, oughtn't I? They may have taken me for the late Mandrin, descending from the mountains of Savoy. By the bye, here are the sixty thousand francs of Her Highness, the Directory." And the young man disdainfully kicked the valise which he had placed on the ground, which emitted a metallic sound indicating the presence of gold. Then he mingled with the group of friends from whom he had been separated by the natural distance between a narrator and his listeners.

One of the monks stooped and lifted the valise.

"Despise gold as much as you please, my dear Morgan, since that doesn't prevent you from capturing it. But I know of some brave fellows who are awaiting these sixty thousand francs, you so disdainfully kick aside, with as much impatience and anxiety as a caravan, lost in the desert, awaits the drop of water which is to save it from dying of thirst."

"Our friends of the Vendée, I suppose?" replied Morgan. "Much good may it do them! Egotists, they are fighting. These gentlemen have chosen the roses and left us the thorns. Come! don't they receive anything from England?"

"Oh, yes," said one of the monks, gayly; "at Quiberon they got bullets and grapeshot."

"I did not say from the English," retorted Morgan; "I said from England."

"Not a penny."

"It seems to me, however," said one of those present, who apparently possessed a more reflective head than his comrades, "it seems to me that our princes might send a little gold to those who are shedding their blood for the monarchy. Are they not afraid the Vendée may weary some day or other of a devotion which up to this time has not, to my knowledge, won her a word of thanks."

"The Vendée, dear friend," replied Morgan, "is a generous land which will not weary, you may be sure. Besides, where is the merit of fidelity unless it has to deal with ingratitude? From the instant devotion meets recognition, it is no longer devotion. It becomes an exchange which reaps its reward. Let us be always faithful, and always devoted, gentlemen, praying Heaven that those whom we serve may remain ungrateful, and then, believe me, we shall bear the better part in the history of our civil wars."

Morgan had scarcely formulated this chivalric axiom, expressive of a desire which had every chance of accomplishment, than three Masonic blows resounded upon the door through which he had entered.

"Gentlemen," said the monk who seemed to fill the rôle of president, "quick, your hoods and masks. We do not know who may be coming to us."

CHAPTER VIII

HOW THE MONEY OF THE DIRECTORY WAS USED

EVERY one hastened to obey. The monks lowered the hoods of their long robes over their faces, Morgan replaced his mask.

"Enter!" said the superior.

The door opened and the serving-brother appeared.

"An emissary from General Georges Cadoudal asks to be admitted," said he.

"Did he reply to the three passwords?"

"Perfectly."

"Then let him in."

The lay brother retired to the subterranean passage, and reappeared a couple of minutes later leading a man easily recognized by his costume as a peasant, and by his square head with its shock of red hair for a Breton. He advanced in the centre of the circle without appearing in the least intimidated, fixing his eyes on each of the monks in turn, and waiting until one of these twelve granite statues should break silence. The president was the first to speak to him.

"From whom do you come?" he asked him.

"He who sent me," replied the peasant, "ordered me to answer, if I were asked that question, that I was sent by Jehu."

"Are you the bearer of a verbal or written message?"

"I am to reply to the questions which you ask me, and exchange a slip of paper for some money."

"Very good; we will begin with the questions. What are our brothers in the Vendée doing?"

"They have laid down their arms and are awaiting only a word from you to take them up again."

"And why did they lay down their arms?"

"They received the order to do so from his Majesty Louis XVIII."

"There is talk of a proclamation written by the King's own hand. Have they received it?"

"Here is a copy."

The peasant gave a paper to the person who was interrogating him. The latter opened it and read:

The war has absolutely no result save that of making the monarchy odious and threatening. Monarchs who return to their own through its bloody succor are never loved; these sanguinary measures must therefore be abandoned; confide in the empire of opinion which returns of itself to its saving principles. "God and the King," will soon be the rallying cry of all Frenchmen. The scattered elements of royalism must be gathered into one formidable sheaf; militant Vendée must be abandoned to its unhappy fate and marched within a more pacific and less erratic path. The royalists of the West have fulfilled their duty; those of Paris, who have prepared everything for the approaching Restoration, must now be relied upon—

The president raised his head, and, seeking Morgan with a flash of the eye which his hood could not entirely conceal, said: "Well, brother, I think this is the fulfilment of your wish of a few moments ago. The royalists of the Vendée and the Midi will have the merit of pure devotion." Then, lowering his eyes to the proclamation, of which there still remained a few lines to read, he continued:

The Jews crucified their King, and since that time they have wandered over the face of the earth. The French guillotined theirs, and they shall be dispersed throughout the land.

Given at Blankenbourg, this 25th of August, 1799, on the day of St. Louis and the sixth year of our reign.

(Signed)   Louis.

The young men looked at each other.

" 'Quos vult perdere Jupiter dementat!' " said Morgan.

"Yes," said the president; "but when those whom Jupiter wishes to destroy represent a principle, they must be sustained not only against Jupiter but against themselves. Ajax, in the midst of the bolts and lightning, clung to a rock, and, threatening Heaven with his clinched hand, he cried, 'I will escape in spite of the gods!' " Then turning toward Cadoudal's envoy, "And what answer did he who sent you make to this proclamation?"

"About what you yourself have just answered. He told me to come and inform myself whether you had decided to hold firm in spite of all, in spite of the King himself."

"By Heavens! yes," said Morgan.

"We are determined," said the President.

"In that case," replied the peasant, "all is well. Here are the real names of our new chiefs, and their assumed names. The general recommends that you use only the latter as far as is possible in your despatches. He observes that precaution when he, on his side, speaks of you."

"Have you the list?" asked the President.

"No; I might have been stopped, and the list taken. Write yourself; I will dictate them to you."

The president seated himself at the table, took a pen, and wrote the following names under the dictation of the Breton peasant:

"Georges Cadoudal, Jehu or Roundhead; Joseph Cadoudal, Judas Maccabeus; Lahaye Saint-Hilaire, David; Burban-Malabry, Brave-la-Mort; Poulpiquez, Royal-Carnage; Bonfils, Brise-Barrière; Dampherné, Piquevers; Duchayla, La Couronne; Duparc, Le Terrible; La Roche, Mithridates; Puisaye, Jean le Blond."

"And these are the successors of Charette, Stofflet, Cathelineau, Bonchamp, d'Elbée, la Rochejaquelin, and Lescure!" cried a voice.

The Breton turned toward him who had just spoken.

"If they get themselves killed like their predecessors," said he, "what more can you ask of them?"

"Well answered," said Morgan, "so that—"

"So that, as soon as our general has your reply," answered the peasant, "he will take up arms again."

"And suppose our reply had been in the negative?" asked another voice.

"So much the worse for you," replied the peasant; "in any case the insurrection is fixed for October 20."

"Well," said the president, "thanks to us, the general will have the wherewithal for his first month's pay. Where is your receipt?"

"Here," said the peasant, drawing a paper from his pocket on which were written these words:

Received from our brothers of the Midi and the East, to be employed for the good of the cause, the sum of . . . .

GEORGES CADOUDAL,
General commanding the Royalist army of Brittany.

The sum was left blank.

"Do you know how to write?" asked the president.

"Enough to fill in the three or four missing words."

"Very well. Then write, 'one hundred thousand francs.'"

The Breton wrote; then extending the paper to the president, he said: "Here is your receipt; where is the money?"

"Stoop and pick up the bag at your feet; it contains sixty thousand francs." Then addressing one of the monks, he asked: "Montbard, where are the remaining forty thousand?"

The monk thus interpellated opened a closet and brought forth a bag somewhat smaller than the one Morgan had brought, but which, nevertheless, contained the good round sum of forty thousand francs.

"Here is the full amount," said the monk.

"Now, my friend," said the president, "get something to eat and some rest; to-morrow you will start."

"They are waiting for me yonder," said the Breton. "I will eat and sleep on horseback. Farewell, gentlemen. Heaven keep you!" And he went toward the door by which he had entered.

"Wait," said Morgan.

The messenger paused.

"News for news," said Morgan; "tell General Cadoudal that General Bonaparte has left the army in Egypt, that he landed at Fréjus, day before yesterday, and will be in Paris in three days. My news is fully worth yours, don't you think so? What do you think of it?"

"Impossible!" exclaimed all the monks with one accord.

"Nevertheless nothing is more true, gentlemen. I have it from our friend the Priest (Leprêtre),[1] who saw him relay at Lyons one hour before me, and recognized him."

"What has he come to France for?" demanded several voices.

"Faith," said Morgan, "we shall know some day. It is probable that he has not returned to Paris to remain there incognito."

"Don't lose an instant in carrying this news to our

---

[1] The name Leprêtre is a contraction of the two words "le prêtre," meaning the priest; hence the name under which this man died.

brothers in the West," said the president to the peasant. "A moment ago I wished to detain you; now I say to you: 'Go!'"

The peasant bowed and withdrew. The president waited until the door was closed.

"Gentlemen," said he, "the news which our brother Morgan has just imparted to us is so grave that I wish to propose a special measure."

"What is it?" asked the Companions of Jehu with one voice.

"It is that one of us, chosen by lot, shall go to Paris and keep the rest informed, with the cipher agreed upon, of all that happens there."

"Agreed!" they replied.

"In that case," resumed the president, "let us write our thirteen names, each on a slip of paper. We put them in a hat. He whose name is first drawn shall start immediately."

The young men, one and all, approached the table, and wrote their names on squares of paper which they rolled and dropped into a hat. The youngest was told to draw the lots. He drew one of the little rolls of paper and handed it to the president, who unfolded it.

"Morgan!" said he.

"What are my instructions?" asked the young man.

"Remember," replied the president, with a solemnity to which the cloistral arches lent a supreme grandeur, "that you bear the name and title of Baron de Sainte-Hermine, that your father was guillotined on the Place de la Révolution and that your brother was killed in Condé's army. Noblesse oblige! Those are your instructions."

"And what else?" asked the young man.

"As to the rest," said the president, "we rely on your royalist principles and your loyalty."

"Then, my friends, permit me to bid you farewell at once. I would like to be on the road to Paris before dawn, and I must pay a visit before my departure."

"Go!" said the president, opening his arms to Morgan.

"I embrace you in the name of the Brotherhood. To another I should say, 'Be brave, persevering and active'; to you I say, 'Be prudent.'"

The young man received the fraternal embrace, smiled to his other friends, shook hands with two or three of them, wrapped himself in his mantle, pulled his hat over his eyes and departed.

CHAPTER IX

ROMEO AND JULIET

UNDER the possibility of immediate departure, Morgan's horse, after being washed, rubbed down and dried, had been fed a double ration of oats and been resaddled and bridled. The young man had only to ask for it and spring upon its back. He was no sooner in the saddle than the gate opened as if by magic; the horse neighed and darted out swiftly, having forgotten its first trip, and ready for another.

At the gate of the Chartreuse, Morgan paused an instant, undecided whether to turn to the right or left. He finally turned to the right, followed the road which leads from Bourg to Seillon for a few moments, wheeled rapidly a second time to the right, cut across country, plunged into an angle of the forest which was on his way, reappeared before long on the other side, reached the main road to Pont-d'Ain, followed it for about a mile and a half, and halted near a group of houses now called the Maison des Gardes. One of these houses bore for sign a cluster of holly, which indicated one of those wayside halting places where the pedestrians quench their thirst, and rest for an instant to recover strength before continuing the long fatiguing voyage of life. Morgan stopped at the door, drew a pistol from its holster and rapped with the butt end as he had done at the Chartreuse. Only as, in all probability, the good folks at the humble tavern were far from being conspirators, the traveller was kept waiting longer than he had been at the monastery. At last he heard the echo of the stable boy's clumsy sabots. The gate creaked, but the worthy man who opened it no sooner perceived the horseman with his drawn pistol than he instinctively tried to close it again.

"It is I, Patout," said the young man; "don't be afraid."

"Ah! sure enough," said the peasant, "it is really you, Monsieur Charles. I'm not afraid now; but you know, as the curé used to tell us, in the days when there was a good God, 'Caution is the mother of safety.' "

"Yes, Patout, yes," said the young man, slipping a piece of silver into the stable boy's hand, "but be easy; the good God will return, and M. le Curé also."

"Oh, as for that," said the good man, "it is easy to see that there is no one left on high by the way things go. Will this last much longer, M. Charles?"

"Patout, I promise, in my honor, to do my best to be rid of all that annoys you. I am no less impatient than you; so I'll ask you not to go to bed, my good Patout."

"Ah! You know well, monsieur, that when you come I don't often go to bed. As for the horse—Goodness! you change them every day? The time before last it was a chestnut, the last time a dapple-gray, now a black one."

"Yes, I'm somewhat capricious by nature. As to the horse, as you say, my dear Patout, he wants nothing. You need only remove his bridle; leave him saddled. Oh, wait; put this pistol back in the holsters and take care of these other two for me." And the young man removed the two from his belt and handed them to the hostler.

"Well," exclaimed the latter, laughing, "any more barkers?"

"You know, Patout, they say the roads are unsafe."

"Ah! I should think they weren't safe! We're up to our necks in regular highway robberies, M. Charles. Why, no later than last week they stopped and robbed the diligence between Geneva and Bourg!"

"Indeed!" exclaimed Morgan; "and whom do they accuse of the robbery?"

"Oh, it's such a farce! Just fancy; they say it was the Companions of Jesus. I don't believe a word of it, of course. Who are the Companions of Jesus if not the twelve apostles?"

"Of course," said Morgan, with his eternally joyous smile, "I don't know of any others."

"Well!" continued Patout, "to accuse the twelve apostles of robbing a diligence, that's the limit. Oh! I tell you, M. Charles, we're living in times when nobody respects anything."

And shaking his head like a misanthrope, disgusted, if not with life, at least with men, Patout led the horse to the stable.

As for Morgan, he watched Patout till he saw him disappear down the courtyard and enter the dark stable; then, skirting the hedge which bordered the garden, he went toward a large clump of trees whose lofty tops were silhouetted against the darkness of the night, with the majesty of things immovable, the while their shadows fell upon a charming little country house known in the neighborhood as the Château des Noires-Fontaines. As Morgan reached the château wall, the hour chimed from the belfry of the village of Montagnac. The young man counted the strokes vibrating in the calm silent atmosphere of the autumn night. It was eleven o'clock. Many things, as we have seen, had happened during the last two hours.

Morgan advanced a few steps farther, examined the wall, apparently in search of a familiar spot, then, having found it, inserted the tip of his boot in a cleft between two stones. He sprang up like a man mounting a horse, seized the top of the wall with the left hand, and with a second spring seated himself astride the wall, from which, with the rapidity of lightning, he lowered himself on the other side. All this was done with such rapidity, such dexterity and agility, that any one chancing to pass at that instant would have thought himself the puppet of a vision. Morgan stopped, as on the other side of the wall, to listen, while his eyes tried to pierce the darkness made deeper by the foliage of poplars and aspens, and the heavy shadows of the little wood. All was silent and solitary. Morgan ventured on his path. We say ventured, because the young man, since nearing the Château des Noires-Fontaines, revealed in all his movements a timidity and hesitation so foreign to his character that it was evident that if he feared it was not for himself alone.

He gained the edge of the wood, still moving cautiously. Coming to a lawn, at the end of which was the little château, he paused. Then he examined the front of the house. Only one of the twelve windows which dotted the three floors was lighted. This was on the second floor at the corner of the house. A little balcony, covered with virgin vines which climbed the walls, twining themselves around the iron railing and falling thence in festoons from the window, overhung the garden. On both sides of the windows, close to the balcony, large-leafed trees met and formed above the cornice a bower of verdure. A Venetian blind, which was raised and lowered by cords, separated the balcony from the window, a separation which disappeared at will. It was through the interstices of this blind that Morgan had seen the light.

The young man's first impulse was to cross the lawn in a straight line; but again, the fears of which we spoke restrained him. A path shaded by lindens skirted the wall and led to the house. He turned aside and entered its dark leafy covert. When he had reached the end of the path, he crossed, like a frightened doe, the open space which led to the house wall, and stood for a moment in the deep shadow of the house. Then, when he had reached the spot he had calculated upon, he clapped his hands three times.

At this call a shadow darted from the end of the apartment and clung, lithe, graceful, almost transparent, to the window.

Morgan repeated the signal. The window was opened immediately, the blind was raised, and a ravishing young girl, in a night dress, her fair hair rippling over her shoulders, appeared in the frame of verdure.

The young man stretched out his arms to her, whose arms were stretched out to him, and two names, or rather two cries from the heart, crossed from one to the other.

"Charles!"

"Amélie!"

Then the young man sprang against the wall, caught at the vine shoots, the jagged edges of the rock, the jutting cornice, and in an instant was on the balcony.

What these two beautiful young beings said to each other was only a murmur of love lost in an endless kiss. Then, by gentle effort, the young man drew the girl with one hand to her chamber, while with the other he loosened the cords of the blind, which fell noisily behind them. The window closed behind the blind. Then the lamp was extinguished, and the front of the Château des Noires-Fontaines was again in darkness.

This darkness had lasted for about a quarter of an hour, when the rolling of a carriage was heard along the road leading from the highway of Pont-d'Ain to the entrance of the château. There the sound ceased; it was evident that the carriage had stopped before the gates.

CHAPTER X

THE FAMILY OF ROLAND

THE carriage which had stopped before the gate was that which brought Roland back to his family, accompanied by Sir John.

The family was so far from expecting him that, as we have said, all the lights in the house were extinguished, all the windows in darkness, even Amélie's. The postilion had cracked his whip smartly for the last five hundred yards, but the noise was insufficient to rouse these country people from their first sleep. When the carriage had stopped, Roland opened the door, sprang out without touching the steps, and tugged at the bell-handle. Five minutes elapsed, and, after each peal, Roland turned to the carriage, saying: "Don't be impatient, Sir John."

At last a window opened and a childish but firm voice cried out: "Who is ringing that way?"

"Ah, is that you, little Edouard?" said Roland. "Make haste and let us in."

The child leaped back with a shout of delight and disappeared. But at the same time his voice was heard in the corridors, crying: "Mother! wake up; it is Roland! Sister! wake up; it is the big brother!"

Then, clad only in his night robe and his little slippers, he ran down the steps, crying: "Don't be impatient, Roland; here I am."

An instant later the key grated in the lock, and the bolts slipped back in their sockets. A white figure appeared in the portico, and flew rather than ran to the gate, which an instant later turned on its hinges and swung open. The child sprang upon Roland's neck and hung there.

"Ah, brother! brother!" he exclaimed, embracing the young man, laughing and crying at the same time. "Ah, big brother Roland! How happy mother will be; and Amélie, too! Everybody is well. I am the sickest—ah! except Michel, the gardener, you know, who has sprained his leg. But why aren't you in uniform? Oh! how ugly you are in citizen's clothes! Have you just come from Egypt? Did you bring me the silver-mounted pistols and the beautiful curved sword? No? Then you are not nice, and I won't kiss you any more. Oh, no, no! Don't be afraid! I love you just the same!"

And the boy smothered the big brother with kisses while he showered questions upon him. The Englishman, still seated in the carriage, looked smilingly through the window at the scene.

In the midst of these fraternal embraces came the voice of a woman; the voice of the mother.

"Where is he, my Roland, my darling son?" asked Madame de Montrevel, in a voice fraught with such violent, joyous emotion that it was almost painful. "Where is he? Can it be true that he has returned; really true that he is not a prisoner, not dead? Is he really living?"

The child, at her voice, slipped from his brother's arms like an eel, dropped upon his feet on the grass, and, as if moved by a spring, bounded toward his mother.

"This way, mother; this way!" said he, dragging his mother, half dressed as she was, toward Roland. When he saw his mother Roland could no longer contain himself. He felt the sort of icicle that had petrified his breast melt, and his heart beat like that of his fellowmen.

"Ah!" he exclaimed, "I was indeed ungrateful to God when life still holds such joys for me."

And he fell sobbing upon Madame de Montrevel's neck without thinking of Sir John, who felt his English phlegm disperse as he silently wiped away the tears that flowed down his cheeks and moistened his lips. The child, the mother, and Roland formed an adorable group of tenderness and emotion.

Suddenly little Edouard, like a leaf tossed about by the wind, flew from the group, exclaiming: "Sister Amélie! Why, where is she?" and he rushed toward the house, repeating: "Sister Amélie, wake up! Get up! Hurry up!"

And then the child could be heard kicking and rapping against a door. Silence followed. Then little Edouard shouted: "Help, mother! Help, brother Roland! Sister Amélie is ill!"

Madame de Montrevel and her son flew toward the house. Sir John, consummate tourist that he was, always carried a lancet and a smelling bottle in his pocket. He jumped from the carriage and, obeying his first impulse, hurried up the portico. There he paused, reflecting that he had not been introduced, an all-important formality for an Englishman.

However, the fainting girl whom he sought came toward him at that moment. The noise her brother had made at the door brought Amélie to the landing; but, without doubt, the excitement which Roland's return had occasioned was too much for her, for after descending a few steps in an almost automatic manner, controlling herself by a violent effort, she gave a sigh, and, like a flower that bends, a branch that droops, like a scarf that floats, she fell, or rather lay, upon the stairs. It was at that moment that the child cried out.

But at his exclamation Amélie recovered, if not her strength, at least her will. She rose, and, stammering, "Be quiet, Edouard! be quite, in Heaven's name! I'm all right," she clung to the balustrade with one hand, and leaning with the other on the child, she had continued to descend. On the last step she met her mother and her brother. Then with a violent, almost despairing movement, she threw both arms around Roland's neck, exclaiming: "My brother! My brother!"

Roland, feeling the young girl's weight press heavily upon his shoulder, exclaimed: "Air! Air! She is fainting!" and carried her out upon the portico. It was this new group, so different from the first, which met Sir John's eyes.

As soon as she felt the fresh air, Amélie revived and raised her head. Just then the moon, in all her splendor, shook off a cloud which had veiled her, and lighted Amélie's face, as pale as her own. Sir John gave a cry of admiration. Never had he seen a marble statue so perfect as this living marble before his eyes.

We must say that Amélie, seen thus, was marvellously beautiful. Clad in a long cambric robe, which defined the outlines of her body, molded on that of the Polyhymnia of antiquity, her pale face gently inclined upon her brother's shoulder, her long golden hair floating around her snowy shoulders, her arm thrown around her mother's neck, its rose-tinted alabaster hand drooping upon the red shawl in which Madame de Montrevel had wrapped herself; such was Roland's sister as she appeared to Sir John.

At the Englishman's cry of admiration, Roland remembered that he was there, and Madame de Montrevel perceived his presence. As for the child, surprised to see this stranger in his mother's home, he ran hastily down the steps of the portico, stopping on the third one, not that he feared to go further, but in order to be on a level with the person he proceeded to question.

"Who are you, sir!" he asked Sir John; "and what are you doing here?"

"My little Edouard," said Sir John, "I am your brother's friend, and I have brought you the silver-mounted pistols and the Damascus blade which he promised you."

"Where are they?" asked the child.

"Ah!" said Sir John, "they are in England, and it will take some time to send for them. But your big brother will answer for me that I am a man of my word."

"Yes, Edouard, yes," said Roland. "If Sir John promises them to you, you will get them." Then turning to Madame de Montrevel and his sister, "Excuse me, my mother; excuse me, Amélie; or rather, excuse yourselves as best you can to Sir John, for you have made me abominably ungrateful." Then grasping Sir John's hand, he continued: "Mother, Sir John took occasion the first time he saw me to render me an inestimable service. I know that you never forget such things. I trust, therefore, that you will always remember that Sir John is one of our best friends; and he will give you the proof of it by saying with me that he has consented to be bored for a couple of weeks with us."

"Madame," said Sir John, "permit me, on the contrary, not to repeat my friend Roland's words. I could wish to spend, not a fortnight, nor three weeks, but a whole lifetime with you."

Madame de Montrevel came down the steps of the portico and offered her hand to Sir John, who kissed it with a gallantry altogether French.

"My lord," said she, "this house is yours. The day you entered it has been one of joy, the day you leave will be one of regret and sadness."

Sir John turned toward Amélie, who, confused by the disorder of her dress before this stranger, was gathering the folds of her wrapper about her neck.

"I speak to you in my name and in my daughter's, who is still too much overcome by her brother's unexpected return to greet you herself as she will do in a moment," continued Madame de Montrevel, coming to Amélie's relief.

"My sister," said Roland, "will permit my friend Sir John to kiss her hand, and he will, I am sure, accept that form of welcome."

Amélie stammered a few words, slowly lifted her arm, and held out her hand to Sir John with a smile that was almost painful.

The Englishman took it, but, feeling how icy and trembling it was, instead of carrying it to his lips he said: "Roland, your sister is seriously indisposed. Let us think only of her health this evening. I am something of a doctor, and if she will deign to permit me the favor of feeling her pulse I shall be grateful."

But Amélie, as if she feared that the cause of her weakness might be surmised, withdrew her hand hastily, exclaiming: "Oh, no! Sir John is mistaken. Joy never causes illness. It is only joy at seeing my brother again which caused this slight indisposition, and it has already passed over." Then turning to Madame de Montrevel, she added with almost feverish haste: "Mother, we are forgetting that these gentlemen have made a long voyage, and have probably eaten nothing since Lyons. If Roland has his usual good appetite he will not object to my leaving you to do the honors of the house, while I attend to the unpoetical but much appreciated details of the housekeeping."

Leaving her mother, as she said, to do the honors of the

house, Amélie went to waken the maids and the man-servant, leaving on the mind of Sir John that sort of fairy-like impression which the tourist on the Rhine brings with him of the Lorelei on her rock, a lyre in her hand, the liquid gold of her hair floating in the evening breezes.

In the meantime, Morgan had remounted his horse, returning at full gallop to the Chartreuse. He drew rein before the portal, pulled out a note-book, and pencilling a few lines on one of the leaves, rolled it up and slipped it through the keyhole without taking time to dismount.

Then pressing in both his spurs, and bending low over the mane of the noble animal, he disappeared in the forest, rapid and mysterious as Faust on his way to the mountain of the witches' sabbath. The three lines he had written were as follows:

"Louis de Montrevel, General Bonaparte's aide-de-camp, arrived this evening at the Château des Noires-Fontaines. Be careful, Companions of Jehu!"

But, while warning his comrades to be cautious about Louis de Montrevel, Morgan had drawn a cross above his name, which signified that no matter what happened the body of the young officer must be considered as sacred by them.

The Companions of Jehu had the right to protect a friend in that way without being obliged to explain the motives which actuated them. Morgan used that privilege to protect the brother of his love.

CHAPTER XI

CHÂTEAU DES NOIRES-FONTAINES

THE Chateau of Noires-Fontaines, whither we have just conducted two of the principal characters of our story, stood in one of the most charming spots of the valley, where the city of Bourg is built. The park, of five or six acres, covered with venerable oaks, was in-

closed on three sides by freestone walls, one of which
opened in front through a handsome gate of wrought-iron,
fashioned in the style of Louis XV.; the fourth side was
bounded by the little river called the Reissouse, a pretty
stream that takes its rise at Journaud, among the foothills
of the Jura, and flowing gently from south to north, joins
the Saône at the bridge of Fleurville, opposite Pont-de-
Vaux, the birthplace of Joubert, who, a month before the
period of which we are writing, was killed at the fatal battle
of Novi.

Beyond the Reissouse, and along its banks, lay, to the
right and left of the Château des Noires-Fontaines, the
village of Montagnac and Saint-Just, dominated further on
by that of Ceyzeriat. Behind this latter hamlet stretched
the graceful outlines of the hills of the Jura, above the
summits of which could be distinguished the blue crests
of the mountains of Bugey, which seemed to be standing
on tiptoe in order to peer curiously over their younger
sisters' shoulder at what was passing in the valley of
the Ain.

It was in full view of this ravishing landscape that Sir
John awoke. For the first time in his life, perhaps, the
morose and taciturn Englishman smiled at nature. He
fancied himself in one of those beautiful valleys of Thessaly celebrated by Virgil, beside the sweet slopes of Lignon
sung by Urfé, whose birthplace, in spite of what the biographers say, was falling into ruins not three miles from the
Chateau des Noires-Fontaines. He was roused by three light
raps at his door. It was Roland who came to see how he had
passed the night. He found him radiant as the sun playing
among the already yellow leaves of the chestnuts and the
lindens.

"Oh! oh! Sir John," cried Roland, "permit me to congratulate you. I expected to find you as gloomy as the
poor monks of the Chartreuse, with their long white robes,
who used to frighten me so much in my childhood; though,
to tell the truth, I was never easily frightened. Instead of

that I find you in the midst of this dreary October, as smiling as a morn of May.''

"My dear Roland," replied Sir John, "I am an orphan; I lost my mother at my birth and my father when I was twelve years old. At an age when children are usually sent to school, I was master of a fortune producing a million a year; but I was alone in the world, with no one whom I loved or who loved me. The tender joys of family life are completely unknown to me. From twelve to eighteen I went to Cambridge, but my taciturn and perhaps haughty character isolated me from my fellows. At eighteen I began to travel. You who scour the world under the shadow of your flag; that is to say, the shadow of your country, and are stirred by the thrill of battle, and the pride of glory, cannot imagine what a lamentable thing it is to roam through cities, provinces, nations, and kingdoms simply to visit a church here, a castle there; to rise at four in the morning at the summons of a pitiless guide, to see the sun rise from Rigi or Etna; to pass like a phantom, already dead, through the world of living shades called men; to know not where to rest; to know no land in which to take root, no arm on which to lean, no heart in which to pour your own! Well, last night, my dear Roland, suddenly, in an instant, in a second, this void in my life was filled. I lived in you; the joys I seek were yours. The family which I never had, I saw smiling around you. As I looked at your mother I said to myself: 'My mother was like that, I am sure.' Looking at your sister, I said: 'Had I a sister I could not have wished her otherwise.' When I embraced your brother, I thought that I, too, might have had a child of that age, and thus leave something behind me in the world, whereas with the nature I know I possess, I shall die as I have lived, sad, surly with others, a burden to myself. Ah! you are happy, Roland! you have a family, you have fame, you have youth, you have that which spoils nothing in a man—you have beauty. You want no joys. You are not deprived of a single delight. I repeat it, Roland, you are a happy man, most happy!"

"Good!" said Roland. "You forget my aneurism, my lord."

Sir John looked at Roland increduously. Roland seemed to enjoy the most perfect health.

"Your aneurism against my million, Roland," said Lord Tanlay, with a feeling of profound sadness, "providing that with this aneurism you give me this mother who weeps for joy on seeing you again; this sister who faints with delight at your return; this child who clings upon your neck like some fresh young fruit to a sturdy young tree; this château with its dewy shade, its river with its verdant flowering banks, these blue vistas dotted with pretty villages and white-capped belfries graceful as swans. I would welcome your aneurism, Roland, and with death in two years, in one, in six months; but six months of stirring, tender, eventful and glorious life!"

Roland laughed in his usual nervous manner.

"Ah!" said he, "so this is the tourist, the superficial traveller, the Wandering Jew of civilization, who pauses nowhere, gauges nothing, judges everything by the sensation it produces in him. The tourist who, without opening the doors of these abodes where dwell the fools we call men, says: 'Behind these walls is happiness!' Well, my dear friend, you see this charming river, don't you? these flowering meadows, these pretty villages? It is the picture of peace, innocence and fraternity; the cycle of Saturn, the golden age returned; it is Eden, Paradise! Well, all that is peopled by beings who have flown at each other's throats. The jungles of Calcutta, the sedges of Bengal are inhabited by tigers and panthers not one whit more ferocious or cruel than the denizens of these pretty villages, these dewy lawns, and these charming shores. After lauding in funeral celebrations the good, the great, the immortal Marat, whose body, thank God! they cast into the common sewer like carrion that he was, and always had been; after performing these funeral rites, to which each man brought an urn into which he shed his tears, behold! our good Bressans, our gentle Bressans, these poultry-fatteners, suddenly decided that the Republicans were all murderers. So they murdered them by the tumbrelful to correct them of that vile defect common to savage and civilized man—the killing his kind. You doubt it? My dear fellow, on the road to Lons-le-Saulnier they will show you, if you are curious, the spot where not six months ago they organized a slaughter fit to turn the stomach of our most ferocious troopers on the battlefield. Picture to yourself a tumbrel of prisoners on their way to Lons-le-Saulnier. It was a staff-sided cart, one of those immense wagons in which they take cattle to market. There were some thirty men in this tumbrel, whose sole crime was foolish exaltation of thought and threatening language. They were bound and gagged; heads hanging, jolted by the bumping of the cart; their throats parched with thirst, despair and terror; unfortunate beings who did not even have, as in the times of Nero and Commodus, the fight in the arena, the hand-to-hand struggle with death. Powerless, motionless, the lust of massacre surprised them in their fetters, and battered them not only in life but in death, their bodies, when their hearts had ceased to beat, still resounded beneath the bludgeons which mangled their flesh and crushed their bones; while women looked on in calm delight, lifting high the children, who clapped their hands for joy. Old men who ought to have been preparing for a Christian death helped, by their goading cries, to render the death of these wretched beings more wretched still. And in the midst of these old men, a little septuagenarian, dainty, powdered, flicking his lace shirt frill if a speck of dust settled there, pinching his Spanish tobacco from a golden snuff-box, with a diamond monogram, eating his amber sugarplums from a Sevres bonbonnière, given him by Madame du Barry, and adorned with the donor's portrait—this septuagenarian—conceive the picture, my dear Sir John—dancing with his pumps upon that mattress of human flesh, wearying his arm, enfeebled by age, in striking repeatedly with his gold-headed cane those of the bodies who seemed not dead enough to him, not properly mangled in that cursed mortar! Faugh! my friend, I have seen Montebello, I have seen Arcole, I have seen Rivoli, I have seen the Pyramids, and I believe I could see nothing more terrible. Well, my mother's mere recital, last night, after you had retired, of what has happened here, made my hair stand on end. Faith! that explains my poor sister's spasms just as my aneurism explains mine."

Sir John watched Roland, and listened with that strange wonderment which his young friend's misanthropical out-bursts always aroused. Roland seemed to lurk in the niches of a conversation in order to fall upon mankind whenever he found an opportunity. Perceiving the im-pression he had made on Sir John's mind, he changed his tone, substituting bitter raillery for his philanthropic wrath.

"It is true," said he, "that, apart from this excellent aristocrat who finished what the butchers had begun, and dyed in blood the red heels of his pumps, the people who performed these massacres belonged to the lower classes, bourgeois and clowns, as our ancestors called those who supported them. The nobles manage things much more daintily. For the rest, you saw yourself what happened at Avignon. If you had been told that, you would never have believed it, would you? Those gentlemen pillagers of stage coaches pique themselves on their great delicacy. They have two faces, not counting their mask. Sometimes they are Cartouche and Mandrin, sometimes Amadis and Galahad. They tell fabulous tales of these heroes of the highways. My mother told me yesterday of one called Laurent. You understand, my dear fellow, that Laurent is a fictitious name meant to hide the real name, just as a mask hides the face. This Laurent combined all the qualities of a hero of romance, all the accomplishments, as you English say, who, under pretext that you were once Normans, allow your-

selves occasionally to enrich your language with a picturesque expression, or some word which has long, poor
beggar! asked and been refused admittance of our own
scholars. This Laurent was ideally handsome. He was
one of seventy-two Companions of Jehu who have lately
been tried at Yssen-geaux. Seventy were acquitted; he and
one other were the only ones condemned to death. The
innocent men were released at once, but Laurent and his
companion were put in prison to await the guillotine. But,
pooh! Master Laurent had too pretty a head to fall under
the executioner's ignoble knife. The judges who condemned him, the curious who expected to witness him
executed, had forgotten what Montaigne calls the cor-
poreal recommendation of beauty. There was a woman
belonging to the jailer of Yssen-geaux, his daughter, sister
or niece; history—for it is history and not romance that
I am telling you—history does not say which. At all
events the woman, whoever she was, fell in love with
the handsome prisoner, so much in love that two hours
before the execution, just as Master Laurent, expecting the
executioner, was sleeping, or pretending to sleep, as usually
happens in such cases, his guardian angel came to him. I
don't know how they managed; for the two lovers, for the
best of reasons, never told the details; but the truth is—now
remember, Sir John, that this is truth and not fiction—that
Laurent was free, but, to his great regret, unable to save his
comrade in the adjoining dungeon. Gensonné, under like
circumstances, refused to escape, preferring to die with the
other Girondins; but Gensonné did not have the head of
Antinous on the body of Apollo. The handsomer the
head, you understand, the more one holds on to it. So
Laurent accepted the freedom offered him and escaped; a
horse was waiting for him at the next village. The young
girl, who might have retarded or hindered his flight, was to
rejoin him the next day. Dawn came, but not the guardian
angel. It seems that our hero cared more for his mistress
than he did for his companion; he left his comrade, but he

would not go without her. It was six o'clock, the very hour for his execution. His impatience mastered him. Three times had he turned his horse's head toward the town, and each time drew nearer and nearer. At the third time a thought flashed through his brain. Could his mistress have been taken, and would she pay the penalty for saving him? He was then in the suburbs. Spurring his horse, he entered the town with face uncovered, dashed through people who called him by name, astonished to see him free and on horseback, when they expected to see him bound and in a tumbrel on his way to be executed. Catching sight of his guardian angel pushing through the crowd, not to see him executed, but to meet him, he urged his horse past the executioner, who had just learned of the disappearance of one of his patients, knocking over two or three bumpkins with the breast of his Bayard. He bounded toward her, swung her over the pommel of his saddle, and, with a cry of joy and a wave of his hat, he disappeared like M. de Condé at the battle of Lens. The people all applauded, and the women thought the action heroic, and all promptly fell in love with the hero on the spot."

Roland, observing that Sir John was silent, paused and questioned him by a look. "Go on," replied the Englishman; "I am listening. And as I am sure you are telling me all this in order to come to something you wish to say, I await your point."

"Well," resumed Roland, laughing, "you are right, my dear friend, and, on my word, you know me as if we had been college chums. Well, what idea do you suppose has been cavorting through my brain all night? It is that of getting a glimpse of these gentlemen of Jehu near at hand."

"Ah, yes, I understand. As you failed to get yourself killed by M. de Barjols, you want to try your chance of being killed by M. Morgan."

"Or any other, my dear Sir John," replied the young officer calmly; "for I assure you that I have nothing in particular against M. Morgan; quite the contrary, though my first impulse when he came into the room and made his little speech—don't you call it a speech—?"

Sir John nodded affirmatively.

"Though my first thought," resumed Roland, "was to spring at his throat and strangle him with one hand, and to tear off his mask with the other."

"Now that I know you, my dear Roland, I do indeed wonder how you refrained from putting such a fine project into execution."

"It was not my fault, I swear! I was just on the point of it when my companion stopped me."

"So there are people who can restrain you?"

"Not many, but he can."

"And now you regret it?"

"Honestly, no! This brave stage-robber did the business with such swaggering bravado that I admired him. I love brave men instinctively. Had I not killed M. de Barjols I should have liked to be his friend. It is true I could not tell how brave he was until I had killed him. But let us talk of something else; that duel is one of my painful thoughts. But why did I come up? It was certainly not to talk of the Companions of Jehu, nor of M. Laurent's exploits— Ah! I came to ask how you would like to spend your time. I'll cut myself in quarters to amuse you, my dear guest, but there are two disadvantages against me: this region, which is not very amusing, and your nationality, which is not easily amused."

"I have already told you, Roland," replied Lord Tanlay, offering his hand to the young man, "that I consider the Château des Noires-Fontaines a paradise."

"Agreed; but still in the fear that you may find your paradise monotonous, I shall do my best to entertain you. Are you fond of archeology—Westminster and Canterbury? We have a marvel here, the church of Brou; a wonder of sculptured lace by Colonban. There is a legend about it which I will tell you some evening when you cannot sleep.

You will see there the tombs of Marguerite de Bourbon, Philippe le Bel, and Marguerite of Austria. I will puzzle you with the problem of her motto: 'Fortune, infortune, fort'une,' which I claim to have solved by a Latinized version: 'Fortuna, infortuna, forti una.' Are you fond of fishing, my dear friend? There's the Reissouse at your feet, and close at hand a collection of hooks and lines belonging to Edouard, and nets belonging to Michel; as for the fish, they, you know, are the last thing one thinks about. Are you fond of hunting? The forest of Seillon is not a hundred yards off. Hunting to hounds you will have perforce to renounce, but we have good shooting. In the days of my old bogies, the Chartreuse monks, the woods swarmed with wild boars, hares and foxes. No one hunts there now, because it belongs to the government; and the government at present is nobody. In my capacity as General Bonaparte's aide-de-camp I'll fill the vacancy, and we'll see who dares meddle with me, if, after chasing the Austrians on the Adige and the Mamelukes on the Nile, I hunt the boars and deer and the hares and foxes on the Reissouse. One day of archeology, one day of fishing, and one of hunting, that's three already. You see, my dear fellow, we have only fifteen or sixteen left to worry about."

"My dear Roland," said Sir John sadly, and without replying to the young officer's wordy sally, "won't you ever tell me about this fever which sears you, this sorrow which undermines you?"

"Ah!" said Roland, with his harsh, doleful laugh, "I have never been gayer than I am this morning; it's your liver, my lord, that is out of order and makes you see everything black."

"Some day I hope to be really your friend," replied Sir John seriously; "then you will confide in me, and I shall help you to bear your burden."

"And half my aneurism! — Are you hungry, my lord?"

"Why do you ask?"

"Because I hear Edouard on the stairs, coming up to tell us that breakfast is ready."

As Roland spoke, the door opened and the boy burst out: "Big brother Roland, mother and sister Amélie are waiting breakfast for Sir John and you."

Then catching the Englishman's right hand, he carefully examined the first joint of the thumb and forefinger.

"What are you looking at, my little friend?" asked Sir John.

"I was looking to see if you had any ink on your fingers."

"And if I had ink on my fingers, what would it mean?"

"That you had written to England, and sent for my pistols and sword."

"No, I have not yet written," said Sir John; "but I will to-day."

"You hear, big brother Roland? I'm to have my sword and my pistols in a fortnight!"

And the boy, full of delight, offered his firm rosy cheek to Sir John, who kissed it as tenderly as a father would have done. Then they went to the dining-room where Madame de Montrevel and Amélie were awaiting them.

CHAPTER XII

PROVINCIAL PLEASURES

THAT same day Roland put into execution part of his plans for his guest's amusement. He took Sir John to see the church of Brou.

Those who have seen the charming little chapel of Brou know that it is known as one of the hundred marvels of the Renaissance; those who have not seen it must have often heard it said. Roland, who had counted on doing the honors of this historic gem to Sir John, and who had not seen it for the last seven or eight years, was much disappointed when, on arriving in front of the building, he found the niches of the saints empty and the carved figures of the portal decapitated.

He asked for the sexton; people laughed in his face. There was no longer a sexton. He inquired to whom he should go for the keys. They replied that the captain of the gendarmerie had them. The captain was not far off, for the cloister adjoining the church had been converted into a barrack.

Roland went up to the captain's room and made himself known as Bonaparte's aide-de-camp. The captain, with the placid obedience of a subaltern to his superior officer, gave him the keys and followed behind him. Sir John was waiting before the porch, admiring, in spite of the mutilation to which they had been subjected, the admirable details of the frontal.

Roland opened the door and started back in astonishment. The church was literally stuffed with hay like a cannon charged to the muzzle.

"What does this mean?" he asked the captain of the gendarmerie.

"A precaution taken by the municipality."

"A precaution taken by the municipality?"

"Yes."

"For what?"

"To save the church. They were going to demolish it; but the mayor issued a decree declaring that, in expiation of the false worship for which it had served, it should be used to store fodder."

Roland burst out laughing, and, turning to Sir John, he said: "My dear Sir John, the church was well worth seeing, but I think what this gentleman has just told us is no less curious. You can always find—at Strasburg, Cologne, or Milan—churches or cathedrals to equal the chapel of Brou; but where will you find an administration idiotic enough to destroy such a masterpiece, and a mayor clever enough to turn it into a barn? A thousand thanks, captain. Here are your keys."

"As I was saying at Avignon, the first time I had the pleasure of seeing you, my dear Roland," replied Sir John, "the French are a most amusing people."

"This time, my lord, you are too polite," replied Roland. "Idiotic is the word. Listen. I can understand the political cataclysms which have convulsed society for the last thousand years; I can understand the communes, the pastorals, the Jacquerie, the maillotins, the Saint Bartholomew, the League, the Fronde, the dragonnades, the Revolution; I can understand the 14th of July, the 5th and 6th of October, the 20th of June, the 10th of August, the 2d and 3d of September, the 21st of January, the 31st of May, the 30th of October, and the 9th Thermidor; I can understand the egregious torch of civil wars, which inflames instead of soothing the blood; I can understand the tidal wave of revolution, sweeping on with its flux, that nothing can arrest, and its reflux, which carries with it the ruins of the institution which it has itself shattered. I can understand all that, but lance against lance, sword against sword, men against men, a people against a people! I can understand the deadly rage of the victors, the sanguinary reaction of the vanquished, the political volcanoes which rumble in the bowels of the globe, shake the earth, topple over thrones, upset monarchies, and roll heads and crowns on the scaffold. But what I cannot understand is this mutilation of the granite, this placing of monuments beyond the pale of the law, the destruction of inanimate things, which belong neither to those who destroy them nor to the epoch in which they are destroyed; this pillage of the gigantic library where the antiquarian can read the archeological history of a country. Oh! the vandals, the barbarians! Worse than that, the idiots! who revenge the Borgia crimes and the debauches of Louis XV. on stone. How well those Pharaohs, Menæs, and Cheops knew man as the most perversive, destructive and evil of animals! They who built their pyramids, not with carved traceries, nor lacy spires, but with solid blocks of granite fifty feet square! How they must have laughed in the depths of those sepulchres as they watched Time dull its scythe and pashas wear out their nails in vain against them. Let us build pyramids, my dear Sir John. They are not difficult as architecture, nor beautiful as art, but they are solid; and that enables a general to say four thousand years later: 'Soldiers, from the apex of these monuments forty centuries are watching you!' On my honor, my lord, I long to meet a windmill this moment that I might tilt against it.''

And Roland, bursting into his accustomed laugh, dragged Sir John in the direction of the château. But Sir John stopped him and asked: ''Is there nothing else to see in the city except the church?''

''Formerly, my lord,'' replied Roland, ''before they made a hay-loft of it, I should have asked you to come down with me into the vaults of the Dukes of Savoy. We could have hunted for that subterranean passage, nearly three miles long, which is said to exist there, and which, according to these rumors, communicates with the grotto of Ceyzeriat. Please observe, I should never offer such a pleasure trip except to an Englishman; it would have been like a scene from your celebrated Anne Radcliffe in the 'Mysteries of Udolpho.' But, as you see, that is impossible, so we will have to be satisfied with our regrets. Come.''

''Where are we going?''

''Faith, I don't know. Ten years ago I should have taken you to the farms where they fatten pullets. The pullets of Bresse, you must know, have a European reputation. Bourg was an annex to the great coop of Strasburg. But during the Terror, as you can readily imagine, these fatteners of poultry shut up shop. You earned the reputation of being an aristocrat if you ate a pullet, and you know the fraternal refrain: 'Ah, ça ira, ça ira—the aristocrats to the lantern!' After Robespierre's downfall they opened up again; but since the 18th of Fructidor, France has been commanded to fast, from fowls and all. Never mind; come on, anyway. In default of pullets, I can show you one thing, the square where they executed those who ate them. But since I was last in the town the streets have changed their names. I know the way, but I don't know the names."

"Look here!" demanded Sir John; "aren't you a Republican?"

"I not a Republican? Come, come! Quite to the contrary. I consider myself an excellent Republican. I am quite capable of burning off my hand, like Mucius Scævola, or jumping into the gulf like Curtius to save the Republic; but I have, unluckily, a keen sense of the ridiculous. In spite of myself, the absurdity of things catches me in the side and tickles me till I nearly die of laughing. I am willing to accept the Constitution of 1791; but when poor Hérault de Séchelles wrote to the superintendent of the National Library to send him a copy of the laws of Minos, so that he could model his constitution on that of the Isle of Crete, I thought it was going rather far, and that we might very well have been content with those of Lycurgus. I find January, February, and March, mythological as they were, quite as good as Nivose, Pluviose, and Ventose. I can't understand why, when one was called Antoine or Chrystomome in 1789, he should be called Brutus or Cassius in 1793. Here, for example, my lord, is an honest street, which was called the Rue des Halles (Market Street). There was nothing indecent or aristocratic about that, was there? Well, now it is called— Just wait (Roland read the inscription). Well, now it is called the Rue de la Révolution. Here's another, which used to be called Notre Dame; it is now the Rue du Temple. Why Rue du Temple? Probably to perpetuate the memory of that place where the infamous Simon tried to teach cobbling to the heir of sixty-three kings. Don't quarrel with me if I am mistaken by one or two! Now here's a third; it was named Crèvecœur, a name famous throughout Bresse, Burgundy and Flanders. It is now the Rue de la Fédération. Federation is a fine thing, but Crèvecœur was a fine name. And then you see to-day it leads straight to the Place de la Guillotine, which is, in my opinion, all wrong. I don't want any streets that lead to such places. This one has its advantages; it is only about a hundred feet from the prison, which economized and still economizes the tumbrel and the horse of M. de Bourg. By the way, have you noticed that the executioner remains noble and keeps his title? For the rest, the square is excellently arranged for spectators, and my ancestor, Montrevel, whose name it bears, doubtless foreseeing its ultimate destiny, solved the great problem, still unsolved by the theatres, of being able to see well from every nook and corner. If ever they cut off my head, which, considering the times in which we are living, would in no wise be surprising, I shall have but one regret: that of being less well-placed and seeing less than the others. Now let us go up these steps. Here we are in the Place des Lices. Our Revolutionists left it its name, because in all probability they don't know what it means. I don't know much better than they, but I think I remember that a certain Sieur d'Estavayer challenged some Flemish count—I don't know who —and that the combat took place in this square. Now, my dear fellow, here is the prison, which ought to give you some idea of human vicissitudes. Gil Blas didn't change his condition more often than this monument its purposes. Before Cæsar it was a Gaelic temple; Cæsar converted it into a Roman fortress; an unknown architect transformed it into a military work during the Middle Ages; the Knights of Baye, following Cæsar's example, re-made it into a fortress; the princes of Savoy used it for a residence; the aunt of Charles V. lived here when she came to visit her church at Brou, which she never had the satisfaction of seeing finished. Finally, after the treaty of Lyons, when Bresse was returned to France, it was utilized both as a prison and a court-house. Wait for me a moment, my lord, if you dislike the squeaking of hinges and the grating of bolts. I have a visit to pay to a certain cell."

"The grating of bolts and the squeaking of hinges is not

a very enlivening sound, but no matter. Since you were kind enough to undertake my education, show me your dungeon.''

''Very well, then. Come in quickly. I see a crowd of persons who look as if they want to speak to me.''

In fact, little by little, a sort of rumor seemed to spread throughout the town. People emerged from the houses, forming groups in the streets, and they all watched Roland with curiosity. He rang the bell of the gate, situated then where it is now, but opening into the prison yard. A jailer opened it for them.

''Ah, ah! so you are still here, Father Courtois?'' asked the young man. Then, turning to Sir John, he added: ''A fine name for a jailer, isn't it, my lord?''

The jailer looked at the young man in amazement.

''How is it,'' he asked through the grating, ''that you know my name, when I don't know yours?''

''Good! I not only know your name, but also your opinions. You are an old royalist, Père Courtois.''

''Monsieur,'' said the jailer, terrified, ''don't make bad jokes if you please, and say what you want.''

''Well, my good Father Courtois, I would like to visit the cell where they put my mother and sister, Madame and Mademoiselle Montrevel.''

''Ah!'' exclaimed the gatekeeper, ''so it's you, M. Louis? You may well say that I know you. What a fine, handsome young man you've grown to be!''

''Do you think so, Father Courtois? Well, I can return the compliment. Your daughter Charlotte is, on my word, a beautiful girl. Charlotte is my sister's maid, Sir John.''

''And she is very happy over it. She is better off there than here, M. Roland. Is it true that you are General Bonaparte's aide-de-camp?''

''Alas! I have that honor, Courtois. You would prefer me to be Comte d'Artois's aide-de-camp, or that of M. le Duc of Angoulême?''

"Oh, do be quiet, M. Louis!" Then putting his lips to the young man's ear, "Tell me, is it true?"

"What, Father Courtois?"

"That General Bonaparte passed through Lyons yesterday?"

"There must be some truth in the rumor, for this is the second time that I have heard it. Ah! I understand now. These good people who were watching me so curiously apparently wanted to question me. They were like you, Father Courtois: they want to know what to make of General Bonaparte's arrival."

"Do you know what they say, M. Louis?"

"Still another rumor, Father Courtois?"

"I should think so, but they only whisper it."

"What is it?"

"They say that he has come to demand the throne of his Majesty Louis XVIII. from the Directory and the king's return to it; and that if Citizen Gohier as president doesn't give it up of his own accord he will take it by force."

"Pooh!" exclaimed the young officer with an incredulous air bordering on irony. But Father Courtois insisted on his news with an affirmative nod.

"Possibly," said the young man; "but as for that, it's news for me. And now that you know me, will you open the gate?"

"Of course I will. I should think so. What the devil am I about?" and the jailer opened the gate with an eagerness equalling his former reluctance. The young man entered, and Sir John followed him. The jailer locked the gate carefully, then he turned, followed by Roland and the Englishman in turn. The latter was beginning to get accustomed to his young friend's erratic character. The spleen he saw in Roland was misanthropy, without the sulkiness of Timon or the wit of Alceste.

The jailer crossed the yard, which was separated from the law courts by a wall fifteen feet high, with an opening let into the middle of the receding wall, closed by a massive oaken door, to admit prisoners without taking them round by the street. The jailer, we say, crossed the yard to a winding stairway in the left angle of the courtyard which led to the interior of the prison.

If we insist upon these details, it is because we shall be obliged to return to this spot later, and we do not wish it to be wholly unfamiliar to our readers when that time comes.

These steps led first to the ante-chamber of the prison, that is to say to the porter's hall of the lower court-room. From that hall ten steps led down into an inner court, separated from a third, which was that of the prisoners, by a wall similar to the one we have described, only this one had three doors. At the further end of the courtyard a passage led to the jailer's own room, which gave into a second passage, on which were the cells which were picturesquely styled cages. The jailer paused before the first of these cages and said, striking the door:

"This is where I put madame, your mother, and your sister, so that if the dear ladies wanted either Charlotte or myself, they need but knock."

"Is there any one in the cell?"

"No one."

"Then please open the door. My friend, Lord Tanlay, is a philanthropic Englishman who is travelling about to see if the French prisons are more comfortable than the English ones. Enter, Sir John."

Père Courtois having opened the door, Roland pushed Sir John into a perfectly square cell measuring ten or twelve feet each way.

"Oh, oh!" exclaimed Sir John, "this is lugubrious."

"Do you think so? Well, my dear friend, this is where my mother, the noblest woman in the world, and my sister, whom you know, spent six weeks with a prospect of leaving it only to make the trip to the Place de Bastion. Just think, that was five years ago, so my sister was scarcely twelve."

"But what crime had they committed?"

"Oh! a monstrous crime. At the anniversary festival with which the town of Bourg considered proper to commemorate the death of the 'Friend of the People,' my mother refused to permit my sister to represent one of the virgins who bore the tears of France in vases. What will you! Poor woman, she thought she had done enough for her country in giving it the blood of her son and her husband, which was flowing in Italy and Germany. She was mistaken. Her country, as it seems, claimed further the tears of her daughter. She thought that too much, especially as those tears were to flow for the citizen Marat. The result was that on the very evening of the celebration, during the enthusiastic exaltation, my mother was declared accused. Fortunately Bourg had not attained the celerity of Paris. A friend of ours, an official in the record-office, kept the affair dragging, until one fine day the fall and death of Robespierre were made known. That interrupted a good many things, among others the guillotinades. Our friend convinced the authorities that the wind blowing from Paris had veered toward clemency; they waited fifteen days, and on the sixteenth they told my mother and sister that they were free. So you understand, my friend —and this involves the most profound philosophical reflection—so that if Mademoiselle Teresa Cabarrus had not come from Spain, if she had not married M. Fontenay, parliamentary counsellor; had she not been arrested and brought before the pro-consul Tallien, son of the Marquis de Bercy's butler, ex-notary's clerk, ex-foreman of a printing-shop, ex-porter, ex-secretary to the Commune of Paris temporarily at Bordeaux; and had the ex-pro-consul not become enamored of her, and had she not been imprisoned, and if on the ninth of Thermidor she had not found means to send a dagger with these words: 'Unless the tyrant dies to-day, I die to-morrow'; had not Saint-Just been arrested in the midst of his discourse; had not Robespierre, on that day, had a frog in his throat; had not Garnier de l'Aube exclaimed: 'It is the blood of Danton choking you!' had not

Louchet shouted for his arrest; had he not been arrested, released by the Commune, recaptured in spite of this, had his jaw broken by a pistol shot, and been executed next day—my mother would, in all probability, have had her head cut off for refusing to allow her daughter to weep for citizen Marat in one of the twelve lachrymal urns which Bourg was desirous of filling with its tears. Good-by, Courtois. You are a worthy man. You gave my mother and sister a little water to put with their wine, a little meat to eat with their bread, a little hope to fill their hearts; you lent them your daughter that they might not have to sweep their cell themselves. That deserves a fortune. Unfortunately I am not rich; but here are fifty louis I happen to have with me. Come, my lord.''

And the young man carried off Sir John before the jailer recovered from his surprise and found time either to thank Roland or refuse the fifty louis; which, it must be said, would have been a remarkable proof of disinterestedness in a jailer, especially when that jailer's opinions were opposed to those of the government he served.

Leaving the prison, Roland and Sir John found the Place des Lices crowded with people who had heard of General Bonaparte's return to France, and were shouting "Vive Bonaparte!" at the top of their lungs—some because they really admired the victor of Arcola, Rivoli, and the Pyramids, others because they had been told, like Père Courtois, that this same victor had vanquished only that Louis XVIII. might profit by his victories.

Roland and Sir John, having now visited all that the town of Bourg offered of interest, returned to the Château des Noires-Fontaines, which they reached before long. Madame de Montrevel and Amélie had gone out. Roland installed Sir John in an easy chair, asking him to wait a few minutes for him. At the end of five minutes he returned with a sort of pamphlet of gray paper, very badly printed, in his hand.

"My dear fellow," said he, "you seemed to have some

doubts about the authenticity of that festival which I just mentioned, and which nearly cost my mother and sister their lives, so I bring you the programme. Read it, and while you are doing so I will go and see what they have been doing with my dogs; for I presume that you would rather hold me quit of our fishing expedition in favor of a hunt."

He went out, leaving in Sir John's hands a copy of the decree of the municipality of the town of Bourg, instituting the funeral rites in honor of Marat, on the anniversary of his death.

CHAPTER XIII

THE WILD-BOAR

SIR JOHN was just finishing that interesting bit of history when Madame de Montrevel and her daughter returned. Amélie, who did not know how much had been said about her between Roland and Sir John, was astounded by the expression with which that gentleman scrutinized her.

To him she seemed more lovely than before. He could readily understand that mother, who at the risk of life had been unwilling that this charming creature should profane her youth and beauty by serving as a mourner in a celebration of which Marat was the deity. He recalled that cold damp cell which he had lately visited, and shuddered at the thought that this delicate white ermine before his eyes had been imprisoned there, without sun or air, for six weeks. He looked at the throat, too long perhaps, but swan-like in its suppleness and graceful in its exaggeration, and he remembered that melancholy remark of the poor Princesse de Lamballe, as she felt her slender neck: "It will not give the executioner much trouble!"

The thoughts which succeeded each other in Sir John's mind gave to his face an expression so different from its customary aspect, that Madame de Montrevel could not refrain from asking what troubled him. He then told her of his visit to the prison, and Roland's pious pilgrimage to the dungeon where his mother and sister had been incarcerated. Just as Sir John had concluded his tale, a view-halloo sounded without, and Roland entered, his hunting-horn in his hands.

"My dear friend," he cried, "thanks to my mother, we shall have a splendid hunt to-morrow."

"Thanks to me?" queried Madame de Montrevel.

"How so?" added Sir John.

"I left you to see about my dogs, didn't I?"

"You said so, at any rate."

"I had two excellent beasts, Barbichon and Ravaude, male and female."

"Oh!" exclaimed Sir John, "are they dead?"

"Well, yes; but just guess what this excellent mother of mine has done?" and, tilting Madame de Montrevel's head, he kissed her on both cheeks. "She wouldn't let them drown a single puppy because they were the dogs of my dogs; so the result is, that to-day the pups, grand-pups, and great-grand-pups of Barbichon and Ravaude are as numerous as the descendant of Ishmael. Instead of a pair of dogs, I have a whole pack, twenty-five beasts, all as black as moles with white paws, fire in their eyes and hearts, and a regiment of cornet-tails that would do you good to see."

And Roland sounded another halloo that brought his young brother to the scene.

"Oh!" shouted the boy as he entered, "you are going hunting to-morrow, brother Roland. I'm going, too, I'm going, too!"

"Good!" said Roland, "but do you know what we are going to hunt?"

"No. All I know is that I'm going, too."

"We're going to hunt a boar."

"Oh, joy!" cried the boy, clapping his little hands.

"Are you crazy?" asked Madame de Montrevel, turning pale.

"Why so, madame mother, if you please?"

"Because boar hunts are very dangerous."

"Not so dangerous as hunting men. My brother got back safe from that, and so will I from the other."

"Roland," cried Madame de Montrevel, while Amélie, lost in thought, took no part in the discussion, "Roland, make Edouard listen to reason. Tell him that he hasn't got common-sense."

But Roland, who recognized himself again in his young brother, instead of blaming him, smiled at his boyish ardor.

"I'd take you willingly," said he, "only to go hunting one must at least know how to handle a gun."

"Oh, Master Roland," cried Edouard, "just come into the garden a bit. Put up your hat at a hundred yards, and I'll show you how to handle a gun."

"Naughty child," exclaimed Madame de Montrevel, trembling, "where did you learn?"

"Why, from the gunsmith at Montagnac, who keeps papa's and Roland's guns. You ask me sometimes what I do with my money, don't you? Well, I buy powder and balls with it, and I am learning to kill Austr ns and Arabs like my brother Roland."

Madame de Montrevel raised her hands to heaven.

"What can you expect, mother?" asked Roland. "Blood will tell. No Montrevel could be afraid of powder. You shall come with us to-morrow, Edouard."

The boy sprang upon his brother's neck.

"And I," said Sir John, "will equip you to-day like a regular huntsman, just as they used to arm the knights of old. I have a charming little rifle that I will give you. It will keep you contented until your sabre and pistols come."

"Well," asked Roland, "are you satisfied now, Edouard?"

"Yes; but when will he give it to me? If you have

to write to England for it, I warn you I shan't believe in it.''

"No, my little friend, we have only to go up to my room and open my gun-case. That's soon done."

''Then, let's go at once.''

"Come on," said Sir John; and he went out, followed by Edouard.

A moment later, Amélie, still absorbed in thought, rose and left the room. Neither Madame de Montrevel nor Roland noticed her departure, so interested were they in a serious discussion. Madame de Montrevel tried to persuade Roland not to take his young brother with him on the morrow's hunt. Roland explained that, since Edouard was to become a soldier like his father and brother, the sooner he learned to handle a gun and become familiar with powder and ball the better. The discussion was not yet ended when Edouard returned with his gun slung over his shoulder.

''Look, brother,'' said he, turning to Roland; "just see what a fine present Sir John has given me." And he looked gratefully at Sir John, who stood in the doorway vainly seeking Amélie with his eyes.

It was in truth a beautiful present. The rifle, designed with that plainness of ornament and simplicity of form peculiar to English weapons, was of the finest finish. Like the pistols, of which Roland had had opportunity to test the accuracy, the rifle was made by the celebrated Manton, and carried a twenty-four calibre bullet. That it had been originally intended for a woman was easily seen by the shortness of the stock and the velvet pad on the trigger. This original purpose of the weapon made it peculiarly suitable for a boy of twelve.

Roland took the rifle from his brother's shoulder, looked at it knowingly, tried its action, sighted it, tossed it from one hand to the other, and then, giving it back to Edouard, said: ''Thank Sir John again. You have a rifle fit for a king's son. Let's go and try it.''

All three went out to try Sir John's rifle, leaving Madame de Montrevel as sad as Thetis when she saw Achilles in his woman's garb draw the sword of Ulysses from its scabbard.

A quarter of an hour later, Edouard returned triumphantly. He brought his mother a bit of pasteboard of the circumference of a hat, in which he had put ten bullets out of twelve. The two men had remained behind in the park conversing.

Madame de Montrevel listened to Edouard's slightly boastful account of his prowess. Then she looked at him with that deep and holy sorrow of mothers to whom fame is no compensation for the blood it sheds. Oh! ungrateful indeed is the child who has seen that look bent upon him and does not eternally remember it. Then, after a few seconds of this painful contemplation, she pressed her second son to her breast, and murmured sobbing: "You, too! you, too, will desert your mother some day."

"Yes, mother," replied the boy, "to become a general like my father, or an aide-de-camp like Roland."

"And to be killed as your father was, as your brother perhaps will be."

For the strange transformation in Roland's character had not escaped Madame de Montrevel. It was but an added dread to her other anxieties, among which Amélie's pallor and abstraction must be numbered.

Amélie was just seventeen; her childhood had been that of a happy laughing girl, joyous and healthy. The death of her father had cast a black veil over her youth and gayety. But these tempests of spring pass rapidly. Her smile, the sunshine of life's dawn, returned like that of Nature, sparkling through that dew of the heart we call tears.

Then, one day about six months before this story opens, Amélie's face had saddened, her cheeks had grown pale, and, like the birds who migrate at the approach of wintry weather, the childlike laughter that escaped her parted lips and white teeth had fled never to return.

Madame de Montrevel had questioned her, but Amélie asserted that she was still the same. She endeavored to smile, but as a stone thrown into a lake rings upon the surface, so the smiles roused by this maternal solicitude faded, little by little, from Amélie's face. With keen maternal instinct Madame de Montrevel had thought of love. But whom could Amélie love? There were no visitors at the Château des Noires-Fontaines, the political troubles had put an end to all society, and Amélie went nowhere alone. Madame de Montrevel could get no further than conjecture. Roland's return had given her a moment's hope; but this hope fled as soon as she perceived the effect which this event had produced upon Amélie.

It was not a sister, but a spectre, it will be recalled, who had come to meet him. Since her son's arrival, Madame de Montrevel had not lost sight of Amélie, and she perceived, with dolorous amazement, that Roland's presence awakened a feeling akin to terror in his sister's breast. She, whose eyes had formerly rested so lovingly upon him, now seemed to view him with alarm. Only a few moments since, Amélie had profited by the first opportunity to return to her room, the one spot in the château where she seemed at ease, and where for the last six months she had spent most of her time. The dinner-bell alone possessed the power to bring her from it, and even then she waited for the second call before entering the dining-room.

Roland and Sir John, as we have said, had divided their time between their visit to Bourg and their preparations for the morrow's hunt. From morn until noon they were to beat the woods; from noon till evening they were to hunt the boar. Michel, that devoted poacher, confined to his chair for the present with a sprain, felt better as soon as the question of the hunt was mooted, and had himself hoisted on a little horse that was used for the errands of the house. Then he sallied forth to collect the beaters from Saint-Just and Montagnac. He, being unable to beat or run, was to remain with the pack, and watch Sir John's and Roland's horse, and Edou-

ard's pony, in the middle of the forest, where it was inter-
sected by one good road and two practicable paths. The
beaters, who could not follow the hunt, were to return to
the château with the game-bags.

The beaters were at the door at six the following morning. Michel was not to leave with the horses and dogs
until eleven. The Château des Noires-Fontaines was just
at the edge of the forest of Seillon, so the hunt could begin
at its very gates.

As the battue promised chiefly deer and hares, the guns
were loaded with balls. Roland gave Edouard a simple little gun which he himself had used as a child. He had not
enough confidence as yet in the boy's prudence to trust him
with a double-barrelled gun. As for the rifle that Sir John
had given him the day before, it could only carry cartridges.
It was given into Michel's safe keeping, to be returned to
him in case they started a boar for the second part of the
hunt. For this Roland and Sir John were also to change
their guns for rifles and hunting knives, pointed as daggers
and sharp as razors, which formed part of Sir John's arsenal, and could be suspended from the belt or screwed
on the point of the gun like bayonets.

From the beginning of the battue it was easy to see that
the hunt would be a good one. A roebuck and two hares
were killed at once. At noon two does, seven roebucks and
two foxes had been bagged. They had also seen two boars,
but these latter had only shaken their bristles in answer to
the heavy balls and made off.

Edouard was in the seventh heaven; he had killed a roebuck. The beaters, well rewarded for their labor, were sent
to the château with the game, as had been arranged. A sort
of bugle was sounded to ascertain Michel's whereabout, to
which he answered. In less than ten minutes the three
hunters had rejoined the gardener with his hounds and
horses.

Michel had seen a boar which he had sent his son to
head off, and it was now in the woods not a hundred paces

distant. Jacques, Michel's eldest son, beat up the woods with Barbichon and Ravaude, the heads of the pack, and in about five minutes the boar was found in his lair. They could have killed him at once, or at least shot at him, but that would have ended the hunt too quickly. The huntsmen launched the whole pack at the animal, which, seeing this troop of pygmies swoop down upon him, started off at a slow trot. He crossed the road, Roland giving the view-halloo, and headed in the direction of the Chartreuse of Seillon, the three riders following the path which led through the woods. The boar led them a chase which lasted until five in the afternoon, turning upon his tracks, evidently unwilling to leave the forest with its thick undergrowth.

At last the violent barking of the dogs warned them that the animal had been brought to bay. The spot was not a hundred paces distant from the pavilion belonging to the Chartreuse, in one of the most tangled thickets of the forest. It was impossible to force the horses through it, and the riders dismounted. The barking of the dogs guided them straight along the path, from which they deviated only where the obstacles they encountered rendered it necessary.

From time to time yelps of pain indicated that members of the attacking party had ventured too close to the animal, and had paid the price of their temerity. About twenty feet from the scene of action the hunters began to see the actors. The boar was backed against a rock to avoid attack in the rear; then, bracing himself on his forepaws, he faced the dogs with his ensanguined eyes and enormous tusks. They quivered around him like a moving carpet; five or six, more or less badly wounded, were staining the battlefield with their blood, though still attacking the boar with a fury and courage that might have served as an example to the bravest men.

Each hunter faced the scene with the characteristic signs of his age, nature and nation. Edouard, at one and the same time, the most imprudent and the smallest, finding the path less difficult, owing to his small stature, arrived first. Roland, heedless of danger of any kind, seeking rather than avoiding it, followed. Finally Sir John, slower, graver, more reflective, brought up the rear.

Once the boar perceived his hunters he paid no further attention to the dogs. He fixed his gleaming, sanguinary eyes upon them; but his only movement was a snapping of the jaws, which he brought together with a threatening sound. Roland watched the scene for an instant, evidently desirous of flinging himself into the midst of the group, knife in hand, to slit the boar's throat as a butcher would that of a calf or a pig. This impulse was so apparent that Sir John caught his arm, and little Edouard exclaimed: "Oh! brother, let me shoot the boar!"

Roland restrained himself, and stacking his gun against a tree, waited, armed only with his hunting-knife, which he had drawn from its sheath.

"Very well," said he, "shoot him; but be careful about it."

"Oh! don't worry," retorted the child, between his set teeth. His face was pale but resolute as he aimed the barrel of his rifle at the animal's head.

"If he misses him, or only wounds him," observed Sir John, "you know that the brute will be upon us before we can see him through the smoke."

"I know it, my lord; but I am accustomed to these hunts," replied Roland, his nostrils quivering, his eyes sparkling, his lips parted: "Fire, Edouard!"

The shot followed the order upon the instant; but after the shot, with, or even before it, the beast, swift as lightning, rushed upon the child. A second shot followed the first, but the animal's scarlet eyes still gleamed through the smoke. But, as it rushed, it met Roland with his knee on the ground, the knife in his hand. A moment later a tangled, formless group, man and boar, boar and man, was rolling on the ground. Then a third shot rang out, followed by a laugh from Roland.

"Ah! my lord," cried the young man, "you've wasted powder and shot. Can't you see that I have ripped him up? Only get his body off of me. The beast weighs at least four hundred pounds, and he is smothering me."

But before Sir John could stoop, Roland, with a vigorous push of the shoulder, rolled the animal's body aside, and rose to his feet covered with blood, but without a single scratch. Little Edouard, either from lack of time or from native courage, had not recoiled an inch. True, he was completely protected by his brother's body, which was between him and the boar. Sir John had sprung aside to take the animal in the flank. He watched Roland, as he emerged from this second duel, with the same amazement that he had experienced after the first.

The dogs—those that were left, some twenty in all—had followed the boar, and were now leaping upon his body in the vain effort to tear the bristles, which were almost as impenetrable as iron.

"You will see," said Roland, wiping the blood from his face and hands with a fine cambric handkerchief, "how they will eat him, and your knife too, my lord."

"True," said Sir John; "where is the knife?"

"In its sheath," replied Roland.

"Ah!" exclaimed the boy, "only the handle shows."

He sprang toward the animal and pulled out the poniard, which, as he said, was buried up to the hilt. The sharp point, guided by a calm eye and a firm hand, had pierced the animal's heart.

There were other wounds on the boar's body. The first, caused by the boy's shot, showed a bloody furrow just over the eye; the blow had been too weak to crush the frontal bone. The second came from Sir John's first shot; it had caught the animal diagonally and grazed his breast. The third, fired at close quarters, went through the body; but, as Roland had said, not until after the animal was dead.

CHAPTER XIV

AN UNPLEASANT COMMISSION

THE hunt was over, darkness was falling, and it was now a question of returning to the château. The horses were nearby; they could hear them neighing impatiently. They seemed to be asking if their courage was so doubted that they were not allowed to share in the exciting drama.

Edouard was bent upon dragging the boar after them, fastening it to the saddle-bow, and so carrying it back to the château; but Roland pointed out that it was simpler to send a couple of men for it with a barrow. Sir John being of the same opinion, Edouard—who never ceased pointing to the wound in the head, and saying, "That's my shot; that's where I aimed"—Edouard, we say, was forced to yield to the majority. The three hunters soon reached the spot where their horses were tethered, mounted, and in less than ten minutes were at the Château des Noires-Fontaines.

Madame de Montrevel was watching for them on the portico. The poor mother had waited there nearly an hour, trembling lest an accident had befallen one or the other of her sons. The moment Edouard espied her he put his pony to a gallop, shouting from the gate: "Mother, mother! We killed a boar as big as a donkey. I shot him in the head; you'll see the hole my ball made; Roland stuck his hunting knife into the boar's belly up to the hilt, and Sir John fired at him twice. Quick, quick! Send the men for the carcass. Don't be frightened when you see Roland. He's all covered with blood—but it's from the boar, and he hasn't a scratch."

This was delivered with Edouard's accustomed volubility while Madame de Montrevel was crossing the clearing between the portico and the road to open the gate. She intended to take Edouard in her arms, but he jumped from his saddle and flung himself upon her neck. Roland and Sir John came up just then, and Amélie appeared on the portico at the same instant.

Edouard left his mother to worry over Roland, who, covered as he was with blood, looked very terrifying, and rushed to his sister with the tale he had rattled off to his mother. Amélie listened in an abstracted manner that probably hurt Edouard's vanity, for he dashed off to the kitchen to describe the affair to Michel, who was certain to listen to him.

Michel was indeed interested; but when, after telling him where the carcass lay, Edouard gave him Roland's order to send a couple of men after the beast, he shook his head.

"What!" demanded Edouard, "are you going to refuse to obey my brother?"

"Heaven forbid! Master Edouard. Jacques shall start this instant for Montagnac."

"Are you afraid he won't find anybody?"

"Goodness, no; he could get a dozen. But the trouble is the time of night. You say the boar lies close to the pavilion of the Chartreuse?"

"Not twenty yards from it."

"I'd rather it was three miles," replied Michel scratching his head; "but never mind. I'll send for them anyway without telling them what they're wanted for. Once here, it's for your brother to make them go."

"Good! Good! Only get them here and I'll see to that myself."

"Oh!" exclaimed Michel, "if I hadn't this beastly sprain I'd go myself. But to-day's doings have made it worse. Jacques! Jacques!"

Jacques came, and Edouard not only waited to hear the

order given, but until he had started. Then he ran upstairs
to do what Roland and Sir John were already doing, that is,
dress for dinner.

The whole talk at table, as may be easily imagined, centred upon the day's prowess. Edouard asked nothing better than to talk about it, and Sir John, astounded by Roland's skill, courage, and good luck, improved upon the
child's narrative. Madame de Montrevel shuddered at
each detail, and yet she made them repeat it twenty
times. That which seemed most clear to her in all this
was that Roland had saved Edouard's life.

"Did you thank him for it?" she asked the boy.

"Thank whom?"

"Your brother."

"Why should I thank him?" retorted Edouard. "I
should have done the same thing."

"Ah, madame, what can you expect!" said Sir John;
"you are a gazelle who has unwittingly given birth to a
race of lions."

Amélie had also paid the closest attention to the account, especially when the hunters spoke of their proximity to the Chartreuse. From that time on she listened with
anxious eyes, and seemed scarcely to breathe, until they
told of leaving the woods after the killing.

After dinner, word was brought that Jacques had returned with two peasants from Montagnac. They wanted
exact directions as to where the hunters had left the animal. Roland rose, intending to go to them, but Madame
de Montrevel, who could never see enough of her son,
turned to the messenger and said: "Bring these worthy men
in here. It is not necessary to disturb M. Roland for that."

Five minutes later the two peasants entered, twirling
their hats in their hands.

"My sons," said Roland, "I want you to fetch the boar
we killed in the forest of Seillon."

"That can be done," said one of the peasants, consulting
his companion with a look.

"Yes, it can be done," answered the other.

"Don't be alarmed," said Roland. "You shall lose nothing by your trouble."

"Oh! we're not," interrupted one of the peasants. "We know you, Monsieur de Montrevel."

"Yes," answered the other, "we know that, like your father, you're not in the habit of making people work for nothing. Oh! if all the aristocrats had been like you, Monsieur Louis, there wouldn't have been any revolution."

"Of course not," said the other, who seemed to have come solely to echo affirmatively what his companion said.

"It remains to be seen now where the animal is," said the first peasant.

"Yes," repeated the second, "remains to be seen where it is."

"Oh! it won't be hard to find."

"So much the better," interjected the peasant.

"Do you know the pavilion in the forest?"

"Which one?"

"Yes, which one?"

"The one that belongs to the Chartreuse of Seillon."

The peasants looked at each other.

"Well, you'll find it some twenty feet distant from the front on the way to Genoud."

The peasants looked at each other once more.

"Hum!" grunted the first one.

"Hum!" repeated the other, faithful echo of his companion.

"Well, what does this 'hum' mean?" demanded Roland.

"Confound it."

"Come, explain yourselves. What's the matter?"

"The matter is that we'd rather that it was the other end of the forest."

"But why the other end?" retorted Roland, impatiently; "it's nine miles from here to the other end, and barely three from here to where we left the boar."

"Yes," said the first peasant, "but just where the boar lies—" And he paused and scratched his head.

"Exactly; that's what," added the other.

"Just what?"

"It's a little too near the Chartreuse."

"Not the Chartreuse; I said the pavilion."

"It's all the same. You know, Monsieur Louis, that there is an underground passage leading from the pavilion to the Chartreuse."

"Oh, yes, there is one, that's sure," added the other.

"But," exclaimed Roland, "what has this underground passage got to do with our boar?"

"This much, that the beast's in a bad place, that's all."

"Oh, yes! a bad place," repeated the other peasant.

"Come, now, explain yourselves, you rascals," said Roland, who was growing angry, while his mother seemed uneasy, and Amélie visibly turned pale.

"Beg pardon, Monsieur Louis," answered the peasant; "we are not rascals; we're God-fearing men, that's all."

"By thunder," cried Roland, "I'm a God-fearing man myself. What of that?"

"Well, we don't care to have any dealings with the devil."

"No, no, no," asserted the second peasant.

"A man can match a man if he's of his own kind," continued the first peasant.

"Sometimes two," said the second, who was built like a Hercules.

"But with ghostly beings phantoms, spectres—no thank you," continued the first peasant.

"No, thank you," repeated the other.

"Oh, mother, sister," queried Roland, addressing the two women, "in Heaven's name, do you understand anything of what these two fools are saying?"

"Fools," repeated the first peasant; "well, possibly. But it's not the less true that Pierre Marey had his neck twisted just for looking over the wall. True, it was of a Saturday—the devil's sabbath."

"And they couldn't straighten it out," affirmed the second peasant, "so they had to bury him with his face turned round looking the other way.

"Oh!" exclaimed Sir John, "this is growing interesting. I'm very fond of ghost stories."

"That's more than sister Amélie is. it seems." cried Edouard.

"What do you mean?"

"Just see how pale she's grown, brother Roland."

"Yes, indeed," said Sir John; "mademoiselle looks as if she were going to faint."

"I? Not at all," exclaimed Amélie, wiping the perspiration from her forehead; "only don't you think it seems a little warm here, mother?"

"No," answered Madame de Montrevel.

"Still," insisted Amélie, "if it would not annoy you, I should like to open the window."

"Do so, my child."

Amélie rose hastily to profit by this permission, and went with tottering steps to a window opening upon the garden. After it was opened, she stood leaning against the sill, half-hidden by the curtains.

"Ah!" she said, "I can breathe here."

Sir John rose to offer her his smelling-salts, but Amélie declined hastily: "No, no, my lord. Thank you, but I am better now."

"Come, come," said Roland, "don't bother about that; it's our boar."

"Well, Monsieur Louis, we will fetch your boar to-morrow."

"That's it," said the second peasant, "to-morrow morning, when it's light."

"But to go there at night—"

"Oh! to go there at night—"

The peasant looked at his comrade and both shook their heads.

"It can't be done at night."

"Cowards."

"Monsieur Louis, a man's not a coward because he's afraid."

"No, indeed; that's not being a coward," replied the other.

"Ah!" said Roland, "I wish some stronger minded men than you would face me with that argument; that a man is not a coward because he's afraid!"

"Well, it's according to what he's afraid of, Monsieur Louis. Give me a good sickle and a good cudgel, and I'm not afraid of a wolf; give me a good gun and I'm not afraid of any man, even if I knew he's waiting to murder me."

"Yes," said Edouard, "but you're afraid of a ghost, even when it's only the ghost of a monk."

"Little Master Edouard," said the peasant, "leave your brother to do the talking; you're not old enough to jest about such things—"

"No," added the other peasant, "wait till your beard is grown, my little gentleman."

"I haven't any beard," retorted Edouard, starting up, "but just the same if I was strong enough to carry the boar, I'd go fetch it myself either by day or night."

"Much good may it do you, my young gentleman. But neither my comrade nor myself would go, even for a whole louis."

"Nor for two?" said Roland, wishing to corner them.

"Nor for two, nor four, nor ten, Monsieur de Montrevel. Ten louis are good, but what could I do with them if my neck was broken?"

"Yes, twisted like Pierre Marey's," said the other peasant.

"Ten louis wouldn't feed my wife and children for the rest of my life, would they?"

"And besides, when you say ten louis," interrupted the second peasant, "you mean really five, because I'd get five, too."

"So the pavilion is haunted by ghosts, is it?" asked Roland.

"I didn't say the pavilion—I'm not sure about the pavilion—but in the Chartreuse—"

"In the Chartreuse, are you sure?"

"Oh! there, certainly."

"Have you seen them?"

"I haven't; but some folks have.'

"Has your comrade?" asked the young officer, turning to the second peasant.

"I haven't seen them; but I did see flames, and Claude Philippon heard chains."

"Ah! so they have flames and chains?" said Roland.

"Yes," replied the first peasant, "for I have seen the flames myself."

"And Claude Philippon heard the chains," repeated the other.

"Very good, my friends, very good," replied Roland, sneering; "so you won't go there to-night at any price?"

"Not at any price."

"Not for all the gold in the world."

"And you'll go to-morrow when it's light?"

"Oh! Monsieur Louis, before you're up the boar will be here."

"Before you're up," said Echo.

"All right," said Roland. "Come back to me the day after to-morrow."

"Willingly, Monsieur Louis. What do you want us to do?"

"Never mind; just come."

"Oh! we'll come."

"That means that the moment you say, 'Come,' you can count upon us, Monsieur Louis."

"Well, then I'll have some information for you."

"What about?"

"The ghosts."

Amélie gave a stifled cry; Madame de Montrevel alone heard it. Louis dismissed the two peasants, and they jostled each other at the door in their efforts to go through together.

Nothing more was said that evening about the Chartreuse or the pavilion, nor of its supernatural tenants, spectres or phantoms who haunted them.

CHAPTER XV

THE STRONG-MINDED MAN

A T TEN o'clock every one was in bed at the Château des Noires-Fontaines, or, at any rate, all had retired to their rooms.

Three or four times in the course of the evening Amélie had approached Roland as if she had something to say to him; but each time the words died upon her lips. When the family left the salon, she had taken his arm, and, although his room was on the floor above hers, she had accompanied him to his very door. Roland had kissed her, bade her good-night, and closed his door, declaring himself very tired.

Nevertheless, in spite of this assertion, Roland, once alone, did not proceed to undress. He went to his collection of arms, selected a pair of magnificent pistols, manufactured at Versailles, and presented to his father by the Convention. He snapped the triggers, and blew into the barrels to see that there were no old charges in them. They were in excellent condition. After which he laid them side by side on the table; then going to the door, looking out upon the stairs, he opened it softly to see if any one were watching. Finding the corridor and stairs empty, he went to Sir John's door and knocked.

"Come in," said the Englishman. Sir John, like himself, was not prepared for bed.

"I guessed from the sign you made me that you had something to say to me," said Sir John, "so I waited for you, as you see."

"Indeed, I have something to say to you," returned Roland, seating himself gayly in an armchair.

"My kind host," replied the Englishman, "I am beginning to understand you. When I see you as gay as you are now, I am like your peasants, I feel afraid."

"Did you hear what they were saying?"

"I heard them tell a splendid ghost story. I, myself, have a haunted castle in England."

"Have you ever seen the ghosts, my lord?"

"Yes, when I was little. Unfortunately, since I have grown up they have disappeared."

"That's always the way with ghosts," said Roland gayly; "they come and go. How lucky it is that I should return just as the ghosts have begun to haunt the Chartreuse of Seillon."

"Yes," replied Sir John, "very lucky. Only are you sure that there are any there?"

"No. But I'll know by the day after to-morrow."

"How so?"

"I intend to spend to-morrow night there."

"Oh!" said the Englishmen, "would you like to have me go with you?"

"With pleasure, my lord. Only, unfortunately, that is impossible."

"Impossible, oh!"

"As I have just told you, my dear fellow."

"But why impossible?"

"Are you acquainted with the manners and customs of ghosts, Sir John?" asked Roland gravely.

"No."

"Well, I am. Ghosts only show themselves under certain conditions."

"Explain that."

"Well, for example, in Italy, my lord, and in Spain, the most superstitious of countries, there are no ghosts, or if there are, why, at the best, it's only once in ten or twenty years, or maybe in a century."

"And to what do you attribute their absence?"

"To the absence of fogs."

"Ah! ah!"

"Not a doubt of it. You understand the native atmosphere of ghosts is fog. Scotland, Denmark and England, regions of fog, are overrun with ghosts. There's the spectre of Hamlet, then that of Banquo, the shadows of Richard III. Italy has only one spectre, Cæsar, and then where did he appear to Brutus? At Philippi, in Macedonia and in Thessaly, the Denmark of Greece, the Scotland of the Orient; where the fog made Ovid so melancholy he named the odes he wrote there Tristia. Why did Virgil make the ghost of Anchises appear to Eneas? Because he came from Mantua. Do you know Mantua? A marsh, a frog-pond, a regular manufactory of rheumatism, an atmosphere of vapors, and consequently a nest of phantoms."

"Go on, I'm listening to you."

"Have you seen the Rhine?"

"Yes."

"Germany, isn't it?"

"Yes."

"Still another country of fairies, water sprites, sylphs, and consequently phantoms ('for whoso does the greater see, can see the less'), and all that on account of the fog. But where the devil can the ghosts hide in Italy and Spain? Not the least bit of mist. And, therefore, were I in Spain or Italy I should never attempt to-morrow's adventure."

"But all that doesn't explain why you refuse my company," insisted Sir John.

"Wait a moment. I've just explained to you that ghosts don't venture into certain countries, because they do not offer certain atmospheric conditions. Now, let me explain the precautions we must take if we wish to see them."

"Explain! explain!" said Sir John, "I would rather hear you talk than any other man, Roland."

And Sir John, stretching himself out in his easy-chair, prepared to listen with delight to the improvisations of this fantastic mind, which he had seen under so many aspects during the few days of their acquaintance.

Roland bowed his head by way of thanks.

"Well, this is the way of it, and you will grasp it readily enough. I have heard so much about ghosts in my life that I know the scamps as if I had made them. Why do ghosts appear?"

"Are you asking me that?" inquired Sir John.

"Yes, I ask you."

"I own that, not having studied ghosts as you have, I am unable to give you a definitive answer."

"You see! Ghosts show themselves, my dear fellow, in order to frighten those who see them."

"That is undeniable."

"Of course! Now, if they don't frighten those to whom they appear, they are frightened by them; witness M. de Turenne, whose ghosts proved to be counterfeiters. Do you know that story?"

"No."

"I'll tell it to you some day; don't let's get mixed up. That is just why, when they decide to appear—which is seldom—ghosts select stormy nights, when it thunders, lightens and blows; that's their scenery."

"I am forced to admit that nothing could be more correct."

"Wait a moment! There are instances when the bravest man feels a shudder run through his veins. Even before I was suffering with this aneurism it has happened to me a dozen times, when I have seen the flash of sabres and heard the thunder of cannon around me. It is true that since I have been subject to this aneurism I rush where the lightning flashes and the thunder growls. Still there is the chance that these ghosts don't know this and believe that I can be frightened."

"Whereas that is an impossibility, isn't it?" asked Sir John.

"What will you! When, right or wrong, one feels that, far from dreading death, one has every reason to seek it, what should he fear? But I repeat, these ghosts, who know so much, may not know that only ghosts know this; they know that the sense of fear increases or diminishes according to the seeing and hearing of exterior things. Thus, for example, where do phantoms prefer to appear? In dark places, cemeteries, old cloisters, ruins, subterranean passages, because the aspect of these localities predisposes the soul to fear. What precedes their appearance? The rattling of chains, groans, sighs, because there is nothing very cheerful in all that? They are careful not to appear in the bright light, or after a strain of dance music. No, fear is an abyss into which you descend step by step, until you are overcome by vertigo; your feet slip, and you plunge with closed eyes to the bottom of the precipice. Now, if you read the accounts of all these apparitions, you'll find they all proceed like this: First the sky darkens, the thunder growls, the wind howls, doors and windows rattle, the lamp—if there is a lamp in the room of the person the ghosts are trying to frighten—the lamp flares, flickers and goes out—utter darkness! Then, in the darkness, groans, wails and the rattling of chains are heard; then, at last, the door opens and the ghost appears. I must say that all the apparitions that I have not seen but read about have presented themselves under similar circumstances. Isn't that so, Sir John?''

"Perfectly."

"And did you ever hear of a ghost appearing to two persons at the same time?"

"I certainly never did hear of it."

"It's quite simple, my dear fellow. Two together, you understand, have no fear. Fear is something mysterious, strange, independent of the will, requiring isolation, darkness and solitude. A ghost is no more dangerous than a cannon ball. Well, a soldier never fears a cannon ball in the daytime, when his elbows touch a comrade to the right and left. No, he goes straight for the battery and is either killed or he kills. That's not what the phantoms want. That's why they never appear to two persons at the same time, and that is the reason I want to go to the Chartreuse alone, my lord. Your presence would prevent the boldest ghost from appearing. If I see nothing, or if I see something worth the trouble, you can have your turn the next day. Does the bargain suit you?"

"Perfectly! But why can't I take the first night?"

"Ah! first, because the idea didn't occur to you, and it is only just that I should benefit by my own cleverness. Besides, I belong to the region; I was friendly with the good monks in their lifetime, and there may be a chance of their appearing to me after death. Moreover, as I know the localities, if it becomes necessary to run away or pursue I can do it better than you. Don't you see the justice of that, my dear fellow?"

"Yes, it couldn't be fairer; but I am sure of going the next night."

"The next night, and the one after, and every day and night if you wish; I only hold to the first. Now," continued Roland rising, "this is between ourselves, isn't it? Not a word to any one. The ghosts might be forewarned and act accordingly. It would never do to let those gay dogs get the best of us; that would be too grotesque."

"Oh, be easy about that. You will go armed, won't you?"

"If I thought I was only dealing with ghosts, I'd go with my hands in my pockets and nothing in my fobs. But, as I told you, M. de Turenne's ghosts were counterfeiters, so I shall take my pistols."

"Do you want mine?"

"No, thanks. Though yours are good, I am about resolved never to use them again." Then, with a smile whose bitterness it would be impossible to describe, he added: "They brought me ill-luck. Good-night! Sir John. I must sleep soundly to-night, so as not to want to sleep to-morrow night."

Then, shaking the Englishman's hand vigorously a second time, he left the room and returned to his own. There he was greatly surprised to find the door, which he was sure he had left closed, open. But as soon as he entered, the sight of his sister explained the matter to him.

"Hello!" he exclaimed, partly astonished, partly uneasy; "is that you, Amélie?"

"Yes, it is I," she said. Then, going close to her brother, and letting him kiss her forehead, she added in a supplicating voice: "You won't go, will you, dear Roland?"

"Go where?" asked Roland.

"To the Chartreuse."

"Good! Who told you that?"

"Oh! for one who knows, how difficult it is to guess!"

"And why don't you want me to go to the Chartreuse?"

"I'm afraid something might happen to you."

"What! So you believe in ghosts, do you?" he asked, looking fixedly into Amélie's eyes.

Amélie lowered her glance, and Roland felt his sister's hand tremble in his.

"Come," said Roland; "Amélie, at least the one I used to know, General de Montrevel's daughter and Roland's sister, is too intelligent to yield to these vulgar terrors. It's impossible that you can believe these tales of apparitions, chains, flames, spectres, and phantoms."

"If I did believe them, Roland, I should not be so alarmed. If ghosts do exist, they must be souls without bodies, and consequently cannot bring their material hatred from the grave. Besides, why should a ghost hate you, Roland; you, who never harmed any one?"

"Good! You forget all those I have killed in war or in duels."

Amélie shook her head. "I'm not afraid of them."

"Then what are you afraid of?"

The young girl raised her beautiful eyes, wet with tears, to Roland, and threw herself in his arms, saying: "I don't know, Roland. But I can't help it, I am afraid."

The young man raised her head, which she was hiding in his breast, with gentle force, and said, kissing her eyelids softly and tenderly: "You don't believe I shall have ghosts to fight with to-morrow, do you?"

"Oh, brother, don't go to the Chartreuse!" cried Amélie, eluding the question.

"Mother told you to say this to me, didn't she?"

"Oh, no, brother! Mother said nothing to me. It is I who guessed that you intended to go."

"Well, if I want to go," replied Roland firmly, "you ought to know, Amélie, that I shall go."

"Even if I beseech you on my knees, brother?" cried Amélie in a tone of anguish, slipping down to her brother's feet; "even if I beseech you on my knees?"

"Oh! women! women!" murmured Roland, "inexplicable creatures, whose words are all mystery, whose lips never tell the real secrets of their hearts, who weep, and pray, and tremble—why? God knows, but man, never! I shall go, Amélie, because I have resolved to go; and when once I have taken a resolution no power on earth can make me change it. Now kiss me and don't be frightened, and I will tell you a secret."

Amélie raised her head, and gazed questioningly, despairingly, at Roland.

"I have known for more than a year," replied the young man, "that I have the misfortune not to be able to die. So reassure yourself, and don't be afraid."

Roland uttered these words so dolefully that Amélie, who had, until then, kept her emotion under control, left the room sobbing.

The young officer, after assuring himself that her door was closed, shut his, murmuring: "We'll see who will weary first, Fate or I."

CHAPTER XVI

THE GHOST

THE next evening, at about the same hour, the young officer, after convincing himself that every one in the Château des Noires-Fontaines had gone to bed, opened his door softly, went downstairs holding his breath, reached the vestibule, slid back the bolts of the outer door noiselessly, and turned round to make sure that all was quiet. Reassured by the darkened windows, he boldly opened the iron gate. The hinges had probably been oiled that day, for they turned without grating, and closed as noiselessly as they had opened behind Roland, who walked rapidly in the direction of Pont d'Ain at Bourg.

He had hardly gone a hundred yards before the clock at Saint-Just struck once; that of Montagnac answered like a bronze echo. It was half-past ten o'clock. At the pace the young man was walking he needed only twenty minutes to reach the Chartreuse; especially if, instead of skirting the woods, he took the path that led direct to the monastery. Roland was too familiar from youth with every nook of the forest of Seillon to needlessly lengthen his walk ten minutes. He therefore turned unhesitatingly into the forest, coming out on the other side in about five minutes. Once there, he had only to cross a bit of open ground to reach the orchard wall of the convent. This took barely another five minutes.

At the foot of the wall he stopped, but only for a few seconds. He unhooked his cloak, rolled it into a ball, and tossed it over the wall. The cloak off, he stood in a velvet coat, white leather breeches, and top-boots. The coat was fastened round the waist by a belt in which were a pair of pistols. A broad-brimmed hat covered his head and shaded his face.

With the same rapidity with which he had removed his garment that might have hindered his climbing the wall, he began to scale it. His foot readily found a chink between the stones; he sprang up, seizing the coping, and was on the other side without even touching the top of the wall over which he bounded. He picked up his cloak, threw it over his shoulder, hooked it, and crossed the orchard to a little door communicating with the cloister. The clock struck eleven as he passed through it. Roland stopped, counted the strokes, and slowly walked around the cloister, looking and listening.

He saw nothing and heard no noise. The monastery was the picture of desolation and solitude; the doors were all open, those of the cells, the chapel, and the refectory. In the refectory, a vast hall where the tables still stood in their places, Roland noticed five or six bats circling around; a frightened owl flew through a broken casement, and perched upon a tree close by, hooting dismally.

"Good!" said Roland, aloud; "I'll make my headquarters here; bats and owls are the vanguards of ghosts."

The sound of that human voice, lifted in the midst of this solitude, darkness and desolation, had something so uncanny, so lugubrious about it, that it would have caused even the speaker to shudder, had not Roland, as he himself said, been inaccessible to fear. He looked about for a place from which he could command the entire hall. An isolated table, placed on a sort of stage at one end of the refectory, which had no doubt been used by the superior of the convent to take his food apart from the monks, to read from pious books during the repast, seemed to Roland best adapted to his needs. Here, backed by the wall, he could not be surprised from behind, and, once his eye grew accustomed to the darkness, he could survey every part of the hall. He looked for a seat, and found an overturned stool about three feet from the table, probably the one occupied by the reader or the person dining there in solitude.

Roland sat down at the table, loosened his cloak to insure greater freedom of movement, took his pistols from his belt, laid one on the table, and striking three blows with the butt-end of the other, he said, in a loud voice: "The meeting is open; the ghosts can appear!"

Those who have passed through churches and cemeteries at night have often experienced, without analyzing it, the supreme necessity of speaking low and reverently which attaches to certain localities. Only such persons can understand the strange impression produced on any one who heard it by that curt, mocking voice which now disturbed the solitude and the shadows. It vibrated an instant in the darkness, which seemed to quiver with it; then it slowly died away without an echo, escaping by all the many openings made by the wings of time.

As he had expected, Roland's eyes had accustomed themselves to the darkness, and now, by the pale light of the rising moon, whose long, white rays penetrated the refectory through the broken windows, he could see distinctly from one end to the other of the vast apartment. Although Roland was as evidently without fear internally as externally, he was not without distrust, and his ear caught the slightest sounds.

He heard the half-hour strike. In spite of himself the sound startled him, for it came from the bell of the convent. How was it that, in this ruin where all was dead, a clock, the pulse of time, was living?

"Oh! oh!" said Roland; "that proves that I shall see something."

The words were spoken almost in an aside. The majesty of the place and the silence acted upon that heart of iron, firm as the iron that had just tolled the call of time upon eternity. The minutes slowly passed, one after the other. Perhaps a cloud was passing between earth and moon, for Roland fancied that the shadows deepened. Then, as midnight approached, he seemed to hear a thousand confused, imperceptible sounds, coming no doubt from the nocturnal universe which wakes while the other sleeps. Nature permits no suspension of life, even for repose. She created her nocturnal world, even as she created her daily world, from the gnat which buzzes about the sleeper's pillow to the lion prowling around the Arab's bivouac.

But Roland, the camp watcher, the sentinel of the desert, Roland, the hunter, the soldier, knew all those sounds; they were powerless to disturb him.

Then, mingling with these sounds, the tones of the clock, chiming the hour, vibrated above his head. This time it was midnight. Roland counted the twelve strokes, one after the other. The last hung, quivering upon the air, like a bird with iron wings, then slowly expired, sad and mournful. Just then the young man thought he heard a moan. He listened in the direction whence it came. Again he heard it, this time nearer at hand.

He rose, his hands resting upon the table, the butt-end of a pistol beneath each palm. A rustle like that of a sheet or a gown trailing along the grass was audible on his right, not ten paces from him. He straightened up as if moved by a spring.

At the same moment a shade appeared on the threshold of the vast hall. This shade resembled the ancient statues lying on the tombs. It was wrapped in an immense winding-sheet which trailed behind it.

For an instant Roland doubted his own eyes. Had the preoccupation of his mind made him see a thing which was not? Was he the dupe of his senses, the sport of those hallucinations which physicians assert, but cannot explain? A moan, uttered by the phantom, put his doubts to flight.

"My faith!" he cried in a burst of laughter, "now for a tussle, friend ghost!"

The spectre paused and extended a hand toward the young officer. "Roland! Roland!" said the spectre in a muffled voice, "it would be a pity not to follow to the grave those you have sent there."

And the spectre, without hastening its step, continued on its way.

Roland, astounded for an instant, came down from the stage, and resolutely followed the ghost. The path was difficult, encumbered with stones, benches awry, and over-turned tables. And yet, through all these obstacles, an in-visible channel seemed open for the spectre, which pursued its way unchecked.

Each time it passed before a window, the light from with-out, feeble as it was, shone upon the winding-sheet and the ghost, outlining the figure, which passed into the obscurity to reappear and vanish again at each succeeding one. Ro-land, his eyes fixed upon the figure, fearing to lose sight of it if he diverted his gaze from it, dared not look at the path, apparently so easy to the spectre, yet bristling with obstacles for him. He stumbled at every step. The ghost was gain-ing upon him. It reached the door opposite to that by which it had entered. Roland saw the entrance to a dark passage. Feeling that the ghost would escape him, he cried: "Man or ghost, robber or monk, halt or I fire!"

"A dead body cannot be killed twice, and death has no power over the spirit," replied the ghost in its muffled voice.

"Who are you?"

"The Shade of him you tore violently from the earth."

The young officer burst into that harsh, nervous laugh, made more terrible by the darkness around him.

"Faith!" said he, "if you have no further indications to give me, I shall not trouble myself to discover you."

"Remember the fountain at Vaucluse," said the Shade, in a voice so faint the words seemed to escape his lips like a sigh rather than articulate speech.

For an instant Roland felt, not his heart failing him, but the sweat pouring from his forehead. Making an effort over himself, he regained his voice and cried, menacingly: "For a last time, apparition or reality, I warn you that, if you do not stop, I shall fire!"

The Shade did not heed him, but continued on its way.

Roland paused an instant to take aim. The spectre was not ten paces from him. Roland was a sure shot; he had himself loaded his pistols, and only a moment before he had looked to the charge to see that it was intact.

As the spectre passed, tall and white, beneath the gloomy vault of the passage, Roland fired. The flash illumined the corridor like lightning, down which the spectre passed with unfaltering, unhastening steps. Then all was blacker than before. The ghost vanished in the darkness. Roland dashed after him, changing his other pistol from the left hand to the right. But short as his stop had been, the ghost had gained ground. Roland saw him at the end of the passage, this time distinctly outlined against the gray background of the night. He redoubled his pace, and as he crossed the threshold of the passage, he fancied that the ghost was plunging into the bowels of the earth. But the torso still remained visible.

"Devil or not," cried Roland, "I follow you!"

He fired a second shot, which filled the cavernous space, into which the ghost had disappeared, with flame and smoke.

When the smoke had cleared away, Roland looked vainly around. He was alone. He sprang into the cistern howling with rage. He sounded the walls with the butt-end of his pistol, he stamped on the ground; but everywhere, earth and stone gave back the sound of solid objects. He tried to pierce the darkness, but it was impossible. The faint moonlight that filtered into the cistern died out at the first steps.

"Oh!" cried Roland, "a torch! a torch!"

No one answered. The only sound to be heard was the spring bubbling close at hand. Realizing that further search would be useless, he emerged from the cavern. Drawing a powder-horn and two balls from his pocket, he loaded his pistols hastily. Then he took the path along which he had just come, found the dark passage, then the vast refectory, and again took his place at the end of the silent hall and waited.

But the hours of the night sounded successively, until the first gleam of dawn cast its pallid light upon the walls of the cloister.

"Well," muttered Roland, "it's over for to-night. Perhaps I shall be more fortunate the next time."

Twenty minutes later he re-entered the Château des Noires-Fontaines.

CHAPTER XVII

INVESTIGATIONS

TWO persons were waiting for Roland's return; one in anguish, the other with impatience. These two persons were Amélie and Sir John. Neither of them had slept for an instant. Amélie displayed her anguish only by the sound of her door, which was furtively closed as Roland came up the staircase. Roland heard the sound. He had not the courage to pass before her door without reassuring her.

"Be easy, Amélie, I am here," he said.

It did not occur to him that his sister might be anxious for any one but him.

Amélie darted from her room in her night-dress. It was easy to see from her pallor and the dark circles which spread nearly to the middle of her cheeks that she had not closed her eyes all night.

"Has nothing happened to you, Roland?" she cried, clasping her brother in her arms and feeling him over anxiously.

"Nothing."

"Nor to any one else?"

"No."

"And you saw nothing?"

"I didn't say that," answered Roland.

"Good God! What did you see?"

"I'll tell that to you later. Meantime, there is no one either killed or wounded."

"Ah! I breathe again!"

"Now, let me give you a bit of advice, little sister. Go to bed and sleep, if you can, till breakfast. I am going to do the same thing, and can assure you I won't need any rocking. Good-night, or rather good-morning."

Roland kissed his sister tenderly. Then affecting to whistle a hunting-air carelessly, he ran up the next flight of steps. Sir John was frankly waiting for him in the hall. He went straight to the young man.

"Well?" he asked.

"Well, I didn't roll my stone entirely for nothing."

"Did you see any ghosts?"

"At any rate I saw something that resembled one very closely."

"Come, tell me all about it."

"I see you won't be able to sleep, or at best only fitfully, if I don't. Here's what happened, in a nutshell."

And Roland gave him a minute account of the night's adventure.

"Excellent," said Sir John, when Roland had finished. "I hope you have left something for me to do."

"I am even afraid," answered Roland, "that I have left you the hardest part."

Then, as Sir John went over each detail, asking many questions about the localities, he said:

"Listen, Sir John. We will pay the Chartreuse a visit in broad daylight after breakfast, which will not interfere in the least with your night-watch. On the contrary, it will acquaint you with the localities. Only you must tell no one."

"Oh!" exclaimed Sir John, "do I look like a gabbler?"

"No, that's true," cried Roland laughing, "you are not a gabbler, but I am a ninny." So saying, he entered his bedchamber.

After breakfast the two young men sauntered down the slopes of the garden, as if to take a walk along the banks of the Reissouse. Then they bore to the left, swung up the hill for about forty paces, struck into the highroad, and crossed the woods, till they reached the convent wall at the very place where Roland had climbed over it on the preceding night.

"My lord," said Roland, "this is the way."

"Very well," replied Sir John, "let us take it."

Slowly, with a wonderful strength of wrist, which betokened a man well trained in gymnastics, the Englishman seized the coping of the wall, swung himself to the top, and dropped down on the other side. Roland followed with the rapidity of one who is not achieving a feat for the first time. They were both on the other side, where the desertion and desolation were more visible by night than by day. The grass was growing knee high in the paths; the espaliers were tangled with vines so thick that the grapes could not ripen in the shadow of the leaves. The wall had given way in several places, and ivy, the parasite rather than the friend of ruins, was spreading everywhere.

As for the trees in the open space, plums, peaches and apricots, they had grown with the freedom of the oaks and beeches in the forest, whose breadth and thickness they seemed to envy. The sap, completely absorbed by the branches which were many and vigorous, produced but little fruit, and that imperfect. By the rustle of the tall grass, Sir John and Roland divined that the lizards, those crawling offsprings of solitude, had established their domicile there, from which they fled in amazement at this disturbance.

Roland led his friend straight to the door between the orchard and the cloister, but before entering he glanced at the clock. That clock, which went at night, was stopped in the day time. From the cloister he passed into the refectory. There the daylight showed under their true aspect the various objects which the darkness had clothed with such fantastic forms the night before. Roland showed Sir John the overturned stools, the table marked by the blow of the pistol, the door by which the phantom had entered. Accompanied by the Englishman, he followed the path he had taken in pursuit of the spectre. He recognized the obstacles which had hindered him, and noted how easily one who knew the locality might cross or avoid them.

At the spot where he had fired, he found the wad, but he looked in vain for the bullet. The arrangement of the passage, which ran slanting, made it impossible for the bullet, if its marks were not on the walls, to have missed the ghost. And yet if the ghost were hit, supposing it to be a solid body, how came it to remain erect? How had it escaped being wounded, and if wounded, why were there no bloodstains on the ground? And there was no trace of either blood or ball.

Sir John was almost ready to admit that his friend had had to do with a veritable ghost.

"Some one came after me," said Roland, "and picked up the ball."

"But if you fired at a man, why didn't the ball go into him?"

"Oh! that's easily explained. The man wore a coat of mail under his shroud."

That was possible, but, nevertheless, Sir John shook his head dubiously. He preferred to believe in a supernatural occurrence; it gave him less trouble.

Roland and he continued their investigations. They reached the end of the passage which opened on the furthest extremity of the orchard. It was there that Roland had seen his spectre for an instant as it glided into the dark vault. He made for the cistern, and so little did he hesitate that he might still have been following the ghost. There he understood how the darkness of the night had seemed to deepen by the absence of all exterior reflection. It was even difficult to see there by day.

Roland took two torches about a foot long from beneath his cloak, took a flint, lighted the tinder, and a match from the tinder. Both torches flared up.

The problem was now to discover the way by which the ghost had disappeared. Roland and Sir John lowered their torches and examined the ground. The cistern was paved with large squares of limestone, which seemed to fit perfectly. Roland looked for his second ball as persistently as for the first. A stone lay loose at his feet, and, pushing it aside, he disclosed an iron ring screwed into one of the limestone blocks.

Without a word Roland seized the ring, braced his feet and pulled. The square turned on its pivot with an ease which proved that it was frequently subjected to the same manipulation. As it turned, it disclosed a subterranean passage.

"Ah!" exclaimed Roland, "this is the way my spectre went."

He entered the yawning cavern, followed by Sir John. They traversed the same path that Morgan took when he returned to give an account of his expedition. At the end of the passage they came upon an iron gate opening into the mortuary vaults. Roland shook the gate, which yielded to his touch. They crossed this subterranean cemetery, and came to a second gate; like the first, it was open. With Roland still in front, they went up several steps, and found themselves in the choir of the chapel, where the scene we have related between Morgan and the Company of Jehu took place. Only now the stalls were empty, the choir was deserted, and the altar, degraded by the abandonment of worship, was no longer covered by the burning tapers or the sacred cloth.

It was evident to Roland that this was the goal of the false ghost, which Sir John persisted in believing a real one. But, real or false, Sir John admitted that its flight had brought it to this particular spot. He reflected a moment and then remarked: "As it is my turn to watch to-night, I have the right to choose my ground; I shall watch here."

And he pointed to a sort of table formed in the centre of the choir by an oaken pedestal which had formerly supported the eagle lectern.

"Indeed," said Roland, with the same heedlessness he showed in his own affairs, "you'll do very well there, only as you may find the gates locked and the stone fastened to-night, we had better look for some more direct way to get here."

In less than five minutes they had found an outlet. The door of the old sacristy opened into the choir, and from the sacristy a broken window gave passage into the forest. The two men climbed through the window and found themselves in the forest thicket some twenty feet from the spot where they had killed the boar.

"That's what we want," said Roland; "only, my dear Sir John, as you would never find your way by night in a forest which, even by day, is so impenetrable, I shall accompany you as far as this."

"Very well. But once I am inside, you are to leave me," said the Englishman. "I remember what you told me about the susceptibility of ghosts. If they know you are near, they may hesitate to appear, and as you have seen one, I insist on seeing at least one myself."

"I'll leave you, don't be afraid," replied Roland, adding, with a laugh, "Only I do fear one thing."

"What is that?"

"That in your double capacity of an Englishman and a heretic they won't feel at ease with you."

"Oh," replied Sir John, gravely, "what a pity I shall not have time to abjure before this evening."

The two friends, having seen all there was to see, returned to the château. No one, not even Amélie, had suspected that their walk was other than an ordinary one. The day passed without questions and without apparent anxiety; besides, it was already late when the two gentlemen returned.

At dinner, to Edouard's great delight, another hunt was proposed, and it furnished a topic for conversation during dinner and part of the evening. By ten o'clock, as usual, all had retired to their rooms, except Roland, who was in that of Sir John.

The difference of character showed itself markedly in the preparations of the two men. Roland had made them joyously, as if for a pleasure trip; Sir John made his gravely, as if for a duel. He loaded his pistols with the utmost care and put them into his belt English fashion. And, instead of a cloak, which might have impeded his movements, he wore a top-coat with a high collar put on over his other coat.

At half-past ten the pair left the house with the same precautions that Roland had observed when alone. It was five minutes before eleven when they reached the broken window, where the fallen stones served as a stepping-block. There, according to agreement, they were to part. Sir John reminded Roland of this agreement.

"Yes," said Roland, "an agreement is an agreement with me. Only, let me give you a piece of advice."

"What is it?"

"I could not find the bullets because some one had been here and carried them off; and that was done beyond doubt to prevent me from seeing the dents on them."

"What sort of dent do you mean?"

"Those of the links of a coat of mail; my ghost was a man in armor."

"That's too bad!" said Sir John; "I hoped for a ghost." Then, after a moment's silence and a sigh expressive of his deep regret in resigning the ghost, he asked: "What was your advice?"

"Fire at his face!"

Sir John nodded assent, pressed the young officer's hand, clambered through the window and disappeared in the sacristy.

"Good-night!" called Roland after him. Then with the indifference to danger which a soldier generally feels for himself and his companions, Roland took his way back to the Château des Noires-Fontaines, as he had promised Sir John.

_____

CHAPTER XVIII

THE TRIAL

THE next day Roland, who had been unable to sleep till about two in the morning, woke about seven. Collecting his scattered wits, he recalled what had passed between Sir John and himself the night before, and was astonished that the Englishman had not wakened him. He dressed hastily and went to Sir John's room at the risk of rousing him from his first sleep.

He knocked at the door. Sir John made no answer. Roland knocked again, louder this time. The same silence. This time some uneasiness mingled with Roland's curiosity. The key was on the outside; the young officer opened the door, and cast a rapid glance around the room. Sir John was not there; he had not returned. The bed was undisturbed. What had happened?

There was not an instant to lose, and we may be sure that, with that rapidity of decision we know in Roland, he lost not an instant. He rushed to his room, finished dressing, put his hunting knife into his belt, slung his rifle over his shoulder and went out. No one was yet awake except the chambermaid. Roland met her on the stairs.

"Tell Madame de Montrevel," said he, "that I have gone into the forest of Seillon with my gun. She must not worry if Sir John and I are not on time for breakfast."

Then he darted rapidly away. Ten minutes later he reached the window where he had left Sir John the night before. He listened, not a sound came from within; the huntsman's ear could detect the morning woodland sounds, but no others. Roland climbed through the window with his customary agility, and rushed through the choir into the sacristy.

One look sufficed to show him that not only the choir but the entire chapel was empty. Had the spectres led the Englishman along the reverse of the way he had come himself? Possibly. Roland passed rapidly behind the altar, into the vaults, where he found the gate open. He entered the subterranean cemetery. Darkness hid its depths. He called Sir John three times. No one answered.

He reached the second gate; it was open like the first. He entered the vaulted passage; only, as it would be impossible to use his gun in such darkness, he slung it over his shoulder and drew out his hunting-knife. Feeling his way, he continued to advance without meeting anybody, but the further he went the deeper became the darkness, which indicated that the stone in the cistern was closed. He reached the steps, and mounted them until his head touched the revolving stone; then he made an effort, and the block turned. Roland saw daylight and leaped into the cistern. The door into the orchard stood open. Roland passed through it, crossed that portion of the orchard which lay between the cistern and the corridor at the other end of which he had fired upon the phantom. He passed along the corridor and entered the refectory. The refectory was empty.

Again, as in the funereal passageway, Roland called three times. The wondering echo, which seemed to have forgotten the tones of the human voice, answered stammering. It was improbable that Sir John had come this way; it was necessary to go back. Roland retraced his steps, and found himself in the choir again. That was where Sir John had intended to spend the night, and there some trace of him must be found.

Roland advanced only a short distance, and then a cry escaped him. A large spot of blood lay at his feet, staining the pavement. On the other side of the choir, a dozen feet from the blood, was another stain, not less large, nor less red, nor less recent. It seemed to make a pendant for the first.

One of these stains was to the right, the other to the left of that sort of pedestal intended, as we have said, to support the eagle lectern—the pedestal which Sir John had selected for his place of waiting. Roland went up to it. It was drenched with blood! Evidently the drama had taken place on that spot; a drama which, if all the signs were true, must have been terrible.

Roland, in his double capacity of huntsman and soldier, was keen at a quest. He could calculate the amount of blood lost by a man who was dead, or by one who was only wounded. That night three men had fallen, either dead or wounded. What were the probabilities?

The two stains in the choir to the right and left of the pedestal were probably the blood of Sir John's two antagonists. That on the pedestal was probably his own. Attacked on both sides, right and left, he had fired with both hands, killing or wounding a man with each shot. Hence these two bloodstains which reddened the pavement. He himself must have been struck down beside the pedestal, on which his blood had spurted.

After a few seconds of examination, Roland was as sure of this as if he had witnessed the struggle with his own eyes. Now, what had been done with the bodies? He cared little enough about two of them; but he was determined to know what had become of that of Sir John.

A track of blood started from the pedestal and led straight to the door. Sir John's body had been carried outside. Roland shook the massive door. It was only latched, and opened at the first pressure. Outside the sill the tracks of blood still continued. Roland could see through the underbrush the path by which the body had been carried. The broken branches, the trampled grass, led Roland to the edge of the wood on the road leading from Pont d'Ain to Bourg. There the body, living or dead, seemed to have been laid on the bank of the ditch. Beyond that no traces whatever.

A man passed just then, coming from the direction of the Château des Noires-Fontaines. Roland went up to him.

"Have you seen anything on the road? Did you meet any one?" he inquired.

"Yes," replied the man, "I saw two peasants carrying a body on a litter."

"Ah!" cried Roland, "was it that of a living man?"

"The man was pale and motionless; he looked as if he were dead."

"Was the blood flowing?"

"I saw some drops on the road."

"In that case, he is living."

Then taking a louis from his pocket he said: "There's a louis for you. Run for Dr. Milliet at Bourg; tell him to get a horse and come at full speed to the Château des Noires-Fontaines. You can add that there is a man there in danger of dying."

While the peasant, stimulated by the reward, made all haste to Bourg, Roland, leaping along on his vigorous legs, was hurrying to the château.

And now, as our readers are, in all probability, as curious as Roland to know what had happened to Sir John, we shall give an account of the events of the night.

A few minutes before eleven, Sir John, as we have seen, entered what was usually known as La Correrie, or the pavilion of the Chartreuse, which was nothing more than a chapel erected in the woods. From the sacristy he entered the choir. It was empty and seemed solitary. A rather brilliant moon, veiled from time to time by a cloud, sent its bluish rays through the stained glass, cracked and broken, of the pointed windows. Sir John advanced to the middle of the choir, where he paused and remained standing beside the pedestal.

The minutes slipped away. But this time it was not the convent clock which marked the time, it was the church at Péronnaz; that is to say, the nearest village to the chapel where Sir John was watching.

Everything happened up to midnight just as it had to

Roland. Sir John heard only the vague rustling and passing noises of the night.

Midnight sounded; it was the moment he awaited with impatience, for it was then that something would happen, if anything was to happen. As the last stroke died away he thought he heard footsteps underground, and saw a light appear behind the iron gate leading to the mortuary vault. His whole attention was fixed on that spot.

A monk emerged from the passage, his hood brought low over his eyes, and carrying a torch in his hand. He wore the dress of a Chartreux. A second one followed, then a third. Sir John counted twelve. They separated before the altar. There were twelve stalls in the choir; six to the right of Sir John, six to his left. The twelve monks silently took their places in the twelve stalls. Each one placed his torch in a hole made for that purpose in the oaken desk, and waited.

A thirteenth monk appeared and took his stand before the altar.

None of the monks affected the fantastic behavior of ghosts or shades; they all belonged undoubtedly to the earth, and were living men.

Sir John, a pistol in each hand, stood leaning against the pedestal in the middle of the choir, and watched with the utmost coolness this manœuvre which tended to surround him. The monks were standing, like him, erect and silent.

The monk at the altar broke the silence.

"Brothers," he asked, "why are the Avengers assembled?"

"To judge a blasphemer!" replied the monks.

"What crime has this blasphemer committed?" continued the interlocutor.

"He has tried to discover the secrets of the Companions of Jehu."

"What penalty has he incurred?"

"Death."

The monk at the altar waited, apparently, to give time for the sentence which had just been pronounced to reach the heart of him whom it concerned. Then turning to the Englishman, who continued as calm as if he were at a comedy, he said: "Sir John Tanlay, you are a foreigner and an Englishman—a double reason why you should leave the Companions of Jehu to fight their own battles with the government, whose downfall they have sworn. You failed in wisdom, you yielded to idle curiosity; instead of keeping away, you have entered the lion's den, and the lion will rend you."

Then after an instant's silence, during which he seemed to await the Englishman's reply, he resumed, seeing that he remained silent: "Sir John Tanlay, you are condemned to death. Prepare to die!"

"Ah! I see that I have fallen into the hands of a band of thieves. If so, I can buy myself off with a ransom." Then turning to the monk at the altar he asked, "How much do you demand, captain?"

A threatening murmur greeted these insolent words. The monk at the altar stretched out his hand.

"You are mistaken, Sir John. We are not a band of thieves," said he in a tone as calm and composed as Sir John's, "and the proof is, that if you have money or jewels upon you, you need only give me your instructions, and they will be remitted either to your family or the person whom you designate."

"And what guarantee shall I have that my last wishes will be carried out?"

"My word."

"The word of the leader of assassins! I don't trust it."

"This time, as before, you are mistaken, Sir John. I am no more the leader of assassins than I am a captain of thieves."

"Who are you, then?"

"The elect of celestial vengeance. I am the envoy of

Jehu, King of Israel, who was anointed by the prophet Elisha to destroy the house of Ahab.''

"If you are what you say, why do you veil your faces? Why do you wear armor under your robes? The elect strike openly; they risk death in giving death. Throw back your hoods, show me your naked breasts, and I will admit that you are what you pretend to be.''

"Brothers, you have heard him,'' said the monk at the altar.

Then, stripping off his gown, he opened his coat, waistcoat and even his shirt. Each monk did the same, and stood with face exposed and bared breast. They were all handsome young men, of whom the eldest was apparently not more than thirty-five. Their dress was elegant, but, strange fact, none was armed. They were judges and nothing more.

"Be satisfied, Sir John Tanlay,'' said the monk at the altar. "You will die, but in dying, you can, as you wished just now, recognize and kill your judges. Sir John, you have five minutes to prepare your soul for death!''

Sir John, instead of profiting by this permission to think of his eternal salvation, coolly cocked his pistols to see that the triggers were all right, and passed a ramrod down the barrels to make sure that the balls were there. Then, without waiting for the five minutes to expire, he said: "Gentlemen, I am ready. Are you?''

The young men looked at each other; then, on a sign from their chief, they walked straight to Sir John, and surrounded him on all sides. The monk at the altar stood immovable, commanding with his eye the scene that was about to take place.

Sir John had only two pistols, consequently he could only kill two men. He selected his victims and fired. Two Companions of Jehu rolled upon the pavement, which they reddened with their blood. The others, as if nothing had happened, still advanced with outstretched hands upon Sir John. Sir John seized his pistols by the muzzle, using them like hammers. He was vigorous and the struggle was long. For ten minutes, a confused group tussled in the centre of the choir; then this violent commotion ceased, and the Companions of Jehu drew away to right and left, and regained their stalls, leaving Sir John bound with their girdles and lying upon the pedestal in the choir.

"Have you commended your soul to God?" asked the monk at the altar.

"Yes, assassin," answered Sir John; "you may strike."

The monk took a dagger from the altar, advanced with uplifted arm, and, standing over Sir John, levelled the dagger at his breast: "Sir John Tanlay," he said, "you are a brave man, and doubtless a man of honor. Swear that you will never breathe a syllable of what you have seen; swear that under no circumstances, whatever they may be, you will recognize us, and we will spare your life."

"As soon as I leave here," replied Sir John, "I shall denounce you. The moment I am free I will trail you down."

"Swear," repeated the monk a second time.

"No," said Sir John.

"Swear," said the monk for the third time.

"Never," replied Sir John.

"Then die, since you will it!"

And he drove his dagger up to the hilt in Sir John's breast; who, whether by force of will, or because the blow killed him at once, did not even sigh. Then the monk in a loud sonorous voice, like a man conscious of having done his duty, exclaimed: "Justice is done!"

Then he returned to the altar, leaving the dagger in the wound and said: "Brothers, you are invited to the ball of the Victims, which takes place in Paris on the 21st of January next, at No. 35 Rue du Bac, in memory of the death of King Louis XVI."

So saying, he re-entered the subterranean passage, followed by the remaining ten monks, each bearing his torch in his hand. Two torches remained to light the three bodies.

A moment later four serving brothers entered, and raised first the bodies of the two monks, which they carried into the vault. Then they returned, lifted that of Sir John, placed it on a stretcher, and carried it out of the chapel by the entrance door, which they closed after them. Two of the monks walked in front of the stretcher, carrying the two torches left in the chapel.

And now, if our readers ask why there was this difference between the treatment received by Roland and that administered to Sir John, why this mansuetude toward one and this rigor toward the other, we reply: Remember that Morgan enjoined on his brethren the safety of Amélie's brother, and thus safeguarded, under no circumstances could Roland die by the hand of a Companion of Jehu.

CHAPTER XIX

THE LITTLE HOUSE IN THE RUE DE LA VICTOIRE

WHILE they are bearing Sir John Tanlay's body to the Château des Noires-Fontaines; while Roland is hurrying in the same direction; while the peasant, despatched by him, is hastening to Bourg to notify Dr. Milliet of the catastrophe which necessitated his immediate presence at Madame de Montrevel's home, let us jump over the distance which separates Bourg from Paris, and the time which elapsed between the 16th of October and the 7th of November; that is to say, between the 24th of Vendemiaire and the 16th Brumaire, and repair to that little house in the Rue de la Victoire rendered historically famous by the conspiracy of the 18th Brumaire, which issued from it fully armed.

It is the same house which stands there to-day on the right of the street at No. 60, apparently astonished to present to the eye, after so many successive changes of government, the consular fasces which may still be seen on the panels of its double oaken doors.

Let us follow the long, narrow alley of lindens that leads from the gate on the street to the door of the house; let us enter the antechamber, take the hall to the right, ascend the twenty steps that lead to a study hung with green paper, and furnished with curtains, easy chairs and couches of the same color. The walls are covered with geographical charts and plans of cities. Bookcases of maple are ranged on either side of the fireplace, which they inclose. The chairs, sofas, tables and desks are piled with books; there is scarcely any room on the chairs to sit down, or on the desks and tables to write.

In the midst of this encumbering mass of reports, letters, pamphlets and books, a man had cleared a space for himself where he was now seated, clutching his hair impatiently from time to time, as he endeavored to decipher a page of notes, compared to which the hieroglyphics on the obelisk of Luxor, would have been transparently intelligible. Just as the secretary's impatience was approaching desperation, the door opened and a young officer wearing an aide's uniform entered.

The secretary raised his head, and a lively expression of satisfaction crossed his face.

"Oh! my dear Roland," said he; "you here at last! I am delighted to see you, for three reasons. First, because I am wearying for you; second, because the general is impatient for your return, and keeps up a hullaballoo about it; and third, because you can help me to read this, with which I have been struggling for the last ten minutes. But first of all, kiss me."

And the secretary and the aide-de-camp embraced each other.

"Well," said the latter, "let us see this word that is troubling you so, my dear Bourrienne!"

"Ah! my dear fellow, what writing! I get a white hair for every page I decipher, and this is my third to-day! Here, read it if you can."

Roland took the sheet from the secretary, and fixing his

eyes on the spot indicated, read quite fluently: "Paragraph XI. The Nile, from Assouan to a distance of twelve miles north of Cairo, flows in a single stream"—"Well," said he, interrupting himself, "that's all plain sailing. What did you mean? The general, on the contrary, took pains when he wrote that."

"Go on, go on," said Bourrienne.

The young man resumed: " 'From that point, which is called'—Ah! ah!"

"There you are! Now what do you say to that?"

Roland repeated: " 'Which is called' — The devil! 'Which is called—' "

"Yes, 'Which is called'—after that?"

"What will you give me, Bourrienne," cried Roland, "if I guess it?"

"The first colonel's commission I find signed in blank."

"By my faith, no! I don't want to leave the general; I'd rather have a good father than five hundred naughty children. I'll give you the three words for nothing."

"What! are there three words there?"

"They don't look as if they were quite three, I admit. Now listen, and make obeisance to me: 'From the point called Ventre della Vacca.' "

"Ha! Ventre de la Vache! Confound it! He's illegible enough in French, but if he takes it into his head to go off in Italian, and that Corsican patois to boot! I thought I only ran the risk of going crazy, but then I should become stupid, too. Well, you've got it," and he read the whole sentence consecutively: " 'The Nile, from Assouan to a distance of twelve miles north of Cairo, flows in a single stream; from that point, which is called Ventre de la Vache, it forms the branches of the Rosetta and the Damietta.' Thank you, Roland," and he began to write the end of the paragraph, of which the first lines were already committed to paper.

"Tell me," said Roland; "is he still got his hobby, the dear general, of colonizing Egypt?"

"Yes; and then, as a sort of offset, a little governing in France; we will colonize from a distance."

"Well, my dear Bourrienne, suppose you post me a little on matters in this country, so that I won't seem to have just arrived from Timbuctoo."

"In the first place, did you come back of your own accord, or were you recalled?"

"Recalled? I should think so!"

"By whom?"

"The general himself."

"Special despatch?"

"Written by himself; see!"

The young man drew a paper from his pocket containing two lines, not signed, in the same handwriting as that which Bourrienne had before him.   These two lines said: " 'Start. Be in Paris 16th Brumaire.   I need you.'"

"Yes," said Bourrienne, "I think it will be on the eighteenth."

"What will be on the eighteenth?"

"On my word, Roland, you ask more than I know.   That man, as you are aware, is not communicative.   What will take place on the 18th Brumaire?   I don't know as yet; but I'll answer for it that something will happen."

"Oh! you must have a suspicion!"

"I think he means to make himself Director in place of Sièyes, or perhaps president in Gohier's stead."

"Good!   How about the Constitution of the year III.?"

"The Constitution of the year III.   What about that?"

"Why, yes, a man must be forty years old to be a Director; and the general lacks just ten of them."

"The deuce! so much the worse for the Constitution. They must violate it."

"It is rather young yet, Bourrienne; they don't, as a rule, violate children of seven."

"My dear fellow, in Barras' hands everything grows old rapidly.   The little girl of seven is already an old prostitute."

Roland shook his head.

"Well, what is it?" asked Bourrienne.

"Why, I don't believe the general will make himself a simple Director with four colleagues. Just imagine it—five kings of France! It wouldn't be a Directory any longer, but a four-in-hand."

"Anyway, up to the present, that is all he has allowed any one to perceive; but you know, my dear friend, if we want to know the general's secrets we must guess them."

"Faith! I'm too lazy to take the trouble, Bourrienne. Besides, I'm a regular Janissary—what is to be, will be. Why the devil should I bother to form an opinion and battle for it. It's quite wearisome enough to have to live." And the young man enforced his favorite aphorism with a long yawn; then he added: "Do you think there will be any sword play?"

"Probably."

"Then there will be a chance of getting killed; that's all I want. Where is the general?"

"With Madame Bonaparte. He went to her about fifteen minutes ago. Have you let him know you are here?"

"No, I wanted to see you first. But I hear his step now."

Just then the door was opened abruptly, and the same historical personage whom we saw playing a silent part incognito at Avignon appeared on the threshold, in the picturesque uniform of the general-in-chief of the army of Egypt, except that, being in his own house, he was bareheaded. Roland thought his eyes were more hollow and his skin more leaden than usual. But the moment he saw the young man, Bonaparte's gloomy, or rather meditative, eye emitted a flash of joy.

"Ah, here you are, Roland!" he said. "True as steel! Called, you come. Welcome, my dear fellow." And he offered Roland his hand. Then he asked, with an imperceptible smile, "What were you doing with Bourrienne?"

"Waiting for you, general."

"And in the meantime gossiping like two old women."

"I admit it, general. I was showing him my order to be here on the 16th Brumaire."

"Did I write the 16th or the 17th?"

"Oh! the 16th, general. The 17th would have been too late."

"Why too late?"

"Why, hang it, Bourrienne says there are to be great doings here on the 18th."

"Capital," muttered Bourrienne; "the scatter-brain will earn me a wigging."

"Ah! So he told you I had planned great doings for the 18th?" Then, approaching Bourrienne, Bonaparte pinched his ear, and said, "Tell-tale!" Then to Roland he added: "Well, it is so, my dear fellow, we have made great plans for the 18th. My wife and I dine with President Gohier; an excellent man, who was very polite to Josephine during my absence. You are to dine with us, Roland."

Roland looked at Bonaparte. "Was it for that you brought me here, general?" he asked, laughing.

"For that, and something else, too, perhaps. Bourrinene, write—"

Bourrienne hastily seized his pen.

"Are you ready?"

"Yes, general."

"'My dear President, I write to let you know that my wife and I, with one of my aides-de-camp, will dine with you the day after to-morrow. This is merely to say that we shall be quite satisfied with a family dinner.'"

"What next?"

"How do you mean?"

"Shall I put, 'Liberty, equality, fraternity'?"

"Or death," added Roland.

"No," said Bonaparte; "give me the pen."

He took the pen from Bourrienne's hands and wrote, "Ever yours, Bonaparte." Then, pushing away the paper, he added: "Address it, Bourrienne, and send an orderly with it."

Bourrienne wrote the address, sealed it, and rang the bell. An officer on duty entered.

"Send an orderly with that," said Bourrienne.

"There is an answer," added Bonaparte.

The officer closed the door.

"Bourrienne," said Bonaparte, pointing to Roland, "look at your friend."

"Well, general, I am looking at him."

"Do you know what he did at Avignon?"

"I hope he didn't make a pope."

"No, he threw a plate at a man's head."

"Oh, that was hasty!"

"That's not all."

"That I can well imagine."

"He fought a duel with that man."

"And, most naturally, he killed him."

"Exactly. Do you know why he did it?"

"No."

The general shrugged his shoulders, and said: "Because the man said that I was a thief." Then looking at Roland with an indefinable expression of raillery and affection, he added: "Ninny!" Then suddenly he burst out: "Oh! by the way, and the Englishman?"

"Exactly, the Englishman, general. I was just going to speak to you about him."

"Is he still in France?"

"Yes, and for awhile even I thought he would remain here till the last trumpet blew its blast through the valley of Jehosaphat."

"Did you miss killing him?"

"Oh! no, not I. We are the best friends in the world. General, he is a capital fellow, and so original to boot that I'm going to ask a bit of a favor for him."

"The devil! For an Englishman?" said Bonaparte, shaking his head. "I don't like the English."

"Good! As a people, but individually—"

"Well, what happened to your friend?"

"He was tried, condemned, and executed."

"What the devil are you telling us?"

"God's truth, general."

"What do you mean when you say, 'He was tried, condemned, and guillotined'?"

"Oh! not exactly that. Tried and condemned, but not guillotined. If he had been guillotined he would be more dangerously ill than he is now."

"Now, what are you gabbling about? What court tried and condemned him?"

"That of the Companions of Jehu!"

"And who are the Companions of Jehu?"

"Goodness! Have you forgotten our friend Morgan already, the masked man who brought back the wine-merchant's two hundred louis?"

"No," replied Bonaparte, "I have not forgotten him. I told you about the scamp's audacity, didn't I, Bourrienne?"

"Yes, general," said Bourrienne, "and I answered that, had I been in your place, I should have tried to find out who he was."

"And the general would know, had he left me alone. I was just going to spring at his throat and tear off his mask, when the general said, in that tone you know so well: 'Friend Roland!'"

"Come back to your Englishman, chatterbox!" cried the general. "Did Morgan murder him?"

"No, not he himself, but his Companions."

"But you were speaking of a court and a trial just now."

"General, you are always the same," said Roland, with their old school familiarity; "you want to know, and you don't give me time to tell you."

"Get elected to the Five Hundred, and you can talk as much as you like."

"Good! In the Five Hundred I should have four hundred and ninety-nine colleagues who would want to talk as much as I, and who would take the words out of my mouth. I'd rather be interrupted by you than by a lawyer."

"Will you go on?"

"I ask nothing better. Now imagine, general, there is a Chartreuse near Bourg—"

"The Chartreuse of Seillon; I know it."

"What! You know the Chartreuse of Seillon?" demanded Roland.

"Doesn't the general know everything?" cried Bourrienne.

"Well, about the Chartreuse; are there any monks there now?"

"No; only ghosts—"

"Are you, perchance, going to tell me a ghost-story?"

"And a famous one at that!"

"The devil! Bourrienne knows I love them. Go on."

"Well, we were told at home that the Chartreuse was haunted by ghosts. Of course, you understand that Sir John and I, or rather I and Sir John, wanted to clear our minds about it. So we each spent a night there."

"Where?"

"Why, at the Chartreuse."

Bonaparte made an imperceptible sign of the cross with his thumb, a Corsican habit which he never lost.

"Ah!" he exclaimed, "did you see any ghosts?"

"One."

"And what did you do to it?"

"Shot at it."

"And then?"

"It walked away."

"And you allowed yourself to be baffled?"

"Good! How well you know me! I followed it, and fired again. But as he knew his way among the ruins better than I, he escaped me."

"The devil!"

"The next day it was Sir John's turn; I mean our Englishman."

"Did he see your ghost?"

"He saw something better. He saw twelve monks enter the church, who tried him for trying to find out their secrets, condemned him to death, and who, on my word of honor, stabbed him."

"Didn't he defend himself?"

"Like a lion. He killed two."

"Is he dead?"

"Almost, but I hope he will recover. Just imagine, general; he was found by the road, and brought home with a dagger in his breast, like a prop in a vineyard."

"Why, it's like a scene of the Sainte-Vehme, neither more nor less."

"And on the blade of the dagger, that there might be no doubt as to who did the deed, were graven the words: 'Companions of Jehu.'"

"Why, it isn't possible that such things can happen in France, in the last year of the eighteenth century. It might do for Germany in the Middle Ages, in the days of the Henrys and the Ottos."

"Not possible, general? But here is the dagger. What do you say to that? Attractive, isn't it?"

And the young man drew from under his coat a dagger made entirely of steel, blade and handle. The handle was shaped like a cross, and on the blade, sure enough, were engraved the words, "Companions of Jehu."

Bonaparte examined the weapon carefully.

"And you say they planted that plaything in your Englishman's breast?"

"Up to the hilt."

"And he's not dead?"

"Not yet, at any rate."

"Have you been listening, Bourrienne?"

"With the greatest interest."

"You must remind me of this, Roland."

"When, general?"

"When?—when I am master. Come and say good-day to Josephine. Come, Bourrienne, you will dine with us, and be careful what you say, you two, for Moreau is coming to dinner. Ah! I will keep the dagger as a curiosity."

He went out first, followed by Roland, who was, soon after, followed by Bourrienne. On the stairs they met the orderly who had taken the note to Gohier.

"Well?" asked the general.

"Here is the President's answer."

"Give it to me."

Bonaparte broke the seal, and read:

The President Gohier is enchanted by the good fortune promised him by General Bonaparte. He will expect him to dinner the day after to-morrow, the 18th Brumaire, with his charming wife, and the aide-de-camp, whoever he may be. Dinner will be served at five o'clock.

If the hour does not suit General Bonaparte, will he kindly make known the one he would prefer.

The President, GOHIER.

16th Brumaire, year VII.

With an indescribable smile, Bonaparte put the letter in his pocket. Then turning to Roland, he asked: "Do you know President Gohier?"

"No, general."

"Ah! you'll see; he's an excellent man."

These words were pronounced in a tone no less indescribable than the smile.

CHAPTER XX

THE GUESTS OF GENERAL BONAPARTE

JOSEPHINE, in spite of her thirty-four years, or possibly because of them (that enchanting age when woman hovers between her passing youth and her coming age), Josephine, always beautiful, more graceful than ever, was still the charming woman we all know. An imprudent remark of Junot's, at the time of her husband's return, had produced a slight coolness between them. But three days had sufficed to restore to the enchantress her full power over the victor of Rivoli and the Pyramids.

She was doing the honors of her salon, when Roland entered the room. Always incapable, like the true Creole she was, of controlling her emotions, she gave a cry of joy, and held out her hand to him. She knew that Roland was devoted to her husband; she knew his reckless bravery, knew that if the young man had twenty lives he would willingly have given them all for Bonaparte. Roland eagerly took the hand she offered him, and kissed it respectfully. Josephine had known Roland's mother in Martinique; and she never failed, whenever she saw Roland, to speak to him of his maternal grandfather, M. de la Clémencière, in whose magnificent garden as a child she was wont to gather those wonderful fruits which are unknown in our colder climates.

A subject of conversation was therefore ready at hand. She inquired tenderly after Madame de Montrevel's health, and that of her daughter and little Edouard. Then, the information given, she said: "My dear Roland, I must now pay attention to my other guests; but try to remain after the other guests, or else let me see you alone to-morrow. I want to talk to you about *him*" (she glanced at Bonaparte) "and have a thousand things to tell you." Then, pressing the young man's hand with a sigh, she added, "No matter what happens, you will never leave him, will you?"

"What do you mean?" asked Roland, amazed.

"I know what I mean," said Josephine, "and when you have talked ten minutes with Bonaparte you will, I am sure, understand me. In the meantime watch, and listen, and keep silence."

Roland bowed and drew aside, resolved, as Josephine had advised, to play the part of observer.

But what was there to observe? Three principal groups occupied the salon. The first, gathered around Madame

Bonaparte, the only woman present, was more a flux and reflux than a group. The second, surrounding Talma, was composed of Arnault, Parseval-Grandmaison, Monge, Berthollet, and two or three other members of the Institute. The third, which Bonaparte had just joined, counted in its circle Talleyrand, Barras, Lucien, Admiral Bruix,[1] Roederer, Regnaud de Saint-Jean-d'Angely, Fouché, Réal, and two or three generals, among whom was Lefebvre.

In the first group they talked ot fashions, music, the theatre; in the second, literature, science, dramatic art; in the third, they talked of everything except that which was uppermost in their minds. Doubtless this reserve was not in keeping with Bonaparte's own feeling at the moment; for after sharing in this commonplace conversation for a short time, he took the former bishop of Autun by the arm and led him into the embrasure of the window.

"Well?" he asked.

Talleyrand looked at Bonaparte with that air which belonged to no one but him.

"What did I tell you of Sièyes, general?"

"You told me to secure the support of those who regarded the friends of the Republic as Jacobins, and to rely upon it that Sièyes was at their head."

"I was not mistaken."

"Then he will yield?"

"Better, he has yielded."

"The man who wanted to shoot me at Fréjus for having landed without being quarantined!"

"Oh, no; not for that."

"But what then?"

"For not having looked at him or spoken to him at Gohier's dinner."

"I must confess that I did it on purpose. I cannot endure that unfrocked monk."

---

[1] AUTHOR'S NÓTE.—Not to be confounded with Rear-Admiral de Brueys, who was killed at Aboukir, August 1, 1798. Admiral Bruix, the negotiator with Talleyrand of the 18th Brumaire, did not die until 1805.

Bonaparte perceived, too late, that the speech he had just made was like the sword of the archangel, double-edged; if Sièyes was unfrocked, Talleyrand was unmitred. He cast a rapid glance at his companion's face; the ex-bishop of Autun was smiling his sweetest smile.

"Then I can count upon him?"

"I will answer for him."

"And Cambacérès and Lebrun, have you seen them?"

"I took Sièyes in hand as the most recalcitrant. Bruix saw the other two."

The admiral, from the midst of the group, had never taken his eyes off of the general and the diplomatist. He suspected that their conversation had a special importance. Bonaparte made him a sign to join them. A less able man would have done so at once, but Bruix avoided such a mistake. He walked about the room with affected in-difference, and then, as if he had just perceived Talleyrand and Bonaparte talking together, he went up to them.

"Bruix is a very able man!" said Bonaparte, who judged men as much by little as by great things.

"And above all very cautious, general!" said Talley-rand.

"Yes. We will need a corkscrew to pull anything out of him."

"Oh, no; on the contrary, now that he has joined us, he will broach the question frankly."

And, indeed, no sooner had Bruix joined them than he began in words as clear as they were concise: "I have seen them; they waver!"

"They waver! Cambacérès and Lebrun waver? Lebrun I can understand—a sort of man of letters, a moderate, a Puritan; but Cambacérès—"

"But it is so."

"But didn't you tell them that I intended to make them each a consul?"

"I didn't get as far as that," replied Bruix, laughing.

"And why not?" inquired Bonaparte.

"Because this is the first word you have told me about your intentions, Citizen General."

"True," said Bonaparte, biting his lips.

"Am I to repair the omission?" asked Bruix.

"No, no," exclaimed Bonaparte hastily; "they might think I needed them. I won't have any quibbling. They must decide to-day without any other conditions than those you have offered them; to-morrow it will be too late. I feel strong enough to stand alone; and I now have Sièyes and Barras."

"Barras?" repeated the two negotiators astonished.

"Yes, Barras, who treated me like a little corporal, and wouldn't send me back to Italy, because, he said, I had made my fortune there, and it was useless to return. Well, Barras—"

"Barras?"

"Nothing." Then, changing his mind, "Faith! I may as well tell you. Do you know what Barras said at dinner yesterday before me? That it was impossible to go on any longer with the Constitution of the year III. He admitted the necessity of a dictatorship; said he had decided to abandon the reins of government, and retire; adding that he himself was looked upon as worn-out, and that the Republic needed new men. Now, guess to whom he thinks of transferring his power. I give it you, as Madame de Sévigné says, in a hundred, thousand, ten thousand. No other than General Hedouville, a worthy man, but I have only to look him in the face to make him lower his eyes. My glance must have been blasting! As the result, Barras came to my bedside at eight o'clock, to excuse himself as best he could for the nonsense he talked the night before, and admitted that I alone could save the Republic, and placed himself at my disposal, to do what I wished, assume any rôle I might assign him, begging me to promise that if I had any plan in my head I would count on him—yes, on him; and he would be true to the crack of doom."

"And yet," said Talleyrand, unable to resist a play

upon words, "doom is not a word with which to conjure liberty."

Bonaparte glanced at the ex-bishop.

"Yes, I know that Barras is your friend, the friend of Fouché and Réal; but he is not mine, and I shall prove it to him. Go back to Lebrun and Cambacérès, Bruix, and let them make their own bargain." Then, looking at his watch and frowning, he added: "It seems to me that Moreau keeps us waiting."

So saying, he turned to the group which surrounded Talma. The two diplomatists watched him. Then Admiral Bruix asked in a low voice: "What do you say, my dear Maurice, to such sentiments toward the man who picked him out, a mere lieutenant, at the siege of Toulon, who trusted him to defend the Convention on the 13th Vendémiaire, and who named him, when only twenty-six, General-in-Chief of the Army in Italy?"

"I say, my dear admiral," replied M. de Talleyrand, with his pallid mocking smile, "that some services are so great that ingratitude alone can repay them."

At that moment the door opened and General Moreau was announced. At this announcement, which was more than a piece of news—it was a surprise to most of those present—every eye was turned toward the door. Moreau appeared.

At this period three men were in the eyes of France. Moreau was one of these three men. The two others were Bonaparte and Pichegru. Each had become a sort of symbol. Since the 18th Fructidor, Pichegru had become the symbol of monarchy; Moreau, since he had been christened Fabius, was the symbol of the Republic; Bonaparte, symbol of war, dominated them both by the adventurous aspect of his genius.

Moreau was at that time in the full strength of his age; we would say the full strength of his genius, if decision were not one of the characteristics of genius. But no one was ever more undecided than the famous cunctator. He was thirty-six years old, tall, with a sweet, calm, firm countenance, and must have resembled Xenophon.

Bonaparte had never seen him, nor had he, on his side, ever seen Bonaparte. While the one was battling on the Adige and the Mincio, the other fought beside the Danube and the Rhine. Bonaparte came forward to greet him, saying: "You are welcome, general!"

"General," replied Moreau, smiling courteously, while all present made a circle around them to see how this new Cæsar would meet the new Pompey, "you come from Egypt, victorious, while I come, defeated, from Italy."

"A defeat which was not yours, and for which you are not responsible, general. It was Joubert's fault. If he had rejoined the Army of Italy as soon as he had been made commander-in-chief, it is more than probable that the Russians and Austrians, with the troops they then had, could not have resisted him. But he remained in Paris for his honeymoon! Poor Joubert paid with his life for that fatal month which gave the enemy time to gather its reinforcements. The surrender of Mantua gave them fifteen thousand men on the eve of the battle. It was impossible that our poor army should not have been overwhelmed by such united forces."

"Alas! yes," said Moreau; "it is always the greater number which defeats the smaller."

"A great truth, general," exclaimed Bonaparte; "an indisputable truth."

"And yet," said Arnault, joining in the conversation, "you yourself, general, have defeated large armies with little ones."

"If you were Marius, instead of the author of 'Marius,' you would not say that, my dear poet. Even when I beat great armies with little ones—listen to this, you young men who obey to-day, and will command to-morrow—it was always the larger number which defeated the lesser."

"I don't understand," said Arnault and Lefebvre together.

But Moreau made a sign with his head to show that he

understood. Bonaparte continued: "Follow my theory, for it contains the whole art of war. When with lesser forces I faced a large army, I gathered mine together, with great rapidity, fell like a thunderbolt on a wing of the great army, and overthrew it; then I profited by the disorder into which this manœuvre never failed to throw the enemy to attack again, always with my whole army, on the other side. I beat them, in this way, in detail; and the victory which resulted was always, as you see, the triumph of the many over the few."

As the able general concluded his definition of his own genius, the door opened and the servant announced that dinner was served.

"General," said Bonaparte, leading Moreau to Josephine, "take in my wife. Gentlemen, follow them."

On this invitation all present moved from the salon to the dining-room.

After dinner, on pretence of showing him a magnificent sabre he had brought from Egypt, Bonaparte took Moreau into his study. There the two rivals remained closeted more than an hour. What passed between them? What compact was signed? What promises were made? No one has ever known. Only, when Bonaparte returned to the salon alone, and Lucien asked him: "Well, what of Moreau?" he answered: "Just as I foresaw; he prefers military power to political power. I have promised him the command of an army." Bonaparte smiled as he pronounced these words; then added, "In the meantime—"

"In the meantime?" questioned Lucien.

"He will have that of the Luxembourg. I am not sorry to make him the jailer of the Directors, before I make him the conqueror of the Austrians."

The next day the following appeared in the "Moniteur":

PARIS, 17th Brumaire. Bonaparte has presented Moreau with a magnificent Damascus sword set with precious stones which he brought from Egypt, the value of which is estimated at twelve thousand francs.

CHAPTER XXI

THE SCHEDULE OF THE DIRECTORY

WE HAVE said that Moreau, furnished no doubt with instructions, left the little house in the Rue de la Victoire, while Bonaparte returned alone to the salon. Everything furnished an object of comment in such a company as was there assembled; the absence of Moreau, the return of Bonaparte unaccompanied, and the visible good humor which animated his countenance, were all remarked upon.

The eyes which fastened upon him most ardently were those of Josephine and Roland. Moreau for Bonaparte added twenty chances to the success of the plot; Moreau against Bonaparte robbed him of fifty. Josephine's eyes were so supplicating that, on leaving Lucien, Bonaparte pushed his brother toward his wife. Lucien understood, and approached Josephine, saying: "All is well."

"Moreau?"

"With us."

"I thought he was a Republican."

"He has been made to see that we are acting for the good of the Republic."

"I should have thought him ambitious," said Roland.

Lucien started and looked at the young man.

"You are right," said he.

"Then," remarked Josephine, "if he is ambitious he will not let Bonaparte seize the power."

"Why not?"

"Because he will want it himself."

"Yes; but he will wait till it comes to him ready-made, inasmuch as he doesn't know how to create it, and is afraid to seize it."

During this time Bonaparte had joined the group which had formed around Talma after dinner, as well as before. Remarkable men are always the centre of attraction.

"What are you saying, Talma?" demanded Bonaparte. "It seems to me they are listening to you very attentively."

"Yes, but my reign is over," replied the artist.

"Why so?"

"I do as citizen Barras has done; I abdicate?"

"So citizen Barras has abdicated?"

"So rumor says."

"Is it known who will take his place?"

"It is surmised."

"Is it one of your friends, Talma?"

"Time was," said Talma, bowing, "when he did me the honor to say I was his."

"Well, in that case, Talma, I shall ask for your influence."

"Granted," said Talma, laughing; "it only remains to ask how it can serve you."

"Get me sent back to Italy; Barras would not let me go."

"The deuce!" said Talma; "don't you know the song, general, 'We won't go back to the woods when the laurels are clipped'?"

"Oh! Roscius, Roscius!" said Bonaparte, smiling, "have you grown a flatterer during my absence?"

"Roscius was the friend of Cæsar, general, and when the conqueror returned from Gaul he probably said to him about the same thing I have said to you."

Bonaparte laid his hand on Talma's shoulder.

"Would he have said the same words after crossing the Rubicon?"

Talma looked Bonaparte straight in the face.

"No," he replied; "he would have said, like the augur, 'Cæsar, beware of the Ides of March!'"

Bonaparte slipped his hand into his breast as if in search of something; finding the dagger of the Companions of Jehu, he grasped it convulsively. Had he a presentiment of the conspiracies of Arena, Saint-Régent, and Cadoudal?

Just then the door opened and a servant announced: "General Bernadotte!"

"Bernadotte," muttered Bonaparte, involuntarily. "What does he want here?"

Since Bonaparte's return, Bernadotte had held aloof from him, refusing all the advances which the general-in-chief and his friends had made him. The fact is, Bernadotte had long since discerned the politician beneath the soldier's greatcoat, the dictator beneath the general, and Bernadotte, for all that he became king in later years, was at that time a very different Republican from Moreau. Moreover, Bernadotte believed he had reason to complain of Bonaparte. His military career had not been less brilliant than that of the young general; his fortunes were destined to run parallel with his to the end, only, more fortunate than that other—Bernadotte was to die on his throne. It is true, he did not conquer that throne; he was called to it.

Son of a lawyer at Pau, Bernadotte, born in 1764—that is to say, five years before Bonaparte—was in the ranks as a private soldier when only eighteen. In 1789 he was only a sergeant-major. But those were the days of rapid promotion. In 1794, Kléber created him brigadier-general on the field of battle, where he had decided the fortunes of the day. Becoming a general of division, he played a brilliant part at Fleurus and Juliers, forced Maestricht to capitulate, took Altdorf, and protected, against an army twice as numerous as his own, the retreat of Joubert. In 1797 the Directory ordered him to take seventeen thousand men to Bonaparte. These seventeen thousand men were his old soldiers, veterans of Kléber, Marceau and Hoche, soldiers of the Sambre-et-Meuse; and yet Bernadotte forgot all rivalry and seconded Bonaparte with all his might, taking part in the passage of the Tagliamento, capturing Gradiska, Trieste, Laybach, Idria, bringing back to the Directory, after the campaign, the flags of the enemy, and accepting, possibly with reluctance, an embassy to Vienna, while Bonaparte secured the command of the army of Egypt.

At Vienna, a riot, excited by the tri-color flag hoisted above the French embassy, for which the ambassador was unable to obtain redress, forced him to demand his passports. On his return to Paris, the Directory appointed him Minister of War. An underhand proceeding of Sièyes, who was offended by Bernadotte's republicanism, induced the latter to send in his resignation. It was accepted, and when Bonaparte landed at Fréjus the late minister had been three months out of office. Since Bonaparte's return, some of Bernadotte's friends had sought to bring about his reinstatement; but Bonaparte had opposed it. The result was a hostility between the two generals, none the less real because not openly avowed.

Bernadotte's appearance in Bonaparte's salon was therefore an event almost as extraordinary as the presence of Moreau. And the entrance of the conqueror of Maestricht caused as many heads to turn as had that of the conqueror of Rastadt. Only, instead of going forward to meet him, as he had Moreau, Bonaparte merely turned round and awaited him.

Bernadotte, from the threshold of the door, cast a rapid glance around the salon. He divided and analyzed the groups, and although he must have perceived Bonaparte in the midst of the principal one, he went up to Josephine, who was reclining on a couch at the corner of the fireplace, like the statue of Agrippina in the Pitti, and, addressing her with chivalric courtesy, inquired for her health; then only did he raise his head as if to look for Bonaparte. At such a time everything was of too much importance for those present not to remark this affectation of courtesy on Bernadotte's part.

Bonaparte, with his rapid, comprehensive intellect, was not the last to notice this; he was seized with impatience, and, instead of awaiting Bernadotte in the midst of the group where he happened to be, he turned abruptly to the embrasure of a window, as if to challenge the ex-minister of war to follow him. Bernadotte bowed graciously to right and left, and controlling his usually mobile face to an expression of perfect calmness, he walked toward Bonaparte, who awaited him as a wrestler awaits his antagonist, the right foot forward and his lips compressed. The two men bowed, but Bonaparte made no movement to extend his hand to Bernadotte, nor did the latter offer to take it.

"Is it you?" asked Bonaparte. "I am glad to see you."

"Thank you, general," replied Bernadotte. "I have come because I wish to give you a few explanations."

"I did not recognize you at first."

"Yet I think, general, that my name was announced by your servant in a voice loud enough to prevent any doubt as to my identity."

"Yes, but he announced General Bernadotte."

"Well?"

"Well, I saw a man in civilian's dress, and though I recognized you, I doubted if it were really you."

For some time past Bernadotte had affected to wear civilian's dress in preference to his uniform.

"You know," said he, laughing, "that I am only half a soldier now. I was retired by citizen Sièyes."

"It seems that it was lucky for me that you were no longer minister of war when I landed at Fréjus."

"How so?"

"You said, so I was told, that had you received the order to arrest me for violating quarantine you would have done so."

"I said it, and I repeat it, general. As a soldier I was always a faithful observer of discipline. As a minister I was a slave to law."

Bonaparte bit his lips. "And will you say, after that, that you have not a personal enmity to me?"

"A personal enmity to you, general?" replied Bernadotte. "Why should I have? We have always gone to-

gether, almost in the same stride; I was even made general
before you. While my campaigns on the Rhine were less
brilliant than yours on the Adige, they were not less profit-
able for the Republic; and when I had the honor to serve
under you, you found in me, I hope, a subordinate devoted,
if not to the man, at least to the country which he served.
It is true that since your departure, general, I have been
more fortunate than you in not having the responsibility of
a great army, which, if one may believe Kléber's despatches,
you have left in a disastrous position.''

"What do you mean? Kléber's last despatches? Has
Kléber written?''

"Are you ignorant of that, general? Has the Directory
not informed you of the complaints of your successor? That
would be a great weakness on their part, and I congratulate
myself to have come here, not only to correct in your mind
what has been said of me, but to tell you what is being said
of you.''

Bonaparte fixed an eye, darkling as an eagle's, on Bernadotte. "And what are they saying of me?'' he asked.

"They say that, as you must come back, you should
have brought the army with you.''

"Had I a fleet? Are you unaware that De Brueys allowed his to be burned?''

"They also say, general, that, being unable to bring
back the army, it would have been better for your renown
had you remained with it.''

"That is what I should have done, monsieur, if events
had not recalled me to France.''

"What events, general?''

"Your defeats.''

"Pardon me, general; you mean to say Schérer's defeats.''

"Yours as well.''

"I was not answerable for the generals commanding our
armies on the Rhine and in Italy until I was minister of
war. If you will enumerate the victories and defeats since
that time you will see on which side the scale turns.''

"You certainly do not intend to tell me that matters are in a good condition?"

"No, but I do say that they are not in so desperate a state as you affect to believe."

"As I affect!—Truly, general, to hear you one would think I had some interest in lowering France in the eyes of foreigners."

"I don't say that; I say that I wish to settle the balance of our victories and defeats for the last three months; and as I came for that, and am now in your house, and in the position of an accused person—"

"Or an accuser."

"As the accused, in the first instance—I begin."

"And I listen," said Bonaparte, visibly on thorns.

"My ministry dates from the 30th Prairial, the 8th of June if you prefer; we will not quarrel over words."

"Which means that we shall quarrel about things."

Bernadotte continued without replying.

"I became minister, as I said, the 8th of June; that is, a short time after the siege of Saint-Jean-d'Acre was raised."

Bonaparte bit his lips. "I did not raise the siege until after I had ruined the fortifications," he replied.

"That is not what Kléber wrote; but that does not concern me." Then he added, smiling: "It happened while Clark was minister."

There was a moment's silence, during which Bonaparte endeavored to make Bernadotte lower his eyes. Not succeeding, he said: "Go on."

Bernadotte bowed and continued: "Perhaps no minister of war—and the archives of the ministry are there for reference—ever received the portfolio under more critical circumstances: civil war within, a foreign enemy at our doors, discouragement rife among our veteran armies, absolute destitution of means to equip new ones. That was what I had to face on the 8th of June, when I entered upon my duties. An active correspondence, dating from the 8th of June, between the civil and military authorities, revived their courage and their hopes. My addresses to the armies—this may have been a mistake—were those, not of a minister to his soldiers, but of a comrade among comrades, just as my addresses to the administrators were those of a citizen to his fellow-citizens. I appealed to the courage of the army, and the heart of the French people; I obtained all that I had asked. The National Guard reorganized with renewed zeal; legions were formed upon the Rhine, on the Moselle. Battalions of veterans took the place of old regiments to reinforce the troops that were guarding our frontiers; to-day our cavalry is recruited by a remount of forty thousand horses, and one hundred thousand conscripts, armed and equipped, have received with cries of 'Vive la Republique!' the flags under which they will fight and conquer—"

"But," interrupted Bonaparte bitterly, "this is an apology you are making for yourself."

"Be it so. I will divide my discourse into two parts. The first will be a contestable apology; the second an array of incontestable facts. I will set aside the apology and proceed to facts. June 17 and 18, the battle of the Trebbia. Macdonald wished to fight without Moreau; he crossed the Trebbia, attacked the enemy, was defeated and retreated to Modena. June 20, battle of Tortona; Moreau defeated the Austrian Bellegarde. July 22, surrender of the citadel of Alexandria to the Austro-Russians. So far the scale turns to defeat. July 30, surrender of Mantua, another check. August 15, battle of Novi; this time it was more than a check, it was a defeat. Take note of it, general, for it is the last. At the very moment we were fighting at Novi, Masséna was maintaining his position at Zug and Lucerne, and strengthening himself on the Aar and on the Rhine; while Lecourbe, on August 14 and 15, took the Saint-Gothard. August 19, battle of Bergen; Brune defeated the Anglo-Russian army, forty thousand strong, and captured the Russian general, Hermann. On the 25th, 26th and 27th of the same month, the battles of Zurich, where

Masséna defeated the Austro-Russians under Korsakoff. Hotze and three other generals are taken prisoners. The enemy lost twelve thousand men, a hundred cannon, and all its baggage; the Austrians, separated from the Russians, could not rejoin them until after they were driven beyond Lake Constance. That series of victories stopped the progress the enemy had been making since the beginning of the campaign; from the time Zurich was retaken, France was secure from invasion. August 30, Molitor defeated the Austrian generals, Jellachich and Luiken, and drove them back into the Grisons. September 1, Molitor attacked and defeated General Rosenberg in the Mutterthal. On the 2d, Molitor forced Souvaroff to evacuate Glarus, to abandon his wounded, his cannon, and sixteen hundred prisoners. The 6th, General Brune again defeated the Anglo-Russians, under the command of the Duke of York. On the 7th, General Gazan took possession of Constance. On the 8th you landed at Fréjus.—Well, general," continued Bernadotte, "as France will probably pass into your hands, it is well that you should know the state in which you find her, and in place of receipt, our possessions bear witness to what we are giving you. What we are now doing, general, is history, and it is important that those who may some day have an interest in falsifying history shall find in their path the denial of Bernadotte."

"Is that said for my benefit, general?"

"I say that for flatterers. You have pretended, it is said, that you returned to France because our armies were destroyed, because France was threatened, the Republic at bay. You may have left Egypt with that fear; but once in France, all such fears must have given way to a totally different belief."

"I ask no better than to believe as you do," replied Bonaparte, with sovereign dignity; "and the more grand and powerful you prove France to be, the more grateful am I to those who have secured her grandeur and her power."

"Oh, the result is plain, general! Three armies defeated: the Russians exterminated, the Austrians defeated and forced to fly, twenty thousand prisoners, a hundred pieces of cannon, fifteen flags, all the baggage of the enemy in our possession, nine generals taken or killed, Switzerland free, our frontiers safe, the Rhine our limit—so much for Masséna's contingent and the situation of Helvetia. The Anglo-Russian army twice defeated, utterly discouraged, abandoning its artillery, baggage, munitions of war and commissariat, even to the women and children who came with the British; eight thousand French prisoners, effective men, returned to France; Holland completely evacuated—so much for Brune's contingent and the situation in Holland. The rearguard of General Klénau forced to lay down its arms at Villanova; a thousand prisoners and three pieces of cannon fallen into our hands, and the Austrians driven back beyond Bormida; in all, counting the combats at la Stura and Pignerol, four thousand prisoners, sixteen cannon, Mondovi, and the occupation of the whole region between la Stura and Tanaro—so much for Championnet's contingent and the situation in Italy. Two hundred thousand men under arms, forty thousand mounted cavalry; that is my contingent, mine, and the situation in France."

"But," asked Bonaparte satirically, "if you have, as you say, two hundred thousand soldiers under arms, why do you want me to bring back the fifteen or twenty thousand men I have in Egypt, who are useful there as colonizers?"

"If I ask you for them, general, it is not for any need we may have of them, but in the fear of some disaster overtaking them."

"What disaster do you expect to befall them, commanded by Kléber?"

"Kléber may be killed, general; and who is there behind Kléber? Menou. Kléber and your twenty thousand men are doomed, general!"

"How doomed?"

"Yes, the Sultan will send troops; he controls by land. The English will send their fleet; they control by sea. We, who have neither land nor sea, will be compelled to take part from here in the evacuation of Egypt and the capitulation of our army."

"You take a gloomy view of things, general!"

"The future will show which of us two have seen things as they are."

"What would you have done in my place?"

"I don't know. But, even had I been forced to bring them back by way of Constantinople, I should never have abandoned those whom France had intrusted to me. Xenophon, on the banks of the Tigris, was in a much more desperate situation than you on the banks of the Nile. He brought his ten thousand back to Ionia, and they were not the children of Athens, not his fellow citizens; they were mercenaries!"

From the instant Bernadotte uttered the word Constantinople, Bonaparte listened no longer; the name seemed to rouse a new train of ideas in his mind, which he followed in solitary thought. He laid his hand on the arm of the astonished Bernadotte, and, with eyes fixed on space, like a man who pursues through space the phantom of a vanished project, he said: "Yes, yes! I thought of it. That is why I persisted in taking that hovel, Saint-Jean-d'Acre. Here you only thought it obstinacy, a useless waste of men sacrificed to the self-love of a mediocre general who feared that he might be blamed for a defeat. What should I have cared for the raising of the siege of Saint-Jean-d'Acre, if Saint-Jean-d'Acre had not been the barrier in the way of the grandest project ever conceived. Cities! Why, good God! I could take as many as ever did Alexander or Cæsar, but it was Saint-Jean-d'Acre that had to be taken! If I had taken Saint-Jean-d'Acre, do you know what I should have done?"

And he fixed his burning eyes upon Bernadotte, who, this time, lowered his under the flame of this genius.

"What I should have done," repeated Bonaparte, and, like Ajax, he seemed to threaten Heaven with his clinched fist; "if I had taken Saint-Jean-d'Acre, I should have found the treasures of the pasha in the city and three thousand stands of arms. With that I should have raised and armed all Syria, so maddened by the ferocity of Djezzar that each time I attacked him the population prayed to God for his overthrow. I should have marched upon Damascus and Aleppo; I should have swelled my army with the malcontents. Advancing into the country, I should, step by step, have proclaimed the abolition of slavery, and the annihilation of the tyrannical government of the pashas. I should have overthrown the Turkish empire, and founded a great empire at Constantinople, which would have fixed my place in history higher than Constantine and Mohammed II. Perhaps I should have returned to Paris by way of Adrianople and Vienna, after annihilating the house of Austria. Well, my dear general, that is the project which that little hovel of a Saint-Jean-d'Acre rendered abortive!"

And he so far forgot to whom he was speaking, as he followed the shadows of his vanished dream, that he called Bernadotte "my dear general." The latter, almost appalled by the magnitude of the project which Bonaparte had unfolded to him, made a step backward.

"Yes," said Bernadotte, "I perceive what you want, for you have just betrayed yourself. Orient or Occident, a throne! A throne? So be it; why not? Count upon me to help you conquer it, but elsewhere than in France. I am a Republican, and I will die a Republican."

Bonaparte shook his head as if to disperse the thoughts which held him in the clouds.

"I, too, am a Republican," said he, "but see what has come of your Republic!"

"What matter!" cried Bernadotte. "It is not to a word or a form that I am faithful, but to the principle. Let the Directors but yield me the power, and I would know how to defend the Republic against her internal enemies, even as I defended her from her foreign enemies."

As he said these words, Bernadotte raised his eyes, and his glance encountered that of Bonaparte. Two naked blades clashing together never sent forth lightning more vivid, more terrible.

Josephine had watched the two men for some time past with anxious attention. She saw the dual glance teeming with reciprocal menace. She rose hastily and went to Bernadotte.

"General," said she.

Bernadotte bowed.

"You are intimate with Gohier, are you not?" she continued.

"He is one of my best friends, madame," said Bernadotte.

"Well, we dine with him the day after to-morrow, the 18th Brumaire; dine there yourself and bring Madame Bernadotte. I should be so glad to know her better."

"Madame," said Bernadotte, "in the days of the Greeks you would have been one of the three graces; in the Middle Ages you would have been a fairy; to-day you are the most adorable woman I know."

And making three steps backward, and bowing, he contrived to retire politely without including Bonaparte in his bow. Josephine followed him with her eyes until he had left the room. Then, turning to her husband, she said: "Well, it seems that it was not as successful with Bernadotte as with Moreau, was it?"

"Bold, adventurous, disinterested, sincere republican, inaccessible to seduction, he is a human obstacle. We must make our way around him, since we cannot overthrow him."

And leaving the salon without taking leave of any one, he went to his study, whither Roland and Bourrienne followed. They had hardly been there a quarter of an hour when the handle of the lock turned softly, the door opened, and Lucien appeared.

CHAPTER XXII

THE OUTLINE OF A DECREE

LUCIEN was evidently expected. Bonaparte had not mentioned his name once since entering the study: but in spite of this silence he had turned his head three or four times with increasing impatience toward the door, and when the young man appeared an exclamation of contentment escaped his lips.

Lucien, the general's youngest brother, was born in 1775, making him now barely twenty-five years old. Since 1797, that is, at the age of twenty-two and a half, he had been a member of the Five Hundred, who, to honor Bonaparte, had made him their president. With the projects he had conceived nothing could have been more fortunate for Bonaparte.

Frank and loyal, republican to the core, Lucien believed that, in seconding his brother's plans, he was serving the Republic better than the future First Consul. In his eyes, no one was better fitted to save it a second time than he who had saved it the first. It was with these sentiments in his heart that he now came to confer with his brother.

"Here you are," said Bonaparte. "I have been waiting for you impatiently."

"So I suspected. But I was obliged to wait until I could leave without being noticed."

"Did you manage it?"

"Yes; Talma was relating a story about Marat and Dumouriez. Interesting as it was, I deprived myself of the pleasure, and here I am."

"I have just heard a carriage driving away; the person who got in it couldn't have seen you coming up my private stairs, could he?"

"The person who drove off was myself, the carriage was mine. If that is not seen every one will think I have left."

Bonaparte breathed freer.

"Well," said he, "let us hear how you have spent your day."

"Oh! I haven't wasted my time, you may be sure."

"Are we to have a decree of the Council?"

"We drew it up to-day, and I have brought it to you— the rough draft at least—so that you can see if you want anything added or changed."

"Let me see it," cried Bonaparte. Taking the paper hastily from Lucien's hand, he read:

Art. I. The legislative body is transferred to the commune of Saint-Cloud; the two branches of the Council will hold their sessions in the two wings of the palace.

"That's the important article," said Lucien. "I had it placed first, so that it might strike the people at once."

"Yes, yes," exclaimed Bonaparte, and he continued:

Art. II. They will assemble there to-morrow, the 20th Brumaire—

"No, no," said Bonaparte, "to-morrow the 19th. Change the date, Bourrienne;" and he handed the paper to his secretary.

"You expect to be ready for the 18th?"

"I shall be. Fouché said day before yesterday, 'Make haste, or I won't answer for the result.'"

"The 19th Brumaire," said Bourrienne, returning the paper to the general.

Bonaparte resumed:

Art. II. They will assemble there to-morrow, the 19th Brumaire, at noon. All deliberations are forbidden elsewhere and before the above date.

Bonaparte read the article a second time.

"Good," said he; "there is no double meaning there." And he continued:

Art. III. General Bonaparte is charged with the enforcement of this decree; he will take all necessary measures for the safety of the National Legislature.

A satirical smile flickered on the stony lips of the reader, but he continued almost immediately.

The general commanding the 17th military division, the guard of the Legislature, the stationary national guard, the troops of the line within the boundaries of the Commune of Paris, and those in the constitutional arrondissement, and throughout the limits of the said 17th division, are placed directly under his orders, and are directed to regard him as their commanding officer.

"Bourrienne, add: 'All citizens will lend him assistance when called upon.' The bourgeois love to meddle in political matters, and when they really can help us in our projects we ought to grant them this satisfaction."

Bourrienne obeyed; then he returned the paper to the general, who went on:

Art. IV. General Bonaparte is summoned before the Council to receive a copy of the present decree, and to make oath thereto. He will consult with the inspecting commissioners of both branches of the Council.

Art. V. The present decree shall be transmitted immediate, by messenger, to all the members of the Council of Five Hundred and to the Executive Directory. It shall be printed and posted, and promulgated throughout the communes of the Republic by special messengers.

Done at Paris this . . . .

"The date is left blank," said Lucien.

"Put 'the 18th Brumaire,' Bourrienne; the decree must take everybody by surprise. It must be issued at seven o'clock in the morning, and at the same hour or even earlier it must be posted on all the walls of Paris."

"But suppose the Ancients won't consent to issue it?" said Lucien.

"All the more reason to have it posted, ninny," said Bonaparte. "We must act as if it had been issued."

"Am I to correct this grammatical error in the last paragraph?" asked Bourrienne, laughing.

"Where?" demanded Lucien, in the tone of an aggrieved author.

"The word 'immediate,'" replied Bourrienne. "You can't say 'transmitted immediate'; it ought to be 'immediately.'"

"It's not worth while," said Bonaparte. "I shall act, you may be sure, as if it were 'immediately.'" Then, after an instant's reflection, he added: "As to what you said just now about their not being willing to pass it, there's a very simple way to get it passed."

"What is that."

"To convoke the members of whom we are sure at six o'clock in the morning, and those of whom we are not sure at eight. Having only our own men, it will be devilishly hard to lose the majority."

"But six o'clock for some, and eight for the others—" objected Lucien.

"Employ two secretaries; one of them can make a mistake." Then turning to Lucien, he said: "Write this."

And walking up and down, he dictated without hesitating, like a man who has long thought over and carefully prepared what he dictates; stopping occasionally beside Bourrienne to see if the secretary's pen were following his every word:

CITIZENS—The Council of the Ancients, the trustee of the nation's wisdom, has issued the subjoined decree: it is authorized by articles 102 and 103 of the Constitution.

This decree enjoins me to take measures for the safety of the National Legislature, and its necessary and momentary removal.

Bourrienne looked at Bonaparte; *instantaneous* was the word the latter had intended to use, but as the general did not correct himself, Bourrienne left *momentary.*

Bonaparte continued to dictate:

The Legislature will find means to avoid the imminent danger into which the disorganization of all parts of the administration has brought us.

But it needs, at this crisis, the united support and confidence of patriots. Rally around it; it offers the only means of establishing the Republic on the bases of civil liberty, internal prosperity, victory and peace.

Bonaparte perused this proclamation, and nodded his head in sign of approval. Then he looked at his watch.

"Eleven o'clock," he said; "there is still time."

Then, seating himself in Bourrienne's chair, he wrote a few words in the form of a note, sealed it, and wrote the address: "To the Citizen Barras."

"Roland," said he, when he had finished, "take a horse out of the stable, or a carriage in the street, and go to Barras' house. I have asked him for an interview to-morrow at midnight. I want an answer."

Roland left the room. A moment later the gallop of a horse resounded through the courtyard, disappearing in the direction of the Rue du Mont-Blanc.

"Now, Bourrienne," said Bonaparte, after listening to the sound, "to-morrow at midnight, whether I am in the house or not, you will take my carriage and go in my stead to Barras."

"In your stead, general?"

"Yes. He will do nothing all day, expecting me to accept him on my side at night. At midnight you will go to him, and say that I have such a bad headache I have had to go to bed, but that I will be with him at seven o'clock in the morning without fail. He will believe you, or he won't believe you; but at any rate it will be too late for him to act against us. By seven in the morning I shall have ten thousand men under my command."

"Very good, general. Have you any other orders for me?"

"No, not this evening," replied Bonaparte. "Be here early to-morrow."

"And I?" asked Lucien.

"See Sièyes; he has the Ancients in the hollow of his hand. Make all your arrangements with him. I don't wish him to be seen here, nor to be seen myself at his house. If by any chance we fail, he is a man to repudiate. After to-morrow I wish to be master of my own actions, and to have no ties with any one."

"Do you think you will need me to-morrow?"

"Come back at night and report what happens."

"Are you going back to the salon?"

"No. I shall wait for Josephine in her own room. Bourrienne, tell her, as you pass through, to get rid of the people as soon as possible."

Then, saluting Bourrienne and his brother with a wave of the hand, he left his study by a private corridor, and went to Josephine's room. There, lighted by a single alabaster lamp, which made the conspirator's brow seem paler than ever, Bonaparte listened to the noise of the carriages, as one after the other they rolled away. At last the sounds ceased, and five minutes later the door opened to admit Josephine.

She was alone, and held a double-branched candlestick in her hand. Her face, lighted by the double flame, expressed the keenest anxiety.

"Well," Bonaparte inquired, "what ails you?"

"I am afraid!" said Josephine.

"Of what? Those fools of the Directory, or the lawyers of the two Councils? Come, come! I have Sièyes with me in the Ancients, and Lucien in the Five Hundred."

"Then all goes well?"

"Wonderfully so!"

"You sent me word that you were waiting for me here, and I feared you had some bad news to tell me."

"Pooh! If I had bad news, do you think I would tell you?"

"How reassuring that is!"

"Well, don't be uneasy, for I have nothing but good news. Only, I have given you a part in the conspiracy."

"What is it?"

"Sit down and write to Gohier."

"That we won't dine with him?"

"On the contrary, ask him to come and breakfast with us. Between those who like each other as we do there can't be too much intercourse."

Josephine sat down at a little rosewood writing desk

"Dictate," said she; "I will write."

"Goodness! for them to recognize my style! Nonsense; you know better than I how to write one of those charming notes there is no resisting."

Josephine smiled at the compliment, turned her forehead to Bonaparte, who kissed it lovingly, and wrote the following note, which we have copied from the original:

To the Citizen Gohier, President of the Executive Directory of the French Republic—

"Is that right?" she asked.

"Perfectly! As he won't wear this title of President much longer, we won't cavil at it."

"Don't you mean to make him something?"

"I'll make him anything he pleases, if he does exactly what I want. Now go on, my dear."

Josephine picked up her pen again and wrote:

Come, my dear Gohier, with your wife, and breakfast with us to-morrow at eight o'clock. Don't fail, for I have some very interesting things to tell you.

Adieu, my dear Gohier! With the sincerest friendship,

Yours,   LA PAGERIE-BONAPARTE.

"I wrote to-morrow," exclaimed Josephine. "Shall I date it the 17th Brumaire?"

"You won't be wrong," said Bonaparte; "there's midnight striking."

In fact, another day had fallen into the gulf of time; the clock chimed twelve. Bonaparte listened gravely and dreamily. Twenty-four hours only separated him from the solemn day for which he had been scheming for a month, and of which he had dreamed for years.

Let us do now what he would so gladly have done, and spring over those twenty-four hours intervening to the day which history has not yet judged, and see what happened in various parts of Paris, where the events we are about to relate produced an overwhelming sensation.

CHAPTER XXIII

ALEA JACTA EST

A T SEVEN in the morning, Fouché, minister of police, entered the bedroom of Gohier, president of the Directory.

"Oh, ho!" said Gohier, when he saw him. "What has happened now, monsieur le ministre, to give me the pleasure of seeing you so early?"

"Don't you know about the decree?" asked Fouché.

"What decree?" asked honest Gohier.

"The decree of the Council of the Ancients."

"When was it issued?"

"Last night."

"So the Council of the Ancients assembles at night now?"

"When matters are urgent, yes."

"And what does the decree say."

"It transfers the legislative sessions to Saint-Cloud."

Gohier felt the blow. He realized the advantage which Bonaparte's daring genius might obtain by this isolation.

"And since when," he asked Fouché, "is the minister of police transformed into a messenger of the Council of the Ancients?"

"That's where you are mistaken, citizen president," replied the ex-Conventional. "I am more than ever minister of police this morning, for I have come to inform you of an act which may have the most serious consequences."

Not being as yet sure of how the conspiracy of the Rue de la Victoire would turn out, Fouché was not averse to keeping open a door for retreat at the Luxembourg. But Gohier, honest as he was, knew the man too well to be his dupe.

"You should have informed me of this decree yesterday, and not this morning; for in making the communication now you are scarcely in advance of the official communication I shall probably receive in a few moments."

As he spoke, an usher opened the door and informed the president that a messenger from the Inspectors of the Council of the Ancients was there, and asked to make him a communication.

"Let him come in," said Gohier.

The messenger entered and handed the president a letter. He broke the seal hastily and read:

CITIZEN PRESIDENT—The Inspecting Commission hasten to inform you of a decree removing the residence of the legislative body to Saint-Cloud.

The decree will be forwarded to you; but measures for public safety are at present occupying our attention.

We invite you to meet the Commission of the Ancients. You will find Sièyes and Ducos already there.

Fraternal greetings,

BARILLON,
FARGUES,
CORNET.

"Very good," said Gohier, dismissing the messenger with a wave of his hand.

The messenger went out. Gohier turned to Fouché.

"Ah!" said he, "the plot is well laid; they inform me of the decree, but they do not send it to me. Happily you are here to tell me the terms of it."

"But," said Fouché, "I don't know them."

"What! do you, the minister of police, mean to tell me that you know nothing about this extraordinary session of the Council of the Ancients, when it has been put on record by a decree?"

"Of course I knew it took place, but I was unable to be present."

"And you had no secretary, no amanuensis to send, who could give you an account, word for word, of this session, when in all probability this session will dispose of the fate of France! Ah, citizen Fouché, you are either a very deep, or a very shallow minister of police!"

"Have you any orders to give me, citizen president?" asked Fouché.

"None, citizen minister," replied the president. "If the Directory judges it advisable to issue any orders, it will be to men whom it esteems worthy of its confidence. You may return to those who sent you," he added, turning his back upon the minister.

Fouché went, and Gohier immediately rang his bell. An usher entered.

"Go to Barras, Sièyes, Ducos, and Moulins, and request them to come to me at once. Ah! And at the same time ask Madame Gohier to come into my study, and to bring with her Madame Bonaparte's letter inviting us to breakfast with her."

Five minutes later Madame Gohier entered, fully dressed, with the note in her hand. The invitation was for eight o'clock. It was then half-past seven, and it would take at least twenty minutes to drive from the Luxembourg to the Rue de la Victoire.

"Here it is, my dear," said Madame Gohier, handing the letter to her husband. "It says eight o'clock."

"Yes," replied Gohier, "I was not in doubt about the hour, but about the day."

Taking the note from his wife's hand, he read it over:

Come, my dear Gohier, with your wife, and breakfast with me to-morrow at eight o'clock. Don't fail, for I have some very interesting things to tell you.

"Ah," said Gohier, "there can be no mistake."

"Well, my dear, are we going?" asked Madame Gohier.

"You are, but not I. An event has just happened about which the citizen Bonaparte is probably well-informed, which will detain my colleagues and myself at the Luxembourg."

"A serious event?"

"Possibly."

"Then I shall stay with you."

"No, indeed; you would not be of any service here. Go to Madame Bonaparte's. I may be mistaken, but, should anything extraordinary happen, which appears to you alarming, send me word some way or other. Anything will do; I shall understand half a word."

"Very good, my dear; I will go. The hope of being useful to you is sufficient."

"Do go!"

Just then the usher entered, and said:

"General Moulins is at my heels; citizen Barras is in his bath, and will soon be here; citizens Sièyes and Ducos went out at five o'clock this morning, and have not yet returned."

"They are the two traitors!" said Gohier; "Barras is only their dupe." Then kissing his wife, he added: "Now, go."

As she turned round, Madame Gohier came face to face with General Moulins. He, for his character was naturally impetuous, seemed furious.

"Pardon me, citizeness," he said. Then, rushing into Gohier's study, he cried: "Do you know what has happened, president?"

"No, but I have my suspicions."

"The legislative body has been transferred to Saint-Cloud; the execution of the decree has been intrusted to General Bonaparte, and the troops are placed under his orders."

"Ha! The cat's out of the bag!" exclaimed Gohier. "Well, we must combine, and fight them."

"Have you heard that Sièyes and Ducos are not in the palace?"

"By Heavens! they are at the Tuileries! But Barras is in his bath; let us go to Barras. The Directory can issue decrees if there is a majority. We are three, and, I repeat it, we must make a struggle!"

"Then let us send word to Barras to come to us as soon as he is out of his bath."

"No; let us go to him before he leaves it."

The two Directors left the room, and hurried toward Barras' apartment. They found him actually in his bath, but they insisted on entering.

"Well?" asked Barras as soon as he saw them.

"Have you heard?"

"Absolutely nothing."

They told him what they themselves knew.

"Ah!" cried Barras, "that explains everything."

"What do you mean?"

"Yes, that is why he didn't come last night."

"Who?"

"Why, Bonaparte."

"Did you expect him last evening?"

"He sent me word by one of his aides-de-camp that he would call on me at eleven o'clock last evening."

"And he didn't come?"

"No. He sent Bourrienne in his carriage to tell me that a violent headache had obliged him to go to bed; but that he would be here early this morning."

The Directors looked at each other.

"The whole thing is plain," said they.

"I have sent Bollot, my secretary, a very intelligent fellow, to find out what he can," continued Barras.

He rang and a servant entered.

"As soon as citizen Bollot returns," said Barras, "ask him to come here."

"He is just getting out of his carriage."

"Send him up! Send him up!"

But Bollot was already at the door.

"Well?" cried the three Directors.

"Well, General Bonaparte, in full uniform, accompanied by Generals Beurnonville, Macdonald and Moreau, are on their way to the Tuileries, where ten thousand troops are awaiting them."

"Moreau! Moreau with him!" exclaimed Gohier.

"On his right!"

"I always told you that Moreau was a sneak, and nothing else!" cried Moulins, with military roughness.

"Are you still determined to resist, Barras?" asked Gohier.

"Yes," replied Barras.

"Then dress yourself and join us in the council-room."

"Go," said Barras, "I follow you."

The two Directors hastened to the council-room. After waiting ten minutes Moulins said: "We should have waited for Barras; if Moreau is a sneak, Barras is a knave."

Two hours later they were still waiting for Barras.

Talleyrand and Bruix had been admitted to Barras' bathroom just after Gohier and Moulins had left it, and in talking with them Barras forgot his appointment.

We will now see what was happening in the Rue de la Victoire.

At seven o'clock, contrary to his usual custom, Bonaparte was up and waiting in full uniform in his bedroom. Roland entered. Bonaparte was perfectly calm; they were on the eve of a battle.

"Has no one come yet, Roland?" he asked.

"No, general," replied the young man, "but I heard the roll of a carriage just now."

"So did I," replied Bonaparte.

At that minute a servant announced: "The citizen Joseph Bonaparte, and the citizen General Bernadotte."

Roland questioned Bonaparte with a glance; was he to go or stay? He was to stay. Roland took his stand at the corner of a bookcase like a sentinel at his post.

"Ah, ha!" exclaimed Bonaparte, seeing that Bernadotte

was still attired in civilian's clothes, "you seem to have a positive horror of the uniform, general!"

"Why the devil should I be in uniform at seven in the morning," asked Bernadotte, "when I am not in active service?"

"You will be soon."

"But I am retired."

"Yes, but I recall you to active service."

"You?"

"Yes, I."

"In the name of the Directory?"

"Is there still a Directory?"

"Still a Directory? What do you mean?"

"Didn't you see the troops drawn up in the streets leading to the Tuileries as you came here?"

"I saw them, and I was surprised."

"Those soldiers are mine."

"Excuse me," said Bernadotte; "I thought they belonged to France."

"Oh, to France or to me; is it not all one?"

"I was not aware of that," replied Bernadotte, coldly.

"Though you doubt it now, you will be certain of it to-night. Come, Bernadotte, this is the vital moment; decide!"

"General," replied Bernadotte, "I am fortunate enough to be at this moment a simple citizen; let me remain a simple citizen."

"Bernadotte, take care! He that is not for me is against me."

"General, pay attention to your words! You said just now, 'Take care.' If that is a threat, you know very well that I do not fear them."

Bonaparte came up to him, and took him by both hands.

"Oh, yes, I know that; that is why I must have you with me. I not only esteem you, Bernadotte, but I love you. I leave you with Joseph; he is your brother-in-law. Between brothers, devil take it, there should be no quarrelling."

"Where are you going?"

"In your character of Spartan you are a rigid observer of the laws, are you not? Well, here is a decree issued by the Council of Five Hundred last night, which confers upon me the immediate command of the troops in Paris. So I was right," he added, "when I told you that the soldiers you met were mine, inasmuch as they are under my orders."

And he placed in Bernadotte's hands the copy of the decree which had been sent to him at six o'clock that morning. Bernadotte read it through from the first line to the last.

"To this," said he, "I have nothing to object. Secure the safety of the National Legislature, and all good citizens will be with you."

"Then be with me now."

"Permit me, general, to wait twenty-four hours to see how you fulfil that mandate."

"Devil of a man!" cried Bonaparte. "Have your own way." Then, taking him by the arm, he dragged him a few steps apart from Joseph, and continued, "Bernadotte, I want to play above-board with you."

"Why so," retorted the latter, "since I am not on your side?"

"Never mind. You are watching the game, and I want the lookers-on to see that I am not cheating."

"Do you bind me to secrecy?"

"No."

"That is well, for in that case I should have refused to listen to your confidences."

"Oh! my confidences are not long! Your Directory is detested, your Constitution is worn-out; you must make a clean sweep of both, and turn the government in another direction. You don't answer me."

"I am waiting to hear what you have to say."

"All I have to say is, Go put on your uniform. I can't wait any longer for you. Join me at the Tuileries among our comrades."

Bernadotte shook his head.

"You think you can count on Moreau, Beurnonville, and Lefebvre," resumed Bonaparte. "Just look out of that window. Who do you see there, and there? Moreau and Beurnonville. As for Lefebvre, I do not see him, but I am certain I shall not go a hundred steps before meeting him. Now will you decide?"

"General," replied Bernadotte, "I am not a man to be swayed by example, least of all when that example is bad. Moreau, Beurnonville, and Lefebvre may do as they wish. I shall do as I ought!"

"So you definitively refuse to accompany me to the Tuileries?"

"I do not wish to take part in a rebellion."

"A rebellion! A rebellion! Against whom? Against a parcel of imbeciles who are pettifogging from morning till night in their hovels."

"These imbeciles, general, are for the moment the representatives of the law. The Constitution protects them; they are sacred to me."

"At least promise me one thing, iron rod that you are."

"What is it?"

"To keep quiet."

"I will keep quiet as a citizen, but—"

"But what? Come, I made a clean breast of it to you; do you do likewise."

"But if the Directory orders me to act, I shall march against the agitators, whoever they may be."

"Ah! So you think I am ambitious?" asked Bonaparte.

"I suspect as much," retorted Bernadotte, smiling.

"Faith," said Bonaparte, "you don't know me. I have had enough of politics, and what I want is peace. Ah, my dear fellow! Malmaison and fifty thousand a year, and I'd willingly resign all the rest. You don't believe me. Well, I invite you to come and see me there, three months hence, and if you like pastorals, we'll do one together. Now, au

revoir! I leave you with Joseph, and, in spite of your refusal, I shall expect you at the Tuileries. Hark! Our
friends are becoming impatient."

They were shouting: "Vive Bonaparte!"

Bernadotte paled slightly. Bonaparte noticed this pallor.

"Ah, ha," he muttered. "Jealous! I was mistaken; he
is not a Spartan, he is an Athenian!"

As Bonaparte had said, his friends were growing impatient. During the hour that had elapsed since the decree
had been posted, the salon, the anterooms, and the courtyard had been crowded. The first person Bonaparte met
at the head of the staircase was his compatriot, Colonel
Sebastiani, then commanding the 9th Dragoons.

"Ah! is that you, Sebastiani?" said Bonaparte.
"Where are your men?"

"In line along the Rue de la Victoire, general."

"Well disposed?"

"Enthusiastic! I distributed among them ten thousand
cartridges which I had in store."

"Yes; but you had no right to draw those cartridges
out without an order from the commandant of Paris. Do
you know that you have burned your vessels, Sebastiani?"

"Then take me into yours, general. I have faith in your
fortunes."

"You mistake me for Cæsar, Sebastiani!"

"Faith! I might make worse mistakes. Besides, down
below in the courtyard there are forty officers or more, of
all classes, without pay, whom the Directory has left in
the most complete destitution for the last year. You are
their only hope, general; they are ready to die for you."

"That's right. Go to your regiment, and take leave
of it."

"Take leave of it? What do you mean, general?"

"I exchange it for a brigade. Go, go!"

Sebastiani did not wait to be told twice. Bonaparte continued his way. At the foot of the stairs he met Lefebvre.

"Here I am, general!" said Lefebvre.

"You? And where is the 17th military division?"

"I am waiting for my appointment to bring it into action."

"Haven't you received your appointment?"

"From the Directory, yes. But as I am not a traitor, I have just sent in my resignation, so that they may know I am not to be counted on."

"And you have come for me to appoint you, so that I may count on you, is that it?"

"Exactly."

"Quick, Roland, a blank commission; fill in the general's name, so that I shall only have to put my name to it. I'll sign it on the pommel of my saddle."

"That's the true sort," said Lefebvre.

"Roland."

The young man, who had already started obediently, came back to the general.

"Fetch me that pair of double-barrelled pistols on my mantel-piece at the same time," said Bonaparte, in a low tone. "One never knows what may happen."

"Yes, general," said Roland; "besides, I shan't leave you."

"Unless I send you to be killed elsewhere."

"True," replied the young man, hastening away to fulfil his double errand.

Bonaparte was continuing on his way when he noticed a shadow in the corridor. He recognized Josephine, and ran to her.

"Good God!" cried she, "is there so much danger?"

"What makes you think that?"

"I overheard the order you gave Roland."

"Serves you right for listening at doors. How about Gohier?"

"He hasn't come."

"Nor his wife?"

"She is here."

Bonaparte pushed Josephine aside with his hand and

entered the salon. He found Madame Gohier alone and very pale.

"What!" said he, without any preamble, "isn't the President coming?"

"He was unable to do so, general," replied Madame Gohier.

Bonaparte repressed a movement of impatience. "He absolutely must come," said he. "Write him that I await him, and I will have the note sent."

"Thank you, general," replied Madame Gohier; "my servants are here, and they can attend to that."

"Write, my dear friend, write," said Josephine, offering her paper and pen and ink.

Bonaparte stood so that he could see over her shoulder what she wrote. Madame Gohier looked fixedly at him, and he drew back with a bow. She wrote the note, folded it, and looked about her for the sealing-wax; but, whether by accident or intention, there was none. Sealing the note with a wafer, she rang the bell. A servant came.

"Give this note to Comtois," said Madame Gohier, "and bid him take it to the Luxembourg at once."

Bonaparte followed the servant, or rather the letter, with his eyes until the door closed. Then, turning to Madame Gohier, he said: "I regret that I am unable to breakfast with you. But if the President has business to attend to, so have I. You must breakfast with my wife. Good appetite to you both."

And he went out. At the door he met Roland.

"Here is the commission, general," said the young man, "and a pen."

Bonaparte took the pen, and using the back of his aide-de-camp's hat, he signed the commission. Roland gave him the pistols.

"Did you look to them?" asked Bonaparte.

Roland smiled. "Don't be uneasy," said he; "I'll answer for them."

Bonaparte slipped the pistols in his belt, murmuring as he did so: "I wish I knew what she wrote her husband."

"I can tell you, word for word, what she wrote, general," said a voice close by.

"You, Bourrienne?"

"Yes. She wrote: 'You did right not to come, my dear; all that is happening here convinces me that the invitation was only a snare. I will rejoin you shortly.'"

"You unsealed the letter?"

"General, Sextus Pompey gave a dinner on his galley to Antony and Lepidus. His freedman said to him: 'Shall I make you emperor of the world?' 'How can you do it?' 'Easily. I will cut the cable of your galley, and Antony and Lepidus are prisoners.' 'You should have done so without telling me,' replied Sextus. 'Now I charge you on your life not to do it.' I remembered those words, general: '*You should have done so without telling me.*'"

Bonaparte thought an instant; then he said: "You are mistaken; it was Octavius and not Antony who was on Sextus' galley with Lepidus." And he went on his way to the courtyard, confining his blame to the historical blunder.

Hardly had the general appeared on the portico than cries of "Vive Bonaparte!" echoed through the courtyard into the street, where they were taken up by the dragoons drawn up in line before the gate.

"That's a good omen, general," said Roland.

"Yes. Give Lefebvre his commission at once; and if he has no horse, let him take one of mine. Tell him to meet me in the court of the Tuileries."

"His division is already there."

"All the more reason."

Glancing about him, Bonaparte saw Moreau and Beurnonville, who were waiting for him, their horses held by orderlies. He saluted them with a wave of his hand, already that of a master rather than that of a comrade. Then, perceiving General Debel out of uniform, he went down the steps and approached him.

"Why are you in civilian's dress?" he asked.

"General, I was not notified. I chanced to be passing along the street, and, seeing the crowd before your house, I came in, fearing you might be in danger."

"Go and put on your uniform quickly."

"But I live the other side of Paris; it would take too long." But, nevertheless, he made as if to retire.

"What are you going to do?"

"Don't be alarmed, general."

Debel had noticed an artilleryman on horseback who was about his size.

"Friend," said he, "I am General Debel. By order of General Bonaparte lend me your uniform and your horse, and I'll give you furlough for the day. Here's a louis to drink the health of the commander-in-chief. To-morrow, come to my house for your horse and uniform. I live in the Rue Cherche-Midi, No. 11."

"Will nothing be done to me?"

"Yes, you shall be made a corporal."

"Good!" said the artilleryman; and he quickly handed over his uniform and horse to General Debel.

In the meantime, Bonaparte heard talking above him. He raised his head and saw Joseph and Bernadotte at a window.

"Once more, general," he said to Bernadotte, "will you come with me?"

"No," said the latter, firmly. Then, lowering his tone, he continued: "You told me just now to take care."

"Yes."

"Well, I say to you, take care."

"Of what?"

"You are going to the Tuileries?"

"Of course."

"The Tuileries are very near the Place de la Révolution."

"Pooh!" retorted Bonaparte, "the guillotine has been moved to the Barrière du Trône."

"Never mind. The brewer Santerre still controls the Faubourg Saint-Antoine, and Santerre is Moulins' friend."

"Santerre has been warned that at the first inimical movement he attempts I will have him shot. Will you come?"

"No."

"As you please. You are separating your fortunes from mine; I do not separate mine from yours." Then, calling to his orderly, he said: "My horse!"

They brought his horse. Seeing an artillery private near him, he said: "What are you doing among the epaulets?"

The artilleryman began to laugh.

"Don't you recognize me, general?" he asked.

"Faith, it's Debel! Where did you get that horse and the uniform?"

"From that artilleryman you see standing there in his shirt. It will cost you a corporal's commission."

"You are wrong, Debel," said Bonaparte; "it will cost me two commissions, one for the corporal, and one for the general of division. Forward, march, gentlemen! We are going to the Tuileries."

And, bending forward on his horse, as he usually did, his left hand holding a slack rein, his right resting on his hip, with bent head and dreamy eyes, he made his first steps along that incline, at once glorious and fatal, which was to lead him to a throne—and to St. Helena.

CHAPTER XXIV

THE EIGHTEENTH BRUMAIRE

ON ENTERING the Rue de la Victoire, Bonaparte found Sebastiani's dragoons drawn up in line of battle. He wished to address them, but they interrupted him at the first words, shouting: "We want no explanations. We know that you seek only the good of the Republic. Vive Bonaparte!"

The cortège followed the streets which led from the Rue

de la Victoire to the Tuileries, amid the cries of "Vive Bonaparte!"

General Lefebvre, according to promise, was waiting at the palace gates. Bonaparte, on his arrival at the Tuileries, was hailed with the same cheers that had accompanied him. Once there, he raised his head and shook it. Perhaps this cry of "Vive Bonaparte!" did not satisfy him. Was he already dreaming of "Vive Napoleon?"

He advanced in front of the troop, surrounded by his staff, and read the decree of the Five Hundred, which transferred the sessions of the Legislature to Saint-Cloud and gave him the command of the armed forces.

Then, either from memory, or offhand—Bonaparte never admitted any one to such secrets—instead of the proclamation he had dictated to Bourrienne two days earlier, he pronounced these words:

"Soldiers—The Council of Ancients has given me the command of the city and the army.

"I have accepted it, to second the measures to be adopted for the good of the people.

"The Republic has been ill governed for two years. You have hoped for my return to put an end to many evils. You celebrated it with a unanimity which imposes obligations that I now fulfil. Fulfil yours, and second your general with the vigor, firmness and strength I have always found in you.

"Liberty, victory, and peace will restore the French Republic to the rank it occupied in Europe, which ineptitude and treason alone caused her to lose!"

The soldiers applauded frantically. It was a declaration of war against the Directory, and soldiers will always applaud a declaration of war.

The general dismounted, amid shouts and bravos, and entered the Tuileries. It was the second time he had crossed the threshold of this palace of the Valois, whose arches had so ill-sheltered the crown and head of the last Bourbon who had reigned there. Beside him walked citizen Roederer. Bonaparte started as he recognized him, and said:

"Ah! citizen Roederer, you were here on the morning of August 10."

"Yes, general," replied the future Count of the Empire.

"It was you who advised Louis XVI. to go before the National Assembly."

"Yes."

"Bad advice, citizen Roederer! I should not have followed it."

"We advise men according to what we know of them. I would not give General Bonaparte the same advice I gave King Louis XVI. When a king has the fact of his flight to Varennes and the 20th of June behind him, it is difficult to save him."

As Roederer said these words, they reached a window opening on the garden of the Tuileries. Bonaparte stopped, and, seizing Roederer by the arm, he said: "On the 20th of June I was there," pointing with his finger to the terrace by the water, "behind the third linden. Through the open window I could see the poor king, with the red cap on his head. It was a piteous sight; I pitied him."

"What did you do?"

"Nothing, I could do nothing; I was only a lieutenant of artillery. But I longed to go in like the others, and whisper: 'Sire, give me four cannon, and I'll sweep the whole rabble out.'"

What would have happened if Lieutenant Bonaparte had followed his impulse, obtained what he wanted from Louis XVI., and *swept the rabble out*, that is to say the people of Paris? Had his cannon made a clean sweep on June 20th, would he have had to make another the 13th Vendemiaire for the benefit of the Convention?

While the ex-Syndic, who had grown grave, was outlining in his mind the opening pages of his future "History of the Consulate," Bonaparte presented himself at the bar of the Council of the Ancients, followed by his staff, and by all those who chose to do likewise. When the tumult caused by this influx of people had subsided, the president read over the decree which invested Bonaparte with the military power. Then, after requesting him to take the oath, the president added:

"He who has never promised his country a victory which he did not win, cannot fail to keep religiously his new promise to serve her faithfully."

Bonaparte stretched forth his hand and said solemnly:

"I swear it!"

All the generals repeated after him, each for himself:

"I swear it!"

The last one had scarcely finished, when Bonaparte recognized Barras' secretary, that same Bollot of whom Barras had spoken that morning to his two colleagues. He had come there solely to give his patron an account of all that was happening there, but Bonaparte fancied he was sent on some secret mission by Barras. He resolved to spare him the first advance, and went straight to him, saying:

"Have you come on behalf of the Directors?" Then, without giving him time to answer, he continued: "What have they done with that France I left so brilliant? I left peace; I find war. I left victories; I find reverses. I left the millions of Italy, and I find spoliation and penury. What have become of the hundred thousand Frenchmen whom I knew by name? They are dead!"

It was not precisely to Barras' secretary that these words should have been said; but Bonaparte wished to say them, needed to say them, and little he cared to whom he said them. Perhaps even, from his point of view, it was better to say them to some one who could not answer him. At that moment Sièyes rose.

"Citizens," said he, "the Directors Moulins and Gohier ask to be admitted."

"They are no longer Directors," said Bonaparte, "for there is no longer a Directory."

"But," objected Sièyes, "they have not yet sent in their resignation."

"Then admit them and let them give it," retorted Bonaparte.

Moulins and Gohier entered. They were pale but calm. They knew they came to force a struggle, but behind their resistance may have loomed the Sinnamary. The exiles they sent there the 18th of Fructidor pointed the way.

"I see with satisfaction," Bonaparte hastened to say, "that you have yielded to our wishes and those of your two colleagues."

Gohier made a step forward and said firmly: "We yield neither to your wishes, nor to those of our two colleagues, who are no longer our colleagues, since they have resigned, but to the Law. It requires that the decree transferring the legislative body to Saint-Cloud shall be proclaimed without delay. We have come here to fulfil the duty which the law imposes on us, fully determined to defend it against all factious persons, whoever they may be, who attempt to attack it."

"Your zeal does not astonish us," replied Bonaparte; "and because you are a man who loves his country you will unite with us."

"Unite with you! And why?"

"To save the Republic."

"To save the Republic! There was a time, general, when you had the honor to be its prop. But to-day the glory of saving it is reserved for us."

"You save it!" retorted Bonaparte. "How will you do that? With the means your Constitution gives you? Why, that Constitution is crumbling on all sides, and even if I did not topple it over, it could not last eight days."

"Ah!" cried Moulins, "at last you avow your hostile intentions."

"My intentions are not hostile!" shouted Bonaparte, striking the floor with the heel of his boot. "The Republic is in peril; it must be saved, and I shall do it."

"You do it?" cried Gohier. "It seems to me it is for the Directory, not you, to say, 'I shall do it!' "

"There is no longer a Directory."

"I did indeed hear that you said so just a moment before we came in."

"There is no longer a Directory, now that Sièyes and Ducos have resigned."

"You are mistaken. So long as there are three Directors, the Directory still exists. Neither Moulins, Barras nor myself, have handed in our resignations."

At that moment a paper was slipped in Bonaparte's hand, and a voice said in his ear: "Read it." He did so; then said aloud: "You, yourself, are mistaken. Barras has resigned, for here is his resignation. The law requires three Directors to make a Directory. You are but two, and, as you said just now, whoever resists the law is a rebel." Then handing the paper to the president, he continued: "Add the citizen Barras' resignation to that of citizens Sièyes and Ducos, and proclaim the fall of the Directory. I will announce it to my soldiers."

Moulins and Gohier were confounded. Barras' resignation sapped the foundations of all their plans. Bonaparte had nothing further to do at the Council of Ancients, but there still remained much to be done in the court of the Tuileries. He went down, followed by those who had accompanied him up. His soldiers no sooner caught sight of him than they burst into shouts of "Vive Bonaparte!" more noisily and more eagerly than ever. He sprang into his saddle and made them a sign that he wished to speak to them. Ten thousand voices that had burst into cries were hushed in a moment. Silence fell as if by enchantment.

"Soldiers," said Bonaparte, in a voice so loud that all could hear it, "your comrades in arms on the frontiers are denuded of the necessaries of life. The people are miserable. The authors of these evils are the factious men against whom I have assembled you to-day. I hope before long to lead you to victory; but first we must deprive those who would stand in the way of public order and general prosperity of their power to do harm."

Whether it was weariness of the government of the Directory, or the fascination exercised by the magic being who called them to victory—so long forgotten in his absence—shouts of enthusiasm arose, and like a train of burning powder spread from the Tuileries to the Carrousel, from the Carrousel to the adjacent streets. Bonaparte profited by this movement. Turning to Moreau, he said:

"General, I will give you proof of the immense confidence I have in you. Bernadotte, whom I left at my house, and who refused to follow us, had the audacity to tell me that if he received orders from the Directory he should execute them against whosoever the agitators might be. General, I confide to you the guardianship of the Luxembourg. The tranquillity of Paris and the welfare of the Republic are in your hands."

And without waiting for a reply he put his horse to a gallop, and rode off to the opposite end of the line.

Moreau, led by military ambition, had consented to play a part in this great drama; he was now forced to accept that which the author assigned him. On returning to the Louvre, Gohier and Moulins found nothing changed apparently. All the sentries were at their posts. They retired to one of the salons of the presidency to consult together. But they had scarcely begun their conference, when General Jubé, the commandant of the Luxembourg, received orders to join Bonaparte at the Tuileries with the guard of the Directory. Their places were filled by Moreau and a portion of the soldiers who had been electrified by Bonaparte. Nevertheless the two Directors drew up a message for the Council of the Five Hundred, in which they protested energetically against what had been done. When this was finished Gohier handed it to his secretary, and Moulins, half dead with exhaustion, returned to his apartments to take some food.

It was then about four o'clock in the afternoon. An

instant later Gohier's secretary returned in great peiturbation.

"Well," said Gohier, "why have you not gone?"

"Citizen president," replied the young man, "we are prisoners in the palace."

"Prisoners? What do you mean?"

"The guard has been changed, and General Jubé is no longer in command."

"Who has replaced him?"

"I think some one said General Moreau."

"Moreau? Impossible! And that coward, Barras, where is he?"

"He has started for his country-place at Grosbois."

"Ah! I must see Moulins!" cried Gohier, rushing to the door. But at the entrance he found a sentry who barred the door. Gohier insisted.

"No one can pass," said the sentry.

"What! not pass?"

"No."

"But I am President Gohier!"

"No one can pass," said the sentry; "that is the order."

Gohier saw it would be useless to say more; force would be impossible. He returned to his own rooms.

In the meantime, General Moreau had gone to see Moulins; he wished to justify himself. Without listening to a word the ex-Director turned his back on him, and, as Moreau insisted, he said: "General, go into the antechamber. That is the place for jailers."

Moreau bowed his head, and understood for the first time into what a fatal trap his honor had fallen.

At five o'clock, Bonaparte started to return to the Rue de la Victoire; all the generals and superior officers in Paris accompanied him. The blindest, those who had not understood the 13th Vendemiaire, those who had not yet understood the return from Egypt, now saw, blazing over the Tuileries, the star of his future, and as everybody could not be a planet, each sought to become a satellite.

The shouts of "Vive Bonaparte!" which came from the lower part of the Rue du Mónt Blanc, and swept like a sonorous wave toward the Rue de la Victoire, told Josephine of her husband's return. The impressionable Creole had awaited him anxiously. She sprang to meet him in such agitation that she was unable to utter a single word.

"Come, come!" said Bonaparte, becoming the kindly man he was in his own home, "calm yourself. We have done to-day all that could be done."

"Is it all over?"

"Oh, no!" replied Bonaparte.

"Must it be done all over again to-morrow?"

"Yes, but to-morrow it will be merely a formality."

That formality was rather rough; but every one knows of the events at Saint-Cloud. We will, therefore, dispense with relating them, and turn at once to the result, impatient as we are to get back to the real subject of our drama, from which the grand historical figure we have introduced diverted us for an instant.

One word more. The 20th Brumaire, at one o'clock in the morning, Bonaparte was appointed First Consul for ten years. He himself selected Cambacérès and Lebrun as his associates under the title of Second Consuls, being firmly resolved this time to concentrate in his own person, not only all the functions of the two consuls, but those of the ministers.

The 20th Brumaire he slept at the Luxembourg in president Gohier's bed, the latter having been liberated with his colleague Moulins.

Roland was made governor of the Luxembourg.

CHAPTER XXV

AN IMPORTANT COMMUNICATION

SOME time after this military revolution, which created a great stir in Europe, convulsing the Continent for a time, as a tempest convulses the ocean—some time after, we say, on the morning of the 30th Nivoise, better and more clearly known to our readers as the 20th of January, 1800, Roland, in looking over the voluminous correspondence which his new office entailed upon him, found, among fifty other letters asking for an audience, the following:

MONSIEUR THE GOVERNOR—I know your loyalty to your word, and you will see that I rely on it. I wish to speak to you for five minutes, during which I must remain masked.

I have a request to make of you. This request you will grant or deny. In either case, as I shall have entered the Palace of the Luxembourg in the interest of the First Consul, Bonaparte, and the royalist party to which I belong, I shall ask for your word of honor that I be allowed to leave it as freely as you allow me to enter.

If to-morrow, at seven in the evening, I see a solitary light in the window over the clock, I shall know that Colonel Roland de Montrevel has pledged me his word of honor, and I shall boldly present myself at the little door of the left wing of the palace, opening on the garden. I shall strike three blows at intervals, after the manner of the free-masons.

In order that you may know to whom you engage or refuse your word, I sign a name which is known to you, that name having been, under circumstances you have probably not forgotten, pronounced before you.

MORGAN,
Chief of the Companions of Jehu.

Roland read the letter twice, thought it over for a few moments, then rose suddenly, and, entering the First Consul's study, handed it to him silently. The latter read it without betraying the slightest emotion, or even surprise; then, with a laconism that was wholly Lacedæmonian, he said: "Place the light."

Then he gave the letter back to Roland.

The next evening, at seven o'clock, the light shone in the window, and at five minutes past the hour, Roland in person was waiting at the little door of the garden. He had scarcely been there a moment when three blows were struck on the door after the manner of the free-masons; first two strokes and then one.

The door was opened immediately. A man wrapped in a cloak was sharply defined against the grayish atmosphere of the wintry night. As for Roland, he was completely hidden in shadow. Seeing no one, the man in the cloak remained motionless for a second.

"Come in," said Roland.

"Ah! it is you, colonel!"

"How do you know it is I?" asked Roland.

"I recognize your voice."

"My voice! But during those few moments we were together in the dining-room at Avignon I did not say a word."

"Then I must have heard it elsewhere."

Roland wondered where the Chief of the Companions of Jehu could have heard his voice, but the other said gayly: "Is the fact that I know your voice any reason why we should stand at the door?"

"No, indeed," replied Roland; "take the lapel of my coat and follow me. I purposely forbade any lights being placed in the stairs and hall which lead to my room."

"I am much obliged for the intention. But on your word I would cross the palace from one end to the other, though it were lighted *à giorno*, as the Italians say."

"You have my word," replied Roland, "so follow me without fear."

Morgan needed no encouragement; he followed his guide fearlessly. At the head of the stairs Roland turned down a corridor equally dark, went twenty steps, opened a door, and entered his own room. Morgan followed him. The room was lighted by two wax candles only. Once there, Morgan took off his cloak and laid his pistols on the table.

"What are you doing?" asked Roland.

"Faith! with your permission," replied Morgan, gayly, "I am making myself comfortable."

"But those pistols you have just laid aside—"

"Ah! did you think I brought them for you?"

"For whom then?"

"Why, that damned police! You can readily imagine that I am not disposed to let citizen Fouché lay hold of me, without burning the mustache of the first of his minions who lays hands on me."

"But once here you feel you have nothing to fear?"

"The deuce!" exclaimed the young man; "I have your word."

"Then why don't you unmask?"

"Because my face only half belongs to me; the other half belongs to my companions. Who knows if one of us being recognized might not drag the others to the guillotine? For of course you know, colonel, we don't hide from ourselves that that is the price of our game!"

"Then why risk it?"

"Ah! what a question. Why do you venture on the field of battle, where a bullet may plow through your breast or a cannon-ball lop off your head?"

"Permit me to say that that is different. On the battlefield I risk an honorable death."

"Ah! do you suppose that on the day I get my head cut off by the revolutionary triangle I shall think myself dishonored? Not the least in the world. I am a soldier like you, only we can't all serve our cause in the same way. Every religion has its heroes and its martyrs; happy the heroes in this world, and happy the martyrs in the next."

The young man uttered these words with a conviction which moved, or rather astonished. Roland.

"But," continued Morgan, abandoning his enthusiasm to revert to the gayety which seemed the distinctive trait of his character, "I did not come here to talk political philosophy. I came to ask you to let me speak to the First Consul."

"What! speak to the First Consul?" exclaimed Roland.

"Of course. Read my letter over; did I not tell you that I had a request to make?"

"Yes."

"Well, that request is to let me speak to General Bonaparte."

"But permit me to say that as I did not expect that request—"

"It surprises you; 'makes you uneasy even. My dear colonel, if you don't believe my word, you can search me from head to foot, and you will find that those pistols are my only weapons. And I haven't even got them, since there they are on your table. Better still, take one in each hand, post yourself between the First Consul and me, and blow out my brains at the first suspicious move I make. Will that suit you?"

"But will you assure me, if I disturb the First Consul and ask him to see you, that your communication is worth the trouble?"

"Oh! I'll answer for that," said Morgan. Then, in his joyous tones, he added: "I am for the moment the ambassador of a crowned, or rather discrowned, head, which makes it no less reverenced by noble hearts. Moreover, Monsieur Roland, I shall take up very little of your general's time; the moment the conversation seems too long, he can dismiss me. And I assure you he will not have to say the word twice."

Roland was silent and thoughtful for a moment.

"And it is to the First Consul only that you can make this communication?"

"To the First Consul only, as he alone can answer me."

"Very well. Wait until I take his orders."

Roland made a step toward the general's room; then he paused and cast an uneasy look at a mass of papers piled on his table. Morgan intercepted this look.

"What!" he said, "you are afraid I shall read those papers in your absence? If you only knew how I detest reading! If my death-warrant lay on that table, I wouldn't take the trouble to read it. I should consider that the clerk's business. And every one to his own task. Monsieur Roland, my feet are cold, and I will sit here in your easy-chair and warm them. I shall not stir till you return."

"Very good, monsieur," said Roland, and he went to the First Consul.

Bonaparte was talking with General Hedouville, commanding the troops of the Vendée. Hearing the door open, he turned impatiently.

"I told Bourrienne I would not see any one."

"So he told me as I came in, but I told him that I was not any one."

"True. What do you want? Be quick."

"He is in my room."

"Who?"

"The man of Avignon."

"Ah, ha! And what does he want?"

"To see you."

"To see me?"

"Yes, you, general. Does that surprise you?"

"No. But what can he want to say to me?"

"He refused obstinately to tell me. But I dare answer for it that he is neither importunate nor a fool."

"No, but he may be an assassin."

Roland shook his head.

"Of course, since you introduce him—"

"Moreover, he is willing that I should be present at the conference and stand between you and him."

Bonaparte reflected an instant.

"Bring him in," he said.

"You know, general, that except me—"

"Yes, General Hedouville will be so kind as to wait a second. Our conversation is of a nature that is not exhausted in one interview. Go, Roland."

Roland left the room, crossed Bourrienne's office, reentered his own room, and found Morgan, as he had said, warming his feet.

"Come, the First Consul is waiting for you," said the young man.

Morgan rose and followed Roland. When they entered Bonaparte's study the latter was alone. He cast a rapid glance on the chief of the Companions of Jehu, and felt no doubt that he was the same man he had seen at Avignon.

Morgan had paused a few steps from the door, and was looking curiously at Bonaparte, convincing himself that he was the man he had seen at the table d'hôte the day he attempted the perilous restoration of the two hundred louis stolen by an oversight from Jean Picot.

"Come nearer," said the First Consul.

Morgan bowed and made three steps forward. Bonaparte partly returned the bow with a slight motion of the head.

"You told my aide-de-camp, Colonel Roland, that you had a communication to make me."

"Yes, citizen First Consul."

"Does that communication require a private interview?"

"No, citizen First Consul, although it is of such importance—"

"You would prefer to be alone."

"Beyond doubt. But prudence—"

"The most prudent thing in France, citizen Morgan, is courage."

"My presence here, general, proves that I agree with you perfectly."

Bonaparte turned to the young colonel.

"Leave us alone, Roland," said he.

"But, general—" objected Roland.

Bonaparte went up to him and said in a low voice: "I see what it is. You are curious to know what this mysterious cavalier of the highroad has to say to me. Don't worry; you shall know."

"That's not it. But suppose, as you said just now, he is an assassin."

"Didn't you declare he was not. Come, don't be a baby; leave us."

Roland went out.

"Now that we are alone, sir," said the First Consul, "speak!"

Morgan, without answering, drew a letter from his pocket and gave it to the general. Bonaparte examined it. It was addressed to him, and the seal bore the three fleurs-de-lis of France.

"Oh!" he said, "what is this, sir?"

"Read it, citizen First Consul."

Bonaparte opened the letter and looked at the signature: "Louis," he said.

"Louis," repeated Morgan.

"What Louis?"

"Louis de Bourbon, I presume."

"Monsieur le Comte de Provençe, brother of Louis XVI."

"Consequently Louis XVIII., since his nephew, the Dauphin, is dead."

Bonaparte looked at the stranger again. It was evident that Morgan was a pseudonym, assumed to hide his real name. Then, turning his eyes on the letter, he read:

January 3, 1800.

Whatever may be their apparent conduct, monsieur, men like you never inspire distrust. You have accepted an exalted post, and I thank you for so doing. You know, better than others, that force and power are needed to make the happiness of a great nation. Save France from her own madness, and you will fulfil the desire of my heart; restore her king, and future generations will bless your memory. If you doubt my gratitude, choose your own place, determine the future of your friends. As for my principles, I am a Frenchman, clement by nature, still more so by judgment. No! the conqueror of Lodi, Castiglione and Arcola, the conqueror of Italy and Egypt, cannot prefer an empty celebrity to fame. Lose no more precious time. We can secure the glory of France. I say *we*, because I have need of Bonaparte for that which he cannot achieve without me. General, the eyes of Europe are upon you, glory awaits you, and I am eager to restore my people to happiness.

LOUIS.

Bonaparte turned to the young man, who stood erect, motionless and silent as a statue.

"Do you know the contents of this letter?" he asked.

The young man bowed. "Yes, citizen First Consul."

"It was sealed, however."

"It was sent unsealed under cover to the person who intrusted it to me. And before doing so he made me read it, that I might know its full importance."

"Can I know the name of the person who intrusted it to you?"

"Georges Cadoudal."

Bonaparte started slightly.

"Do you know Georges Cadoudal?" he asked.

"He is my friend."

"Why did he intrust it to you rather than to another?"

"Because he knew that in telling me to deliver the letter to you with my own hand it would be done."

"You have certainly kept your promise, sir."

"Not altogether yet, citizen First Consul."

"How do you mean? Haven't you delivered it to me?"

"Yes, but I promised to bring back an answer."

"But if I tell you I will not give one."

"You will have answered; not precisely as I could have wished, but it will be an answer."

Bonaparte reflected for a few moments. Then shaking his shoulders to rid himself of his thoughts, he said: "They are fools."

"Who, citizen?" asked Morgan.

"Those who write me such letters—fools, arch fools. Do they take me for a man who patterns his conduct by the past? Play Monk! What good would it do? Bring back another Charles II.? No, faith, it is not worth while. When a man has Toulon, the 13th Vendemiaire, Lodi, Castiglione, Arcola, Rivoli and the Pyramids behind him, he's no Monk. He has the right to aspire to more than a duchy of Albemarle, and the command by land and sea of the forces of his Majesty King Louis XVIII."

"For that reason you are asked to make your own conditions, citizen First Consul."

Bonaparte started at the sound of that voice as if he had forgotten that any one was present.

"Not counting," he went on, "that it is a ruined family, a dead branch of a rotten trunk. The Bourbons have so intermarried with one another that the race is depraved; Louis XIV. exhausted all its sap, all its vigor.—You know history, sir?" asked Bonaparte, turning to the young man.

"Yes, general," he replied; "at least as well as a ci-devant can know it."

"Well, you must have observed in history, especially in that of France, that each race has its point of departure, its culmination, and its decadence. Look at the direct line of the Capets; starting from Hugues Capet, they attained their highest grandeur in Philippe Auguste and Louis XI., and fell with Philippe V. and Charles IV. Take the Valois; starting with Philippe VI., they culminated in François I. and fell with Charles IX. and Henry III. See the Bourbons; starting with Henry IV., they have their culminating point in Louis XIV. and fall with Louis XV. and Louis XVI.—only they fall lower than the others; lower in debauchery with Louis XV., lower in misfortune with Louis XVI. You talk to me of the Stuarts, and show me the example of Monk. Will you tell me who succeeded Charles II.? James II. And who to James II.? William of Orange, a usurper. Would it not have been better, I ask you, if Monk had put the crown on his own head? Well, if I was fool enough to restore Louis XVIII. to the throne, like Charles II. he would have no children, and, like James II., his brother Charles X. would succeed him, and like him would be driven out by some William of Orange. No, no! God has not put the destiny of this great and glorious country we call France into my hands that I should cast it back to those who have gambled with it and lost it.''

"Permit me, general, to remark that I did not ask you for all this."

"But I, I ask you—"

"I think you are doing me the honor to take me for posterity."

Bonaparte started, turned round, saw to whom he was speaking, and was silent.

"I only want," said Morgan, with a dignity which surprised the man whom he addressed, "a yes or a no."

"And why do you want that?"

"To know whether we must continue to war against you as an enemy, or fall at your feet as a savior."

"War," said Bonaparte, "war! Madmen, they who war with me! Do they not see that I am the elect of God?"

"Attila said the same thing."

"Yes; but he was the elect of destruction; I, of the new era. The grass withered where he stepped; the harvest will ripen where I pass the plow. War? Tell me what has become of those who have made it against me? They lie upon the plains of Piedmont, of Lombardy and Cairo!"

"You forget the Vendée; the Vendée is still afoot."

"Afoot, yes! but her leaders? Cathelineau, Lescure, La Rochejaquelin, d'Elbée, Bonchamps, Stofflet, Charette?"

"You are speaking of men only; the men have been mown down, it is true; but the principle is still afoot, and for it are fighting Autichamp, Suzannet, Grignon, Frotté, Châtillon, Cadoudal. The younger may not be worth the elder, but if they die as their elders died, what more can you ask?"

"Let them beware! If I determine upon a campaign

against the Vendée I shall send neither Santerre nor Rossignol!''

''The Convention sent Kléber, and the Directory, Hoche!''

''I shall not send; I shall go myself.''

''Nothing worse can happen to them than to be killed like Lescure, or shot like Charette.''

''It may happen that I pardon them.''

''Cato taught us how to escape the pardon of Cæsar.''

''Take care; you are quoting a Republican!''

''Cato was one of those men whose example can be followed, no matter to what party they belong.''

''And suppose I were to tell you that I hold the Vendée in the hollow of my hand?''

''You!''

''And that within three months she will lay down her arms if I choose?''

The young man shook his head.

''You don't believe me?''

''I hesitate to believe you.''

''If I affirm to you that what I say is true; if I prove it by telling you the means, or rather the men, by whom I shall bring this about?''

''If a man like General Bonaparte affirms a thing, I shall believe it; and if that thing is the pacification of the Vendée, I shall say in my turn: 'Beware! Better the Vendée fighting than the Vendée conspiring. The Vendée fighting means the sword, the Vendée conspiring means the dagger.' ''

''Oh! I know your dagger,'' said Bonaparte. ''Here it is.''

And he drew from a drawer the dagger he had taken from Roland and laid it on the table within reach of Morgan's hand.

''But,'' he added, ''there is some distance between Bonaparte's breast and an assassin's dagger. Try.''

And he advanced to the young man with a flaming eye.

''I did not come here to assassinate you,'' said the young man, coldly. ''Later, if I consider your death indispensable to the cause, I shall do all in my power, and if I fail it will not be because you are Marius and I the Cimbrian. Have you anything else to say to me, citizen First Consul?'' concluded the young man, bowing.

"Yes. Tell Cadoudal that when he is ready to fight the enemy, instead of Frenchmen, I have a colonel's commission ready signed in my desk for him.''

"Cadoudal commands, not a regiment, but an army. You were unwilling to retrograde from Bonaparte to Monk; why should you expect him to descend from general to colonel? Have you nothing else to say to me, citizen First Consul?''

"Yes. Have you any way of transmitting my reply to the Comte de Provençe?''

"You mean King Louis XVIII.?''

"Don't let us quibble over words. To him who wrote to me.''

"His envoy is now at the camp at Aubiers.''

"Well, I have changed my mind; I shall send him an answer. These Bourbons are so blind that this one would misinterpret my silence.''

And Bonaparte, sitting down at his desk, wrote the following letter with a care that showed he wished to make it legible:

I have received your letter, monsieur. I thank you for the good opinion you express in it of me. You must not wish for your return to France; it could only be over a hundred thousand dead bodies. Sacrifice your own interests to the repose and welfare of France. History will applaud you. I am not insensible to the misfortunes of your family, and I shall hear with pleasure that you are surrounded with all that could contribute to the tranquillity of your retreat.   BONAPARTE.

Then, folding and sealing the letter, he directed it to "Monsieur le Comte de Provençe,'' and handed it to Morgan. Then he called Roland, as if he knew the latter were not far off.

"General?'' said the young officer, appearing instantly.

"Conduct this gentleman to the street,'' said Bonaparte. "Until then you are responsible for him.''

Roland bowed in sign of obedience, let the young man, who said not a word, pass before him, and then followed. But before leaving, Morgan cast a last glance at Bonaparte.

The latter was still standing, motionless and silent, with folded arms, his eyes fixed upon the dagger, which occupied his thoughts far more than he was willing to admit even to himself.

As they crossed Roland's room, the Chief of the Companions of Jehu gathered up his cloak and pistols. While he was putting them in his belt, Roland remarked: "The citizen First Consul seems to have shown you a dagger which I gave him."

"Yes, monsieur," replied Morgan.

"Did you recognize it?"

"Not that one in particular; all our daggers are alike."

"Well," said Roland, "I will tell you whence it came."

"Ah! where was that?"

"From the breast of a friend of mine, where your Companions, possibly you yourself, thrust it."

"Possibly," replied the young man carelessly. "But your friend must have exposed himself to punishment."

"My friend wished to see what was happening at night in the Chartreuse."

"He did wrong."

"But I did the same wrong the night before, and nothing happened to me."

"Probably because some talisman protects you."

"Monsieur, let me tell you something. I am a straightforward man who walks by daylight. I have a horror of all that is mysterious."

"Happy those who can walk the highroads by daylight, Monsieur de Montrevel!"

"That is why I am going to tell you the oath I made, Monsieur Morgan. As I drew the dagger you saw from my friend's breast, as carefully as possible, that I might not draw his soul with it, I swore that henceforward it should be war to the death between his assassins and myself. It was largely to tell you that that I gave you a pledge of safety.''

"That is an oath I hope to see you forget, Monsieur de Montrevel.''

"It is an oath I shall keep under all circumstances, Monsieur Morgan; and you would be most kind if you would furnish me with an opportunity as soon as possible.''

"In what way, sir?''

"Well, for example, by accepting a meeting with me, either in the Bois de Boulogne or at Vincennes. We don't need to say that we are fighting because you or one of your friends stabbed Lord Tanlay. No; we can say anything you please.'' (Roland reflected a moment.) "We can say the duel is on account of the eclipse that takes place on the 12th of next month. Does the pretext suit you?''

"The pretext would suit me,'' replied Morgan, in a tone of sadness of which he seemed incapable, "if the duel itself could take place. You have taken an oath, and you mean to keep it, you say. Well, every initiate who enters the Company of Jehu swears that he will not expose in any personal quarrel a life that belongs to the cause and not to himself.''

"Oh! So that you assassinate, but will not fight.''

"You are mistaken. We sometimes fight.''

"Have the goodness to point out an occasion when I may study that phenomenon.''

"Easily enough. If you and five or six men, as resolute as yourself, will take your places in some diligence carrying government money, and will defend it against our attack, the occasion you seek will come. But, believe me, do better than that; do not come in our way.''

"Is that a threat, sir?'' asked the young man, raising his head.

"No,'' replied Morgan, in a gentle, almost supplicating voice, "it is an entreaty.''

"Is it addressed to me in particular, or would you include others?''

"I make it to you in particular;" and the chief of the
Companions of Jehu dwelt upon the last word.

"Ah!" exclaimed the young man, "then I am so fortunate as to interest you?"

"As a brother," replied Morgan, in the same soft, caress-
ing tone.

"Well, well," said Roland, "this is decidedly a wager."
Bourrienne entered at that moment.

"Roland," he said, "the First Consul wants you."

"Give me time to conduct this gentleman to the street,
and I'll be with him."

"Hurry up; you know he doesn't like to wait."

"Will you follow me, sir?" Roland said to his mysterious
companion.

"I am at your orders, sir."

"Come, then."   And Roland, taking the same path by
which he had brought Morgan, took him back, not to the
door opening on the garden (the garden was closed), but to
that on the street.   Once there, he stopped and said: "Sir,
I gave you my word, and I have kept it faithfully.   But
that there may be no misunderstanding between us, have
the goodness to tell me that you understand it to have been
for this one time and for to-day only."

"That was how I understood it, sir."

"You give me back my word then?"

"I should like to keep it, sir; but I recognize that you
are free to take it back."

"That is all I wish to know.   Au revoir! Monsieur
Morgan."

"Permit me not to offer you the same wish, Monsieur de
Montrevel."

The two young men bowed with perfect courtesy.   Roland re-entered the Luxembourg, and Morgan, following
the line of shadow projected by the walls, took one of the
little streets to the Place Saint-Sulpice.

It is he whom we are now to follow.

CHAPTER XXVI

THE BALL OF THE VICTIMS

AFTER taking about a hundred steps Morgan removed his mask. He ran more risk of being noticed in the streets of Paris as a masked man than with uncovered face.

When he reached the Rue Taranne he knocked at the door of a small furnished lodging-house at the corner of that street and the Rue du Dragon, took a candlestick from a table, a key numbered 12 from a nail, and climbed the stairs without exciting other attention than a well-known lodger would returning home. The clock was striking ten as he closed the door of his room. He listened attentively to the strokes, the light of his candle not reaching as far as the chimney-piece. He counted ten.

"Good!" he said to himself; "I shall not be too late."

In spite of this probability, Morgan seemed determined to lose no time. He passed a bit of tinder-paper under the heater on the hearth, which caught fire instantly. He lighted four wax-candles, all there were in the room, placed two on the mantel-shelf and two on a bureau opposite, and spread upon the bed a complete dress of the Incroyable of the very latest fashion. It consisted of a short coat, cut square across the front and long behind, of a soft shade between a pale-green and a pearl-gray; a waistcoat of buff plush, with eighteen mother-of-pearl buttons; an immense white cravat of the finest cambric; light trousers of white cashmere, decorated with a knot of ribbon where they buttoned above the calves, and pearl-gray silk stockings, striped transversely with the same green as the coat, and delicate pumps with diamond buckles. The inevitable eye-glass was not forgotten. As for the hat, it was precisely the same in which Carle Vernet painted his dandy of the Directory.

When these things were ready, Morgan waited with seeming impatience. At the end of five minutes he rang the bell. A waiter appeared.

"Hasn't the wig-maker come?" asked Morgan.

In those days wig-makers were not yet called hair-dressers.

"Yes, citizen," replied the waiter, "he came, but you had not yet returned, so he left word that he'd come back. Some one knocked just as you rang; it's probably—"

"Here, here," cried a voice on the stairs.

"Ah! bravo," exclaimed Morgan. "Come in, Master Cadanette; you must make a sort of Adonis of me."

"That won't be difficult, Monsieur le Baron," replied the wig-maker.

"Look here, look here; do you mean to compromise me, citizen Cadenette?"

"Monsieur le Baron, I entreat you, call me Cadenette; you'll honor me by that proof of familiarity; but don't call me citizen. Fie; that's a revolutionary denomination! Even in the worst of the Terror I always called my wife *Madame* Cadenette. Now, excuse me for not waiting for you; but there's a great ball in the Rue du Bac this evening, the ball of the Victims (the wig-maker emphasized this word). I should have thought that M. le Baron would be there."

"Why," cried Morgan, laughing; "so you are still a royalist, Cadenette?"

The wig-maker laid his hand tragically on his heart.

"Monsieur le Baron," said he, "it is not only a matter of conscience, but a matter of state."

"Conscience, I can understand that, Master Cadenette, but state! What the devil has the honorable guild of wig-makers to do with politics?"

"What, Monsieur le Baron?" said Cadenette, all the

while getting ready to dress his client's hair; "you ask me that? You, an aristocrat!"

"Hush, Cadenette!"

"Monsieur le Baron, we *ci-devants* can say that to each other."

"So you are a *ci-devant?*"

"To the core! In what style shall I dress M. le Baron's hair?"

"Dog's ears, and tied up behind."

"With a dash of powder?"

"Two, if you like, Cadenette."

"Ah! monsieur, when one thinks that for five years I was the only man who had an atom of powder '*à la maréchale.*' Why, Monsieur le Baron, a man was guillotined for owning a box of powder!"

"I've known people who were guillotined for less than that, Cadenette. But explain how you happen to be a *ci-devant*. I like to understand everything."

"It's very simple, Monsieur le Baron. You admit, don't you, that among the guilds there were some that were more or less aristocratic."

"Beyond doubt; accordingly as they were nearer to the higher classes of society."

"That's it, Monsieur le Baron. Well, we had the higher classes by the hair of their head. I, such as you see me, I have dressed Madame de Polignac's hair; my father dressed Madame du Barry's; my grandfather, Madame de Pompadour's. We had our privileges, Monsieur; we carried swords. It is true, to avoid the accidents that were liable to crop up among hotheads like ourselves, our swords were usually of wood; but at any rate, if they were not the actual thing, they were very good imitations. Yes, Monsieur le Baron," continued Cadenette with a sigh, "those days were the good days, not only for the wig-makers, but for all Trance. We were in all the secrets, all the intrigues; nothing was hidden from us. And there is no known instance, Monsieur le Baron, of a wig-maker betraying a secret. Just look at our poor queen; to whom did she trust her diamonds? To the great, the illustrious Leonard, the prince of wig-makers. Well, Monsieur le Baron, two men alone overthrew the scaffolding of a power that rested on the wigs of Louis XIV., the puffs of the Regency, the frizettes of Louis XV., and the cushions of Marie Antoinette."

"And those two men, those levellers, those two revolutionaries, who were they, Cadenette? that I may doom them, so far as it lies in my power, to public execration."

"M. Rousseau and citizen Talma: Monsieur Rousseau, who said that absurdity, 'We must return to Nature,' and citizen Talma, who invented the Titus head-dress."

"That's true, Cadenette; that's true."

"When the Directory came in there was a moment's hope. M. Barras never gave up powder, and citizen Moulins stuck to his queue. But, you see, the 18th Brumaire has knocked it all down; how could any one friz Bonaparte's hair! Ah! there," continued Cadenette, puffing out the dog's ears of his client—"there's aristocratic hair for you, soft and fine as silk, and takes the tongs so well one would think you wore a wig. See, Monsieur le Baron, you wanted to be as handsome as Adonis! Ah! if Venus had seen you, it's not of Adonis that Mars would have been jealous!"

And Cadenette, now at the end of his labors and satisfied with the result, presented a hand-mirror to Morgan, who examined himself complacently.

"Come, come!" he said to the wig-maker, "you are certainly an artist, my dear fellow! Remember this style, for if ever they cut off my head I shall choose to have it dressed like that, for there will probably be women at my execution."

"And M. le Baron wants them to regret him," said the wig-maker gravely.

"Yes, and in the meantime, my dear Cadenette, here, is a crown to reward your labors. Have the goodness to tell them below to call a carriage for me."

Cadenette sighed.

"Monsieur le Baron," said he, "time was when I should have answered: 'Show yourself at court with your hair dressed like that, and I shall be paid.' But there is no court now, Monsieur le Baron, and one must live. You shall have your carriage."

With which Cadenette sighed again, slipped Morgan's crown in his pocket, made the reverential bow of wig-makers and dancing-masters, and left the young man to complete his toilet.

The head being now dressed, the rest was soon done; the cravat alone took time, owing to the many failures that occurred; but Morgan concluded the difficult task with an experienced hand, and as eleven o'clock was striking he was ready to start. Cadenette had not forgotten his errand; a hackney-coach was at the door. Morgan jumped into it, calling out: "Rue du Bac, No. 60."

The coach turned into the Rue de Grenelle, went up the Rue du Bac, and stopped at No. 60.

"Here's a double fare, friend," said Morgan, "on condition that you don't stand before the door."

The driver took the three francs and disappeared around the corner of the Rue de Varennes. Morgan glanced up the front of the house; it seemed as though he must be mistaken, so dark and silent was it. But he did not hesitate; he rapped in a peculiar fashion.

The door opened. At the further end of the courtyard was a building, brilliantly lighted. The young man went toward it, and, as he approached, the sound of instruments met his ear. He ascended a flight of stairs and entered the dressing-room. There he gave his cloak to the usher whose business it was to attend to the wraps.

"Here is your number," said the usher. "As for your weapons, you are to place them in the gallery where you can find them easily."

Morgan put the number in his trousers pocket, and entered the great gallery transformed into an arsenal. It contained a complete collection of arms of all kinds, pistols, muskets, carbines, swords, and daggers. As the ball might at any moment be invaded by the police, it was necessary that every dancer be prepared to turn defender at an instant's notice. Laying his weapons aside, Morgan entered the ballroom.

We doubt if any pen could give the reader an adequate idea of the scene of that ball. Generally, as the name "Ball of the Victims" indicated, no one was admitted except by the strange right of having relatives who had either been sent to the scaffold by the Convention or the Commune of Paris, blown to pieces by Collot d'Herbois, or drowned by Carrier. As, however, the victims guillotined during the three years of the Terror far outnumbered the others, the dresses of the majority of those who were present were the clothes of the victims of the scaffold. Thus, most of the young girls, whose mothers and older sisters had fallen by the hands of the executioner, wore the same costume their mothers and sisters had worn for that last lugubrious ceremony; that is to say, a white gown and red shawl, with their hair cut short at the nape of the neck. Some added to this costume, already so characteristic, a detail that was even more significant; they knotted around their necks a thread of scarlet silk, fine as the blade of a razor, which, as in Faust's Marguerite, at the Witches' Sabbath, indicated the cut of the knife between the throat and the collar bone.

As for the men who were in the same case, they wore the collars of their coats turned down behind, those of their shirt wide open, their necks bare, and their hair cut short.

But many had other rights of entrance to this ball besides that of having Victims in their families; some had made victims themselves. These latter were increasing. There were present men of forty or forty-five years of age, who had been trained in the boudoirs of the beautiful courtesans of the seventeenth century—who had known Madame du Barry in the attics of Versailles, Sophie Arnoult with M. de Lauraguais, La Duthé with the Comte d'Artois

—who had borrowed from the courtesies of vice the polish with which they covered their ferocity. They were still young and handsome; they entered a salon, tossing their perfumed locks and their scented handkerchiefs; nor was it a useless precaution, for if the odor of musk or verbena had not masked it they would have smelled of blood.

There were men there twenty-five or thirty years old, dressed with extreme elegance, members of the association of Avengers, who seemed possessed with the mania of assassination, the lust of slaughter, the frenzy of blood, which no blood could quench—men who, when the order came to kill, killed all, friends or enemies; men who carried their business methods into the business of murder, giving their bloody checks for the heads of such or such Jacobins, and paying on sight.

There were younger men, eighteen and twenty, almost children, but children fed, like Achilles, on the marrow of wild beasts, like Pyrrhus, on the flesh of bears; here were the pupil-bandits of Schiller, the apprentice-judges of the Sainte-Vehme—that strange generation that follows great political convulsions, like the Titans after chaos, the hydras after the Deluge; as the vultures and crows follow the carnage.

Here was the spectre of iron impassible, implacable, inflexible, which men call Retaliation; and this spectre mingled with the guests. It entered the gilded salons; it signalled with a look, a gesture, a nod, and men followed where it led. It was, as says the author from whom we have borrowed these hitherto unknown but authentic details, "a merry lust for extermination."

The Terror had affected great cynicism in clothes, a Spartan austerity in its food, the profound contempt of a barbarous people for arts and enjoyments. The Thermidorian reaction was, on the contrary, elegant, opulent, adorned; it exhausted all luxuries, all voluptuous pleasures, as in the days of Louis XV.; with one addition, the luxury of vengeance, the lust of blood.

Fréron's name was given to the youth of the day, which was called the jeunesse Fréron, or the *jéunesse dorée* (gilded youth). Why Fréron? Why should he rather than others receive that strange and fatal honor?

I cannot tell you—my researches (those who know me will do me the justice to admit that when I have an end in view, I do not count them)—my researches have not discovered an answer. It was a whim of Fashion, and Fashion is the one goddess more capricious than Fortune.

Our readers will hardly know to-day who Fréron was. The Fréron who was Voltaire's assailant was better known than he who was the patron of these elegant assassins; one was the son of the other. Louis Stanislas was son of Elie-Catherine. The father died of rage when Miromesnil, Keeper of the Seals, suppressed his journal. The other, irritated by the injustices of which his father had been the victim, had at first ardently embraced the revolutionary doctrines. Instead of the "Année Littéraire," strangled to death in 1775, he created the "Orateur du Peuple," in 1789. He was sent to the Midi on a special mission, and Marseilles and Toulon retain to this day the memory of his cruelty. But all was forgotten when, on the 9th Thermidor, he proclaimed himself against Robespierre, and assisted in casting from the altar the Supreme Being, the colossus who, being an apostle, had made himself a god. Fréron, repudiated by the Mountain, which abandoned him to the heavy jaws of Moise Bayle; Fréron, disdainfully repulsed by the Girondins, who delivered him over to the imprecations of Isnard; Fréron, as the terrible and picturesque orator of the Var said, "Fréron naked and covered with the leprosy of crime," was accepted, caressed and petted by the Thermidorians. From them he passed into the camp of the royalists, and without any reason whatever for obtaining that fatal honor, found himself suddenly at the head of a powerful party of youth, energy and vengeance, standing between the passions of the day, which led to all, and the impotence of the law, which permitted all.

It was to the midst of this *jeunesse* Fréron, mouthing its words, slurring its r's, giving its "word of honor" about everything, that Morgan now made his way.

It must be admitted that this *jeunesse*, in spite of the clothes it wore, in spite of the memories these clothes evoked, was wildly gay. This seems incomprehensible, but it is true. Explain if you can that Dance of Death at the beginning of the fifteenth century, which, with all the fury of a modern galop, led by Musard, whirled its chain through the very Cemetery of the Innocents, and left amid its tombs fifty thousand of its votaries.

Morgan was evidently seeking some one.

A young dandy, who was dipping into the silver-gilt comfit-box of a charming victim, with an ensanguined finger, the only part of his delicate hand that had escaped the almond paste, tried to stop him, to relate the particulars of the expedition from which he had brought back this bloody trophy. But Morgan smiled, pressed his other hand which was gloved, and contented himself with replying: "I am looking for some one."

"Important?"

"Company of Jehu."

The young man with the bloody finger let him pass.

An adorable Fury, as Corneille would have called her, whose hair was held up by a dagger with a blade as sharp as a needle, barred his way, saying: "Morgan, you are the handsomest, the bravest, the most deserving of love of all the men present. What have you to say to the woman who tells you that?"

"I answer that I love," replied Morgan, "and that my heart is too narrow to hold one hatred and two loves." And he continued on his search.

Two young men who were arguing, one saying, "He was English," the other, "He was German," stopped him.

"The deuce," cried one; "here is the man who can settle it for us."

"No," replied Morgan, trying to push past them; "I'm in a hurry."

"There's only a word to say," said the other. "We have made a bet, Saint-Amand and I, that the man who was tried and executed at the Chartreuse du Seillon, was, according to him, a German, and, according to me, an Englishman."

"I don't know," replied Morgan; "I wasn't there. Ask Hector; he presided that night."

"Tell us where Hector is?"

"Tell me rather where Tiffauges is; I am looking for him."

"Over there, at the end of the room," said the young man, pointing to a part of the room where the dance was more than usually gay and animated. "You will recognize him by his waistcoat; and his trousers are not to be despised. I shall have a pair like them made with the skin of the very first hound I meet."

Morgan did not take time to ask in what way Tiffauges' waistcoat was remarkable, or by what queer cut or precious material his trousers had won the approbation of a man as expert in such matters as he who had spoken to him. He went straight to the point indicated by the young man, saw the person he was seeking dancing an été, which seemed, by the intricacy of its weaving, if I may be pardoned for this technical term, to have issued from the salons of Vestris himself.

Morgan made a sign to the dancer. Tiffauges stopped instantly, bowed to his partner, led her to her seat, excused himself on the plea of the urgency of the matter which called him away, and returned to take Morgan's arm.

"Did you see him," Tiffauges asked Morgan.

"I have just left him," replied the latter.

"Did you deliver the King's letter?"

"To himself."

"Did he read it?"

"At once."

"Has he sent an answer?"

"Two; one verbal, one written; the second dispenses with the first."

"You have it?"

"Here it is."

"Do you know the contents?"

"A refusal."

"Positive?"

"Nothing could be more positive."

"Does he know that from the moment he takes all hope away from us we shall treat him as an enemy?"

"I told him so."

"What did he answer?"

"He didn't answer; he shrugged his shoulders."

"What do you think his intentions are?"

"It's not difficult to guess."

"Does he mean to keep the power himself?"

"It looks like it."

"The power, but not the throne?"

"Why not the throne?"

"He would never dare to make himself king."

"Oh! I can't say he means to be absolutely king, but I'll answer for it that he means to be something."

"But he is nothing but a soldier of fortune!"

"My dear fellow, better in these days to be the son of his deeds, than the grandson of a king."

The young man thought a moment.

"I shall report it all to Cadoudal," he said.

"And add that the First Consul said these very words: 'I hold the Vendée in the hollow of my hand, and if I choose in three months not another shot will be fired.' "

"It's a good thing to know."

"You know it; let Cadoudal know it, and take measures."

Just then the music ceased; the hum of the dancers died away; complete silence prevailed; and, in the midst of this silence, four names were pronounced in a sonorous and emphatic voice.

These four names were Morgan, Montbar, Adler and d'Assas.

"Pardon me," Morgan said to Tiffauges, "they are probably arranging some expedition in which I am to take part. I am forced, therefore, to my great regret, to bid you farewell. Only before I leave you let me look closer at your waistcoat and trousers, of which I have heard—curiosity of an amateur; I trust you will excuse it."

"Surely!" exclaimed the young Vendéan, "most willingly."

CHAPTER XXVII

THE BEAR'S SKIN

WITH a rapidity and good nature that did honor to his courtesy, he went close to the candelabra, which were burning on the chimney-piece. The waistcoat and trousers seemed to be of the same stuff; but what was that stuff? The most experienced connoisseur would have been puzzled.

The trousers were tight-fitting as usual, of a light tint between buff and flesh color; the only remarkable thing about them was the absence of the seam, and the closeness with which they clung to the leg. The waistcoat, on the other hand, had two characteristic signs which attracted attention; it had been pierced by three balls, which had the holes gaping, and these were stained a carmine, so like blood, that it might easily have been mistaken for it. On the left side was painted a bloody heart, the distinguishing sign of the Vendéans. Morgan examined the two articles with the closest attention, but without result.

"If I were not in such a hurry," said he, "I should like to look into the matter for myself. But you heard for yourself; in all probability, some news has reached the committee; government money probably. You can announce it to Cadoudal; only we shall have to take it first. Ordinarily,

I command these expeditions; if I delay, some one may take my place. So tell me what your waistcoat and trousers are made of."

"My dear Morgan," replied the Vendéan, "perhaps you have heard that my brother was captured near Bressure, and shot by the Blues?"

"Yes, I know that."

"The Blues were retreating; they left the body at the corner of the hedge. We were pursuing them so closely that we arrived just after them. I found the body of my brother still warm. In one of his wounds a sprig was stuck with these words: 'Shot as a brigand by me, Claude Flageolet, corporal of the Third Battalion of Paris.' I took my brother's body, and had the skin removed from his breast. I vowed that this skin, pierced with three holes, should eternally cry vengeance before my eyes. I made it my battle waistcoat."

"Ah!" exclaimed Morgan, with a certain astonishment, in which, for the first time, was mingled something akin to terror—"Ah! then that waistcoat is made of your brother's skin? And the trousers?"

"Oh!" replied the Vendéan, "the trousers, that's another matter. They are made of the skin of Claude Flageolet, corporal of the Third Battalion of Paris."

At that moment the voice again called out, in the same order, the names of Morgan, Montbar, Adler and d'Assas.

Morgan rushed out of the study, crossed the dancing-hall from end to end, and made his way to a little salon on the other side of the dressing-room. His three companions, Montbar, Adler and d'Assas, were there already. With them was a young man in the government livery of a bearer of despatches, namely a green and gold coat. His boots were dusty, and he wore a visored cap and carried the despatch-box, the essential accoutrements of a cabinet courier.

One of Cassini's maps, on which could be followed the whole lay of the land, was spread on the table.

Before saying why this courier was there, and with what

object the map was unfolded, let us cast a glance at the three new personages whose names had echoed through the ballroom, and who are destined to play an important part in the rest of this history.

The reader already knows Morgan, the Achilles and the Paris of this strange association; Morgan, with his blue eyes, his black hair, his tall, well-built figure, graceful, easy, active bearing; his eye, which was never without animation; his mouth, with its fresh lips and white teeth, that was never without a smile; his remarkable countenance, composed of mingling elements that seemed so foreign to each other—strength and tenderness, gentleness and energy; and, through it all, that bewildering expression of gayety that was at times. alarming when one remembered that this man was perpetually rubbing shoulders with death, and the most terrifying of all deaths—that of the scaffold.

As for d'Assas, he was a man from thirty-five to thirty-eight years of age, with bushy hair that was turning gray, and mustaches as black as ebony. His eyes were of that wonderful shade of Indian eyes, verging on maroon. He was formerly a captain of dragoons, admirably built for struggle, whether physical or moral, his muscles indicating strength, and his face, obstinacy. For the rest, a noble bearing, great elegance of manners, scented like a dandy, carrying, either from caprice or luxury, a bottle of English smelling-salts, or a silver-gilt vinaigrette containing the most subtle perfumes.

Montbar and Adler, whose real names were unknown, like those of d'Assas and Morgan, were commonly called by the Company "the inseparables." Imagine Damon and Pythias, Euryalus and Nisus, Orestes and Pylades at twenty-two—one joyous, loquacious, noisy, the other melancholy, silent, dreamy; sharing all things, dangers, money, mistresses; one the complement of the other; each rushing to all extremes, but forgetting self when in peril to watch over the other, like the Spartan youths on the sacred legions—and you will form an idea of Montbar and Adler.

It is needless to say that all three were Companions of Jehu. They had been convoked, as Morgan suspected, on business of the Company.

On entering the room, Morgan went straight to the pretended bearer of despatches and shook hands with him.

"Ah! the dear friend," said the latter, with a stiff movement, showing that the best rider cannot do a hundred and fifty miles on post-hacks with impunity. "You are taking it easy, you Parisians. Hannibal at Capua slept on rushes and thorns compared to you. I only glanced at the ball-room in passing, as becomes a poor cabinet courier bearing despatches from General Masséna to the citizen First Consul; but it seemed to me you were a fine lot of victims! Only, my poor friends, you will have to bid farewell to all that for the present; disagreeable, unlucky, exasperating, no doubt, but the House of Jehu before all."

"My dear Hastier—" began Morgan.

"Stop!" cried Hastier. "No proper names, if you please, gentlemen. The Hastiers are an honest family in Lyons, doing business, it is said, on the Place des Terreaux, from father to son, and would be much humiliated to learn that their heir had become a cabinet courier, and rode the highways with the national pack on his back. Lecoq as much as you please, but not Hastier. I don't know Hastier; and you, gentlemen," continued the young man, addressing Montbar, Adler and d'Assas, "do you know him?"

"No," replied the three young men, "and we ask pardon for Morgan, who did wrong."

"My dear Lecoq," exclaimed Morgan.

"That's right," interrupted Hastier. "I answer to that name! Well, what did you want to tell me?"

"I wanted to say that if you are not the antipodes of the god Harpocrates, whom the Egyptians represent with a finger on his lips, you will, instead of indulging in a lot of declamations, more or less flowery, tell us why this costume, and why that map?"

"The deuce!" retorted the young man. "If you don't

know already, it's your fault and not mine. If I hadn't
been obliged to call you twice, caught as you doubtless
were in the toils of some beautiful Eumenides imploring
vengeance of a fine young man for the death of her old
parents, you'd know as much as these gentlemen, and I
wouldn't have to sing an encore. Well, here's what it is:
simply of the remaining treasure of the Berne bears, which
General Lecourbe is sending to the citizen First Consul by
order of General Masséna. A trifle, only a hundred thousand francs, that they don't dare send over the Jura on
account of M. Teysonnet's partisans, who, they pretend, are
likely to seize it; so it will be sent by Geneva, Bourg,
Mâcon, Dijon, and Troyes; a much safer way, as they will
find when they try it."

"Very good!"

"We were informed of this by Renard, who started from
Gex at full speed, and transmitted the news to l'Hirondelle,
who is at present stationed at Châlon-sur-Saône. He transmitted it to me, Lecoq, at Auxerre, and I have done a hundred and fifty miles to transmit it in turn to you. As for
the secondary details, here they are. The treasure left
Berne last octodi, 28th Nivôse, year VIII. of the Republic
triple and indivisible. It should reach Genoa to-day, duodi,
and leave to-morrow, tridi, by the diligence from Geneva to
Bourg; so that, by leaving this very night, by the day after
to-morrow, quintide, you can, my dear sons of Israel, meet
the treasure of messires the bears between Dijon and Troyes,
near Bar-sur-Seine or Châtillon. What say you?"

"By heavens!" cried Morgan, "we say that there seems
to be no room for argument left; we say we should never
have permitted ourselves to touch the money of their High-
nesses the bears of Berne so long as it remained in their
coffers; but as it has changed hands once, I see no objec-
tion to its doing so a second time. Only how are we to
start?"

"Haven't you a post-chaise?"

"Yes. it's here in the coach-house."

"Haven't you horses to get you to the next stage ?"

"They are in the stable."

"Haven't you each your passports."

"We have each four."

"Well, then ?"

"Well, we can't stop the diligence in a post-chaise. We don't put ourselves to too much inconvenience, but we don't take our ease in that way."

"Well, and why not ?" asked Montbar; "it would be original. I can't see why, if sailors board from one vessel to another, we couldn't board a diligence from a post-chaise. We want novelty; shall we try it, Adler ?"

"I ask nothing better," replied the latter, "but what will we do with the postilion ?"

"That's true," replied Montbar.

"The difficulty is foreseen, my children," said the courier; "a messenger has been sent to Troyes. You will leave your post-chaise at Delbauce; there you will find four horses all saddled and stuffed with oats. You will then calculate your time, and the day after to-morrow, or rather to-morrow, for it is past midnight, between seven and eight in the morning, the money of Messires Bruin will pass an anxious quarter of an hour."

"Shall we change our clothes ?" inquired d'Assas.

"What for ?" replied Morgan. "I think we are very presentable as we are. No diligence could be relieved of unnecessary weight by better dressed fellows. Let us take a last glance at the map, transfer a pâté, a cold chicken, and a dozen of champagne from the supper-room to the pockets of the coach, arm to the teeth in the arsenal, wrap ourselves in warm cloaks, and—clack! postilion !"

"Yes !" cried Montbar, "that's the idea."

"I should think so," added Morgan. "We'll kill the horses if necessary, and be back at seven in the evening, in time to show ourselves at the opera."

"That will establish an alibi," observed d'Assas.

"Precisely," said Morgan, with his imperturbable gayety. "How could men who applaud Mademoiselle Clotilde and M. Vestris at eight o'clock in the evening have been at Bar and Châtillon in the morning settling accounts with the conductor of a diligence? Come, my sons, a last look at the map to choose our spot."

The four young men bent over Cassini's map.

"If I may give you a bit of topographical advice," said the courier, "it would be to put yourselves in ambush just beyond Massu; there's a ford opposite to the Riceys — see, there!"

And the young man pointed out the exact spot on the map.

"I should return to Chacource, there; from Chacource you have a department road, straight as an arrow, which will take you to Troyes; at Troyes you take carriage again, and follow the road to Sens instead of that to Coulommiers. The donkeys—there are plenty in the provinces—who saw you in the morning won't wonder at seeing you again in the evening; you'll get to the opera at ten instead of eight —a more fashionable hour—neither seen nor recognized, I'll warrant you."

"Adopted, so far as I am concerned," said Morgan.

"Adopted!" cried the other three in chorus.

Morgan pulled out one of the two watches whose chains were dangling from his belt; it was a masterpiece of Petitot's enamel, and on the outer case which protected the painting was a diamond monogram. The pedigree of this beautiful trinket was as well established as that of an Arab horse; it had been made for Marie-Antoinette, who had given it to the Duchesse de Polastron, who had given it to Morgan's mother.

"One o'clock," said Morgan; "come, gentlemen, we must relay at Lagny at three."

From that moment the expedition had begun, and Morgan became its leader; he no longer consulted, he commanded.

D'Assas, who in Morgan's absence commanded, was the first to obey on his return.

Half an hour later a closed carriage containing four young men wrapped in their cloaks was stopped at the Fontainebleau barrier by the post-guard, who demanded their passports.

"Oh, what a joke!" exclaimed one of them, putting his head out of the window and affecting the pronunciation of the day. "Passpawts to dwive to Gwobois to call on citizen *Ba-as?* 'Word of fluted honor!' you're cwazy, fwend! Go on, dwiver!"

The coachman whipped up his horses and the carriage passed without further opposition.

CHAPTER XXVIII

FAMILY MATTERS

LET us leave our four *hunters* on their way to Lagny —where, thanks to the passports they owed to the obligingness of certain clerks in citizen Fouché's employ, they exchanged their own horses for post-horses and their coachman for a postilion—and see why the First Consul had sent for Roland.

After leaving Morgan, Roland had hastened to obey the general's orders. He found the latter standing in deep thought before the fireplace. At the sound of his entrance General Bonaparte raised his head.

"What were you two saying to each other?" asked Bonaparte, without preamble, trusting to Roland's habit of answering his thought.

"Why," said Roland, "we paid each other all sorts of compliments, and parted the best friends in the world."

"How does he impress you?"

"As a perfectly well-bred man."

"How old do you take him to be?"

"About my age, at the outside."

"So I think; his voice is youthful. What now, Roland,

can I be mistaken? Is there a new royalist generation grow-ing up?"

"No, general," replied Roland, shrugging his shoulders; "it's the remains of the old one."

"Well, Roland, we must build up another, devoted to my son—if ever I have one."

Roland made a gesture which might be translated into the words, "I don't object." Bonaparte understood the ges-ture perfectly.

"You must do more than not object," said he; "you must contribute to it."

A nervous shudder passed over Roland's body.

"In what way, general?" he asked.

"By marrying."

Roland burst out laughing.

"Good! With my aneurism?" he asked.

Bonaparte looked at him, and said: "My dear Roland, your aneurism looks to me very much like a pretext for re-maining single."

"Do you think so?"

"Yes; and as I am a moral man I insist upon marriage."

"Does that mean that I am immoral," retorted Roland, "or that I cause any scandal with my mistresses?"

"Augustus," answered Bonaparte, "created laws against celibates, depriving them of their rights as Roman citizens."

"Augustus—"

"Well?"

"I'll wait until you are Augustus; as yet, you are only Cæsar."

Bonaparte came closer to the young man, and, laying his hands on his shoulders, said: "Roland, there are some names I do not wish to see extinct, and among them is that of Montrevel."

"Well, general, in my default, supposing that through caprice or obstinacy I refuse to perpetuate it, there is my little brother."

"What! Your brother? Then you have a brother?"

"Why, yes; I have a brother! Why shouldn't I have a brother?"

"How old is he?"

"Eleven or twelve."

"Why did you never tell me about him?"

"Because I thought the sayings and doings of a youngster of that age could not interest you."

"You are mistaken, Roland; I am interested in all that concerns my friends. You ought to have asked me for something for your brother."

"Asked what, general?"

"His admission into some college in Paris."

"Pooh! You have enough beggars around you without my swelling their number."

"You hear; he is to come to Paris and enter college. When he is old enough, I will send him to the Ecole Militaire, or some other school which I shall have founded before then."

"Faith, general," said Roland, "just as if I had guessed your good intentions, he is this very day on the point of starting for Paris."

"What for?"

"I wrote to my mother three days ago to bring the boy to Paris. I intended to put him in college without mentioning it, and when he was old enough to tell you about him—always supposing that my aneurism had not carried me off in the meantime. But in that case—"

"In that case?"

"Oh! in that case I have left a bit of a will addressed to you, and recommending to your kindness my mother, and the boy and the girl—in short, the whole raft."

"The girl! Who is she?"

"My sister."

"So you have a sister also?"

"Yes."

"How old is she?

"Seventeen."

"Pretty ?"

"Charming."

"I'll take charge of her establishment."

Roland began to laugh.

"What's the matter?" demanded the First Consul.

"General, I'm going to put a placard over the grand entrance to the Luxembourg."

"What will you put on the placard?"

" 'Marriages made here.' "

"Why not? Is it any reason because you don't wish to marry for your sister to remain an old maid? I don't like old maids any better than I do old bachelors."

"I did not say, general, that my sister should remain an old maid; it's quite enough for one member of the Montrevel family to have incurred your displeasure."

"Then what do you mean?"

"Only that, as the matter concerns my sister, she must, if you will allow it, be consulted."

"Ah, ha! Some provincial love-affair, is there?"

"I can't say. I left poor Amélie gay and happy, and I find her pale and sad. I shall get the truth out of her; and if you wish me to speak to you again about the matter, I will do so."

"Yes, do so—when you get back from the Vendée."

"Ah! So I am going to the Vendée?"

"Why, is that, like marriage, repugnant to you?"

"Not in the least."

"Then you are going to the Vendée."

"When?"

"Oh, you need not hurry, providing you start to-morrow."

"Excellent; sooner if you wish. Tell me what I am to do there."

"Something of the utmost importance, Roland."

"The devil! It isn't a diplomatic mission, I presume?"

"Yes; it is a diplomatic mission for which I need a man who is not a diplomatist."

"Then I'm your man, general! Only, you understand,

the less a diplomatist I am, the more precise my instructions must be."

"I am going to give them to you. Do you see that map?"

And he showed the young man a large map of Piedmont stretched out on the floor, under a lamp suspended from the ceiling.

"Yes, I see it," replied Roland, accustomed to follow the general along the unexpected dashes of his genius; "but it is a map of Piedmont."

"Yes, it's a map of Piedmont."

"So there is still a question of Italy?"

"There is always a question of Italy."

"I thought you spoke of the Vendée?"

"Secondarily."

"Why, general, you are not going to send me to the Vendée and go yourself to Italy, are you?"

"No; don't be alarmed."

"All right; but I warn you, if you did, I should desert and join you."

"I give you permission to do so; but now let us go back to Mélas."

"Excuse me, general; this is the first time you have mentioned him."

"Yes; but I have been thinking of him for a long time. Do you know where I shall defeat him?"

"The deuce! I do."

"Where?"

"Wherever you meet him."

Bonaparte laughed.

"Ninny!" he said, with loving familiarity. Then, stooping over the map, he said to Roland, "Come here."

Roland stooped beside him. "There," resumed Bonaparte; "that is where I shall fight him."

"Near Alessandria?"

"Within eight or nine miles of it. He has all his supplies, hospitals, artillery and reserves in Alessandria; and he will not leave the neighborhood. I shall have to strike

a great blow; that's the only condition on which I can get
peace. I shall cross the Alps"—he pointed to the great
Saint-Bernard—"I shall fall upon Mélas when he least expects me, and rout him utterly."

"Oh! trust you for that!"

"Yes; but you understand, Roland, that in order to quit
France with an easy mind, I can't leave it with an inflamma-
tion of the bowels—I can't leave war in the Vendée."

"Ah! now I see what you are after. No Vendée! And
you are sending me to the Vendée to suppress it."

"That young man told me some serious things about the
Vendée. They are brave soldiers, those Vendéans, led by
a man of brains, Georges Cadoudal. I have sent him the
offer of a regiment, but he won't accept."

"Jove! He's particular."

"But there's one thing he little knows."

"Who, Cadoudal?"

"Yes, Cadoudal. That is that the Abbé Bernier has
made me overtures."

"The Abbé Bernier?"

"Yes."

"Who is the Abbé Bernier?"

"The son of a peasant from Anjou, who may be now
about thirty-three or four years of age. Before the insurrection he was curate of Saint-Laud at Angers. He refused
to take the oath and sought refuge among the Vendéans.
Two or three times the Vendée was pacificated; twice she
was thought dead. A mistake! the Vendée was pacificated,
but the Abbé Bernier had not signed the peace; the Vendée
was dead, but the Abbé Bernier was still alive. One day
the Vendée was ungrateful to him. He wished to be appointed general agent to the royalist armies of the interior;
Stofflet influenced the decision and got his old master,
Comte Colbert de Maulevrier, appointed in Bernier's stead.
When, at two o'clock in the morning, the council broke
up, the Abbé Bernier had disappeared. What he did that
night, God and he alone can tell; but at four o'clock in

the morning a Republican detachment surrounded the
farmhouse where Stofflet was sleeping, disarmed and de-
fenceless. At half-past four Stofflet was captured; eight
days later he was executed at Angers. The next day
Autichamp took command, and, to avoid making the same
blunder as Stofflet, he appointed the Abbé Bernier general
agent. Now, do you understand?"

"Perfectly."

"Well, the Abbé Bernier, general agent of the belligerent forces, and furnished with plenary powers by the
Comte d'Artois—the Abbé Bernier has made overtures
to me."

"To you, to Bonaparte, to the First Consul he deigns
to—? Why, that's very kind of the Abbé Bernier? Have
you accepted them?"

"Yes, Roland; if the Vendée will give me peace, I will
open her churches and give her back her priests."

"And suppose they chant the *Domine, salvum fac
regem?*"

"That would be better than not singing at all. God is
omnipotent, and he will decide. Does the mission suit you,
now that I have explained it?"

"Yes, thoroughly."

"Then, here is a letter for General Hédouville. He is
to treat with the Abbé Bernier as the general-in-chief of the
Army of the West. But you are to be present at all these
conferences; he is only my mouthpiece, you are to be my
thought. Now, start as soon as possible; the sooner you
get back, the sooner Mélas will be defeated."

"General, give me time to write to my mother,
that's all."

"Where will she stop?"

"At the Hôtel des Ambassadeurs."

"When do you think she will arrive?"

"This is the night of the 21st of January; she will be
here the evening of the 23d, or the morning of the 24th."

"And she stops at the Hôtel des Ambassadeurs?"

"Yes, general."

"I take it all on myself."

"Take it all on yourself, general?"

"Certainly; your mother can't stay at a hotel."

"Where should she stay?"

"With a friend."

"She knows no one in Paris."

"I beg your pardon, Monsieur Roland; she knows citizen Bonaparte, First Consul, and his wife."

"You are not going to lodge my mother at the Luxembourg. I warn you that that would embarrass her very much."

"No; but I shall lodge her in the Rue de la Victoire."

"Oh, general!"

"Come, come; that's settled. Go, now, and get back as soon as possible."

Roland took the First Consul's hand, meaning to kiss it; but Bonaparte drew him quickly to him.

"Embrace me, my dear Roland," he said, "and good luck to you."

Two hours later Roland was rolling along in a post-chaise on the road to Orleans. The next day, at nine in the morning, he entered Nantes, after a journey of thirty-three hours.

CHAPTER XXIX

THE GENEVA DILIGENCE

ABOUT the hour when Roland was entering Nantes, a diligence, heavily loaded, stopped at the inn of the Croix-d'Or, in the middle of the main street of Châtillon-sur-Seine.

In those days the diligences had but two compartments, the coupé and the interior; the rotunda is an adjunct of modern times.

The diligence had hardly stopped before the postilion

jumped down and opened the doors. The travellers dismounted. There were seven in all, of both sexes. In the
interior, three men, two women, and a child at the breast;
in the coupé, a mother and her son.

The three men in the interior were, one a doctor from
Troyes, the second a watchmaker from Geneva, the third
an architect from Bourg. The two women were a lady's
maid travelling to Paris to rejoin her mistress, and the
other a wet-nurse; the child was the latter's nursling,
which she was taking back to its parents.

The mother and son in the coupé were people of position; the former, about forty years of age, still preserving
traces of great beauty, the latter a boy between eleven and
twelve. The third place in the coupé was occupied by the
conductor.

Breakfast was waiting, as usual, in the dining-room; one
of those breakfasts which conductors, no doubt in collusion
with the landlords, never give travellers the time to eat.
The woman and the nurse got out of the coach and went to
a baker's shop nearby, where each bought a hot roll and a
sausage, with which they went back to the coach, settling
themselves quietly to breakfast, thus saving the cost, probably too great for their means, of a meal at the hotel.

The doctor, the watchmaker, the architect and the
mother and son entered the inn, and, after warming themselves hastily at the large kitchen-fire, entered the dining-
room and took seats at the table.

The mother contented herself with a cup of coffee with
cream, and some fruit. The boy, delighted to prove himself a man by his appetite at least, boldly attacked the
viands. The first few moments were, as usual, employed
in satisfying hunger. The watchmaker from Geneva was
the first to speak.

"Faith, citizen," said he (the word citizen was still used
in public places), "I tell you frankly I was not at all sorry
to see daylight this morning."

"Cannot monsieur sleep in a coach?" asked the doctor.

"Oh, yes, sir," replied the compatriot of Jean-Jacques; "on the contrary, I usually sleep straight through the night. But anxiety was stronger than fatigue this time."

"Were you afraid of upsetting?" asked the architect.

"No. I'm very lucky in that respect; it seems enough for me to be in a coach to make it unupsettable. No, that wasn't it."

"What was it, then?" questioned the doctor.

"They say in Geneva that the roads in France are not safe."

"That's according to circumstances," said the architect.

"Ah! how's that?" inquired the watchmaker.

"Oh!" replied the architect; "if, for example, we were carrying government money, we would surely be stopped, or rather we would have been already."

"Do you think so?" queried the watchmaker.

"That has never failed. I don't know how those devils of Companions of Jehu manage to keep so well posted; but they never miss an opportunity."

The doctor nodded affirmatively.

"Ah!" exclaimed the watchmaker, addressing the doctor; "do you think so, too?"

"I do."

"And if you knew there was government money in the coach, would you be so imprudent as to take passage in it?"

"I must admit," replied the doctor, "that I should think twice about it."

"And you, sir?" said the questioner to the architect.

"Oh, I," replied the latter—"as I am on important business, I should have started anyway."

"I am tempted," said the watchmaker, "to take off my valise and my cases, and wait for to-morrow's diligence, because my boxes are filled with watches worth something like twenty thousand francs. We've been lucky so far, but there's no use tempting Providence."

"Did you not hear these gentlemen say," remarked the

lady, joining in the conversation for the first time, "that we run the risk of being stopped only when the coach carries government money?"

"That's exactly it," replied the watchmaker, looking anxiously around. "We are carrying it."

The mother blanched visibly and looked at her son. Before fearing for herself every mother fears for her child.

"What! we are carrying it?" asked the doctor and the architect in varying tones of excitement. "Are you sure of what you are saying?"

"Perfectly sure, gentlemen."

"Then you should either have told us before, or have told us in a whisper now."

"But perhaps," said the doctor, "the gentleman is not quite sure of what he says."

"Or perhaps he is joking," added the architect.

"Heaven forbid!"

"The Genevese are very fond of a laugh," persisted the doctor.

"Sir," replied the Genevese, much hurt that any one should think he liked to laugh, "I saw it put on the coach myself."

"What?"

"The money."

"Was there much?"

"A good many bags."

"But where does the money come from?"

"The treasury of the bears of Berne. You know, of course, that the bears of Berne received an income of fifty or even sixty thousand francs."

The doctor burst out laughing.

"Decidedly, sir, you are trying to frighten us," said he.

"Gentlemen," said the watchmaker, "I give you my word of honor—"

"Take your places, gentlemen," shouted the conductor, opening the door. "Take your places! We are three-quarters of an hour late."

"One moment, conductor, one moment," said the architect; "we are consulting."

"About what?"

"Close the door, conductor, and come over here."

"Drink a glass of wine with us, conductor."

"With pleasure, gentlemen; a glass of wine is never to be refused."

The conductor held out his glass, and the three travellers touched it; but just as he was lifting it to his lips the doctor stopped his arm.

"Come, conductor, frankly, is it true?"

"What?"

"What this gentleman says?" And he pointed to the Genevese.

"Monsieur Féraud?"

"I don't know if that is his name."

"Yes, sir, that is my name—Féraud & Company, No. 6 Rue du Rempart, Geneva, at your service," replied the watchmaker, bowing.

"Gentlemen," repeated the conductor, "take your places!"

"But you haven't answered."

"What the devil shall I answer? You haven't asked me anything."

"Yes, we asked you if it is true that you are carrying a large sum of money belonging to the French Government?"

"Blabber!" said the conductor to the watchmaker, "did you tell that?"

"Confound it, my worthy fellow—"

"Come, gentlemen, your places."

"But before getting in we want to know—"

"What? Whether I have government money? Yes I have. Now, if we are stopped, say nothing and all will be well."

"Are you sure?"

"Leave me to arrange matters with these gentry."

"What will you do if we are stopped?" the doctor asked the architect.

"Faith! I shall follow the conductor's advice."

"That's the best thing to do," observed the latter.

"Well, I shall keep quiet," repeated the architect.

"And so shall I," added the watchmaker.

"Come, gentlemen, take your seats, and let us make haste."

The boy had listened to this conversation with frowning brow and clinched teeth.

"Well," he said to his mother, "if we are stopped, I know what I'll do."

"What will you do?" she asked.

"You'll see."

"What does this little boy say?" asked the watchmaker.

"I say you are all cowards," replied the child unhesitatingly.

"Edouard!" exclaimed his mother, "what do you mean?"

"I wish they'd stop the diligence, that I do!" cried the boy, his eye sparkling with determination.

"Come, come, gentlemen, in Heaven's name, take your places," called the conductor once more.

"Conductor," said the doctor, "I presume you have no weapons!"

"Yes, I have my pistols."

"Unfortunate!"

The conductor stooped to the doctor's ear and whispered: "Don't be alarmed, doctor; they're only loaded with powder."

"Good!"

"Forward, postilion, forward!" shouted the conductor, closing the door of the interior. Then, while the postilion snapped his whip and started the heavy vehicle, he also closed that of the coupé.

"Are you not coming with us, conductor?" asked the lady.

"Thank you, no, Madame de Montrevel," replied the conductor; "I have something to do on the imperial." Then, looking into the window, he added: "Take care the Monsieur Edouard does not touch the pistols in the pocket of the carriage; he might hurt himself."

"Pooh!" retorted the boy, "as if I didn't know how to handle a pistol. I have handsomer ones than yours, that my friend Sir John had sent me from England; haven't I, mamma?"

"Never mind, Edouard," replied Madame de Montrevel, "I entreat you not to touch them."

"Don't worry, little mother." Then he added softly, "All the same, if the Companions of Jehu stop us, I know what I shall do."

The diligence was again rolling heavily on its way to Paris.

It was one of those fine winter days which makes those who think that nature is dead at that season admit that nature never dies but only sleeps. The man who lives to be seventy or eighty years of age has his nights of ten or twelve hours, and often complains that the length of his nights adds to the shortness of his days. Nature, which has an everlasting existence; trees, which live a thousand years; have sleeping periods of four or five months, which are winters for us but only nights for them. The poets, in their envious verse, sing the immortality of nature, which dies each autumn and revives each spring. The poets are mistaken; nature does not die each autumn, she only falls asleep; she is not resuscitated, she awakens. The day when our globe really dies, it will be dead indeed. Then it will roll into space or fall into the abysses of chaos, inert, mute, solitary, without trees, without flowers, without verdure, without poets.

But on this beautiful day of the 23d of February, 1800, sleeping nature dreamed of spring; a brilliant, almost joyous sun made the grass in the ditches on either side of the road sparkle with those deceptive pearls of the hoarfrost which vanish at a touch, and rejoice the heart of a tiller of the earth when he sees them glittering at the points of his wheat as it pushes bravely up through the soil. All the windows of the diligence were lowered, to give entrance to this earliest smile of the Divine, as though all hearts were saying: "Welcome back, traveller long lost in the clouds of the West, or beneath the heaving billows of Ocean!"

Suddenly, about an hour after leaving Châtillon, the diligence stopped at a bend of the river without any apparent cause. Four horsemen quietly approached, walking their horses, and one of them, a little in advance of the others, made a sign with his hand to the postilion, ordering him to draw up. The postilion obeyed.

"Oh, mamma!" cried Edouard, standing up and leaning out of the window in spite of Madame de Montrevel's protestations; "oh, mamma, what fine horses! But why do these gentlemen wear masks? This isn't carnival."

Madame de Montrevel was dreaming. A woman always dreams a little; young, of the future; old, of the past. She started from her revery, put her head out of the window, and gave a little cry.

Edouard turned around hastily.

"What ails you, mother?" he asked.

Madame de Montrevel turned pale and took him in her arms without a word. Cries of terror were heard in the interior.

"But what is the matter?" demanded little Edouard, struggling to escape from his mother's encircling arms.

"Nothing, my little man," said one of the masked men in a gentle voice, putting his head through the window of the coupé; "nothing but an account we have to settle with the conductor, which does not in the least concern you travellers. Tell your mother to accept our respectful homage, and to pay no more heed to us than if we were not here." Then passing to the door of the interior, he added: "Gentlemen, your servant. Fear nothing for your money or jewels, and reassure that nurse—we have not come here to turn her milk.'' Then to the conductor: "Now, then, Père Jérôme, we have a hundred thousand francs on the imperial and in the boxes, haven't we?"

"Gentlemen, I assure you—"

"That the money belongs to the government. It did belong to the bears of Berne; seventy thousand francs in gold, the rest in silver. The silver is on the top of the coach, the gold in the bottom of the coupé. Isn't that so? You see how well informed we are."

At the words "bottom of the coupé" Madame de Montrevel gave another cry of terror; she was about to come in contact with men who, in spite of their politeness, inspired her with the most profound terror.

"But what is the matter, mother, what is the matter?" demanded the boy impatiently.

"Be quiet, Edouard; be quiet!"

"Why must I be quiet?"

"Don't you understand?"

"No."

"The coach has been stopped."

"Why? Tell me why? Ah, mother, I understand."

"No, no," said Madame de Montrevel, "you don't understand."

"Those gentlemen are robbers."

"Take care you don't say so."

"What, you mean they are not robbers? Why, see they are taking the conductor's money."

Sure enough, one of the four was fastening to the saddle of his horse the bags of silver which the conductor threw down from the imperial.

"No," repeated Madame de Montrevel, "no, they are not robbers." Then lowering her voice, she added: "They are Companions of Jehu."

"Ah!" cried the boy, "they are the ones who assassinated my friend, Sir John."

And the child turned very pale, and his breath came hissing through his clinched teeth.

At that moment one of the masked men opened the door of the coupé, and said with exquisite politeness: "Madame la Comtesse, to our great regret we are obliged to disturb you; but we want, or rather the conductor wants, a package from the bottom of the coupé. Will you be so kind as to get out for a moment? Jérôme will get what he wants as quickly as possible." Then, with that note of gayety which was never entirely absent from that laughing voice, he added, "Won't you, Jérôme?"

Jérôme replied from the top of the diligence, confirming these words.

With an instinctive movement to put herself between the danger and her son, Madame de Montrevel, while complying with that request, pushed Edouard behind her. That instant sufficed for the boy to seize the conductor's pistols.

The young man with the laughing voice assisted Madame de Montrevel from the coach with the greatest care, then signed to one of his companions to give her an arm, and returned to the coach.

But at that instant a double report was heard. Edouard had fired a pistol with each hand at the Companion of Jehu, who disappeared in the smoke.

Madame de Montrevel screamed, and fainted away. Various cries, expressive of diverse sentiments, echoed that of the mother.

From the interior came one of terror; they had all agreed to offer no resistance, and now some one had resisted. From the three young men came a cry of surprise—it was the first time such a thing had happened.

They rushed to their companion, expecting to find him reduced to pulp; but they found him safe and sound, laughing heartily, while the conductor, with clasped hands, was exclaiming: "Monsieur, I swear there were no balls; monsieur, I protest, they were only charged with powder."

"The deuce," said the young man, "don't I see that? But the intention was good, wasn't it, my little Edouard?" Then, turning to his companions, he added: "Confess, gentlemen, that he is a fine boy—a true son of his father, and brother of his brother. Bravo, Edouard! you'll make a man some day!"

Taking the boy in his arms, he kissed him, in spite of his struggles, on both cheeks.

Edouard fought like a demon, thinking no doubt that it was very humiliating to be embraced by a man at whom he had just fired two pistols.

In the meantime one of the Companions had carried Edouard's mother to the bank by the roadside a little distance from the diligence. The man who had kissed Edouard with so much affection and persistence now looked around for her.

"Ah!" cried he, on perceiving her, "Madame de Montrevel still unconscious? We can't leave a woman in that condition, gentlemen. Conductor, take Master Edouard." Placing the boy in Jérôme's arms, he turned to one of his companions: "Man of precautions," said he, "haven't you smelling salts or a bottle of essence with you?"

"Here!" said the young man he had addressed, pulling a flask of toilet vinegar from his pocket.

"Good," said the other, who seemed to be the leader of the band. "Do you finish up the matter with Master Jérôme; I'll take charge of Madame de Montrevel."

It was indeed time. The fainting fit was giving place to a violent nervous attack; spasmodic movements shook her whole body and strangled cries came from her throat.

The young man leaned over her and made her inhale the salts.

Madame de Montrevel presently opened her frightened eyes, and called out: "Edouard! Edouard!" With an involuntary movement she knocked aside the mask of the man who was supporting her, exposing his face.

The courteous, laughing young man—our readers have already recognized him—was Morgan.

Madame de Montrevel paused in amazement at sight of those beautiful blue eyes, the lofty brow, and the gracious lips smiling at her. She realized that she ran no danger

from such a man, and that no harm could have befallen
Edouard. Treating Morgan as a gentleman who had suc-
cored her, and not as a bandit who had caused her fainting-
fit, she exclaimed: "Ah, sir! how kind you are."

In the words, in the tones in which she uttered them,
there lay a world of thanks, not only for herself, but for
her child.

With singular delicacy, entirely in keeping with his chivalric nature, Morgan, instead of picking up his fallen mask
and covering his face immediately, so that Madame de Montrevel could only have retained a fleeting and confused impression of it—Morgan replied to her compliment by a low
bow, leaving his features uncovered long enough to produce
their impression; then, placing d'Assas' flask in Madame de
Montrevel's hand—and then only—he replaced his mask.
Madame de Montrevel understood the young man's delicacy.

"Ah! sir," said she, "be sure that, in whatever place or
situation I see you again, I shall not recognize you."

"Then, madame," replied Morgan, "it is for me to
thank you and repeat, 'How kind you are.' "

"Come, gentlemen, take your seats!" said the conductor, in his customary tone, as if nothing unusual had
happened.

"Are you quite restored, madame, or should you like a
few minutes more to rest?" asked Morgan. "The diligence
shall wait."

"No, that is quite unnecessary; I feel quite well, and am
much indebted to you."

Morgan offered Madame de Montrevel his arm, and she
leaned upon it to reach the diligence. The conductor had
already placed little Edouard inside. When Madame de
Mortrevel had resumed her seat, Morgan, who had already
made his peace with the mother, wished to do so with the
son.

"Without a grudge, my young hero," he said, offering
his hand.

But the boy drew back.

"I don't give my hand to a highway robber," he replied.

Madame de Montrevel gave a start of terror.

"You have a charming boy, madame," said Morgan; "only he has his prejudices." Then, bowing with the utmost courtesy, he added, "A prosperous voyage, madame," and closed the door.

"Forward!" cried the conductor.

The carriage gave a lurch.

"Oh! pardon me, sir!" exclaimed Madame de Montrevel; "your flask!"

"Keep it, madame," said Morgan; "although I trust you are sufficiently recovered not to need it."

But Edouard, snatching the flask from his mother's hands, flung it out of the window, crying: "Mamma doesn't receive presents from robbers."

"The devil!" murmured Morgan, with the first sigh his Companions had ever heard him give. "I think I am right not to ask for my poor Amélie in marriage." Then, turning to his Companions, he said: "Well, gentlemen, is it finished?"

"Yes," they answered with one voice.

"Then let us mount and be off. Don't forget we have to be at the Opera at nine o'clock this evening."

Springing into his saddle, he was the first to jump the ditch, reach the river, and there unhesitatingly took the ford which the pretended courier had pointed out on Cassini's map.

When he reached the opposite bank, followed by the other young men, d'Assas said to him: "Say, didn't your mask fall off?"

"Yes; but no one saw my face but Madame de Montrevel."

"Hum!" muttered d'Assas. "Better no one had seen it."

Putting their horses to a gallop, all four disappeared across the fields in the direction of Chacource.

CHAPTER XXX

CITIZEN FOUCHÉ'S REPORT

ON ARRIVING the next day, toward eleven in the morning, at the Hôtel des Ambassadeurs, Madame de Montrevel was astonished to find, instead of Roland, a stranger awaiting her. The stranger approached her.

"Are you the widow of General de Montrevel, madame?" he asked.

"Yes, monsieur," replied Madame de Montrevel, not a little astonished.

"And you are looking for your son?"

"Yes; and I do not understand, after the letter he wrote me—"

"Man proposes, the First Consul disposes," replied the stranger, laughing. "The First Consul has disposed of your son for a few days, and has sent me to receive you in his stead."

Madame de Montrevel bowed.

"To whom have I the honor of speaking?" she asked.

"To citizen Fauvelet de Bourrienne, his first secretary," replied the stranger.

"Will you thank the First Consul for me," replied Madame de Montrevel, "and have the kindness to express to him the profound regret I feel at not being able to do so myself?"

"But nothing can be more easy, madame."

"How so?"

"The First Consul has ordered me to bring you to the Luxembourg."

"Me?"

"You and your son."

"Oh! I am going to see General Bonaparte; I am going to see General Bonaparte!" cried the child, jumping for joy and clapping his hands. "What happiness!"

"Edouard, Edouard!" exclaimed Madame de Montrevel. Then, turning to Bourrienne, "You must excuse him, sir; he is a little savage from the Jura Mountains."

Bourrienne held out his hand to the boy.

"I am a friend of your brother's," said he. "Will you ki s me?"

"Oh! willingly, sir," replied Edouard. "You are not a th'ef, I know."

"Why, no; I trust not," replied the secretary, laughing.

"You must excuse him once again, sir. Our diligence was stopped on the way."

"Stopped?"

"Yes."

"By robbers?"

"Not exactly."

"Monsieur," asked Edouard, "when people take other people's money, are they not thieves?"

"That is what they are generally called, my dear child."

"There, you see, mamma."

"Come, Edouard, be quiet, I beg of you."

Bourrienne glanced at Madame de Montrevel, and saw clearly from the expression of her face that the subject was disagreeable to her; he therefore dropped it.

"Madame," said he, "may I remind you that I have orders to take you to the Luxembourg, and to add that Madame Bonaparte is expecting you?"

"Pray give me time to change my gown and to dress Edouard, sir."

"How long will that take, madame?"

"Is half an hour too much to ask?"

"No, indeed; if half an hour really suffices I shall think you most reasonable."

"Be easy, sir; it will be sufficient."

"Well, madame," said the secretary, bowing, "I will attend to an errand, and return in half an hour to place myself at your orders."

"Thank you, sir."

"Don't be annoyed if I should be punctual."

"I shall not keep you waiting."

Bourrienne left. Madame de Montrevel dressed Edouard first, then herself, and was ready five minutes before Bourrienne reappeared.

"Take care, madame," said Bourrienne laughing, "lest I tell the First Consul of your extreme punctuality."

"What should I have to fear if you did?"

"He would keep you near him to give lessons in punctuality to Madame Bonaparte."

"Oh!" exclaimed Madame de Montrevel, "you must forgive unpunctuality in a Creole."

"But I believe you are a Creole also, madame."

"Madame Bonaparte sees her husband every day," said Madame de Montrevel, laughing, "whereas I am to see the First Consul for the first time."

"Come, mother, let us go!" said Edouard.

The secretary drew aside to allow Madame de Montrevel to pass out. Fifteen minutes later they had reached the Luxembourg.

Bonaparte occupied the suite of rooms on the ground floor to the right. Josephine's chamber and boudoir were on the first floor; a stairway led from the First Consul's study to her room.

She was expecting Madame de Montrevel, for as soon as she saw her she opened her arms as to a friend. Madame de Montrevel had stopped respectfully at the door.

"Oh! come in, come in, madame!" said Josephine. "To-day is not the first that I know you; I have long known you through your excellent son, Roland. Shall I tell you what comforts me when Bonaparte leaves me? It is that Roland goes with him; for I fancy that, so long as Roland is with him, no harm will befall him. Well, won't you kiss me?"

Madame de Montrevel was confused by so much kindness.

"We are compatriots, you know," continued Josephine. "Oh! how well I remember M. de la Clémencière, and his beautiful gardens with the splendid fruit. I remember having seen a young girl who seemed its queen. You must have married very young, madame?"

"At fourteen."

"Yes, you could not have been older to have a son of Roland's age. But pray sit down."

She led the way, making a sign to Madame de Montrevel to sit beside her.

"And that charming boy," she said, pointing to Edouard, "is he also your son?" And she gave a sigh. "God has been prodigal to you, madame, and as He has given you all you can desire, will you not implore Him to send me a son."

She pressed her lips enviously to Edouard's forehead.

"My husband will be delighted to see you, he is so fond of your son, madame! You would not have been brought to me in the first instance, if he were not engaged with the minister of police. For that matter," she added, laughing, "you have arrived at an unfortunate moment; he is furious!"

"Oh!" cried Madame de Montrevel, frightened; "if that is so, I would rather wait."

"No, no! On the contrary, the sight of you will calm him. I don't know just what is the matter; but it seems a diligence was stopped on the outskirts of the Black Forest in broad daylight. Fouché will find his credit in danger if the thing goes on."

Madame de Montrevel was about to answer when the door opened and an usher appeared.

"The First Consul awaits Madame de Montrevel," he said.

"Go," said Josephine; "Bonaparte's time is so precious that he is almost as impatient as Louis XV., who had nothing to do. He does not like to wait."

Madame de Montrevel rose hastily and turned to take Edouard with her.

"No," said Josephine; "leave this beautiful boy with me. You will stay and dine with us, and Bonaparte can see him then. Besides, if my husband takes a fancy to see him, he can send for him. For the time, I am his second mamma. Come, what shall we do to amuse ourselves?"

"The First Consul must have a fine lot of weapons, madame," replied the boy.

"Yes, very fine ones. Well, I will show you the First Consul's arms."

Josephine, leading the child, went out of one door, and Madame de Montrevel followed the usher through the other.

On the way the countess met a fair man, with a pale face and haggard eye, who looked at her with an uneasiness that seemed habitual to him. She drew hastily aside to let him pass. The usher noticed her movement.

"That is the minister of police," he said in a low voice.

Madame de Montrevel watched him as he disappeared, with a certain curiosity. Fouché was already at that time fatally celebrated. Just then the door of Bonaparte's study opened and his head was seen through the aperture. He caught sight of Madame de Montrevel.

"Come in, madame," he said; "come in."

Madame de Montrevel hastened her steps and entered the study.

"Come in," said Bonaparte, closing the door himself. "I have kept you waiting much against my will; but I had to give Fouché a scolding. You know I am very well satisfied with Roland, and that I intend to make a general of him at the first opportunity. When did you arrive?"

"This very moment, general."

"Where from? Roland told me, but I have forgotten."

"From Bourg."

"What road?"

"Through Champagne."

"Champagne! Then when did you reach Châtillon?"

"Yesterday morning at nine o'clock."

"In that case, you must have heard of the stoppage of the diligence."

"General—"

"Yes, a diligence was stopped at ten in the morning, between Châtillon and Bar-sur-Seine."

"General, it was ours."

"Yours?"

"Yes."

"You were in the diligence that was stopped?"

"I was."

"Ah! now I shall get the exact details! Excuse me, but you understand my desire for correct information, don't you? In a civilized country which has General Bonaparte for its chief magistrate, diligences can't be stopped in broad daylight on the highroads with impunity, or—"

"General, I can tell you nothing, except that those who stopped it were on horseback and masked."

"How many were there?"

"Four."

"How many men were there in the diligence?"

"Four, including the conductor."

"And they didn't defend themselves?"

"No, general."

"The police report says, however, that two shots were fired."

"Yes, general, but those two shots—"

"Well?"

"Were fired by my son."

"Your son? Why, he is in Vendée!"

"Roland, yes; but Edouard was with me."

"Edouard! Who is Edouard?"

"Roland's brother."

"True, he spoke of him; but he is only a child."

"He is not yet twelve, general."

"And it was he who fired the two shots?"

"Yes, general."

"Why didn't you bring him with you?"

"I did."

"Where is he?"

"I left him with Madame Bonaparte."

Bonaparte rang, and an usher appeared.

"Tell Josephine to bring the boy to me." Then, walking up and down his study, he muttered, "Four men! And a child taught them courage! Were any of the robbers wounded?"

"There were no balls in the pistols."

"What! no balls?"

"No; they belonged to the conductor, and he had taken the precaution to load them with powder only."

"Very good; his name shall be known."

Just then the door opened, and Madame Bonaparte entered, leading the boy by the hand.

"Come here," Bonaparte said to him.

Edouard went up to him without hesitation and made a military salute.

"So you fired at the robbers twice, did you?"

"There, you see, mamma, they were robbers!" interrupted the child.

"Of course they were robbers; I should like to hear any one declare they were not! Was it you who fired at them, when the men were afraid?"

"Yes, it was I, general. But unfortunately that coward of a conductor had loaded his pistols only with powder; otherwise I should have killed their leader."

"Then you were not afraid?"

"I?" replied the boy. "No, I am never afraid."

"You ought to be named Cornelia, madame," exclaimed Bonaparte, turning to Madame de Montrevel, who was leaning on Josephine's arm. Then he said to the child, kissing him: "Very good; we will take care of you. What would you like to be?"

"Soldier first."

"What do you mean by first?"

"Why, first a soldier, then later a colonel like my brother, and then a general like my father."

"It won't be my fault if you are not," answered the First Consul.

"Nor mine," retorted the boy.

"Edouard!" exclaimed Madame de Montrevel, timidly.

"Now don't scold him for answering properly;" and Bonaparte, lifting the child to the level of his face, kissed him.

"You must dine with us," said he, "and to-night Bourrienne, who met you at the hotel, will install you in the Rue de la Victoire. You must stay there till Roland gets back; he will then find you suitable lodgings. Edouard shall go to the Prytanée, and I will marry off your daughter."

"General!"

"That's all settled with Roland." Then, turning to Josephine, he said: "Take Madame de Montrevel with you, and try not to let her be bored.—And, Madame de Montrevel, if *your friend* (he emphasized the words) wishes to go to a milliner, prevent it; she can't want bonnets, for she bought thirty-eight last month."

Then, giving Edouard a friendly tap, he dismissed the two women with a wave of the hand.

CHAPTER XXXI

THE SON OF THE MILLER OF LEGUERNO

WE HAVE said that at the very moment when Morgan and his three companions stopped the Geneva diligence between Bar-sur-Seine and Châtillon, Roland was entering Nantes.

If we are to know the result of his mission we must not grope our way, step by step, through the darkness in which the Abbé Bernier wrapped his ambitious projects, but we must join him later at the village of Muzillac, between

Ambon and Guernic, six miles above the little bay into which the Vilaine River falls.

There we find ourselves in the heart of the Morbihan; that is to say, in the region that gave birth to the Chouan-nerie. It was close to Laval, on the little farm of the Poiriers, that the four Chouan brothers were born to Pierre Cottereau and Jeanne Moyné. One of their ances-tors, a misanthropical woodcutter, a morose peasant, kept himself aloof from the other peasants as the *chat-huant* (screech-owl) keeps aloof from the other birds; hence the name Chouan, a corruption of *chat-huant.*

The name became that of a party. On the right bank of the Loire they said Chouans when they meant Bretons, just as on the left bank they said brigands when they meant Vendéans.

It is not for us to relate the death and destruction of that heroic family, nor follow to the scaffold the two sisters and a brother, nor tell of battlefields where Jean and René, martyrs to their faith, lay dying or dead. Many years have elapsed since the executions of Perrine, René and Pierre, and the death of Jean; and the martyrdom of the sisters, the exploits of the brothers have passed into legends. We have now to do with their successors.

It is true that these gars (lads) are faithful to their tradi-tions. As they fought beside la Rouërie, Bois-Hardy and Bernard de Villeneuve, so did they fight beside Bourmont, Frotté, and Georges Cadoudal. Theirs was always the same courage, the same devotion—that of the Christian soldier, the faithful royalist. Their aspect is always the same, rough and savage; their weapons, the same gun or cudgel, called in those parts a "ferte." Their garments are the same; a brown woollen cap, or a broad-brimmed hat scarcely covering the long straight hair that fell in tangles on their shoulders, the old *Aulerci Cenomani*, as in Cæsar's day, *promisso capillo;* they are the same Bretons with wide breeches of whom Martial said:

> *Tam laxa est . . .*
> *Quam veteres braccæ Britonis pauperis.*

To protect themselves from rain and cold they wore goatskin garments, made with the long hair turned outside; on the breasts of which, as countersign, some wore a scapulary and chaplet, others a heart, the heart of Jesus; this latter was the distinctive sign of a fraternity which withdrew apart each day for common prayer.

Such were the men, who, at the time we are crossing the borderland between the Loire-Inférieure and Morbihan, were scattered from La Roche-Bernard to Vannes, and from Quertemberg to Billiers, surrounding consequently the village of Muzillac.

But it needed the eye of the eagle soaring in the clouds, or that of the screech-owl piercing the darkness, to distinguish these men among the gorse and heather and underbrush where they were crouching.

Let us pass through this network of invisible sentinels, and after fording two streams, the affluents of a nameless river which flows into the sea near Billiers, between Arzal and Dangau, let us boldly enter the village of Muzillac.

All is still and sombre; a single light shines through the blinds of a house, or rather a cottage, which nothing distinguishes from its fellows. It is the fourth to the right on entering the village.

Let us put our eye to one of these chinks and look in.

We see a man dressed like the rich peasants of Morbihan, except that gold lace about a finger wide stripes the collar and buttonholes of his coat and also the edges of his hat. The rest of his dress consists of leathern trousers and high-topped boots. His sword is thrown upon a chair. A brace of pistols lies within reach of his hand. Within the fireplace the barrels of two or three muskets reflect the light of a blazing fire.

The man is seated before a table; a lamp lights some papers which he is reading with great attention, and illuminates his face at the same time.

The face is that of a man of thirty. When the cares of a partisan warfare do not darken it, its expression must surely be frank and joyous. Beautiful blond hair frames it; great blue eyes enliven it; the head, of a shape peculiarly Breton, seems to show, if we believe in Gall's system, an exaggerated development of the organs of self-will. And the man has two names. That by which he is known to his soldiers, his familiar name, is Round-head; and his real name, received from brave and worthy parents, Georges Cadudal, or rather Cadoudal, tradition having changed the orthography of a name that is now historic.

Georges was the son of a farmer of the parish of Kerléano in the commune of Brech. The story goes that this farmer was once a miller. Georges had just received at the college of Vannes—distant only a few leagues from Brech —a good and solid education when the first appeals for a royalist insurrection were made in Vendée. Cadoudal listened to them, gathered together a number of his companions, and offered his services to Stofflet. But Stofflet insisted on seeing him at work before he accepted him. Georges asked nothing better. Such occasions were not long to seek in the Vendéan army. On the next day there was a battle; Georges went into it with such determination and made so desperate a rush that M. de Maulevrier's former huntsman, on seeing him charge the Blues, could not refrain from saying aloud to Bonchamp, who was near him:

"If a cannon ball doesn't take off that *Big Round Head*, it will roll far, I warrant you."

The name clung to Cadoudal—a name by which, five centuries earlier, the lords of Malestroit, Penhoël, Beaumanoir and Rochefort designated the great Constable, whose ransom was spun by the women of Brittany.

"There's the Big Round Head," said they; "now we'll exchange some good sword-play with the English."

Unfortunately, at this time it was not Breton swordthrusts against English, but Frenchmen against Frenchmen.

Georges remained in Vendée until after the defeat of Savenay. The whole Vendéan army was either left upon the battlefield or vanished in smoke. For three years,

Georges had performed prodigies of valor, strength and dexterity; he now crossed the Loire and re-entered Morbihan with only one man left of all who had followed him.

That man became his aide-de-camp, or rather his brother-in-arms. He never left him, and in memory of the hard campaign they had made together he changed his name from Lemercier to Tiffauges. We have seen him at the ball of the Victims charged with a message to Morgan.

As soon as Cadoudal returned to his own part of the country, he fomented insurrection on his own responsibility. Bullets respected that big round head, and the big round head justified Stofflet's prediction. He succeeded La Rochejacquelin, d'Elbée, Bonchamp, Lescure, even Stofflet himself, and became their rival for fame, their superior in power; for it happened (and this will give an idea of his strength) that Cadoudal, almost single-handed, had been able to resist the government of Bonaparte, who had been First Consul for the last three months. The two leaders who continued with him, faithful to the Bourbon dynasty, were Frotté and Bourmont.

At the time of which we are now speaking, that is to say, the 26th of January, 1800, Cadoudal commanded three or four thousand men with whom he was preparing to blockade General Hatry in Vannes.

During the time that he awaited the First Consul's answer to the letter of Louis XVIII. he had suspended hostilities; but Tiffauges had arrived a couple of days before with it.

That letter was already on the way to England, whence it would be sent to Mittau; and since the First Consul would not accept peace on the terms dictated by Louis XVIII., Cadoudal, commander-in-chief of Louis XVIII. in the West, renewed his warfare against Bonaparte, intending to carry it on alone, if necessary, with his friend Tiffauges. For the rest, the latter was at Pouancé, where conferences were being held between Châtillon, d'Autichamp, the Abbé Bernier, and General Hédouville.

He was reflecting—this last survivor of the great warriors

of the civil war—and the news he had just received was indeed a matter for deep reflection.

General Brune, the conqueror of Alkmaar and Castricum, the savior of Holland, had just been appointed to the command of the Republican forces in the West. He had reached Nantes three days previous, intending, at any cost, to annihilate Cadoudal and his Chouans.

At any cost, therefore, Cadoudal and his Chouans must prove to the commander-in-chief that they knew no fear, and had nothing to expect from intimidation.

Just then the gallop of a horse was heard; the rider no doubt had the countersign, for he passed without difficulty the various patrols stationed along the road to La Roche-Bernard, and entered the village of Muzillac, also without difficulty.

He stopped before the door of the cottage in which Georges was sitting. The latter raised his head, listened, and, by way of precaution, laid his hands on his pistols, though it was probable that the new-comer was a friend.

The rider dismounted, strode up the path, and opened the door of the room where Georges was waiting.

"Ah! it's you, Cœur-de-Roi," said Cadoudal. "Where do you come from?"

"From Pouancé, general."

"What news?"

"A letter from Tiffauges."

"Give it to me."

Georges snatched the letter hastily from Cœur-de-Roi's hand and read it.

"Ah!" he exclaimed.

Then he read it a second time.

"Have you seen the man whose coming he speaks of?" inquired Cadoudal.

"Yes, general," replied the courier.

"What sort of a man is he?"

"A handsome young fellow of twenty-six or seven."

"What manner?"

"Determined."

"That's it. When does he arrive?"

"Probably to-night."

"Did you safe-guard him along the road?"

"Yes; he'll come safely."

"Do it again. Nothing must happen to him; he is protected by Morgan."

"That's understood, general."

"Anything more to say?"

"The advanced guard of the Republicans has reached La Roche-Bernard."

"How many men?"

"About a thousand. They have a guillotine with them, and the commissioner of the executive power, Millière."

"Are you sure?"

"I met them on the road. The commissioner was riding near the colonel, and I recognized him perfectly. He executed my brother, and I have sworn he shall die by my own hand."

"And you'll risk your life to keep your oath?"

"At the first opportunity."

"Perhaps it won't be long coming."

The gallop of a horse echoed through the street.

"Ah!" said Cœur-de-Roi, "that is probably the man you expect."

"No," replied Cadoudal, "this rider comes from the direction of Vannes."

The sound became more distinct, and it proved that Cadoudal was right.

The second horseman, like the first, halted at the gate, dismounted, and came into the room. The royalist leader recognized him at once, in spite of the large cloak in which he was wrapped.

"Is it you, Bénédicité?" he asked.

"Yes, general."

"Where do you come from?"

"From Vannes, where you sent me to watch the Blues."

"Well, what are the Blues doing?"

"Scaring themselves about dying of hunger if you blockade the town. In order to procure provisions General Hatry intends to carry off the supplies at Grandchamp. The general is to command the raid in person; and, to act more quickly, only a hundred men are to go."

"Are you tired, Bénédicité?"

"Never, general."

"And your horse?"

"He came fast, but he can do twelve or fifteen miles more without killing himself."

"Give him two hours' rest, a double feed of oats, and make him do thirty."

"On those conditions he can do them."

"Start in two hours. Be at Grandchamp by daybreak. Give the order in my name to evacuate the village. I'll take care of General Hatry and his column. Is that all you have to say?"

"No, I heard other news."

"What is it?"

"That Vannes has a new bishop."

"Ha! so they are giving us back our bishops?"

"So it seems; but if they are all like this one, they can keep them."

"Who is he?"

"Audrein!"

"The regicide?"

"Audrein the renegade."

"When is he coming?"

"To-night or to-morrow."

"I shall not go to meet him; but let him beware of falling into my men's hands."

Bénédicité and Cœur-de-Roi burst into a laugh which completed Cadoudal's thought.

"Hush!" cried Cadoudal.

The three men listened.

"This time it is probably he," observed Georges.

The gallop of a horse could be heard coming from the direction of La Roche-Bernard.

"It is certainly he," repeated Cœur-de-Roi.

"Then, my friends, leave me alone. You, Bénédicité, get to Grandchamp as soon as possible. You, Cœur-de-Roi, post thirty men in the courtyard; I want messengers to send in different directions. By the way, tell some one to bring the best that can be got for supper in the village."

"For how many, general?"

"Oh! two."

"Are you going out?"

"No, only to meet the man who is coming."

Two or three men had already taken the horses of the messengers into the courtyard. The messengers themselves disappeared.

Georges reached the gate on the street just as a horseman, pulling up his horse, looked about him and seemed to hesitate.

"He is here, sir," said Georges.

"Who is here?"

"He whom you seek."

"How do you know whom I am seeking?"

"I presume it is Georges Cadoudal, otherwise called Round-head."

"Exactly."

"Then I bid you welcome, Monsieur Roland de Montrevel, for I am the person you seek."

"Ah, ah!" exclaimed the young man, amazed.

Then, dismounting, he looked about as if for some one to take his mount.

"Throw the bridle over your horse's neck, and don't be uneasy about him. You will find him when you want him. Nothing is ever lost in Brittany; you are in the land of honesty."

The young man made no remark, threw the bridle over his horse's neck as he had been told, and followed Cadoudal, who walked before him.

"Only to show you the way, colonel," said the leader of the Chouans.

They both entered the cottage, where an invisible hand had just made up the fire.

CHAPTER XXXII

WHITE AND BLUE

ROLAND entered, as we have said, behind Georges, and as he entered cast a glance of careless curiosity around him. That glance sufficed to show him that they were alone.

"Are these your quarters, general?" asked Roland with a smile, turning the soles of his boots to the blaze.

"Yes, colonel."

"They are singularly guarded."

Georges smiled in turn.

"Do you say that because you found the road open from La Roche-Bernard here?" he asked.

"I did not meet a soul."

"That does not prove that the road was not guarded."

"Unless by the owls, who seemed to fly from tree to tree, and accompanied me all the way, general. In that case, I withdraw my assertion."

"Exactly," replied Cadoudal. "Those owls were my sentinels, sentinels with good eyes, inasmuch as they have this advantage over the eyes of men, they can see in the dark."

"It is not the less true that I was fortunate in having inquired my way at La Roche-Bernard; for I didn't meet even a cat who could have told me where to find you."

"But if you had raised your voice at any spot on the road and asked: 'Where shall I find Georges Cadoudal?' a voice would have answered: 'At the village of Muzillac, fourth house to the right.' You saw no one, colonel; but at that very moment fifteen hundred men, or thereabout, knew that Colonel Roland, the First Consul's aide-de-camp, was on his way to a conference with the son of the miller of Leguerno."

"But if they knew that I was a colonel in the Republican service and aide-de camp to the First Consul, how came they to let me pass?"

"Because they were ordered to do so."

"Then you knew that I was coming?"

"I not only knew that you were coming, but also why you have come."

Roland looked at him fixedly.

"Then it is useless for me to tell you; and you will answer me even though I say nothing?"

"You are about right."

"The deuce! I should like to have a proof of this superiority of your police over ours."

"I will supply it, colonel."

"I shall receive it with much satisfaction, especially before this excellent fire, which also seems to have been expecting me."

"You say truer than you know, colonel; and it is not the fire only that is striving to welcome you warmly."

"Yes, but it does not tell me, any more than you have done, the object of my mission."

"Your mission, which you do me the honor to extend to me, was primarily intended for the Abbé Bernier alone. Unhappily the Abbé Bernier, in the letter he sent his friend Martin Duboys, presumed a little on his strength. He offered his mediation to the First Consul."

"Pardon me," interrupted Roland, "you tell me something I did not know; namely, that the Abbé Bernier had written to General Bonaparte."

"I said he wrote to his friend Martin Duboys, which is very different. My men intercepted the letter and brought it to me. I had it copied, and forwarded the original, which I am certain reached the right hands. Your visit to General Hédouville proves it."

"You know that General Hédouville is no longer in command at Nantes. General Brune has taken his place."

"You may even say that General Brune commands at La Roche-Bernard, for a thousand Republican soldiers entered that town to-night about six o'clock, bringing with them a guillotine and the citizen commissioner-general Thomas Millière. Having the instrument, it was necessary to have the executioner."

"Then you say, general, that I came to see the Abbé Bernier?"

"Yes; the Abbé Bernier had offered his mediation. But he forgot that at the present there are two Vendées—the Vendée of the left bank, and the Vendée of the right bank—and that, after treating with d'Autichamp, Châtillon, and Suzannet at Pouancé, it would still be necessary to negotiate with Frotté, Bourmont and Cadoudal—and where? That no one could tell—"

"Except you, general."

"So, with the chivalry that is the basis of your nature, you undertook to bring me the treaty signed on the 25th. The Abbé Bernier, d'Autichamp, Châtillon, and Suzannet signed your pass, and here you are."

"On my word, general, I must admit that you are perfectly well-informed. The First Consul desires peace with all his heart. He knows that in you he has a brave and honorable adversary, and being unable to meet you himself, since you were not likely to come to Paris, he expedited me to you in his behalf."

"That is to say, to the Abbé Bernier."

"That can hardly matter to you, general, if I bind myself to make the First Consul ratify what may be agreed upon between you and me. What are your conditions of peace?"

"They are very simple, colonel: that the First Consul shall restore his Majesty Louis XVIII. to the throne; that he himself be constable, lieutenant-general, general-in-chief by land and sea, and I his first subordinate."

"The First Consul has already replied to that demand."

"And that is why I have decided to reply myself to his response."

"When?"

"This very night, if occasion offers."

"In what way?"

"By resuming hostilities."

"But are you aware that Châtillon, d'Autichamp and Suzannet have laid down their arms?"

"They are the leaders of the Vendéans, and in the name of the Vendéans they can do as they see fit. I am the leader of the Chouans, and in the name of the Chouans I shall do what suits me."

"Then you condemn this unhappy land to a war of extermination, general!"

"It is a martyrdom to which I summon all Christians and royalists."

"General Brune is at Nantes with the eight thousand prisoners just returned to us by the English after their defeats at Alkmaar and Castricum."

"That is the last time they will have the chance. The Blues have taught us the bad habit of not making prisoners. As for the number of our enemies, we don't care for that; it is a mere detail."

"If General Brune with his eight thousand men, joined to the twenty thousand he has received from General Hédouville, is not sufficient, the First Consul has decided to march against you in person with one hundred thousand men."

Cadoudal smiled.

"We will try to prove to him," he said, "that we are worthy to fight against him."

"He will burn your towns."

"We shall retire to our huts."

"He will burn your huts."

"We will live in the woods."

"Reflect, general."

"Do me the honor to remain here forty-eight hours,

colonel, and you will see that my reflections are already made."

"I am tempted to accept."

"Only, colonel, don't ask for more than I can give; a night's sleep beneath a thatched roof or wrapped in a cloak under an oak tree, a horse to follow me, and a safe-guard when you leave me."

"I accept."

"Have I your word, colonel, that you will not interfere with any orders I give, and will do nothing to defeat the surprises I may attempt?"

"I am too curious to see for that. You have my word, general."

"Whatever takes place before your eyes?"

"Whatever takes place before my eyes. I renounce the rôle of actor and confine myself wholly to that of spectator. I wish to say to the First Consul: 'I have seen.' "

Cadoudal smiled.

"Well, you shall see," said he.

At that moment the door opened, and two peasants brought in a table all laid, on which stood a smoking bowl of cabbage-soup and a piece of lard; an enormous pot of cider, just drawn from the cask, was foaming over the edges of the jug between two glasses. A few buckwheat cakes served as a desert to this modest repast. The table was laid for two.

"You see, Monsieur de Montrevel, that my lads hoped you would do me the honor to sup with me."

"Faith! they were not far wrong. I should have asked for supper, had you not invited me; and I might have been forced to seize some had you not invited me."

"Then fall to!"

The young colonel sat down gayly.

"Excuse the repast I offer you," said Cadoudal; "unlike your generals, I don't make prize money; my soldiers feed me. Have you anything else for us, Brise-Bleu?"

"A chicken fricassee, general."

"That's your dinner, Monsieur de Montrevel."

"A feast! Now, I have but one fear, general."

"What is it?"

"All will go well for the eating, but when it comes to drinking—"

"Don't you like cider? The devil! I'm sorry; cider or water, that's my cellar."

"Oh! that's not it; but whose health are we going to drink?"

"Is that all, sir?" said Cadoudal, with great dignity. "We will drink to the health of our common mother, France. We are serving her with different minds, but, I hope, the same hearts. To *France*, Monsieur," said Cadoudal, filling the two glasses.

"To *France*, general!" replied Roland, clinking his glass against that of Georges.

And both gayly reseated themselves, their consciences at rest, and attacked the soup with appetites that were not yet thirty years old.

CHAPTER XXXIII

THE LAW OF RETALIATION

"NOW, general," said Roland, when supper was over and the two young men, with their elbows on the table and their legs stretched out before the blazing fire, began to feel that comfortable sensation that comes of a meal which youth and appetite have seasoned. "Now for your promise to show me things which I can report to the First Consul."

"You promised, remember, not to object to them."

"Yes, but I reserve the right, in case you wound my conscience too severely, to withdraw."

"Only give time to throw a saddle on the back of your horse, or of mine, if yours is too tired, colonel, and you are free."

"Very good."

"As it happens," said Cadoudal, "events will serve you. I am here, not only as general, but as judge, though it is long since I have had a case to try. You told me, colonel, that General Brune was at Nantes; I knew it. You told me his advanced guard was only twelve miles away, at La Roche-Bernard; I knew that also. But a thing you may not know is that this advanced guard is not commanded by a soldier like you and me, but by citizen Thomas Millière, Commissioner of the Executive authorities. Another thing of which you may perhaps be ignorant is that citizen Thomas Millière does not fight like us with cannon, guns, bayonets, pistols and swords, but with an instrument invented by your Republican philanthropists, called the guillotine."

"It is impossible, sir," cried Roland, "that under the First Consul any one can make that kind of war."

"Ah! let us understand each other, colonel. I don't say that the First Consul makes it; I say it is made in his name."

"And who is the scoundrel that abuses the authority given him, to make war with a staff of executioners?"

"I have told you his name; he is called Thomas Millière. Question whom you please, colonel, and throughout all Vendée and Brittany you'll hear but one voice on that man. From the day of the rising in Vendée and Brittany, now six years ago, Millière has been, always and everywhere, the most active agent of the Terror. For him the Terror did not end with Robespierre. He denounced to his superiors, or caused to be denounced to himself, the Breton and Vendéan soldiers, their parents, friends, brothers, sisters, wives, even the wounded and dying; he shot or guillotined them all without a trial. At Daumeray, for instance, he left a trail of blood behind him which is not yet, can never be, effaced. More than eighty of the inhabitants were slaughtered before his eyes. Sons were killed in the arms of their mothers, who vainly stretched those bloody arms to Heaven imploring vengeance. The successive pacifications of Brittany and Vendée have never slaked the thirst for murder which burns his entrails. He is the same in 1800 that he was in 1793. Well, this man—''

Roland looked at the general.

"This man," continued the general, with the utmost calmness, "is to die. Seeing that society did not condemn him, I have condemned him."

"What! Die at La Roche-Bernard, in the midst of the Republicans; in spite of his bodyguard of assassins and executioners?"

"His hour has struck; he is to die."

Cadoudal pronounced these words with such solemnity that no doubt remained in Roland's mind, not only as to the sentence, but also the execution of it. He was thoughtful for an instant.

"And you believe that you have the right to judge and condemn that man, guilty as he is?"

"Yes; for that man has judged and condemned, not the guilty but the innocent."

"If I said to you: 'On my return to Paris I will demand the arrest and trial of that man,' would you not trust my word?"

"I would trust your word; but I should say to you: 'A maddened wild beast escapes from its cage, a murderer from his prison; men are men, subject to error. They have sometimes condemned the innocent, they might spare the guilty.' My justice is more certain than yours, colonel, for it is the justice of God. The man will die."

"And by what right do you claim that your justice, the justice of a man liable to error like other men, is the justice of God?"

"Because I have made God a sharer in that justice. Oh! my condemnation of that man is not of yesterday."

"How do you mean?"

"In the midst of a storm when thunder roared without cessation, and the lightning flashed from minute to minute,

I raised my arms to heaven, and I said to God: 'O God! whose look is that lightning, whose voice is that thunder, if this man ought to die, extinguish that lightning, still the thunder for ten minutes. The silence of the skies, the darkness of the heavens shall be thy answer!' Watch in hand, I counted eleven minutes without a flash or a sound. I saw at the point of a promontory a boat, tossed by a terrible tempest, a boat with but one man in it, in danger every minute of sinking; a wave lifted it as the breath of an infant lifts a plume, and cast it on the rocks. The boat flew to pieces; the man clung to the rock, and all the people cried out: 'He is lost!' His father was there, his two brothers were there, but none dared to succor him. I raised my arms to the Lord and said: 'If Millière is condemned by Thee as by me, O God, let me save that man; with no help but thine let me save him!' I stripped, I knotted a rope around my arm, and I swam to the rock. The water seemed to subside before my breast. I reached the man. His father and brothers held the rope. He gained the land. I could have returned as he did, fastening the rope to the rocks. I flung it away from me ; I trusted to God and cast myself into the waves. They floated me gently and surely to the shore, even as the waters of the Nile bore Moses' basket to Pharaoh's daughter. The enemy's outposts were stationed around the village of Saint-Nolf; I was hidden in the woods of Grandchamp with fifty men. Recommending my soul to God, I left the woods alone. 'Lord God,' I said, 'if it be Thy will that Millière die, let that sentry fire upon me and miss me; then I will return to my men and leave that sentry unharmed, for Thou wilt have been with him for an instant.' I walked to the Republican; at twenty paces he fired and missed me. Here is the hole in my hat, an inch from my head; the hand of God had aimed that weapon. That happened yesterday. I thought that Millière was at Nantes. To-night they came and told me that Millière and his guillotine were at La Roche-Bernard. Then I said: 'God has brought him to me; he shall die.' "

Roland listened with a certain respect to the superstitious narrative of the Breton leader. He was not surprised to find such beliefs and such poetry in a man born in face of a savage sea, among the Druid monuments of Karnac. He realized that Millière was indeed condemned, and that God, who had thrice seemed to approve his judgment, alone could save him. But one last question occurred to him.

"How will you strike him?" he asked.

"Oh!" said Georges, "I do not trouble myself about that; he will be executed."

One of the two men who had brought in the supper table now entered the room.

"Brise-Bleu," said Cadoudal, "tell Cœur-de-Roi that I wish to speak to him."

Two minutes later the Breton presented himself.

"Cœur-de-Roi," said Cadoudal, "did you not tell me that the murderer Thomas Millière was at Roche-Bernard?"

"I saw him enter the town side by side with the Republican colonel, who did not seem particularly flattered by such companionship."

"Did you not add that he was followed by his guillotine?"

"I told you his guillotine followed between two cannon, and I believe if the cannon could have got away the guillotine would have been left to go its way alone."

"What precautions does Millière take in the towns he visits?"

"He has a special guard about him, and the streets around his house are· barricaded. He carries pistols always at hand."

"In spite of that guard, in spite of that barricade and the pistols, will you undertake to reach him?"

"I will, general."

"Because of his crimes, I have condemned that man; he must die."

"Ah!" exclaimed Cœur-de-Roi, "the day of justice has come at last!"

"Will you undertake to execute my sentence, Cœur-de-Roi?"

"I will, general."

"Go then, Cœur-de-Roi. Take the number of men you need; devise what stratagem you please, but reach the man, and strike."

"If I die, general—"

"Fear not; the curate of Leguerno shall say enough masses in your behalf to keep your poor soul out of purgatory. But you will not die, Cœur-de-Roi."

"That's all right, general. Now that I am sure of the masses, I ask nothing more. I have my plan."

"When will you start?"

"To-night."

"When will he die?"

"To-morrow."

"Go. See that three hundred men are ready to follow me in half an hour."

Cœur-de-Roi went out as simply as he had entered.

"You see," said Cadoudal, "the sort of men I command. Is your First Consul as well served as I, Monsieur de Montrevel?"

"By some, yes."

"Well, with me it is not some, but all."

Bénédicité entered and questioned Georges with a look.

"Yes," replied Georges, with voice and nod.

Bénédicité went out.

"Did you see any one on your way here?" asked Cadoudal.

"Not one."

"I asked for three hundred men in half an hour, and they will be here in that time. I might have asked for five hundred, a thousand, two thousand, and they would have responded as promptly."

"But," said Roland, "you have, in number at least, a limit you cannot exceed."

"Do you want to know my effective? It is easily told,

I won't tell you myself, for you wouldn't believe me. Wait. I will have some one tell you."

He opened the door and called out: "Branche-d'Or!"

Two seconds later Branche-d'Or appeared.

"This is my major-general," said Cadoudal, laughing. "He fulfils the same functions for me that General Berthier does for the First Consul. Branche-d'Or—"

"General."

"How many men are stationed along the road from here to La Roche-Bernard, which the gentleman followed in coming to see me?"

"Six hundred on the Arzal moor, six hundred among the Marzan gorse, three hundred at Péaule, three hundred at Billiers."

"Total, eighteen hundred. How many between Noyal and Muzillac?"

"Four hundred."

"Two thousand two hundred. How many between here and Vannes?"

"Fifty at Theix, three hundred at the Trinité, six hundred between the Trinité and Muzillac."

"Three thousand two hundred. And from Ambon to Leguerno?"

"Twelve hundred."

"Four thousand four hundred. And in the village around me, in the houses, the gardens, the cellars?"

"Five to six hundred, general."

"Thank you, Bénédicité."

He made a sign with his head and Bénédicité went out.

"You see," said Cadoudal, simply, "about five thousand. Well, with those five thousand men, all belonging to this country, who know every tree, every stone, every bush, I can make war against the hundred thousand men the First Consul threatens to send against me."

Roland smiled.

"You think that is saying too much, don't you?"

"I think you are boasting a little, general; boasting of your men, rather."

"No; for my auxiliaries are the whole population. None of your generals can make a move unknown to me; send a despatch without my intercepting it; find a retreat where I shall not pursue him. The very soil is royalist and Christian! In default of the inhabitants, it speaks and tells me: 'The Blues passed here; the slaughterers are hidden there!' For the rest, you can judge for yourself."

"How?"

"We are going on an expedition about twenty-four miles from here. What time is it?"

Both young men looked at their watches.

"Quarter to twelve," they said together.

"Good!" said Georges, "our watches agree; that is a good sign. Perhaps some day our hearts will do the same."

"You were saying, general?"

"I was saying that it was a quarter to twelve, colonel; and that at six o'clock, before day, we must be twenty miles from here. Do you want to rest?"

"I!"

"Yes; you can sleep an hour."

"Thanks; it's unnecessary."

"Then we will start whenever you are ready."

"But your men?"

"Oh! my men are ready."

"Where?"

"Everywhere."

"I should like to see them."

"You shall."

"When?"

"Whenever agreeable to you. My men are very discreet, and never show themselves till I make the signal."

"So that whenever I want to see them—"

"You will tell me; I shall give the signal and they'll appear."

"Let us start, general."

"Yes, let us start."

The two young men wrapped themselves in their cloaks and went out. At the door Roland collided against a small group of five men. These five men wore Republican uniforms; one of them had sergeant stripes on his sleeve.

"What is all this?" asked Roland.

"Nothing," replied Cadoudal, laughing.

"But who are these men?"

"Cœur-de-Roi and his party; they are starting on that expedition you know of."

"Then they expect by means of this uniform—"

"Oh! you shall know all, colonel; I have no secrets from you." Then, turning to the little group, Cadoudal called: "Cœur-de-Roi!"

The man with the stripes on his sleeves left the group, and came to Cadoudal.

"Did you call me, general?" asked the pretended sergeant.

"Yes, I want to know your plan."

"Oh! general, it is very simple."

"Let me judge of that."

"I put this paper in the muzzle of my gun." Cœur-de-Roi showed a large envelope with an official red seal, which had once, no doubt, contained some Republican despatch intercepted by the Chouans. "I present myself to the sentries, saying: 'Despatch from the general of division.' I enter the first guardhouse and ask to be shown the house of the citizen-commissioner; they show me, I thank them; always best to be polite. I reach the house, meet a second sentry to whom I tell the same tale as to the first; I go up or down to citizen Millière accordingly as he lives in the cellar or the garret. I enter without difficulty, you understand—'Despatch from the general of division'. I find him in his study or elsewhere, present my paper, and while he opens it, I kill him with this dagger, here in my sleeve."

"Yes, but you and your men?"

"Ah, faith! In God's care; we are defending his cause, it is for him to take care of us."

"Well, you see, colonel," said Cadoudal, "how easy it all is. Let us mount, colonel! Good luck, Cœur-de-Roi!"

"Which of these two horses am I to take?" asked Roland.

"Either; one is as good as the other; each has an excellent pair of English pistols in its holsters."

"Loaded?"

"And well-loaded, colonel; that's a job I never trust to any one."

"Then we'll mount."

The two young men were soon in their saddles, and on the road to Vannes; Cadoudal guiding Roland, and Branche-d'Or, the major-general of the army, as Georges called him, following about twenty paces in the rear.

When they reached the end of the village, Roland darted his eyes along the road, which stretches in a straight line from Muzillac to the Trinité. The road, fully exposed to view, seemed absolutely solitary.

They rode on for about a mile and a half, then Roland said: "But where the devil are your men?"

"To right and left, before and behind us."

"Ha, what a joke!"

"It's not a joke, colonel; do you think I should be so rash as to risk myself thus without scouts?"

"You told me, I think, that if I wished to see your men I had only to say so."

"I did say so."

"Well, I wish to see them."

"Wholly, or in part?"

"How many did you say were with you?"

"Three hundred."

"Well, I want to see one hundred and fifty."

"Halt!" cried Cadoudal.

Putting his hands to his mouth he gave the hoot of the

screech-owl, followed by the cry of an owl; but he threw the hoot to the right and the cry to the left.

Almost instantly, on both sides of the road, human forms could be seen in motion, bounding over the ditch which separated the bushes from the road, and then ranging themselves beside the horses.

"Who commands on the right?" asked Cadoudal.

"I, Moustache," replied a peasant, coming near.

"Who commands on the left?" repeated the general.

"I, Chante-en-hiver," replied another peasant, also approaching him.

"How many men are with you, Moustache?"

"One hundred."

"How many men are with you, Chante-en-hiver?"

"Fifty."

"One hundred and fifty in all, then?" asked Georges.

"Yes," replied the two Breton leaders.

"Is that your number, colonel?" asked Cadoudal laughing.

"You are a magician, general."

"No; I am a poor peasant like them; only I command a troop in which each brain knows what it does, each heart beats singly for the two great principles of this world, religion and monarchy." Then, turning to his men, Cadoudal asked: "Who commands the advanced guard?"

"Fend-l'air," replied the two Chouans.

"And the rear-guard?"

"La Giberne."

The second reply was made with the same unanimity as the first.

"Then we can safely continue our way?"

"Yes, general; as if you were going to mass in your own village."

"Let us ride on then, colonel," said Cadoudal to Roland. Then turning to his men he cried: "Be lively, my lads."

Instantly every man jumped the ditch and disappeared. For a few seconds the crackling of twigs on the bushes, and the sound of steps among the underbrush, was heard. Then all was silent.

"Well," asked Cadoudal, "do you think that with such men I have anything to fear from the Blues, brave as they may be?"

Roland heaved a sigh; he was of Cadoudal's opinion.

They rode on. About three miles from Trinité they caught sight of a black spot approaching along the road with great rapidity. As it became more distinct this spot stopped suddenly.

"What is that?" asked Roland.

"As you see, a man," replied Cadoudal.

"Of course; but who is this man?"

"You might have guessed from the rapidity of his coming; he is a messenger."

"Why does he stop?"

"Because he has seen us, and does not know whether to advance or retreat."

"What will he do?"

"Wait before deciding."

"For what?"

"A signal."

"Will he answer the signal?"

"He will not only answer but obey it. Will you have him advance or retreat; or will you have him step aside."

"I wish him to advance; by that means we shall know the news he brings."

Cadoudal gave the call of the cuckoo with such perfection that Roland looked about him for the bird.

"It was I," said Cadoudal, "you need not look for it."

"Is the messenger going to come?"

"Not going to, he is coming."

The messenger had already started, and was rapidly approaching; in a few seconds he was beside his general.

"Ah!" said the latter, "is that you, Monte-à-l'assaut?"

The general stooped, and Monte-à-l'assaut said a few words in his ear.

"Bénédicité has already warned me," said Georges. Then turning to Roland, he said, "Something of importance is to happen in the village of the Trinité in a quarter of an hour, which you ought to see. Come, hurry up."

And, setting the example, he put his horse to a gallop. Roland did the same.

When they reached the village they could see from a distance, by the light of some pine torches, a tumultuous mob in the market square. The cries and movements of this mob bespoke some grave occurrence.

"Fast, fast!" cried Cadoudal.

Roland asked no better; he dug his spurs in his horse's belly.

At the clatter of horses' hoofs the peasants scattered. There were five or six hundred of them at least, all armed.

Cadoudal and Roland found themselves in a circle of light in the midst of cries and agitation.

The crowd was pressing more particularly toward the opening of a street which led to the village of Tridon. A diligence was coming down that street escorted by a dozen Chouans; two on either side of the postilion, ten others guarding the doors. The carriage stopped in the middle of the market-square. All were so intent upon the diligence that they paid but scant attention to Cadoudal.

"Hola," shouted Georges. "What is all this?"

At this well known voice, every one turned round, and heads were uncovered.

"The Big Round Head!" they murmured.

"Yes," said Cadoudal.

A man went up to Georges.

"Didn't Bénédicité and Monte-à-l'assaut notify you?" he inquired.

"Yes. Is that the diligence from Ploermel to Vannes that you are bringing back?"

"Yes, general. It was stopped between Tréfléon and Saint-Nolf."

"Is he in it?"

"We think so."

"Act according to your consciences; if it is a crime toward God, take it on yourselves; I take only the responsibility toward men. I will be present at what takes place; but I will not share in it—either to hinder or help."

"Well," demanded a hundred voices, "what does he say, Sabre-tout?"

"He says we must act according to our consciences, and that he washes his hands of it."

"Long live the Big Round Head!" cried all the people, rushing toward the diligence.

Cadoudal remained motionless in the midst of this crowd. Roland stood near him, also motionless, but full of curiosity; for he was completely ignorant of who, or what, was in question.

The man who had just spoken to Cadoudal, and whom his companions called Sabre-tout, opened the door. The travellers were huddled together and trembling in the darkness within.

"If you have nothing to reproach yourselves with against God or the king," said Sabre-tout in a full sonorous voice, "descend without fear. We are not brigands, we are Christians and royalists."

This declaration no doubt reassured the travellers, for a man got out, then two women, then a mother pressing her child in her arms, and finally another man. The Chouans examined them attentively as they came down the carriage steps; not finding the man they wanted, they said to each traveller, "Pass on."

One man alone remained in the coach. A Chouan thrust a torch in the vehicle, and by its light they could see he was a priest.

"Minister of the Lord," said Sabre-tout, "why did you not descend with the others? Did you not hear me say we were Christians and royalists?"

The priest did not move; but his teeth chattered.

"Why this terror?" continued Sabre-tout. "Does not

your cloth plead for you? The man who wears a cassock can have done nothing against royalty or religion."

The priest crouched back, murmuring: "Mercy! mercy!"

"Why mercy?" demanded Sabre-tout, "do you feel that you are guilty, wretch?"

"Oh! oh!" exclaimed Roland, "is that how you royalists and Christians speak to a man of God!"

"That man," said Cadoudal, "is not a man of God, but a man of the devil."

"Who is he, then?"

"Both an atheist and a regicide; he denied his God and voted for the death of the king. That is the Conventional Audrein."

Roland shuddered. "What will they do?" he asked.

"He gave death, he will receive death," answered Cadoudal.

During this time the Chouans had pulled Audrein out of the diligence.

"Ha! is it you, bishop of Vannes?" cried Sabre-tout.

"Mercy!" begged the bishop.

"We were informed of your arrival, and were waiting for you."

"Mercy!" repeated the bishop for the third time.

"Have you your pontifical robes with you?"

"Yes, my friends, I have."

"Then dress yourself as a prelate; it is long since we have seen one."

A trunk marked with the prelate's name was taken from the diligence and opened. They took the bishop's robes from it, and handed them to Audrein, who put them on. Then, when every vestment was in its place, the peasants ranged themselves in a circle, each with his musket in his hand. The glare of the torches was reflected on the barrels, casting evil gleams.

Two men took the priest and led him into the circle, supporting him beneath his arms. He was pale as death. There was a moment of lugubrious silence.

A voice broke it. It was that of Sabre-tout.

"We are about to judge you," said the Chouan. "Priest of God, you have betrayed the Church; child of France, you have condemned your king to death."

"Alas! alas!" stammered the priest.

"Is it true?"

"I do not deny it."

"Because it is impossible to deny. What have you to say in justification?"

"Citizens—"

"We are not citizens," cried Sabre-tout, in a voice of thunder, "we are royalists."

"Gentlemen—"

"We are not gentlemen; we are Chouans."

"My friends—"

"We are not your friends; we are your judges. Your judges are questioning you; answer."

"I repent of what I did, and I ask pardon of God and men."

"Men cannot pardon you," replied the same implacable voice; "for, pardoned to-day, you would sin to-morrow. You may change your skin, but never your heart. You have nothing to expect from men but death; as for God, implore his mercy."

The regicide bowed his head; the renegade bent his knee. But suddenly drawing himself up, he cried: "I voted the king's death, it is true, but with a reservation—"

"What reservation?"

"The time of the execution."

"Sooner or later, it was still the king's death which you voted, and the king was innocent."

"True, true," said the priest, "but I was afraid."

"Then you are not only a regicide, and an apostate, but also a coward. We are not priests, but we are more just than you. You voted the death of the innocent; we vote the death of the guilty. You have ten minutes in which to prepare to meet your God."

The bishop gave a cry of terror and fell upon both knees; the church bells rang, as if of their own impulse, and two of the men present, accustomed to the offices of the church, intoned the prayers for the dying. It was some time before the bishop found words with which to respond. He turned affrighted glances in supplication to his judges one after the other, but not one face met his with even the consolation of mere pity. The torches, flickering in the wind, lent them, on the contrary, a savage and terrible expression. Then at last he mingled his voice with the voices that were praying for him.

The judges allowed him time to follow the funeral prayer to its close. In the meantime others were preparing a pile of wood.

"Oh!" cried the priest, beholding these preparations with growing terror; "would you have the cruelty to kill me thus?"

"No," replied his inflexible accuser, "flames are the death of martyrs; you are not worthy of such a death. Apostate, the hour has come!"

"Oh, my God! my God!" cried the priest, raising his arms to heaven.

"Stand up!" said the Chouan.

The priest tried to obey, but his strength failed him, and he fell again to his knees.

"Will you let that murder be done before your eyes?" Roland asked Cadoudal.

"I said that I washed my hands of it," replied the latter.

"Pilate said that, and Pilate's hands are to this day red with the blood of Jesus Christ."

"Because Jesus Christ was a righteous man; this man is a Barabbas."

"Kiss your cross! kiss your cross!" cried Sabre-tout.

The prelate looked at him with a terrified air, but without obeying. It was evident that he no longer saw, no longer heard.

"Oh!" cried Roland, making an effort to dismount, "it shall never be said that I let a man be murdered before me, and did not try to save him."

A threatening murmur rose around him; his words had been overheard. That was all that was needed to excite the young man.

"Ah! is that the way of it?" he cried, carrying his hand to one of his holsters.

But with a movement rapid as thought, Cadoudal seized his hand, and, while Roland struggled vainly to free himself from this grip of iron, he shouted: "Fire!"

Twenty shots resounded instantly, and the bishop fell, an inert mass.

"Ah!" cried Roland. "What have you done?"

"Forced you to keep your promise," replied Cadoudal; "you swore to see all and hear all without offering any opposition."

"So perish all enemies of God and the king," said Sabretout, in a solemn voice.

"Amen!" responded the spectators with one voice of sinister unanimity.

Then they stripped the body of its sacerdotal ornaments, which they flung upon the pile of wood, invited the other travellers to take their places in the diligence, replaced the postilion in his saddle, and, opening their ranks to give passage to the coach, cried: "Go with God!"

The diligence rolled rapidly away.

"Come, let us go," cried Cadoudal, "we have still twelve miles to do, and we have lost an hour here." Then, addressing the executioners, he said: "That man was guilty; that man is punished. Human justice and divine justice are satisfied. Let prayers for the dead be said over his body, and give him Christian burial; do you hear?" And sure of being obeyed, Cadoudal put his horse to a gallop.

Roland seemed to hesitate for a moment whether to follow him or not; then, as if resolving to accomplish a duty, he said: "I will go to the end."

Spurring his horse in the direction taken by Cadoudal, he reached the Chouan leader in a few strides. Both disappeared in the darkness, which grew thicker and thicker as the men left the place where the torches were illuminating the dead priest's face and the fire was consuming his vestments.

CHAPTER XXXIV

THE DIPLOMACY OF GEORGES CADOUDAL

THE feeling that Roland experienced as he followed Georges Cadoudal resembled that of a man halfawakened, who is still under the influence of a dream, and returns gradually from the confines which separate night from day. He strives to discover whether the ground he walks on is that of fiction or reality, and the more he burrows in the dimness of his brain the further he buries himself in doubt.

A man existed for whom Roland felt a worship almost divine. Accustomed to live in the atmosphere of glory which surrounded that man, to see others obey his orders, and to obey them himself with a promptness and abnegation that were almost Oriental, it seemed amazing to him to encounter, at the opposite ends of France, two organized powers, enemies of the power of that man, and prepared to struggle against it. Suppose a Jew of Judas Maccabeus, a worshipper of Jehovah, having, from his infancy, heard him called the King of kings, the God of strength, of vengeance, of armies, the Eternal, coming suddenly face to face with the mysterious Osiris of the Egyptians, or the thundering Jupiter of the Greeks.

His adventures at Avignon and Bourg with Morgan and the Company of Jehu, his adventures in the villages of Muzillac and the Trinité with Cadoudal and his Chouans, seemed to him some strange initiation in an unknown religion; but like those courageous neophytes who risk death to learn the secrets of initiation, he resolved to follow to the end.

Besides he was not without a certain admiration for these exceptional characters; nor did he measure without a certain amazement these revolted Titans, challenging his god; he felt they were in no sense common men—neither those who had stabbed Sir John in the Chartreuse of Seillon, nor those who had shot the bishop of Vannes at the village of the Trinité.

And now, what was he to see? He was soon to know, for they had ridden five hours and a half and the day was breaking.

Beyond the village of Tridon they turned across country; leaving Vannes to the left, they reached Tréfléon. At Tréfléon, Cadoudal, still followed by his major-general, Branche-d'Or, had found Monte-à-l'assaut and Chante-en-hiver. He gave them further orders, and continued on his way, bearing to the left and skirting the edges of a little wood which lies between Grandchamp and Larré. There Cadoudal halted, imitated, three separate times in succession, the cry of an owl, and was presently surrounded by his three hundred men.

A grayish light was spreading through the sky beyond Tréfléon and Saint-Nolf; it was not the rising of the sun, but the first rays of dawn. A heavy mist rose from the earth and prevented the eye from seeing more than fifty feet beyond it.

Cadoudal seemed to be expecting news before risking himself further.

Suddenly, about five hundred paces distant, the crowing of a cock was heard. Cadoudal pricked up his ears; his men looked at each other and laughed.

The cock crowed again, but nearer.

"It is he," said Cadoudal; "answer him."

The howling of a dog came from within three feet of Roland, but so perfectly imitated that the young man, although aware of what it was, looked about him for the animal that was uttering such lugubrious plaints. Almost at the same moment he saw a man coming rapidly through the mist, his form growing more and more distinct as he approached. The new-comer saw the two horsemen, and went toward them.

Cadoudal rode forward a few paces, putting his finger to his lips, as if to request the man to speak low. The latter, therefore, did not pause until he was close beside his general.

"Well, Fleur-d'épine," asked Georges, "have we got them?"

"Like a mouse in a trap; not one can re-enter Vannes, if you say the word."

"I desire nothing better. How many are there?"

"One hundred men, commanded by the general himself."

"How many wagons?"

"Seventeen."

"When did they start?"

"They must be about a mile and three-quarters from here."

"What road have they taken?"

"Grandchamp to Vannes."

"So that, if I deploy from Meucon to Plescop—"

"You'll bar the way."

"That's all."

Cadoudal called his four lieutenants, Chante-en hiver, Monte-à-l'assaut, Fend-l'air, and La Giberne, to him, gave each of them fifty men, and each with his men disappeared like shadows in the heavy mist, giving the well-known hoot as they vanished. Cadoudal was left with a hundred men, Branche-d'Or and Fleur-d'épine. He returned to Roland.

"Well, general," said the latter, "is everything satisfactory?"

"Yes, colonel, fairly so," replied the Chouan; "but you can judge for yourself in half an hour."

"It will be difficult to judge of anything in that mist."

Cadoudal looked about him.

"It will lift in half an hour," said he. "Will you utilize the time by eating a mouthful and drinking a glass?"

"Faith!" said the young man, "I must admit that the ride has hollowed me."

"I make a point," said Georges, "of eating the best breakfast I can before fighting."

"Then you are going to fight?"

"I think so."

"Against whom?"

"Why, the Republicans, and as we have to do with General Hatry, I doubt if he surrenders without resistance."

"Do the Republicans know they are going to fight you?"

"They haven't the least idea."

"So it is to be a surprise?"

"Not exactly, inasmuch as when the fog lifts they will see us as soon as we see them." Then, turning to the man who seemed to be in charge of the provisions, Cadoudal added, "Brise-Bleu, is there anything for breakfast?"

Brise-Bleu nodded affirmatively, went into the wood, and came out dragging after him a donkey loaded with two baskets. He spread a cloak on a rise of the ground, and placed on it a roast chicken, a bit of cold salt pork, some bread and buckwheat cakes. This time Brise-Bleu had provided luxury in the shape of a bottle of wine and a glass.

Cadoudal motioned Roland to the table and the improvised repast. The young man sprang from his horse, throwing the bridle to a Chouan. Cadoudal did likewise.

"Now," said the latter, turning to his men, "you have half an hour to do as we do. Those who have not breakfasted in half an hour are notified that they must fight on empty stomachs."

The invitation seemed equivalent to an order, so promptly and precisely was it executed. Every man pulled from his bag or his pocket a bit of bread or a buckwheat cake, and followed the example of his general, who had already divided the chicken between Roland and himself. As there was but one glass, both officers shared it.

While they were thus breakfasting, side by side, like two friends on a hunt, the sun rose, and, as Cadoudal had predicted, the mist became less and less dense. Soon the nearest trees could be distinguished; then the line of the woods, stretching to the right from Meucon to Grandchamp, while to the left the plain of Plescop, threaded by a rivulet, sloped gradually toward Vannes. This natural declivity of the ground became more and more perceptible as it neared the ocean.

On the road from Grandchamp to Plescop, a line of wagons were now visible, the tail of which was still hidden in the woods. This line was motionless; evidently some unforeseen obstacle had stopped it.

In fact, about a quarter of a mile before the leading wagon they perceived the two hundred Chouans, under Monte-à-l'assaut, Chante-en-hiver, Fend-l'air, and Giberne, barring the way.

The Republicans, inferior in number—we said that there were but a hundred—had halted and were awaiting the complete dispersion of the fog to determine the number and character of the men they were about to meet. Men and wagons were now in a triangle, of which Cadoudal and his hundred men formed one of the angles.

At sight of this small number of men thus surrounded by triple forces, and of the well-known uniform, of which the color had given its name to the Republican forces, Roland sprang hastily to his feet. As for Cadoudal, he remained where he was, nonchalantly finishing his meal. Of the hundred men surrounding the general, not one seemed to perceive the spectacle that was now before their eyes; it seemed almost as if they were waiting for Cadoudal's order to look at it.

Roland had only to cast his eyes on the Republicans to see that they were lost. Cadoudal watched the various emotions that succeeded each other on the young man's face.

"Well," asked the Chouan, after a moment's silence, "do you think my dispositions well taken?"

"You might better say your precautions, general," replied Roland, with a sarcastic smile.

"Isn't it the First Consul's way to make the most of his advantages when he gets them?" asked Cadoudal.

Roland bit his lips; then, instead of replying to the royalist leader's question, he said: "General, I have a favor to ask which I hope you will not refuse."

"What is it?"

"Permission to let me go and be killed with my comrades."

Cadoudal rose. "I expected that request," he said.

"Then you will grant it?" cried Roland, his eyes sparkling with joy.

"Yes; but, first, I have a favor to ask of you," said the royalist leader, with supreme dignity.

"Ask it, sir."

"To bear my flag of truce to General Hatry."

"For what purpose?"

"I have several proposals to make to him before the fight begins."

"I presume that among those proposals which you deign to intrust to me you do not include that of laying down his arms?"

"On the contrary, colonel, you understand that that is the first of my proposals."

"General Hatry will refuse it."

"That is probable."

"And then?"

"Then I shall give him his choice between two others, either of which he can, I think, accept without forfeiting his honor."

"What are they?"

"I will tell you in due time. Begin with the first."

"State it."

"General Hatry and his hundred men are surrounded by a triple force. I offer them their lives; but they must lay down their arms, and make oath not to serve again in the Vendée for five years."

Roland shook his head.

"Better that than to see his men annihilated."

"Maybe so; but he would prefer to have his men anni-hilated, and be annihilated with them."

"Don't you think," asked Cadoudal, laughing, "that it might be as well, in any case, to ask him?"

"True," said Roland.

"Well, colonel, be so good as to mount your horse, make yourself known to him, and deliver my proposal."

"Very well," replied Roland.

"The colonel's horse," said Cadoudal, motioning to the Chouan who was watching it. The man led it up. The young man sprang upon it, and rapidly covered the dis-tance which separated him from the convoy.

A group of men were gathered on its flank, evidently composed of General Hatry and his officers. Roland rode toward them, scarcely three gunshots distant from the Chouans. General Hatry's astonishment was great when he saw an officer in the Republican uniform approaching him. He left the group and advanced three paces to meet the messenger.

Roland made himself known, related how he came to be among the Whites, and transmitted Cadoudal's proposal to General Hatry.

As he had foreseen, the latter refused it. Roland re-turned to Cadoudal with a proud and joyful heart.

"He refuses!" he cried, as soon as his voice could be heard.

Cadoudal gave a nod that showed he was not surprised by the refusal.

"Then, in that case," he answered, "go back with my second proposition. I don't wish to have anything to re-proach myself with in answering to such a judge of honor as you."

Roland bowed. "What is the second proposition?"

"General Hatry shall meet me in the space that separates the two troops, he shall carry the same arms as I—that is, his sabre and pistols—and the matter shall be decided between us. If I kill him, his men are to submit to the conditions already named, for we cannot take prisoners; if he kills me, his men shall pass free and be allowed to reach Vannes safely. Come, I hope that's a proposition you would accept, colonel?"

"I would accept it myself," replied Roland.

"Yes," exclaimed Cadoudal, "but you are not General Hatry. Content yourself with being a negotiator this time, and if this proposition, which, if I were he, I wouldn't let escape me, does not please him, come to me. I'm a good fellow, and I'll make him a third."

Roland rode off a second time; his coming was awaited by the Republicans with visible impatience. He transmitted the message to General Hatry.

"Citizen," replied the general, "I must render account of my conduct to the First Consul. You are his aide-decamp, and I charge you on your return to Paris to bear testimony on my behalf to him. What would you do in my place? Whatever you would do, that I shall do."

Roland started; his face assumed the grave expression of a man who is arguing a point of honor in his own mind. Then, at the end of a few seconds, he said: "General, I should refuse."

"Your reasons, citizen?" demanded the general.

"The chances of a duel are problematic; you cannot subject the fate of a hundred brave men to a doubtful chance. In an affair like this, where all are concerned, every man had better defend his own skin as best he can."

"Is that your opinion, colonel?"

"On my honor."

"It is also mine; carry my reply to the royalist general."

Roland galloped back to Cadoudal, and delivered General Hatry's reply.

Cadoudal smiled. "I expected it," he said.

"You couldn't have expected it, because it was I who advised him to make it."

"You thought differently a few moments ago."

"Yes; but you yourself reminded me that I was not General Hatry. Come, what is your third proposition?" said Roland impatiently; for he began to perceive, or rather he had perceived from the beginning, that the noble part in the affair belonged to the royalist general.

"My third proposition," said Cadoudal, "is not a proposition but an order; an order for two hundred of my men to withdraw. General Hatry has one hundred men; I will keep one hundred. My Breton forefathers were accustomed to fight foot to foot, breast to breast, man to man, and oftener one to three than three to one. If General Hatry is victorious, he can walk over our bodies and tranquilly enter Vannes; if he is defeated, he cannot say it is by numbers. Go, Monsieur de Montrevel, and remain with your friends. I give them thus the advantage of numbers, for you alone are worth ten men."

Roland raised his hat.

"What are you doing, sir?" demanded Cadoudal.

"I always bow to that which is grand, general; I bow to you."

"Come, colonel," said Cadoudal, "a last glass of wine; let each of us drink to what we love best, to that which we grieve to leave behind, to that we hope to meet in heaven."

Taking the bottle and the one glass, he filled it half full, and offered it to Roland. "We have but one glass, Monsieur de Montrevel; drink first."

"Why first?"

"Because, in the first place, you are my guest, and also because there is a proverb that whoever drinks after another knows his thought." Then, he added, laughing: "I want to know your thought, Monsieur de Montrevel."

Roland emptied the glass and returned it to Cadoudal. The latter filled his glass half full, as he had done for Roland, and emptied it in turn.

"Well," asked Roland, "now do you know my thought, general?"

"No," replied Cadoudal, "the proverb is false."

"My thought," said Roland, with his usual frankness, "is that you are a brave man, general. I shall feel honored if, at this moment when we are going to fight against each other, you will give me your hand."

The two young men clasped hands, more like friends parting for a long absence than two enemies about to meet on the battlefield. There was a simple grandeur, full of majesty, in this action. Each raised his hat.

"Good luck!" said Roland to Cadoudal; "but allow me to doubt it. I must even confess that it is from my lips, not my heart."

"God keep you, sir," said Cadoudal, "and I hope that my wish will be realized. It is the honest expression of my thoughts."

"What is to be the signal that you are ready?" inquired Roland.

"A musket shot fired in the air, to which you will reply in the same way."

"Very good, general," replied Roland. And putting his horse to a gallop, he crossed the space between the royalist general and the Republican general for the third time.

"Friends," said Cadoudal, pointing to Roland, "do you see that young man?"

All eyes were bent upon Roland. "Yes," came from every mouth.

"He came with a safe-guard from our brothers in the Midi; his life is sacred to you; he may be captured, but it must be living—not a hair of his head must be touched."

"Very good, general," replied the Chouans.

"And now, my friends, remember that you are the sons of those thirty Bretons who fought the thirty British between Ploermel and Josselin, ten leagues from here, and conquered them." Then, in a low voice, he added with a sigh, "Unhappily we have not to do with the British this time."

The fog had now lifted completely, and, as usually happens, a few rays of the wintry sun tinged the plain of Plescop with a yellow light.

It was easy therefore to distinguish the movements of the two troops. While Roland was returning to the Republicans, Branche-d'Or galloped toward the two hundred men who were blocking the way. He had hardly spoken to Cadoudal's four lieutenants before a hundred men were seen to wheel to the right and a hundred more to wheel to the left and march in opposite directions, one toward Plumergat, the other toward Saint-Ave, leaving the road open. Each body halted three-quarters of a mile down the road, grounded arms and remained motionless. Branche-d'Or returned to Cadoudal.

"Have you any special orders to give me, general?" he asked.

"Yes, one," answered Cadoudal, "take eight men and follow me. When you see the young Republican, with whom I breakfasted, fall under his horse, fling yourself upon him, you and your eight men, before he has time to free himself, and take him prisoner."

"Yes, general."

"You know that I must have him safe and sound."

"That's understood, general."

"Choose your eight men. Monsieur de Montrevel once captured, and his parole given, you can do as you like."

"Suppose he won't give his parole?"

"Then you must surround him so that he can't escape, and watch him till the fight is over."

"Very well," said Branche-d'Or, heaving a sigh; "but it'll be a little hard to stand by with folded arms while the others are having their fun."

"Pooh! who knows?" said Cadoudal; "there'll probably be enough for everybody."

Then, casting a glance over the plain and seeing his own men stationed apart, and the Republicans massed for battle, he cried: "A musket!"

They brought one. Cadoudal raised it above his head

and fired in the air. Almost at the same moment, a shot fired in the same manner from the midst of the Republicans answered like an echo to that of Cadoudal.

Two drums beating the advance and a bugle were heard. Cadoudal rose in his stirrups.

"Children," he cried, "have you all said your morning prayers?"

"Yes, yes!" answered almost every voice.

"If any of you forgot them, or did not have time, let them pray now."

Five or six peasants knelt down and prayed.

The drums and bugle drew nearer.

"General, general," cried several voices impatiently, "they are coming."

The general motioned to the kneeling peasants.

"True," replied the impatient ones.

Those who prayed rose one by one, according as their prayers had been long or short. By the time they were all afoot, the Republicans had crossed nearly one-third of the distance. They marched, bayonets fixed, in three ranks, each rank three abreast.

Roland rode at the head of the first rank, General Hatry between the first and second. Both were easily recognized, being the only men on horseback. Among the Chouans, Cadoudal was the only rider, Branche-d'Or having dismounted to take command of the eight men who were to follow Georges.

"General," said a voice, "the prayer is ended, and every one is standing."

Cadoudal looked around him to make sure it was true; then he cried in a loud voice: "Forward! Enjoy yourselves, my lads!"

This permission, which to Vendéans and Chouans, was equivalent to sounding a charge, was scarcely given before the Chouans spread over the fields to cries of "Vive le roi!" waving their hats with one hand and their guns with the other.

Instead of keeping in rank like the Republicans, they

scattered like sharpshooters, forming an immense crescent, of which Georges and his horse were the centre.

A moment later the Republicans were flanked and the firing began. Cadoudal's men were nearly all poachers, that is to say, excellent marksmen, armed with English carbines, able to carry twice the length of the army musket. Though the first shots fired might have seemed wide of range, these messengers of death nevertheless brought down several men in the Republican ranks.

"Forward!" cried the general.

The soldiers marched on, bayonets fixed; but in a few moments there was no enemy before them. Cadoudal's hundred men had turned skirmishers; they had separated, and fifty men were harassing both of the enemy's flanks.

General Hatry ordered his men to wheel to the right and left. Then came the order: "Fire!"

Two volleys followed with the precision and unanimity of well-disciplined troops; but they were almost without result, for the Republicans were firing upon scattered men. Not so with the Chouans, who fired on a mass; with them every shot told.

Roland saw the disadvantage of the position. He looked around and, amid the smoke, distinguished Cadoudal, erect and motionless as an equestrian statue. He understood that the royalist leader was waiting for him.

With a cry he spurred his horse toward him. As if to save him part of the way, Cadoudal put his horse to a gallop. But a hundred feet from Cadoudal he drew rein.

"Attention!" he said to Branche-d'Or and his companions.

"Don't be alarmed, general; here we are," said Branche-d'Or.

Cadoudal drew a pistol from his holster and cocked it.

Roland, sabre in hand, was charging, crouched on his horse's neck. When they were twenty paces apart, Cadoudal slowly raised his hand in Roland's direction. At ten paces he fired.

The horse Roland was riding had a white star on its forehead. The ball struck the centre of that star, and the horse, mortally wounded, rolled over with its rider at Cadoudal's feet.

Cadoudal put spurs to his own horse and jumped both horse and rider.

Branche-d'Or and his men were ready. They sprang, like a pack of jaguars, upon Roland, entangled under the body of his horse. The young man dropped his sword and tried to seize his pistols, but before he could lay hand upon the holsters two men had him by the arms, while the four others dragged his horse from between his legs. The thing was done with such unanimity that it was easy to see the manœuvre had been planned.

Roland roared with rage. Branche-d'Or came up to him and put his hat in his hand.

"I do not surrender!" shouted Roland.

"Useless to do so, Monsieur de Montrevel," replied Branche-d'Or with the utmost politeness.

"What do you mean?" demanded Roland, exhausting his strength in a struggle as desperate as it was useless.

"Because you are captured, sir."

It was so true that there could be no answer.

"Then kill me!" cried Roland.

"We don't want to kill you, sir," replied Branche-d'Or.

"Then what do you want?"

"Give us your parole not to fight any more, and you are free."

"Never!" exclaimed Roland.

"Excuse me, Monsieur de Montrevel," said Branche-d'Or, "but that is not loyal!"

"What!" shrieked Roland, in a fury, "not loyal! You insult me, villain, because you know I can't defend myself or punish you."

"I am not a villain, and I didn't insult you, Monsieur de Montrevel; but I do say that by not giving your word, you deprive the general of nine men, who might be useful to him and who are obliged to stay here to guard you. That's not the way the Big Round Head acted toward you. He had two hundred men more than you, and he sent them away. Now we are only eighty-nine against one hundred."

A flame crossed Roland's face; then almost as suddenly he turned pale as death.

"You are right, Branche-d'Or," he replied. "Succor or no succor, I surrender. You and your men can go and fight with your comrades."

The Chouans gave a cry of joy, let go their hold of Roland, and rushed toward the Republicans, brandishing their hats and muskets, and shouting: "Vive le roi!"

Roland, freed from their grip, but disarmed physically by his fall, morally by his parole, went to the little eminence, still covered by the cloak which had served as a tablecloth for their breakfast, and sat down. From there he could see the whole combat; not a detail was lost upon him.

Cadoudal sat erect upon his horse amid fire and smoke, like the Demon of War, invulnerable and implacable.

Here and there the bodies of a dozen or more Chouans lay stretched upon the sod. But it was evident that the Republicans, still massed together, had lost double that number. Wounded men dragged themselves across the open space, meeting, rearing their bodies like mangled snakes, to fight, the Republicans with their bayonets, and the Chouans with their knives. Those of the wounded Chouans who were too far off to fight their wounded enemies hand to hand, reloaded their guns, and, struggling to their knees, fired and fell again.

On either side the struggle was pitiless, incessant, furious; civil war—that is war without mercy or compassion—waved its torch above the battlefield.

Cadoudal rode his horse around these living breastworks, firing at twenty paces, sometimes his pistols, sometimes a musket, which he discharged, cast aside, and picked up again reloaded. At each discharge a man fell. The third time he made this round General Hatry honored him with a fusillade. He disappeared in the flame and smoke, and Roland saw him go down, he and his horse, as if annihilated.

Ten or a dozen Republicans sprang from the ranks and met as many Chouans; the struggle was terrible, hand to hand, body to body, but the Chouans, with their knives, were sure of the advantage.

Suddenly Cadoudal appeared, erect, a pistol in each hand; it was the death of two men; two men fell. Then through the gap left by these ten or twelve he flung himself forward with thirty men. He had picked up an army musket, and, using it like a club, he brought down a man with each blow. He broke his way through the battalion, and reappeared at the other side. Then, like a boar which returns upon the huntsman he has ripped up and trampled, he rushed back through the gaping wound and widened it.

From that moment all was over.

General Hatry rallied a score of men, and, with bayonets down, they fell upon the circle that enveloped them. He marched at the head of his soldiers on foot; his horse had been killed. Ten men had fallen before the circle was broken, but at last he was beyond it. The Chouans wanted to pursue them, but Cadoudal, in a voice of thunder, called them back.

"You should not have allowed him to pass," he cried, "but having passed he is free to retreat."

The Chouans obeyed with the religious faith they placed in the words of their chief.

"And now," said Cadoudal, "cease firing; no more dead; make prisoners."

The Chouans drew together and surrounded the heaps of dead, and the few living men, more or less wounded, who lay among the dead.

Surrendering was still fighting in this fatal war, where on both sides the prisoners were shot—on the one side, because Chouans and Vendéans were considered brigands; on the other, because they knew not where to put the captives.

The Republicans threw their guns away, that they might not be forced to surrender them. When their captors approached them every cartridge-box was open; every man had fired his last shot.

Cadoudal walked back to Roland.

During the whole of this desperate struggle the young man had remained on the mound. With his eyes fixed on the battle, his hair damp with sweat, his breast heaving, he waited for the result. Then, when he saw the day was lost, his head fell upon his hands, and he still sat on, his forehead bowed to the earth.

Cadoudal reached him before he seemed to hear the sound of footsteps. He touched the young man's shoulder. Roland raised his head slowly without attempting to hide the two great tears that were rolling down his cheeks.

"General," said Roland, "do with me what you will. I am your prisoner."

"I can't make the First Consul's ambassador a prisoner," replied Cadoudal, laughing, "but I can ask him to do me a service."

"Command me, general."

"I need a hospital for the wounded, and a prison for prisoners; will you take the Republican soldiers, wounded and prisoners, back to Vannes."

"What do you mean, general?" exclaimed Roland.

"I give them, or rather I confide them to you. I regret that your horse was killed; so is mine. But there is still that of Brise-Bleu; accept it."

The young man made a motion of rejection.

"Until you can obtain another, of course," added Cadoudal, bowing.

Roland felt that he must put himself, at least in simplicity, on a level with the man with whom he was dealing.

"Shall I see you again, general?" he asked, rising.

"I doubt it, sir. My operations call me to the coast near Port-Louis; your duty recalls you to the Luxembourg."

"What shall I tell the First Consul, general?"

"What you have seen, sir. He must judge between the Abbé Bernier's diplomacy and that of Georges Cadoudal."

"After what I have seen, sir, I doubt if you ever have need of me," said Roland; "but in any case remember that you have a friend near the First Consul."

And he held out his hand to Cadoudal. The royalist took it with the same frankness and freedom he had shown before the battle.

"Farewell, Monsieur de Montrevel," said he, "I need not ask you to justify General Hatry. A defeat like that is fully as glorious as a victory."

During this time Brise-Bleu's horse had been led up for the Republican colonel.

He sprang into the saddle.

"By the bye," said Cadoudal, "as you go through La Roche-Bernard, just inquire what has happened to citizen Thomas Millière."

"He is dead," said a voice.

Cœur-de-Roi and his four men, covered with mud and sweat, had just arrived, but too late for the battle.

Roland cast a last glance at the battlefield, sighed, and, waving a last farewell to Cadoudal, started at a gallop across the fields to await, on the road to Vannes, the wagon-load of wounded and the prisoners he was asked to deliver to General Hatry.

Cadoudal had given a crown of six ecus to each man.

Roland could not help reflecting that the gift was made with the money of the Directory sent to the West by Morgan and the Companions of Jehu.

CHAPTER XXXV

A PROPOSAL OF MARRIAGE

ROLAND'S first visit on arriving in Paris was to the First Consul. He brought him the twofold news of the pacification of the Vendée, and the increasingly bitter insurrection in Brittany.

Bonaparte knew Roland; consequently the triple narrative of Thomas Millière's murder, the execution of Bishop Audrein, and the fight at Grandchamp, produced a deep impression upon him. There was, moreover, in the young man's manner a sombre despair in which he could not be mistaken.

Roland was miserable over this lost opportunity to get himself killed. An unknown power seemed to watch over him, carrying him safe and sound through dangers which resulted fatally to others. Sir John had found twelve judges and a death-warrant, where he had seen but a phantom, invulnerable, it is true, but inoffensive.

He blamed himself bitterly for singling out Cadoudal in the fight, thus exposing himself to a pre-arranged plan of capture, instead of flinging himself into the fray and killing or being killed.

The First Consul watched him anxiously as he talked; the longing for death still lingered in his mind, a longing he hoped to cure by this return to his native land and the endearments of his family.

He praised and defended General Hatry, but, just and impartial as a soldier should be, he gave full credit to Cadoudal for the courage and generosity the royalist general had displayed.

Bonaparte listened gravely, almost sadly; ardent as he was for foreign war with its glorious halo, his soul revolted at the internecine strife which drained the life-blood of the nation and rent its bowels. It was a case in which, to his thinking, negotiation should be substituted for war. But how negotiate with a man like Cadoudal?

Bonaparte was not unaware of his own personal seductions when he chose to exercise them. He resolved to see Cadoudal, and without saying anything on the subject to Roland, he intended to make use of him for the interview when the time came. In the meantime he wanted to see if Brune, in whose talent he had great confidence, would be more successful than his predecessors.

He dismissed Roland, after telling him of his mother's arrival and her installation in the little house in the Rue de la Victoire.

Roland sprang into a coach and was driven there at once. He found Madame de Montrevel as happy and as proud as a woman and a mother could be. Edouard had gone, the day before, to the Prytanée Français, and she herself was preparing to return to Amélie, whose health continued to give her much anxiety.

As for Sir John, he was not only out of danger, but almost well again. He was in Paris, had called upon Madame de Montrevel, and, finding that she had gone with Edouard to the Prytanée, he had left his card. It bore his address, Hôtel Mirabeau, Rue de Richelieu.

It was eleven o'clock, Sir John's breakfast hour, and Roland had every chance of finding him at that hour. He got back into his carriage, and ordered the coachman to stop at the Hôtel Mirabeau.

He found Sir John sitting before an English breakfast, a thing rarely seen in those days, drinking large cups of tea and eating bloody chops.

As soon as the Englishman saw Roland he gave a cry of joy and ran to meet him. Roland himself had acquired a deep affection for that exceptional nature, where the noblest qualities of the heart seemed striving to hide themselves beneath national eccentricities.

Sir John was pale and thin, but in other respects he was well. His wound had completely healed, and except for a slight oppression, which was diminishing daily and would soon disappear altogether, he had almost recovered his former health. He now welcomed Roland with a tenderness scarcely to be expected from that reserved nature, declaring that the joy he felt in seeing him again was all he wanted for his complete recovery.

He begged Roland to share the meal, telling him to order his own breakfast, à la Française. Roland accepted. Like all soldiers who had fought the hard wars of the Revolution, when bread was often lacking, Roland cared little for what he ate; he had acquired the habit of eating whatever was put before him as a precaution against the days when there might be nothing at all. Sir John's attention in asking him to make a French breakfast was scarcely noticed by him at all.

But what Roland did notice was Sir John's preoccupation of mind. It was evident that Sir John had something on his lips which he hesitated to utter. Roland thought he had better help him.

So, when breakfast was nearly over, Roland, with his usual frankness, which almost bordered upon brutality at times, leaned his elbows on the table, settled his chin in his hands, and said: "Well, my dear Sir John, you have something to say to your friend Roland that you don't dare put into words."

Sir John started, and, from pale as he was, turned crimson.

"Confound it!" continued Roland, "it must be hard to get out; but, Sir John, if you have many things to ask me, I know but few that I have the right to refuse you. So, go on; I am listening."

And Roland closed his eyes as if to concentrate all his attention on what Sir John was about to say. But the matter was evidently, from Sir John's point of view, so extremely difficult to make known, that at the end of a dozen seconds, finding that Sir John was still silent, Roland opened his eyes.

The Englishman was pale again; but this time he was paler than before. Roland held out his hand to him.

"Why," he said, "I see you want to make some compliment about the way you were treated at the Château des Noires-Fontaines."

"Precisely, my friend; for the happiness or misery of my life will date from my sojourn at the château."

Roland looked fixedly at Sir John. "The deuce!" he exclaimed, "can I be so fortunate—" Then he stopped, remembering that what he was about to say was most unconventional from the social point of view.

"Oh!" exclaimed Sir John, "my dear Roland, finish what you were saying."

"You wish it?"

"I implore you."

"But if I am mistaken; if I should say something nonsensical."

"My friend, my friend, go on."

"Well, as I was saying, my lord, can I be so fortunate as to find your lordship in love with my sister?"

Sir John gave a cry of joy, and with a rapid movement, of which so phlegmatic a man might have been thought incapable, he threw himself in Roland's arms.

"Your sister is an angel, my dear Roland," he exclaimed, "and I love her with all my heart."

"Are you entirely free to do so, my lord?"

"Entirely. For the last twelve years, as I told you, I have had my fortune under my own control; it amounts to twenty-five thousand pounds sterling a year."

"Too much, my dear fellow, for a woman who can only bring you fifty thousand francs."

"Oh!" said the Englishman, with that national accent that returned to him occasionally in moments of strong excitement, "if I must get rid of a part of it, I can do so."

"No," replied Roland, laughing, "that's not necessary.

You're rich; it's unfortunate, but what's to be done ?—No, that's not the question.   Do you love my sister ?''

"I adore her."

"And she," resumed Roland, "does she love you ?"

"Of course you understand," returned Sir John, "that I have not asked her.   I was bound, my dear Roland, to speak to you first, and if the matter were agreeable, to beg you to plead my cause with your mother.   After I have obtained the consent of both, I shall make my offer.   Or rather, you will make it for me, for I should never dare.''

"Then I am the first to receive your confidence ?"

"You are my best friend, and it ought to be so."

"Well, my dear friend, as far as I am concerned, your suit is won—naturally."

"Your mother and sister remain."

"They will be one.   You understand that my mother will leave Amélie free to make her own choice; and I need not tell you that if it falls upon you she will be delighted. But there is a person whom you have forgotten."

"Who is that?" said Sir John, in the tone of a man who, having weighed all chances for and against, believes he knows them all, and is met by an obstacle he has never thought of.

"The First Consul," said Roland.

"God—" ejaculated the Englishman, swallowing the last words of the national oath.

"He spoke to me just before I left for the Vendée of my sister's marriage," continued Roland, "saying that it no longer concerned my mother and myself, for he would take charge of it.''

"Then," said Sir John, "I am lost."

"Why so ?"

"The First Consul does not like the English."

"Say rather that the English do not like the First Consul.''

"But who will present my wishes to the First Consul ?"

"I will."

"And will you speak of them as agreeable to yourself?"

"I'll turn you into a dove of peace between the two nations," said Roland, rising.

"Oh! thank you," cried Sir John, seizing the young man's hand. Then he added, regretfully, "Must you leave me?"

"My friend, I have only a few hours' leave. I have given one to my mother, two to you, and I owe one to your friend Edouard. I want to kiss him and ask his masters to let him scuffle as he likes with his comrades. Then I must get back to the Luxembourg."

"Well, take him my compliments, and tell him I have ordered another pair of pistols for him, so that the next time he is attacked by bandits he needn't use the conductor's."

Roland looked at Sir John.

"Now, what is it?" he asked.

"What! Don't you know?"

"No. What is it I don't know?"

"Something that nearly killed our poor Amélie?"

"What thing?"

"The attack on the diligence."

"But what diligence?"

"The one which your mother was in."

"The diligence my mother was in?"

"Yes."

"The diligence my mother was in was attacked?"

"You have seen Madame de Montrevel, and she didn't tell you?"

"Not a word about that, anyway."

"Well, my dear Edouard proved a hero; as no one else defended the coach, he did. He took the conductor's pistols and fired."

"Brave boy!" exclaimed Roland.

"Yes, but unluckily or luckily the conductor had taken the precaution to remove the bullets. Edouard was praised and petted by the Companions of Jehu as the bravest of the brave: but he neither killed nor wounded them."

"Are you sure of what you are telling me?"

"I tell you your sister almost died of fright."

"Very good," said Roland.

"How very good?" exclaimed Sir John.

"I mean, all the more reason why I should see Edouard."

"What makes you say that."

"A plan."

"Tell me what it is."

"Faith! no. My plans don't turn out well for you."

"But you know, my dear Roland, that if there are any reprisals to make—"

"I shall make them for both. You are in love, my dear fellow; live in your love."

"You promise me your support?"

"That's understood! I am most anxious to call you brother."

"Are you tired of calling me friend?"

"Faith, yes; it is too little."

"Thanks."

They pressed each other's hands and parted.

A quarter of an hour later Roland reached the Prytanée Français, which stood then on the present site of the Lyceum of Louis-le-Grand—that is to say, at the head of the Rue Saint-Jacques, behind the Sorbonne.

At the first words of the director, Roland saw that his young brother had been especially recommended to the authorities. The boy was sent for. Edouard flung himself into the arms of his "big brother" with that passionate adoration he had for him.

After the first embraces were over, Roland inquired about the stoppage of the diligence. Madame de Montrevel had been chary of mentioning it; Sir John had been sober in statement, but not so Edouard. It was his Iliad, his very own. He related it with every detail—Jérôme's connivance with the bandits, the pistols loaded with powder only, his mother's fainting-fit, the attention paid to her by those who had caused it, his own name known to the bandits.

the fall of the mask from the face of the one who was restoring his mother, his certainty that she must have seen the man's face.

Roland was above all struck with this last particular.

Then the boy related their audience with the First Consul, and told how the latter had kissed and petted him, and finally recommended him to the director of the Prytanée Français.

Roland learned from the child all that he wished to know, and as it took but five minutes to go from the Rue Saint Jacques to the Luxembourg, he was at the palace in that time.

CHAPTER XXXVI

SCULPTURE AND PAINTING

WHEN Roland returned to the Luxembourg, the clock of the palace marked one hour and a quarter after mid-day.

The First Consul was working with Bourrienne.

If we were merely writing a novel, we should hasten to its close, and in order to get there more expeditiously we should neglect certain details, which, we are told, historical figures can do without. That is not our opinion. From the day we first put pen to paper—now some thirty years ago—whether our thought were concentrated on a drama, or whether it spread itself into a novel, we have had a double end—to instruct and to amuse.

And we say instruct first, for amusement has never been to our mind anything but a mask for instruction. Have we succeeded? We think so. Before long we shall have covered with our narratives an enormous period of time; between the ''Comtesse de Salisbury'' and the ''Comte de Monte-Cristo'' five centuries and a half are comprised. Well, we assert that we have taught France as much history about those five centuries and a half as any historian.

More than that; although our opinions are well known; although, under the Bourbons of the elder branch as under the Bourbons of the younger branch, under the Republic as under the present government, we have always proclaimed them loudly, we do not believe that that opinion has been unduly manifested in our books and dramas.

We admire the Marquis de Posa in Schiller's "Don Carlos"; but, in his stead, we should not have anticipated the spirit of that age to the point of placing a philosopher of the eighteenth century among the heroes of the sixteenth, an encyclopedist at the court of Philippe II. Therefore, just as we have been—in literary parlance—monarchical under the Monarchy, republican under the Republic, we are to-day reconstructionists under the Consulate.

That does not prevent our thought from hovering above men, above their epoch, and giving to each the share of good and evil they do. Now that share no one, except God, has the right to award from his individual point of view. The kings of Egypt who, at the moment they passed into the unknown, were judged upon the threshold of their tombs, were not judged by a man, but by a people. That is why it is said: "The judgment of a people is the judgment of God."

Historian, novelist, poet, dramatic author, we are nothing more than the foreman of a jury who impartially sums up the arguments and leaves the jury to give their verdict. The book is the summing up; the readers are the jury.

That is why, having to paint one of the most gigantic figures, not only of modern times but of all times; having to paint the period of his transition, that is to say the moment when Bonaparte transformed himself into Napoleon, the general into an emperor—that is why we say, in the fear of becoming unjust, we abandon interpretations and substitute facts.

We are not of those who say with Voltaire that, "no one is a hero to his valet."

It may be that the valet is near-sighted or envious—two

infirmities that resemble each other more closely than people think. We maintain that a hero may become a kind man, but a hero, for being kind, is none the less a hero.

What is a hero in the eyes of the public? A man whose genius is momentarily greater than his heart. What is a hero in private life? A man whose heart is momentarily greater than his genius.

Historians, judge the genius!

People, judge the heart!

Who judged Charlemagne? The historians. Who judged Henri IV.? The people. Which, in your opinion, was the most righteously judged?

Well, in order to render just judgment, and compel the court of appeals, which is none other than posterity, to confirm contemporaneous judgments, it is essential not to light up one side only of the figure we depict, but to walk around it, and wherever the sunlight does not reach, to hold a torch, or even a candle.

Now, let us return to Bonaparte.

He was working, as we said, with Bourrienne. Let us inquire into the usual division of the First Consul's time.

He rose at seven or eight in the morning, and immediately called one of his secretaries, preferably Bourrienne, and worked with him until ten. At ten, breakfast was announced; Josephine, Hortense and Eugène either waited or sat down to table with the family, that is with the aides-de-camp on duty and Bourrienne. After breakfast he talked with the usual party, or the invited guests, if there were any; one hour was devoted to this intercourse, which was generally shared by the First Consul's two brothers, Lucien and Joseph, Regnault de Saint-Jean-d'Angely, Boulay (de la Meurthe), Monge, Berthollet, Laplace and Arnault. Toward noon Cambacérès arrived. As a general thing Bonaparte devoted half an hour to his chancellor; then suddenly, without warning, he would rise and say: "Au revoir, Josephine! au revoir, Hortense! Come, Bourrienne, let us go to work."

This speech, which recurred almost regularly in the same words, was no sooner uttered than Bonaparte left the salon and returned to his study. There, no system of work was adopted; it might be some urgent matter or merely a caprice. Either Bonaparte dictated or Bourrienne read, after which the First Consul went to the council.

In the earlier months of the Consulate, he was obliged to cross the courtyard of the little Luxembourg to reach the council-chamber, which, if the weather were rainy, put him in bad humor; but toward the end of December he had the courtyard covered; and from that time he almost always returned to his study singing. Bonaparte sang almost as false as Louis XV.

As soon as he was back he examined the work he had ordered done, signed his letters, and stretched himself out in his armchair, the arms of which he stabbed with his penknife as he talked. If he was not inclined to talk, he reread the letters of the day before, or the pamphlets of the day, laughing at intervals with the hearty laugh of a great child. Then suddenly, as one awakening from a dream, he would spring to his feet and cry out: "Write, Bourrienne!"

Then he would sketch out the plan for some building to be erected, or dictate some one of those vast projects which have amazed—let us say rather, terrified the world.

At five o'clock he dined; after dinner the First Consul ascended to Josephine's apartments, where he usually received the visits of the ministers, and particularly that of the minister of foreign affairs, M. de Talleyrand. At midnight, sometimes earlier, but never later, he gave the signal for retiring by saying, brusquely: "Let us go to bed."

The next day, at seven in the morning, the same life began over again, varied only by unforeseen incidents.

After these details of the personal habits of the great genius we are trying to depict under his first aspect, his personal portrait ought, we think, to come.

Bonaparte, First Consul, has left fewer indications of his personal appearance than Napoleon, Emperor. Now, as nothing less resembles the Emperor of 1812 than the First Consul of 1800, let us endeavor, if possible, to sketch with a pen those features which the brush has never fully portrayed, that countenance which neither bronze nor marble has been able to render. Most of the painters and sculptors who flourished during this illustrious period of art—Gros, David, Prud'hon, Girodet and Bosio—have endeavored to transmit to posterity the features of the Man of Destiny, at the different epochs when the vast providential vistas which beckoned him first revealed themselves. Thus, we have portraits of Bonaparte, commander-in-chief, Bonaparte, First Consul, and Napoleon, Emperor; and although some painters and sculptors have caught more or less successfully the type of his face, it may be said that there does not exist, either of the general, the First Consul, or the emperor, a single portrait or bust which perfectly resembles him.

It was not within the power of even genius to triumph over an impossibility. During the first part of Bonaparte's life it was possible to paint or chisel Bonaparte's protuberant skull, his brow furrowed by the sublime line of thought, his pale elongated face, his granite complexion, and the meditative character of his countenance. During the second part of his life it was possible to paint or to chisel his broadened forehead, his admirably defined eyebrows, his straight nose, his close-pressed lips, his chin modelled with rare perfection, his whole face, in short, like a coin of Augustus. But that which neither his bust nor his portrait could render, which was utterly beyond the domain of imitation, was the mobility of his look; that look which is to man what the lightning is to God, namely, the proof of his divinity.

In Bonaparte, that look obeyed his will with the rapidity of lightning; in one and the same minute it dared from beneath his eyelids, now keen and piercing as the blade of a dagger violently unsheathed, now soft as a sun ray or a kiss, now stern as a challenge, or terrible as a threat.

Bonaparte had a look for every thought that stirred his soul. In Napoleon, this look, except in the momentous circumstances of his life, ceased to be mobile and became fixed, but even so it was none the less impossible to render; it was a drill sounding the heart of whosoever he looked upon, the deepest, the most secret thought of which he meant to sound. Marble or painting might render the fixedness of that look, but neither the one nor the other could portray its life—that is to say, its penetrating and magnetic action. Troubled hearts have veiled eyes.

Bonaparte, even in the days of his leanness, had beautiful hands, and he displayed them with a certain coquetry. As he grew stouter his hands became superb; he took the utmost care of them, and looked at them when talking, with much complacency. He felt the same satisfaction in his teeth, which were handsome, though not with the splendor of his hands.

When he walked, either alone or with some one, whether in a room or in a garden, he always bent a little forward, as though his head were heavy to carry, and crossed his hands behind his back. He frequently made an involuntary movement with the right shoulder, as if a nervous shudder had passed through it, and at the same time his mouth made a curious movement from right to left, which seemed to result from the other. These movements, however, had nothing convulsive about them, whatever may have been said notwithstanding; they were a simple trick indicative of great preoccupation, a sort of congestion of the mind. It was chiefly manifested when the general, the First Consul, or the Emperor, was maturing vast plans. It was after such promenades, accompanied by this twofold movement of the shoulders and lips, that he dictated his most important notes. On a campaign, with the army, on horseback, he was indefatigable; he was almost as much so in ordinary life, and would often walk five or six hours in succession without perceiving it.

When he walked thus with some one with whom he was

familiar, he commonly passed his arm through that of his companion and leaned upon him.

Slender and thin as he was at the period when we place him before our readers' eyes, he was much concerned by the fear of future corpulence; it was to Bourrienne that he usually confided this singular dread.

"You see, Bourrienne, how slim and abstemious I am. Well, nothing can rid me of the idea that when I am forty I shall be a great eater and very fat. I foresee that my constitution will undergo a change. I take exercise enough, but what will you!—it's a presentiment; and it won't fail to happen."

We all know to what obesity he attained when a prisoner at Saint Helena.

He had a positive passion for baths, which no doubt contributed not a little to make him fat; this passion became an irresistible need. He took one every other day, and stayed in it two hours, during which time the journals and pamphlets of the day were read to him. As the water cooled he would turn the hot-water faucet until he raised the temperature of his bathroom to such a degree that the reader could neither bear it any longer, nor see to read. Not until then would he permit the door to be opened.

It has been said that he was subject to epileptic attacks after his first campaign in Italy. Bourrienne was with him eleven years, and never saw him suffer from an attack of this malady.

Bonaparte, though indefatigable when necessity demanded it, required much sleep, especially during the period of which we are now writing. Bonaparte, general or First Consul, kept others awake, but he slept, and slept well. He retired at midnight, sometimes earlier, as we have said, and when at seven in the morning they entered his room to awaken him he was always asleep. Usually at the first call he would rise; but occasionally, still half asleep, he would mutter: "Bourrienne, I beg of you, let me sleep a little longer."

Then, if there was nothing urgent, Bourrienne would return at eight o'clock; if it was otherwise, he insisted, and then, with much grumbling, Bonaparte would get up. He slept seven, sometimes eight, hours out of the twenty-four, taking a short nap in the afternoon. He also gave particular instruction for the night.

"At night," he would say, "come in my room as seldom as possible. Never wake me if you have good news to announce—good news can wait; but if there is bad news, wake me instantly, for then there is not a moment to be lost in facing it."

As soon as Bonaparte had risen and made his morning ablutions, which were very thorough, his valet entered and brushed his hair and shaved him; while he was being shaved, a secretary or an aide-de-camp read the newspapers aloud, always beginning with the "Moniteur." He gave no real attention to any but the English and German papers.

"Skip that," he would say when they read him the French papers; "*I know what they say, because they only say what I choose.*"

His toilet completed, Bonaparte went down to his study. We have seen above what he did there. At ten o'clock the breakfast as announced, usually by the steward, in these words: "The general is served." No title, it will be observed, not even that of First Consul.

The repast was a frugal one. Every morning a dish was served which Bonaparte particularly liked—a chicken fried in oil with garlic; the same dish that is now called on the bills of fare at restaurants "Chicken à la Marengo."

Bonaparte drank little, and then only Bordeaux or Burgundy, preferably the latter. After breakfast, as after dinner, he drank a cup of black coffee; never between meals. When he chanced to work until late at night they brought him, not coffee, but chocolate, and the secretary who worked with him had a cup of the same. Most historians, narrators, and biographers, after saying that Bonaparte drank a great deal of coffee, add that he took snuff to excess.

They are doubly mistaken. From the time he was twenty-four, Bonaparte had contracted the habit of taking snuff; but only enough to keep his brain awake. He took it habitually, not, as biographers have declared, from the pocket of his waistcoat, but from a snuff-box which he changed almost every day for a new one—having in this matter of collecting snuff-boxes a certain resemblance to the great Frederick. If he ever did take snuff from his waistcoat pocket, it was on his battle days, when it would have been difficult, while riding at a gallop under fire, to hold both reins and snuff-box. For those days he had special waistcoats, with the right-hand pocket lined with perfumed leather; and, as the sloping cut of his coat enabled him to insert his thumb and forefinger into this pocket without unbuttoning his coat, he could, under any circumstances and at any gait, take snuff when he pleased.

As general or First Consul, he never wore gloves, contenting himself with holding and crumpling them in his left hand. As Emperor, there was some advance in this propriety; he wore one glove, and as he changed his gloves, not once, but two or three times a day, his valet adopted the habit of giving him alternate gloves; thus making one pair serve as two.

Bonaparte had two great passions which Napoleon inherited — for war and architectural monuments to his fame.

Gay, almost jolly in camp, he was dreamy and sombre in repose. To escape this gloom he had recourse to the electricity of art, and saw visions of those gigantic monumental works of which he undertook many, and completed some. He realized that such works are part of the life of peoples; they are history written in capitals, landmarks of the ages, left standing long after generations are swept away. He knew that Rome lives in her ruins, that Greece speaks by her statues, that Egypt, splendid and mysterious spectre, appeared through her monuments on the threshold of civilized existence.

What he loved above everything, what he hugged in preference to all else, was renown, heroic uproar; hence his need of war, his thirst for glory. He often said:

"A great reputation is a great noise; the louder it is, the further it is heard. Laws, institutions, monuments, nations, all fall; but sound remains and resounds through other generations. Babylon and Alexandria are fallen; Semiramis and Alexander stand erect, greater perhaps through the echo of their renown, waxing and multiplying through the ages, than they were in their lifetimes." Then he added, connecting these ideas with himself: "My power depends on my fame and on the battles I win. Conquest has made me what I am, and conquest alone can sustain me. A new-born government must dazzle, must amaze. The moment it no longer flames, it dies out; once it ceases to grow, it falls."

He was long a Corsican, impatient under the conquest of his country; but after the 13th Vendemiaire he became a true Frenchman, and ended by loving France with true passion. His dream was to see her great, happy, powerful, at the head of the nations in glory and in art. It is true that, in making France great, he became great with her, and attached his name indissolubly to her grandeur. To him, living eternally in this thought, actuality disappeared in the future; wherever the hurricane of war may have swept him, France, above all things else, above all nations, filled his thoughts. "What will my Athenians think?" said Alexander, after Issus and Arbela. "I hope the French will be content with me," said Bonaparte, after Rivoli and the Pyramids.

Before battle, this modern Alexander gave little thought to what he should do in case of victory, but much in case of defeat. He, more than any man, was convinced that trifles often decide the greatest events; he was therefore more concerned in foreseeing such events than in producing them. He watched them come to birth, and ripen; then, when the right time came, he appeared, laid his hand on them, mastered and guided them, as an able rider masters and guides a spirited horse.

His rapid rise in the midst of revolutions and political changes he had brought about, or seen accomplished, the events which he had controlled, had given him a certain contempt for men; moreover, he was not inclined by nature to think well of them. His lips were often heard to utter the grievous maxim—all the more grievous because he personally knew its truth—"There are two levers by which men are moved, fear and self-interest."

With such opinions Bonaparte did not, in fact, believe in friendship.

"How often," said Bourrienne, "has he said to me, 'Friendship is only a word; I love no one, not even my brothers—Joseph a little possibly; but if I love him it is only from habit, and because he is my elder. Duroc, yes, I love him; but why? Because his character pleases me; because he is stern, cold, resolute; besides, Duroc never sheds a tear. But why should I love any one? Do you think I have any true friends? As long as I am what I am, I shall have friends—apparently at least; but when my luck ceases, you'll see! Trees don't have leaves in winter. I tell you, Bourrienne, we must leave whimpering to the women, it's their business; as for me, no feelings. I need a vigorous hand and a stout heart; if not, better let war and government alone.'"

In his familiar intercourse, Bonaparte was what schoolboys call a tease; but his teasings were never spiteful, and seldom unkind. His ill-humor, easily aroused, disappeared like a cloud driven by the wind; it evaporated in words, and disappeared of its own will. Sometimes, however, when matters of public import were concerned, and his lieutenants or ministers were to blame, he gave way to violent anger; his outbursts were then hard and cruel, and often humiliating. He gave blows with a club, under which, willingly or unwillingly, the recipient had to bow his head; witness his scene with Jomini and that with the Duc de Bellune.

Bonaparte had two sets of enemies, the Jacobins and the royalists; he detested the first and feared the second. In speaking of the Jacobins, he invariably called them the murderers of Louis XVI.; as for the royalists, that was another thing; one might almost have thought he foresaw the Restoration. He had about him two men who had voted the death of the king, Fouché and Cambacérès.

He dismissed Fouché, and, if he kept Cambacérès, it was because he wanted the services of that eminent legist; but he could not endure him, and he would often catch his colleague, the Second Consul, by the ear, and say: "My poor Cambacérès, I'm so sorry for you; but your goose is cooked. If ever the Bourbons get back they will hang you."

One day Cambacérès lost his temper, and with a twist of his head he pulled his ear from the living pincers that held it.

"Come," he said, "have done with your foolish joking."

Whenever Bonaparte escaped any danger, a childish habit, a Corsican habit, reappeared; he always made a rapid sign of the cross on his breast with the thumb.

Whenever he met with any annoyance, or was haunted with a disagreeable thought, he hummed—what air? An air of his own that was no air at all, and which nobody ever noticed, he sang so false. Then, still singing, he would sit down before his writing desk, tilting in his chair, tipping it back till he almost fell over, and mutilating, as we have said, its arms with a penknife, which served no other purpose, inasmuch as he never mended a pen himself. His secretaries were charged with that duty, and they mended them in the best manner possible, mindful of the fact that they would have to copy that terrific writing, which, as we know, was not absolutely illegible.

The effect produced on Bonaparte by the ringing of bells is known. It was the only music he understood, and it went straight to his heart. If he was seated when the vibrations began he would hold up his hand for silence, and lean toward the sound. If he was walking, he would stop, bend his head, and listen. As long as the bell rang he remained motionless; when the sound died away in space, he resumed his work, saying to those who asked him to explain this singular liking for the iron voice: "It reminds me of my first years at Brienne; I was happy then!"

At the period of which we are writing, his greatest personal interest was the purchase he had made of the domain of Malmaison. He went there every night like a schoolboy off for his holiday, and spent Sunday and often Monday there. There, work was neglected for walking expeditions, during which he personally superintended the improvements he had ordered. Occasionally, and especially at first, he would wander beyond the limits of the estate; but these excursions were thought dangerous by the police, and given up entirely after the conspiracy of the Aréna and the affair of the infernal machine.

The revenue derived from Malmaison, calculated by Bonaparte himself, on the supposition that he should sell his fruits and vegetables, did not amount to more than six thousand francs.

"That's not bad," he said to Bourrienne; "but," he added with a sigh, "one must have thirty thousand a year to be able to live here."

Bonaparte introduced a certain poesy in his taste for the country. He liked to see a woman with a tall flexible figure glide through the dusky shrubberies of the park; only that woman must be dressed in white. He hated gowns of a dark color and had a horror of stout women. As for pregnant women, he had such an aversion for them that it was very seldom he invited one to his soirées or his fêtes. For the rest, with little gallantry in his nature, too overbearing to attract, scarcely civil to women, it was rare for him to say, even to the prettiest, a pleasant thing; in fact, he often produced a shudder by the rude remarks he made even to Josephine's best friends. To one he remarked: "Oh! what red arms you have!" To another, "What an ugly head-dress you are wearing!" To a third, "Your gown is dirty; I have seen you wear it twenty times"; or, "Why don't you change your dressmaker; you are dressed like a fright."

One day he said to the Duchesse de Chevreuse, a charming blonde, whose hair was the admiration of every one: "It's queer how red your hair is!"

"Possibly," replied the duchess, "but this is the first time any man has told me so."

Bonaparte did not like cards; when he did happen to play it was always vingt-et-un. For the rest, he had one trait in common with Henry IV., he cheated; but when the game was over he left all the gold and notes he had won on the table, saying:

"You are ninnies! I have cheated all the time we've been playing, and you never found out. Those who lost can take their money back."

Born and bred in the Catholic faith, Bonaparte had no preference for any dogma. When he re-established divine worship it was done as a political act, not as a religious one. He was fond, however, of discussions bearing on the subject; but he defined his own part in advance by saying: "My reason makes me a disbeliever in many things; but the impressions of my childhood and the inspirations of my early youth have flung me back into uncertainty."

Nevertheless he would never hear of materialism; he cared little what the dogma was, provided that dogma recognized a Creator. One beautiful evening in Messidor, on board his vessel, as it glided along between the twofold azure of the sky and sea, certain mathematicians declared there was no God, only animated matter. Bonaparte looked at the celestial arch, a hundred times more brilliant between Malta and Alexandria than it is in Europe, and, at a moment when they thought him unconscious of the conversation, he exclaimed, pointing to the stars: "You may say what you please, but it was a God who made all that."

Bonaparte, though very exact in paying his private

debts, was just the reverse about public expenses. He was firmly convinced that in all past transactions between ministers and purveyors or contractors, that if the minister who had made the contract was not a dupe, the State at any rate was robbed; for this reason he delayed the period of payment as long as possible; there were literally no evasions, no difficulties he would not make, no bad reasons he would not give. It was a fixed idea with him, an immutable principle, that every contractor was a cheat.

One day a man who had made a bid that was accepted was presented to him.

"What is your name?" he asked, with his accustomed brusqueness.

"Vollant, citizen First Consul."

"Good name for a contractor."

"I spell it with two l's, citizen."

"To rob the better, sir," retorted Bonaparte, turning his back on him.

Bonaparte seldom changed his decisions, even when he saw they were unjust. No one ever heard him say: "I was mistaken." On the contrary, his favorite saying was: "I always believe the worst"—a saying more worthy of Simon than Augustus.

But with all this, one felt that there was more of a desire in Bonaparte's mind to seem to despise men than actual contempt for them. He was neither malignant nor vindictive. Sometimes, it is true, he relied too much upon necessity, that iron-tipped goddess; but for the rest, take him away from the field of politics and he was kind, sympathetic, accessible to pity, fond of children (great proof of a kind and pitying heart), full of indulgence for human weakness in private life, and sometimes of a good-humored heartiness, like that of Henri IV. playing with his children in the presence of the Spanish ambassador.

If we were writing history we should have many more things to say of Bonaparte without counting those which—after finishing with Bonaparte—we should still have to say of Napoleon. But we are writing a simple narrative, in which Bonaparte plays a part; unfortunately, wherever Bonaparte shows himself, if only for a moment, he becomes, in spite of himself, a principal personage.

The reader must pardon us for having again fallen into digression; that man, who is a world in himself, has, against our will, swept us along in his whirlwind.

Let us return to Roland, and consequently to our legitimate tale.

CHAPTER XXXVII

THE AMBASSADOR

WE HAVE seen that Roland, on returning to the Luxembourg, asked for the First Consul and was told that he was engaged with Fouché, the minister of police.

Roland was a privileged person; no matter what functionary was with Bonaparte, he was in the habit, on his return from a journey, or merely from an errand, of half opening the door and putting in his head. The First Consul was often so busy that he paid no attention to this head. When that was the case, Roland would say "General!" which meant, in the close intimacy which still existed between the two schoolmates: "General, I am here; do you need me? I'm at your orders." If the First Consul did not need him, he replied: "Very good." If on the contrary he did need him, he said, simply: "Come in." Then Roland would enter, and wait in the recess of a window until the general told him what he wanted.

On this occasion, Roland put his head in as usual, saying: "General!"

"Come in," replied the First Consul, with visible satisfaction; "come in, come in!"

Roland entered. Bonaparte was, as he had been told, busy with the minister of police. The affair on which the

First Consul was engaged, and which seemed to absorb him a great deal, had also its interest for Roland.

It concerned the recent stoppages of diligences by the Companions of Jehu.

On the table lay three *procès-verbaux* relating the stoppage of one diligence and two mail-coaches. Tribier, the paymaster of the Army of Italy, was in one of the latter. The stoppages had occurred, one on the highroad between Meximieux and Montluel, on that part of the road which crosses the commune of Belignieux; the second, at the extremity of the lake of Silans, in the direction of Nantua; the third, on the highroad between Saint-Etienne and Bourg, at a spot called Les Carronnières.

A curious fact was connected with these stoppages. A sum of four thousand francs and a case of jewelry had been mixed up by mistake with the money-bags belonging to the government. The owners of the money had thought them lost, when the justice of the peace at Nantua received an unsigned letter telling him the place where these objects had been buried, and requesting him to return them to their rightful owners, as the Companions of Jehu made war upon the government and not against private individuals.

In another case, that of the Carronnières—where the robbers, in order to stop the mail-coach, which had continued on its way with increased speed in spite of the order to stop, were forced to fire at a horse—the Companions of Jehu had felt themselves obliged to make good this loss to the postmaster, who had received five hundred francs for the dead horse. That was exactly what the animal had cost eight days before; and this valuation proved that they were dealing with men who understood horses.

The *procès-verbaux* sent by the local authorities were accompanied by the affidavits of the travellers.

Bonaparte was singing that mysterious tune of which we have spoken; which showed that he was furious. So, as Roland might be expected to bring him fresh information, he had called him three times to come in.

"Well," said he, "your part of the country is certainly in revolt against me; just look at that."

Roland glanced at the papers and understood at once.

"Exactly what I came to speak to you about, general," said he.

"Then begin at once; but first go ask Bourrienne for my department atlas."

Roland fetched the atlas, and, guessing what Bonaparte desired to look at, opened it at the department of the Ain.

"That's it," said Bonaparte; "show me where these affairs happened."

Roland laid his finger on the edge of the map, in the neigborhood of Lyons.

"There, general, that's the exact place of the first attack, near the village of Bellignieux."

"And the second?"

"Here," said Roland, pointing to the other side of the department, toward Geneva; "there's the lake of Nantua, and here's that of Silans."

"Now the third?"

Roland laid his finger on the centre of the map.

"General, there's the exact spot. Les Carronnières are not marked on the map because of their slight importance."

"What are Les Carronnières?" asked the First Consul.

"General, in our part of the country the manufactories of tiles are called *carronnières;* they belong to citizen Terrier. That's the place they ought to be on the map."

And Roland made a pencil mark on the paper to show the exact spot where the stoppage occurred.

"What!" exclaimed Bonaparte; "why, it happened less than a mile and a half from Bourg!"

"Scarcely that, general; that explains why the wounded horse was taken back to Bourg and died in the stables of the Belle-Alliance."

"Do you hear all these details, sir!" said Bonaparte, addressing the minister of police.

"Yes, citizen First Consul," answered the latter.

"You know I want this brigandage to stop?"

"I shall use every effort—"

"It's not a question of your efforts, but of its being done."

The minister bowed.

"It is only on that condition," said Bonaparte, "that I shall admit you are the able man you claim to be."

"I'll help you, citizen," said Roland.

"I did not venture to ask for your assistance," said the minister.

"Yes, but I offer it; don't do anything that we have not planned together."

The minister looked at Bonaparte.

"Quite right," said Bonaparte; "you can go. Roland will follow you to the ministry."

Fouché bowed and left the room.

"Now," continued the First Consul, "your honor depends upon your exterminating these bandits, Roland. In the first place, the thing is being carried on in your department; and next, they seem to have some particular grudge against you and your family."

"On the contrary," said Roland, "that's what makes me so furious; they spare me and my family."

"Let's go over it again, Roland. Every detail is of importance; it's a war of Bedouins over again."

"Just notice this, general. I spend a night in the Chartreuse of Seillon, because I have been told that it was haunted by ghosts. Sure enough, a ghost appears, but a perfectly inoffensive one. I fire at it twice, and it doesn't even turn around. My mother is in a diligence that is stopped, and faints away. One of the robbers pays her the most delicate attentions, bathes her temples with vinegar, and gives her smelling-salts. My brother Edouard fights them as best he can; they take him in their arms, kiss him, and make him all sorts of compliments on his courage; a little more and they would have given him sugar-plums as a reward for his gallant conduct. Now, just the reverse; my friend Sir John follows my example, goes where I have been; he is treated as a spy and stabbed, as they thought, to death.''

"But he didn't die.''

"No. On the contrary, he is so well that he wants to marry my sister.''

"Ah, ha! Has he asked for her?''

"Officially.''

"And you answered?''

"I answered that the matter depended on two persons.''

"Your mother and you; that's true.''

"No; my sister herself—and you.''

"Your sister I understand; but I?''

"Didn't you tell me, general, that you would take charge of marrying her?''

Bonaparte walked up and down the room with his arms crossed; then, suddenly stopping before Roland, he said: "What is your Englishman like?''

"You have seen him, general.''

"I don't mean physically; all Englishmen are alike—blue eyes, red hair, white skin, long jaws.''

"That's their *th*,'' said Roland, gravely.

"Their *th*?''

"Yes. Did yon ever learn English, general?''

"Faith! I tried to learn it.''

"Your teacher must have told you that the *th* was sounded by pressing the tongue against the teeth. Well, by dint of punching their teeth with their tongues the English have ended by getting those elongated jaws, which, as you said just now, is one of the distinctive characteristics of their physiognomy.''

Bonaparte looked at Roland to see if that incorrigible jester were laughing or speaking seriously. Roland was imperturbable.

"Is that your opinion?'' said Bonaparte.

"Yes, general, and I think that physiologically it is as good as any other. I have a lot of opinions like it, which I bring to light as the occasion offers.''

"Come back to your Englishman."

"Certainly, general."

"I asked you what he was like."

"Well, he is a gentleman; very brave, very calm, very impassible, very noble, very rich, and, moreover—which may not be a recommendation to you—a nephew of Lord Grenville, prime minister to his Britannic Majesty."

"What's that?"

"I said, prime minister to his Britannic Majesty."

Bonaparte resumed his walk; then, presently returning to Roland, he said: "Can I see your Englishman?"

"You know, general, that you can do anything."

"Where is he?"

"In Paris."

"Go find him and bring him here."

Roland was in the habit of obeying without reply; he took his hat and went toward the door.

"Send Bourrienne to me," said the First Consul, just as Roland passed into the secretary's room.

Five minutes later Bourrienne appeared.

"Sit down there, Bourrienne," said the First Consul, "and write."

Bourrienne sat down, arranged his paper, dipped his pen in the ink, and waited.

"Ready?" asked the First Consul, sitting down upon the writing table, which was another of his habits; a habit that reduced his secretary to despair, for Bonaparte never ceased swinging himself back and forth all the time he dictated—a motion that shook the table as much as if it had been in the middle of the ocean with a heaving sea.

"I'm ready," replied Bourrienne, who had ended by forcing himself to endure, with more or less patience, all Bonaparte's eccentricities.

"Then write." And he dictated:

Bonaparte, First Consul of the Republic, to his Majesty the King of Great Britain and Ireland.

Called by the will of the French nation to the chief magistracy of the Republic, I think it proper to inform your Majesty personally of this fact.

Must the war, which for two years has ravaged the four quarters of the globe, be perpetuated? Is there no means of staying it?

How is it that two nations, the most enlightened of Europe, more powerful and strong than their own safety and independence require; how is it that they sacrifice to their ideas of empty grandeur or bigoted antipathies the welfare of commerce, internal prosperity, the happiness of families? How is it that they do not recognize that peace is the first of needs and the first of a nation's glories?

These sentiments cannot be foreign to the heart of a king who governs a free nation with the sole object of rendering it happy.

Your Majesty will see in this overture my sincere desire to contribute efficaciously, for the second time, to a general pacification, by an advance frankly made and free of those formalities which, necessary perhaps to disguise the dependence of feeble states, only disclose in powerful nations a mutual desire to deceive.

France and England can, for a long time yet, by the abuse of their powers, and to the misery of their peoples, carry on the struggle without exhaustion; but, and I dare say it, the fate of all the civilized nations depends on the conclusion of a war which involves the universe.

Bonaparte paused. "I think that will do," said he. "Read it over, Bourrienne."

Bourrienne read the letter he had just written. After each paragraph the First Consul nodded approvingly, and said: "Go on."

Before the last words were fairly uttered, he took the letter from Bourrienne's hands and signed it with a new pen. It was a habit of his never to use the same pen twice. Nothing could be more disagreeable to him than a spot of ink on his fingers.

"That's good," said he. "Seal it and put on the address: 'To Lord Grenville.'"

Bourrienne did as he was told. At the same moment the noise of a carriage was heard entering the courtyard of the Luxembourg. A moment later the door opened and Roland appeared.

"Well?" asked Bonaparte.

"Didn't I tell you you could have anything you wanted, general?"

"Have you brought your Englishman?"

"I met him in the Place de Buci; and, knowing that you don't like to wait, I caught him just as he was, and made him get into the carriage. Faith! I thought I should have to drive round to the Rue Mazarine, and get a guard to bring him. He's in boots and a frock-coat."

"Let him come in," said Bonaparte.

"Come in, Sir John," cried Roland, turning round.

Lord Tanlay appeared on the threshold. Bonaparte had only to glance at him to recognize a perfect gentleman. A trifling emaciation, a slight pallor, gave Sir John the characteristics of great distinction. He bowed, awaiting the formal introduction, like the true Englishman he was.

"General," said Roland, "I have the honor to present to you Sir John Tanlay, who proposed to go to the third cataract for the purpose of seeing you, but who has, to-day, obliged me to drag him by the ear to the Luxembourg."

"Come in, my lord; come in," said Bonaparte. "This is not the first time we have seen each other, nor the first that I have expressed the wish to know you; there was therefore positive ingratitude in trying to evade my desire."

"If I hesitated," said Sir John, in excellent French, as usual, "it was because I could scarcely believe in the honor you do me."

"And besides, very naturally, from national feeling, you detest me, don't you, like the rest of your countrymen?"

"I must confess, general," answered Sir John, smiling, "that they have not got beyond admiration."

"And do you share the absurd prejudice that claims that national honor requires you to hate to-day the enemy who may be a friend to-morrow?"

"France has been almost a second mother country to me,

and my friend Roland will tell you that I long for the moment when, of my two countries, the one to which I shall owe the most will be France."

"Then you ought to see France and England shaking hands for the good of the world, without repugnance."

"The day when I see that will be a happy day for me."

"If you could contribute to bring it about would you do so?"

"I would risk my life to do it."

"Roland tells me you are a relative of Lord Grenville."

"His nephew."

"Are you on good terms with him?"

"He was very fond of my mother, his eldest sister."

"Have you inherited the fondness he bore your mother?"

"Yes; only I think he holds it in reserve till I return to England."

"Will you deliver a letter for me?"

"To whom?"

"King George III."

"I shall be greatly honored."

"Will you undertake to soy to your uncle that which cannot be written in a letter?"

"Without changing a syllable; the words of General Bonaparte are history."

"Well, tell him—" but, interrupting himself, he turned to Bourrienne, saying: "Bourrienne, find me the last letter from the Emperor of Russia."

Bourrienne opened a box, and, without searching, laid his hand on a letter that he handed to Bonaparte.

The First Consul cast his eye over the paper and then gave it to Lord Tanlay.

"Tell him," said he, "first and before all, that you have read this letter."

Sir John bowed and read as follows:

CITIZEN FIRST CONSUL—I have received, each armed and newly clothed in the uniform of his regiment, the nine thousand Russians, made prisoners in Holland, whom you

have returned to me without ransom, exchange, or condition of any kind.

This is pure chivalry, and I boast of being chivalrous.

I think that which I can best offer you in exchange for
this magnificent present, citizen First Consul, is my friendship. Will you accept it?

As an earnest of that friendship, I am sending his passports to Lord Whitworth, the British Ambassador to Saint
Petersburg.

Furthermore, if you will be, I do not say my second, but
my witness, I will challenge personally every king who will
not take part against England and close his ports to her.

I begin with my neighbor the King of Denmark, and
you will find in the "Gazette de la Cour" the ultimatum
I have sent him.

What more can I say to you? Nothing, unless it be that
you and I together can give laws to the world.

I am your admirer and sincere friend,   PAUL.

Lord Tanlay turned to the First Consul. "Of course
you know," said he, "that the Emperor of Russia is mad."

"Is it that letter that makes you think so, my lord?"
asked Bonaparte.

"No; but it confirms my opinion."

"It was a madman who gave Henry VI. of Lancaster the
crown of Saint-Louis, and the blazon of England still bears
—until I scratch them out with my sword—the fleur-de-lis
of France."

Sir John smiled; his national pride revolted at this as-
sumption in the conqueror of the Pyramids.

"But," said Bonaparte, "that is not the question to-day;
everything in its own time."

"Yes," murmured Sir John, "we are too near Aboukir."

"Oh, I shall never defeat you at sea," said Bonaparte;
"it would take fifty years to make France a maritime nation; but over there," and he motioned with his hand to
the East, "at the present moment, I repeat, that the question is not war but peace. I must have peace to accomplish
my dream, and, above all, peace with England. You see,
I play aboveboard; I am strong enough to speak frankly.

If the day ever comes when a diplomatist tells the truth, he will be the first diplomatist in the world; for no one will believe him, and he will attain, unopposed, his ends."

"Then I am to tell my uncle that you desire peace."

"At the same time letting him know that I do not fear war. If I can't ally myself with King George, I can, as you see, do so with the Emperor Paul; but Russia has not reached that point of civilization that I desire in an ally."

"A tool is sometimes more useful than an ally."

"Yes; but, as you said, the Emperor is mad, and it is better to disarm than to arm a madman. I tell you that two nations like France and England ought to be inseparable friends or relentless enemies; friends, they are the poles of the world, balancing its movements with perfect equilibrium; enemies, one must destroy the other and become the world's sole axis."

"But suppose Lord Grenville, not doubting your genius, still doubts your power; if he holds the opinion of our poet Coleridge, that our island needs no rampart, no bulwark, other than the raucous murmur of the ocean, what shall I tell him?"

"Unroll the map of the world, Bourrienne," said Bonaparte.

Bourrienne unrolled a map; Bonaparte stepped over to it.

"Do you see those two rivers?" said he, pointing to the Volga and the Danube. "That's the road to India," he added.

"I thought Egypt was, general," said Sir John.

"So did I for a time; or, rather, I took it because I had no other. But the Czar opens this one; your government can force me to take it. Do you follow me?"

"Yes, citizen; go on."

"Well, if England forces me to fight her, if I am obliged to accept this alliance with Catherine's successor, this is what I shall do: I shall embark forty thousand Russians on the Volga; I shall send them down the river to Astrakhan; they will cross the Caspian and await me at Asterabad."

Sir John bowed in sign of deep attention. Bonaparte continued: "I shall embark forty thousand Frenchmen on the Danube."

"Excuse me, citizen First Consul, but the Danube is an Austrian river."

"I shall have taken Vienna."

Sir John stared at Bonaparte.

"I shall have taken Vienna," continued the latter. "I shall then embark forty thousand Frenchmen on the Danube; I find Russian vessels at its mouth ready to transport them to Taganrog; I march them by land along the course of the Don to Pratisbianskaïa, whence they move to Tzaritsin; there they descend the Volga in the same vessels that have transported the forty thousand Russians to Asterabad; fifteen days later I have eighty thousand men in western Persia. From Asterabad, these united corps will march to the Indus; Persia, the enemy of England, is our natural ally."

"Yes; but once in the Punjab, the Persian alliance will do you no good; and an army of eighty thousand men cannot drag its provisions along with it."

"You forget one thing," said Bonaparte, as if the expedition were already under way, "I have left bankers at Teheran and Caboul. Now, remember what happened nine years ago in Lord Cornwallis' war with Tippo Saïb. The commander-in-chief fell short of provisions, and a simple captain—I forget his name."

"Captain Malcolm," said Lord Tanlay.

"That's it!" cried Bonaparte. "You know the story! Captain Malcolm had recourse to the Brinjaries, those Bohemians of India, who cover the whole Hindostan peninsula with their encampments, and control the grain supplies. Well, those Bohemians are faithful to the last penny to those who pay them; they will feed me."

"You must cross the Indus."

"What of that!" exclaimed Bonaparte, "I have a hundred and eighty miles of bank between Déra-Ismaël-Khan and Attok to choose from. I know the Indus as well as I do the Seine. It is a slow current flowing about three miles an hour; its medium depth is, I should say, at the point I mentioned, from twelve to fifteen feet, and there are ten or more fords on the line of my operations."

"Then your line is already traced out?" asked Sir John smiling.

"Yes, in so far as it follows a broad uninterrupted stretch of fertile, well-watered provinces; that I avoid the sandy deserts which separate the lower valley of the Indus from Rajputana; and also that I follow the general bases of all invasions of India that have had any success, from Mahmoud of Ghazni, in the year 1000, to Nadir Shah, in 1739. And how many have taken the route I mean to take between the two epochs! Let us count them. After Mahmoud of Ghazni came Mohammed Ghori, in 1184, with one hundred and twenty thousand men; after him, Timur Tang, or Timur the Lame, whom we call Tamerlane, with sixty thousand men; after Tamerlane, Babar; after Babar, Humajan, and how many more I can't remember. Why, India is there for whoever will go and take it!"

"You forget, citizen First Consul, that all the conquerors you have named had only the aboriginal populations to deal with, whereas you have the English. We hold India—"

"With from twenty to twenty-two thousand men."

"And a hundred thousand Sepoys."

"I have counted them all, and I regard England and India, the one with the respect, the other with the contempt, they merit. Wherever I meet European infantry, I prepare a second, a third, and if necessary, a fourth line of reserves, believing that the first three might give way before the British bayonets; but wherever I find the Sepoys, I need only the postilion's whip to scatter the rabble. Have you any other questions to put to me, my lord?"

"One, citizen First Consul: are you sincerely desirous of peace?"

"Here is the letter in which I ask it of your king, my

lord, and it is to be quite sure that it reaches his Britannic Majesty that I ask Lord Grenville's nephew to be my messenger.''

"It shall be done as you desire, citizen; and were I the uncle, instead of the nephew, I should promise more."

"When can you start?"

"In an hour I shall be gone."

"You have no wish to express to me before leaving?"

"None. In any case, if I have any, I leave my affairs to my friend, Roland."

"Shake hands with me, my lord; it will be a good omen, as you represent England and I France."

Sir John accepted the honor done him by Bonaparte, with the exact measure of cordiality that indicated both his sympathy for France, and his mental reserves for the honor of his own nation.

Then, having pressed Roland's hand with fraternal effusion, he bowed again to the First Consul and went out. Bonaparte followed him reflectively with his eyes; then he said suddenly: "Roland, I not only consent to your sister's marriage with Lord Tanlay, but I wish it. Do you understand? *I wish it.*"

He laid such emphasis upon those three words, that to any one who knew him they signified plainly, not "I wish," but "I will."

The tyranny was sweet to Roland, and he accepted it with grateful thanks.

CHAPTER XXXVIII

THE TWO SIGNALS

LET us now relate what happened at the Château des Noires-Fontaines three days after the events we have just described took place in Paris.

Since the successive departures of Roland, then Madame de Montrevel and her son, and finally Sir John—Roland to rejoin his general, Madame de Montrevel to place Edouard in school, and Sir John to acquaint Roland with his matrimonial plans—Amélie had remained alone with Charlotte at the Château des Noires-Fontaines. We say *alone*, because Michel and his son Jacques did not live in the house, but in the little lodge at the gate where he added the duties of porter to those of gardener.

It therefore happened that at night all the windows, excepting those of Amélie, which, as we have said, were on the first floor overlooking the garden, and that of Charlotte in the attic, were left in darkness.

Madame de Montrevel had taken the second chambermaid with her. The two young girls were perhaps rather isolated in their part of the house, which consisted of a dozen bedrooms on three floors, especially at a time when so many rumors of robberies on the highroads reached them. Michel, therefore, proposed to his young mistress that he sleep in the main building, so as to be near her in case of need. But she, in a firm voice, assured him that she felt no fear, and desired no change in the customary routine of the château.

Michel did not insist, and retired, saying that Mademoiselle might, in any case, sleep in peace, for he and Jacques would make the rounds of the house during the night.

Amélie at first seemed anxious about those rounds; but she soon noticed that Michel and Jacques contented themselves with watching on the edge of the forest of Seillon, and the frequent appearance of a jugged hare, or a haunch of venison on the table, proved to her that Michel kept his word regarding the promised rounds.

She therefore ceased to trouble about Michel's rounds, which were always on the side of the house opposite to that where she feared them.

Now, as we have said, three days after the events we have just related, or, to speak more correctly, during the night following the third day, those who were accustomed to see no light save in Amélie's windows on the first floor and Charlotte's on the third, might have observed with surprise that, from eleven o'clock until midnight, the four windows on the first floor were illuminated. It is true that each was lighted by a single wax-candle. They might also have seen the figure of a young girl through the shades, staring in the direction of the village of Ceyzeriat.

This young girl was Amélie, pale, breathing with difficulty, and seeming to watch anxiously for a signal.

At the end of a few minutes she wiped her forehead and drew a joyous breath. A fire was lighted in the direction she had been watching. Then she passed from room to room, putting out the three candles one after the other, leaving only the one which was burning in her own room. As if the fire awaited this return signal, it was now extinguished.

Amélie sat down by her window and remained motionless, her eyes fixed on the garden. The night was dark, without moon or stars, and yet at the end of a quarter of an hour she saw, or rather divined, a shadow crossing the lawn and approaching the window. She placed her single candle in the furthest corner of her room, and returned to open her window.

He whom she was awaiting was already on the balcony.

As on the first night when we saw him climb it, the young man put his arm around the girl's waist and drew her into the room. She made but slight resistance; her hand sought the cord of the Venetian blind, unfastened it from the hook that held it, and let it fall with more noise than prudence would have counselled.

Behind the blind, she closed the window; then she fetched the candle from the corner where she had hidden it. The light illuminated her face, and the young man gave a cry of alarm, for it was covered with tears.

"What has happened?" he asked.

"A great misfortune!" replied the young girl.

"Oh, I feared it when I saw the signal by which you recalled me after receiving me last night. But is it irreparable?"

"Almost," answered Amélie.

"I hope, at least, that it threatens only me."

"It threatens us both."

The young man passed his hand over his brow to wipe away the sweat that covered it.

"Tell me," said he; "you know I am strong."

"If you have the strength to hear it," said she, "I have none to tell it." Then, taking a letter from the chimney-piece, she added: "Read that; that is what I received by the post to-night."

The young man took the letter, opened it, and glanced hastily at the signature.

"From Madame de Montrevel," said he.

"Yes, with a postscript from Roland."

The young man read:

MY DEAREST DAUGHTER—I hope that the news I announce will give you as much joy as it has already given our dear Roland and me. Sir John, whose heart you doubted, claiming that it was only a mechanical contrivance, manufactured in the workshops at Vaucanson, admits that such an opinion was a just one until the day he saw you; but he maintains that since that day he has a heart, and that that heart adores you.

Did you suspect it, my dear Amélie, from his aristocratic and polished manners, when your mother's eyes failed to discern this tenderness.

This morning, while breakfasting with your brother, he formally asked your hand. Your brother received the offer with joy, but he made no promises at first. The First Consul, before Roland's departure for the Vendée, had already spoken of making himself responsible for your establishment. But since then he has asked to see Lord Tanlay, and Sir John, though he maintained his national reserve, was taken into the First Consul's good graces at once, to such a degree that he received from him, at their first interview, a mission to his uncle, Lord Grenville. Sir John started for England immediately.

I do not know how many days Sir John will be absent, but on his return he is certain to present himself to you as your betrothed.

Lord Tanlay is still young, pleasing in appearance, and

immensely rich; he is highly connected in England, and Roland's friend. I do not know a man who has more right, I will not say to your love, but to your profound esteem.

The rest of my news I can tell you in two words. The First Consul is still most kind to me and to your two brothers, and Madame Bonaparte has let me know that she only awaits your marriage to place you near her.

There is talk of leaving the Luxembourg, and removing to the Tuileries. Do you understand the full meaning of this change of domicile?

Your mother, who loves you,

CLOTILDE DE MONTREVEL.

Without pausing, the young man turned to Roland's postscript. It was as follows:

You have read, my dear little sister, what our good mother has written. This marriage is a suitable one under all aspects. It is not a thing to be childish about; the First Consul *wishes* you to become Lady Tanlay; that is to say, he *wills* it.

I am leaving Paris for a few days. Though you may not see me, you will hear of me.

I kiss you, ROLAND.

"Well, Charles," asked Amélie, when the young man had finished reading, "what do you think of that?"

"That it is something we had to expect from day to day, my poor angel, but it is none the less terrible."

"What is to be done?"

"There are three things we can do."

"Tell me."

"In the first place, resist if you have the strength; it is the shortest and surest way."

Amélie dropped her head.

"You will never dare, will you?"

"Never."

"And yet you are my wife, Amélie; a priest has blessed our union."

"But they say that marriage before a priest is null before the law."

"Is it not enough for you, the wife of a proscribed man?" asked Morgan, his voice trembling as he spoke.

Amélie flung herself into his arms.

"But my mother," said she; "our marriage did not have her presence and blessing."

"Because there were too many risks to run, and we wished to run them alone."

"But that man— Did you notice that my brother says he *wills* it?"

"Oh, if you loved me, Amélie, that man would see that he may change the face of the State, carry war from one end of the world to the other, make laws, build a throne, but that he cannot force lips to say yes when the heart says no."

"If I loved you!" said Amélie, in a tone of soft reproach. "It is midnight, you are here in my room, I weep in your arms—I, the daughter of General de Montrevel and the sister of Roland—and you say, 'If you loved me.'"

"I was wrong, I was wrong, my darling Amélie. Yes, I know that you were brought up in adoration of that man; you cannot understand that any one should resist him, and whoever does resist him is a rebel in your eyes."

"Charles, you said there were three things that we could do. What is the second?"

"Accept apparently the marriage they propose to you, and gain time by delaying under various pretexts. The man is not immortal."

"No; but is too young for us to count on his death. The third way, dear friend?"

"Fly—but that is a last resource, Amélie; there are two objections: first, your repugnance."

"I am yours, Charles; I will surmount my repugnance."

"And," added the young man, "my engagements."

"Your engagements?"

"My companions are bound to me, Amélie; but I, too, am bound to them. We also have a man to whom we have sworn obedience. That man is the future king of France.

If you accept your brother's devotion to Bonaparte, accept ours to Louis XVIII.''

Amélie let her face drop into her hands with a sigh.

"Then,'' said she, "we are lost.''

"Why so? On various pretexts, your health above all, you can gain a year. Before the year is out Bonaparte will probably be forced to begin another war in Italy. A single defeat will destroy his prestige; in short, a great many things can happen in a year.''

"Did you read Roland's postscript, Charles?''

"Yes; but I didn't see anything in it that was not in your mother's letter.''

"Read the last sentence again.'' And Amélie placed the letter before him. He read:

I am leaving Paris for a few days; though you may not see me, you will hear of me.

"Well?''

"Do you know what that means?''

"No.''

"It means that Roland is in pursuit of you.''

"What does that matter? He cannot die by the hand of any of us.''

"But you, unhappy man, you can die by his!''

"Do you think I should care so very much if he killed me, Amélie?''

"Oh! even in my gloomiest moments I never thought of that.''

"So you think your brother is on the hunt for us?''

"I am sure of it.''

"What makes you so certain?''

"Because he swore over Sir John's body, when he thought him dead, to avenge him.''

"If he had died,'' exclaimed the young man, bitterly, "we should not be where we are, Amélie.''

"God saved him, Charles; it was therefore good that he did not die.''

"For us?"

"I cannot fathom the ways of the Lord. I tell you, my beloved Charles, beware of Roland; Roland is close by."

Charles smiled incredulously.

"I tell you that he is not only near here, but he has been seen."

"He has been seen! Where? Who saw him?"

"Who saw him?"

"Yes."

"Charlotte, my maid, the jailer's daughter. She asked permission to visit her parents yesterday, Sunday; you were coming, so I told her she could stay till this morning."

"Well?"

"She therefore spent the night with her parents. At eleven o'clock the captain of the gendarmerie brought in some prisoners. While they were locking them up, a man, wrapped in a cloak, came in and asked for the captain. Charlotte thought she recognized the new-comer's voice. She looked at him attentively; his cloak slipped from his face, and she saw that it was my brother."

The young man made a movement.

"Now do you understand, Charles? My brother comes to Bourg, mysteriously, without letting me know; he asks for the captain of the gendarmerie, follows him into the prison, speaks only to him, and disappears. Is that not a threatening outlook for our love? Tell me, Charles!"

As Amélie spoke, a dark cloud spread slowly over her lover's face.

"Amélie," said he, "when my companions and I bound ourselves together, we did not deceive ourselves as to the risks we ran."

"But, at least," said Amélie, "you have changed your place of refuge; you have abandoned the Chartreuse of Seillon?"

"None but our dead are there now."

"Is the grotto of Ceyzeriat perfectly safe?"

"As safe as any refuge can be that has two exits."

"The Chartreuse of Seillon had two exits; yet, as you say, you left your dead there."

"The dead are safer than the living; they are sure not to die on the scaffold."

Amélie felt a shudder go through her.

"Charles!" she murmured.

"Listen," said the young man. "God is my witness, and you too, that I have always put laughter and gayety between your presentiments and my fears; but to-day the aspect of things has changed; we are coming face to face with the crisis. Whatever the end brings us, it is approaching. I do not ask of you, my Amélie, those selfish, unreasonable things that lovers in danger of death exact from their mistresses; I do not ask you to bind your heart to the dead, your love to a corpse—"

"Friend," said the young girl, laying her hand on his arm, "take care; you are doubting me."

"No; I do you the highest honor in leaving you free to accomplish the sacrifice to its full extent; but I do not want you to be bound by an oath; no tie shall fetter you."

"So be it," said Amélie.

"What I ask of you," continued the young man, "and I ask you to swear it on our love, which has been, alas! so fatal to you, is this: if I am arrested and disarmed, if I am imprisoned and condemned to death, I implore you, Amélie, I exact of you, that in some way you will send me arms, not only for myself, but for my companions also, so that we may still be masters of our lives."

"But in such a case, Charles, may I not tell all to my brother? May I not appeal to his tenderness; to the generosity of the First Consul?"

Before the young girl had finished, her lover seized her violently by the wrist.

"Amélie," said he, "it is no longer one promise I ask of you, there are two. Swear to me, in the first place, and above all else, that you will not solicit my pardon. Swear it, Amélie; swear it!''

"Do I need to swear, dear?'' asked the young girl, bursting into tears. "I promise it.''

"Promise it on the hour when I first said I loved you, on the hour when you answered that I was loved!''

"On your life, on mine, on the past, on the future, on our smiles, on our tears.''

"I should die in any case, you see, Amélie, even though I had to beat my brains out against the wall; but I should die dishonored.''

"I promise you, Charles.''

"Then for my second request, Amélie: if we are taken and condemned, send me arms—arms or poison, the means of dying, any means. Coming from you, death would be another joy.''

"Far or near, free or a prisoner, living or dead, you are my master, I am your slave; order and I obey.''

"That is all, Amélie; it is simple and clear, you see, no pardon, and the means of death.''

"Simple and clear, but terrible.''

"You will do it, will you not?''

"You wish me to?''

"I implore you.''

"Order or entreaty, Charles, your will shall be done.''

The young man held the girl, who seemed on the verge of fainting, in his left arm, and approached his mouth to hers. But, just as their lips were about to touch, an owl's cry was heard, so close to the window that Amélie started and Charles raised his head. The cry was repeated a second time, and then a third.

"Ah!'' murmured Amélie, "do you hear that bird of ill-omen? We are doomed, my friend.''

But Charles shook his head.

"That is not an owl, Amélie,' he said; "it is the call of our companions. Put out the light.''

Amélie blew it out while her lover opened the window.

"Even here," she murmured; "they seek you even here!"

"It is our friend and confidant, the Comte de Jayat; no one else knows where I am." Then, leaning from the balcony, he asked: "Is it you, Montbar?"

"Yes; is that you, Morgan?"

"Yes."

A man came from behind a clump of trees.

"News from Paris; not an instant to lose; a matter of life and death to us all."

"Do you hear, Amélie?"

Taking the young girl in his arms, he pressed her convulsively to his heart.

"Go," she said, in a faint voice, "go. Did you not hear him say it was a matter of life and death for all of you?"

"Farewell, my Amélie, my beloved, farewell!"

"Oh! don't say farewell."

"No, no; au revoir!"

"Morgan, Morgan!" cried the voice of the man waiting below in the garden.

The young man pressed his lips once more to Amélie's; then, rushing to the window, he sprang over the balcony at a bound and joined his friend.

Amélie gave a cry, and ran to the balustrade; but all she saw was two moving shadows entering the deepening shadows of the fine old trees that adorned the park.

CHAPTER XXXIX

THE GROTTO OF CEYZERIAT

THE two young men plunged into the shadow of the trees. Morgan guided his companion, less familiar than he with the windings of the park, until they reached the exact spot where he was in the habit of scaling the wall. It took but an instant for both of them to accomplish that feat. The next moment they were on the banks of the Reissouse.

A boat was fastened to the foot of a willow; they jumped into it, and three strokes of the oar brought them to the other side. There a path led along the bank of the river to a little wood which extends from Ceyzeriat to Etrez, a distance of about nine miles, and thus forms, on the other side of the river, a pendant to the forest of Seillon.

On reaching the edge of the wood they stopped. Until then they had been walking as rapidly as it was possible to do without running, and neither of them had uttered a word. The whole way was deserted; it was probable, in fact certain, that no one had seen them. They could breathe freely.

"Where are the Companions?" asked Morgan.

"In the grotto," replied Montbar.

"Why don't we go there at once?"

"Because we shall find one of them at the foot of that beech, who will tell us if we can go further without danger."

"Which one?"

"D'Assas."

A shadow came from behind the tree.

"Here I am," it said.

"Ah! there you are," exclaimed the two young men.

"Anything new?" inquired Montbar.

"Nothing; they are waiting for you to come to a decision."

"In that case, let us hurry."

The three young men continued on their way. After going about three hundred yards, Montbar stopped again, and said softly: "Armand!"

The dry leaves rustled at the call, and a fourth shadow stepped from behind a clump of trees, and approached his companions.

"Anything new?" asked Montbar.

"Yes; a messenger from Cadoudal."

"The same one who came before?"

"Yes."

"Where is he?"

"With the brothers, in the grotto."

"Come."

Montbar rushed on ahead; the path had grown so narrow that the four young men could only walk in single file. It rose for about five hundred paces with an easy but winding slope. Coming to an opening, Montbar stopped and gave, three times, the same owl's cry with which he had called Morgan. A single hoot answered him; then a man slid down from the branches of a bushy oak. It was the sentinel who guarded the entrance to the grotto, which was not more than thirty feet from the oak. The position of the trees surrounding it made it almost impossible of detection.

The sentinel exchanged a few whispered words with Montbar, who seemed, by fulfilling the duties of leader, desirous of leaving Morgan entirely to his thoughts. Then, as his watch was probably not over, the bandit climbed the oak again, and was soon so completely blended with the body of the tree that those he had left might have looked for him in vain in that aërial bastion.

The glade became narrower as they neared the entrance to the grotto. Montbar reached it first, and from a hiding-place known to him he took a flint, a steel, some tinder, matches, and a torch. The sparks flew, the tinder caught fire, the match cast a quivering bluish flame, to which succeeded the crackling, resinous flames of the torch.

Three or four paths were then visible. Montbar took one without hesitation. The path sank, winding into the earth, and turned back upon itself, as if the young men were retracing their steps underground, along the path that had brought them. It was evident that they were following the windings of an ancient quarry, probably the one from which were built, nineteen hundred years earlier, the three Roman towns which are now mere villages, and Cæsar's camp which overlooked them.

At intervals this subterraneous path was cut entirely across by a deep ditch, impassable except with the aid of a plank, that could, with a kick, be precipitated into the hollow beneath. Also, from place to place, breastworks could still be seen, behind which men could intrench themselves and fire without exposing their persons to the sight or fire of the enemy. Finally, at five hundred yards from the entrance, a barricade of the height of a man presented a final obstacle to those who sought to enter a circular space in which ten or a dozen men were now seated or lying around, some reading, others playing cards.

Neither the readers nor the players moved at the noise made by the new-comers, or at the gleam of their light playing upon the walls of the quarry, so certain were they that none but friends could reach this spot, guarded as it was.

For the rest, the scene of this encampment was extremely picturesque; wax candles were burning in profusion (the Companions of Jehu were too aristocratic to make use of any other light) and cast their reflection upon stands of arms of all kinds, among which double-barrelled muskets and pistols held first place. Foils and masks were hanging here and there upon the walls; several musical instruments were lying about, and a few mirrors in gilt frames proclaimed the fact that dress was a pastime by no means unappreciated by the strange inhabitants of that subterranean dwelling.

They all seemed as tranquil as though the news which had drawn Morgan from Amélie's arms was unknown to them, or considered of no importance.

Nevertheless, when the little group from outside approached, and the words: "The captain! the captain!" were heard, all rose, not with the servility of soldiers toward their approaching chief, but with the affectionate deference of strong and intelligent men for one stronger and more intelligent than they.

Then Morgan shook his head, raised his eyes, and, passing before Montbar, advanced to the centre of the circle which had formed at his appearance, and said:

"Well, friends, it seems you have had some news."

"Yes, captain," answered a voice; "the police of the First Consul does us the honor to be interested in us."

"Where is the messenger?" asked Morgan.

"Here," replied a young man, wearing the livery of a cabinet courier, who was still covered with mud and dust.

"Have you any despatches?"

"Written, no; verbal, yes."

"Where do they come from?"

"The private office of the minister of police."

"Can they be trusted?"

"I'll answer for them; they are positively official."

("It's a good thing to have friends everywhere," observed Montbar, parenthetically.)

"Especially near M. Fouché," resumed Morgan; "let us hear the news."

"Am I to tell it aloud, or to you privately?"

"I presume we are all interested, so tell it aloud."

"Well, the First Consul sent for citizen Fouché at the Louvre, and lectured him on our account."

"Capital! what next?"

"Citizen Fouché replied that we were clever scamps, very difficult to find, and still more difficult to capture when we had been found. In short, he praised us highly."

"Very amiable of him. What next?"

"Next, the First Consul replied that that did not concern him, that we were brigands, and that it was our brigandage which maintained the war in Vendée, and that the day we ceased sending money to Brittany there would be no more Brittany."

"Excellent reasoning, it seems to me."

"He said the West must be fought in the East and the Midi."

"Like England in India."

"Consequently he gave citizen Fouché full powers, and, even if it cost a million and he had to kill five hundred men, he must have our heads."

"Well, he knows his man when he makes his demand; remains to be seen if we let him have them."

"So citizen Fouché went home furious, and vowed that before eight days passed there should not be a single Companion of Jehu left in France."

"The time is short."

"That same day couriers started for Lyons, Mâcon, Sons-le-Saulnier, Besançon and Geneva, with orders to the garrison commanders to do personally all they could for our destruction; but above all to obey unquestioningly M. Roland de Montrevel, aide-de-camp to the First Consul, and to put at his disposal as many troops as he thought needful."

"And I can add," said Morgan, "that M. Roland de Montrevel is already in the field. He had a conference with the captain of the gendarmerie, in the prison at Bourg, yesterday."

"Does any one know why?" asked a voice.

"The deuce!" said another, "to engage our cells."

"Do you still mean to protect him?" asked d'Assas.

"More than ever."

"Ah! that's too much!" muttered a voice.

"Why so," retorted Morgan imperiously, "isn't it my right as a Companion?"

"Certainly," said two other voices.

"Then I use it; both as a Companion and as your leader."

"But suppose in the middle of the fray a stray ball should take him?" said a voice.

"Then, it is not a right I claim, nor an order that I give, but an entreaty I make. My friends, promise me, on your honor, that the life of Roland de Montrevel will be sacred to you."

With unanimous voice, all stretching out their hands, they replied: "We swear on our honor!"

"Now," resumed Morgan, "let us look at our position under its true aspect, without deluding ourselves in any way. Once an intelligent police force starts out to pursue us, and makes actual war against us, it will be impossible for us to resist. We may trick them like a fox, or double like a boar, but our resistance will be merely a matter of time, that's all. At least that is my opinion."

Morgan questioned his companions with his eyes, and their acquiescence was unanimous, though it was with a smile on their lips that they recognized their doom. But that was the way in those strange days. Men went to their death without fear, and they dealt it to others without emotion.

"And now," asked Montbar, "have you anything further to say?"

"Yes," replied Morgan, "I have to add that nothing is easier than to procure horses, or even to escape on foot; we are all hunters and more or less mountaineers. It will take us six hours on horseback to get out of France, or twelve on foot. Once in Switzerland we can snap our fingers at citizen Fouché and his police. That's all I have to say."

"It would be very amusing to laugh at citizen Fouché," said Montbar, "but very dull to leave France."

"For that reason, I shall not put this extreme measure to a vote until after we have talked with Cadoudal's messenger."

"Ah, true," exclaimed two or three voices; "the Breton! where is the Breton?"

"He was asleep when I left," said Montbar.

"And he is still sleeping," said Adler, pointing to a man lying on a heap of straw in a recess of the grotto.

They wakened the Breton, who rose to his knees, rubbing his eyes with one hand and feeling for his carbine with the other.

"You are with friends," said a voice; "don't be afraid."

"Afraid!" said the Breton; "who are you, over there, who thinks I am afraid?"

"Some one who probably does not know what fear is,

my dear Branche-d'Or," said Morgan, who recognized in Cadoudal's messenger the same man whom they had received at the Chartreuse the night he himself arrived from Avignon. "I ask pardon on his behalf."

Branche-d'Or looked at the young men before him with an air that left no doubt of his repugnance for a certain sort of pleasantry; but as the group had evidently no offensive intention, their gayety having no insolence about it, he said, with a tolerably gracious air: "Which of you gentlemen is captain? I have a letter for him from my captain."

Morgan advanced a step and said: "I am."

"Your name?"

"I have two."

"Your fighting name?"

"Morgan."

"Yes, that's the one the general told me; besides, I recognize you. You gave me a bag containing sixty thousand francs the night I saw the monks. The letter is for you then."

"Give it to me."

The peasant took off his hat, pulled out the lining, and from between it and the felt he took a piece of paper which resembled another lining, and seemed at first sight to be blank. Then, with a military salute, he offered the paper to Morgan, who turned it over and over and could see no writing; at least none was apparent.

"A candle," he said.

They brought a wax light; Morgan held the paper to the flame. Little by little, as the paper warmed, the writing appeared. The experience appeared familiar to the young men; the Breton alone seemed surprised. To his naïve mind the operation probably seemed like witchcraft; but so long as the devil was aiding the royalist cause the Chouan was willing to deal with him.

"Gentlemen," said Morgan, "do you want to know what the master says?"

All bowed and listened, while the young man read:

My dear Morgan—If you hear that I have abandoned the cause, and am in treaty with the government of the First Consul and the Vendéan leaders, do not believe it. I am a Breton of Brittany, and consequently as stubborn as a true Breton. The First Consul sent one of his aides-de-camp to offer me an amnesty for all my men, and the rank of colonel for myself. I have not even consulted my men, I refused for them and for me.

Now, all depends on us; as we receive from the princes neither money nor encouragement, you are our only treasurer; close your coffers, or rather cease to open those of the government for us, and the royalist opposition, the heart of which beats only in Brittany, will subside little by little, and end before long.

I need not tell you that my life will have ended first.

Our mission is dangerous; probably it will cost us our heads; but what can be more glorious than to hear posterity say of us, if one can hear beyond the grave: "All others despaired; but they, never!"

One of us will survive the other, but only to succumb later. Let that survivor say as he dies: *Etiamsi omnes, ego non.*

Count on me as I count on you.   Cadoudal.

P.S.—You know that you can safely give Branche-d'Or all the money you have for the Cause. He has promised me not to let himself be taken, and I trust his word.

A murmur of enthusiasm ran through the group, as Morgan finished the last words of the letter.

"You have heard it, gentlemen?" he said.

"Yes, yes, yes," repeated every voice.

"In the first place, how much money have we to give to Branche-d'Or?"

"Thirteen thousand francs from the Lake of Silans, twenty-two thousand from Les Carronnières, fourteen thousand from Meximieux, forty-nine thousand in all," said one of the group.

"You hear, Branche-d'Or?" said Morgan; "it is not much—only half what we gave you last time, but you know the proverb: 'The handsomest girl in the world can only give what she has.'"

"The general knows what you risk to obtain this money, and he says that, no matter how little you send, he will receive it gratefully."

"All the more, that the next will be better," said a young man who had just joined the group, unperceived, so absorbed were all present in Cadoudal's letter. "More especially if we say two words to the mail-coach from Chambéry next Saturday."

"Ah! is that you, Valensolle?" said Morgan.

"No real names, if you please, baron; let us be shot, guillotined, drawn and quartered, but save our family honor. My name is Adler; I answer to no other."

"Pardon me, I did wrong—you were saying?"

"That the mail-coach from Paris to Chambéry will pass through Chapelle-de-Guinchay and Belleville next Saturday, carrying fifty thousand francs of government money to the monks of Saint-Bernard; to which I may add that there is between those two places a spot called the Maison-Blanche, which seems to me admirably adapted for an ambuscade."

"What do you say, gentlemen?" asked Morgan. "Shall we do citizen Fouché the honor to worry about his police? Shall we leave France? Or shall we still remain faithful Companions of Jehu?"

There was but one reply—"We stay."

"Right!" said Morgan. "Brothers, I recognize you there. Cadoudal points out our duty in that admirable letter we have just received. Let us adopt his heroic motto: *Etiamsi omnes, ego non.*" Then, addressing the peasant, he said, "Branche-d'Or, the forty-nine thousand francs are at your disposal; you can start when you like. Promise something better next time, in our name, and tell the general for me that, wherever he goes, even though it be to the scaffold, I shall deem it an honor to follow, or to precede him. Au revoir, Branche-d'Or." Then, turning to the young man who seemed so anxious to preserve his incognito, "My dear Adler," he said, like a man who has recovered his gayety, lost for an instant, "I undertake to feed and lodge you this night, if you will deign to accept me as a host."

"Gratefully, friend Morgan," replied the new-comer. "Only let me tell you that I could do without a bed, for I am dropping with fatigue, but not without supper, for I am dying of hunger."

"You shall have a good bed and an excellent supper."

"Where must I go for them."

"Follow me."

"I'm ready."

"Then come on. Good-night, gentlemen! Are you on watch, Montbar?"

"Yes."

"Then we can sleep in peace."

So saying, Morgan passed his arm through that of his friend, took a torch in his other hand, and passed into the depths of the grotto, where we will follow him if our readers are not too weary of this long session.

It was the first time that Valensolle, who came, as we have said, from the neighborhood of Aix, had had occasion to visit the grotto of Ceyzeriat, recently adopted as the meeting-place of the Companions of Jehu. At the preceding meetings he had occasion to explore only the windings and intricacies of the Chartreuse of Seillon, which he now knew so well that in the farce played before Roland the part of ghost was intrusted to him. Everything was, therefore, curious and unknown to him in this new domicile, where he now expected to take his first sleep, and which seemed likely to be, for some days at least, Morgan's headquarters.

As is always the case in abandoned quarries—which, at the first glance, partake somewhat of the character of subterranean cities—the different galleries excavated by the removal of the stone end in a cul de sac; that is to say, at a point in the mine where the work stops. One of these streets seemed to prolong itself indefinitely. Nevertheless, there came a point where the mine would naturally have ended, but there, in the angle of the tunnelled way, was cut (For what purpose? The thing remains a mystery to this day among the people of the neighborhood) an opening two-thirds the width of the gallery, wide enough, or nearly so, to give passage to two men abreast.

The two friends passed through this opening. The air there became so rarefied that their torch threatened to go out at every step. Vallensolle felt drops of ice-cold water falling on his hands and face.

"Bless me," said he, "does it rain down here?"

"No," replied Morgan, laughing; "only we are passing under the Reissouse."

"Then we are going to Bourg?"

"That's about it."

"All right; you are leading me; you have promised me supper and a bed, so I have nothing to worry about—unless that light goes out," added the young man, looking at the paling flame of the torch.

"That wouldn't matter; we can always find ourselves here."

"In the end!" said Valensolle. "And when one reflects that we are wandering through a grotto under rivers at three o'clock in the morning, sleeping the Lord knows where, with the prospect of being taken, tried, and guillotined some fine morning, and all for princes who don't even know our names, and who if they did know them one day would forget them the next—I tell you, Morgan, it's stupid!"

"My dear fellow," said Morgan, "what we call stupid, what ordinary minds never do understand in such a case, has many a chance to become sublime."

"Well, well," said Valensolle, "I see that you will lose more than I do in this business; I put devotion into it, but you put enthusiasm."

Morgan sighed.

"Here we are," said he, letting the conversation drop,

like a burden too heavy to be carried longer. In fact, his foot had just struck against the first step of a stairway.

Preceding Valensolle, for whom he lighted the way, Morgan went up ten steps and reached the gate. Taking a key from his pocket, he opened it. They found themselves in the burial vault. On each side of the vault stood coffins on iron tripods: ducal crowns and escutcheons, blazoned azure, with the cross argent, indicated that these coffins belonged to the family of Savoy before it came to bear the royal crown. A flight of stairs at the further end of the cavern led to an upper floor.

Valensolle cast a curious glance around him, and by the vacillating light of the torch, he recognized the funereal place he was in.

"The devil!" said he, "we are just the reverse of the Spartans, it seems."

"Inasmuch as they were Republicans and we are royalists?" asked Morgan.

"No; because they had skeletons at the end of their suppers, and we have ours at the beginning."

"Are you sure it was the Spartans who proved their philosophy in that way?" asked Morgan, closing the door.

"They or others — what matter?" said Vallensolle. "Faith! my citation is made, and like the Abbé Vertot, who wouldn't rewrite his siege, I'll not change it."

"Well, another time you had better say the Egyptians."

"Well," said Valensolle, with an indifference that was not without a certain sadness, "I'll probably be a skeleton myself before I have another chance to display my erudition. But what the devil are you doing? Why did you put out the torch? You're not going to make me eat and sleep here I hope?"

Morgan had in fact extinguished the torch at the foot of the steps leading to the upper floor.

"Give me your hand," said the young man.

Valensolle seized his friend's hand with an eagerness that showed how very slight a desire he had to make a longer stay in the gloomy vaults of the dukes of Savoy, no matter what honor there might be in such illustrious companionship.

Morgan went up the steps. Then, by the tightening of his hand, Valensolle knew he was making an effort. Presently a stone was raised, and through the opening a trembling gleam of twilight met the eyes of the young men, and a fragrant aromatic odor came to comfort their sense of smell after the mephitic atmosphere of the vaults.

"Ah!" cried Valensolle, "we are in a barn; I prefer that."

Morgan did not answer; he helped his companion to climb out of the vault, and then let the stone drop back in its place.

Valensolle looked about him. He was in the midst of a vast building filled with hay, into which the light filtered through windows of such exquisite form that they certainly could not be those of a barn.

"Why!" said Valensolle, "we are not in a barn!"

"Climb up the hay and sit down near that window," replied Morgan.

Valensolle obeyed and scrambled up the hay like a schoolboy in his holidays; then he sat down, as Morgan had told him, before a window. The next moment Morgan placed between his friend's legs a napkin containing a paté, bread, a bottle of wine, two glasses, two knives and two forks.

"The deuce!" cried Valensolle, ' "Lucullus sups with Lucullus.' "

Then gazing through the panes at a building with numberless windows, which seemed to be a wing of the one they were in, and before which a sentry was pacing, he exclaimed: "Positively, I can't eat my supper till I know where we are. What is this building? And why that sentry at the door?"

"Well," said Morgan, "since you absolutely must know, I will tell you. We are in the church of Brou, which was converted into a fodder storehouse by a decree of the Municipal Council. That adjoining building is now the barracks of the gendarmerie, and that sentry is posted to prevent any one from disturbing our supper or surprising us while we sleep."

"Brave fellows," said Valensolle, filling his glass; "their health, Morgan!"

"And ours!" said the young man, laughing; "the devil take me if any one could dream of finding us here."

Morgan had hardly drained his glass, when, as if the devil had accepted the challenge, the sentinel's harsh, strident voice cried: "*Qui vive!*"

"Hey!" exclaimed the two young men, "what does this mean?"

A body of thirty men came from the direction of Pont d'Aın, and, after giving the countersign to the sentry, at once dispersed; the larger number, led by two men, who seemed to be officers, entered the barracks; the others continued on their way.

"Attention!" said Morgan.

And both young men, on their knees, their ears alert, their eyes at the window, waited.

Let us now explain to the reader the cause of this interruption of a repast which, though taken at three o'clock in the morning, was not, as we have seen, over-tranquil.

CHAPTER XL

A FALSE SCENT

THE jailer's daughter had not been mistaken; it was indeed Roland whom she had seen in the jail speaking to the captain of the gendarmerie. Neither was Amélie wrong in her terror. Roland was really in pursuit of Morgan.

Although he avoided going to the Château des Noires-Fontaines, it was not that he had the slightest suspicion of the interest his sister had in the leader of the Companions of Jehu; but he feared the indiscretion of one of his servants. He had recognized Charlotte at the jail, but as the girl showed no astonishment, he believed she had not recognized him, all the more because, after exchanging a few words with the captain, he went out to wait for the latter on the Place du Bastion, which was always deserted at that hour.

His duties over, the captain of gendarmerie joined him. He found Roland impatiently walking back and forth. Roland had merely made himself known at the jail, but here he proceeded to explain the matter, and to initiate the captain into the object of his visit.

Roland had solicited the First Consul, as a favor to himself, that the pursuit of the Companions of Jehu be intrusted to him personally, a favor he had obtained without difficulty. An order from the minister of war placed at his disposal not only the garrison of Bourg, but also those of the neighboring towns. An order from the minister of police enjoined all the officers of the gendarmerie to render him every assistance.

He naturally applied in the first instance to the captain of the gendarmerie at Bourg, whom he had long known personally as a man of great courage and executive ability. He found what he wanted in him. The captain was furious against the Companions of Jehu, who had stopped diligences within a mile of his town, and on whom he was unable to lay his hand. He knew of the reports relating to the last three stoppages that had been sent to the minister of police, and he understood the latter's anger. But Roland brought his amazement to a climax when he told him of the night he had spent at the Chartreuse of Seillon, and of what had happened to Sir John at that same Chartreuse during the succeeding night.

The captain had heard by common rumor that Madame de Montrevel's guest had been stabbed; but as no one had lodged a complaint, he did not think he had the right to investigate circumstances which it seemed to him Roland wished to keep in the dark. In those troublous days more indulgence was shown to officers of the army than they might have received at other times.

As for Roland, he had said nothing because he wished to reserve for himself the satisfaction of pursuing the assassins and sham ghosts of the Chartreuse when the time came. He now arrived with full power to put that design into execution, firmly resolved not to return to the First Consul until it was accomplished. Besides, it was one of those adventures he was always seeking, at once dangerous and picturesque, an opportunity of pitting his life against men who cared little for their own, and probably less for his. Roland had no conception of Morgan's safe-guard which had twice protected him from danger—once on the night he had watched at the Chartreuse, and again when he had fought against Cadoudal. How could he know that a simple cross was drawn above his name, and that this symbol of redemption guaranteed his safety from one end of France to the other?

For the rest, the first thing to be done was to surround the Chartreuse of Seillon, and to search thoroughly into its most secret places—a thing Roland believed himself perfectly competent to do.

The night was now too far advanced to undertake the expedition, and it was postponed until the one following. In the meantime Roland remained quietly in hiding in the captain's room at the barracks that no one might suspect his presence at Bourg nor its cause. The following night he was to guide the expedition. In the course of the morrow, one of the gendarmes, who was a tailor, agreed to make him a sergeant's uniform. He was to pass as a member of the brigade at Sons-le-Saulnier, and, thanks to the uniform, could direct the search at the Chartreuse without being recognized.

Everything happened as planned. Roland entered the barracks with the captain about one o'clock, ascended to the latter's room, where he slept on a bed on the floor like a man who has just passed two days and two nights in a post-chaise. The next day he restrained his impatience by drawing a plan of the Chartreuse of Seillon for the captain's instruction, with which, even without Roland's help, that worthy officer could have directed the expedition without going an inch astray.

As the captain had but eighteen men under him, and it was not possible to surround the monastery completely with that number, or rather, to guard the two exits and make a thorough search through the interior, and, as it would have taken three or four days to bring in all the men of the brigade scattered throughout the neighborhood, the officer, by Roland's order, went to the colonel of dragoons, garrisoned at Bourg, told him of the matter in hand, and asked for twelve men, who, with his own, made thirty in all.

The colonel not only granted the twelve men, but, learning that the expedition was to be commanded by Colonel Roland de Montrevel, aide-de-camp to the First Consul, he proposed that he himself should join the party at the head of his twelve men.

Roland accepted his co-operation, and it was agreed that the colonel (we employ the words colonel and chief of brigade indifferently, both being interchangeable terms indicating the same rank) and his twelve dragoons should pick up Roland, the captain, and his eighteen men, the barracks being directly on their road to the Chartreuse. The time was set for eleven that night.

At eleven precisely, with military punctuality, the colonel of dragoons and his twelve men joined the gendarmes, and the two companies, now united in one, began their march. Roland, in his sergeant's uniform, made himself known to his brother colonel; but to the dragoons and gendarmes he remained, as agreed upon, a sergeant detached from the brigade at Sons-le-Saulnier. Only, as it might otherwise have seemed extraordinary that a sergeant, wholly unfamiliar with these localities, should be their guide, the men were told that Roland had been in his youth a novice at Seillon, and was therefore better acquainted than most persons with the mysterious nooks of the Chartreuse.

The first feeling of these brave soldiers had been a slight humiliation at being guided by an ex-monk; but, on the other hand, as that ex-monk wore the three-cornered hat jauntily, and as his whole manner and appearance was that of a man who has completely forgotten that he formerly wore a cowl, they ended by accepting the humiliation, and reserved their final judgment on the sergeant until they could see how he handled the musket he carried on his arm, the pistols he wore in his belt, and the sword that hung at his side.

The party was supplied with torches, and started in perfect silence. They were divided into three squads; one of eight men, led by the captain of gendarmerie, another of ten, commanded by the colonel, and the third of twelve men, with Roland at its head. On leaving the town they separated.

The captain of the gendarmerie, who knew the localities better than the colonel of dragoons, took upon himself to guard the window of La Correrie, giving upon the forest of Seillon, with his eight men. The colonel of dragoons was commissioned by Roland to watch the main entrance of the Chartreuse; with him were five gendarmes and five dragoons. Roland was to search the interior, taking with him five gendarmes and seven dragoons.

Half an hour was allowed each squad to reach its post; it was more than was needed. Roland and his men were to scale the orchard wall when half-past eleven was ringing from the belfry at Péronnaz. The captain of gendarmerie followed the main road from Pont d'Ain to the edge of the woods, which he skirted until he reached his appointed station. The colonel of dragoons took the crossroad which branches from the highway of Pont d'Ain and leads to the great portal of the Chartreuse. Roland crossed the fields to the orchard wall which, as the reader will remember, he had already climbed on two occasions.

Punctually at half-past eleven he gave the signal to his men to scale the wall. By the time they reached the other side the men, if they did not yet know that Roland was brave, were at least sure that he was active.

Roland pointed in the dusk to a door—the one that led from the orchard into the cloister. Then he sprang ahead through the rank grasses; first, he opened the door; first, he entered the cloister.

All was dark, silent and solitary. Roland, still guiding his men, reached the refectory. Absolute solitude; utter silence.

They crossed the hall obliquely, and returned to the garden without alarming a living creature except the owls and the bats. There still remained the cistern, the mortuary vault, and the pavilion, or rather, the chapel in the forest, to be searched. Roland crossed the open space between the cistern and the monastery. After descending the steps, he lighted three torches, kept one, and handed the other two, one to a dragoon, the other to a gendarme; then he raised the stone that concealed the stairway.

The gendarmes who followed Roland began to think him as brave as he was active.

They followed the subterranean passage to the first gate; it was closed but not locked. They entered the funereal vault. Here was more than solitude, more than silence; here was death. The bravest felt a shiver in the roots of their hair.

Roland went from tomb to tomb, sounding each with the butt of the pistol he held in his hand. Silence everywhere. They crossed the vault, reached the second gate, and entered the chapel. The same silence, the same solitude; all was deserted, as it seemed, for years. Roland went straight to the choir; there lay the blood on the stones; no one had taken the trouble to efface it. Here was the end of his search, which had proved futile. Roland could not bring himself to retreat. He fancied he was not attacked because of his numerous escort; he therefore left ten men and a torch in the chapel, told them to put themselves in communication, through the ruined window, with the captain of the gendarmerie, who was ambushed in the forest within a few feet of the window, while he himself, with two men, retraced his steps.

This time the two men who followed Roland thought him more than brave, they considered him foolhardy. But Roland, caring little whether they followed or not, retraced his own steps in default of those of the bandits. The two men, ashamed, followed him.

Undoubtedly the Chartreuse was deserted. When Roland reached the great portal, he called to the colonel of dragoons; he and his men were at their post. Roland opened the door and joined them. They had seen nothing, heard nothing. The whole party entered the monastery, closing and barricading the door behind them to cut off the bandits' retreat, if they were fortunate enough to meet any. Then they hastened to rejoin their comrades, who, on their side, had united with the captain and his eight men, and were waiting for them in the choir.

There was nothing for it but to retire. Two o'clock had just struck; nearly three hours had been spent in fruitless search. Roland, rehabilitated in the estimation of the gendarmes and the dragoons, who saw that the ex-novice did not shirk danger, regretfully gave the signal for retreat by opening the door of the chapel which looked toward the forest.

This time Roland merely closed the door behind him, there being no longer any hope of encountering the brigands. Then the little troop returned to Bourg at a quick step. The captain of gendarmerie, with his eighteen men and Roland, re-entered the barracks, while the colonel and his twelve men continued on their way toward the town.

It was the sentinel's call, as he challenged the captain and his party, which had attracted the attention of Morgan and Valensolle; and it was the noise of their return to the barracks which interrupted the supper, and caused Morgan to cry out at this unforeseen circumstance: "Attention!"

In fact, in the present situation of these young men,

every circumstance merited attention. So the meal was interrupted. Their jaws ceased to work to give the eyes and
ears full scope. It soon became evident that the services
of their eyes were alone needed.

Each gendarme regained his room without light. The
numerous barrack windows remained dark, so that the
watchers were able to concentrate their attention on a
single point.

Among those dark windows, two were lighted. They
stood relatively back from the rest of the building, and
directly opposite to the one where the young men were
supping. These windows were on the first floor, but in
the position the watchers occupied at the top of bales of
hay, Morgan and Valensolle were not only on a level, but
could even look down into them. These windows were
those of the room of the captain of gendarmes.

Whether from indifference on the worthy captain's part,
or by reason of State penury, the windows were bare of curtains, so that, thanks to the two candles which the captain
had lighted in his guest's honor, Morgan and Valensolle
could see everything that took place in this room.

Suddenly Morgan grasped Valensolle's arm, and pressed
it with all his might.

"Hey," said Valensolle, "what now?"

Roland had just thrown his three-cornered hat on a chair
and Morgan had recognized him.

"Roland de Montrevel!" he exclaimed, "Roland in a
sergeant's uniform! This time we are on his track while
he is still seeking ours. It behooves us not to lose it."

"What are you going to do?" asked Valensolle, observing that his friend was preparing to leave him.

"Inform our companions. You stay here and do not
lose sight of him. He has taken off his sword, and laid
his pistols aside, therefore it is probable he intends to
spend the night in the captain's room. To-morrow I defy
him to take any road, no matter which, without one of
us at his heels."

And Morgan sliding down the declivity of the hay, disappeared from sight, leaving his companion crouched like a sphinx, with his eyes fixed on Roland de Montrevel.

A quarter of an hour later Morgan returned. By this time the officer's windows were dark like all the others of the barracks.

"Well?" asked Morgan.

"Well," replied Valensolle, "it ended most prosaically. They undressed themselves, blew out the candles, and lay down, the captain on his bed, Roland on a mattress. They are probably trying to outsnore each other at the present moment."

"In that case," said Morgan, "good-night to them, and to us also."

Ten minutes later the wish was granted, and the two young men were sleeping, as if they did not have danger for a bed-fellow.

CHAPTER XLI

THE HÔTEL DE LA POSTE

THAT same morning, about six o'clock, at the cold gray breaking of a February day, a rider, spurring a post-hack and preceded by a postilion who was to lead back the horse, left Bourg by the road to Mâcon or Saint-Julien.

We say Mâcon *or* Saint-Julien, because about three miles from the capital of Bresse the road forks; the one to the right keeping straight on to Saint-Julien, the other, which deviates to the left, leading to Mâcon.

When the rider reached this bifurcation, he was about to take the road leading to Mâcon, when a voice, apparently coming from beneath an upset cart, implored his pity. The rider called to the postilion to see what the matter was.

A poor market-man was pinned down under a load of vegetables. He had evidently attempted to hold up the cart just as the wheel, sinking into the ditch, overbalanced the vehicle. The cart had fallen on him, but fortunately, he said, he thought no limbs were broken, and all he wanted was to get the cart righted, and then he could recover his legs.

The rider was compassionate to his fellow being, for he not only allowed the postilion to stop and help the market-man, but he himself dismounted, and with a vigor one would hardly have expected from so slight a man, he assisted the postilion not only to right the cart, but to replace it on the roadbed. After which he offered to help the man to rise; but the latter had said truly; he really was safe and sound, and if there were a slight shaking of the legs, it only served to prove the truth of the proverb that God takes care of drunkards. The man was profuse in his thanks, and took his horse by the bridle, as much, it was evident, to hold himself steady as to lead the animal.

The riders remounted their horses, put them to a gallop, and soon disappeared round a bend which the road makes a short distance before it reaches the woods of Monnet.

They had scarcely disappeared when a notable change took place in the demeanor of our market-man. He stopped his horse, straightened up, put the mouthpiece of a tiny trumpet to his lips, and blew three times. A species of groom emerged from the woods which line the road, leading a gentleman's horse by the bridle. The market-man rapidly removed his blouse, discarded his linen trousers, and appeared in vest and breeches of buckskin, and top boots. He searched in his cart, drew forth a package which he opened, shook out a green hunting coat with gold braidings, put it on, and over it a dark-brown overcoat; took from the servant's hands a hat which the latter presented him, and which harmonized with his elegant costume, made the man screw his spurs to his boots, and sprang upon his horse with the lightness and skill of an experienced horseman.

"To-night at seven," he said to the groom, "be on the

road between Saint-Just and Ceyzeriat. You will meet
Morgan. Tell him that he *whom he knows of* has gone
to Mâcon, but that I shall be there before him."

Then, without troubling himself about his cart and vegetables, which he left in his servant's charge, the ex-market-
man, who was none other than our old acquaintance Montbar, turned his horse's head toward the Monnet woods, and
set out at a gallop. His mount was not a miserable post
hack, like that on which Roland was riding. On the contrary, it was a blooded horse, so that Montbar easily overtook the two riders, and passed them on the road between
the woods of Monnet and Polliat. The horse, except for
a short stop at Saint-Cyr-sur-Menthon, did the twenty-eight
or thirty miles between Bourg and Mâcon, without resting,
in three hours.

Arrived at Mâcon, Montbar dismounted at the Hôtel de
la Poste, the only one which at that time was fitted to receive guests of distinction. For the rest, from the manner
in which Montbar was received it was evident that the host
was dealing with an old acquaintance.

"Ah! is it you, Monsieur de Jayat?" said the host.
"We were wondering yesterday what had become of you.
It's more than a month since we've seen you in these
parts."

"Do you think it's as long as that, friend?" said the
young man, affecting to drop his r's after the fashion of
the day. "Yes, on my honor, that's so! I've been with
friends, the Trefforts and the Hautecourts. You know
those gentlemen by name, don't you?"

"By name, and in person."

"We hunted to hounds. They're finely equipped, word
of honor! Can I breakfast here this morning?"

"Why not?"

"Then serve me a chicken, a bottle of Bordeaux, two
cutlets, fruit—any trifle will go."

"At once. Shall it be served in your room, or in the
common room?"

"In the common room, it's more amusing; only give me a table to myself. Don't forget my horse. He is a fine beast, and I love him better than I do certain Christians, word of honor!"

The landlord gave his orders. Montbar stood before the fire, his coat-tails drawn aside, warming his calves.

"So you still keep to the posting business?" he said to the landlord, as if desirous of keeping up the conversation.

"I should think so!"

"Then you relay the diligences?"

"Not the diligences, but the mail-coaches."

"Ah! tell me—I want to go to Chambéry some of these days—how many places are there in the mail-coach?"

"Three; two inside, and one out with the courier."

"Do I stand any chance of finding a vacant seat?"

"It may happen; but the safest way is to hire your own conveyance."

"Can't I engage a place beforehand?"

"No; for don't you see, Monsieur de Jayat, that if travellers take places from Paris to Lyons, they have the first right."

"See, the aristocrats!" said Montbar, laughing. "Apropos of aristocrats, there is one behind me posting here. I passed him about a mile the other side of Polliat. I thought his hack a little wind-broken."

"Oh!" exclaimed the landlord, "that's not astonishing; my brothers in the business have a poor lot of horses."

"Why, there's our man!" continued Montbar; "I thought I had more of a lead of him."

Roland was, in fact, just passing the windows at a gallop.

"Do you still want chamber No. 1, Monsieur de Jayat?" asked the landlord.

"Why do you ask?"

"Because it is the best one, and if you don't take it, I shall give it to that man, provided he wants to make any stay."

"Oh! don't bother about me; I shan't know till later in the day whether I go or stay. If the new-comer means to remain give him No. 1. I will content myself with No. 2."

"The gentleman is served," said the waiter, looking through the door which led from the kitchen to the common room.

Montbar nodded and accepted the invitation. He entered the common room just as Roland came into the kitchen. The dinner was on the table. Montbar changed his plate and sat down with his back to the door. The precaution was useless. Roland did not enter the common room, and Montbar breakfasted without interruption. When dessert was over, however, the host himself brought in his coffee. Montbar understood that the good man was in talkative humor; a fortunate circumstance, for there were certain things he was anxious to hear about.

"Well," said Montbar, "what became of our man? Did he only change horses?"

"No, no, no," said the landlord; "as you said, he's an aristocrat. He ordered breakfast in his own room."

"His room or my room?" asked Montbar; "for I'm certain you put him in that famous No. 1."

"Confound it! Monsieur de Jayat, it's your own fault. You told me I could do as I liked."

"And you took me at my word; that was right. I shall be satisfied with No. 2."

"You'll be very uncomfortable. It's only separated from No. 1 by a partition, and you can hear everything that happens from one room to the other."

"Nonsense, my dear man, do you think I've come here to do improper things, or sing seditious songs, that you are afraid the stranger should hear or see what I do?"

"Oh! that's not it."

"What is it, then?"

"I'm not afraid you'll disturb others. I'm afraid they'll disturb you."

"So your new guest is a roisterer?"

"No; he looks to me like an officer."

"What makes you think so?"

"His manner, in the first place. Then he inquired what regiment was in garrison at Mâcon; and when I told him it was the 7th mounted Chasseurs, he said: 'Good! the colonel is a friend of mine. Can a waiter take him my card and ask him to breakfast with me?'"

"Ah, ha!"

"So you see how it is. When officers get together they make so much racket and noise. Perhaps they'll not only breakfast, but dine and sup together."

"I've told you already, my good man, that I am not sure of passing the night here. I am expecting letters from Paris, *poste restante*, which will decide me. In the meantime, light a fire in No. 2, and make as little noise as possible, to avoid annoying my neighbors. And, at the same time, send me up pen and ink, and some paper. I have letters to write."

Montbar's orders were promptly executed, and he himself followed the waiter to see that Roland was not disturbed by his proximity.

The chamber was just what the landlord had said. Not a movement could be made, not a word uttered in the next room, that was not heard. Consequently Montbar distinctly heard the waiter announce Colonel Saint-Maurice, then the resounding steps of the latter in the corridor, and the exclamations of the two friends, delighted to meet again.

On the other hand, Roland, who had been for a moment disturbed by the noise in the adjoining room, forgot it as soon as it had ceased, and there was no danger of its being renewed. Montbar, left alone, seated himself at the table, on which were paper, pen and ink, and remained perfectly motionless.

The two officers had known each other in Italy, where Roland was under the command of Saint-Maurice, the latter being then a captain and Roland a lieutenant. At present their rank was equal, but Roland had beside a double commission from the First Consul and the minister of police, which placed all officers of his own rank under his command, and even, within the limits of his mission, those of a higher rank.

Morgan had not been mistaken in supposing that Amélie's brother was in pursuit of the Companions of Jehu. If Roland's nocturnal search at the Chartreuse of Seillon was not convincing, the conversation between the young officer and his colleague was proof positive. In it, it developed that the First Consul was really sending fifty thousand francs as a gift to the monks of Saint-Bernard, by post; but that this money was in reality a trap devised for the capture of the Companions of Jehu, if all means failed to surprise them in the Chartreuse of Seillon or some other refuge.

It now remained to be seen how these bandits should be captured. The case was eagerly debated between the two officers while they had breakfast. By the time dessert was served they were both agreed upon a plan.

That same evening, Morgan received the following letter:

Just as Adler told us, next Friday at five o'clock the mail-coach will leave Paris with fifty thousand francs for the fathers of Saint-Bernard.

The three places, the one in the coupé and the two in the interior, are already engaged by three travellers who will join the coach, one at Sens, the other two at Tonnerre. The travellers are, in the coupé, one of citizen Fouché's best men; in the interior M. Roland de Montrevel and the colonel of the 7th Chasseurs, garrisoned at Mâcon. They will be in civilians' clothes not to excite suspicion, but armed to the teeth.

Twelve mounted Chasseurs, with muskets, pistols, and sabres, will escort the coach, but at some distance behind it, so as to arrive during the fray. The first pistol fired will be the signal for putting their horses to a gallop and falling upon us.

Now my advice is that, in spite of these precautions, in fact because of these precautions, the attack should be made at the place agreed upon, namely the Maison-Blanche. If that is also the opinion of the comrades, let me know it. I will myself take the coach, as postilion, from Mâcon to Belleville. I will undertake to settle the colonel, and one of you must be responsible for Fouché's agent.

As for M. Roland de Montrevel, no harm will befall him, for I have a means, known to me alone and by me invented, by which he can be prevented from leaving the coach.

The precise day and hour at which the mail to Chambéry will pass the Maison-Blanche is Saturday at six in the evening. Answer in these words, "Saturday, six of the evening," and all will go on rollers.   MONTBAR.

At midnight Montbar, who had complained of the noise his neighbor made, and had removed to a room at the opposite end of the inn, was awakened by a courier, who was none other than the groom who had brought him his horse ready bridled and saddled in the morning. The letter contained only these words, followed by a postscript:

Saturday, six of the evening.   MORGAN.

P.S.—Do not forget, even when fighting, above all when fighting, that Roland de Montrevel's life is safeguarded.

The young man read this reply with visible satisfaction. The matter was no longer a mere stoppage of a diligence, but a species of affair of honor among men of differing opinions, with clashes of courage and bravery. It was no longer a matter of gold spilled upon the highroad, but of blood to be shed—not of pistols loaded with powder, and wielded by a child's hands, but of deadly weapons handled by soldiers accustomed to their use.

For the rest, as Montbar had all the day that was dawning and the morrow before him in which to mature his plans, he contented himself with asking his groom to inquire which postilion would take the coach at Mâcon at five o'clock for the two stages between Mâcon and Belleville. He also sent him to buy four screw-rings and two padlocks fastening with keys.

He already knew that the mail was due at Mâcon at half past four, waited for the travellers to dine, and started again punctually at five. No doubt all his plans were previously laid, for, after giving these directions, Montbar dismissed his servant and went to sleep like a man who has long arrears of slumber to make up.

The next morning he did not wake, or rather did not come downstairs until nine o'clock. He asked casually what had become of his noisy neighbor, and was told that he had started in the Lyons mail at six in the morning, with his friend the colonel of the Chasseurs; but the landlord thought they had only engaged places as far as Tonnerre.

If Monsieur de Jayat had interested himself in the young officer, the latter, in turn, had made inquiries about him, asking who he was, whether he came habitually to the hotel, and whether he would be willing to sell his horse. The landlord had replied that he knew Monsieur de Jayat well, for he was in the habit of coming to the hotel whenever business brought him to Mâcon, and that, as for the horse, he did not believe, considering the affection the young gentleman showed for the animal, that he would consent to part with him for any price. On which the traveller had departed without saying any more.

After breakfast M. de Jayat, who seemed to find time hanging heavily on his hands, ordered his horse, mounted it, and rode out from Mâcon by the Lyons road. As long as he was in the town he allowed his horse to take the pace his fancy dictated, but once beyond it, he gathered up the reins and pressed the animal with his knees. The hint sufficed, and the animal broke into a gallop.

Montbar passed through the villages of Varennes, La Crèche, and Chapelle-de-Guinchay, and did not stop until he reached the Maison-Blanche. The spot was exactly as Valensolle had described it, and was admirably adapted for an ambuscade.

The Maison-Blanche stood in a tiny valley between a sharp declivity and a rise in the ground. A little rivulet without a name flowed past the corner of the garden and made its way to the Saône just above Challe. Tall bushy trees followed the course of the little stream, and described a half-circle, inclosing the house on three sides. The house itself was formerly an inn which proved unproductive to the innkeeper. It had been closed for seven or eight years, and was beginning to fall into decay. Before reaching it, the main road coming from Mâcon made a sharp turn.

Montbar examined the locality with the care of an engineer choosing his ground for a battlefield. He drew a pencil and a note-book from his pocket and made an accurate plan of the position. Then he returned to Mâcon.

Two hours later his groom departed, carrying the plan to Morgan, having informed his master that Antoine was the name of the postilion who was to take the coach from Mâcon to Belleville. The groom also gave him the four screw-rings and the two padlocks he had purchased.

Montbar ordered up a bottle of old Burgundy, and sent for Antoine.

Ten minutes later Antoine appeared. He was a fine, handsome fellow, twenty-five or six years of age, about Montbar's height; a fact which the latter, in looking him over from head to foot, remarked with satisfaction. The postilion paused at the threshold, and, carrying his hand to his hat in a military salute, he said: "Did the citizen send for me?"

"Are you the man they call Antoine?" asked Montbar.

"At your service, and that of your company."

"Well, you can serve me, friend. But close the door and come here."

Antoine closed the door, came within two steps of Montbar, saluted again, and said: "Ready, master."

"In the first place," said Montbar, "if you have no objections, we'll drink a glass of wine to the health of your mistress."

"Oh! oh! My mistress!" cried Antoine. "Can fellows like me afford mistresses? They're all very well for gentlemen such as you."

"Come, you scamp!" said Montbar. "You can't make

me believe that, with your make-up, you've made a vow of chastity."

"Oh! I don't say I'm a monk in that particular. I may have a bit of a love-affair here and there along the high-road."

"Yes, at every tavern; and that's why we stop so often with our return horses to drink a drop or fill a pipe."

"Confound it!" said Antoine, with an indescribable twist of the shoulders. "A fellow must have his fun."

"Well, taste the wine, my lad. I'll warrant it won't make you weep." And filling a glass, Montbar signed to the postilion to fill the other.

"A fine honor for me! To your health and that of your company!"

This was an habitual phrase of the worthy postilion, a sort of extension of politeness which did not need the presence of others to justify it in his eyes.

"Ha!" said he, after drinking and smacking his lips, "there's vintage for you—and I have gulped it down at a swallow as if it were heel-taps!"

"That was a mistake, Antoine."

"Yes, it was a mistake."

"Luckily," said Montbar, refilling his glass, "you can repair it."

"No higher than my thumb, citizen," said the facetious postilion, taking care that his thumb touched the rim of the glass.

"One minute," said Montbar, just as Antoine was putting his glass to his lips.

"Just in time," said the postilion; "it was on its way. What is it?"

"You wouldn't let me drink to the health of your mistress, but I hope you won't refuse to drink to mine."

"Oh! that's never refused, especially with such wine. To the health of your mistress and her company."

Thereupon citizen Antoine swallowed the crimson liquor, tasting and relishing it this time.

"Hey!" exclaimed Montbar, "you're in too much of a hurry, my friend."

"Pooh!" retorted the postilion.

"Yes. Suppose I have several mistresses. If I don't name the one we drink to what good will it do her?"

"Why, that's true!"

"Sad; but you'll have to try again, my friend."

"Ha! Try again, of course! Can't do things half-way with a man like you. The sin's committed; we'll drink again." And Antoine held out his glass. Montbar filled it to the brim.

"Now," said Antoine, eying the bottle, and making sure it was empty, "there must be no mistake. Her name?"

"To the beautiful Josephine!" said Montbar.

"To the beautiful Josephine!" repeated Antoine.

And he swallowed the Burgundy with increasing satisfaction. Then, after drinking, and wiping his lips on his sleeve, he said, as he set the glass on the table: "Hey! one moment, citizen."

"What now?" exclaimed Montbar. "Anything wrong this time?"

"I should say so. We've made a great blunder; but it's too late now."

"Why so?"

"The bottle is empty."

"That one, yes; but not this one."

So saying, Montbar took from the chimney corner another bottle, already uncorked.

"Ah! ah!" exclaimed Antoine, a radiant smile lighting his face.

"Is there any remedy for it?" asked Montbar.

"There is," replied Antoine, holding out his glass.

Montbar filled it as scrupulously full as he had the first three.

"Well," said the postilion, holding the ruby liquid to the light and admiring its sparkle, "as I was saying, we drank to the health of the beautiful Josephine—"

"Yes," said Montbar.

"But," said Antoine, "there are a devilish lot of Josephines in France."

"True. How many do you suppose there are, Antoine?"

"Perhaps a hundred thousand."

"Granted. What then?"

"Well, out of that hundred thousand a tenth of them must be beautiful."

"That's a good many."

"Say a twentieth."

"All right."

"That makes five thousand."

"The devil! You're strong in arithmetic!"

"I'm the son of a schoolmaster."

"Well?"

"Well, to which of those five thousand did we drink, hey?"

"You're right, Antoine. The family name must follow. To the beautiful Josephine—"

"Stop. This glass was begun; it won't do. If the health is to do her any good, we'll have to empty it and fill it again."

He put the glass to his lips.

"There, it's empty," he said.

"And full," added Montbar, putting the bottle to the glass.

"I'm ready. To the beautiful Josephine—"

"To the beautiful Josephine—Lollier!"

And Montbar emptied his glass.

"By the Lord!" exclaimed Antoine. "Wait a moment. Josephine Lollier! Why, I know her."

"I didn't say you didn't."

"Josephine Lollier! Why, she's the daughter of the man who keeps the post-horses at Belleville."

"Exactly."

"Damn it!" exclaimed the postilion, "you're not to be pitied—a pretty slip of a girl! To the health of beautiful Josephine Lollier."

And he swallowed his fifth glass of Burgundy.

"Now," asked Montbar, "do you understand why I had you sent up here, my lad?"

"No; but I don't bear you any grudge for it, all the same."

"That's very kind of you."

"Oh! I'm a pretty good devil."

"Well, I'll tell you why I sent for you."

"I'm all ears."

"Wait. You'll hear better if your glass is full than if it's empty."

"Are you a doctor for deaf folk?" asked the postilion, banteringly.

"No; but I've lived a good deal among drunkards," replied Montbar, filling Antoine's glass again.

"A man is not a drunkard because he likes wine," said Antoine.

"I agree with you, my good fellow," replied Montbar. "A man is only a drunkard when he can't carry his liquor."

"Well said," cried Antoine, who seemed to carry his pretty well. "I'm listening."

"You told me that you didn't understand why I had sent for you."

"That's what I said."

"Still, you must have suspected that I had an object?"

"Every man has an object, good or bad, according to our priest," observed Antoine, sententiously.

"Well, my friend," resumed Montbar, "mine is to make my way by night, without being recognized, into the courtyard of Master Nicolas-Denis Lollier, postmaster at Belleville."

"At Belleville," repeated Antoine, who had followed Montbar's words with all the attention he was capable of. "You wish to make your way by night, without being recognized, into the courtyard of Master Nicolas-Denis Lollier, postmaster at Belleville, in order to see the beautiful Josephine? Ah, ha! my sly dog!"

"You have it, my dear Antoine; and I wish to get in without being recognized, because Father Lollier has discovered everything, and has forbidden his daughter to see me."

"You don't say so. Well, what can I do about it?"

"Your wits are still muddled, Antoine. Drink another glass of wine to brighten them up."

"Right you are," exclaimed Antoine.

And he swallowed his sixth glass of wine.

"You ask what you can do, Antoine?"

"Yes, what can I do? That's what I ask."

"Everything, my friend."

"I?"

"You."

"Ha! I'm curious to know what. Clear it up, clear it up!" And he held out his glass.

"You drive the mail to Chambéry to-morrow, don't you?"

"Yes; at six o'clock."

"Well, suppose that Antoine is a good fellow?"

"No supposing about it; he is!"

"Well, this is what Antoine does—"

"Go on; what does he do?"

"In the first place, he empties his glass."

"Done! that's not difficult."

"Then he takes these ten louis."

Montbar spread ten louis on the table.

"Ah, ha!" exclaimed Antoine, "yellow boys, real ones. I thought those little devils had all emigrated."

"You see there are some left."

"And what is Antoine to do to put them in his pocket?"

"Antoine must lend me his best postilion's suit."

"To you?"

"And let me take his place to-morrow night."

"Ah, yes; so that you can see the beautiful Josephine to-morrow night."

"Of course. I reach Belleville at eight, drive into the

courtyard, and say the horses are tired and must rest from eight till ten, and from eight to ten—''

"You can fool Père Lollier."

"Well, there you are, Antoine!"

"There I am! When a fellow's young he goes with the young 'uns; when he's a bachelor he's in with the bachelors; when he's old and a papa, he can go with the papas, and cry, 'Long live the papas.' ''

"Then, my good Antoine, you'll lend me your best jacket and breeches?"

"I've just got a new jacket and breeches that I've never worn."

"And you'll let me take your place?"

"With pleasure."

"Then I'll give you five louis for earnest money."

"And the rest?"

"To-morrow, when I pull on the boots; only—there's one precaution you must take."

"What is it?"

"There's talk of brigands robbing diligences; you'll be careful to put the holsters on the saddle."

"What for?"

"For pistols."

"No, no! Don't you go and shoot those fine young fellows."

"What! do you call robbers who pillage diligences fine young men?"

"A man's not a robber because he takes government money."

"Is that your opinion?"

"I should say so; besides, it's the opinion of a good many other people, too. As for me, if I were a judge, I'd never in the world condemn them."

"Perhaps you would drink to their health?"

"Of course, if the wine was good."

"I dare you to do it," said Montbar, emptying the last of the second bottle into Antoine's glass.

"You know the proverb?" said the postilion.

"What is it?"

"Never defy a fool to commit his folly. To the health of the Companions of Jehu."

"Amen!" responded Montbar.

"And the five louis?" asked Antoine, putting his glass on the table.

"There they are."

"Thank you; you shall have the holsters on your saddle; but take my advice and don't put pistols in 'em; or if you do, follow Père Jérôme's example—he's the conductor of the Geneva diligence—and put powder and no balls in 'em."

And with that philanthropic advice, the postilion took his leave, and went down the stairway singing a postilion's song in a vinous voice.

Montbar followed the song conscientiously through two verses, then, as the voice died away in the distance, he was obliged to forego the rest of the song, however interesting he may have found it.

CHAPTER XLII

THE CHAMBÉRY MAIL-COACH

THE next day, at five in the afternoon, Antoine, anxious, no doubt, not to be late, was in the courtyard of the Hôtel de la Poste, harnessing the three horses which were to relay the mail-coach.

Shortly after, the coach rumbled into the courtyard at a gallop, and was pulled up under the windows of a room close to the servants' stairway, which had seemed greatly to occupy Antoine's attention. If any one had paid attention to so slight a detail it might have been observed that the window-curtain was somewhat imprudently drawn aside to permit the occupant of the room to see the persons who got out of the coach. There were three men, who, with the haste of famished travellers, made their way toward the brilliantly lighted windows of the common room.

They had scarcely entered, when a smart postilion came down the kitchen staircase, shod simply with thin pumps over which he intended to pull his heavy riding-boots. These he received from Antoine, slipping five louis into his hand at the same time, and turned for the man to throw his riding cape over his shoulders, a protection rendered necessary by the severity of the weather.

This completed, Antoine returned hastily to the stables and hid in the darkest corner. As for the man who had taken his place, reassured no doubt by the high collar of the cape that concealed half of his face, he went straight to the horses which stood ready harnessed, slipped his pistols into the holsters, and, profitting by the moment when the other horses were being led into the stable by their postilion, he took a gimlet, which might in case of need serve as a dagger, from his pocket, and screwed the four rings into the woodwork of the coach, one into each door, and the other two into the body of the coach. After which he put the horses to with a rapidity and skill which bespoke in him a man familiar from childhood with all the details of an art pushed to extremes in our day by that honorable class of society which we call "gentlemen riders."

That done, he waited, quieting his restless horses by voice and whip, judiciously combined, or used in turn.

Every one knows the rapidity with which the meals of the unhappy beings condemned to travel by mail are hurried through. The half-hour was not up, when the voice of the conductor was heard, calling:

"Come, citizen travellers, take your places."

Montbar placed himself close to the carriage door and recognized Roland and the colonel of the 7th Chasseurs, perfectly, in spite of their disguise, as they jumped into the coach, paying no attention whatever to the postilion.

The latter closed the door upon them, slipped the padlock through the two rings and turned the key. Then, walking around the coach, he pretended to drop his whip before the other door, and, in stooping for it, slipped the second padlock through the rings, deftly turned the key as he straightened up, and, assured that the two officers were securely locked in, he sprang upon his horse, grumbling at the conductor who had left him to do his work. In fact the conductor was still squabbling with the landlord over his bill when the third traveller got into his place in the coupé.

"Are you coming this evening, to-night, or to-morrow morning, Père François?" cried the pretended postilion, imitating Antoine as best he could.

"All right, all right, I'm coming," answered the conductor; then, looking around him: "Why, where are the travellers?" he asked.

"Here," replied the two officers from the interior and the agent from the coupé.

"Is the door properly closed?" persisted Père François.

"I'll answer for that," said Montbar.

"Then off you go, baggage!" cried the conductor, as he climbed into the coupé and closed the door behind him.

The postilion did not wait to be told twice; he started his horses, digging his spurs into the belly of the one he rode and lashing the others vigorously. The mail-coach dashed forward at a gallop.

Montbar drove as if he had never done anything else in his life; as he crossed the town the windows rattled and the houses shook; never did real postilion crack his whip with greater science.

As he left Mâcon he saw a little troop of horse; they were the twelve chasseurs told off to follow the coach without seeming to escort it. The colonel passed his head through the window and made a sign to the sergeant who commanded them.

Montbar did not seem to notice anything; but after going some four or five hundred yards, he turned his head, while executing a symphony with his whip, and saw that the escort had started.

"Wait, my babes!" said Montbar, "I'll make you see the country." And he dug in his spurs and brought down his whip. The horses seemed to have wings, and the coach flew over the cobblestones like the chariot of thunder rumbling past. The conductor became alarmed.

"Hey, Master Antoine," cried he, "are you drunk?"

"Drunk? fine drinking!" replied Montbar; "I dined on a beetroot salad."

"Damn him! If he goes like that," cried Roland, thrusting his head through the window, "the escort can't keep up."

"You hear what he says!" shrieked the conductor.

"No," replied Montbar, "I don't."

"Well, he says that if you keep this up the escort can't follow."

"Is there an escort?" asked Montbar.

"Of course; we're carrying government money."

"That's different; you ought to have said so at first."

But instead of slacking his pace the coach was whirled along as before; if there was any change, it was for greater velocity than before.

"Antoine, if there's an accident, I'll shoot you through the head," shouted the conductor.

"Run along!" exclaimed Montbar; "everybody knows those pistols haven't any balls in them."

"Possibly not; but mine have!" cried the police agent.

"That remains to be seen," replied Montbar, keeping on his way at the same pace without heed to these remonstrances.

On they went with the speed of lightning through the village of Varennes, then through that of La Crêche and the little town of Chapelle-de-Guinchay; only half a mile further and they would reach the Maison-Blanche. The horses were dripping, and tossed the foam from their mouths as they neighed with excitement.

Montbar glanced behind him; more than a mile back the sparks were flying from the escort's horses. Before him was the mountainous declivity. Down it he dashed, gathering the reins to master his horses when the time came.

The conductor had ceased expostulating, for he saw that the hand which guided the horses was firm and capable. But from time to time the colonel thrust his head through the window to look for his men.

Half-way down the slope Montbar had his horses under control, without, however, seeming to check their course. Then he began to sing, at the top of his voice, the "Réveil du Peuple," the song of the royalists, just as the "Marseillaise" was the song of the Jacobins.

"What's that rogue about?" cried Roland, putting his head through the window. "Tell him to hold his tongue, conductor, or I'll put a ball through his loins."

Perhaps the conductor might have repeated Roland's threat to Montbar, but he suddenly saw a black line blocking the road. "Halt, conductor!" thundered a voice the next moment.

"Postilion, drive over the bellies of those bandits!" shouted the police agent.

"Drive on yourself!" said Montbar. "Do you suppose I'm going over the stomachs of friends? Who-o-ah!"

The mail coach stopped as if by magic.

"Go on! go on!" cried Roland and the colonel, aware that the escort was too far behind to help them.

"Ha! you villain of a postilion," cried the police agent, springing out of the coupé, and pointing his pistol at Montbar, "you shall pay for this."

The words were scarcely uttered when Montbar, forestalling him, fired, and the agent rolled, mortally wounded, under the wheels of the coach. His fingers, convulsed by death, touched the trigger and the pistol went off, but the ball touched no one.

"Conductor," shouted the two officers, "by all the powers of heaven, open, open, open quickly!"

"Gentlemen," said Morgan, advancing, "we are not

attacking your persons, we merely want the government money. Conductor! that fifty thousand francs, and quickly too!"

Two shots from the interior made answer for the officers, who, after vainly shaking the doors, were still more fruitlessly attempting to force themselves through the windows. No doubt one of their shots took effect, for a cry of rage was heard and a flash illuminated the road. The colonel gave a sigh, and fell back against Roland. He was killed outright.

Roland fired again, but no one replied to him. His pistols were both discharged; locked in as he was he could not use his sabre, and he howled with rage.

Meantime the conductor was forced, with a pistol at his throat, to give up the money. Two men took the bags containing the fifty thousand francs, and fastened them on Montbar's horse, which his groom had brought ready saddled and bridled, as if to a meet. Montbar kicked off his heavy boots and sprang into the saddle.

"My compliments to the First Consul, Monsieur de Montrevel!" cried Morgan. Then, turning to his companions, he cried: "Scatter which way you will, you know the rendezvous for to-morrow night."

"Yes, yes," replied ten or a dozen voices.

And the band dispersed like a flock of birds, disappearing down the valley into the shadow of the trees that lined the banks of the little river and surrounded the Maison-Blanche.

At that moment the gallop of horses was heard, and the escort, alarmed by the pistol shots, appeared on the crest of the hill and came down the slope like an avalanche. But it came too late; it found only the conductor sitting dazed by the roadside, the bodies of the colonel and of Fouche's agent, and Roland a prisoner, roaring like a lion gnawing at the bars of its cage.

CHAPTER XLIII

LORD GRENVILLE'S REPLY

WHILE the events we have just recorded were trans-
piring, and occupying the minds and newspapers
of the provinces, other events, of very different
import, were maturing in Paris, which were destined to
occupy the minds and newspapers of the whole world.

Lord Tanlay had returned, bringing the reply of his
uncle, Lord Grenville. This reply consisted of a letter addressed to M. de Talleyrand, inclosing a memorandum for
the First Consul. The letter was couched in the following
terms:

DOWNING STREET, February 14, 1800

SIR—I have received and placed before the King the letter which you transmitted to me through my nephew, Lord
Tanlay. His Majesty, seeing no reason to depart from the
long-established customs of Europe in treating with foreign
States, directs me to forward you in his name the official
reply which is herewith inclosed.

I have the honor to be, with the highest esteem, your
very humble and obedient servant, GRENVILLE.

The letter was dry; the memorandum curt. Moreover,
the First Consul's letter to King George was autographic,
and King George, not "departing from the long-established
customs of Europe in treating with foreign States," replied
by a simple memorandum written by a secretary.

True, the memorandum was signed "Grenville." It was
a long recrimination against France; against the spirit of
disorder, which disturbed the nation; against the fears
which that spirit of disorder inspired in all Europe; and
on the necessity imposed on the sovereigns of Europe, for

the sake of their own safety, to repress it.   In short, the memorandum was virtually a continuation of the war.

The reading of such a dictum made Bonaparte's eyes flash with the flame which, in him, preceded his great decisions, as lightning precedes thunder.

"So, sir," said he, turning to Lord Tanlay, "this is all you have obtained?"

"Yes, citizen First Consul."

"Then you did not repeat verbally to your uncle all that I charged you to say to him?"

"I did not omit a syllable."

"Did you tell him that you had lived in France three years, that you had seen her, had studied her; that she was strong, powerful, prosperous and desirous of peace while prepared for war?"

"I told him all that."

"Did you add that the war which England is making against France is a senseless war; that the spirit of disorder of which they speak, and which, at the worst, is only the effervescence of freedom too long restrained, which it were wiser to confine to France by means of a general peace; that that peace is the sole *cordon sanitaire* which can prevent it from crossing our frontiers; and that if the volcano of war is lighted in France, France will spread like lava over foreign lands.   Italy is delivered, says the King of England; but from whom?   From her liberators.   Italy is delivered, but why?   Because I conquered Egypt from the Delta to the third Cataract; Italy is delivered because I was no longer in Italy.   But—I am here; in a month I can be in Italy.   What do I need to win her back from the Alps to the Adriatic?   A single battle.   Do you know what Masséna is doing in defending Genoa?   Waiting for me. Ha! the sovereigns of Europe need war to protect their crowns?   Well, my lord, I tell you that I will shake Europe until their crowns tremble on their heads.   Want war, do they?   Just wait—Bourrienne!   Bourrienne!"

The door between the First Consul's study and the secretary's office opened precipitately, and Bourrienne rushed in, his face terrified, as though he thought Bonaparte were calling for help. But when he saw him highly excited, crumpling the diplomatic memorandum in one hand and striking with the other on his desk, while Lord Tanlay was standing calm, erect and silent near him, he understood immediately that England's answer had irritated the First Consul.

"Did you call me, general?" he asked.

"Yes," said the First Consul, "sit down there and write."

Then in a harsh, jerky voice, without seeking his words, which, on the contrary, seemed to crowd through the portals of his brain, he dictated the following proclamation:

SOLDIERS!—In promising peace to the French people, I was your mouthpiece; I know your power.

You are the same men who conquered the Rhine, Holland and Italy, and granted peace beneath the walls of astounded Vienna.

Soldiers, it is no longer our own frontiers that you have to defend; it is the enemy's country you must now invade.

Soldiers, when the time comes, I shall be among you, and astounded Europe shall remember that you belong to the race of heroes!

Bourrienne raised his head, expectant, after writing the last words.

"Well, that's all," said Bonaparte.

"Shall I add the sacramental words: 'Vive la République!'?"

"Why do you ask that?"

"Because we have issued no proclamation during the last four months, and something may be changed in the ordinary formulas."

"The proclamation will do as it is," said Bonaparte, "add nothing to it."

Taking a pen, he dashed rather than wrote his signature at the bottom of the paper, then handing it to Bourrienne, he said: "See that it appears in the 'Moniteur' to-morrow."

Bourrienne left the room, carrying the proclamation with him.

Bonaparte, left alone with Lord Tanlay, walked up and down the room for a moment, as though he had forgotten the Englishman's presence; then he stopped suddenly before him.

"My lord," he asked, "do you think you obtained from your uncle all that another man might have obtained in your place?"

"More, citizen First Consul."

"More! more! Pray, what have you obtained?"

"I think that the citizen First Consul did not read the royal memorandum with all the attention it deserves."

"Heavens!" exclaimed Bonaparte, "I know it by heart."

"Then the citizen First Consul cannot have weighed the meaning and the wording of a certain paragraph."

"You think so?"

"I am sure of it; and if the citizen First Consul will permit me to read him the paragraph to which I allude—"

Bonaparte relaxed his hold upon the crumpled note, and handed it to Lord Tanlay, saying: "Read it."

Sir John cast his eyes over the document, with which he seemed to be familiar, paused at the tenth paragraph, and read:

The best and surest means for peace and security, and for their continuance, would be the restoration of that line of princes who for so many centuries have preserved to the French nation its internal prosperity and the respect and consideration of foreign countries. Such an event would have removed, and at any time will remove, the obstacles which are now in the way of negotiations and peace; it would guarantee to France the tranquil possession of her former territory, and procure for all the other nations of Europe, through a like tranquillity and peace, that security which they are now obliged to seek by other means.

"Well," said Bonaparte, impatiently, "I have read all that, and perfectly understood it. Be Monk, labor for another man, and your victories, your renown, your genius will be forgiven you; humble yourself, and you shall be allowed to remain great!"

"Citizen First Consul," said Lord Tanlay, "no one knows better than I the difference between you and Monk, and how far you surpass him in genius and renown."

"Then why do you read me that?"

"I only read that paragraph," replied Sir John, "to lead you to give to the one following its due significance."

"Let's hear it," said Bonaparte, with repressed impatience.

Sir John continued:

But, however desirable such an event may be for France and for the world, it is not to this means alone that his Majesty restricts the possibility of a safe and sure pacification.

Sir John emphasized the last words.

"Ah! ah!" exclaimed Bonaparte, stepping hastily to Sir John's side.

The Englishman continued:

His Majesty does not presume to prescribe to France her form of government, nor the hands into which she may place the necessary authority to conduct the affairs of a great and powerful nation.

"Read that again, sir," said Bonaparte, eagerly.

"Read it yourself," replied Sir John.

He handed him the note, and Bonaparte re-read it.

"Was it you, sir," he asked, "who added that paragraph?"

"I certainly insisted on it."

Bonaparte reflected.

"You are right," he said; "a great step has been taken; the return of the Bourbons is no longer a condition *sine quâ non*. I am accepted, not only as a military, but also as a political power." Then, holding out his hand to Sir John, he added: "Have you anything to ask of me, sir?"

"The only thing I seek has been asked of you by my friend Roland."

"And I answered, sir, that I shall be pleased to see you the husband of his sister. If I were richer, or if you were less so, I would offer to dower her"—Sir John made a motion—"but as I know your fortune will suffice for two," added Bonaparte, smiling, "or even more, I leave you the joy of giving not only happiness, but also wealth to the woman you love. Bourrienne!" he called.

Bourrienne appeared.

"I have sent it, general," he said.

"Very good," replied the First Consul; "but that is not what I called you for."

"I await your orders."

"At whatever hour of the day or night Lord Tanlay presents himself, I shall be happy to receive him without delay; you hear me, my dear Bourrienne? You hear me, my lord?"

Lord Tanlay bowed his thanks.

"And now," said Bonaparte, "I presume you are in a hurry to be off to the Château des Noires-Fontaines. I won't detain you, but there is one condition I impose."

"And that is, general?"

"If I need you for another mission—"

"That is not a condition, citizen First Consul; it is a favor."

Lord Tanlay bowed and withdrew.

Bourrienne prepared to follow him, but Bonaparte called him back. "Is there a carriage below?" he asked.

Bourrienne looked into the courtyard. "Yes, general."

"Then get ready and come with me."

"I am ready, general; I have only my hat and overcoat to get, and they are in the office."

"Then let us go," said Bonaparte.

He took up his hat and coat, went down the private staircase, and signed to the carriage to come up. Notwithstanding Bourrienne's haste, he got down after him. A footman opened the door; Bonaparte sprang in.

"Where are we going, general?" asked Bourrienne.

"To the Tuileries," replied Bonaparte.

Bourrienne, amazed, repeated the order, and looked at the First Consul as if to seek an explanation; but the latter was plunged in thought, and the secretary, who at this time was still the friend, thought it best not to disturb him.

The horses started at gallop—Bonaparte's usual mode of progression—and took the way to the Tuileries.

The Tuileries, inhabited by Louis XVI. after the days of the 5th and 6th of October, and occupied successively by the Convention and the Council of Five Hundred, had remained empty and devastated since the 18th Brumaire. Since that day Bonaparte had more than once cast his eyes on that ancient palace of royalty; but he knew the importance of not arousing any suspicion that a future king might dwell in the palace of the abolished monarchy.

Bonaparte had brought back from Italy a magnificent bust of Junius Brutus; there was no suitable place for it at the Luxembourg, and toward the end of November, Bonaparte had sent for the Republican, David, and ordered him to place the bust in the gallery of the Tuileries. Who could suppose that David, the friend of Marat, was preparing the dwelling of a future emperor by placing the bust of Cæsar's murderer in the gallery of the Tuileries? No one did suppose, nor even suspect it.

When Bonaparte went to see if the bust were properly placed, he noticed the havoc committed in the palace of Catherine of Medicis. The Tuileries were no longer the abode of kings, it is true, but they were a national palace, and the nation could not allow one of its palaces to become dilapidated. Bonaparte sent for citizen Lecomte, the architect, and ordered him to *clean* the · Tuileries. The word might be taken in both senses—moral and physical.

The architect was requested to send in an estimate of the cost of the cleaning. It amounted to five hundred thousand francs. Bonaparte asked if, for that sum, the Tuileries could be converted into a suitable "palace for the government."

The architect replied that the sum named would suffice not only to restore the Tuileries to their former condition, but to make them habitable.

A habitable palace, that was all Bonaparte wanted. How should he, a Republican, need regal luxury? The "palace of the government" ought to be severely plain, decorated with marbles and statues only. But what ought those statues to be? It was the First Consul's duty to select them.

Accordingly, Bonaparte chose them from the three great ages and the three great nations: from the Greeks, from the Romans, from France and her rivals. From the Greeks he chose Alexander and Demosthenes; the genius of conquest and the genius of eloquence. From the Romans he chose Scipio, Cicero, Cato, Brutus and Cæsar, placing the great victim side by side with the murderer, as great almost as himself. From the modern world he chose Gustavus Adolphus, Turenne, the great Condé, Duguay-Trouin, Marlborough, Prince Eugène, and the Maréchal de Saxe; and, finally, the great Frederick and George Washington—false philosophy upon a throne, and true wisdom founding a free state.

To these he added warlike heroes—Dampierre, Dugommier, Joubert—to prove that, while he did not fear the memory of a Bourbon in the great Condé, neither was he jealous of his brothers-in-arms, the victims of a cause already no longer his.

Matters were in this state at the period of which we are now speaking; that is, the last of February, 1800. The Tuileries had been cleaned, the busts were in their niches, the statues were on their pedestals; and only a favorable occasion was wanting.

That occasion came when the news of Washington's death was received. The founder of the liberty of the United States had ceased to breathe on the 14th of December, 1799.

It was that event of which Bonaparte was thinking,

when Bourrienne saw by the expression of his face that he must be left entirely to the reflections which absorbed him.

The carriage stopped before the Tuileries. Bonaparte sprang out with the same haste with which he had entered it; went rapidly up the stairs, and through the apartments, examining more particularly those which had been inhabited by Louis XVI. and Marie-Antoinette. In the private study of Louis XVI. he stopped short.

"Here's where we will live, Bourrienne," he said, suddenly, as if the latter had followed him through the mental labyrinth in which he wandered, following the thread of Ariadne which we call thought. "Yes, we will lodge here; the Third Consul can have the Pavilion of Flora, and Cambacérès will remain at the Chancellerie."

"In that way," said Bourrienne, "when the time comes, you will have only one to turn out."

"Come, come," said Bonaparte, catching Bourrienne by the ear, "that's not bad."

"When shall we move in, general?" asked Bourrienne.

"Oh, not to-morrow; it will take at least a week to prepare the Parisians to see me leave the Luxembourg for the Tuileries."

"Eight days," exclaimed Bourrienne; "that will do."

"Especially if we begin at once. Come, Bourrienne, to the Luxembourg."

With the rapidity that characterized all his movements when serious matters were in question, he passed through the suites of apartments he had already visited, ran down the stairs, and sprang into the carriage, calling out: "To the Luxembourg!"

"Wait, wait," cried Bourrienne, still in the vestibule; "general, won't you wait for me?"

"Laggard!" exclaimed Bonaparte. And the carriage started, as it had come, at a gallop.

When Bonaparte re-entered his study he found the minister of police awaiting him.

"Well, what now, citizen Fouché? You look upset. Have I, perchance, been assassinated?"

"Citizen First Consul," said the minister, "you seemed to attach the utmost importance to the destruction of those bands who call themselves the Companions of Jehu."

"Evidently, since I sent Roland himself to pursue them. Have you any news of them?"

"We have."

"From whom?"

"Their leader himself."

"Their leader?"

"He has had the audacity to send me a report of their last exploit."

"Against whom?"

"The fifty thousand francs you sent to the Saint-Bernard fathers."

"What became of them?"

"The fifty thousand francs?"

"Yes."

"They are in the possession of those brigands, and their leader informs me he will transfer them shortly to Cadoudal."

"Then Roland is killed?"

"No."

"How do you mean, no?"

"My agent is killed; Colonel Maurice is killed; but your aide-de-camp is safe and sound."

"Then he will hang himself," said Bonaparte.

"What good would that do? The rope would break; you know his luck."

"Or his misfortune, yes— Where is the report?"

"You mean the letter?"

"Letter, report, thing—whatever it was that told you this news."

The minister handed the First Consul a paper inclosed in a perfumed envelope.

"What's this?"

"The thing you asked for."

Bonaparte read the address: "To the citizen Fouché, minister of police. Paris." Then he opened the letter, which contained the following.

CITIZEN MINISTER—I have the honor to inform you that the fifty thousand francs intended for the monks of Saint-Bernard came into our hands on the night of February 25, 1800 (old style), and that they will reach those of citizen Cadoudal within the week.

The affair was well-managed, save for the deaths of your agent and Colonel Saint-Maurice. As for M. Roland de Montrevel, I have the satisfaction of informing you that nothing distressing has befallen him. I did not forget that he was good enough to receive me at the Luxembourg.

I write you, citizen minister, because I presume that M. Roland de Montrevel is just now too much occupied in pursuing us to write you himself. But I am sure that at his first leisure moment you will receive from him a report containing all the details into which I cannot enter for lack of time and facilities for writing.

In exchange for the service I render you, citizen minister, I will ask you to do one for me; namely, inform Madame de Montrevel, without delay, that her son is in safety.   MORGAN.

Maison-Blanche, on the road from Mâcon to Lyons, Saturday, 9 P.M.

"Ha, the devil!" said Bonaparte; "a bold scamp!" Then he added, with a sigh: "What colonels and captains those men would make me!"

"What are your orders, citizen First Consul?" asked the minister of police.

"None; that concerns Roland. His honor is at stake; and, as he is not killed, he will take his revenge."

"Then the First Consul will take no further notice of the affair?"

"Not for the present, at any rate." Then, turning to his secretary, he added, "We have other fish to fry, haven't we, Bourrienne?"

Bourrienne nodded affirmatively.

"When does the First Consul wish to see me again?" asked the minister.

"To-night, at ten o'clock. We move out in eight days."

"Where are you going?"

"To the Tuileries."

Fouché gave a start of amazement.

"Against your opinion, I know," said the First Consul; "but I'll take the whole business on myself; you have only to obey."

Fouché bowed, and prepared to leave the room.

"By the way!" exclaimed Bonaparte.

Fouché turned round.

"Don't forget to notify Madame de Montrevel that her son is safe and sound; that's the least you can do for citizen Morgan after the service he has rendered you."

And he turned his back on the minister of police, who retired, biting his lips till the blood came.

CHAPTER XLIV

CHANGE OF RESIDENCE

THAT same day, the First Consul, left alone with Bourrienne, dictated the following order, addressed to the Consulate guard and to the army at large:

Washington is dead! That great man fought against tyranny. He consolidated the liberty of America. His memory will ever be dear to the French people, to all free men in both hemispheres, but especially to the French soldiers, who, like Washington and his soldiers, have fought for Liberty and Equality. Consequently, the First Consul orders that the flags and banners of the Republic shall be hung with crape for ten days.

But the First Consul did not intend to confine himself to this order of the day.

Among the means he took to facilitate his removal from the Luxembourg to the Tuileries was one of those fêtes by which he knew, none better, how to amuse the eyes and also direct the minds of the spectator. This fête was to take place at the Invalides, or, as they said in those days, the Temple of Mars. A bust of Washington was to be crowned, and the flags of Aboukir were to be received from the hands of General Lannes.

It was one of those combinations which Bonaparte thoroughly understood—a flash of lightning drawn from the contact of contrasting facts. He presented the great man of the New World, and a great victory of the old; young America coupled with the palms of Thebes and Memphis.

On the day fixed for the ceremony, six thousand cavalry were in line from the Luxembourg to the Invalides. At eight o'clock, Bonaparte mounted his horse in the main courtyard of the Consular palace; issuing by the Rue de Tournon he took the line of the quays, accompanied by a staff of generals, none of whom were over thirty-five years of age.

Lannes headed the procession; behind him were sixty Guides bearing the sixty captured flags; then came Bonaparte about two horse's-lengths ahead of his staff.

The minister of war, Berthier, awaited the procession under the dome of the temple. He leaned against a statue of Mars at rest, and the ministers and councillors of state were grouped around him. The flags of Denain and Fontenoy, and those of the first campaign in Italy, were already suspended from the columns which supported the roof. Two centenarian "Invalids" who had fought beside Maréchal Saxe were standing, one to the right and one to the left of Berthier, like caryatides of an ancient world, gazing across the centuries. To the right, on a raised platform, was the bust of Washington, which was now to be draped with the flags of Aboukir. On another platform, opposite to the former, stood Bonaparte's armchair.

On each side of the temple were tiers of seats in which was gathered all the elegant society of Paris, or rather that portion of it which gave its adhesion to the order of ideas then to be celebrated.

When the flags appeared, the trumpets blared, their metallic sounds echoing through the arches of the temple.

Lannes entered first. At a sign from him, the Guides mounted two by two the steps of the platform and placed the staffs of the flags in the holders prepared for them. During this time Bonaparte took his place in the chair.

Then Lannes advanced to the minister of war, and, in that voice that rang out so clearly on the battlefield, crying "Forward!" he said:

"Citizen minister, these are the flags of the Ottoman army, destroyed before your eyes at Aboukir. The army of Egypt, after crossing burning deserts, surviving thirst and hunger, found itself before an enemy proud of his numbers and his victories, and believing that he saw an easy prey in our troops, exhausted by their march and incessant combats. He had yet to learn that the French soldier is greater because he knows how to suffer than because he knows how to vanquish, and that his courage rises and augments in danger. Three thousand Frenchmen, as you know, fell upon eighteen thousand barbarians, broke their ranks, forced them back, pressed them between our lines and the sea; and the terror of our bayonets is such that the Mussulmans, driven to choose a death, rushed into the depths of the Mediterranean.

"On that memorable day hung the destinies of Egypt, France and Europe, and they were saved by your courage.

"Allied Powers! if you dare to violate French territory, and if the general who was given back to us by the victory of Aboukir makes an appeal to the nation—Allied Powers! I say to you, that your successes would be more fatal to you than disasters! What Frenchman is there who would not march to victory again under the banners of the First Consul, or serve his apprenticeship to fame with him?"

Then, addressing the "Invalids," for whom the whole lower gallery had been reserved, he continued in a still more powerful voice:

"And you, brave veterans, honorable victims of the fate of battles, you will not be the last to flock under the orders of him who knows your misfortunes and your glory, and who now delivers to your keeping these trophies won by your valor. Ah, I know you, veterans, you burn to sacrifice the half of your remaining lives to your country and its freedom!''

This specimen of the military eloquence of the conqueror of Montebello was received with deafening applause. Three times the minister of war endeavored to make reply; and three times the bravos cut him short. At last, however, silence came, and Berthier expressed himself as follows:

''To raise on the banks of the Seine these trophies won on the banks of the Nile; to hang beneath the domes of our temples, beside the flags of Vienna, of Petersburg, of London, the banners blessed in the mosques of Byzantium and Cairo; to see them here, presented by the same warriors, young in years, old in glory, whom Victory has so often crowned—these things are granted only to Republican France.

''Yet this is but a part of what he has done, that hero, in the flower of his age covered with the laurels of Europe, he, who stood a victor before the Pyramids, from the summits of which forty centuries looked down upon him while, surrounded by his warriors and learned men, he emancipated the native soil of art and restored to it the lights of civilization.

''Soldiers, plant in this temple of the warrior virtues those ensigns of the Crescent, captured on the rocks of Canopus by three thousand Frenchmen from eighteen thousand Ottomans, as brave as they were barbarous. Let them bear witness, not to the valor of the French soldier—the universe itself resounds to that—but to his unalterable constancy, his sublime devotion. Let the sight of these banners console you, veteran warriors, you, whose bodies, gloriously mutilated on the field of honor, deprive your courage of other exercise than hope and prayer. Let them proclaim from that dome above us, to all the enemies of France, the influence of genius, the value of the heroes who captured them; forewarning of the horrors of war all those who are deaf to our offers of peace. Yes, if they will have war, they shall have it—war, terrible and unrelenting!

''The nation, satisfied, regards the Army of the East with pride.

''That invincible army will learn with joy that the First Consul is watchful of its glory. It is the object of the

keenest solicitude on the part of the Republic. It will hear
with pride that we have honored it in our temples, while
awaiting the moment when we shall imitate, if need be, on
the fields of Europe, the warlike virtues it has displayed
on the burning sands of Africa and Asia.

"Come, in the name of that army, intrepid general, come
in the name of those heroes among whom you now appear,
and receive an embrace in token of the national gratitude.

"And in the moment when we again take up our arms
in defence of our independence (if the blind fury of kings
refuses the peace we offer), let us cast a branch of laurel on
the ashes of Washington, that hero who freed America from
the yoke of our worst and most implacable enemy. Let his
illustrious shade tell us of the glory which follows a nation's
liberator beyond the grave!"

Bonaparte now came down from his platform, and in the
name of France was embraced by Berthier.

M. de Fontanes, who was appointed to pronounce the
eulogy on Washington, waited courteously until the echoes
of the torrent of applause, which seemed to fall in cascades
through the vast amphitheatre, had died away. In the
midst of these glorious individualities, M. de Fontanes
was a curiosity, half political, half literary. After the
18th Fructidor he was proscribed with Suard and Laharpe;
but, being perfectly hidden in a friend's house, and never
going out except at night, he managed to avoid leaving
France. Nevertheless, an accident, impossible to foresee,
had betrayed him. He was knocked down one night on
the Place du Carrousel by a runaway horse, and was recognized by a policeman, who ran to his assistance. But
Fouché, who was at once informed, not only of his presence
in France, but also of his actual hiding-place, pretended to
know nothing of him.

A few days after the 18th Brumaire, Maret, who became
later the Duc de Bassano, Laplace, who continued to be
simply a man of science, and Regnault de Saint-Jean-
d'Angely, who died mad, spoke to the First Consul of
M. de Fontanes and of his presence in Paris.

"Present him to me," replied the First Consul simply.

M. de Fontanes was presented to Bonaparte, who, recognizing his supple nature and the unctuous flattery of his eloquence, chose him to deliver the eulogy on Washington, and perhaps something of his own at the same time.

M. de Fontanes' address was too long to be reported here; all that we shall say about it is, that it was precisely what Bonaparte desired.

That evening there was a grand reception at the Luxembourg. During the ceremony a rumor was spread that the First Consul contemplated removing to the Tuileries. Persons who were either bold or curious ventured on a few words to Josephine. She, poor woman, who still saw before her the tumbrel and the scaffold of Marie Antoinette, had an instinctive horror of all that might connect her with royalty; she therefore hesitated to reply and referred all questions to her husband.

Then another rumor began to be bruited about which served as a counterpoise to the former. Murat, it was said, had asked the hand of Mademoiselle Caroline Bonaparte in marriage. But this marriage was not without its obstacles; Bonaparte had had a quarrel, lasting over a year, with the man who aspired to the honor of becoming his brother-in-law. The cause of this quarrel will seem rather strange to our readers.

Murat, the lion of the army; Murat, whose courage had become proverbial; Murat, who might well have been taken by a sculptor as a model for the god of war; Murat, on one occasion, when he must have slept ill or breakfasted badly, had a moment of weakness.

It happened before Mantua, in which city Wurmser, after the battle of Rivoli, was forced to shut himself up with twenty-eight thousand men; General Miollis, with four thousand only, was investing the place. During a sortie attempted by the Austrians, Murat, at the head of five hundred men, received an order to charge three thousand. Murat charged, but feebly. Bonaparte, whose aide-de-camp he then was, was so irritated that he would not suffer him to remain about him. This was a great blow to Murat, all the more because he was at that time desirous of becoming the general's brother-in-law; he was deeply in love with Caroline Bonaparte.

How had that love come about? It can be told in two words. Perhaps those who read our books singly are surprised that we sometimes dwell on certain details which seem somewhat long drawn out for the book in which they appear. The fact is, we are not writing isolated books, but, as we have already said, we are filling, or trying to fill, an immense frame. To us, the presence of our characters is not limited to their appearance in one book. The man you meet in one book may be a king in a second volume, and exiled or shot in a third.

Balzac did a great and noble work with a hundred aspects, and he called it the "Comédie Humaine." Our work, begun at the same time as his—although, be it understood, we do not praise it—may fitly be called "The Drama of France."

Now, let us return to Murat, and tell how this love, which had so glorious and, possibly, so fatal an influence on his destiny, came to him.

In 1796, Murat was sent to Paris, charged with the duty of presenting to the Directory the flags and banners taken by the French army at the battles of Dego and Mondovi. During this voyage he made the acquaintance of Madame Bonaparte and Madame Tallien. At Madame Bonaparte's house he again met Mademoiselle Caroline Bonaparte. We say *again*, for that was not the first time he had met the woman who was to share the crown of Naples with him. They had met in Rome, at her brother's house, and, in spite of the rivalry of a young and handsome Roman prince, she had shown him a marked preference.

The three women combined to obtain for him the rank of general of brigade from the Directory. Murat returned to the Army of Italy, more in love than ever, and, in spite of his new rank, he solicited and obtained the favor of re-

maining with the general-in-chief as aide-de-camp. Unhappily, the fatal sortie took place soon after, in consequence
of which he fell in disgrace with Bonaparte. This disgrace
had for awhile all the characteristics of actual enmity.
Bonaparte dismissed him from his service as aide-de-camp,
and transferred him to Neille's division, and then to that
of Baraguey-d'Hilliers. The result was, that when Bonaparte returned to Paris after the treaty of Tolentino, Murat
did not accompany him.

This did not at all suit the female triumvirate, who had
taken the young general under its direction. The beautiful
intriguers entered into the campaign, and as the expedition
to Egypt was then preparing, they induced the minister of
war to send Murat with it. He embarked in the same ship
as Bonaparte, namely the "Orient," but the latter did not
address a single word to him during the voyage. After
they reached Alexandria, Murat was at first unable to break
the icy barrier opposed to him by the general, who, more to
put him at a distance from his own person than to give him
an opportunity to distinguish himself, confronted him with
Mourad Bey. But, during that campaign, Murat performed
such prodigies of valor that he effaced, by such bravery,
the memory of that momentary weakness; he charged so
intrepidly, so madly at Aboukir, that Bonaparte had not
the heart to bear him further malice.

Consequently Murat had returned to France with Bonaparte. He had powerfully co-operated with him on the
18th and especially on the 19th Brumaire. He was, therefore, restored to full favor, and, as a proof of that favor,
had received the command of the Consular guard.

He thought this the moment to declare his love, a love
already well-known to Josephine, who favored it; for which
she had two reasons. In the first place, she was a woman
in the most charming acceptation of the word; that is to
say, all the gentler passions of women were attractive to
her. Joachim loved Caroline, Caroline loved Joachim; that
was enough to make her wish to protect their love. In

the second place, Bonaparte's brothers detested Josephine; Joseph and Lucien were her bitterest enemies, and she was not sorry to make herself two ardent friends in Caroline and Murat. She therefore encouraged the latter to approach Bonaparte on the subject.

Three days before the ceremony we have just described, Murat had entered Bonaparte's study, and, after endless hesitation and circumlocution, had proffered his request.

It is probable that the love of the young pair was no news to Bonaparte, who, however, received it with stern gravity, and contented himself with replying that he would think it over. The matter, in fact, required thinking over. Bonaparte came of a noble family, Murat was the son of an innkeeper. The alliance at such a moment might have great significance. Was the First Consul, in spite of his noble birth, in spite of the exalted rank to which he had raised himself, not only sufficiently republican, but also sufficiently democratic to mingle his blood with that of the common people.

He did not reflect long; his strong, good sense, and his logical mind, told him that he had every interest in allowing the marriage, and he gave his consent to it the same day.

The double news of this marriage and of the removal to the Tuileries was launched on the public at the same time; the one was to counterpoise the other. The First Consul was about to occupy the palace of the former kings, to sleep in the bed of the Bourbons, as they said at that time, but he gave his sister to the son of an innkeeper!

And now, it may be asked, what dowry did the future Queen of Naples bring to the hero of Aboukır? Thirty thousand francs and a diamond necklace, which the First Consul took from his wife, being too poor to buy one. Josephine, who was very fond of her necklace, pouted a little; but the gift, thus obtained, was a triumphant reply to those who claimed that Bonaparte had made a fortune in Italy; besides, why had she taken the interests of the young couple so to heart? She had insisted on marrying them, and she ought to contribute to the dowry.

The result of this clever combination was that on the day when the Consuls left the Luxembourg for the "palace of the government," escorted by the *son of an innkeeper*, soon to be Bonaparte's brother-in-law, it did not occur to those who saw the procession pass to do otherwise than admire and applaud. And, in truth, what could be more admirable and worthy of applause than those processions, which had at their head such men as Murat, Moreau, Junot, Duroc, Augereau, and Masséna?

A grand review had been ordered to take place that same day in the square of the Carrousel. Madame Bonaparte was to be present—not, to be sure, in the balcony of the clock-tower, that being evidently too royal, but at the window of Lebrun's apartment in the Pavilion of Flora.

Bonaparte started at one o'clock precisely from the Luxembourg, escorted by three thousand picked men, among them the splendid regiment of the Guides, created three years earlier as a bodyguard to Bonaparte during the Italian campaign, in consequence of a great danger he had escaped on one occasion. He was resting in a small château, after the exhaustion attendant upon the passage of the Mincio, and was preparing to take a bath, when a retreating Austrian detachment, losing its way, invaded the château, which had no other guard than the sentries. Bonaparte had barely time to escape in his shirt.

A curious difficulty, which deserves to be recorded, arose on the morning of this removal, which took place the 30th Pluviose, year VIII. The generals, of course, had their horses and the ministers their carriages, but the other functionaries had not yet judged it expedient to go to such an expense. Carriages were therefore lacking. They were supplied from the hackney coach-stands, and slips of paper of the same color as the carriages were pasted over their numbers.

The carriage of the First Consul alone was harnessed

with six white horses, but as the three consuls were in the same carriage, Bonaparte and Cambacérès on the front seat, and Lebrun on the back, it was, after all, but two horses apiece. Besides, were not these six white horses given to the commander-in-chief by the Emperor Francis himself, after the treaty of Campo-Formio, a trophy in themselves?

The carriage crossed a part of Paris, following the Rue de Thionville, the Quai Voltaire, and the Pont-Royal. From the archway of the Carrousel to the great portal of the Tuileries the Consular guard lined the way. As Bonaparte passed through the archway, he raised his head and read the inscription it bore. That inscription was as follows:

AUGUST 10, 1792.

ROYALTY IS ABOLISHED IN FRANCE

AND SHALL NEVER RISE AGAIN.

An almost imperceptible smile flickered on the First Consul's lips.

At the door of the Tuileries, Bonaparte left the carriage and sprang into the saddle to review the troops. When he appeared on his war-horse the applause burst forth wildly on all sides.

After the review was over, he placed himself in front of the clock-tower, with Murat on his right, Lannes at his left, and the glorious staff of the Army of Italy behind him. Then began the march past.

And now it was that one of those inspirations came to him which engrave themselves forever on the hearts of soldiers. As the flags of the 30th, the 96th, and the 33d demi-brigades were borne past him, and he saw that, of those banners, there remained but a stick and a few rags, riddled with balls and blackened with powder, he took his hat from his head and bowed.

Then, when the march was over, he dismounted from his horse, and, with a firm step, he walked up the grand stairway of the Valois and the Bourbons.

That night, when he was alone with Bourrienne, the latter asked: "Well, general, are you satisfied?"

"Yes," replied Bonaparte, dreamily, "everything went off nicely, didn't it?"

"Wonderfully well."

"I saw you standing near Madame Bonaparte at the ground-floor window of the Pavilion of Flora."

"I saw you, too, general; you were reading the inscription on the arch of the Carrousel."

"Yes," said Bonaparte, " 'August 10, 1792. Royalty is abolished in France, and shall never rise again.' "

"Shall I have it removed?" asked Bourrienne.

"Useless," replied the First Consul, "it will fall of itself." Then, with a sigh, he added: "Bourrienne, do you know whom I missed to-day?"

"No, general."

"Roland. What the devil is he doing that he doesn't give me any news of himself?"

We are about to see what Roland was doing.

CHAPTER XLV

THE FOLLOWER OF TRAILS

THE reader will not have forgotten the situation in which the escort of chasseurs found the Chambéry mail-coach.

The first thing they did was to look for the obstacle which prevented Roland from getting out. They found the padlock and wrenched off the door.

Roland bounded from the coach like a tiger from its cage. We have said that the ground was covered with snow. Roland, hunter and soldier, had but one idea—to follow the trail of the Companions of Jehu. He had seen them disappear in the direction of Thoissy; but he believed they were not likely to continue in that direction because, between them and the little town ran the Saône, and there were no bridges across the river between Belleville and Mâcon. He ordered the escort and the conductor to wait for him on the highroad, and alone and on foo, witthout even waiting to reload his pistols, he started on the tracks of Morgan and his companions.

He was not mistaken. A mile from the highroad the fugitives had come to the river; there they had halted, probably deliberating, for the trampling of their horses' hoofs was plainly visible; then they had separated into two troops, one going up the river to Mâcon, and the other descending it in the direction of Belleville.

This separation was doubtless intended to puzzle their pursuers, if they were pursued. Roland had heard the parting call of the leader: "To-morrow night, you know where!" He had no doubt, therefore, that whichever trail he followed, whether up or down—if the snow did not melt too fast—would lead him to the rendezvous, where, either together or singly, the Companions of Jehu were certain to assemble.

He returned upon his own tracks, ordered the conductor to put on the boots thrown aside by the pretended postilion, mount the horse and take the coach to the next relay, namely Belleville. The sergeant of chasseurs and four of his men, who knew how to write, were to accompany the conductor and sign his report of what had occurred. Roland forbade all mention of himself and where he had gone, lest the brigands should get word of his future plans. The rest of the escort were to carry back their colonel's body, and make deposition on their own account, along the same lines as the conductor, to the authorities, and equally without mention of Roland.

These orders given, the young man dismounted a chasseur and took his horse, selecting the one he thought most serviceable. Then he reloaded his pistols, and put them in the holsters in place of the regulation weapons of the dismounted chasseur. Having done this, and promised the

conductor and the chasseurs a speedy vengeance, condi-
tioned, however, on their keeping his present proceedings
secret, he mounted the horse and rode off in the direction
he had already investigated.

When he reached the spot where the two troops had
separated, he had to decide between the different trails.
He chose that which descended the Saône toward Belleville. He had excellent reason for making this choice, although it might possibly take him out of his way for six
or eight miles. In the first place he was nearer Belleville
than Mâcon; then he had spent twenty-four hours at Mâcon,
and might be recognized there, whereas he had never
stopped at Belleville longer than the time required to
change horses when accident brought him there by post.

The events we have just recorded had taken barely an
hour to happen. Eight o'clock was striking from the
church clock at Thoissy when Roland started in pursuit
of the fugitives. The way was plain; five or six horses
had left their imprint on the snow; one of these horses
had paced.

Roland jumped the two or three brooks which watered
the space he had to cross to reach Belleville. A hundred
yards from the town he paused, for here the trail separated
again; two of the six travellers had turned to the right,
that is to say, they had struck away from the river, the four
others to the left, continuing on their way to Belleville.
At the outskirts of the town, another secession had taken
place; three of the riders had gone round the town, one
had entered it.

Roland followed the latter, sure that he could recover
the traces of the others. The one who had entered the
town and followed the main street had stopped at a pretty
house between court and garden, numbered 67. He had
rung and some one had let him in; for through the iron
grating could be seen traces of footsteps, and beside them
the tracks of a horse being led to the stable.

It was quite evident that one, at least, of the Compan-

ions of Jehu had stopped there. By going to the mayor
of the town, exhibiting his authority, and asking for gendarmes, Roland could have arrested him at once. But that
was not his object; he did not wish to arrest a solitary individual; he wanted to catch the whole company in a trap.

He made a note in his mind of No. 67, and continued on
his way. He crossed the entire town and rode a few hundred paces beyond it without meeting any fresh traces. He
was about to return, when it occurred to him that, if the
tracks of the three riders reappeared anywhere, it would
be at the head of the bridge. And there, sure enough, he
found the hoof-prints of three horses, which were undoubtedly those he sought, for one of them paced.

Roland galloped in pursuit. On reaching Monceaux
—same precaution, the riders had skirted the village; but
Roland was too good a scout to trouble himself about that.
He kept on his way, and at the other end of Monceaux he
recovered the fugitives' tracks. Not far from Châtillon one
of the three horses had left the highroad, turning to the
right toward a little château, standing on a hill a short
distance from the road between Châtillon and Trévoux.
This time the three remaining riders, evidently believing
they had done enough to mislead any one who might be
following, had kept straight on through Châtillon and taken
the road to Neuville.

The direction taken by the fugitives was eminently satisfactory to Roland; they were undoubtedly on their way to
Bourg; if they had not intended to go there they would
have taken the road to Marlieux. Now, Bourg was the
headquarters Roland had himself chosen for the centre of
his own operations; it was his own town, and he knew, with
the minuteness of boyish knowledge, every bush, every ruin,
every cavern in the neighborhood.

At Neuville the riders had skirted the village. Roland
did not trouble himself about a ruse, already known and
thwarted; but on the other side he found but one trail.
He could not be mistaken in that horse, however; it was

the pacer. Certain of recovering the trail again, Roland retraced his steps. The two riders had separated at a road leading off to Vannes; one had taken that road, the other had skirted the village, which, as we have said, was on the road to Bourg. This was the one to follow; besides, the gait of the horse made it easier, as it could not be confused with any other. Moreover, he was on his way to Bourg, and between Neuville and Bourg there was but one other village, that of Saint-Denis. For the rest, it was not probable that the solitary rider intended to go further than Bourg.

Roland continued on his way with more eagerness than ever, convinced that he was nearing the end. In fact the rider had not skirted Bourg, but had boldly entered the town. There, it seemed to Roland that the man had hesitated, unless this hesitation were a last ruse to hide his tracks. But after ten minutes spent in following his devious tracks Roland was sure of his facts; it was not trickery but hesitation.

The print of a man's steps came from a side street; the traveller and the pedestrian had conferred together for a moment, and then the former had evidently employed the latter as a guide. From that point on, the footsteps of a man went side by side with those of the horse. Both came to an end at the hôtel de la Belle-Alliance. Roland remembered that the horse wounded in the attack at Les Carronnières had been brought to this inn. In all probability there was some connivance between the inn-keeper and the Companion of Jehu. For the rest, in all probability the rider would stay there until the next evening. Roland felt by his own fatigue that the man he was following must need rest. And Roland, in order not to force his horse and the better to reconnoitre the tracks he was following, had taken six hours to do thirty miles.

Three o'clock was striking from the truncated bell-tower of Nôtre-Dame. Roland debated what to do. Should he stop at some inn in the town? Impossible, he was too well known in Bourg; besides, his horse with its cavalry saddle-cloth would excite suspicion. It was one of the conditions of success that his presence at Bourg should remain unknown.

He could hide at the Château des Noires-Fontaines and keep on the watch, but could he trust the servants? Michel and Jacques would hold their tongues, Roland was sure of them; but Charlotte, the jailer's daughter, she might gossip. However, it was three o'clock in the morning, every one was asleep, and the safest plan was certainly to put himself in communication with Michel. Michel would find some way of concealing his presence.

To the deep regret of his horse, who had no doubt scented a stable, Roland wheeled about and rode off in the direction of Pont-d'Ain. As he passed the church of Brou he glanced at the barrack of the gendarmes, where, in all probability, they and their captain were sleeping the sleep of the righteous.

Roland cut through the little strip of forest which jutted into the road. The snow deadened the sound of his horse's hoofs. Branching into the road from the other side, he saw two men slinking along in the ditch, carrying a deer slung by its forelegs to a sapling. He thought he recognized the cut of the two men, and he spurred his horse to overtake them. The men were on the watch; they turned, saw the rider, who was evidently making for them, flung the animal into the ditch, and made for the shelter of the forest of Seillon.

"Hey, Michel!" cried Roland, more and more convinced that he had to do with his own gardener.

Michel stopped short; the other man kept on his way across the fields.

"Hey, Jacques!" shouted Roland.

The other man stopped. If they were recognized, it was useless to fly; besides, there was nothing hostile in the call; the voice was friendly, rather than threatening.

"Bless me!" said Jacques, "it sounds like M. Roland."

"I do believe it is he," said Michel.

And the two men, instead of continuing their flight, returned to the highroad.

Roland had not heard what the two poachers had said, but he had guessed.

"Hey, the deuce! of course it is I," he shouted.

A minute more and Michel and Jacques were beside him. The questions of father and son were a crossfire, and it must be owned they had good reason for amazement. Roland, in civilian's dress, on a cavalry horse, at three in the morning, on the road from Bourg to the château! The young officer cut short all questions.

"Silence, poachers!" said he, "put that deer behind me and be off at trot to the château. No one must know of my presence there, not even my sister."

Roland spoke with military precision, and both men knew that when he gave an order there was no replying. They picked up the deer, put it behind his saddle, and followed the gentle trot of the horse at a run. There was less than a mile to do, and it took but ten minutes. At a short distance from the château, Roland pulled up. The two men went forward as scouts to see if all were quiet. Satisfied on that point, they made a sign to Roland to advance.

Roland came, dismounted, found the door of the lodge open, and entered. Michel took the horse to the stable and carried the deer to the kitchen; for Michel belonged to that honorable class of poachers, who kill game for the pleasure of killing, and not for the selfish interest of sale. There was no need for precaution, either for horse or deer; for Amélie took no more notice of what went on in the stable than of what they served her to eat.

During this time Jacques lighted the fire. When Michel returned he brought the remains of a leg of mutton and some eggs for an omelet. Jacques made up a bed in the office.

Roland warmed himself and ate his supper without saying a word. The two men looked at each other with an astonishment that was not devoid of a certain degree of anxiety. A rumor of the expedition to Seillon had got about, and it was whispered that Roland had led it. Apparently, he had returned for another similar expedition.

When Roland had finished his supper he looked up and saw Michel.

"Ah! so there you are?" he exclaimed.

"I am waiting for Monsieur's orders."

"Here they are; listen carefully."

"I'm all ears."

"It's a question of life or death; of more than that, of my honor."

"Speak, Monsieur Roland."

Roland pulled out his watch.

"It is now five o'clock. When the inn of the Belle-Alliance opens, be there, as if you were just sauntering by; then stop a minute to chat with whoever opens it."

"That will probably be Pierre."

"Pierre or another; find out from him who the traveller is who arrived last night on a pacing horse. You know what pacing is, don't you?"

"The deuce! You mean a horse that goes like a bear, both feet forward at the same time."

"Bravo! You can also find out whether the traveller is leaving this morning, or whether he proposes to spend the day at the hotel, can't you?"

"Of course I can find that out."

"Well, when you have found out all that, come and tell me; but remember, not a word about my being here. If any one asks about me, say that they had a letter from me yesterday, and that I was in Paris with the First Consul."

"That's understood."

Michel departed. Roland went to bed and to sleep, leaving Jacques to guard the building.

When Roland awoke Michel had returned. He had found out all that his master desired to know. The horseman who had arrived in the night was to leave the next morning, and on the travellers' register, which every innkeeper was obliged by law to keep in those days, was entered: "Saturday, 30th Pluviose, *ten at night;* the citizen Valensolle, from Lyons going to Geneva." Thus the alibi was prepared; for the register would prove that the citizen Valensolle had arrived at ten o'clock, and it was impossible that he could have assisted in robbing the mail-coach near the Maison-Blanche at half-past eight and yet have reached the Hotel de la Belle-Alliance at ten.

But what impressed Roland the most was that the man he had followed through the night, and whose name and retreat he had just discovered, was none other than the second of Alfred de Barjols, whom he himself had killed in a duel near the fountain of Vaucluse; and that that second was, in all probability, the man who had played the part of ghost at the Chartreuse of Seillon.

So, then, the Companions of Jehu were not mere thieves, but, on the contrary, as rumor said, gentlemen of good family, who, while the noble Bretons were laying down their lives for the royalist cause in the West, were, here in the East, braving the scaffold to send to the combatants the money they took from the government.

CHAPTER XLVI

AN INSPIRATION

WE HAVE seen that during the pursuit of the preceding night Roland could have arrested one or two of the men he was pursuing. He could now do the same with M. de Valensolle, who was probably, like Roland himself, taking a day's rest after a night of great fatigue.

To do it he had only to write a line to the captain of gendarmes, or to the colonel of dragoons, who had assisted him during that ineffectual search at Seillon. Their honor was concerned in the affair. They could instantly surprise M. de Valensolle in bed, and at the cost of two pistol shots—two men killed or wounded—he would be taken.

But M. de Valensolle's arrest would give warning to the

rest of the band, who would instantly put themselves in safety beyond the frontier. It was better, therefore, to keep to his first idea; to go slowly, to follow the different trails which must converge to one centre, and, at the risk of a general engagement, throw a net over the whole company.

To do that, M. de Valensolle must not be arrested. It was better to follow him on his pretended journey to Geneva, which was probably but a blind to foil investigation. It was therefore agreed that Roland, whose disguise, however good, was liable to be penetrated, should remain at the lodge, and Michel and Jacques should head off the game. In all probabilities, M. de Valensolle would not set out from the inn before nightfall.

Roland made inquiries of Michel about the life his sister had led since her mother's departure. He learned that she had never once left the grounds during that time. Her habits were still the same, except for the walks and visits she had made with Madame de Montrevel.

She rose at seven or eight in the morning, sketched or practiced her music till breakfast, and afterward read or employed herself at some kind of embroidery, or took advantage of the sunshine to go out with Charlotte to the river. Sometimes she bade Michel unfasten the little boat, and then, well wrapped in furs, would row up the Reissouse as far as Montagnac or down to Saint-Just. During these trips she spoke to no one. Then she dined. After dinner, she retired to her bedroom and did not appear again.

By half-past six, therefore, Michel and Jacques could decamp without arousing any suspicion as to their whereabout; and, accordingly, at that hour they took their blouses, game-bags and guns, and started. Roland had given them their instructions. They were to follow the pacing horse until they had ascertained his destination, or until they had lost all trace of him. Michel was to lie in wait opposite the inn of the Belle-Alliance; Jacques was to station himself outside of Bourg, just where the main road divides into three branches, one going to Saint-

Amour, another to Saint-Claude, and the third to Nantua. This last was at the same time the highroad to Geneva. It was evident that unless M. de Valensolle returned upon his steps, which was not probable, he would take one or another of these three roads.

The father started in one direction, the son in another. Michel went toward the town by the road to Pont-d'Ain, passing the church of Brou. Jacques crossed the Reissouse, followed the right bank of the little river, and found himself, after walking a few hundred yards beyond the town, at the sharp angle made by the parting of the three roads. Father and son reached their separate posts at about the same time.

At this particular moment, that is to say, about seven o'clock, the stillness and solitude surrounding the Château des Noires-Fontaines was broken by the arrival of a post-chaise, which stopped before the iron gate. A servant in livery got off the box and pulled the chain of the bell.

It was Michel's business to open the gate, but Michel was away, as we know. Amélie and Charlotte probably counted on him, for the bell was rung three times before any one answered it. At last the maid appeared at the head of the stairs calling Michel. Michel made no reply. Finally, protected by the locked gates, Charlotte ventured to approach them. In spite of the obscurity she recognized the servant.

"Ah, is it you, Monsieur James?" she cried, somewhat reassured. James was Sir John's confidential valet.

"Yes, mademoiselle, it is I, or rather it is Sir John."

The carriage door opened at this moment, and his master's voice was heard saying: "Mademoiselle Charlotte, will you tell your mistress that I have just arrived from Paris, that I have called to leave my card, and to ask permission, not to be received this evening, but to be allowed to call to-morrow, if she will grant me that favor. Ask her at what hour I shall least inconvenience her."

Mademoiselle Charlotte had a high opinion of Sir John,

consequently she acquitted herself of the commission with
the utmost alacrity. Five minutes later she returned to
announce that Sir John would be received the next day
between twelve and one o'clock.

Roland knew what the Englishman had come for. In
his mind the marriage was an accomplished fact, and he
regarded Sir John already as his brother-in-law. He hesitated a moment as to whether he should or should not
make himself known to Sir John, and tell his friend about
his projects; but he reflected that Sir John was not a man
to let him work them out alone. He, too, had a revenge to
take on the Companions of Jehu; he would certainly insist
on taking part in the expedition, whatever it was. And
that expedition, however it might result, was certain to be
dangerous, and another disaster might befall him. Roland's
luck, as Roland well knew, did not extend to his friends.
Sir John, grievously wounded, had barely escaped with his
life, and the colonel of dragoons had been killed outright.
He therefore allowed Sir John to drive away without giving
any sign of his own proximity.

As for Charlotte, she did not seem in the least surprised
that Michel was not there to open the gate. Evidently they
were accustomed to his absences, and they did not disturb
either the mistress or the maid. For the rest, Roland knew
his sister well enough to understand this indifference. Amélie, feeble under a moral suffering wholly unsuspected by
Roland, who attributed to simple nervous crises the fluc-
tuations of his sister's character, Amélie was strong and
brave before real danger. That was no doubt why she felt
no fear about remaining with Charlotte alone in the lonely
house, without other protection than that afforded by the
two gardeners, who spent their nights in poaching.

As for ourselves, we know that Michel and his son did
really serve their mistress' desire more in absenting themselves thus frequently from the château than in staying
near it. Their absence left the coast clear for Morgan,
and that was all Amélie really cared about.

That evening and part of the night went by without bringing Roland any news. He tried to sleep, but succeeded ill. He fancied every minute that he heard some one at the door. The day was just beginning to glimmer through the shutters when the door did actually open. Michel and Jacques were returning, and this is what had happened to them:

They had each gone to his post, Michel at the inn door, Jacques to the junction of the roads. Twenty paces from the door Michel had met Pierre, and three words sufficed to show him that M. de Valensolle was still at the inn. The latter had announced that, as he had a long journey before him, he would let his horse rest and would not start until nightfall. Pierre did not doubt that he was going to Geneva, as he said.

Michel proposed a glass of wine to Pierre. Pierre accepted. After that, Michel was sure of being warned of any change. Pierre was the hostler, and nothing could be done in the stable without his knowledge. A lad attached to the inn promised to convey the news to Michel, in return for which Michel gave him three charges of powder with which to make firecrackers.

At midnight the traveller had not yet started; they had drunk four bottles of wine, but Michel had partaken sparingly of them. He had found means to pour three of the four bottles into Pierre's glass, where they did not long remain. At midnight the wine-shop closed, and Michel having nowhere to go for the four hours that still remained until daybreak, Pierre offered him a bed of straw in the stable. Michel accepted. The two friends went back arm-in-arm; Pierre staggering, Michel pretending to stagger.

At three o'clock in the morning the servant of the hotel awakened Michel. The traveller wanted his horse. Michel, pretending that he must be off to see to his game, also rose. His toilet was not long in making; he had only to shake the straw from his hair, game-bag, and blouse, after which he took leave of his friend Pierre and hid himself at the corner of the street.

Fifteen minutes later the gate opened and a man rode out on a pacing horse. It was M. de Valensolle. He took the street that led to the Geneva road. Michel followed without concealment, whistling a hunting air. Only, as Michel could not run for fear of attracting the rider's notice, he lost sight of him before long. But Jacques was there, thought he, waiting at the fork of the roads. Yes, Jacques had been there, but he had been there for over six hours of a winter's night, in five degrees of cold. Had he the courage to stand six hours in the snow and kick his soles against a tree?

Thinking thus, Michel took a short cut through the streets and lanes, running at full speed; but horse and rider, in spite of his haste, had gone faster than he. He reached the fork of the roads. All was silent and solitary. The snow, trampled the day before, a Sunday, no longer showed distinct tracks. The steps of the horse were lost in the mud of the road. Nor did he waste further time in vain searching. He wondered what had become of Jacques; but his poacher's eye soon told him.

Jacques had stood on watch at the foot of a tree. For how long? It was difficult to say, but long enough to become very cold. The snow was well beaten down by his heavy hunting-boots. He had evidently tried to keep warm by walking up and down. Then suddenly he must have remembered a little mud hut on the other side of the road, such as the road-menders build as a shelter against the rain. He had gone down the ditch and crossed the road. His trail, lost for a moment in the centre of the road, was visible on the snow at either side. This trail formed a diagonal line, making straight for the hut. It was evidently in the hut that Jacques had passed the night. But when had he left it? and why had he left it? The first question was unanswerable. But to the most inexperienced scout the second was plain enough. He had left it to follow M. de

Valensolle. The same footsteps that had approached the hut were to be seen going, as they left it, in the direction of Ceyzeriat.

The traveller had really taken the road to Geneva. Jacques' footsteps showed it plainly. The stride was long, like that of a man running, and he had followed the road behind the trees, evidently to conceal himself from the rider. At a wretched tavern, one of those with the legend inscribed over its door: "Here we give food and drink, equestrian and pedestrian lodgings," the trail stopped. It was clear that the rider had stopped before this inn, for Jacques had also paused behind a tree some twenty feet distant, where the snow was trampled. Then, probably after the gate had closed on horse and rider, Jacques had left his tree, crossed the road, this time with hesitation, his short steps leading, not to the door, but to the window.

Michel put his own feet in his son's footprints and reached the window. Through the chinks in the shutter the interior, when lighted, could be seen; but now all was dark, and Michel could see nothing. But Jacques had certainly looked through the window; no doubt it was then lighted, and he had been able to see something.

Where had he gone on leaving the window? Round the house, close to the wall. This excursion was easy to follow. The snow was virgin. As for his purpose in going round the house that was not difficult to make out. Jacques, like a lad of sense, had concluded that the traveller had not left a good hotel, saying that he was going to Geneva, to put up at a miserable tavern a mile from the town.

He must have ridden through the yard and gone out by some other exit. Jacques had, therefore, skirted the house in the hope of recovering the trail, if not of the horse, at least of the rider on the other side.

Sure enough, from a small gate in the rear, opening toward the forest that extends from Coterz to Ceyzeriat, footsteps could be seen advancing in a straight line to the edge of the woods. They were those of a man elegantly shod, wearing spurs on his heels, for the spurs had left their marks upon the snow.

Jacques had not hesitated to follow these marks. The track of his heavy shoes could be seen near the prints of the delicate boot—the large foot of the peasant near the slender foot of the city man.

It was now five o'clock. Day was breaking, and Michel resolved to go no further. Jacques was on the trail, and the young poacher was worth as much as the old one. Michel circled the open as if he were returning from Ceyzeriat, resolving to enter the inn and wait for Jacques' return; certain that his son would know he had followed him and had stopped short at this isolated house.

Michel knocked on the window-shutter and was soon admitted. He knew the landlord, who was well accustomed to his nocturnal habits, asked for a bottle, complaining bitterly of his poor luck, and asked permission to wait for his son, who was in the woods on the other side, and who, he hoped, had been more successful in tracking the game. It goes without saying that this permission was readily accorded. Michel opened the window-shutters, in order to look out on the road.

It was not long before some one knocked on the glass. It was Jacques. His father called him.

Jacques had been as unfortunate as his father. No game; and he was frozen. An armful of wood was thrown on the fire and a second bottle of wine was brought. Jacques warmed himself and drank.

Then, as it was necessary that the two poachers should be back at the château before daylight, that their absence might not be noticed, Michel paid for the wine and the wood, and the pair departed.

Neither had said one word before the landlord of the subject that filled their minds. He was not to suspect that they were on other trail than that of game. But no sooner were they outside of the house than Michel drew close to his son. Jacques recounted how he had followed the tracks until they had reached a crossroad in the forest. There a man, armed with a gun, had suddenly appeared and asked him what he was doing in the forest at that hour. Jacques replied that he was watching for game. "Then go further," said the man; "don't you see that this place is taken?"

Jacques admitted the justice of this claim, and went on about a hundred rods further, but, just as he was slanting to the left to return to the crossroad, another man, armed like the first, had suddenly started up with the same inopportune question. Jacques gave him the same answer: "Watching for game." The man had then pointed to the edge of the woods, saying in a threatening manner: "If I have any advice to give you, my young friend, it is to go over there. It will be safer for you than here."

Jacques had taken this advice, or at least had pretended to take it, for as soon as he had reached the edge of the woods he had crept along in the ditch, until, convinced that it would be impossible to recover M. de Valensolle's track, he had struck into the open, and returned by fields and the highroad to the tavern, where he hoped to, and in fact did, find his father.

They reached the Château des Noires-Fontaines, as we have seen, just as day was breaking.

All that we have related was repeated to Roland with a multiplicity of detail which we must omit, and convinced the young officer that the two armed men, who had warned off Jacques, were not poachers as they seemed, but Companions of Jehu. But where was their haunt located? There was no deserted convent, no ruin, in that direction.

Suddenly Roland clapped his hand to his head. "Idiot that I am!" he cried, "why did I never think of that?"

A smile of triumph crossed his lips, and addressing the two men, who were mortified at having brought him no more definite news, he cried: "My lads, I know all I want to know. Go to bed and sleep sound; my word, you deserve to!" He himself, setting the example, slept like a man whose brain has solved a problem of the utmost importance which has long harassed it.

The thought had just flashed through his mind that the Companions of Jehu had abandoned the Chartreuse of Seillon for the grottoes of Ceyzeriat; and at the same time he recalled the subterranean passage leading from these grottoes to the church of Brou.

CHAPTER XLVII

A RECONNOISSANCE

THAT same day, Sir John, making use of the permission accorded him the night before, presented himself at the Château des Noires-Fontaines between twelve and one o'clock.

Everything occurred as Morgan had advised. Sir John was received as the friend of the family, Lord Tanlay as a suitor whose attentions were most flattering. Amélie made no opposition to the wishes of her mother and brother, and to the commands of the First Consul, further than to dwell on the state of her health and to ask for delay on that account. Sir John bowed and submitted; he had obtained more than he had hoped to obtain. He was accepted.

He felt that his presence in Bourg, if prolonged, would be an impropriety, Amélie being (still on the plea of ill-health) parted from her mother and brother. He therefore announced that he would pay her a second visit on the morrow, and leave Bourg that same evening. He would delay further visits until Amélie came to Paris, or until Madame de Montrevel returned to Bourg. The latter arrangement was the more probable of the two, for Amélie assured him she needed the country air and the spring-like weather to assist her in recovering her health.

Thanks to Sir John's considerate delicacy, the plan arranged between Amélie and Morgan was thus carried out, and the two lovers had before them a period of solitude and a respite in which to form their plans.

Michel learned these details from Charlotte and imparted them in turn to Roland. The latter determined to await Sir John's departure before he took any decisive steps against the Companions of Jehu. But this did not prevent him from endeavoring to set at rest any remaining doubts.

When night came he put on a hunting-suit, and over it Michel's blouse, concealed his face beneath a broad-brimmed hat, slipped a pair of pistols in his knife-belt, hidden by the blouse, and boldly took the road from Noires-Fontaines to Bourg. He stopped at the barracks of the gendarmerie and asked to see the captain.

The captain was in his room. Roland went up and made himself known. Then, as it was only eight o'clock, and some one passing might recognize him, he blew out the light, and the two men talked in the dark. The captain knew already what had happened on the Lyons road three days earlier, and, certain that Roland was not killed, was expecting him. To his great astonishment, Roland asked him for only one, or rather for two things: the key of the church of Brou and a crowbar.

The captain gave him the required articles, and offered to accompany him, but Roland refused. It was evident to his mind that he had been betrayed by some one connected with the affair of the Maison-Blanche, and he would not expose himself to a second defeat. He therefore begged the captain to tell no one of his presence in Bourg, and to await his return, even if it were delayed some hours. The captain agreed.

Roland, the key in his right hand, the crowbar in his left, reached the side door of the church without making any noise. This he unlocked, entered, relocked it behind him, and found himself facing a wall of hay. He listened. The most profound silence reigned.

He remembered his boyish habits, took his bearings, put

the key in his pocket, and scrambled up the wall of hay, which was about fifteen feet high and formed a sort of platform. When he reached the top he slid down on the other side, as though he were descending the scarp of a fortification, and reached the flooring of the church, which was almost wholly composed of mortuary stones.

The choir was empty, thanks to a rood-screen which protected it on one side, and also to the walls which inclosed it to right and left. The door of the screen was open and Roland entered the choir without difficulty. He came face to face with the monument of Philippe le Beau. At the head of the tomb was a large square flagstone. It covered the steps which led to the burial vaults.

Roland must have known the way, for as soon as he reached the stone he knelt down and felt with his hand for the edge of it. When he found it he stood up, inserted his lever and raised the slab. With one hand he held it up while he went down the steps. Then he lowered it slowly. It seemed as though this nocturnal visitor were voluntarily separating himself from the land of the living, and descending into the world of the dead. And strange indeed to him, who sees by night as by day, on the earth and beneath it, must the impassibility of this young man have seemed, who passed among the dead in search of the living, and who, in spite of darkness and solitude, did not shudder at the touch of the mortuary marbles.

He walked on, feeling his way among the tombs, until he came to the iron gate leading to the subterranean passage. He looked for the lock. It was only bolted. He inserted the end of his lever between the bolt and the staple, and pushed it gently. The gate opened. He drew it close after him, but did not lock it, so as to avoid delay on his return. The crowbar he left at the corner of the gate.

Then, with straining ears, dilated pupils, every sense tense with this effort to hear, the need to breathe, the impossibility of seeing, he advanced slowly, a pistol in one hand, touching the wall with the other to guide himself.

He walked thus for fifteen minutes. A few drops of ice-cold water fell through the roof on his hands and shoulders, and told him he was passing under the river.

At the end of this time he found the door which opened from the passage into the quarry. There he halted a moment. He could now breathe more freely, and, moreover, he fancied that he heard distant sounds, and could see flickering lights, like will-o'-the-wisps, on the pillars that supported the roof. An observer might have thought, not distinguishing the face of the silent listener, that he showed hesitation; but the moment his countenance was seen, no one could have mistaken its expression of hope.

He then resumed his way, heading toward the light he thought he had seen. As he advanced, the lights and the noises grew more distinct. It was evident that the quarry was inhabited. By whom? He did not yet know, but he would know.

He was already within ten feet of that open clearing in the midst of the granite walls which we described on our first visit to the grotto of Ceyzeriat. Roland clung closely to the wall, and moved forward almost imperceptibly. In the dim half-light he looked like a gliding bass-relief.

At last his head passed beyond an angle of the wall, and his glance rested upon what we may call the camp of the Companions of Jehu.

A dozen or more of the members sat there at supper. Roland was seized with a wild desire to precipitate himself into their midst, attacking them singly, and fighting until he died. But he repressed the insensate thought, withdrew his head as slowly as he had advanced it, and, with beaming eyes and heart full of joy, returned, unseen and unsuspected, along the way he had come. Everything was now explained; the deserted Chartreuse, M. de Valensolle's disappearance, and the counterfeit poachers near the entrance to the grotto of Ceyzeriat.

This time he was sure of his vengeance, his deadly, terrible vengeance—deadly, because, in like manner as he had been spared (he suspected intentionally), he meant to spare others; with this difference that, whereas he had been spared for life, he would order these men spared for death, death on the scaffold.

Half-way back he thought he heard a noise behind him. He turned and was certain he saw a gleam of light. He quickened his steps. The gate once passed, there was no danger of losing his way. It was no longer a quarry with a thousand windings; it was a straight and narrow vaulted passage leading to the mortuary grating. At the end of ten minutes he again passed under the river; a couple of minutes later, his outstretched hand touched the iron gate.

He took the crowbar from the place where he had left it, entered the vault, pulled the gate to, closed it gently and noiselessly, and, guiding himself by the tombs, he regained the staircase, pushed up the flagstone with his head, and stood once more in the land of the living.

There it was comparative daylight. He left the choir, closed the door of the screen as he had found it, scaled the hay, crossed the platform, and slid down the other side. The key was still in his pocket. He unlocked the door and stepped out into the street.

The captain of gendarmerie was anxiously awaiting him. They conferred together for a few moments, and then they returned to Bourg by the outer road to avoid being seen. Here they entered the town through the market-gate, and followed the Rue de la Révolution, the Rue de la Liberté, and the Rue d'Espagne, since called the Rue Simonneau. There Roland ensconced himself in a corner of the Rue du Greffe and waited. The captain continued on his way alone. He went down the Rue des Ursules (for the last seven years called the Rue des Casernes). This was where the colonel of dragoons lived. He had just gone to bed when the captain of the gendarmerie entered his room; in two words the latter told all, and he rose at once and dressed in haste.

When the colonel of dragoons and the captain of gendarmerie appeared in the square, a shadow detached itself from the opposite wall and came up to them. That shadow was Roland. The three men stood talking for about ten minutes, Roland giving his orders, the other two listening and approving.

Then they separated. The colonel returned home. Roland and the captain followed the Rue de l'Etoile, climbed the steps of the Jacobins, passed down the Rue du Bourgneuf, and reached the outer road once more. Then they struck diagonally across to the highroad of Pont-d'Ain. The captain stopped at the barracks, which were on the way, and Roland continued alone to the château.

Twenty minutes later—in order not to awaken Amélie—instead of ringing the bell he knocked on Michel's window-blind. Michel opened, and with one bound Roland, devoured by that fever which took possession of him whenever he incurred, or merely dreamed of some danger, sprang into the room.

He would not have awakened Amélie had he rung, for Amélie was not asleep. Charlotte had been into town ostensibly to see her father, but really to take a letter from her mistress to Morgan. She had seen Morgan and brought back his answer.

Amélie was reading that answer, which was as follows:

DEAR LOVE OF MINE—Yes, all goes well on your side, for you are an angel; but I greatly fear that all may go ill on mine, for I am the demon.

I must see you, I must hold you in my arms and press you to my heart. I know not what presentiment hangs over me; but I am sad, sad as death.

Send Charlotte to-morrow to make sure that Sir John is gone, and then, if you are certain, make the accustomed signal. Do not be alarmed; do not talk to me of the snow, or tell me that my footsteps will be seen. This time it is not I who will go to you, but you who must come to me. Do you understand? You can safely walk in the park, and no one will notice your footsteps.

Put on your warmest shawl and your thickest furs. Then we will spend an hour in the boat under the willows together, and change our rôles for once. Usually I tell you of my hopes and you tell me of your fears; but to-morrow, you will tell me of your hopes and I will tell you of my fears, my darling Amélie.

Only, be sure to come out as soon as you have made the signal. I will await it at Montagnac, and from Montagnac to the Reissouse it will not take a love like mine five minutes to reach you.

Au revoir, my poor Amélie; had you never met me you would have been the happiest of the happy. Fatality placed me in your path, and I have made a martyr of you.

Your CHARLES.

P.S.—To-morrow without fail, unless some insurmountable obstacle prevents.

CHAPTER XLVIII

IN WHICH MORGAN'S PRESENTIMENTS ARE VERIFIED

IT OFTEN happens that the skies are never so calm or so serene as before a storm. The day was beautiful and still; one of those glorious days of February when, in spite of the tingling cold of the atmosphere, in spite of a winding-sheet of snow covering the earth, the sun smiles down upon mankind with a promise of spring.

Sir John came at noon to make his farewell visit to Amélie. He had, or thought he had, her promise, and that satisfied him. His impatience was altogether personal; but Amélie, in accepting his suit, even though she relegated the period of her marriage to the vaguest possible future, had crowned his hopes. He trusted to the First Consul and to Roland's friendship for the rest. He therefore returned to Paris to do much of his courting with Madame de Montrevel, not being able to remain at Bourg and carry it on with Amélie.

A quarter of an hour after he had left the Château des Noires-Fontaines, Charlotte was also on her way to Bourg. At four o'clock she returned, bringing word that she had seen Sir John with her own eyes getting into his travelling carriage, and that he had taken the road to Mâcon.

Amélie could therefore feel perfectly at ease on that score. She breathed freer. She had tried to inspire Morgan with a peace of mind which she herself did not share. Since the day that Charlotte had brought back the news of Roland's presence at Bourg, she had had a presentiment, like that of Morgan himself, that they were approaching some terrible crisis. She knew all that had happened at the Chartreuse of Seillon. She foresaw the struggle between her brother and her lover, and, with her mind at rest about her brother, thanks to Morgan's protection, she, knowing Roland's character, trembled for her lover's life.

Moreover, she had heard of the stoppage of the Chambéry mail-coach and the death of the colonel of Chasseurs. She also knew that her brother had escaped, but that he had disappeared since that time. She had received no letter from him herself. This disappearance and silence, to her who knew her brother so well, was even worse than open and declared war.

As for Morgan, she had not seen him since the scene we have narrated, when she promised to send him arms wherever he might be, in case he were condemned to death. Amélie therefore awaited this interview, for which Morgan had asked, with as much impatience as he who had asked it. As soon as she thought Michel and his son were in bed, she lighted the four windows with the candles which were to summon Morgan to her.

Then, following her lover's injunctions, she wrapped herself in a cashmere shawl, which Roland had brought her from the battlefield of the Pyramids, and which he had unwound from the head of a chieftain whom he had killed. Over this she flung a fur mantle, left Charlotte behind to keep her informed in case of eventualities, which she trusted would not be forthcoming, opened the park gate, and hastened toward the river.

During the day she had gone to the Reissouse and back

several times to trace a line of footsteps, among which the nocturnal ones would not be noticed. She now descended, if not tranquilly at least boldly, the slope leading to the river. Once there, she looked about her for the boat beneath the willows. A man was waiting in it—Morgan. With two strokes of the oar he reached a spot where Amélie could come to him. The young girl sprang down and he caught her in his arms.

The first thing the young girl noticed was the joyous radiance which illuminated, if we may say so, the face of her lover.

"Oh!" she cried, "you have something nice to tell me."

"What makes you think so, dearest?" asked Morgan with his tenderest smile.

"There is something in your face, my darling Charles, something more than the mere happiness of seeing me."

"You are right," said Morgan, throwing the boat-chain around a willow and letting the oars float idly beside the boat. Then, taking Amélie in his arms, he said, "You were right, my Amélie. Oh! blind weak beings! It is at the very moment that happiness knocks at our door that we despair and doubt."

"Oh, speak, speak!" said Amélie, "tell me what has happened."

"Do you remember, my Amélie, how you answered me the last time we met, when I asked you to fly and spoke to you of your probable repugnance to the step?"

"Yes, I remember, Charles. I said that I was yours, and that, though I felt that repugnance, I would conquer it for your sake."

"And I replied that I had engagements which would prevent my leaving the country; that I was bound to others, and they to me; that our duty was to one man to whom we owed absolute obedience—the future King of France, Louis XVIII."

"Yes, you told me that."

"Well, we are now released from our pledges, Amélie,

not only by the King, but by our general, Georges Cadoudal.''

''Oh! my friend, then you will be as other men, only above all others.''

''I shall become a simple exile, Amélie. There is no hope of our being included in the Breton or Vendéan amnesty.''

''Why not?''

''We are not soldiers, my darling child. We are not even rebels. We are Companions of Jehu.''

Amélie sighed.

''We are bandits, brigands, highwaymen,'' said Morgan, dwelling on the words with evident intention.

''Hush!'' said Amélie, laying her hand on her lover's lips. ''Hush! don't let us speak of that. Tell me how it is that your king has released you, and your general also.''

''The First Consul wished to see Cadoudal. In the first place, he sent your brother to him with certain proposals. Cadoudal refused to come to terms; but, like ourselves, he received orders from Louis XVIII. to cease hostilities. Coincident with that order came another message from the First Consul to Cadoudal. It was a safeguard for the Vendéan general, and an invitation to come to Paris; an over ture from one power to another power. Cadoudal accepted, and is now on his way to Paris. If it is not peace, it is at least a truce.''

''Oh, what joy, my Charles!''

''Don't rejoice too much, my love.''

''Why not?''

''Do you know why they have issued this order to suspend hostilities?''

''No.''

''Because M. Fouché is a long-headed man. He realized that, since he could not defeat us, he must dishonor us. He has organized false companies of Jehu, which he has set loose in Maine and Anjou, who don't stop at the government money, but pillage and rob travellers, and invade the châteaux and farms by night, and roast the feet of the owners to make them tell where their treasure is hidden. Well, these men, these bandits, these *roasters*, have taken our name, and claim to be fighting for the same principles, so that M. Fouché and his police declare that we are not only beyond the pale of the law, but beyond that of honor.''

"Oh!"

"That is what I wished to tell you before I ask you to fly with me, my Amélie. In the eyes of France, in the eyes of foreigners, even in the eyes of the prince we have served, and for whom we have risked the scaffold, we shall be hereafter, and probably are now, dishonored men worthy of the scaffold.''

"Yes; but to me you are my Charles, the man of devoted convictions, the firm royalist, continuing to struggle for a cause when other men have abandoned it. To me you are the loyal Baron de Sainte-Hermine, or, if you like it better, you are to me the noble, courageous, invincible Morgan.''

"Ah! that is what I longed to hear, my darling. If you feel thus, you will not hesitate, in spite of the cloud of infamy that hangs over our honor, you will not hesitate—I will not say to give yourself to me, for that you have already done—but to become my wife.''

"Hesitate! No, not for an instant, not for a second! To do it is the joy of my soul, the happiness of my life! Your wife? I am your wife in the sight of God, and God will have granted my every prayer on the day that he enables me to be your wife before men.''

Morgan fell on his knees.

"Then,'' he said, "here at your feet, with clasped hands and my whole heart supplicating, I say to you, Amélie, will you fly with me? Will you leave France with me? Will you be my wife in other lands?''

Amélie sprang erect and clasped her head in her hands, as though her brain were bursting with the force of the blood that rushed to it. Morgan caught both her hands and looked at her anxiously.

"Do you hesitate?" he asked in a broken, trembling voice.

"No, not an instant!" she cried resolutely. "I am yours in the past, in the present, in the future, here, everywhere. Only the thought convulses me. It is so unexpected."

"Reflect well, Amélie. What I ask of you is to abandon country and family, all that is dear to you, all that is sacred. If you follow me, you leave the home where you were born, the mother who nurtured you, the brother who loves you, and who, perhaps, when he hears that you are the wife of a brigand, will hate you. He will certainly despise you."

As he spoke, Morgan's eyes were anxiously questioning Amélie's face. Over that face a tender smile stole gradually, and then it turned from heaven to earth, and bent upon Morgan, who was still on his knees before her.

"Oh, Charles!" she murmured, in a voice as soft as the clear limpid river flowing at her feet, "the love that comes direct from the Divine is very powerful indeed, since, in spite of those dreadful words you have just uttered, I say to you without hesitation, almost without regret: Charles, I am here; Charles, I am yours. Where shall we go?"

"Amélie, our fate is not one to discuss. If we go, if you follow me, it must be at once. To-morrow we must be beyond the frontier."

"How do we go?"

"I have two horses, ready saddled at Montagnac, one for you, Amélie, and one for me. I have letters of credit for two hundred thousand francs on London and Vienna. We will go wherever you prefer."

"Wherever you are, Charles. What difference does it make so long as you are there?"

"Then come."

"Can I have five minutes, Charles; is that too much?"

"Where are you going?"

"To say good-by to many things, to fetch your precious letters and the ivory chaplet used at my first communion. Oh! there are many sacred cherished souvenirs of my childhood which will remind me over there of my mother, of France. I will fetch them and return."

"Amélie!"

"What is it?"

"I cannot leave you. If I part with you an instant now I feel that I shall lose you forever. Amélie, let me go with you."

"Yes, come. What matter if they see your footsteps now? We shall be far enough away to-morrow. Come!"

The young man sprang from the boat and gave his hand to Amélie to help her out. Then he folded his arm about her and they walked to the house.

On the portico Charles stopped.

"Go on alone," said he; "memory is a chaste thing. I know that, and I will not embarrass you by my presence. I will wait here and watch for you. So long as I know you are close by me I do not fear to lose you. Go, dear, and come back quickly."

Amélie answered with a kiss. Then she ran hastily up to her room, took the little coffer of carved oak clamped with iron, her treasury, which contained her lover's letters from first to last, unfastened from the mirror above her bed the white and virginal chaplet that hung there; put into her belt a watch her father had given her, and passed into her mother's bedchamber. There she stooped and kissed the pillow where her mother's head had lain, knelt before the Christ at the foot of the bed, began a thanksgiving she dared not finish, changed it to a prayer, and then suddenly stopped—she fancied she heard Charles calling her.

She listened and heard her name a second time, uttered in a tone of agony she could not understand. She quivered, sprang to her feet, and ran rapidly down the stairs.

"What is it?" cried Amélie, seizing the young man's hand.

"Listen, listen!" said he.

Amélie strained her ears to catch the sound which

seemed to her like musketry. It came from the direction of Ceyzeriat.

"Oh!" cried Morgan, "I was right in doubting my happiness to the last. My friends are attacked. Adieu, Amélie, adieu!"

"Adieu!" cried Amélie, turning pale. "What, will you leave me?"

The sound of the firing grew more distinct.

"Don't you hear them? They are fighting, and I am not there to fight with them."

Daughter and sister of a soldier, Amélie understood him and she made no resistance.

"Go!" she said, letting her hands drop beside her. "You were right, we are lost."

The young man uttered a cry of rage, caught her to his breast, and pressed her to him as though he would smother her. Then, bounding from the portico, he rushed in the direction of the firing with the speed of a deer pursued by hunters.

"I come! I come, my friends!" he cried. And he disappeared like a shadow beneath the tall trees of the park.

Amélie fell upon her knees, her hands stretched toward him without the strength to recall him, or, if she did so, it was in so faint a voice that Morgan did not stop or even check his speed to answer her.

CHAPTER XLIX

ROLAND'S REVENGE

IT IS easy to guess what had happened. Roland had not wasted his time with the captain of gendarmerie and the colonel of dragoons. They on their side did not forget that they had their own revenge to take.

Roland had informed them of the subterranean passage that led from the church of Brou to the grotto of Ceyzeriat. At nine in the evening the captain and the eighteen men under his command were to go to the church, descend into the burial vault of the Dukes of Savoy, and prevent with their bayonets all communication between the subterranean passage and the quarry.

Roland, at the head of twenty men, was to inclose the woods in a semicircle, drawing in upon it until the two ends should meet at the grotto of Ceyzeriat. The first movement of the party was to be made at nine o'clock, in conjunction with the captain of the gendarmerie.

We have seen, from what Morgan told Amélie, the nature of the present intentions of the Companions of Jehu. The news brought from Mittau and from Brittany had put them at ease. Each man felt that he was free, and, knowing that the struggle had been a hopeless one, he rejoiced in his liberty.

There was therefore a full meeting at the grotto of Ceyzeriat, almost a fête. At twelve o'clock the Companions of Jehu were to separate, and each one, according to his facilities, was to cross the frontier and leave France.

We know how their leader employed his last moments. The others, who had not the same ties of the heart, were supping together in the broad open space of the quarry, brilliantly illuminated—a feast of separation and farewell; for, once out of France, the Vendée and Brittany pacificated, Condé's army destroyed, who knew when and where they should meet again in foreign lands.

Suddenly the report of a shot fell upon their ears.

Every man sprang to his feet as if moved by an electric shock. A second shot, and then through the depths of the quarry rang the cry, quivering on the wings of the bird of ill-omen, "To arms!"

To the Companions of Jehu, subjected to all the vicissitudes of life of an outlaw, the occasional rest they snatched was never that of peace. Pistols, daggers, carbines, were ever near at hand. At the cry, given no doubt by the sentinel, each man sprang to his weapons and stood with panting breast and strained ears, waiting.

In the midst of the silence a step as rapid as well could be in the darkness was heard. Then, within the circle of light thrown by the torches and candles, a man appeared.

"To arms!" he cried again, "we are attacked!"

The two shots the Companions of Jehu had heard were from the double-barrelled gun of the sentry. It was he who now appeared, his smoking gun in his hand.

"Where is Morgan?" cried twenty voices.

"Absent," replied Montbar; "consequently I command. Put out the lights and retreat to the church. A fight is useless now. It would only be waste of blood."

He was obeyed with an alacrity that showed that every one appreciated the danger. The little company drew together in the darkness.

Montbar, who knew the windings of the subterranean passage almost as well as Morgan, directed the troop, and, followed by his companions, he plunged into the heart of the quarry. Suddenly, as he neared the gate of the passage, he fancied he heard an order given in a low tone not fifty feet away, then a sound like the cocking of guns. He stretched out both arms and muttered in a low voice:

"Halt!" At the same instant came the command, this time perfectly audible: "Fire!"

It was hardly given before the cavern was lighted with a glare, followed by a frightful volley. Ten carbines had been discharged at once into the narrow passage. By their light Montbar and his companions recognized the uniform of the gendarmes.

"Fire!" cried Montbar in turn.

Seven or eight shots answered the command. Again the darkness was illuminated. Two of the Companions of Jehu lay upon the ground, one killed outright, the other mortally wounded.

"Our retreat is cut off, my friends," cried Montbar. "To the right-about! If we have a chance, it is through the forest."

The movement was executed with the precision of a

military manœuvre. Montbar, again at the head of his companions, retraced his steps. At that moment the gendarmes fired again. But no one replied. Those who had discharged their guns reloaded them. Those who had not, reserved their fire for the real struggle which was to come. One or two sighs alone told that the last volley of the gendarmes had not been without result.

At the end of five minutes Montbar stopped. The little party had reached the open space of the quarry.

"Are your pistols and guns all loaded?" he asked.

"Yes," answered a dozen voices.

"Remember the order for those who fall into the hands of the police. We belong to the army of M. de Teyssonnet, and we are here to recruit men for the royalist cause. If they talk to us of mail-coaches and diligences, we don't know what they mean."

"Agreed."

"In either case it will be death. We know that well enough; but the death of a soldier is better than that of thieves—the volley of a platoon rather than the guillotine."

"Yes, yes," cried a mocking voice, "we know what that is—Vive la fusillade!"

"Forward, friends!" said Montbar, "and let us sell our lives for what they are worth; that is to say, as dearly as possible."

"Forward!" they all cried.

Then, as rapidly as was possible in the profound darkness, the little troop resumed its march, still under the guidance of Montbar. As they advanced, the leader noticed a smell of smoke which alarmed him. At the same time gleams of light began to flicker on the granite walls at the angles of the path, showing that something strange was happening at the opening of the grotto.

"I believe those scoundrels are smoking us out," exclaimed Montbar.

"I fear so," replied Adler.

"They think we are foxes."

"Oh!" replied the same voice, "they shall know by our claws that we are lions."

The smoke became thicker and thicker, the light more and more vivid.

They turned the last corner. A pile of dried wood had been lighted in the quarry about fifty feet from the entrance, not for the smoke, but for the light it gave. By the blaze of that savage flame the weapons of the dragoons could be seen gleaming at the entrance of the grotto.

Ten steps in advance of the men stood an officer, waiting. He was leaning on his carbine, not only exposed to attack, but apparently courting it. It was Roland. He was easily recognized. He had flung his cap away, his head was bare, and the fitful light of the flames played upon his features. But that which should have cost him his life saved him. Montbar recognized him and stepped backward.

"Roland de Montrevel!" he said. "Remember Morgan's injunction."

"Yes," replied the other Companions, in muffled tones.

"And now," said Montbar, "let us die, but dearly!"

And he sprang forward into the space illuminated by the fire, and discharged one barrel of his gun at the dragoons, who replied with a volley.

It would be impossible to relate all that followed. The grotto was filled with smoke, which the flame of each weapon pierced like a flash of lightning. The two bands clinched and fought hand to hand, pistols and daggers serving them in turn. At the noise of the struggle, the gendarmes poured in from the rear—a few more demons added to this fight of devils—but the groups of friends and enemies were so confused they dared not fire. They struggled in the red and lurid atmosphere, fell down and rose again; a roar of rage was heard, then a cry of agony—the death sigh of a man. The survivor sought another man, and the struggle was renewed.

This work of death lasted fifteen minutes, perhaps

twenty. At the end of those twenty minutes twenty corpses could be counted in the grotto of Ceyzeriat. Thirteen were those of the gendarmes and the dragoons, nine belonged to the Companions of Jehu. Five of the latter were still living; overwhelmed by numbers, crippled by wounds, they were taken alive. The gendarmes and the dragoons, twenty-five in number, surrounded them.

The captain of gendarmes had his arm shattered, the colonel of dragoons was wounded in the thigh. Roland alone, covered with blood that was not his own, had not a scratch. Two of the prisoners were so grievously wounded that it was impossible for them to walk, and the soldiers were obliged to carry them on an improvised litter. Torches were lighted, and the whole troop, with the prisoners, took the road to the town.

As they were leaving the forest to branch into the high-road, the gallop of a horse was heard. It came on rapidly.

"Go on," said Roland; "I will stay here and find out what this means."

It was a rider, who, as we have said, was advancing at full speed.

"Who goes there?" cried Roland, raising his carbine when the rider was about twenty paces from him.

"One more prisoner, Monsieur de Montrevel," replied the rider, "I could not be in at the fight, but I will at least go to the scaffold. Where are my friends?"

"There, sir," replied Roland, who had recognized, not the face, but the voice of the rider, a voice which he now heard for the third time. As he spoke, he pointed to the little group in the centre of the soldiers who were making their way along the road from Ceyzeriat to Bourg.

"I am glad to see that no harm has befallen you, M. de Montrevel," said the young man, with great courtesy; "I assure you it gives me much happiness." And spurring his horse, he was beside the soldiers and gendarmes in a few strides. "Pardon me, gentlemen," he said, springing from his horse, "I claim a place among my three friends, the Vicomte de Jayat, the Comte de Valensolle, and the Marquis de Ribier."

The three prisoners gave a cry of admiration and held out their hands to their friend. The two wounded men lifted themselves up on their litters, and murmured: "Well done, Sainte-Hermine, well done!"

"I do believe, God help me!" cried Roland, "that those brigands will have the nobler side of the affair!"

CHAPTER L

CADOUDAL AT THE TUILERIES

THE day but one after the events which we have just related took place, two men were walking side by side up and down the grand salon of the Tuileries. They were talking eagerly, accompanying their words with hasty and animated gestures. These men were the First Consul, Bonaparte, and Cadoudal.

Cadoudal, impelled by the misery that might be entailed by a prolonged struggle in Brittany, had just signed a peace with Brune. It was after this signing of the peace that he had released the Companions of Jehu from their obligations. Unhappily, this release had reached them, as we have seen, twenty-four hours too late.

When treating with Brune, Cadoudal had asked nothing for himself save the liberty to go immediately to England. But Brune had been so insistent, that he had consented to an interview with the First Consul. He had, in consequence, come to Paris. The very morning of his arrival he went to the Tuileries, sent in his name, and had been received. It was Rapp who, in Roland's absence, introduced him. As the aide-de-camp withdrew, he left both doors open, so as to see everything from Bourrienne's room, and to be able to go to the assistance of the First Consul if necessary.

But Bonaparte, who perfectly understood Rapp's motive, closed the door. Then, returning hastily to Cadoudal's side, he said: "Ah! so it is you at last! One of your enemies, my aide-de-camp, Roland de Montrevel, has told me fine things of you."

"That does not surprise me," replied Cadoudal. "During the short time I saw M. de Montrevel, I recognized in him a most chivalrous nature."

"Yes; and that touched you?" asked the First Consul, fixing his falcon eye on the royalist chief. "Listen, Georges. I need energetic men like you to accomplish the work I have undertaken. Will you be one of them? I have already offered you the rank of colonel, but you are worth more than that. I now offer you the rank of general of division."

"I thank you from the bottom of my heart, citizen First Consul," replied Cadoudal; "but you would despise me if I accepted."

"Why so?" queried Bonaparte, hastily.

"Because I have pledged myself to the House of Bourbon; and I shall remain faithful to it under all circumstances."

"Let us discuss the matter," resumed the First Consul. "Is there no way to bind you?"

"General," replied the royalist leader, "may I be permitted to repeat to you what has been said to me?"

"Why not?"

"Because it touches upon the deepest political interests."

"Pooh! some nonsense," said the First Consul, smiling uneasily.

Cadoudal stopped short and looked fixedly at his companion.

"It is said that an agreement was made between you and Commodore Sidney Smith at Alexandria, the purport of which was to allow you to return to France on the condition, accepted by you, of restoring the throne to our former kings."

Bonaparte burst out laughing.

"How astonishing you are, you plebeians!" he said,
"with your love for your former kings! Suppose that I
did re-establish the throne (a thing, I assure you, I have
not the smallest desire to do), what return will you get, you
who have shed your blood for the cause? Not even the
confirmation of the rank you have won in it, colonel. Have
you ever known in the royalist ranks a colonel who was
not a noble? Did you ever hear of any man rising by his
merits into that class of people? Whereas with me, Georges,
you can attain to what you will. The higher I raise myself,
the higher I shall raise those who surround me. As for
seeing me play the part of Monk, dismiss that from your
mind. Monk lived in an age in which the prejudices we
fought and overthrew in 1789 were in full force. Had Monk
wished to make himself king, he could not have done so.
Dictator? No! It needed a Cromwell for that! Richard
could not have maintained himself. It is true that he was
the true son of a great man—in other words a fool. If I had
wished to make myself king, there was nothing to hinder
me; and if ever the wish takes me there will be nothing to
hinder. Now, if you have an answer to that, give it."

"You tell me, citizen First Consul, that the situation in
France in 1800 is not the same as England in 1660. Charles
I. was beheaded in 1649, Louis XVI. in 1793. Eleven years
elapsed in England between the death of the king and the
restoration of his son. Seven years have already elapsed in
France since the death of Louis XVI. Will you tell me
that the English revolution was a religious one, whereas
the French revolution was a political one? To that I reply
that a charter is as easy to make as an abjuration."

Bonaparte smiled.

"No," he said, "I should not tell you that. I should
say to you simply this: that Cromwell was fifty years old
when Charles I. died. I was twenty-four at the death of
Louis XVI. Cromwell died at the age of fifty-nine. In ten
years' time he was able to undertake much, but to accomplish little. Besides, his reform was a total one—a vast

political reform by the substitution of a republican government for a monarchical one. Well, grant that I live to be Cromwell's age, fifty-nine; that is not too much to expect; I shall still have twenty years, just the double of Cromwell. And remark, I change nothing, I progress; I do not overthrow, I build up. Suppose that Cæsar, at thirty years of age, instead of being merely the first roué of Rome, had been its greatest citizen; suppose his campaign in Gaul had been made; that his campaign in Egypt was over, his campaign in Spain happily concluded; suppose that he was thirty years old instead of fifty—don't you think he would have been both Cæsar and Augustus?"

"Yes, unless he found Brutus, Cassius, and Casca on his path."

"So," said Bonaparte, sadly, "my enemies are reckoning on assassination, are they? In that case the thing is easy, and you, my enemy, have the first chance. What hinders you at this moment, if you feel like Brutus, from striking me as he struck Cæsar? I am alone with you, the doors are shut; and you would have the time to finish me before any one could reach you."

Cadoudal made a step backward.

"No," said he, "we do not count upon assassination, and I think our extremity must be great indeed before any of us would become a murderer; but there are the chances of war. A single reverse would destroy your prestige. One defeat would bring the enemy to the heart of France. The camp-fires of the Austrians can already be seen from the frontiers of Provence. A cannon-ball may take off your head, as it did that of Marshal Berwick, and then what becomes of France? You have no children, and your brothers—"

"Oh!" cried Bonaparte, "from that point of view you are right enough; but, if you don't believe in Providence, I do. I believe that nothing happens by chance. I believe that when, on the 15th of August, 1769 (one year, day for day, after Louis XV. issued the decree reuniting Corsica to

France), a child was born in Ajaccio, destined to bring about the 13th Vendémiaire and the 18th Brumaire, and that Providence had great designs, mighty projects, in view for that child. I am that child. If I have a mission, I have nothing to fear. My mission is a buckler. If I have no mission, if I am mistaken, if, instead of living the twenty-five or thirty years I need to accomplish my work, I am stabbed to the heart like Cæsar, or knocked over by a cannon-ball like Berwick, Providence will have had its reasons for acting so, and on Providence will devolve the duty of providing for France. We spoke just now of Cæsar. When Rome followed his body, mourning, and burned the houses of his murderers, when the Eternal City turned its eyes to the four quarters of the globe, asking whence would come the genius to stay her civil wars, when she trembled at the sight of drunken Antony and treacherous Lepidus, she never thought of the pupil of Apollonius, the nephew of Cæsar, the young Octavius. Who then remembered that son of the Velletri banker, whitened with the flour of his ancestors? No one; not even the far-sighted Cicero. '*Orandum et tollendum*,' he said. Well, that lad fooled all the graybeards in the Senate, and reigned almost as long as Louis XIV. Georges, Georges! don't struggle against the Providence which created me, or that Providence will destroy you."

"Then I shall be destroyed while following the path and the religion of my fathers," replied Cadoudal, bowing; "and I hope that God will pardon my error, which will be that of a fervent Christian and a faithful son."

Bonaparte laid his hands on the shoulders of the young leader.

"So be it," said he; "but at least remain neuter. Leave events to complete themselves. Watch the thrones as they topple, the crowns as they fall. Usually spectators pay for a show; I will pay you to look on."

'And what will you pay me for that, citizen First Consul?" asked Cadoudal, laughing.

"One hundred thousand francs a year," replied Bonaparte.

"If you would give a hundred thousand francs to one poor rebel leader," said Cadoudal, "what would you give to the prince for whom he fought?"

"Nothing, sir. I pay you for your courage, not for the principle for which you fought. I prove to you that I, man of my own works, judge men solely by theirs. Accept, Georges, I beg of you."

"And suppose I refuse?"

"You will do wrong."

"Will I still be free to depart when I please?"

Bonaparte went to the door and opened it.

"The aide-de-camp on duty," he said.

He waited, expecting to see Rapp. Roland appeared.

"Ah, is it you!" he cried. Then, turning to Cadoudal, he said: "Colonel, I do not need to present to you my aide-de-camp, M. Roland de Montrevel. He is already one of your acquaintances. Roland, tell the colonel that he is as free in Paris as you were in his camp at Muzillac, and that if he wishes a passport for any country in the world, Fouché has orders to give it to him."

"Your word suffices, citizen First Consul," replied Cadoudal, bowing. "I leave to-night."

"May I ask where you are going?"

"To London, general."

"So much the better."

"Why so much the better?"

"Because there you will be near the men for whom you have fought."

"And then?"

"Then, when you have seen them—"

"What?"

"You will compare them with those against whom you have fought. But, once out of France, colonel—"

Bonaparte paused.

"I am waiting," said Cadoudal.

"Do not return without warning me, or, if you do, do not be surprised if I treat you as an enemy."

"That would be an honor, general. By treating me so you will show that you consider me a man to be feared."

So saying, Georges bowed to the First Consul, and retired.

"Well, general," asked Roland, after the door had closed on the Breton leader, "is he the man I represented him to be?"

"Yes," responded Bonaparte, thoughtfully; "only he sees things awry. But the exaggeration of his ideas arises from noble sentiments, which must give him great influence over his own people." Then he added, in a low voice, "But we must make an end of him. And now what have you been doing, Roland?"

"Making an end of my work," replied Roland.

"Ah, ha! Then the Companions of Jehu—"

"No longer exist, general. Three-fourths are dead, the rest prisoners."

"And you are safe and sound?"

"Don't speak of it, general. I do verily believe I have a compact with the devil."

That same evening Cadoudal, as he said, left Paris for England. On receiving the news that the Breton leader was in London, Louis XVIII. wrote him the following letter:

I have learned with the greatest satisfaction, general, that you have at last *escaped* from the hands of the tyrant who misconceived you so far as to offer you service under him. I deplore the unhappy circumstances which obliged you to treat with him; but I did not feel the slightest uneasiness; the heart of my faithful Bretons, and yours in particular, are too well known to me. To-day you are free, you are near my brother, all my hopes revive. I need not say more to such a Frenchman as you.

Louis.

To this letter were added a lieutenant-general's commission and the grand cordon of Saint-Louis.

CHAPTER LI

THE ARMY OF THE RESERVES

THE First Consul had reached the point he desired. The Companions of Jehu were destroyed and the Vendée was pacificated.

When demanding peace from England he had hoped for war. He understood very well that, born of war, he could exist only by war. He seemed to foresee that a poet would arise and call him "The Giant of War."

But war—what war? Where should he wage it? An article of the constitution of the year VIII. forbade the First Consul to command the armies in person, or to leave France.

In all constitutions there is inevitably some absurd provision. Happy the constitutions that have but one! The First Consul found a means to evade this particular absurdity.

He established a camp at Dijon. The army which occupied this camp was called the Army of the Reserves. The force withdrawn from Brittany and the Vendée, some thirty thousand men in all, formed the nucleus of this army. Twenty thousand conscripts were incorporated in it; General Berthier was appointed commander-in-chief. The plan which Bonaparte explained to Roland in his study one day was still working in his mind. He expected to recover Italy by a single battle, but that battle must be a great victory.

Moreau, as a reward for his co-operation on the 18th Brumaire, received the command he had so much desired. He was made commander-in-chief of the Army of the Rhine, with eighty thousand men under him. Augereau, with twenty-five thousand more, was on the Dutch frontier. And Masséna, commanding the Army of Italy, had withdrawn to the country about Genoa, where he was tenaciously maintaining himself against the land forces of the Austrian General Ott, and the British fleet under Admiral Keith.

While the latter movements were taking place in Italy, Moreau had assumed the offensive on the Rhine, and defeated the enemy at Stockach and Moeskirch. A single victory was to furnish an excuse to put the Army of Reserves under waiting orders. Two victories would leave no doubt as to the necessity of co-operation. Only, how was this army to be transported to Italy?

Bonaparte's first thought was to march up the Valais and to cross the Simplon. He would thus turn Piedmont and enter Milan. But the operation was a long one, and must be done overtly. Bonaparte renounced it. His plan was to surprise the Austrians and to appear with his whole army on the plains of Piedmont before it was even suspected that he had crossed the Alps. He therefore decided to make the passage of the Great Saint-Bernard. It was for this purpose that he had sent the fifty thousand francs, seized by the Companions of Jehu, to the monks whose monastery crowns that mountain. Another fifty thousand had been sent since, which had reached their destination safely. By the help of this money the monastery was to be amply provisioned for an army of fifty thousand men halting there for a day.

Consequently, toward the end of April the whole of the artillery was advanced to Lauzanne, Villeneuve, Martigny, and Saint-Pierre. General Marmont, commanding the artillery, had already been sent forward to find a means of transporting cannon over the Alps. It was almost an impracticable thing to do; and yet it must be achieved. No precedent existed as a guide. Hannibal with his elephants, Numidians, and Gauls; Charlemagne with his Franks, had no such obstacles to surmount.

During the campaign in Italy in 1796, the army had not crossed the Alps, but turned them, descending from Nice to Cerasco by the Corniche road. This time a truly titanic work was undertaken.

In the first place, was the mountain unoccupied? The mountain without the Austrians was in itself difficult enough to conquer! Lannes was despatched like a forlorn hope with a whole division. He crossed the peak of the Saint-Bernard without baggage or artillery, and took possession of Châtillon. The Austrians had left no troops in Piedmont, except the cavalry in barracks and a few posts of observation. There were no obstacles to contend with except those of nature. Operations were begun at once.

Sledges had been made to transport the guns; but narrow as they might be, they were still too wide for the road. Some other means must be devised. The trunks of pines were hollowed and the guns inserted. At one end was a rope to pull them, at the other a tiller to guide them. Twenty grenadiers took the cables. Twenty others carried the baggage of those who drew them. An artillery-man commanded each detachment with absolute power, if need be, over life and death. The iron mass in such a case was far more precious than the flesh of men.

Before leaving each man received a pair of new shoes and twenty biscuits. Each put on his shoes and hung his biscuits around his neck. The First Consul, stationed at the foot of the mountain, gave to each cannon detachment the word to start.

A man must traverse the same roads as a tourist, on foot or on mule-back, he must plunge his eye to the depth of the precipice, before he can have any idea of what this crossing was. Up, always up those beetling slopes, by narrow paths, on jagged stones, which cut the shoes first, the feet next!

From time to time they stopped, drew breath, and then on again without a murmur. The ice-belt was reached. Before attempting it the men received new shoes; those of the morning were in shreds. A biscuit was eaten, a drop of brandy from the canteen was swallowed, and on they went. No man knew whither he was climbing. Some asked how many more days it would take; others if they might stop for a moment at the moon. At last they came to the eternal snows. There the toil was less severe. The gun-logs slid upon the snow, and they went faster.

One fact will show the measure of power given to the artilleryman who commanded each gun.

General Chamberlhac was passing. He thought the advance not fast enough. Wishing to hasten it, he spoke to an artilleryman in a tone of command.

"You are not in command here," replied the man; "I am. I am responsible for the gun; I direct its march. Pass on."

The general approached the artilleryman as if to take him by the throat. But the man stepped back, saying: "General, don't touch me, or I will send you to the bottom of that precipice with a blow of this tiller."

After unheard-of toil they reached the foot of the last rise, at the summit of which stands the convent. There they found traces of Lannes' division. As the slope was very steep, the soldiers had cut a sort of stairway in the ice. The men now scaled it. The fathers of Saint-Bernard were awaiting them on the summit. As each gun came up the men were taken by squads into the hospice. Tables were set along the passage with bread and Gruyère cheese and wine.

When the soldiers left the convent they pressed the hands of the monks and embraced the dogs.

The descent at first seemed easier than the ascent, and the officers declared it was their turn to drag the guns. But now the cannon outstripped the teams, and some were dragged down faster than they wished. General Lannes and his division were still in the advance. He had reached the valley before the rest of the army, entered the Aosta, and received his orders to march upon Ivrea, at the entrance to the plains of Piedmont. There, however, he encountered an obstacle which no one had foreseen.

The fortress of Bard is situated about twenty-four miles from Aosta. On the road to Ivrea, a little behind the village, a small hill closes the valley almost hermetically. The river Dora flows between this hill and the mountain on the right. The river, or rather, the torrent, fills the whole space. The mountain on the left presents very much the same aspect; only, instead of the river, it is the highroad which passes between the hill and the mountain. It is there that the fortress of Bard stands. It is built on the summit of the hill, and extends down one side of it to the highroad.

How was it that no one had thought of this obstacle which was wellnigh insurmountable? There was no way to assault it from the bottom of the valley, and it was impossible to scale the rocks above it.

Yet, by dint of searching, they did find a path that they were able to level sufficiently for the cavalry and the infantry to pass; but they tried in vain to get the artillery over it, although they took the guns apart as at the Mont Saint-Bernard.

Bonaparte ordered two cannon levelled on the road, and opened fire on the fortress; but it was soon evident that these guns made no effect. Moreover, a cannon ball from the fortress struck one of the two cannon and shattered it. The First Consul then ordered an assault by storm.

Columns formed in the village, and armed with ladders dashed up at a run and reached the fortress at several points; but to insure success, not only celerity, but silence was needed. It ought to have been a surprise; but Colonel Dufour, who commanded one column, ordered the advance to be sounded, and marched boldly to the assault. The column was repulsed, and the colonel received a ball through his body.

Then a company of picked marksmen were chosen. They were supplied with provisions and cartridges, and crept between the rocks until they reached a ledge, from which they commanded the fort. From this ledge they discovered another, not quite so high, but which also overlooked the fort. To this they contrived, with extreme difficulty, to hoist two guns, with which they formed a battery. These two pieces on one side, and the sharpshooters on the other, began to make the enemy uneasy.

In the meantime, General Marmont proposed a plan to the First Consul, so bold that the enemy could not suspect it. It was nothing less than to move the artillery along the highroad, notwithstanding that the enemy could rake it.

Manure and wool from the mattresses were found in the villages and were spread upon the road. The wheels and chains, and all the jingling portions of the gun-carriages were swathed in hay. The horses belonging to the guns and caissons were taken out, and fifty men supplied their places. This latter precaution had two advantages: first, the horses might neigh, while the men had every interest in keeping dead silence; secondly, a dead horse will stop a whole convoy, whereas a dead man, not being fastened to the traces, can be pushed aside and his place taken without even stopping the march. An officer and a subordinate officer of artillery were placed in charge of each carriage or caisson, with the promise of six hundred francs for the transport of each gun or wagon beyond the range of the fort.

General Marmont, who had proposed the plan, superintended the first operation himself. Happily, a storm prevailed and made the night extremely dark. The first six cannon and the first six caissons passed without a single shot from the fortress. The men returned, picking their steps silently, one after another, in single file; but this time the enemy must have heard some noise, and, wishing to know the cause, threw hand-grenades. Fortunately, they fell beyond the road.

Why should these men, who had once passed, return ?

Merely to get their muskets and knapsacks. This might have been avoided had they been stowed on the caissons; but no one can think of everything, and, as it happened, no one in the fort at Bard had thought at all.

As soon as the possibility of the passage was demonstrated, the transport of the artillery became a duty like any other; only, now that the enemy were warned, it was more dangerous. The fort resembled a volcano with its belching flames and smoke; but, owing to the vertical direction in which it was forced to fire, it made more noise than it did harm. Five or six men were killed to each wagon; that is to say, a tenth of each fifty; but the cannon once safely past, the fate of the campaign was secure.

Later it was discovered that the pass of the Little Saint-Bernard would have been practicable, and that the whole artillery could have crossed it without dismounting a gun or losing a man. It is true, however, that the feat would have been less glorious because less difficult.

The army was now in the fertile plains of Piedmont. It was reinforced on the Ticino by a corps of twelve thousand men detached from the Army of the Rhine by Moreau, who, after the two victories he had just won, could afford to lend this contingent to the Army of Italy. He had sent them by the Saint-Gothard. Thus strengthened, the First Consul entered Milan without striking a blow.

By the bye, how came the First Consul, who, according to a provision of the constitution of the year VIII., could not assume command of the army, nor yet leave France, to be where he was? We shall now tell you.

The evening before the day on which he left Paris—that is to say, the 15th of May, or, according to the calendars of the time, the 15th Floréal—he had sent for the two other consuls and all the ministers, saying to Lucien: "Prepare a circular letter to the prefects to-morrow." Then he said to Fouché: "You will publish the circular in all the newspapers. You are to say that I have left for Dijon to inspect the Army of the Reserves. Add, but without affirming it positively, that I may go as far as Geneva. In any case, let it be well impressed on every one that I shall not be absent more than a fortnight. If anything unusual happens I shall return like a thunderclap. I commend to your keeping all the great interests of France; and I hope you will soon hear of me by way of Vienna and London."

On the 6th he started. From that moment his strong determination was to make his way to the plains of Piedmont, and there to fight a decisive battle. Then, as he never doubted that he would conquer, he would answer, like Scipio, to those who accused him of violating the constitution: "On such a day, at such an hour, I fought the Carthagenians; let us go to the capitol, and render thanks to the gods."

Leaving France on the 6th of May, the First Consul was encamped with his whole army between Casale and Turin on the 26th of the same month. It had rained the whole day; but, as often happens in Italy, toward evening the sky had cleared, changing in a few moments from murky darkness to loveliest azure, and the stars came sparkling out.

The First Consul signed to Roland to follow him, and together they issued from the little town of Chivasso and walked along the banks of the river. About a hundred yards beyond the last house a tree, blown down by the wind, offered a seat to the pedestrians. Bonaparte sat down and signed to Roland to join him. He apparently had something to say, some confidence to make to his young aide-de-camp.

Both were silent for a time, and then Bonaparte said: "Roland, do you remember a conversation we had together at the Luxembourg?"

"General," said Roland, laughing, "we had a good many conversations together at the Luxembourg; in one of which you told me we were to cross into Italy in the spring, and fight General Mélas at Torre di Gallifolo or San-Guiliano. Does that still hold good?"

"Yes: but that is not the conversation I mean."

"What was it, general?"

"The day we talked of marriage."

"Ah, yes! My sister's marriage. That has probably taken place by this time, general."

"I don't mean your sister's marriage; I mean yours."

"Good!" said Roland, with a bitter smile. "I thought that had been disposed of, general." And he made a motion as if to rise. Bonaparte caught him by the arm.

"Do you know whom I meant you to marry at that time, Roland?" he said, with a gravity that showed he was determined to be heard.

"No, general."

"Well, my sister Caroline."

"Your sister?"

"Yes. Does that astonish you?"

"I had no idea you had ever thought of doing me that honor."

"Either you are ungrateful, Roland, or you are saying what you do not mean. You know that I love you."

"Oh! my general!"

He took the First Consul's two hands and pressed them with the deepest gratitude.

"Yes, I should have liked you for my brother-in-law."

"Your sister and Murat love each other, general," said Roland. "It is much better that the plan should have gone no further. Besides," he added, in muffled tones, "I thought I told you that I did not care to marry."

Bonaparte smiled. "Why don't you say offhand that you intend becoming a Trappist father?"

"Faith, general, re-establish the cloisters and remove these opportunities for me to try to get myself killed, which, thank God! are not lacking, and you have guessed what my end will be."

"Are you in love? Is this the result of some woman's faithlessness?"

"Good!" said Roland, "so you think I am in love! That is the last straw!"

"Do you complain of my affection when I wished to marry you to my sister?"

"But the thing is impossible now! Your three sisters are all married—one to General Leduc, one to Prince Bacciocchi, and the third to Murat."

"In short," said Bonaparte, laughing, "you feel easy and settled in your mind. You think yourself rid of my alliance."

"Oh, general!" exclaimed Roland.

"You are not ambitious, it seems?"

"General, let me love you for all the good you have done to me, and not for what you seek to do."

"But suppose it is for my own interests that I seek to bind you to me, not by the ties of friendship alone, but also by those of matrimony. Suppose I say to you: In my plans for the future I cannot rely upon my two brothers, whereas I could never for one instant doubt you?"

"In heart, yes, you are right."

"In all respects! What can I do with Leclerc—a commonplace man; with Bacciocchi—who is not French; with Murat—lion-hearted and feather-brained? And yet some day I shall have to make princes of them because they are my sisters' husbands. When that time comes, what can I make of you?"

"A marshal of France."

"And afterward?"

"Afterward? I should say that was enough."

"And then you would be one of twelve, and not a unity of your own."

"Let me be simply your friend. Let me always thresh out the truth with you, and then I'll warrant I shall be out of the crowd."

"That may be enough for you, Roland, but it is not enough for me," persisted Bonaparte. Then, as Roland said nothing, he continued: "I have no more sisters, Roland, it is true; but I have dreamed that you might be something more to me than a brother." Then, as Roland still said nothing, he went on: "I know a young girl, Roland, a charming child, whom I love as a daughter. She is just seventeen. You are twenty-six, and a brigadier-general *de facto*. Before the end of the campaign you will be general of division. Well, Roland, when the campaign is over, we will return together to Paris, and you shall marry her—"

"General," interrupted Roland, "I think I see Bourrienne looking for you."

And in fact the First Consul's secretary was already within two feet of the friends.

"Is that you, Bourrienne?" asked Bonaparte, somewhat impatiently.

"Yes, general, a courier from France."

"Ah!"

"And a letter from Madame Bonaparte."

"Good!" said the First Consul, rising eagerly, "give it to me." And he almost snatched the letter from Bourrienne's hand.

"And for me?" asked Roland. "Nothing for me?"

"Nothing."

"That is strange," said the young man, pensively.

The moon had risen, and by its clear, beautiful light Bonaparte was able to read his letters. Through the first two pages his face expressed perfect serenity. Bonaparte adored his wife; the letters published by Queen Hortense bear witness to that fact. Roland watched these expressions of the soul on his general's face. But toward the close of the letter Bonaparte's face clouded; he frowned and cast a furtive glance at Roland.

"Ah!" exclaimed the young man, "it seems there is something about me in the letter."

Bonaparte did not answer and continued to read. When he had finished, he folded the letter and put it in the side pocket of his coat. Then, turning to Bourrienne, he said: "Very well, we will return. I shall probably have to despatch a courier. Go mend some pens while you are waiting for me."

Bourrienne bowed and returned to Chivasso.

Bonaparte then went up to Roland and laid his hand on his shoulder, saying: "I have no luck with the marriages I attempt to make."

"How so?" asked Roland.

"Your sister's marriage is off."

"Has she refused?"

"No; she has not."

"She has not? Can it be Sir John?"

"Yes."

"Refused to marry my sister after asking her of me, of my mother, of you, of herself?"

"Come, don't begin to get angry. Try to see that there is some mystery in all this."

"I don't see any mystery, I see an insult!"

"Ah! there you are, Roland. That explains why your mother and sister did not write to you. But Josephine thought the matter so serious that you ought to be in-formed. She writes me this news and asks me to tell you of it if I think best. You see I have not hesitated."

"I thank you sincerely, general. Does Lord Tanlay give any reason for this refusal?"

"A reason that is no reason."

"What is it?"

"It can't be the true one."

"But what is it?"

"It is only necessary to look at the man and to talk with him for five minutes to understand that."

"But, general, what reason does he give for breaking his word?"

"That your sister is not as rich as he thought she was."

Roland burst into that nervous laugh which was a sign with him of violent agitation.

"Ha!" said he, "that was the very first thing I told him."

"What did you tell him?"

"That my sister hadn't a penny. How can the children of republican generals be rich?"

"And what did he answer?"

"That he was rich enough for two."

"You see, therefore, that that was not the real reason for his refusal."

"And it is your opinion that one of your aides-de-camp can receive such an insult, and not demand satisfaction?"

"In such situations the person who feels affronted must judge of the matter for himself, my dear Roland."

"General, how many days do you think it will be before we have a decisive action?"

Bonaparte calculated.

"Not less than fifteen days, or three weeks," he answered.

"Then, general, I ask you for a furlough of fifteen days."

"On one condition."

"What is it?"

"That you will first go to Bourg and ask your sister from which side the refusal came."

"That is my intention."

"In that case you have not a moment to lose."

"You see I lose none," said the young man, already on his way to the village.

"One moment," said Bonaparte; "you will take my despatches to Paris, won't you?"

"Ah! I see; I am the courier you spoke of just now to Bourrienne."

"Precisely."

"Come then."

"Wait one moment. The young men you arrested—"

"The Companions of Jehu?"

"Yes. Well, it seems that they were all of noble families. They were fanatics rather than criminals. It appears that your mother has been made the victim of some judicial trick or other in testifying at their trial and has caused their conviction."

"Possibly. My mother was in the coach stopped by them, as you know, and saw the face of their leader."

"Well, your mother implores me, through Josephine,

to pardon those poor madmen—that is the very word she uses. They have appealed their case. You will get there before the appeal can be rejected, and, if you think it desirable, tell the minister of justice for me to suspend matters. After you get back we can see what is best to be done."

"Thank you, general. Anything more?"

"No," said Bonaparte, "except to think over our conversation."

"What was it about?"

"Your marriage."

CHAPTER LII

THE TRIAL

"WELL, I'll say as you did just now, we'll talk about it when I return, if I do."

"Bless me!" exclaimed Bonaparte, "I'm not afraid; you'll kill him as you have the others; only this time, I must admit, I shall be sorry to have him die."

"If you are going to feel so badly about it, general, I can easily be killed in his stead."

"Don't do anything foolish, ninny!" cried Bonaparte, hastily; "I should feel still worse if I lost you."

"Really, general, you are the hardest man to please that I know of," said Roland with his harsh laugh.

And this time he took his way to Chivasso without further delay.

Half an hour later, Roland was galloping along the road to Ivrae in a post-chaise. He was to travel thus to Aosta, at Aosta take a mule, cross the Saint-Bernard to Martigny, thence to Geneva, on to Bourg, and from Bourg to Paris.

While he is galloping along let us see what has happened in France, and clear up the points in the conversation between Bonaparte and his aide-de-camp which must be obscure to the reader's mind.

The prisoners which Roland had made at the grotto of

Ceyzeriat had remained but one night in the prison at Bourg. They had been immediately transferred to that of Besançon, where they were to appear before a council of war.

It will be remembered that two of these prisoners were so grievously wounded that they were carried into Bourg on stretchers. One of them died that same night, the other, three days after they reached Besançon. The number of prisoners was therefore reduced to four; Morgan, who had surrendered himself voluntarily and who was safe and sound, and Montbar, Adler, and d'Assas, who were more or less wounded in the fight, though none of them dangerously. These four aliases hid, as the reader will remember, the real names of the Baron de Sainte-Hermine, the Comte de Jayat, the Vicomte de Valensolle, and the Marquis de Ribier.

While the evidence was being taken against the four prisoners before the military commission at Besançon, the time expired when under the law such cases were tried by courts-martial. The prisoners became accountable therefore to the civil tribunals. This made a great difference to them, not only as to the penalty if convicted, but in the mode of execution. Condemned by a court-martial, they would be shot; condemned by the courts, they would be guillotined. Death by the first was not infamous; death by the second was.

As soon as it appeared that their case was to be brought before a jury, it belonged by law to the court of Bourg. Toward the end of March the prisoners were therefore transferred from the prison of Besançon to that of Bourg, and the first steps toward a trial were taken.

But here the prisoners adopted a line of defence that greatly embarrassed the prosecuting officers. They declared themselves to be the Baron de Sainte-Hermine, the Comte de Jayat, the Vicomte de Valensolle, and the Marquis de Ribier, and to have no connection with the pillagers of diligences, whose names were Morgan, Montbar, Adler, and d'Assas. They acknowledged having belonged to armed bands; but these forces belonged to the army of M. de Teyssonnet and were a ramification of the army of Brittany intended to operate in the East and the Midi, while the army of Brittany, which had just signed a peace, operated in the North. They had waited only to hear of Cadoudal's surrender to do likewise, and the despatch of the Breton leader was no doubt on its way to them when they were attacked and captured.

It was difficult to disprove this. The diligences had invariably been pillaged by masked men, and, apart from Madame de Montrevel and Sir John Tanlay, no one had ever seen the faces of the assailants.

The reader will recall those circumstances: Sir John, on the night they had tried, condemned, and stabbed him; Madame de Montrevel, when the diligence was stopped, and she, in her nervous struggle, had struck off the mask of the leader.

Both had been summoned before the preliminary court and both had been confronted with the prisoners; but neither Sir John nor Madame de Montrevel had recognized any of them. How came they to practice this deception? As for Madame de Montrevel, it was comprehensible. She felt a double gratitude to the man who had come to her assistance, and who had also forgiven, and even praised, Edouard's attack upon himself. But Sir John's silence was more difficult to explain, for among the four prisoners he must have recognized at least two of his assailants.

They had recognized him, and a certain quiver had run through their veins as they did so, but their eyes were none the less resolutely fixed upon him, when, to their great astonishment, Sir John, in spite of the judge's insistence, had calmly replied: "I have not the honor of knowing these gentlemen."

Amélie—we have not spoken of her, for there are sorrows no pen can depict—Amélie, pale, feverish, almost expiring since that fatal night when Morgan was arrested, awaited the return of her mother and Sir John from the preliminary trial with dreadful anxiety. Sir John arrived first. Madame de Montrevel had remained behind to give some orders to Michel. As soon as Amélie saw him she rushed forward, crying out: "What happened?"

Sir John looked behind him, to make sure that Madame de Montrevel could neither see nor hear him, then he said: "Your mother and I recognized no one."

"Ah! how noble you are! how generous! how good, my lord!" cried the young girl, trying to kiss his hand.

But he, withdrawing his hand, said hastily: "I have only done as I promised you; but hush—here is your mother."

Amélie stepped back. "Ah, mamma!" she said, "so you did not say anything to compromise those unfortunate men?"

"What!" replied Madame de Montrevel; "would you have me send to the scaffold a man who had helped me, and who, instead of punishing Edouard, kissed him?"

"And yet," said Amélie, trembling, "you recognized him, did you not?"

"Perfectly," replied Madame de Montrevel. "He is the fair man with the black eyebrows who calls himself the Baron de Sainte-Hermine."

Amélie gave a stifled cry. Then, making an effort to control herself, she said: "Is that the end of it for Sir John and you? Will you be called to testify again?"

"Probably not," replied Madame de Montrevel.

"In any case," observed Sir John, "as neither your mother nor I recognized any one, she will persist in that declaration."

"Oh! most certainly," exclaimed Madame de Montrevel. "God keep me from causing the death of that unhappy young man. I should never forgive myself. It is bad enough that Roland should have been the one to capture him and his companions."

Amélie sighed, but nevertheless her face assumed a calmer expression. She looked gratefully at Sir John,

and then went up to her room, where Charlotte was waiting for her. Charlotte had become more than a maid, she
was now Amélie's friend. Every day since the four young
men had returned to the prison at Bourg she had gone there
to see her father for an hour or so. During these visits
nothing was talked of but the prisoners, whom the worthy
jailer, royalist as he was, pitied with all his heart. Charlotte made him tell her everything, even to their slightest
words, and later reported all to Amélie.

Matters stood thus when Madame de Montrevel and Sir
John arrived at Noires-Fontaines. Before leaving Paris,
the First Consul had informed Madame de Montrevel, both
through Josephine and Roland, that he approved of her
daughter's marriage, and wished it to take place during
his absence, and as soon as possible. Sir John had declared to her that his most ardent wishes were for this
union, and that he only awaited Amélie's commands to
become the happiest of men. Matters having reached this
point, Madame de Montrevel, on the morning of the day
on which she and Sir John were to give their testimony, had
arranged a private interview between her daughter and Sir
John.

The interview lasted over an hour, and Sir John did not
leave Amélie until the carriage came to the door which was
to take Madame de Montrevel and himself to the court.

We have seen that his deposition was all in the prisoners' favor, and we have also seen how Amélie received
him on his return.

That evening Madame de Montrevel had a long conversation with her daughter. To her mother's pressing inquiries,
Amélie merely replied that the state of her health was such
that she desired a postponement of her marriage, and that
she counted on Sir John's delicacy to grant it.

The next day Madame de Montrevel was obliged to return to Paris, her position in Madame Bonaparte's household not admitting of longer absence. The morning of her
departure she urged Amélie to accompany her; but again

the young girl dwelt upon the feebleness of her health.
The sweetest and most reviving months in the year were
just opening, and she begged to be allowed to spend them
in the country, for they were sure, she said, to do her good.

Madame de Montrevel, always unable to deny Amélie
anything, above all where it concerned her health, granted
her request.

On her return to Paris, Madame de Montrevel travelled
as before, with Sir John. Much to her surprise, during the
two days' journey he did not say anything to her about his
marriage to Amélie. But Madame Bonaparte, as soon as
she saw her friend, asked the usual question: "Well, when
shall we marry Amélie and Sir John? You know how
much the First Consul desires it."

To which Madame de Montrevel replied: "It all depends on Sir John."

This response furnished Madame Bonaparte with much
food for reflection. Why should a man who had been so
eager suddenly grow cold? Time alone could explain the
mystery.

Time went by, and the trial of the prisoners began.
They were confronted with all the travellers who had
signed the various depositions, which, as we have seen,
were in the possession of the minister of police. No one
had recognized them, for no one had seen their faces uncovered. Moreover, the travellers asserted that none of
their property, either money or jewels, had been taken.
Jean Picot testified that the two hundred louis which had
been taken from him by accident had been returned.

These preliminary inquiries lasted over two months.
At the end of that time the accused, against whom there
was no evidence connecting them with the pillage of the
coaches, were under no accusation but that of their own
admissions; that is to say, of being affiliated with the
Breton and Vendéan insurrection. They were simply
one of the armed bands roaming the Jura under the
orders of M. de Teyssonnet.

The judges delayed the final trial as long as possible, hoping that some more direct testimony might be discovered. This hope was balked. No one had really suffered from the deeds imputed to these young men, except the Treasury, whose misfortunes concerned no one. The trial could not be delayed any longer.

The prisoners, on their side, had made the best of their time. By means, as we have seen, of an exchange of passports, Morgan had travelled sometimes as Ribier, and Ribier as Sainte-Hermine, and so with the others. The result was a confusion in the testimony of the innkeepers, which the entries in their books only served to increase. The arrival of travellers, noted on the registers an hour too early or an hour too late, furnished the prisoners with irrefutable alibis. The judges were morally convinced of their guilt; but their conviction was impossible against such testimony.

On the other hand, it must be said that public sympathy was wholly with the prisoners.

The trial began. The prison at Bourg adjoins the court-room. The prisoners could be brought there through the interior passages. Large as the hall was, it was crowded on the opening day. The whole population of Bourg thronged about the doors, and persons came from Mâcon, Sons-le-Saulnier, Besançon, and Nantua, so great was the excitement caused by the stoppages, and so popular were the exploits of the Companions of Jehu.

The entrance of the four prisoners was greeted by a murmur in which there was nothing offensive. Public sentiment seemed equally divided between curiosity and sympathy. Their presence, it must be admitted, was well calculated to inspire both. Very handsome, dressed in the latest fashion of the day, self-possessed without insolence, smiling toward the audience, courteous to their judges, though at times a little sarcastic, their personal appearance was their best defence.

The oldest of the four was barely thirty. Questioned as

to their names, Christian and family, their age, and places
of birth, they answered as follows:

"Charles de Sainte-Hermine, born at Tours, department
of the Indre-et-Loire, aged twenty-four."

"Louis-André de Jayat, born at Bage-le-Château, department of the Ain, aged twenty-nine."

"Raoul-Frederic-Auguste de Valensolle, born at Sainte-
Colombe, department of the Rhone, aged twenty-seven."

"Pierre-Hector de Ribier, born at Bollène, department of
Vaucluse, aged twenty-six."

Questioned as to their social condition and state, all four
said they were of noble rank and royalists.

These fine young men, defending themselves against
death on the scaffold, not against a soldier's death before
the guns—who asked the death they claimed to have merited as insurrectionists, but a death of honor—formed a
splendid spectacle of youth, courage, and gallant bearing.

The judges saw plainly that on the accusation of being
insurrectionists, the Vendée having submitted and Brittany
being pacificated, they would have to be acquitted. That
was not a result to satisfy the minister of police. Death
awarded by a council of war would not have satisfied him;
he had determined that these men should die the death of
malefactors, a death of infamy.

The trial had now lasted three days without proceeding
in the direction of the minister's wishes. Charlotte, who
could reach the courtroom through the prison, was there
each day, and returned each night to Amélie with some
fresh word of hope. On the fourth day, Amélie could
bear the suspense no longer. She dressed herself in a
costume similar to the one that Charlotte wore, except
that the black lace of the head-dress was longer and
thicker than is usual with the Bressan peasant woman.
It formed a veil and completely hid her features.

Charlotte presented Amélie to her father as one of her
friends who was anxious to see the trial. The good man
did not recognize Mademoiselle de Montrevel, and in order

to enable the young girls to see the prisoners well he placed them in the doorway of the porter's room, which opened upon the passage leading to the courtroom. This passage was so narrow at this particular point that the four gendarmes who accompanied the prisoners changed the line of march. First came two officers, then the prisoners one by one, then the other two officers. The girls stood in the doorway.

When Amélie heard the doors open she was obliged to lean upon Charlotte's shoulder for support, the earth seemed to give way under her feet and the wall at her back. She heard the sound of feet and the rattle of the gendarmes' sabres, then the door of the prison opened.

First one gendarme appeared, then another, then Sainte-Hermine, walking first, as though he were still Morgan, the captain of the Companions of Jehu.

As he passed Amélie murmured: "Charles!"

The prisoner recognized the beloved voice, gave a faint cry, and felt a paper slip into his hand. He pressed that precious hand, murmured her name, and passed on.

The others who followed did not, or pretended not to, notice the two girls. As for the gendarmes, they had seen and heard nothing.

As soon as the party stepped into the light, Morgan unfolded the note and read as follows:

Do not be anxious, my beloved Charles; I am and ever will be your faithful Amélie, in life or death. I have told all to Lord Tanlay. He is the most generous man on earth; he has promised me to break off the marriage and to take the whole responsibility on himself. I love you.

Morgan kissed the note and put it in his breast. Then he glanced down the corridor and saw the two Bressan women leaning against the door. Amélie had risked all to see him once more. It is true, however, that at this last session of the court no additional witnesses were expected who could injure the accused, and in the absence of proof it was impossible to convict them.

The best lawyers in the department, those of Lyons and Besançon, had been retained by the prisoners for their defence. Each had spoken in turn, destroying bit by bit the indictment, as, in the tournaments of the Middle Ages, a strong and dexterous knight was wont to knock off, piece by piece, his adversary's armor. Flattering applause had followed the more remarkable points of their arguments, in spite of the usher's warnings and the admonitions of the judge.

Amélie, with clasped hands, was thanking God, who had so visibly manifested Himself in the prisoners' favor. A dreadful weight was lifted from her tortured breast. She breathed with joy, and looked through tears of gratitude at the Christ which hung above the judge's head.

The arguments were all made, and the case about to be closed. Suddenly an usher entered the courtroom, approached the judge, and whispered something in his ear.

"Gentlemen," said the judge, "the court is adjourned for a time. Let the prisoners be taken out."

There was a movement of feverish anxiety among the audience. What could have happened? What unexpected event was about to take place? Every one looked anxiously at his neighbor. Amélie's heart was wrung by a presentiment. She pressed her hand to her breast; it was as though an ice-cold iron had pierced it to the springs of life.

The gendarmes rose. The prisoners did likewise, and were then marched back to their cells. One after the other they passed Amélie. The hands of the lovers touched each other; those of Amélie were as cold as death.

"Whatever happens, thank you," said Charles, as he passed.

Amélie tried to answer, but the words died on her lips.

During this time the judge had risen and passed into the council-chamber. There he found a veiled woman, who had just descended from a carriage at the door of the court-house, and had not spoken to any one on her way in.

"Madame," said the judge, "I offer you many excuses for the way in which I have brought you from Paris; but the life of a man depends upon it, and before that consideration everything must yield."

"You have no need to excuse yourself, sir," replied the veiled lady, "I know the prerogatives of the law, and I am here at your orders."

"Madame," said the judge, "the court and myself recognize the feeling of delicacy which prompted you, when first confronted with the prisoners, to decline to recognize the one who assisted you when fainting. At that time the prisoners denied their identity with the pillagers of the diligences. Since then they have confessed all; but it is our wish to know the one who showed you that consideration, in order that we may recommend him to the First Consul's clemency."

"What!" exclaimed the lady, "have they really confessed?"

"Yes, madame, but they will not say which of their number helped you, fearing, no doubt, to contradict your testimony, and thus cause you embarrassment."

"What is it you request of me, sir?"

"That you will save the gentleman who assisted you."

"Oh! willingly," said the lady, rising; "what am I to do?"

"Answer a question which I shall ask you."

"I am ready, sir."

"Wait here a moment. You will be sent for presently."

The judge went back into the courtroom. A gendarme was placed at each door to prevent any one from approaching the lady. The judge resumed his seat.

"Gentlemen," said he, "the session is reopened."

General excitement prevailed. The ushers called for silence, and silence was restored.

"Bring in the witness," said the judge.

An usher opened the door of the council-chamber, and the lady, still veiled, was brought into court. All eyes turned upon her. Who was she? Why was she there? What had she come for? Amélie's eyes fastened upon her at once.

"O my God!" she murmured, "grant that I be mistaken."

"Madame," said the judge, "the prisoners are about to be brought in. Have the goodness to point out the one who, when the Geneva diligence was stopped, paid you those attentions."

A shudder ran through the audience. They felt that some fatal trap had been laid for the prisoners.

A dozen voices began to shout: "Say nothing!" but the ushers, at a sign from the judge, cried out imperatively: "Silence!"

Amélie's heart turned deadly cold. A cold sweat poured from her forehead. Her knees gave way and trembled under her.

"Bring in the prisoners," said the judge, imposing silence by a look as the usher had with his voice. "And you, madame, have the goodness to advance and raise your veil."

The veiled lady obeyed.

"My mother!" cried Amélie, but in a voice so choked that only those near her heard the words.

"Madame de Montrevel!" murmured the audience.

At that moment the first gendarme appeared at the door, then the second. After him came the prisoners, but not in the same order as before. Morgan had placed himself third, so that, separated as he was from the gendarmes by Montbar and Adler in front and d'Assas behind, he might be better able to clasp Amélie's hand.

Montbar entered first.

Madame de Montrevel shook her head.

Then came Adler.

Madame de Montrevel made the same negative sign.

Just then Morgan passed before Amélie.

"We are lost!" she said.

He looked at her in astonishment as she pressed his hand convulsively. Then he entered.

"That is he," said Madame de Montrevel, as soon as she saw Morgan—or, if the reader prefers it, Baron Charles de Sainte-Hermine—who was now proved one and the same man by means of Madame de Montrevel's identification.

A long cry of distress burst from the audience. Montbar burst into a laugh.

"Ha! by my faith!" he cried, "that will teach you, dear friend, to play the gallant with fainting women." Then, turning to Madame de Montrevel, he added: "With three short words, madame, you have decapitated four heads."

A terrible silence fell, in the midst of which a groan was heard.

"Usher," said the judge, "have you warned the public that all marks of approbation or disapproval are forbidden?"

The usher inquired who had disobeyed the order of the court. It was a woman wearing the dress of a Bressan peasant, who was being carried into the jailer's room.

From that moment the accused made no further attempt at denial; but, just as Morgan had united with them when arrested, they now joined with him. Their four heads should be saved, or fall together.

That same day, at ten in the evening, the jury rendered a verdict of guilty, and the court pronounced the sentence of death.

Three days later, by force of entreaties, the lawyers obtained permission for the accused to appeal their case; but they were not admitted to bail.

CHAPTER LIII

IN WHICH AMÉLIE KEEPS HER WORD

THE verdict rendered by the jury of the town of Bourg had a terrible effect, not only in the courtroom, but throughout the entire town. The four prisoners had shown such chivalric brotherhood, such noble bearing, such deep conviction in the faith they professed, that their enemies themselves admired the devotion which had made robbers and highwaymen of men of rank and family.

Madame de Montrevel, overwhelmed by the part she had been made to play at the crucial point of this drama, saw but one means of repairing the evil she had done, and that was to start at once for Paris and fling herself at the feet of the First Consul, imploring him to pardon the four condemned men. She did not even take time to go to the Château des Noires-Fontaines to see Amélie. She knew that Bonaparte's departure was fixed for the first week in May, and this was already the 6th. When she last left Paris everything had been prepared for that departure.

She wrote a line to Amélie explaining by what fatal deception she had been instrumental in destroying the lives of four men, when she intended to save the life of one. Then, as if ashamed of having broken the pledge she had made to Amélie, and above all to herself, she ordered fresh post-horses and returned to Paris.

She arrived there on the morning of the 8th of May. Bonaparte had started on the evening of the 6th. He said on leaving that he was only going to Dijon, possibly as far as Geneva, but in any case he should not be absent more than three weeks. The prisoners' appeal, even if rejected, would not receive final consideration for five or six weeks. All hope need not therefore be abandoned.

But, alas! it became evident that the review at Dijon was only a pretext, that the journey to Geneva had never been seriously thought of, and that Bonaparte, instead of going to Switzerland, was really on his way to Italy.

Then Madame de Montrevel, unwilling to appeal to her son, for she had heard his oath when Lord Tanlay had been left for dead, and knew the part he had played in the capture of the Companions of Jehu—then Madame de Montrevel appealed to Josephine, and Josephine promised to write to the First Consul. That same evening she kept her promise.

But the trial had made a great stir. It was not with these prisoners as with ordinary men. Justice made haste, and thirty-five days after the verdict had been rendered the appeal was rejected. This decision was immediately sent to Bourg with an order to execute the prisoners within twenty-four hours. But notwithstanding the haste of the minister of police in forwarding this decision, the first intimation of the fatal news was not received by the judicial authorities at Bourg. While the prisoners were taking their daily walk in the courtyard a stone was thrown over the outer wall and fell at their feet. Morgan, who still retained in relation to his comrades the position of leader, picked it up, opened the letter which inclosed the stone, and read it. Then, turning to his friends, he said: "Gentlemen, the appeal has been rejected, as we might have expected, and the ceremony will take place in all probability to-morrow."

Valensolle and Ribier, who were playing a species of quoits with crown-pieces and louis, left off their game to hear the news. Having heard it they returned to their game without remark.

Jayat, who was reading "La Nouvelle Héloïse," resumed his book, saying: "Then, I shall not have time to finish M. Jean-Jacques Rousseau's masterpiece, and

upon my word I don't regret it, for it is the most utterly
false and wearisome book I ever read in my life!''

Sainte-Hermine passed his hand over his forehead, murmuring: "Poor Amélie!" Then observing Charlotte, who
was at the window of the jailer's room overlooking the
courtyard, he went to her. "Tell Amélie that she must
keep the promise she made me, to-night.''

The jailer's daughter closed the window, kissed her
father, and told him that in all probability he would see
her there again that evening. Then she returned to Noires-
Fontaines, a road she had taken twice every day for the last
two months, once at noon on her way to the prison, once in
the evening on returning to the château.

Every night she found Amélie in the same place, sitting
at the window which, in happier days, had given admittance
to her beloved Charles. Since the day she had fainted in
the courtroom she had shed no tears, and, we may almost
add, had uttered no word. Unlike the marble of antiquity
awakening into life, she might have been compared to a
living woman petrifying into stone. Every day she grew
paler.

Charlotte watched her with astonishment. Common
minds, always impressed by noisy demonstrations, that is
to say, by cries and tears, are unable to understand a mute
sorrow. Dumbness to them means indifference. She was
therefore astonished at the calmness with which Amélie
received the message she was charged to deliver. She did
not see in the dimness of the twilight that Amélie's face
from being pale grew livid. She did not feel the deadly
clutch which, like an iron wrench, had seized her heart.
She did not know that as her mistress walked to the door
an automatic stiffness was in her limbs. Nevertheless she
followed her anxiously. But at the door Amélie stretched
out her hand.

"Wait for me there,'' she said.

Charlotte obeyed. Amélie closed the door behind her,
and went up to Roland's room.

Roland's room was veritably that of a soldier and a hunts-man, and its chief adornments were trophies and weapons. Arms of all kinds were here, French and foreign, from the blue-barrelled pistol of Versailles to the silver-handled pistol of Cairo, from the tempered blade of Catalonia to the Turkish cimeter.

Amélie took down from this arsenal four daggers, sharp-edged and pointed, and eight pistols of different shapes. She put balls in a bag and powder in a horn. Thus sup-plied she returned to her own room. There Charlotte as-sisted her in putting on the peasant gown. Then she waited for the night.

Night comes late in June. Amélie stood motionless, mute, leaning against the chimney-piece, and looking through the open window at the village of Ceyzeriat, which was slowly disappearing in the gathering shades of night. When she could no longer distinguish any-thing but the lights which were being lighted one by one, she said:

"Come, it is time to go."

The two young girls went out. Michel paid no attention to Amélie, supposing her to be some friend of Charlotte's, who had called to see her and whom the jailer's daughter was now escorting home.

Ten o'clock was striking as they passed the church of Brou. It was quarter past when Charlotte knocked at the prison door. Old Courtois opened it.

We have already shown the political opinions of the worthy jailer. He was a royalist. He therefore felt the deepest sympathy for the four condemned men, and had hoped, like nearly every one in Bourg—like Madame de Montrevel, whose despair at what she had done was known to him—that the First Consul would pardon them. He had therefore mitigated their captivity as much as possible, without failing in his duty, by relieving them of all need-less restrictions. On the other hand, it is true that he had refused a gift of sixty thousand francs (a sum which in those

days was worth nearly treble what it is now) to allow them
to escape.

We have seen how, being taken into confidence by his
daughter, he had allowed Amélie, disguised as a Bressan
peasant, to be present at the trial. The reader will also
remember the kindness the worthy man had shown to
Amélie and her mother when they themselves were prisoners. This time, as he was still ignorant of the rejection
of the appeal, he allowed his feelings to be worked upon.
Charlotte had told him that her young mistress was to start
that night for Paris to endeavor to hasten the pardon, and
that she desired before leaving to see the Baron de Sainte-
Hermine and obtain his last instructions.

There were five doors to break through to reach the
street, a squad of guards in the courtyard, and sentinels
within and without the prison. Consequently Père Courtois
felt no anxiety lest his prisoners escape. He therefore consented that Amélie should see Morgan.

We trust our readers will excuse us if we use the names
Morgan, Charles, and the Baron de Sainte-Hermine, inter-
changeably, since they are aware that by that triple appel-
lation we intend to designate the same man.

Courtois took a light and walked before Amélie. The
young girl, as though prepared to start by the mail-coach
at once on leaving the prison, carried a travelling bag in
her hand. Charlotte followed her mistress.

"You will recognize the cell, Mademoiselle de Montrevel," said Courtois. "It is the one in which you were confined with your mother. The leader of these unfortunate
young men, the Baron Charles de Sainte-Hermine, asked
me as a favor to put them in cage No. 1. You know that's
the name we give our cells. I did not think I ought to
refuse him that consolation, knowing how the poor fellow
loved you. Oh, don't be uneasy, Mademoiselle Amélie, I
will never breathe your secret. Then he questioned me,
asking which had been your mother's bed, and which
yours. I told him, and then he wanted his to stand just

where yours did. That wasn't hard, for the bed was not only in the same place, but it was the very one you had used. So, since the poor fellow entered your cell, he has spent nearly all his time lying on your bed."

Amélie gave a sigh that resembled a groan. She felt —and it was long since she had done so—a tear moisten her eyelids. Yes! she was loved as she loved, and the lips of a disinterested stranger gave her the proof of it. At this moment of eternal separation this conviction shone like a diamond of light in its setting of sorrow.

The doors opened one by one before Père Courtois. When they reached the last one, Amélie laid her hand on the jailer's shoulder. She thought she heard a chant. Listening attentively, she became aware that it was a voice repeating verses.

But the voice was not Morgan's; it was unknown to her. Here is what it said:

> I have bared all my heart to the God of the just,
>   He has witnessed my penitent tears;
> He has stilled my remorse, He has armed me with trust,
>   He has pitied and calmed all my fears.
>
> My enemies, scoffing, have said in their rage:
>   "Let him die, be his mem'ry accursed!"
> Saith the merciful Father, my grief to assuage,
>   "Their hatred hath now done its worst.
>
> "I have heard thy complaints, and I know that the ban
>   Of remorse hath e'en brought thee so low;
> I can pity the soul of the penitent man
>   That was weak in this valley of woe;
>
> "I will crown thy lost name with the just acclaim
>   Of the slow-judging righteous years;
> Their pity and justice in time shall proclaim
>   Thine honor; then lay off thy fears!"
>
> I bless thee, O God! who hast deigned to restore
>   Mine honor that Thou hast made whole
> From shame and remorse; as I enter Death's door
>   To Thee I commend my poor soul!

> To the banquet of life, an unfortunate guest,
>   I came for a day, and I go—
> I die in my vigor; I sought not to rest
>   In the grave where the weary lie low.
>
> Farewell to thee, earth! farewell, tender verdure
>   Of woodland! Farewell, sunny shore!
> Green fields that I love, azure skies, smiling Nature,
>   Farewell! I shall see thee no more.
>
> May thy beauty still gladden the friends that I love,
>   Whom I long for—but stern fate denies;
> May they pass full of years, though I wait them above;
>   May a last loving hand close their eyes.

The voice was silent; no doubt the last verse was finished. Amélie, who would not interrupt the last meditations of the doomed men, and who had recognized Gilbert's beautiful ode written on a hospital bed the night before his death, now signed to the jailer to open the door. Père Courtois, jailer as he was, seemed to share the young girl's emotion, for he put the key in the lock and turned it as softly as he could. The door opened.

Amélie saw at a glance the whole interior of the cell, and the persons in it.

Valensolle was standing, leaning against the wall, and still holding the book from which he had just read the lines that Amélie had overheard. Jayat was seated near a table with his head resting on his hands. Ribier was sitting on the table itself. Near him, but further back, Sainte-Hermine, his eyes closed as if in sleep, was lying on the bed.

At sight of the young girl, whom they knew to be Amélie, Ribier and Jayat rose. Morgan did not move; he had heard nothing.

Amélie went directly to him, and, as if the love she felt for him were sanctified by the nearness of death, she gave no heed to the presence of his friends, but pressed her lips to his, murmuring: "Awake, my Charles, it is I, Amélie. I have come to keep my promise."

Morgan gave a cry of joy and clasped her in his arms.

"Monsieur Courtois," said Montbar, "you are a worthy man. Leave those poor young people alone. It would be sacrilege to trouble their last moments together on earth by our presence."

Père Courtois, without a word, opened the door of the adjoining cell. Valensolle, Jayat and Ribier entered it, and the door was closed upon them. Then, making a sign to Charlotte, Courtois himself went away. The lovers were alone.

There are scenes that should not be described, words that must not be repeated. God, who sees and hears them from his immortal throne, alone knows what sombre joys, what bitter pleasures they contain.

At the end of an hour the two young people heard the key turn once more in the lock. They were sad but calm. The conviction that their separation would not be for long gave them a sweet serenity. The worthy jailer seemed more grieved and distressed at his second appearance than at his first; but Morgan and Amélie thanked him with a smile.

He went to the cell where the others were locked up and opened it, murmuring to himself: "Faith! It would have been hard if they couldn't have been alone together on their last night."

Valensolle, Jayat and Ribier returned. Amélie, with her left arm wound around Morgan, held out her right hand to them. All three, one after the other, kissed that cold, damp hand. Then Morgan led her to the door.

"Au revoir!" he said.

"Soon!" she answered.

And then this parting at the gates of death was sealed by a long kiss, followed by a groan so terrible that it seemed to rend their hearts in twain.

The door closed again, the bolts and bars shot into their places.

"Well?" cried Valensolle, Jayat and Ribier with one accord.

"Here!" replied Morgan, emptying the travelling bag upon the table.

The three young men gave a cry of joy as they saw the shining pistols and gleaming blades. It was all that they desired next to liberty—the joy, the dolorous precious joy of knowing themselves masters of their own lives, and, if need be, that of others.

During this time the jailer led Amélie to the street. When they reached it he hesitated a moment, then he touched Amélie's arm, saying as he did so: "Mademoiselle de Montrevel, forgive me for causing you so much pain, but it is useless for you to go to Paris."

"Because the appeal has been rejected and the execution takes place to-morrow, I suppose you mean," said Amélie.

The jailer in his astonishment stepped back a pace.

"I knew it, my friend," said Amélie. Then turning to Charlotte, she said: "Take me to the nearest church and come for me to-morrow after all is over."

The nearest church was not far off. It was that of Sainte-Claire. For the last three months it had been opened for public worship under the decree of the First Consul. As it was now nearly midnight, the doors were closed; but Charlotte knew where the sexton lived and she went to wake him. Amélie waited, leaning against the walls as motionless as the marble figures that adorned its frontal.

The sexton arrived at the end of half an hour. During that time the girl had seen a dreadful sight. Three men had passed her, dragging a cart, which she saw by the light of the moon was painted red. Within this cart she perceived shapeless objects, long planks and singular ladders, all painted the same color. They were dragging it toward the bastion Montrevel, the place used for the executions.

Amélie divined what it was, and, with a cry, she fell upon her knees.

At that cry the men in black turned round. They fancied for a moment that one of the sculptured figures of the porch had descended from its niche and was kneeling there.

The one who seemed to be the leader stepped close to the young girl.

"Don't come near me!" she cried. "Don't come near me!"

The man returned humbly to his place and continued on his way. The cart disappeared round the corner of the Rue des Prisons; but the noise of its wheels still sounded on the stones and echoed in the girl's heart.

When the sacristan and Charlôtte returned they found the young girl on her knees. The man raised some objections against opening the church at that hour of the night; but a piece of gold and Mademoiselle de Montrevel's name dispelled his scruples. A second gold piece decided him to light a little chapel. It was the one in which Amélie had made her first communion. There, kneeling before the altar, she implored them to leave her alone.

Toward three in the morning she saw the colored window above the altar of the Virgin begin to lighten. It looked to the east, so that the first ray of light came direct to her eyes as a messenger from God.

Little by little the town awoke. To Amélie the noise seemed louder than ever before. Soon the vaulted ceiling of the church shook with the tramp of a troop of horsemen. This troop was on its way to the prison.

A little before nine the young girl heard a great noise, and it seemed to her that the whole town must be rushing in the same direction. She strove to lose herself in prayer, that she might not hear these different sounds that spoke to her in an unknown language of which her anguish told her she understood every word.

In truth, a terrible thing was happening at the prison. It was no wonder that the whole town had rushed thither.

At nine o'clock Père Courtois entered the jail to tell the prisoners at one and the same time that their appeal had been rejected and that they must prepare for immediate death. He found the four prisoners armed to the teeth.

The jailer, taken unawares, was pulled into the cell and

the door locked behind him. Then the young men, without any defence on his part, so astonished was he, seized his keys, and passing through the door opposite to the one by which he had entered they locked it on him. Leaving him in their cell, they found themselves in the adjoining one, in which he had placed three of them during Amélie's interview with Morgan.

One of the keys on the jailer's bunch opened the other door of this cell, and that door led to the inner courtyard of the prison. This courtyard was closed by three massive doors, all of which led to a sort of lobby, opening upon the porter's lodge, which in turn adjoined the law-courts. From this lodge fifteen steps led down into a vast courtyard closed by an iron gate and railing. Usually this gate was only locked at night. If it should happen to be open on this occasion it would offer a possibility of escape.

Morgan found the key of the prisoners' court, opened the door, and rushed with his companions to the porter's lodge and to the portico, from which the fifteen steps led down into the courtyard. From there the three young men could see that all hope was lost.

The iron gate was closed, and eighty men, dragoons and gendarmes, were drawn up in front of it.

When the four prisoners, free and armed to the teeth, sprang from the porter's lodge to the portico, a great cry, a cry of astonishment and terror, burst from the crowd in the street beyond the railing.

Their aspect was formidable, indeed; for to preserve the freedom of their movements, perhaps to hide the shedding of blood, which would have shown so quickly on their white linen, they were naked to the waist. A handkerchief knotted around their middle bristled with weapons.

A glance sufficed to show them that they were indeed masters of their own lives, but not of their liberty. Amid the clamoring of the crowd and the clanking of the sabres, as they were drawn from their scabbards, the young men paused an instant and conferred together. Then Montbar, after shaking hands with his companions, walked down the fifteen steps and advanced to the gate.

When he was within four yards of the gate he turned, with a last glance at his comrades, bowed graciously to the now silent mob, and said to the soldiers: "Very well, gentlemen of the gendarmerie! Very well, dragoons!"

Then, placing the muzzle of his pistol to his mouth, he blew out his brains.

Confused and frantic cries followed the explosion, but ceased almost immediately as Valensolle came down the steps, holding in his hand a dagger with a straight and pointed blade. His pistols, which he did not seem inclined to use, were still in his belt.

He advanced to a sort of shed supported on three pillars, stopped at the first pillar, rested the hilt of his dagger upon it, and, with a last salutation to his friends, clasped the column with one arm till the blade had disappeared in his breast. For an instant he remained standing, then a mortal pallor overspread his face, his arm loosened its hold, and he fell to the ground, stone-dead.

The crowd was mute, paralyzed with horror.

It was now Ribier's turn. He advanced to the gate, and, once there, aimed the two pistols he held at the gendarmes. He did not fire, but the gendarmes did. Three or four shots were heard, and Ribier fell, pierced by two balls.

Admiration seized upon the spectators at sight of these successive catastrophes. They saw that the young men were willing to die, but to die with honor, and as they willed, and also with the grace of the gladiators of antiquity. Silence therefore reigned when Morgan, now left alone, came smiling down the steps of the portico and held up his hand in sign that he wished to speak. Besides, what more could it want—this eager mob, watching for blood? A greater sight had been given to it than it came to see. Four dead men had been promised to it; four heads were to be cut off; but here was variety in death, unexpected, picturesque. It was natural, therefore, that the crowd should keep silence when Morgan was seen to advance.

He held neither pistols nor daggers in his hands; they were in his belt. He passed the body of Valensolle, and placed himself between those of Jayat and Ribier.

"Gentlemen," said he, "let us negotiate."

The hush that followed was so great that those present seemed scarcely to breathe. Morgan said: "There lies a man who has blown out his brains [he pointed to Jayat]; here lies one who stabbed himself [he designated Valensolle]; a third who has been shot [he indicated Ribier]; you want to see the fourth guillotined. I understand that."

A dreadful shudder passed through the crowd.

"Well," continued Morgan, "I am willing to give you that satisfaction. I am ready, but I desire to go to the scaffold in my own way. No one shall touch me; if any one does come near me I shall blow out his brains—except that gentleman," continued Morgan, pointing to the executioner. "This is his affair and mine only."

The crowd apparently thought this request reasonable, for from all sides came the cry, "Yes, yes, yes."

The officer saw that the quickest way to end the matter was to yield to Morgan's demand.

"Will you promise me," he asked, "that if your hands and feet are not bound you will not try to escape?"

"I give my word of honor," replied Morgan.

"Then," said the officer, "stand aside, and let us take up the bodies of your comrades."

"That is but right," said Morgan, and he turned aside to a wall about ten paces distant and leaned against it.

The gate opened. Three men dressed in black entered the courtyard and picked up the bodies one after the other. Ribier was not quite dead; he opened his eyes and seemed to look for Morgan.

"Here I am," said the latter. "Rest easy, dear friend, I follow."

Ribier closed his eyes without uttering a word.

When the three bodies had been removed, the officer of the gendarmerie addressed Morgan.

"Are you ready, sir?" he asked.

"Yes," replied Morgan, bowing with exquisite politeness.

"Then come."

"I come."

And he took his place between a platoon of gendarmerie and a detachment of dragoons.

"Will you mount the cart, sir, or go on foot?" asked the captain.

"On foot, on foot, sir. I am anxious that all shall see it is my pleasure to be guillotined, and that I am not afraid."

The sinister procession crossed the Place des Lisses and skirted the walls of the Hôtel Montbazon. The cart bearing the three bodies came first, then the dragoons, then Morgan walking alone in a clear space of some ten feet before and behind him, then the gendarmes. At the end of the wall they turned to the left.

Suddenly, through an opening that existed at that time between the wall and the market-place, Morgan saw the scaffold raising its two posts to heaven like two bloody arms.

"Faugh!" he exclaimed, "I have never seen a guillotine, and I had no idea it was so ugly."

Then, without further remark, he drew his dagger and plunged it into his breast up to the hilt.

The captain of the gendarmerie saw the movement without being in time to prevent it. He spurred his horse toward Morgan, who, to his own amazement and that of every one else, remained standing. But Morgan, drawing a pistol from his belt, and cocking it, exclaimed: "Stop! It was agreed that no one should touch me. I shall die alone, or three of us will die together."

The captain reined back his horse.

"Forward!" said Morgan.

They reached the foot of the guillotine. Morgan drew

out his dagger and struck again as deeply as before. A cry of rage rather than pain escaped him.

"My soul must be riveted to my body," he said.

Then, as the assistants wished to help him mount the scaffold on which the executioner was awaiting him, he cried out: "No, I say again, let no one touch me."

Then he mounted the three steps without staggering.

When he reached the platform, he drew out the dagger again and struck himself a third time. Then a frightful laugh burst from his lips; flinging the dagger, which he had wrenched from the third ineffectual wound, at the feet of the executioner, he exclaimed: "By my faith! I have done enough. It is your turn; do it if you can."

A minute later the head of the intrepid young man fell upon the scaffold, and by a phenomenon of that unconquerable vitality which he possessed it rebounded and rolled forward beyond the timbers of the guillotine.

Go to Bourg, as I did, and they will tell you that, as the head rolled forward, it was heard to utter the name of Amélie.

The dead bodies were guillotined after the living one; so that the spectators, instead of losing anything by the events we have just related, enjoyed a double spectacle.

CHAPTER LIV

THE CONFESSION

THREE days after the events we have just recited, a carriage covered with dust and drawn by two horses white with foam stopped about seven of the evening before the gate of the Château des Noires-Fontaines. To the great astonishment of the person who was in such haste to arrive, the gates were open, a crowd of peasants filled the courtyard, and men and women were kneeling on the portico. Then, his sense of hearing being rendered more acute by astonishment at what he had seen, he fancied he heard the ringing of a bell.

He opened the door of the chaise, sprang out, crossed the courtyard rapidly, went up the portico, and found the stairway leading to the first floor filled with people.

Up the stairs he ran as he had up the portico, and heard what seemed to him a murmured prayer from his sister's bedroom. He went to the room. The door was open. Madame de Montrevel and little Edouard were kneeling beside Amélie's pillow; Charlotte, Michel, and his son Jacques were close at hand. The curate of Sainte-Claire was administering the last sacraments; the dismal scene was lighted only by the light of the wax-tapers.

The reader has recognized Roland in the traveller whose carriage stopped at the gate. The bystanders made way for him; he entered the room with his head uncovered and knelt beside his mother.

The dying girl lay on her back, her hands clasped, her head raised on her pillows, her eyes fixed upon the sky, in a sort of ecstasy. She seemed unconscious of Roland's arrival. It was as though her soul were floating between heaven and earth, while the body still belonged to this world.

Madame de Montrevel's hand sought that of Roland, and finding it, the poor mother dropped her head on his shoulder, sobbing. The sobs passed unnoticed by the dying girl, even as her brother's arrival had done. She lay there perfectly immovable. Only when the viaticum had been administered, when the priest's voice promised her eternal blessedness, her marble lips appeared to live again, and she murmured in a feeble but intelligible voice: "Amen!"

Then the bell rang again; the choir-boy, who was carrying it, left the room first, followed by the two acolytes who bore the tapers, then the cross-bearer, and lastly the priest with the Host. All the strangers present followed

the procession, and the family and household were left
alone.   The house, an instant before so full of sound and
life, was silent, almost deserted.

The dying girl had not moved; her lips were closed,
her hands clasped, her eyes raised to heaven.   After a
few minutes Roland stooped to his mother's ear, and whispered: "Come out with me, mother, I must speak to you."

Madame de Montrevel rose.   She pushed little Edouard
toward the bed, and the child stood on tiptoe to kiss his sister on the forehead.   Then the mother followed him, and,
leaning over, with a sob she pressed a kiss upon the same
spot.   Roland, with dry eyes but a breaking heart—he
would have given much for tears in which to drown his
sorrow—kissed his sister as his mother and little brother
had done.   She seemed as insensible to this kiss as to the
preceding ones.

Edouard left the room, followed by Madame de Montrevel and Roland.   Just as they reached the door they stopped,
quivering.   They had heard the name of Roland, uttered in
a low but distinct tone.

Roland turned.   Amélie called him a second time.

"Did you call me, Amelie?" he asked.

"Yes," replied the dying girl.

"Alone, or with my mother?"

"Alone."

That voice, devoid of emphasis, yet perfectly intelligible,
had something glacial about it; it was like an echo from another world.

"Go, mother," said Roland.   "You see that she wishes
to be alone with me."

"O my God!" murmured Madame de Montrevel, "can
there still be hope?"

Low as these words were, the dying girl heard them.

"No, mother," she said.   "God has permitted me to see
my brother again; but to-night I go to Him."

Madame de Montrevel groaned.

"Roland, Roland!" she said, "she is there already."

Roland signed to her to leave them alone, and she went away with little Edouard. Roland closed the door, and returned to his sister's bedside with unutterable emotion.

Her body was already stiffening in death; the breath from her lips would scarcely have dimmed a mirror; the eyes only, wide-open, were fixed and brilliant, as though the whole remaining life of the body, dead before its time, were centred there. Roland had heard of this strange state called ecstasy, which is nothing else than catalepsy. He saw that Amélie was a victim of that preliminary death.

"I am here, sister," he said. "What can I do for you?"

"I knew you would come," she replied, still without moving, "and I waited for you."

"How did you know that I was coming?" asked Roland.

"I saw you coming."

Roland shuddered.

"Did you know why I was coming?" he asked.

"Yes; I prayed God so earnestly in my heart that He gave me strength to rise and write to you."

"When was that?"

"Last night."

"Where is the letter?"

"Under my pillow. Take it, and read it."

Roland hesitated an instant. Was his sister delirious?

"Poor Amélie!" he murmured.

"Do not pity me," she said, "I go to join him."

"Whom?" asked Roland.

"Him whom I loved, and whom you killed."

Roland uttered a cry. This was delirium; or else—what did his sister mean?

"Amélie," said he, "I came to question you—"

"About Lord Tanlay; yes, I know," replied the young girl.

"You knew! How could you know?"

"Did I not tell you I saw you coming, and knew why you came?"

"Then answer me."

"Do not turn me from God and from him, Roland. I have written it all; read my letter."

Roland slipped his hand beneath the pillow, convinced that his sister was delirious.

To his great astonishment he felt a paper, which he drew out. It was a sealed letter; on it were written these words: "For Roland, who will come to-morrow."

He went over to the night-light in order to read the letter, which was dated the night before at eleven o'clock in the evening.

My brother, we have each a terrible thing to forgive the other.

Roland looked at his sister; she was still motionless. He continued to read:

I loved Charles de Sainte-Hermine; I did more than love him, he was my lover.

"Oh!" muttered the young man between his teeth, "he shall die."

"He is dead," said Amélie.

The young man gave a cry of astonishment. He had uttered the words to which Amélie had replied too low even to hear them himself. His eyes went back to the letter.

There was no legal marriage possible between the sister of Roland de Montrevel and the leader of the Companions of Jehu: that was the terrible secret which I bore—and it crushed me.

One person alone had to know it, and I told him; that person was Sir John Tanlay.

May God forever bless that noble-hearted man, who promised to break off an impossible marriage, and who kept his word. Let his life be sacred to you, Roland; he has been my only friend in sorrow, and his tears have mingled with mine.

I loved Charles de Saint-Hermine; I was his mistress; that is the terrible thing you must forgive.

But, in exchange, you caused his death; that is the terrible thing I now forgive you.

Oh! come fast, Roland, for I cannot die till you are here.

To die is to see him again; to die is to be with him and never to leave him again. I am glad to die.

All was clearly and plainly written; there was no sign of delirium in the letter.

Roland read it through twice, and stood for an instant silent, motionless, palpitating, full of bitterness; then pity got the better of his anger. He went to Amélie, stretched his hand over her, and said: "Sister, I forgive you."

A slight quiver shook the dying body.

"And now," she said, "call my mother, that I may die in her arms."

Roland opened the door and called Madame de Montrevel. She was waiting and came at once.

"Is there any change?" she asked, eagerly.

"No," replied Roland, "only Amélie wishes to die in your arms."

Madame de Montrevel fell upon her knees beside her daughter's bed.

Then Amélie, as though an invisible hand had loosened the bonds that held her rigid body to the bed, rose slowly, parted the hands that were clasped upon her breast, and let one fall slowly into those of her mother.

"Mother," she said, "you gave me life and you have taken it from me; I bless you. It was a mother's act. There was no happiness possible for your daughter in this life."

Then, letting her other hand fall into that of Roland, who was kneeling on the other side of the bed, she said: "We have forgiven each other, brother?"

"Yes, dear Amélie," he replied, "and from the depths of our hearts, I hope."

"I have still one last request to make."

"What is it?"

"Do not forget that Lord Tanlay has been my best friend."

"Fear nothing," said Roland; "Lord Tanlay's life is sacred to me."

Amélie drew a long breath; then in a voice which showed her growing weakness, she said: "Farewell, mother; farewell, Roland; kiss Edouard for me."

Then with a cry from her soul, in which there was more of joy than sadness, she said: "Here I am, Charles, here I am!"

She fell back upon her bed, withdrawing her two hands as she did so, and clasping them upon her breast again.

Roland and his mother rose and leaned over her. She had resumed her first position, except that her eyelids were closed and her breath extinguished. Amélie's martyrdom was over, she was dead.

CHAPTER LV

INVULNERABLE

AMÉLIE died during the night of Monday and Tuesday, that is to say, the 2d and 3d of June. On the evening of Thursday, the 5th of June, the Grand Opera at Paris was crowded for the second presentation of "Ossian, or the Bards."

The great admiration which the First Consul professed for the poems of Macpherson was universally known; consequently the National Academy, as much in flattery as from literary choice, had brought out an opera, which, in spite of all exertions, did not appear until a month after General Bonaparte had left Paris to join the Army of the Reserves.

In the balcony to the left sat a lover of music who was noticeable for the deep attention he paid to the performance. During the interval between the acts, the door-keeper came to him and said in a low voice:

"Pardon me, sir, are you Sir John Tanlay?"

"I am."

"In that case, my lord, a gentleman has a message to give you; he says it is of the utmost importance, and asks if you will speak to him in the corridor."

"Oh!" said Sir John, "is he an officer?"

"He is in civilian's dress, but he looks like an officer."

"Very good," replied Sir John; "I know who he is."

He rose and followed the woman. Roland was waiting in the corridor. Lord Tanlay showed no surprise on seeing him, but the stern look on the young man's face repressed the first impulse of his deep affection, which was to fling himself upon his friend's breast.

"Here I am, sir," said Sir John.

Roland bowed.

"I have just come from your hotel," he said. "You have, it seems, taken the precaution to inform the porter of your whereabout every time you have gone out, so that persons who have business with you should know where to find you."

"That is true, sir."

"The precaution is a good one, especially for those who, like myself, come from a long distance and are hurried and have no time to spare."

"Then," said Sir John, "was it to see me that you left the army and came to Paris?"

"Solely for that honor, sir; and I trust that you will guess my motives, and spare me the necessity of explaining them."

"From this moment I am at your service, sir," replied Sir John.

"At what hour to-morrow can two of my friends wait upon you?"

"From seven in the morning until midnight; unless you prefer that it should be now."

"No, my lord; I have but just arrived, and I must have time to find my friends and give them my instructions. If it will not inconvenience you, they will probably call upon you to-morrow between ten and eleven. I shall be very much obliged to you if the affair we have to settle could be arranged for the same day.''

"I believe that will be possible, sir; as I understand it to be your wish, the delay will not be from my side.''

"That is all I wished to know, my lord; pray do not let me detain you longer.''

Roland bowed, and Sir John returned the salutation. Then the young man left the theatre and Sir John returned to his seat in the balcony. The words had been exchanged in such perfectly well modulated voices, and with such an impassible expression of countenance on both sides, that no one would have supposed that a quarrel had arisen between the two men who had just greeted each other so courteously.

It happened to be the reception day of the minister of war. Roland returned to his hotel, removed the traces of his journey, jumped into a carriage, and a little before ten he was announced in the salon of the citizen Carnot.

Two purposes took him there: in the first place, he had a verbal communication to make to the minister of war from the First Consul; in the second place, he hoped to find there the two witnesses he was in need of to arrange his meeting with Sir John.

Everything happened as Roland had hoped. He gave the minister of war all the details of the crossing of the Mont Saint-Bernard and the situation of the army; and he himself found the two friends of whom he was in search. A few words sufficed to let them know what he wished; soldiers are particularly open to such confidences.

Roland spoke of a grave insult, the nature of which must remain a secret even to his seconds. He declared that he was the offended party, and claimed the choice of weapons and mode of fighting—advantages which belong to the challenger.

The young fellows agreed to present themselves to Sir John the following morning at the Hôtel Mirabeau, Rue de

Richelieu, at nine o'clock, and make the necessary arrangements with Sir John's seconds. After that they would join Roland at the Hôtel de Paris in the same street.

Roland returned to his room at eleven that evening, wrote for about an hour, then went to bed and to sleep.

At half-past nine the next morning his friends came to him. They had just left Sir John. He admitted all Roland's contentions; declared that he would not discuss any of the arrangements; adding that if Roland regarded himself as the injured party, it was for him to dictate the conditions. To their remark that they had hoped to discuss such matters with two of his friends and not with himself, he replied that he knew no one in Paris intimately enough to ask their assistance in such a matter, and that he hoped, once on the ground, that one of Roland's seconds would consent to act in his behalf. The two officers were agreed that Lord Tanlay had conducted himself with the utmost punctiliousness in every respect.

Roland declared that Sir John's request for the services of one of his two seconds was not only just but suitable, and he authorized either one of them to act for Sir John and to take charge of his interests. All that remained for Roland to do was to dictate his conditions. They were as follows!

Pistols were chosen. When loaded the adversaries were to stand at five paces. At the third clap of the seconds' hands they were to fire. It was, as we see, a duel to the death, in which, if either survived, he would be at the mercy of his opponent. Consequently the young officers made many objections; but Roland insisted, declaring that he alone could judge of the gravity of the insult offered him, and that no other reparation than this would satisfy him. They were obliged to yield to such obstinacy. But the friend who was to act as Sir John's second refused to bind himself for his principal, declaring that unless Sir John ordered it he would refuse to be a party to such a murder.

"Don't excite yourself, dear friend," said Roland, "I know Sir John, and I think he will be more accommodating than you."

The seconds returned to Sir John; they found him at his English breakfast of beefsteak, potatoes and tea. On seeing them he rose, invited them to share his repast, and, on their refusing, placed himself at their disposal. They began by assuring him that he could count upon one of them to act as his second. The one acting for Roland announced the conditions. At each stipulation Sir John bowed his head in token of assent and merely replied: "Very good!"

The one who had taken charge of his interests attempted to make some objections to a form of combat that, unless something impossible to foresee occurred, must end in the death of both parties; but Lord Tanlay begged him to make no objections.

"M. de Montrevel is a gallant man," he said; "I do not wish to thwart him in anything; whatever he does is right."

It only remained to settle the hour and the place of meeting. On these points Sir John again placed himself at Roland's disposal. The two seconds left even more delighted with him after this interview than they had been after the first. Roland was waiting for them and listened to what had taken place.

"What did I tell you?" he asked.

They requested him to name the time and place. He selected seven o'clock in the evening in the Allée de la Muette. At that hour the Bois was almost deserted, but the light was still good enough (it will be remembered that this was in the month of June) for the two adversaries to fight with any weapon.

No one had spoken of the pistols. The young men proposed to get them at an armorer's.

"No," said Roland, "Sir John has an excellent pair of duelling pistols which I have already used. If he is not unwilling to fight with those pistols I should prefer them to all others."

The young man who was now acting as Sir John's second went to him with the three following questions: Whether the time and place suited him, and whether he would allow his pistols to be used.

Lord Tanlay replied by regulating his watch by that of his second and by handing him the box of pistols.

"Shall I call for you, my lord?" asked the young man.

Sir John smiled sadly.

"Needless," he replied; "you are M. de Montrevel's friend, and you will find the drive pleasanter with him than with me. I will go on horseback with my servant. You will find me on the ground."

The young officer carried this reply to Roland.

"What did I tell you?" observed Roland again.

It was then mid-day, there were still seven hours before them, and Roland dismissed his friends to their various pleasures and occupations. At half-past six precisely they were to be at his door with three horses and two servants. It was necessary, in order to avoid interference, that the trip should appear to be nothing more than an ordinary promenade.

At half-past six precisely the waiter informed Roland that his friends were in the courtyard. Roland greeted them cordially and sprang into his saddle. The party followed the boulevards as far as the Place Louis XV. and then turned up the Champs Elysées. On the way the strange phenomenon that had so much astonished Sir John at the time of Roland's duel with M. de Barjols recurred. Roland's gayety might have been thought an affectation had it not been so evidently genuine. The two young men acting as seconds were of undoubted courage, but even they were bewildered by such utter indifference. They might have understood it had this affair been an ordinary duel, for coolness and dexterity insure their possessor a great advantage over his adversary; but in a combat like this to which they were going neither coolness nor dexterity would avail to save the combatants, if not from death at least from some terrible wound.

Furthermore, Roland urged on his horse like a man in haste, so that they reached the end of the Allée de la Muette five minutes before the appointed time.

A man was walking in the allée. Roland recognized Sir John. The seconds watched the young man's face as he caught sight of his adversary. To their great astonishment it expressed only tender good-will.

A few more steps and the four principal actors in the scene that was about to take place met.

Sir John was perfectly calm, but his face wore a look of profound sadness. It was evident that this meeting grieved him as deeply as it seemed to rejoice Roland.

The party dismounted. One of the seconds took the box of pistols from the servants and ordered them to lead away the horses, and not to return until they heard pistol-shots. The principals then entered the part of the woods that seemed the thickest, and looked about them for a suitable spot. For the rest, as Roland had foreseen, the Bois was deserted; the approach of the dinner hour had called every one home.

They found a small open spot exactly suited to their needs. The seconds looked at Roland and Sir John. They both nodded their heads in approval.

"Is there to be any change?" one of the seconds asked Sir John.

"Ask M. de Montrevel," replied Lord Tanlay; "I am entirely at his disposal."

"Nothing," said Roland.

The seconds took the pistols from the box and loaded them. Sir John stood apart, switching the heads of the tall grasses with his riding-whip.

Roland watched him hesitatingly for a moment, then taking his resolve, he walked resolutely toward him. Sir John raised his head and looked at him with apparent hope.

"My lord," said Roland, "I may have certain grievances against you, but I know you to be, none the less, a man of your word."

"You are right," replied Sir John.

"If you survive me will you keep the promise that you made me at Avignon?"

"There is no possibility that I shall survive you, but so long as I have any breath left in my body, you can count upon me."

"I refer to the final disposition to be made of my body."

"The same, I presume, as at Avignon?"

"The same, my lord."

"Very well, you may set your mind at rest."

Roland bowed to Sir John and returned to his friends.

"Have you any wishes in case the affair terminates fatally?" asked one of them.

"One only."

"What is it?"

"That you permit Sir John to take entire charge of the funeral arrangements. For the rest, I have a note in my left hand for him. In case I have not time to speak after the affair is over, you are to open my hand and give him the note."

"Is that all?"

"Yes."

"The pistols are loaded, then."

"Very well, inform Sir John."

One of the seconds approached Sir John. The other measured off five paces. Roland saw that the distance was greater than he had supposed.

"Excuse me," he said, "I said three paces."

"Five," replied the officer who was measuring the distance.

"Not at all, dear friend, you are wrong."

He turned to Sir John and to the other second questioningly.

"Three paces will do very well," replied Sir John, bowing.

There was nothing to be said if the two adversaries were agreed. The five paces were reduced to three. Then two sabres were laid on the ground to mark the limit. Sir John and Roland took their places, standing so that their toes touched the sabres. A pistol was then handed to each of them.

They bowed to say that they were ready. The two seconds stepped aside. They were to give the signal by clapping their hands three times. At the first clap the principals were to cock their pistols; at the second to take aim; at the third to fire.

The three claps were given at regular intervals amid the most profound silence; the wind itself seemed to pause and the rustle of the trees was hushed. The principals were calm, but the seconds were visibly distressed.

At the third clap two shots rang out so simultaneously that they seemed but one. But to the utter astonishment of the seconds the combatants remained standing. At the signal Roland had lowered his pistol and fired into the ground. Sir John had raised his and cut the branch of a tree three feet behind Roland. Each was clearly amazed —amazed that he himself was still living, after having spared his antagonist.

Roland was the first to speak.

"Ah!" he cried, "my sister was right in saying that you were the most generous man on earth."

And throwing his pistol aside he opened his arms to Sir John, who rushed into them.

"Ah! I understand," he said. "You wanted to die; but, God be thanked, I am not your murderer."

The two seconds came up.

"What is the matter?" they asked together.

"Nothing," said Roland, "except that I could not die by the hand of the man I love best on earth. You saw for yourselves that he preferred to die rather than kill me."

Then throwing himself once more into Sir John's arms, and grasping the hands of his two friends, he said: "I see that I must leave that to the Austrians. And now, gentlemen, you must excuse me. The First Consul is on the eve of a great battle in Italy, and I have not a moment to lose if I am to be there."

Leaving Sir John to make what explanations he thought suitable to the seconds, Roland rushed to the road, sprang upon his horse, and returned to Paris at a gallop.

CHAPTER LVI

CONCLUSION

IN THE meantime the French army continued its march, and on the 5th of June it entered Milan.

There was little resistance. The fort of Milan was invested. Murat, sent to Piacenza, had taken the city without a blow. Lannes had defeated General Ott at Montebello. Thus disposed, the French army was in the rear of the Austrians before the latter were aware of it.

During the night of the 8th of June a courier arrived from Murat, who, as we have said, was occupying Piacenza. Murat had intercepted a despatch from General Melas, and was now sending it to Bonaparte. This despatch announced the capitulation of Genoa; Masséna, after eating horses, dogs, cats and rats, had been forced to surrender. Melas spoke of the Army of the Reserves with the utmost contempt; he declared that the story of Bonaparte's presence in Italy was a hoax; and asserted that he knew for certain that the First Consul was in Paris.

Here was news that must instantly be imparted to Bonaparte, for it came under the category of bad news. Consequently, Bourrienne woke him up at three o'clock in the morning and translated the despatch. Bonaparte's first words were as follows:

"Pooh! Bourrienne, you don't understand German."

But Bourrienne repeated the translation word for word. After this reading the general rose, had everybody waked up, gave his orders, and then went back to bed and to sleep.

That same day he left Milan and established his headquarters at Stradella; there he remained until June 12th, left on the 13th, and marched to the Scrivia through Montebello, where he saw the field of battle, still torn and bleeding after Lannes' victory. The traces of death were everywhere; the church was still overflowing with the dead and wounded.

"The devil!" said the First Consul to the victor, "you must have made it pretty hot here."

"So hot, general, that the bones in my division were cracking and rattling like hail on a skylight."

Desaix joined the First Consul on the 11th of June, while he was still at Stradella. Released by the capitulation of El-Arish, he had reached Toulon the 6th of May, the very day on which Bonaparte left Paris. At the foot of the Mont Saint-Bernard Bonaparte received a letter from him, asking whether he should march to Paris or rejoin the army.

"Start for Paris, indeed!" exclaimed Bonaparte; "write him to rejoin the army at headquarters, wherever that may be."

Bourrienne had written, and, as we have seen, Desaix joined the army the 11th of June, at Stradella. The First Consul received him with twofold joy. In the first place, he regained a man without ambition, an intelligent officer and a devoted friend. In the second place, Desaix arrived just in the nick of time to take charge of the division lately under Boudet, who had been killed. Through a false report, received through General Gardannes, the First Consul was led to believe that the enemy refused to give battle and was retiring to Genoa. He sent Desaix and his division on the road to Novi to cut them off.

The night of the 13th passed tranquilly. In spite of a heavy storm, an engagement had taken place the preceding evening in which the Austrians had been defeated. It seemed as though men and nature were wearied alike, for all was still during the night. Bonaparte was easy in his mind; there was but one bridge over the Bormida, and he had been assured that that was down. Pickets were stationed as far as possible along the Bormida, each with four scouts.

The whole of the night was occupied by the enemy in crossing the river. At two in the morning two parties of scouts were captured; seven of the eight men were killed, the eighth made his way back to camp crying: "To arms!"

A courier was instantly despatched to the First Consul, who was sleeping at Torre di Galifo. Meanwhile, till orders could be received, the drums beat to arms all along the line. A man must have shared in such a scene to understand the effect produced on a sleeping army by the roll of drums calling to arms at three in the morning. The bravest shuddered. The troops were sleeping in their clothes; every man sprang up, ran to the stacked arms, and seized his weapons.

The lines formed on the vast plains of Marengo. The noise of the drums swept on like a train of lighted powder. In the dim half-light the hasty movements of the pickets could be seen. When the day broke, the French troops were stationed as follows:

The division Gardannes and the division Chamberlhac, forming the extreme advance, were encamped around a little country-place called Petra Bona, at the angle formed by the highroad from Marengo to Tortona, and the Bormida, which crosses the road on its way to the Tanaro.

The corps of General Lannes was before the village of San Giuliano, the place which Bonaparte had pointed out to Roland three months earlier, telling him that on that spot the fate of the campaign would be decided.

The Consular guard was stationed some five hundred yards or so in the rear of Lannes.

The cavalry brigade, under General Kellermann, and a

few squadrons of chasseurs and hussars, forming the left, filled up, along the advanced line, the gap between the divisions of Gardannes and Chamberlhac.

A second brigade, under General Champeaux, filled up the gap on the right between General Lannes' cavalry.

And finally the twelfth regiment of hussars, and the twenty-first chasseurs, detached by Murat under the orders of General Rivaud, occupied the opening of the Valley of Salo and the extreme right of the position.

These forces amounted to about twenty-five or six thousand men, not counting the divisions Monnet and Boudet, ten thousand men in all, commanded by Desaix, and now, as we have said, detached from the main army to cut off the retreat of the enemy to Genoa. Only, instead of making that retreat, the enemy were now attacking.

During the day of the 13th of June, General Melas, commander-in-chief of the Austrian army, having succeeded in reuniting the troops of Generals Haddich, Kaim and Ott, crossed the Tanaro, and was now encamped before Alessandria with thirty-six thousand infantry, seven thousand cavalry, and a numerous well-served and well-horsed artillery.

At four o'clock in the morning the firing began and General Victor assigned all to their line of battle. At five Bonaparte was awakened by the sound of cannon. While he was dressing, General Victor's aide-de-camp rode up to tell him that the enemy had crossed the Bormida and was attacking all along the line of battle.

The First Consul called for his horse, and, springing upon it, galloped off toward the spot where the fighting was going on. From the summit of the hill he could overlook the position of both armies.

The enemy was formed in three columns; that on the left, comprising all the cavalry and light infantry, was moving toward Castel-Ceriolo by the Salo road, while the columns of the right and centre, resting upon each other and comprising the infantry regiments under Generals Haddich, Kaim and O'Reilly, and the reserve of grenadiers under command of General Ott, were advancing along the Tortona road and up the Bormida.

The moment they crossed the river the latter columns came in contact with the troops of General Gardannes, posted, as we have said, at the farmhouse and the ravine of Petra Bona. It was the noise of the artillery advancing in this direction that had brought Bonaparte to the scene of battle. He arrived just as Gardannes' division, crushed under the fire of that artillery, was beginning to fall back, and General Victor was sending forward Chamberlhac's division to its support. Protected by this move, Gardannes' troops retreated in good order, and covered the village of Marengo.

The situation was critical; all the plans of the commander-in-chief were overthrown. Instead of attacking, as was his wont, with troops judiciously massed, he was attacked himself before he could concentrate his forces. The Austrians, profiting by the sweep of land that lay before them, ceased to march in columns, and deployed in lines parallel to those of Gardannes and Chamberlhac—with this difference, that they were two to the French army's one. The first of these lines was commanded by General Haddich, the second by General Melas, the third by General Ott.

At a short distance from the Bormida flows a stream called the Fontanone, which passes through a deep ravine forming a semicircle round the village of Marengo, and protecting it. General Victor had already divined the advantages to be derived from this natural intrenchment, and he used it to rally the divisions of Gardannes and Chamberlhac.

Bonaparte, approving Victor's arrangements, sent him word to defend Marengo to the very last extremity. He himself needed time to prepare his game on this great chess-board inclosed between the Bormida, the Fontanone, and Marengo.

His first step was to recall Desaix, then marching, as

we have said, to cut the retreat to Genoa. General Bonaparte sent off two or three aides-de-camp with orders not
to stop until they had reached that corps. Then he waited,
seeing clearly that there was nothing to do but to fall back
in as orderly a manner as possible, until he could gather a
compact mass that would enable him, not only to stop the
retrograde movement, but to assume the offensive.

But this waiting was horrible.

Presently the action was renewed along the whole line.
The Austrians had reached one bank of the Fontanone, of
which the French occupied the other. Each was firing on
the other from either side of the ravine; grape-shot flew
from side to side within pistol range. Protected by its terrible artillery, the enemy had only to extend himself a little
more to overwhelm Bonaparte's forces. General Rivaud, of
Gardannes' division, saw the Austrians preparing for this
manœuvre. He marched out from Marengo, and placed a
battalion in the open with orders to die there rather than
retreat, then, while that battalion drew the enemy's fire,
he formed his cavalry in column, came round the flank of
the battalion, fell upon three thousand Austrians advancing
to the charge, repulsed them, threw them into disorder, and,
all wounded as he was by a splintered ball, forced them back
behind their own lines. After that he took up a position to
the right of the battalion, which had not retreated a step.

But during this time Gardannes' division, which had
been struggling with the enemy from early morning, was
driven back upon Marengo, followed by the first Austrian
line, which forced Chamberlhac's division to retreat in like
manner. There an aide-de-camp sent by Bonaparte ordered
the two divisions to rally and retake Marengo at any cost.

General Victor reformed them, put himself at their head,
forced his way through the streets, which the Austrians had
not had time to barricade, retook the village, lost it again,
took it a third time, and then, overwhelmed by numbers,
lost it for the third time.

It was then eleven o'clock. Desaix, overtaken by Bonaparte's aide-de-camp, ought at that hour to be on his way to the battle.

Meanwhile, Lannes with his two divisions came to the help of his struggling comrades. This reinforcement enabled Gardannes and Chamberlhac to reform their lines parallel to the enemy, who had now debouched, through Marengo, to the right and also to the left of the village.

The Austrians were on the point of overwhelming the French.

Lannes, forming his centre with the divisions rallied by Victor, deployed with his two least exhausted divisions for the purpose of opposing them to the Austrian wings. The two corps—the one excited by the prospect of victory, the other refreshed by a long rest—flung themselves with fury into the fight, which was now renewed along the whole line.

After struggling an hour, hand to hand, bayonet to bayonet, General Kaim's corps fell back; General Champeaux, at the head of the first and eighth regiments of dragoons, charged upon him, increasing his disorder. General Watrin, with the sixth light infantry and the twenty-second and fortieth of the line, started in pursuit and drove him nearly a thousand rods beyond the rivulet. But this movement separated the French from their own corps; the centre divisions were endangered by the victory on the right, and Generals Watrin and Champeaux were forced to fall back to the lines they had left uncovered.

At the same time Kellermann was doing on the left wing what Champeaux and Watrin had done on the right. Two cavalry charges made an opening through the enemy's line; but behind that first line was a second. Not daring to go further forward, because of superior numbers, Kellermann lost the fruits of that momentary victory.

It was now noon. The French army, which undulated like a flaming serpent along a front of some three miles, was broken in the centre. The centre, retreating, abandoned the wings. The wings were therefore forced to follow the retrograde movement. Kellermann to the left,

Watrin to the right, had given their men the order to fall back. The retreat was made in squares, under the fire of eighty pieces of artillery which preceded the main body of the Austrian army. The French ranks shrank visibly; men were borne to the ambulances by men who did not return.

One division retreated through a field of ripe wheat; a shell burst and fired the straw, and two or three thousand men were caught in the midst of a terrible conflagration; cartridge-boxes exploded, and fearful disorder reigned in the ranks.

It was then that Bonaparte sent forward the Consular guard.

Up they went at a charge, deployed in line of battle, and stopped the enemy's advance. Meantime the mounted grenadiers dashed forward at a gallop and overthrew the Austrian cavalry.

Meanwhile the division which had escaped from the conflagration received fresh cartridges and reformed in line. But this movement had no other result than to prevent the retreat from becoming a rout.

It was two o'clock.

Bonaparte watched the battle, sitting on the bank of a ditch beside the highroad to Alessandria. He was alone. His left arm was slipped through his horse's bridle; with the other he flicked the pebbles in the road with the tip of his riding-whip. Cannon-balls were plowing the earth about him. He seemed indifferent to this great drama on which hung all his hopes. Never had he played so desperate a game—six years of victory against the crown of France!

Suddenly he roused from his revery. Amid the dreadful roar of cannon and musketry his ear caught the hoofbeats of a galloping horse. He raised his head. A rider, dashing along at full speed, his horse covered with white froth, came from the direction of Novi. When he was within fifty feet, Bonaparte gave one cry:

"Roland!"

The latter dashed on, crying: "Desaix! Desaix! Desaix!"

Bonaparte opened his arms; Roland sprang from his horse, and flung himself upon the First Consul's neck.

There was a double joy for Bonaparte in this arrival—that of again seeing a man whom he knew would be devoted to him unto death, and because of the news he brought.

"And Desaix?" he questioned.

"Is within three miles; one of your aides met him retracing his steps toward the cannon."

"Then," said Bonaparte, "he may yet come in time."

"How? In time?"

"Look!"

Roland glanced at the battlefield and grasped the situation in an instant.

During the few moments that had elapsed while they were conversing, matters had gone from bad to worse. The first Austrian column, the one which had marched on Castel-Ceriolo and had not yet been engaged, was about to fall on the right of the French army. If it broke the line the retreat would be flight—Desaix would come too late.

"Take my last two regiments of grenadiers," said Bonaparte. "Rally the Consular guard, and carry it with you to the extreme right—you understand? in a square, Roland!—and stop that column like a stone redoubt."

There was not an instant to lose. Roland sprang upon his horse, took the two regiments of grenadiers, rallied the Consular guard, and dashed to the right. When he was within fifty feet of General Elsnitz's column, he called out: "In square! The First Consul is looking at us!"

The square formed. Each man seemed to take root in his place.

General Elsnitz, instead of continuing his way in the movement to support Generals Melas and Kaim—instead of despising the nine hundred men who present no cause for fear in the rear of a victorious army—General Elsnitz paused and turned upon them with fury.

Those nine hundred men were indeed the stone redoubt that General Bonaparte had ordered them to be. Artillery, musketry, bayonets, all were turned upon them, but they yielded not an inch.

Bonaparte was watching them with admiration, when, turning in the direction of Novi, he caught the gleam of Desaix's bayonets. Standing on a knoll raised above the plain, he could see what was invisible to the enemy.

He signed to a group of officers who were near him, awaiting orders; behind stood orderlies holding their horses. The officers advanced. Bonaparte pointed to the forest of bayonets, now glistening in the sunlight, and said to one of the officers: "Gallop to those bayonets and tell them to hasten. As for Desaix, tell him I am waiting for him here."

The officer galloped off. Bonaparte again turned his eyes to the battlefield. The retreat continued; but Roland and his nine hundred had stopped General Elsnitz and his column. The stone redoubt was transformed into a volcano; it was belching fire from all four sides. Then Bonaparte, addressing three officers, cried out: "One of you to the centre; the other two to the wings! Say everywhere that the reserves are at hand, and that we resume the offensive."

The three officers departed like arrows shot from a bow, their ways parting in direct lines to their different destinations. Bonaparte watched them for a few moments, and when he turned round he saw a rider in a general's uniform approaching.

It was Desaix—Desaix, whom he had left in Egypt, and who that very morning had said, laughing: "The bullets of Europe don't recognize me; some ill-luck is surely impending over me."

One grasp of the hand was all that these two friends needed to reveal their hearts.

Then Bonaparte stretched out his arm toward the battlefield.

A single glance told more than all the words in the world.

Twenty thousand men had gone into the fight that morning, and now scarcely more than ten thousand were left within a radius of six miles—only nine thousand infantry, one thousand cavalry, and ten cannon still in condition for use. One quarter of the army was either dead or wounded, another quarter was employed in removing the wounded; for the First Consul would not suffer them to be abandoned. All of these forces, save and excepting Roland and his nine hundred men, were retreating.

The vast space between the Bormida and the ground over which the army was now retreating was covered with the dead bodies of men and horses, dismounted cannon and shattered ammunition wagons. Here and there rose columns of flame and smoke from the burning fields of grain.

Desaix took in these details at a glance.

"What do you think of the battle?" asked Bonaparte.

"I think that this one is lost," answered Desaix; "but as it is only three o'clock in the afternoon, we have time to gain another."

"Only," said a voice, "we need cannon!"

This voice belonged to Marmont, commanding the artillery.

"True, Marmont; but where are we to get them?"

"I have five pieces still intact from the battlefield; we left five more at Scrivia, which are just coming up."

"And the eight pieces I have with me," said Desaix.

"Eighteen pieces!" said Marmont; "that is all I need."

An aide-de-camp was sent to hasten the arrival of Desaix's guns. His troops were advancing rapidly, and were scarcely half a mile from the field of battle. Their line of approach seemed formed for the purpose at hand; on the left of the road was a gigantic perpendicular hedge protected by a bank. The infantry was made to file in a narrow line along it, and it even hid the cavalry from view.

During this time Marmont had collected his guns and

stationed them in battery on the right front of the army. Suddenly they burst forth, vomiting a deluge of grapeshot and canister upon the Austrians.   For an instant the enemy wavered.

Bonaparte profited by that instant of hesitation to send forward the whole front of the French army.

"Comrades!" he cried, "we have made steps enough backward; remember, it is my custom to sleep on the battlefield!"

At the same moment, and as if in reply to Marmont's cannonade, volleys of musketry burst forth to the left, taking the Austrians in flank.   It was Desaix and his division, come down upon them at short range and enfilading the enemy with the fire of his guns.

The whole army knew that this was the reserve, and that it behooved them to aid this reserve by a supreme effort.

"Forward!" rang from right to left.   The drums beat the charge.   The Austrians, who had not seen the reserves, and were marching with their guns on their shoulders, as if at parade, felt that something strange was happening within the French lines; they struggled to retain the victory they now felt to be slipping from their grasp.

But everywhere the French army had resumed the offensive.   On all sides the ominous roll of the charge and the victorious Marseillaise were heard above the din.   Marmont's battery belched fire; Kellermann dashed forward with his cuirassiers and cut his way through both lines of the enemy.

Desaix jumped ditches, leaped hedges, and, reaching a little eminence, turned to see if his division were still following him.   There he fell; but his death, instead of diminishing the ardor of his men, redoubled it, and they charged with their bayonets upon the column of General Zach.

At that moment Kellermann, who had broken through both of the enemy's lines, saw Desaix's division struggling with a compact, immovable mass.   He charged in flank, forced his way into a gap, widened it, broke the square, quartered it, and in less than fifteen minutes the five thousand Austrian grenadiers who formed the mass were overthrown, dispersed, crushed, annihilated. They disappeared like smoke. General Zach and his staff, all that was left, were taken prisoners.

Then, in turn, the enemy endeavored to make use of his immense cavalry corps; but the incessant volleys of musketry, the blasting canister, the terrible bayonets, stopped short the charge. Murat was manœuvring on the flank with two light-battery guns and a howitzer, which dealt death to the foe.

He paused for an instant to succor Roland and his nine hundred men. A shell from the howitzer fell and burst in the Austrian ranks; it opened a gulf of flame. Roland sprang into it, a pistol in one hand, his sword in the other. The whole Consular guard followed him, opening the enemy's ranks as a wedge opens the trunk of an oak. Onward he dashed, till he reached an ammunition wagon surrounded by the enemy; then, without pausing an instant, he thrust the hand holding the pistol through the opening of the wagon and fired. A frightful explosion followed, a volcano had burst its crater and annihilated those around it.

General Elsnitz's corps was in full flight; the rest of the Austrian army swayed, retreated, and broke. The generals tried in vain to stop the torrent and form up for a retreat. In thirty minutes the French army had crossed the plain it had defended foot by foot for eight hours.

The enemy did not stop until Marengo was reached. There they made a vain attempt to reform under fire of the artillery of Carra-Saint-Cyr (forgotten at Castel-Ceriolo, and not recovered until the day was over); but the Desaix, Gardannes, and Chamberlhac divisions, coming up at a run, pursued the flying Austrians through the streets.

Marengo was carried. The enemy retired on Petra Bona, and that too was taken. Then the Austrians rushed toward the bridge of the Bormida; but Carra-

Saint-Cyr was there before them. The flying multitudes sought the fords, or plunged into the Bormida under a devastating fire, which did not slacken before ten that night.

The remains of the Austrian army regained their camp at Alessandria. The French army bivouacked near the bridge. The day had cost the Austrian army four thousand five hundred men killed, six thousand wounded, five thousand prisoners, besides twelve flags and thirty cannon.

Never did fortune show herself under two such opposite aspects as on that day. At two in the afternoon, the day spelt defeat and its disastrous consequences to Bonaparte; at five, it was Italy reconquered and the throne of France in prospect.

That night the First Consul wrote the following letter to Madame de Montrevel:

MADAME—I have to-day won my greatest victory; but it has cost me the two halves of my heart, Desaix and Roland.

Do not grieve, madame; your son did not care to live, and he could not have died more gloriously.

BONAPARTE.

Many futile efforts were made to recover the body of the young aide-de-camp: like Romulus, he had vanished in a whirlwind.

None ever knew why he had pursued death with such eager longing.

THE END

www.ingramcontent.com/pod-product-compliance
Lightning Source LLC
Chambersburg PA
CBHW011349010726
47494CB00008B/2228